Dear Reader,

I always love revisiting the McKettricks, especially at Christmas! If you missed it in hardcover, here's your chance to spend the holidays with these folks of Blue River, Texas. You'll find a bonus story included, *Daring Moves*—one of my favorites. I also hope you'll be watching for the final installment of my newest trilogy set in Parable, Montana, when *Big Sky River* hits stores in January.

In *A Lawman's Christmas,* who should appear in Blue River as the new marshal but Clay McKettrick, Jeb and Chloe's son from *Secondhand Bride.* His arrival puts Dara Rose Nolan in a tailspin…. What if the young widow with two daughters—and no way to earn a living—is forced out of her home by the new lawman? But 'tis the season for miracles, if only Dara Rose can allow herself to wish for the gift she needs most—Christmas in Clay's arms.

I would also like to write today to tell you about the scholarship program I personally finance—Linda Lael Miller Scholarships for Women, awarded to those seeking to improve their lot in life through education. You can find more information about this program on my website, www.lindalaelmiller.com.

With love,

Linda Lael Miller

Praise for the novels of
#1 *New York Times* bestselling author
Linda Lael Miller

"Miller is one of the finest American writers in the genre."
—*RT Book Reviews*

"Miller tugs at the heartstrings as few authors can."
—*Publishers Weekly*

"After reading this book your heart will be so full of Christmas cheer you'll want to stuff a copy in the stocking of every romance fan you know!"
—*USA TODAY Happy Ever After blog*
on *A Lawman's Christmas*

"We are again treated to another tale involving one of my favorite families by the amazing Miller, who just steals your heart with good stories about good people. Her overall theme of strength in family never fails to grab your attention and keep you coming back for more."
—*Fresh Fiction* on *A Lawman's Christmas*

"Miller's attention to small details makes her stories a delight to read. With engaging characters and loveable animals, this second story in the Creed Cowboys trilogy is a sure hit for the legions of cowboy fans out there."
—*RT Book Reviews* on *Creed's Honor*

"A passionate love too long denied drives the action in this multifaceted, emotionally rich reunion story that overflows with breathtaking sexual chemistry."
—*Library Journal* on *McKettricks of Texas: Tate*

"Strong characterization and a vivid western setting make for a fine historical romance."
—*Publishers Weekly* on *McKettrick's Choice*

LINDA LAEL MILLER

A Lawman's Christmas:
A McKettricks of Texas Novel

HARLEQUIN®
entertain, enrich, inspire™

ISBN-13: 978-0-373-77787-7

A LAWMAN'S CHRISTMAS:
A McKETTRICKS OF TEXAS NOVEL
Copyright © 2012 by Harlequin Books S.A.

The publisher acknowledges the copyright holder of the individual works as follows:

A LAWMAN'S CHRISTMAS:
A McKETTRICKS OF TEXAS NOVEL
Copyright © 2011 by Linda Lael Miller

DARING MOVES
Copyright © 1990 by Linda Lael Miller

Recycling programs for this product may not exist in your area.

This edition published by arrangement with Harlequin Books S.A.

For questions and comments about the quality of this book, please contact us at CustomerService@Harlequin.com.

www.Harlequin.com

Printed in U.S.A.

CONTENTS

Also available from Linda Lael Miller and Harlequin HQN

McKettricks of Texas

The McKettricks

The Montana Creeds

The Mojo Sheepshanks

The Stone Creek series

The Creed Cowboys

The Parable series

Coming soon

A LAWMAN'S CHRISTMAS: A McKETTRICKS OF TEXAS NOVEL

In memory of Kathy Bannon.
We sure do miss you, Teach.

Chapter 1

<svg>⤔⤍⤏</svg>

Early December, 1914

IF THE SPARK-THROWING SCREECH of iron-on-iron hadn't wrenched Clay McKettrick out of his uneasy sleep, the train's lurching stop—which nearly pitched him onto the facing seat—would surely have done the trick.

Grumbling, Clay sat up straight and glowered out the window, shoving splayed fingers through his dark hair.

Blue River, Texas. His new home. And more, for as the new marshal, he'd be responsible for protecting the town and its residents.

Not that he could see much of it just then, with all that steam from the smokestack billowing between the train and the depot.

The view didn't particularly matter to him, anyhow, since he'd paid a brief visit to the town a few months back and seen what there was to see—which hadn't been much, even in the sun-spangled, blue-sky days of summer. Now that winter was coming on—Clay's granddad, Angus, claimed it snowed dust and chiggers in that part of Texas—

the rutted roads and weathered facades of the ramshackle buildings would no doubt be of bleak appearance.

With an inward sigh, Clay stood to retrieve his black, round-brimmed hat and worn duster from the wooden rack overhead. In the process, he allowed himself to ponder, yet again, all he'd left behind to come to this place at the hind end of beyond and carve out a life of his own making.

He'd left plenty.

A woman, to start with. And then there was his family, the sprawling McKettrick clan, including his ma and pa, Chloe and Jeb, his two older sisters and the thriving Triple M Ranch, with its plentitude of space and water and good grass.

A fragment of a Bible verse strayed across his brain. *The cattle on a thousand hills...*

There were considerably fewer than a thousand hills on the Triple M, big as it was, but the cattle were legion.

To his granddad's way of thinking, those hills and the land they anchored might have been on loan from the Almighty, but everything else—cows, cousins, mineral deposits and timber included—belonged to Angus McKettrick, his four sons and his daughter, Katie.

Clay shrugged into the long coat and put on his hat. His holster and pistol were stowed in his trunk in the baggage compartment, and his paint gelding, Outlaw, rode all alone in the car reserved for livestock.

The only other passenger on board, an angular woman with severe features and no noticeable inclination toward small talk, remained seated, with the biggest Bible Clay had ever seen resting open on her lap. She seemed poised to leap right into the pages at the first hint of sin and disappear into all those apocalyptic threats and grand promises. According to the conductor, a fitful little fellow bearing the pitted scars of a long-ago case of smallpox, the lady had come all the way from Cincinnati with the express purpose of saving the heathen.

Clay—bone-tired, homesick for the ranch and for his kinfolks, and wryly amused, all of a piece—nodded a respectful farewell to the woman as he passed her seat, resisting the temptation to stop and inquire about the apparent shortage of heathens in Cincinnati.

Most likely, he decided, reaching the door, she'd already converted the bunch of them, and now she was out to wrestle the devil for the whole state of Texas. He wouldn't have given two cents for old Scratch's chances.

A chill wind, laced with tiny flakes of snow, buffeted Clay as he stepped down onto the small platform, where all three members of the town council, each one stuffed into his Sunday best and half-strangled by a celluloid collar, waited to greet the new marshal.

Mayor Wilson Ponder spoke for the group. "Welcome to Blue River, Mr. McKettrick," the fat man boomed, a blustery old cuss with white muttonchop whiskers and piano-key teeth that seemed to operate independently of his gums.

Clay, still in his late twenties and among the youngest of the McKettrick cousins, wasn't accustomed to being addressed as "mister"—around home, he answered to "hey, you"—and he sort of liked the novelty of it. "Call me Clay," he said.

There were handshakes all around.

The conductor lugged Clay's trunk out of the baggage car and plunked it down on the platform, then busily consulted his pocket watch.

"Better unload that horse of yours," he told Clay, in the officious tone so often adopted by short men who didn't weigh a hundred pounds sopping wet, "if you don't want him going right on to Fort Worth. This train pulls out in five minutes."

Clay nodded, figuring Outlaw would be ready by now for fresh air and a chance to stretch his legs, since he'd been cooped up in a rolling box ever since Flagstaff.

Taking his leave from the welcoming committee with a touch to the brim of his hat and a promise to meet them later at the marshal's office, he crossed the small platform, descended the rough-hewn steps and walked through cinders and lingering wisps of steam to the open door of the livestock car. He lowered the heavy ramp himself and climbed into the dim, horse-scented enclosure.

Outlaw nickered a greeting, and Clay smiled and patted the horse's long neck before picking up his saddle and other gear and tossing the lot of it to the ground beside the tracks.

That done, he loosed the knot in Outlaw's halter rope and led the animal toward the ramp.

Some horses balked at the unfamiliar, but not Outlaw. He and Clay had been sidekicks for more than a decade, and they trusted each other in all circumstances.

Outside, in the brisk, snow-dappled wind, having traversed the slanted iron plate with no difficulty, Outlaw blinked, adjusting his unusual blue eyes to the light of midafternoon. Clay meant to let the gelding stand untethered while he put the ramp back in place, but before he could turn around, a little girl hurried around the corner of the brick depot and took a competent hold on the lead rope.

She couldn't have been older than seven, and she was small even for that tender age. She wore a threadbare calico dress, a brown bonnet and a coat that, although clean, had seen many a better day. A blond sausage curl tumbled from inside the bonnet to gleam against her forehead, and she smiled with the confidence of a seasoned wrangler.

"My name is Miss Edrina Nolan," she announced importantly. "Are you the new marshal?"

Amused, Clay tugged at his hat brim to acknowledge her properly and replied, "I am. Name's Clay McKettrick."

Edrina put out her free hand. "How do you do, Mr. McKettrick?" she asked.

"I do just fine," he said, with a little smile. Growing up on the Triple M, he and all his cousins had been around horses all their lives, so the child's remarkable ease with a critter many times her size did not surprise him.

It was impressive, though.

"I'll hold your horse," she said. "You'd better help the railroad man with that ramp. He's liable to hurt himself if you don't."

Clay looked back over one shoulder and, sure enough, there was the banty rooster of a conductor, struggling to hoist that heavy slab of rust-speckled iron off the ground so the train could get under way again. He lent his assistance, figuring he'd just spared the man a hernia, if not a heart attack, and got a glare for his trouble, rather than thanks.

Since the fellow's opinion made no real never-mind to Clay either way, he simply turned back to the little girl, ready to reclaim his horse.

She was up on the horse's back, her faded skirts billowing around her, and with the snow-strained sunlight framing her, she looked like one of those cherub-children gracing the pages of calendars, Valentines and boxes of ready-made cookies.

"Whoa, now," he said, automatically taking hold of the lead rope. Given that he hadn't saddled Outlaw yet, he was somewhat mystified as to how she'd managed to mount up the way she had. Maybe she really was a cherub, with little stubby wings hidden under that thin black coat.

Up ahead, the engineer blew the whistle to signal imminent departure, and Outlaw started at the sound, though he didn't buck, thank the good Lord.

"Whoa," Clay repeated, very calmly but with a note of sternness. It was then that he spotted the stump on the other side of the horse and realized that Edrina must have scrambled up on that to reach Outlaw's back.

They all waited—man, horse and cherub—until the train pulled out and the racket subsided somewhat.

Edrina smiled serenely down at him. "Mama says we'll all have to go to the poorhouse, now that you're here," she announced.

"Is that so?" Clay asked mildly, as he reached up, took the child by the waist and lifted her off the horse, setting her gently on her feet. Then he commenced to collecting Outlaw's blanket, saddle and bridle from where they'd landed when he tossed them out of the railroad car, and tacking up. Out of the corner of his eye, he saw the town-council contingent straggling off the platform.

Edrina nodded in reply to his rhetorical question, still smiling, and the curl resting on her forehead bobbed with the motion of her head. "My papa was the marshal a while back," she informed Clay matter-of-factly, "but then he died in the arms of a misguided woman in a room above the Bitter Gulch Saloon and left us high and dry."

Clay blinked, wondering if he'd mistaken Edrina Nolan for a child when she was actually a lot older. Say, forty.

"I see," he said, after clearing his throat. "That's unfortunate. That your papa passed on, I mean." Clay had known the details of his predecessor's death, having been regaled with the story the first time he set foot in Blue River, but it took him aback that Edrina knew it, too.

She folded her arms and watched critically as he threw on Outlaw's beat-up saddle and put the cinch through the buckle. "Can you shoot a gun and everything?" she wanted to know.

Clay spared her a sidelong glance and a nod. Why wasn't this child in school? Did her mother know she was running loose like a wild Indian and leaping onto the backs of other people's horses when they weren't looking?

And where the heck had a kid her age learned to ride like that?

"Good," Edrina said, with a relieved sigh, her little arms still folded. "Because Papa couldn't be trusted with a firearm. Once, when he was cleaning a pistol, meaning to go out and hunt rabbits for stew, it went off by accident and made a big hole in the floor. Mama put a chair over it—she said it was so my sister, Harriet, and I wouldn't fall in and wind up under the house, with all the cobwebs and the mice, but I know it was really because she was embarrassed for anybody to see what Papa had done. Even Harriet has more sense than to fall in a hole, for heaven's sake, and she's only five."

Clay suppressed a smile, tugged at the saddle to make sure it would hold his weight, put a foot into the stirrup and swung up. Adjusted his hat in a gesture of farewell. "I'll be seeing you, chatterbox," he said kindly.

"What about your trunk?" Edrina wanted to know. "Are you just going to leave it behind, on the platform?"

"I mean to come back for it later in the day," Clay explained, wondering why he felt compelled to clarify the matter at all. "This horse and I, we've been on that train for a goodly while, and right now, we need to stretch our muscles a bit."

"I could show you where our house is," Edrina persisted, scampering along beside Outlaw when Clay urged the horse into a walk. "Well, I guess it's *your* house now."

"Maybe you ought to run along home," Clay said. "Your mama's probably worried about you."

"No," Edrina said. "Mama has no call to worry. She thinks I'm in school."

Clay bit back another grin.

They'd climbed the grassy embankment leading to the street curving past the depot and on into Blue River by then. The members of the town's governing body waddled just ahead, single file, along a plank sidewalk like a trio of black ducks wearing top hats.

"And why *aren't* you in school?" Clay inquired affably, adjusting his hat again, and squaring his shoulders against the nippy breeze and the swirling specks of snow, each one sharp-edged as a razor.

She shivered slightly, but that was the only sign that she'd paid any notice at all to the state of the weather. While Miss Edrina Nolan pondered her reply, Clay maneuvered the horse to her other side, hoping to block the bitter wind at least a little.

"I already know everything they have to teach at that school," Edrina said at last, in a tone of unshakable conviction. "And then some."

Clay chuckled under his breath, though he refrained from comment. It wasn't as if anybody were asking his opinion.

The first ragtag shreds of Blue River were no more impressive than he recalled them to be—a livery on one side of the road, and an abandoned saloon on the other. Waist-high grass, most of it dead, surrounded the latter; craggy shards of filthy glass edged its one narrow window, and the sign above the door dangled by a lone, rusty nail.

Last Hope: Saloon and Games of Chance, it read in painted letters nearly worn away by time and weather.

"You shouldn't be out in this weather," Clay told Edrina, who was still hiking along beside him and Outlaw, eschewing the broken plank sidewalk for the road. "Too cold."

"I like it," she said. "The cold is very bracing, don't you think? Makes a body feel wide-awake."

The town's buildings, though unpainted, began to look a little better as they progressed. Smoke curled from twisted chimneys and doors were closed up tight.

There were few people on the streets, Clay noticed, though he glimpsed curious faces at various windows as they went by.

He raised his collar against the rising wind, figuring he'd had all the "bracing" he needed, thank you very much, and he was sure enough "wide-awake" now that he was off the train and back in the saddle.

He was hungry, too, and he wanted a bath and barbering.

And ten to twelve hours of sleep, lying prone instead of sitting upright in a hard seat.

"I reckon maybe you ought to show me where you live, after all," he said, at some length. At least that way, he could steer the child homeward, where she belonged, make sure she got there, and rest easy thereafter, where her welfare was concerned.

Edrina pointed past a general store, a telegraph and telephone office, the humble jailhouse where he would soon be officiating and a tiny white church surrounded by a rickety picket fence, much in need of whitewash. "It's one street over," she said, already veering off a little, as though she meant to duck between buildings and take off. "Our place, that is. It's the one with an apple tree in the yard and a chicken house out back."

Clay drew up his horse with a nearly imperceptible tug of the reins. "Hold it right there," he said, with quiet authority, when Edrina started to turn away.

She froze. Turned slowly to look at him with huge china-blue eyes. "You're going to tell Mama I haven't been at school, aren't you?" she asked, sounding sadly resigned to whatever fate awaited her.

"I reckon it's *your* place to tell her that, not mine."

Edrina blinked, and a series of emotions flashed across her face—confusion, hope and, finally, despair. "She'll be sorely vexed when she finds out," the girl said. "Mama places great store in learning."

"Most sensible people do," Clay observed, biting the inside of his lower lip so he wouldn't laugh out loud. Edrina might have been little more than a baby, but she sat a horse like a Comanche brave—he'd seen that for himself back at the depot—and carried herself with a dignity out of all proportion to her size, situation and hand-me-down clothes. "Maybe from now on, you ought to pay better heed to what your mama says. She has your best interests at heart, you know."

Edrina gave a great, theatrical sigh, one that seemed to involve her entire small personage. "I suppose Miss Krenshaw will tell Mama I've been absent since recess, anyway," she said. "Even if *you* don't."

Miss Krenshaw, Clay figured, was probably the schoolmarm.

Outlaw's well-shod hooves made a lonely, *clompety-clip* kind of sound on the hard dirt of the road. The horse turned a little, to go around a trough with a lacy green scum floating atop the water.

"Word's sure to get out," Clay agreed reasonably, thinking of all those faces, at all those windows, "one way or another."

"Thunderation and spit!" Edrina exclaimed, with the vigor of total sincerity. "I don't know why folks can't just tend to their own affairs and leave me to do as I please."

Clay made a choking sound, disguised it as a cough, as best he could, anyway. "How old are you?" he asked, genuinely interested in the answer.

"Six," Edrina replied.

He'd have bet she was a short ten, maybe even eleven. "So you're in the first grade at school?"

"I'm in the second," Edrina said, trudging along beside his horse. "I already knew how to read when I started in September, and I can cipher, too, so Miss Krenshaw let me skip a grade. Actually, she suggested I enter *third* grade, but Mama said no, that wouldn't do at all, because I needed time to be a child. As if I could *help* being a child."

She sounded wholly exasperated.

Clay hid yet another grin by tilting his head, in hopes that his hat brim would cast a shadow over his face. "You'll be all grown up sooner than you think," he allowed. "I reckon if asked, I'd be inclined to take your mama's part in the matter."

"You weren't asked, though," Edrina pointed out thoughtfully, and with an utter lack of guile or rancor.

"True enough," Clay agreed moderately.

They were quiet, passing by the little white church, then the adjoining graveyard, where, Clay speculated, the last marshal, Parnell Nolan, must be buried. Edrina hurried

ahead when they reached the corner, and Clay and Outlaw followed at an easy pace.

Clay hadn't bothered to visit the house that came with
the marshal's job on his previous stopover in Blue River. At
the time, he'd just signed the deed for two thousand acres
of raw ranch land, and his thoughts had been on the house
and barn he meant to build there, the cattle and horses he
would buy, the wells he would dig and the fences he would
put up. He could have waited, of course, bided on the Triple
M until spring, living the life he'd always lived, but he'd
been too impatient and too proud to do that.

Besides, it was his nature to be restless, and so, in order
to keep himself occupied until spring, he'd accepted the
town's offer of a laughable salary and a star-shaped badge
to pin on his coat until they could rustle up some damn
fool to take up the occupation for good.

"There it is," Edrina said, with a note of sadness in her
voice that caught and pulled at Clay's heart like a fishhook
snagging on something underwater.

Clay barely had time to take in the ramshackle place—
the council referred to it as a "cottage," though he would
have called it a shack—before one of the prettiest women
he'd ever laid eyes on shot out through the front door like
a bullet and stormed down the path toward them.

Chickens scattered, clucking and squawking, as she
passed.

Her hair was the color of pale cider, pinned up in back
and fluffing out around her flushed face, as was the fashion among his sisters and female cousins back home in
Arizona. Her eyes might have been blue, but they might
have been green, too, and right now, they were shooting
fire hot enough to brand the toughest hide.

Reaching the rusty-hinged gate in the falling-down

fence, she stopped suddenly, fixed those changeable eyes on him and glared.

Clay felt a jolt inside, as though Zeus had flung a lightning bolt his way and he'd caught it with both hands instead of sidestepping it, like a wiser man would have done.

The woman's gaze sliced to the little girl.

"Edrina Louise Nolan," she said, through a fine set of straight white teeth, "what am I going to do with you?" Her skin was good, too, Clay observed, with that part of his brain that usually stood back and assessed things. Smooth, with a peachy glow underneath.

"Let me go to third grade?" Edrina ventured bravely.

Clay gave an appreciative chuckle, quickly quelled by a glare from the lady. He didn't wither easily, though he knew that was the result she'd intended, and he did take some pleasure in thwarting her.

At that, the woman gave a huffy little sigh and turned her attention back to her daughter. She threw out one arm—like Edrina, she wore calico—and pointed toward the gaping door of the shack. "That will be quite enough of your nonsense, young lady," she said, with a reassuring combination of affection and anger, thrusting open the creaky gate. "Get yourself into the house *now* and prepare to contemplate the error of your ways!"

Before obeying her mother's command, Edrina paused just long enough to look up at Clay, who was still in the saddle, as though hoping he'd intercede.

That was a thing he had no right to do, of course, but he felt a pang on the little girl's behalf just the same. And against his own better judgment he dismounted, took off his hat, holding it in one hand and shoving the other through his hair, fingers splayed.

"You go on and do what your mama tells you," he said

to Edrina, though his words had the tone of a suggestion, rather than a command.

Edrina's very fetching mother looked him over again, this time with something that might have been chagrin. Then she bristled again, like a little bird ruffling up faded feathers. "You're *him,* aren't you?" she accused. "The new marshal?"

"Yes, ma'am," Clay said, confounded by the strange mixture of terror and jubilation rising up within him. "I am the new marshal. And you are...?"

"Dara Rose Nolan. You may address me as *Mrs.* Nolan, if you have any further *reason* to address me, which I do not anticipate."

With that, she turned on one shabby-heeled shoe and pointed herself toward the "cottage," with its sagging roof, leaking rain barrel and sparkling-clean windows.

Edrina and another little girl—the aforementioned Harriet, no doubt—darted out of the doorway as their mother approached, vanishing into the interior of the house.

Clay watched appreciatively as the widow Nolan retreated hurriedly up the walk, with nary a backward glance.

Chickens, pecking peacefully at the ground, squawked and flapped their wings as they fled.

The door slammed behind her.

Clay smiled, resettled his hat and got back on his horse.

Before, he'd dreaded the long and probably idle months ahead, expecting the season to be a lonesome one, and boring, to boot, since he knew nothing much ever happened in Blue River, when it came to crime. That was the main reason the town fathers hadn't been in any big rush to replace Parnell Nolan.

Now, reining Outlaw away toward the edge of town,

and the open country beyond, meaning to ride up onto a ridge he knew of, where the view extended for miles in every direction, Clay figured the coming winter might not be so dull, after all.

INSIDE THE HOUSE, Dara Rose drew a deep breath and sighed it out hard.

Heaven knew, she hadn't been looking forward to the new marshal's arrival, given the problems that were sure to result, but she hadn't planned on losing her composure and behaving rudely, either. Poor as she was, Dara Rose still had high standards, and she believed in setting a good example for her children, prided herself on her good manners and even temperament.

Imagining how she must have looked to Clay McKettrick, rushing out of the house, scaring the chickens half to death in the process, she closed her eyes for a moment, then sighed again.

Edrina and Harriet watched her from the big rocking chair over by the wood-burning stove, Edrina wisely holding her tongue, Harriet perched close beside her, her rag doll, Molly, resting in the curve of one small arm.

The regulator clock ticked ponderously on the wall, lending a solemn rhythm to the silence, and snow swirled past the windows, as if trying to find a way in.

Dara Rose shivered.

"What are we going to do, Mama?" Edrina asked reasonably, and at some length. She was a good child, normally, helpful and even tempered, but her restlessness and curiosity often led her straight into mischief.

Dara Rose looked up at the oval-framed image of her late husband, Parnell Nolan, and her throat thickened as fresh despair swept over her. Despite the scandalous way he died, she missed him, missed the steadiness of his presence, missed his quiet ways and his wit.

"I don't rightly know," Dara Rose admitted, after swallowing hard and blinking back the scalding tears that were always so close to the surface these days. "But never you mind—I'll think of something."

Edrina slipped a reassuring arm around Harriet, who was sucking her thumb.

Dara Rose didn't comment on the thumb-sucking, though it was worrisome to her. Harriet had left that habit behind when she was three, but after Parnell's death, nearly a year ago now, she'd taken it up again. It wasn't hard to figure out why—the poor little thing was frightened and confused.

So was Dara Rose, for that matter, though of course she didn't let on. With heavy-handed generosity, Mayor Ponder and the town council had allowed her and the children to remain in the cottage on the stipulation that they'd have to vacate when a marshal was hired to take Parnell's place.

"Don't worry," Edrina told her sister, tightening her little arm around the child, just briefly. "Mama *always* thinks of something."

It was true that Dara Rose had managed to put food on the table by raising vegetables in her garden patch, taking in sewing and the occasional bundle of laundry and sometimes sweeping floors in the shops and businesses along Main Street. As industrious as she was, however, the pickings were already slim; without the house, the situation would go from worrisome to destitute.

Oh, she had choices—there were always choices, weren't there?—but they were wretched ones.

She could become a lady of the evening over at the Bitter Gulch Saloon and maybe—*maybe*—earn enough to board her children somewhere nearby, where she could see them now and then. How long would it be before they realized how she was earning their living and came to despise her? A year, two years? Three?

Her second option was only slightly more palatable; Ezra Maddox had offered her a job as his cook and housekeeper, on his remote ranch, but he'd plainly stipulated that she couldn't bring her little girls along. In fact, he'd come right out and said she ought to just put Edrina and Harriet in an orphans' home or farm them out to work for their keep. It would be good for their character, he'd claimed.

In fact, the last time he'd come to call, the previous Sunday after church, he'd stood in this very room, beaming at his own generosity, and announced that if Dara Rose measured up, he might even marry her.

The mere thought made her shudder.

And the *audacity* of the man. He expected her to turn her daughters over to strangers and spend the rest of her days darning his socks and cooking his food, and in return, he offered room, board and a pittance in wages. If she "measured up," as he put it, she'd be required to share his bed and give up the salary he'd been paying her, too.

Dara Rose's final prospect was to take her paltry savings—she kept them in a fruit jar, hidden behind the cookstove in the tiny kitchen—purchase train tickets for herself and her children and travel to San Antonio or Dallas or Houston, where she might find honest work and decent lodgings.

But suppose she *didn't* find work? Times were hard. The little bit of money she had would soon be eaten up by living expenses, and *then* what?

Dara Rose knew she'd be paralyzed by these various scenarios if she didn't put them out of her head and get busy doing something constructive, so she headed for the kitchen, meaning to start supper.

Last fall, someone had given her the hindquarter of a deer, and she'd cut the meat into strips and carefully preserved it in jars. There were green beans and corn and stubby orange carrots from the garden, too, along with apples and pears from the fruit trees growing behind the church, and berries she and the girls had gathered during the summer and brought home in lard tins and baskets. Thanks to the chickens, there were plenty of eggs, some of which she sold, and some she traded over at the mercantile for small amounts of sugar and flour and other staples. Once in a great while, she bought tea, but that was a luxury.

She straightened her spine when she realized Edrina had followed her into the little lean-to of a kitchen.

"I like Mr. McKettrick," the child said conversationally. "Don't you?"

Keeping her back to the child, Dara Rose donned her apron and tied it in back with brisk motions of her hands. "My opinion of the new marshal is neither here nor there," she replied. "And don't think for one moment, Edrina Louise Nolan, that I've forgotten that you ran away from school again. You are in serious trouble."

Edrina gave a philosophical little sigh. "How serious?" she wanted to know.

"*Very* serious," Dara Rose answered, adding wood to the fire in the cookstove and jabbing at it with a poker.

"I think we're *all* in serious trouble," Edrina observed sagely.

Out of the mouths of babes, Dara Rose thought.

"Do we have to be orphans now, Mama?" Harriet asked. As usual, she'd followed Edrina.

Dara Rose put the poker back in its stand beside the stove and turned to look at her daughters. Harriet clung to her big sister's hand, looking up at her mother with enormous, worried eyes.

"We are a family," she said, kneeling and wrapping an arm around each of them, pulling them close, drawing in the sweet scent of their hair and skin, "and we are going to stay together. I promise."

Now to find a way to *keep* that promise.

Chapter 2

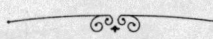

THE SNOW WAS COMING down harder and faster when Clay returned to Blue River from the high ridge, where he'd breathed in the sight of his land, the wide expanse of it and the sheer potential, Outlaw strong and steady beneath him.

Dusk was fast approaching now, and lamps glowed in some of the windows on Main Street, along with the occasional stark dazzle of a lightbulb. Clay had yet to decide whether or not he'd have his place wired for electricity when the time came; like the telephone, it was still a new-fangled invention as far as he was concerned, and he wasn't entirely sure it would last.

At the livery stable, Clay made arrangements for Outlaw and then headed in the direction of the Bitter Gulch Saloon, where he figured the mayor and the town council were most likely to be waiting for him.

Most of the businesses were sealed up tight against the weather, but the saloon's swinging doors were all that stood between the crowded interior and the sidewalk. A piano tinkled a merry if discordant tune somewhere in all that roiling blue cigar smoke, and bottles rattled against the rims of glasses.

The floor was covered in sawdust; the bar was long and ornately carved with various bare-breasted women pouring water into urns decorated with all sorts of flowers and mythical animals and assorted other decorations.

Clay removed his hat, thumped the underside of the brim with one forefinger to knock off the light coating of snow and caught a glimpse of his own reflection in the chipped and murky glass of the mirror in back of the bar.

He didn't commonly frequent saloons, not being much of a drinker, but he knew he'd be dropping in at the Bitter Gulch on a regular basis, once he'd been sworn in as marshal and taken up his duties. Douse the seeds of trouble with enough whiskey and they were bound to take root, break ground and sprout foliage faster than the green beans his ma liked to plant in her garden every spring.

One glance told him he'd been right to look for Mayor Ponder and his cronies here—they'd gathered around a table over in the corner, near the potbellied stove, each with his own glass and his own bottle.

Inwardly, Clay sighed, but he managed a smile as he approached the table, snow melting on the shoulders of his duster.

"Good to see you, Clay," Mayor Ponder said cordially, as one of the others in the party dragged a chair over from a nearby table. "Sent a boy to fetch your trunk from the depot," the older man went on, as Clay joined them, taking the offered seat without removing his coat. He didn't plan on staying long. "You didn't say where you wanted your gear sent, so I told Billy to haul it over to the jailhouse for the time being."

"Thanks," Clay said mildly, setting his hat on the table.

At home, the McKettrick women enforced their own private ordinance against such liberties, on the grounds that it was not only unmannerly, but bad luck and a mite on the slovenly side, too.

"Have a drink with us?" Ponder asked, studying Clay thoughtfully through the shifting haze of smoke. The smell of unwashed bodies and poor dental hygiene was so thick it was nearly visible, and he felt a strong and sudden yearning to be outside again, in the fresh air.

Clay shook his head. "Not now," he said. "It's been a long day, and I'm ready for a meal, a hot bath and a bed."

Ponder cleared his throat. "Speaking of, well, beds, I'm afraid the house we offered you is still occupied. We've been telling Dara Rose that she'd have to move when we found a replacement for Parnell, but so far, she's stayed put."

Dara Rose. Clay smiled slightly at the reminder of the fiery little woman who'd burst through the door of that shack a couple of hours before when he showed up with Edrina, stormed through a flock of cacophonous chickens and let him know, in no uncertain terms, that she wasn't at all glad to see him.

There had been no shortage of women in Clay McKettrick's life—he'd even fallen in love with one, to his eventual sorrow—but none of them had affected him quite the way the widow Nolan did.

"No hurry," Clay said easily, resting his hands on his thighs. "I can get a room at the hotel, or bunk in at the jailhouse."

"The town of Blue River cannot stand good for the cost of lodgings," Ponder said, looking worried. "Having that power line strung all the way out here from Austin depleted our treasury."

One of the other men huffed at that, and poured himself another shot of whiskey. "Hell," he said, with a hiccup, "we're flat busted and up to our hind ends in debt."

Ponder flushed, and his big whiskers quivered along with those heavy jowls of his. "We *can* pay the agreed-upon salary," he stated, after glaring over at his colleague for a long moment. "Seventy-five dollars a month and living quarters, as agreed." He paused, flushed. "I'll speak to Mrs. Nolan in the morning," he clarified. "Tell her she needs to make other arrangements immediately."

"Don't do that," Clay said, quietly but quickly, too. He took a breath, slowed himself down on the inside. "I don't mind paying for a hotel room or sleeping at the jail, for the time being."

The little group exchanged looks.

Snow spun at the few high windows the Bitter Gulch Saloon boasted, like millions of tiny ghosts in search of someplace to haunt.

"A deal," Ponder finally blustered, "is a deal. We offered you a place to live as part of your salary, and we intend to keep our word."

Clay rubbed his chin thoughtfully. His beard was coming in again, even though he'd shaved that morning, on board the train. Nearly cut his own throat in the process, as it happened, because of the way the car jostled along the tracks. "Where are Mrs. Nolan and her little girls likely to wind up?" he asked, hoping he didn't sound too concerned. "Once they've moved out of that house, I mean."

"Ezra Maddox offered for her," said another member of the council. "He's a hard man, old Ezra, but he's got a farm and a herd of dairy cows and money in the bank, and she could do a lot worse when it comes to husbands."

Clay felt a strange stab at the news, deep inside, but he

was careful not to let his reaction show. He felt *something* for Dara Rose Nolan, but what that something was exactly was a matter that would require some sorting out.

"Ezra ain't willing to take the girls along with their mama, though," imparted the first man, pouring himself yet another dose of whiskey and throwing it back without so much as a shudder or a wince. The stuff might have been creek water, for all the effect it seemed to have going down the fellow's gullet. "And he didn't actually offer to marry up with Dara Rose right there at the beginning, either. He means to try her out as a housekeeper before he makes her his wife. Ezra likes to know what he's getting."

Someplace in the middle of Clay's chest, one emotion broke away from the tangle and filled all the space he occupied.

It was pure anger, cold and urgent and prickly around the edges.

What kind of man expects a woman to part with her own children? he wondered, silently furious. His neck turned hot, and he had to release his jaw muscles by force of will.

"Dara Rose is a bit shy on choices at the moment, if you ask me," Ponder put in, taking a defensive tone suggesting he was a friend of Ezra Maddox's and meant to take the man's part if a controversy arose. With a wave of one hand, he indicated their surroundings, including the half dozen saloon girls, waiting tables in their moth-eaten finery. "If she turns Ezra down, she'll wind up right here." He paused to indulge in a slight smile, and Clay underwent another internal struggle just to keep from backhanding the mayor of Blue Creek hard enough to send him sprawling in the dirty sawdust. "Can't say as I'd mind that, really."

Clay seethed, but his expression was schooled to quiet amusement. He'd grown up playing poker with his granddad, his pa and uncles, his many rambunctious cousins, male and female. He knew how to keep his emotions to himself.

Mostly.

"And you a married man," scolded one of the other council members, but his tone was indulgent. "For shame."

Clay pushed his chair back, slowly, and stood. Stretched before retrieving his hat from its place on the table. "I will leave you gentlemen to your discussion," he said, with a slight but ironic emphasis on the word *gentlemen*.

"But we meant to swear you in," Ponder protested. "Make it official."

"Morning will be here soon enough," Clay said, putting his hat on. "I'll meet you at the jailhouse at eight o'clock. Bring a badge and a Bible."

Ponder did not look pleased; he was used to piping the tune, it was obvious, and most folks probably danced to it.

Most folks weren't McKettricks, though.

Clay smiled an idle smile, tugged at the brim of his hat in a gesture of farewell and turned to leave the saloon. Just beyond the swinging doors, he paused on the sidewalk to draw in some fresh air and look up at the sky.

It was snow-shrouded and dark, that sky, and Clay wished for a glimpse, however brief, of the stars.

He'd come to Blue River to start a ranch of his own, marry some good woman and raise a bunch of kids with her, build a legacy comparable to the one his granddad had established on the Triple M. Figuring he'd never love anybody but Annabel Carson, who had made up her mind to wed his cousin Sawyer, come hell or high water, he hadn't been especially stringent with his requirements for a bride.

He wanted a wife and a partner, somebody loyal who'd stand shoulder to shoulder with him in good times and bad.

She had to be smart and have a sense of humor—ranching was too hard a life for folks lacking in those characteristics, in his opinion—but she didn't necessarily have to be pretty.

Annabel was mighty easy on the eyes, after all, and look where *that* got him. Up shit creek without a paddle, that was where. She'd claimed to love Clay with her whole heart, but at the first disagreement, she'd thrown his promise ring in his face and gone chasing after Sawyer.

Even now, all these months later, the recollection carried a powerful sting, racing through Clay's veins like snake venom.

Crossing the street to the town's only hotel, its electric lights glowing a dull gold at the downstairs windows, Clay rode out the sensation, the way he'd trained himself to do, but a remarkable thing happened at the point when Annabel's face usually loomed up in his mind's eye.

He saw Dara Rose Nolan there instead.

BY THE TIME DARA ROSE got up the next morning, washed and dressed and built up the fires, then headed out to feed and water the chickens and gather the eggs, the snow had stopped, the ground was bare and the sky was a soft blue.

She hadn't slept well, but the crisp bite of approaching winter cleared some of the cobwebs from her beleaguered brain, and she smiled as she worked. Her situation was as dire as ever, of course, but daylight invariably raised her hopes and quieted her fears.

When the sun was up, she could believe things would work out in the long run if she did her best and maintained her faith.

She *would* find a way to earn an honest living and keep

her family together. She had to believe that to keep putting one foot in front of the other.

This very day, as soon as the children had had their breakfast and Edrina had gone off to school, Dara Rose decided, flinging out ground corn for the chickens, now clucking and flapping around her skirts and pecking at the ground, she and her youngest daughter would set out to knock on every respectable door in town if they had to.

Someone in Blue River surely needed a cook, a house-keeper, a nurse or some combination thereof. She'd work for room and board, for herself and the girls, and they wouldn't take up much space, the three of them. What little cash they needed, she could earn by taking in sewing.

The idea wasn't new, and it wasn't likely to come to fruition, either, given that most people in town were only a little better off than she was and therefore not in the market for household help, but it heartened Dara Rose a little, just the same, as she finished feeding the chickens, dusted her hands together and went to retrieve the egg basket, hanging by its handle from a nail near the back door.

Holding her skirts up with one hand, Dara Rose ducked into the tumbledown chicken coop and began gathering eggs from the straw where the hens roosted.

That morning, there were more than a dozen—fifteen, by her count—which meant she and Edrina and Harriet could each have one for breakfast. The remainder could be traded at the mercantile for salt—she was running a little low on that—and perhaps some lard and a small scoop of white sugar.

Thinking these thoughts, Dara Rose was humming under her breath as she left the chicken coop, carrying the egg basket.

She nearly dropped the whole bunch of them right to

the ground when she caught sight of the new marshal, riding his fancy spotted horse, reining in just the other side of the fence, a shiny nickel star gleaming on his worn coat.

It made him look like a gunslinger, that long coat, and the round-brimmed hat only added to the rakish impression.

Already bristling, Dara Rose drew a deep breath and rustled up a smile. It wasn't as if the man existed merely to irritate and inconvenience *her,* after all.

The marshal, swinging down out of the saddle and approaching the rickety side gate to stroll, bold as anything, into her yard, did not smile back.

Dara Rose's high hopes shriveled instantly as the obvious finally struck her: Clay McKettrick had come to send her and the children packing. He'd want to move himself—and possibly a family—in, and soon. The fact that he had a fair claim to the house did nothing whatsoever to make her feel better.

"Mornin'," he said, standing directly in front of her now, and pulling politely at the brim of his hat before taking it off.

"Good morning," Dara Rose replied cautiously, still mindful of her rudeness the day before and the regret it had caused her. Her gaze moved to the polished star pinned to his coat, and she felt an achy twinge of loss, remembering Parnell.

Poor, well-meaning, chivalrous Parnell.

Greetings exchanged, both of them just stood there looking at each other, for what seemed like a long time.

Finally, Marshal McKettrick cleared his throat, holding his hat in both hands now, and the wintry sun caught in his dark hair. He looked as clean as could be, standing there, his clothes fresh, except for the coat, and his boots brushed to a shine.

Dara Rose felt a small, peculiar shift in a place behind her heart.

"I just wanted to say," the man began awkwardly, inclining his head toward the house, "that there's no need for you and the kids to clear out right away. I spent last night at the hotel, but there's a cot and a stove at the jailhouse, and that will suit me fine for now."

Dara Rose's throat tightened, and the backs of her eyes burned. She didn't quite dare to believe her own ears. "But you're entitled to live here," she reminded him, and then could have nipped off her tongue. "And surely your wife wouldn't want to set up housekeeping in a—"

In that instant, the awkwardness was gone. The marshal's mouth slanted in a grin, and mischief sparkled in his eyes. They were the color of new denim, those eyes.

"I don't have a wife," he said simply. "Not yet, anyhow."

That grin. It did something unnerving to Dara Rose's insides.

Her heartbeat quickened inexplicably, nearly racing, then fairly lurched to a stop. Did Clay McKettrick expect something in return for his kindness? If he was looking for favors, he was going to be disappointed, because she wasn't that kind of woman.

Not anymore.

"It's almost Christmas," Clay said, assessing the sky briefly before meeting her gaze again.

Confused, Dara Rose squinted up at him. Christmas was important to Edrina and Harriet, as it was to most children, but it was the least of her own concerns.

"Do you need spectacles?" Clay asked.

Taken aback by the question, Dara Rose opened her

mouth to speak, found herself at a complete loss for words and pressed her lips together. Then she shook her head.

Clay McKettrick chuckled and reached for the egg basket.

It wasn't heavy, and the contents were precious, but Dara Rose offered no resistance. She let him take it.

"Where did Edrina learn to ride a horse?" he asked.

They were moving now, heading slowly toward the house, as though it were the least bit proper for the two of them to be behind closed doors together.

Dara Rose blinked, feeling as muddled as if he'd spoken to her in a foreign language instead of plain English. "I beg your pardon?"

They stepped into the small kitchen, with its slanted wall and iron cookstove, Dara Rose in the lead, and the marshal set the basket of eggs on the table, which was comprised of two barrels with a board nailed across their tops.

"Edrina was there to meet Outlaw and me when we got off the train yesterday," Clay explained quietly, keeping his distance and folding his arms loosely across his chest. "The child has a way with horses."

Dara Rose heard the girls stirring in the tiny room the three of them shared, just off the kitchen, and such a rush of love for her babies came over her that she almost teared up. "Yes," she said. "Parnell—my husband—kept a strawberry roan named Gawain. Edrina's been quite at home in the saddle since she was a tiny thing."

"What happened to him?" Clay asked.

"Parnell?" Dara Rose asked stupidly, feeling her cheeks go crimson.

"I know what happened to your husband, ma'am," Clay said quietly. "I was asking about the horse."

Dara Rose felt dazed, but she straightened her spine

and looked Clay McKettrick in the eye. "We had to sell Gawain after my husband died," she said. It was the simple truth, and almost as much of a sore spot as Parnell's death. They'd all loved the gelding, but Ezra Maddox had offered a good price for him, and Dara Rose had needed the money for food and firewood and kerosene for the lamps.

Edrina, already mourning the man she'd believed to be her father, had cried for days.

"I see," Clay said gravely, a bright smile breaking over his handsome face like a sunrise as Edrina and Harriet hopped into the room and hurried to stand by the stove, wearing their calico dresses but no shoes or stockings.

"Do we have to go live in the poorhouse now?" Harriet asked, groping for Edrina's hand, finding it and evidently forgetting that the floor was cold enough to sting her bare feet. In the dead of winter, the planks sometimes frosted over.

To Dara Rose's surprise, Clay crouched, putting himself nearly at eye level with both children. He kept his balance easily, still holding his hat, and when his coat opened a ways, she caught an ominous glimpse of the gun belt buckled around his lean hips.

"You don't have to go anywhere," he said, very solemnly.

Edrina's eyes widened. Her unbrushed curls rioted around her face, like gold in motion, and her bow-shaped lips formed a smile. "Really and truly?" she asked. "We can stay here?"

Clay nodded.

"But where will *you* live?" Harriet wanted to know. Like her sister, she was astute and well-spoken. Dara Rose had never used baby talk with her girls, and she'd been reading aloud to them since before they were born.

"I'll be fine over at the jailhouse, at least until spring," Clay replied, rising once again to his full height. He was tall, this man from Arizona, broad through the shoulders and thick in the chest, but the impression he gave was of leanness and agility. He was probably fast with that pistol he carried, Dara Rose thought, and was disturbed by the knowledge.

It was the twentieth century, after all, and the West was no longer wild. Hardly anyone, save sheriffs and marshals, carried a firearm.

"I'm going to school today," Edrina announced happily, "and I plan on staying until Miss Krenshaw rings the bell at three o'clock, too."

Clay crooked a smile, but his gaze, Dara Rose discovered, had found its way back to her. "That's good," he said.

"Why don't you stay for breakfast?" Edrina asked the man wearing her father's badge pinned to his coat.

"Edrina," Dara Rose almost whispered, embarrassed.

"I've already eaten," Clay replied. "Had the ham and egg special in the hotel dining room before Mayor Ponder swore me in."

"Oh," Edrina said, clearly disappointed.

"That's a fine horse, mister," Harriet chimed in, her head tipped way back so she could look up into Clay's recently shaven face.

Dara Rose was still trying to bring the newest blush in her cheeks under control, and she could only manage that by avoiding Clay McKettrick's eyes.

"Yes, indeed," Clay answered the child. "His name's Outlaw, but you can't go by that. He's a good old cayuse."

"I got to ride him yesterday, down by the railroad tracks," Edrina boasted. Then her face fell a little. "Sort of."

"If it's all right with your mother," Clay offered, "and you go to school like you ought to, you can ride Outlaw again."

"Me, too?" Harriet asked, breathless with excitement at the prospect.

Clay caught Dara Rose's gaze again. "That's your mother's decision to make, not mine," he said, so at home in his own skin that she wondered what kind of life he'd led, before his arrival in Blue River. An easy one, most likely.

But something in his eyes refuted that.

"We'll see," Dara Rose said.

Both girls groaned, wanting a "yes" instead of a "maybe."

"I'd best be getting on with my day," Clay said, with another slow, crooked grin.

And then he was at the door, ducking his head so he wouldn't bump it, putting on his hat and walking away.

Dara Rose watched through the little window over the sink until he'd gone through the side gate and mounted his horse.

"We don't have to go to the orphanage!" Harriet crowed, clapping her plump little hands in celebration.

"There will be no more talk of orphanages," Dara Rose decreed briskly, pumping water at the rusty sink to wash her hands.

"Does Mr. McKettrick have a wife?" Edrina piped up. "Because if he doesn't, you could marry him. I don't think he'd send Harriet and me away, like Mr. Maddox wants to do."

Dara Rose kept her back to her daughters as she began breakfast preparations, using all her considerable willpower to keep her voice calm and even. "That's none of your business," she said firmly. "Nor mine, either. And don't you *dare* pry into Mr. McKettrick's private affairs by asking, either one of you."

Both girls sighed at this.

"Go get your shoes and stockings on," Dara Rose ordered, setting the cast-iron skillet on the stove, plopping in the last smidgeon of bacon grease to keep the eggs from sticking.

"I need to go to the outhouse," Harriet said.

"Put your shoes on first," Dara Rose countered. "It's a nice day out, but the ground is cold."

The children obeyed readily, which threw her a little. She was raising her daughters to have minds of their own, but that meant they were often obstinate and sometimes even defiant.

Parnell had accused her of spoiling them, though he'd indulged the girls plenty himself, buying them hair ribbons and peppermint sticks and letting them ride his horse. Edrina, rough and tumble as any boy but at the same time all girl, was virtually fearless as well as outspoken, and trying as the child sometimes was, Dara Rose wouldn't have changed anything about her. Except, of course, for her tendency to play hooky from school.

Harriet, just a year younger than her sister, was more tentative, less likely to take risks than Edrina was. Too small to really understand death, Harriet very probably expected her papa to come home one day, riding Gawain, his saddlebags bulging with presents.

Dara Rose's eyes smarted again and, inwardly, she brought herself up short.

She and the girls had been given a reprieve, that was all. They could go on living in the marshal's house for a while, but other arrangements would have to be made eventually, just the same.

Which was why, when she and the girls had eaten, and the dishes had been washed and the fires banked, Dara Rose followed through with her original plan.

She and Harriet walked Edrina to the one-room schoolhouse at the edge of town, and then took the eggs to the mercantile, to be traded for staples.

It was warm inside the general store, and Harriet became so captivated by the lovely doll on display in the tinsel-draped front window that Dara Rose feared the child would refuse to leave the place at all.

"Look, Mama," she breathed, without taking her eyes from the beautiful toy when Dara Rose approached and took her hand. "Isn't she pretty? She's almost as tall as *I am*."

"She's pretty," Dara Rose conceded, trying to keep the sadness out of her voice. "But not nearly as pretty as you are."

Harriet looked up at her, enchanted. "Edrina says there's no such person as St. Nicholas," she said. "She says it was you and Papa who filled our stockings last Christmas Eve."

Dara Rose's throat ached. She had to swallow before she replied, "Edrina is right, sweetheart," she said hoarsely. Other people could afford to pretend that magical things happened, at least while their children were young, but she did not have that luxury.

"I guess the doll probably costs a lot," Harriet said, her voice small and wistful.

Dara Rose checked the price tag dangling from the doll's delicate wrist, though she already knew it would be far out of her reach.

Two dollars and fifty cents.

What was the world coming to?

"She comes with a trunk full of clothes," the storekeeper

put in helpfully. Philo Bickham meant well, to be sure, but he wasn't the most thoughtful man on earth. "That's real human hair on her head, too, and she came all the way from Germany."

Harriet's eyes widened with something that might have been alarm. "But didn't the hair *belong* to someone?" she asked, no doubt picturing a bald child wandering sadly through the Black Forest.

"People sometimes sell their hair," Dara Rose explained, giving Mr. Bickham a less than friendly glance as she drew her daughter toward the door. "And then it grows back."

Harriet immediately brightened. "Could we sell *my* hair? For two dollars and fifty cents?"

"No," Dara Rose said, and instantly regretted speaking so abruptly. She dropped to her haunches, tucked stray golden curls into Harriet's tattered bonnet. "Your hair is much too beautiful to sell, sweetheart."

"But I could grow more," Harriet reasoned. "You said so yourself, Mama."

Dara Rose smiled, mainly to keep from crying, and stood very straight, juggling the egg basket, now containing a small tin of lard, roughly three-quarters of a cup of sugar scooped into a paper sack and a box of table salt, from one wrist to the other.

"We'll be on our way now, Harriet," she said. "We have things to do."

Chapter 3

<hr>

AS HE RODE SLOWLY ALONG every street in Blue River that morning, touching his hat brim to all he encountered so the town folks would know they had a marshal again, one who meant to live up to the accompanying responsibilities, Clay found himself thinking about Parnell Nolan. Blessed with a beautiful wife and two fine daughters, and well-liked from what little Clay had learned about him, Nolan had still managed to be in a whorehouse when he drew his last breath.

Yes, plenty of men indulged themselves in brothels—bachelors and husbands, sons and fathers alike—but they usually exercised some degree of discretion, in Clay's experience.

Always inclined to give somebody the benefit of the doubt, at least until they'd proven themselves unworthy of the courtesy, Clay figured Parnell might have done his sinning in secret, with the notion that he was therefore protecting his wife and children from scandal. But Blue River was a small place, like Clay's hometown of Indian

Rock, and stories that were too good not to tell had a way
of getting around. Fast.

Of course, Nolan surely hadn't planned on dying that
particular night, in the midst of awkward circumstances.

Reaching the end of the last street in town, near the
schoolhouse, Clay stopped to watch, leaning on the pom-
mel of his saddle and letting Outlaw nibble at the patchy
grass, as children spilled out the door of the little red building, shouting to one another, eager to make the most of
recess.

He spotted Edrina right away—her bonnet hung down
her back by its laces, revealing that unmistakable head of
spun-gold hair, and her cheeks glowed with exuberance
and good health and the nippy coolness of the weather.

As Clay watched, she found a stick, etched the squares
for a game of hopscotch in the bare dirt and jumped right
in. Within moments, the other little girls were clamoring
to join her, while the boys played kick-the-can at an artfully disdainful distance, making as much racket as they
could muster up.

The schoolmarm—a plain woman, spare and tall, and
probably younger than she looked—surveyed the melee
from the steps of the building, but she was quick to notice
the horse and rider looking on from the road.

Clay tugged at his hat brim and nodded a silent greeting. His ma, Chloe, had been a schoolteacher when she
was younger, and he had an ingrained respect for the profession. It was invariably a hard row to hoe.

The teacher nodded back, descended the schoolhouse
steps with care, lest she trip over the hem of her brown
woolen dress. Instead of a coat or a cloak, she wore a dark
blue shawl to keep warm.

Clay waited as she approached, then dismounted to meet

her at the gate, though he kept to his own side and she kept to hers, as was proper.

The lady introduced herself. "Miss Alvira Krenshaw," she said, putting out a bony hand. She hadn't missed the star pinned to his coat, of course; her eyes had gone right to it. "You must be our new town marshal."

Clay shook her hand and acknowledged her supposition with another nod and, "Clay McKettrick."

"How do you do?" she said, not expecting an answer.

Clay gave her one, anyway. "So far, so good," he replied, with a slight grin. Miss Alvira Krenshaw looked like a sturdy, no-nonsense soul, and although she wasn't pretty, she wasn't homely, either. She'd probably make some man a good wife, given half a chance, and though thin, she looked capable of carrying healthy babies to full-term, delivering them without a lot of fuss and raising them to competent adulthood.

Wanting a wife to carry over the threshold of his new house, come spring, and impregnate as soon as possible, Clay might have set right to courting Miss Alvira, provided she was receptive to such attentions, if not for one problem. He'd gone and met Dara Rose Nolan.

Stepping off the train the day before, he'd been sure of almost everything that concerned him. What he wanted, what sort of man he was, all of it. Now, after just two brief encounters with his predecessor's widow, he wasn't sure of much of *anything*.

Considerable figuring out would be called for before he undertook to win himself a bride, and that was for certain.

Over Alvira's shoulder, he saw a boy run over to where the girls were playing hopscotch, grab at Edrina's dangling bonnet and yank on it hard enough to knock her down.

The bonnet laces held, though, and the boy ran, laughing, his friends shouting a mingling of mockery and encouragement, while a disgruntled, flaming-faced Edrina got back to her feet, dusting off her coat as she glared at the transgressor.

"Looks like trouble," Clay observed dryly, causing Miss Alvira to flare out her long, narrow nostrils and then spin around to see for herself.

Edrina, still flushed with fury, marched right into the middle of that cluster of small but earnest rascals, stood face-to-face with the primary mischief-maker and landed a solid punch to his middle. Knocked the wind right out of him.

Miss Alvira was on the run by then, blowing shrill toots through the whistle every schoolmarm seemed to come equipped with, but the damage, such as it was, was done.

The thwarted bonnet thief was on his knees now, clutching his belly and gasping for breath, and though his dignity had certainly suffered, he didn't look seriously hurt.

Clay suppressed a smile and lingered there by the gate, watching.

Edrina looked a mite calmer by then, but she was still pink in the face and her fists remained clenched. She stood her ground, spotted Clay when she turned her head toward Miss Alvira and that earsplitting whistle of hers.

"What is going on here?" Alvira demanded, her voice carrying, almost as shrill as the whistle. She reached down, caught the gasping boy from behind, where his suspenders crossed, and wrenched him unceremoniously to his feet.

Clay felt a flash of sympathy for the little fellow. Like as not, he'd taken a shine to Edrina and, boys being what boys have always been, hoped to gain her notice by snatching her bonnet and running off with it—the equivalent of tugging at a girl's pigtail or surprising her with a close-up look at a bullfrog or a squirmy garter snake, and glory be and hallelujah if she squealed.

Miss Alvira, still gripping the boy's suspenders, turned to frown at Edrina.

"Edrina Nolan," she said, "young ladies do not strike others with their fists."

Edrina, who had been looking in Clay's direction until that moment, faced her accuser, folded her arms and staunchly replied, "He had it coming."

"Go inside this instant," Alvira ordered both children, indicating the open door of the schoolhouse with a pointing of her index finger. "Thomas, you will stand in the corner behind my desk, by the bookcase. Edrina, you will occupy the one next to the cloakroom."

"For how long?" Edrina wanted to know.

Clay had to admire the child's spirit.

"Until I tell you that you may take your seats," Miss Alvira answered firmly, shooing the rest of her brood toward the hallowed halls of learning with a waving motion of her free arm. "Inside," she called. "All of you. Recess is over."

The command elicited groans of protest, but the children obeyed.

Thomas, clearly humiliated because he'd been publicly bested by a girl, slunk, head down, toward the schoolhouse, and Edrina followed in her own time, literally dragging her feet by scuffing the toe of first one shoe and then the other in the dirt as she walked. Finally, she looked back over one shoulder, caught Clay's eye and gave an eloquent little shrug of resignation.

He hoped the distance and the shadow cast by the brim of his hat would hide his smile.

That kid should have been born a McKettrick.

DARA ROSE MADE THE ROUNDS that morning just as she'd planned, swallowing her pride and knocking on each door to ask for work, with little Harriet trudging along, uncomplaining, at her side.

There were only half a dozen real *houses* in Blue River; the rest were mostly hovels and shanties, shacks like the one she lived in. The folks there were no better off than she was and, in many cases, things were worse for them. Thin smoke wafted from crooked chimneys and scrawny chickens pecked at the small expanses of bare dirt that passed for yards.

Mrs. O'Reilly, whose husband had run off with a dance hall girl six months ago and left her with three children to look after, all of them under five years old, was outside. The woman was probably in her early twenties, but she looked a generation older; there were already streaks of gray at her temples and she'd lost one of her eye teeth.

She had a bonfire going, with a big tin washtub teetering atop the works, full of other people's laundry. Steam boiled up into the crisp air as she stirred the soapy soup, and Peg O'Reilly managed a semblance of a smile when she caught sight of Dara Rose and Harriet.

Two of the O'Reilly children, both boys, ran whooping around their mother like Sioux braves on the warpath, both of them barefoot and coatless. Their older sister, Addie, must have been inside, where it was, Dara Rose devoutly hoped, comparatively warm.

"Mornin', Miz Nolan," Peg called, though she didn't smile. She was probably self-conscious about that missing tooth, Dara Rose figured, with a stab of well-hidden pity.

Dara Rose smiled, offered a wave and paused at the edge of the road, even though she'd meant to keep going. Lord knew, she had reason enough to be discouraged herself, after being turned away from all those doors, but she just couldn't bring herself to pass on by.

Harriet, no doubt weary from keeping up with Dara Rose all morning, tugged reluctantly at her mother's hand, wanting to go on.

"How's Addie?" Dara Rose asked.

"She's poorly," Peg replied. "Been abed since yesterday, so she's not much help with these little yahoos." Still tending to the wash, which was just coming to a simmer, she indicated the boys with a nod of her head.

They had both stopped their chasing game to stare at Harriet in abject wonder. Even in her poor clothes and the shoes she would outgrow all too soon, she probably looked as pretty to them as that doll over at the mercantile did to her.

"Mama," Harriet whispered, looking up at Dara Rose from beneath the drooping brim of her bonnet, "what's that smell?"

"Hush," Dara Rose whispered back, hoping Peg hadn't heard the little girl's voice over the crackling of the fire and the barking of a neighbor's dog.

Peg let go of the old broomstick she used to stir the shirts and trousers and small clothes as they soaked, and wiped a forearm across her brow. The sleeves of her calico dress were rolled up to her elbows, and her apron was little more than a rag.

"Could you use some eggs?" Dara Rose asked, in the manner of one asking a favor. "I've got plenty put by."

A flicker of yearning showed in Peg O'Reilly's careworn face before she squared her shoulders and raised her chin a notch. "I'd say no, on grounds that I've got my pride and I know you're having a hard time of it, too, but for the young'uns," she replied. "The last of the oatmeal is used up, and we're almost out of pinto beans, but a nice fried egg might put some color in Addie's cheeks and that's for sure."

"I'll send Edrina over with a basket right after she gets home from school," Dara Rose said.

"You understand that I can't pay you nothin'," Peg warned, stiffening her backbone.

"I understand," Dara Rose confirmed lightly, though every egg her hens laid was precious, since it could be sold for cash money or traded for things she couldn't raise, like flour. "I've got too many, and I don't want them to go to waste."

"Mama," Harriet interjected, "we don't—"

This time, Dara Rose didn't hush her daughter out loud, but simply squeezed the child's hand a little more tightly than she might otherwise have done.

"Obliged, then," Peg said, and went back to her stirring.

Dara Rose nodded and started off toward home again, poor Harriet scrambling to keep up.

"Mama," the child insisted, half-breathless, "you already traded away all the eggs, remember? Over at the mercantile? And the hens probably haven't laid any new ones yet."

"There are nearly two dozen in the crock on the pantry shelf," Dara Rose reminded her daughter. Like the potatoes, carrots, turnips and onions she'd squirreled away down in the root cellar, along with a few bushels of apples from the tree in her yard, the eggs suspended in water glass were part of her skimpy reserves, something she and the girls could eat if the hens stopped laying or the hawks got them.

"Yes," Harriet reasoned, intrepidly logical, "but what if there's a hard winter and *we* need to eat them?"

"Harriet," Dara Rose replied, walking a little faster because it was almost time for Edrina to come home for the midday meal, "there are times when a person simply has to help somebody who needs a hand and hope the good Lord pays heed and makes recompense." Parting with a few eggs didn't trouble her nearly as much as the realization that her five-year-old daughter had obviously been worrying about whether or not there would be enough food to get them through.

"What's 'recompense'?" Harriet asked.

"Never mind," Dara Rose answered.

They reached the house, removed their bonnets and their wraps—Dara Rose's cloak and Harriet's coat—and Dara Rose ladled warm water out of the stove reservoir for the washing of hands.

In her mind, she heard Peg O'Reilly's words of brave despair. *The last of the oatmeal is used up, and we're almost out of pinto beans....*

Peg earned a pittance taking in laundry as it was, and what little money she earned probably went to pay for starvation rations and to meet the rent on that converted chicken coop of a house they all lived in.

As she reheated the canned venison leftover from last night's supper, then sliced and thinly buttered the last of the bread she'd made a few days before, Dara Rose silently reminded herself of something Parnell had often told her. "No matter how tough things get," he used to say, "you won't have to look far to find somebody else who'd be glad to trade places with you."

Her children were healthy, unlike Peg's eldest, and the three of them had a roof over their heads. And Parnell, at least, hadn't left them willingly, the way Jack O'Reilly had done.

Harriet, her mother's busy little helper, set three places

at the table and then dragged a chair over to the side window so she could stand on the seat and keep a lookout for her sister. Although they had their scuffles and tiffs, like all children, Harriet's admiration for Edrina knew no bounds.

"There she is!" Harriet shouted gleefully, after a few moments of peering through the glass. "There's Edrina!"

Dara Rose smiled and began ladling warm venison and broth into enamel-coated bowls. She'd just set the bread plate in the middle of the improvised table when Edrina dragged in, looking despondent.

"You might as well know straightaway that I'm in trouble again," she immediately confessed. "Thomas Phillips tried to steal my bonnet at recess, and near strangled me with the ties while he was at it, and I socked him in the stomach. Miss Krenshaw made me stand in the corner for a whole hour, and I have to stay after school to wash the blackboard every day this week."

Dara Rose sighed, shook her head in feigned dismay and placed her hands on her hips. "Edrina," she said, on a long breath, and shook her head again.

"Did Thomas have to stand in the corner, too?" Harriet inquired, already a great believer in fair play.

"Yes," Edrina answered, with precious little satisfaction. "He has to carry in the drinking water for the whole school."

"Wash your hands," Dara Rose said mildly, when her elder daughter would have sat down to her meal instead.

Edrina obeyed, with a sigh of her own, and pulled the stool out from under the sink to climb up and plunge her small hands into the basin of warm water Dara Rose had set there.

"Mr. McKettrick came by the schoolhouse today," the child announced. "That sure is a fine horse he rides."

Dara Rose felt an odd little catch at the mention of the new marshal and, to her shame, caught herself wondering if he'd found Alvira Krenshaw at all fetching. She was certainly eligible, Miss Krenshaw was, and while she wouldn't win any prizes for looks, most people agreed that she was a handsome woman with a good head on her shoulders.

"Was there some kind of trouble? Besides your disagreement with Thomas?"

Edrina had finished washing up, and she climbed deftly back down off the stool, drying her hands on her skirts as she approached the table. "No," she replied, "but he talked to Miss Krenshaw at the gate for a long time."

Dara Rose, who had long since learned to choose her battles, decided to let the hand-drying incident pass. She hoisted Harriet onto the stool, helped her lather to her elbows and then rinse and lifted her down again.

The three of them gathered at the table.

It was Harriet's turn to say grace. "Thank you for the venison and the bread," she said, in her direct way, her bright head bowed and her eyes squeezed shut. "And if there's any way I could get that pretty doll in the window of the mercantile for my very own, I would appreciate the kindness. Amen."

Dara Rose suppressed a smile even as she endured another pang to her heart. Much as she'd have loved to give her daughters toys for Christmas, she couldn't afford to do it. And even if she'd had any spare money at all, Edrina and Harriet needed shoes and warm clothes and nourishing food, like milk.

"What do you want St. Nicholas to bring you for Christmas?" Harriet asked Edrina, with companionable interest, as they all began to eat.

Edrina answered without hesitation, a note of gentle tolerance in her voice. "You know there isn't any St. Nicholas, Harriet," she reminded her sister. "He's just a story person, made up by that Mr. Moore."

"Couldn't we just *pretend* he's real?" Harriet wanted to know. "Just 'til lunch is over?" She sounded more like an adult than a little girl and Dara Rose, though proud of her bright daughters, hoped they weren't growing up too fast.

"It wouldn't hurt to pretend," she put in quietly.

Harriet's face lit up. "What do *you* want for Christmas, Mama?" she asked eagerly, forgetting all about her food.

Dara Rose pretended to think very hard for a few moments. "A cow, I think," she finally decided. "Then we'd have milk and butter of our own. Maybe even cheese."

Harriet looked nonplussed. "A cow?" she repeated.

Edrina glanced at Dara Rose, her expression almost conspiratorial, and considered the question under discussion. "I know what *I'd* want," she said presently. "Books. Exciting ones, with bears and outlaws and spooks in them."

Again, Dara Rose's heart pinched. She'd be lucky to afford peppermint sticks to drop into the girls' Christmas stockings this year, never mind dolls and books.

She cleared her throat. "Harriet and I stopped by the O'Reilly place today," she said. "Little Addie's under the weather again, and those boys looked hungry enough to dip spoons into the laundry kettle."

"And something smells bad there," Harriet added.

Dara Rose didn't scold her, but went right on. "I think they'd be grateful to have firewood and enough to eat, like we do," she said, hoping she'd made her point and wouldn't have to follow up with a sermon on Christian charity.

"Mama's giving them some of our eggs," Harriet said matter-of-factly. "She says sometimes a person just has to help somebody else and hope the good Lord pays heed and makes competition."

Edrina didn't say anything, since she had a mouthful of bread.

Dara Rose wondered if Harriet even knew what it meant to pay heed. "The two of you can take a basket over to the O'Reillys', as soon as school's out for the day," she said. "And furthermore, Harriet Nolan, you will *not* remark on the bad smell."

"It's probably the outhouse that stinks," Edrina said. "Ours might get that way, too, without Papa around to shovel lye into it once in a while."

"Edrina," Dara Rose said, "we are at the table."

A long pause ensued.

"I have to stay after to wash the blackboard," Edrina reminded her mother.

"Fine," Dara Rose answered, pushing back her chair and carrying her bowl and spoon to the sink. "I'll wash the eggs and put them in the basket and you can drop them off at the O'Reilly place on your way back to school."

"There will be hell to pay if I'm late for class," Edrina said frankly. "Don't forget, I'm already in trouble for slugging Thomas Phillips in the stomach."

Dara Rose bit the inside of her lower lip to keep from smiling. "I won't forget," she said, heading for the single shelf that served as a pantry, bowl in hand, and fishing eight perfect brown ovals out of the crock filled to the brim with water glass. "If you hurry, you can deliver the eggs and still get back to school before Miss Krenshaw rings the bell. *And* I will thank you not to swear, Edrina Nolan."

Harriet, who staunchly maintained that she was too

old to take naps, was already getting heavy-lidded, chin drooping, and yawning a little.

Dara Rose washed the eggs and put them into the basket, covering them with a flour-sack dish towel. She handed them to Edrina, who was already buttoning her coat. "Wear your bonnet," she instructed. "The sky may be blue as summer, but the wind has a bite to it."

Edrina nodded, resigned, and let herself out, taking the egg basket with her.

"Bring that basket home," Dara Rose called after her. "And the dish towel, too."

Edrina replied, but Dara Rose didn't hear what she said. She was already scooping up her sleepy child and carrying her to bed.

CLAY CHECKED THE BITTER Gulch Saloon and looked in at the bank, but there was no malfeasance afoot in either place.

Figuring it was indeed going to be a long winter, he walked back to the jailhouse, where he had a tiny office, a potbellied stove and a cot, and helped himself to a cup of the passable coffee he'd made earlier.

The stuff was stale and lukewarm, but stout enough to rouse a dead man from his eternal rest.

That, he supposed, was what this coming winter was going to feel like. Eternal rest.

He sighed, crossed to the single cell and peered through the bars, almost wishing he had a prisoner. That way, there would have been somebody to talk to, at least.

Alas, lawbreakers seemed to be pretty thin on the ground around those parts at the moment, a fact he supposed he should have been grateful to note.

Clay sat down in the creaky wooden chair behind the

scarred wooden table that served as a desk and reached for the dusty stack of wanted posters and old mail piled on one corner.

If anybody stopped by, he'd like to give the impression that he was working, even if he wasn't. It made him smile to imagine what his granddad would think if he could see him now, collecting seventy-five dollars a month for doing not much of anything except drinking bad coffee and flipping through somebody else's correspondence.

He set aside the older wanted posters and read the few missives that looked even remotely official—none of them were, it turned out—and he was thinking maybe he ought to meander over to the livery stable and brush old Outlaw down, when he came to the last two letters and realized they were addressed to Mrs. Parnell B. Nolan.

The first, from an outfit called the Wildflower Salve Company, was most likely a sales pitch of some kind, but the second looked personal and smelled faintly of lemon verbena. The envelope was fat, made of good vellum, and the handwriting on the front was flowing cursive, with all kinds of loops and swirls.

Clay looked at the postmark, but couldn't make out where the letter had been mailed, or when, and there wasn't any return address.

Not that any of this was his concern in the first place.

Clay frowned, wondering how long the letters had been moldering in that pile, and then he smiled, holding the envelopes in one hand and lightly slapping them against the opposite palm.

Maybe it wasn't his sworn duty to make sure the mail got delivered, but it was as good an excuse as any for calling on Dara Rose Nolan.

Clay rose from his chair, fetched his coat and hat and set out on foot.

THERE HE STOOD, on her front doorstep this time, looking affably handsome.

For the briefest fraction of a moment, Dara Rose feared that Clay McKettrick had changed his mind, decided he wanted the house, after all. Her stomach quivered in a peculiar way that didn't seem to have much to do with the fear of eviction.

"I found these letters over at the office," he said, and produced two envelopes from an inside pocket of his duster. "They're addressed to you."

Dara Rose's eyes rounded. Getting a letter was a rare thing indeed. Getting two at once was virtually unheard-of.

She opened the door a little wider, extended a hand for the envelopes and spoke very quietly because Harriet was napping. "Thank you," she said.

He let her take the envelopes, but he held on to them for a second longer than necessary, too.

Although her curiosity was great, Dara Rose wanted to savor the prospect of those letters for a little while. She'd read them later, by lamplight, when the girls were both down for the night and the house was quiet.

She tucked them into the pocket of her apron, blushing a little.

"Come in," she heard her own voice say, much to her surprise.

It simply wasn't proper for a widow to invite a man into her home, even in broad daylight, but she'd done just that and already stepped back so he could pass, and the marshal didn't hesitate to step over the threshold.

He stood in the middle of the front room, seeming to fill it to capacity with the width of his shoulders and the sheer unwieldy substance of his presence. His gaze went straight to the oversize daguerreotype of Parnell on one wall.

He seemed to consider her late husband's visage for a few moments, before turning to meet her eyes.

"He doesn't look like the kind of man who'd die in a brothel," he remarked.

Dara Rose was jangled, but not offended. Everyone knew what had happened to Parnell, and the scandal, though still alive, had long since died down to an occasional whisper, especially since Jack O'Reilly had left his wife and children for a sloe-eyed girl from the Bitter Gulch Saloon.

"He wasn't," she said, very softly, and then colored up again. "That kind of man, I mean. Not really."

Dara Rose had never confided the truth about her marriage to Parnell Nolan to a single living soul west of the Mississippi River, and she was confounded by a sudden urge to tell Marshal McKettrick everything.

Not a chance, she thought, running her hands down the front of her apron as if they'd been wet.

"It must have been hard for you and the children," Clay said quietly. His eyes, blue as cornflowers in high summer, took on a solemn expression. "Not just his dying, but being left on your own and all."

"We manage," Dara Rose said.

"I reckon you do," he agreed, and he looked more puzzled than solemn now.

She knew he was wondering why she hadn't found another husband, but she wasn't about to volunteer an explanation. Maybe she hadn't actually loved Parnell Nolan, but she'd liked him. Depended on him. Even respected him.

Parnell had been kind to her, cherished the girls like they were his daughters instead of his nieces, and married her.

She would have felt disloyal, discussing Parnell with

a relative stranger; though, oddly enough, in some ways she felt as if she'd always known Clay McKettrick, and known him well. He stirred vague memories in her, like dreams that left only an echo behind when the sun rose.

The silence was awkward.

Dara Rose didn't ask the marshal to sit down, and she couldn't offer him coffee because she didn't have any.

So the two of them just stood there, each one waiting for the other to speak.

Finally, Clay grinned ever so slightly and turned his hat decisively in his hands. He went to the door and opened it, pausing to look back at Dara Rose, his impressive form rimmed in wintry light.

"Good day to you, Mrs. Nolan," he said.

Dara Rose swallowed. "Good day, Mr. McKettrick," she replied formally. "And, once again, thank you."

"Anytime," he said, and then he left the house, closed the door behind him.

Dara Rose resisted the temptation to rush to the window and watch him heading down the walk.

Harriet appeared in the doorway to the bedroom, hair rumpled, rubbing her eyes with the backs of her hands. "I thought I heard Papa's voice," she said.

Dara Rose's heart cracked and then split down the middle. "Sweetheart," she said, bending her knees so she could look directly into the child's sleep-flushed face, "Papa's gone to heaven, remember?"

Harriet's lower lip wobbled, which further bruised Dara Rose's already injured heart. How could such a small child be expected to understand the permanence of death?

"Is heaven a real place?" Harriet asked. "Or is it just pretend, like St. Nicholas?"

"I believe it's a real place," Dara Rose said.

Harriet frowned, obviously puzzled. "Is it like here? Are there trees and kittens and trains to ride?"

Dara Rose blinked rapidly and rose back to her full height. "I don't know, sweetheart. One day, a long, long time from now, we'll find out for sure, but right now, we have to live in *this* world, and we might as well make the best of it."

"I think I would like this world better," Harriet told her, "if there was a St. Nicholas in it."

Dara Rose gave a small, strangled chuckle at that, and pulled her daughter close for a hug. "We don't need St. Nicholas, you and Edrina and me," she said. "We have one another."

Chapter 4

~~~

A~~fter the chickens were fed~~ and had retreated into their coop to roost for the night, Dara Rose made a simple supper of baked potatoes and last summer's string beans, boiled with bits of salt pork and onion, for herself and the girls, and the three of them sat at the table in the kitchen, eating by the light of a kerosene lantern and chatting quietly.

The subject of St. Nicholas did not come up again, thankfully. In Dara Rose's humble opinion, Clement C. Moore had a lot to answer for. By writing that lengthy and admittedly charming poem, "'Twas the Night Before Christmas," he'd created expectations in children that many parents couldn't hope to meet.

Instead, Edrina recounted her visit to the O'Reillys' after lunch, and fretted that it wasn't fair that she had to wash the blackboard every single day for a week when all she'd done was defend herself against that wretched Thomas. Large flakes of snow drifted, like benevolent ghosts, past the darkened window next to the back door, and brought a sigh to hover in the back of Dara Rose's throat.

Winter. As a privileged only child, back in Massachusetts, she'd loved everything about that season, even the cold. It was a time to skate and sled and build castles out of snow and then drink hot chocolate by the fire while Nanny told stories or recited long, exciting poems about shipwrecks and ghosts and Paul Revere's ride.

Had she ever really lived such a life? Dara Rose wondered now, as she did whenever her childhood came to mind.

"Mama?" Edrina said, breaking the sudden spell the sight of snowflakes had cast over Dara Rose. "Did you hear what I said about Addie O'Reilly?"

Dara Rose gave herself an inward shake and sat up a little straighter in her chair. "I'm sorry," she said, because she was always truthful with the children. "I'm afraid I was woolgathering."

Edrina's perfect little face glowed, heart-shaped, in the light of love and a kerosene lantern. "She's really sick," she informed her mother, in a tone of good-natured patience, as though she were the parent and Dara Rose the child. "Mrs. O'Reilly told me she has romantic fever."

Dara Rose did not correct Edrina. She was too stricken by the tragedy of it, the patent unfairness. *Rheumatic fever.* Was there no end to the sorrows and hardships visited on that poor family?

"That's dreadful," she said.

"And Addie gets lonely, staying inside all the time," Edrina went on. "So I said Harriet and I would come to visit on Saturday morning. We can, can't we, Mama? Because I promised."

Dara Rose's heart swelled with affection for her daughter, and then sank a little. It was like her spirited Edrina to make such an offer, and follow through on it, too, whether or not she had her mother's permission. When Edrina made a promise, she kept it, which meant she was really asking if Harriet could go with her.

As far as Dara Rose knew, rheumatic fever wasn't contagious, but heaven only knew what other diseases her children might contract during a visit to the O'Reilly house—diphtheria, the dreaded influenza, perhaps even typhoid or cholera.

"You mustn't promise such things, in the future, without speaking to me first," Dara Rose told Edrina, hedging. "I feel as sorry for the O'Reillys as you do, Edrina, but there are other considerations."

"And it stinks over there," Harriet interjected solemnly, her nose twitching a little at the memory.

Dara Rose had lost her appetite, which was fine, because she'd had enough to eat, anyway. "Harriet," she said. "That will be enough of that sort of talk. It is not suitable for the supper table."

Harriet sighed. "It's *never* suitable," she lamented.

"Hush," Dara Rose told her, her attention focused, for the moment, on her elder daughter. "You may visit the O'Reillys on Saturday morning," she stated, rising to begin clearing the table. "But only because you gave your word and I would not ask you to break it."

"If I hadn't promised, you wouldn't let me go?" Edrina pressed. She'd never been one to quit while the quitting was good, a trait she came by honestly, Dara Rose had to admit. She had the same shortcoming herself.

"That's right," she replied, at some length. "I have to think about your safety, Edrina, and that of your sister."

"My safety? The O'Reillys wouldn't hurt us."

"Not deliberately," Dara Rose allowed, "but it isn't the most sanitary place in the world, and you might catch something."

Although she didn't mention it, she was thinking of the diphtheria outbreak two years before, during which four children had perished, all of them from one family.

"Is that suitable talk for the supper table?" Harriet asked sincerely.

"Never mind," Dara Rose said. "It's time you both got ready for bed. Shall I walk with you to the outhouse, or are you brave enough to go on your own?"

Edrina scraped back her chair, rose to fetch her coat and Harriet's from the pegs near the back door. Her expression said she was brave enough to do anything, and protect her little sister in the bargain.

"Maybe that's why Addie's so lonesome," Edrina said, opening the door to the chilly night, with its flurries of snow. "Because everybody is afraid of catching something if they visit."

Chagrin swept over Dara Rose—*out of the mouths of babes*—but she assumed a stern countenance. "Don't stand there with the door open," she said.

Later, when the children were in bed, and she'd read them a story from their one dog-eared book of fairy tales and heard their prayers—Harriet put in another request for the doll from the mercantile—kissed them good-night and tucked them in, Dara Rose returned to the kitchen.

There, she took the two letters Mr. McKettrick had delivered earlier from her apron pocket, and sat down.

The kerosene in the lamp was getting low, and the wick was smoking a little, but Dara Rose did not hurry.

She knew the plump missive was from her cousin, Piper, who taught school in a small town in Maine. She meant to save that one for last, and she took the time to weigh it in her hand, run her fingers over the vellum and examine the stamp before setting it carefully aside.

She opened the letter from the Wildflower Salve Company first, even though she knew it was an advertisement and nothing more, and carefully smoothed the single page on the tabletop.

Her eyes widened a little as she read, and her heart fluttered up into her throat as her excitement grew.

Bold print declared that Dara Rose was holding the key to financial security right there in her hand. She could win prizes, it fairly shouted. She could earn money. And all she had to do was introduce her friends and neighbors to the wonders of Wildflower Salve. Each colorfully decorated round tin—an elegant keepsake in its own right, according to the Wildflower Salve people—sold for a mere fifty cents. And she would get to keep a whopping twenty-five cents for her commission.

Dara Rose sat back, thinking.

Twenty-five cents was a lot of money.

And there were prizes. All sorts of prizes—toys, household goods, luxuries of all sorts—could be had in lieu of commissions, if the "independent business person" preferred.

Out of the goodness of their hearts, the folks at the Wildflower Salve Company, of Racine, Wisconsin, would be happy to send her a full twenty tins of this "medicinal miracle" in good faith. If for some incomprehensible reason her "friends and relations" didn't snap up the whole shipment practically as soon as she opened the parcel, she could return the merchandise and owe nothing.

Five dollars, Dara Rose thought. If she sold twenty

tins of Wildflower Salve, she would earn *five dollars*—a virtual fortune.

The kerosene lamp flickered, reminding her that she'd soon be sitting in the dark, and Dara Rose set aside "the opportunity of a lifetime" to open the letter from Piper.

A crisp ten-dollar bill fell out, nearly stopping Dara Rose's heart.

She set it carefully aside, and her hands trembled as she unfolded the clump of pages covered in Piper's lovely cursive. The date was nearly eight months in the past.

"Dearest Cousin," the missive began. "News of your tragic misfortune reached me yesterday, via the telegraph…"

Piper's letter, misplaced all this time, went on to say that she hoped Dara Rose could put the money enclosed to good use—that the weather was fine in Maine, with the spring coming, but she already dreaded the winter. How were the girls faring? Did Dara Rose intend to stay on in "that little Texas town," or would she and the children consider coming to live with her? The teacher's quarters were small, she wrote, bringing tears to Dara Rose's eyes, but they could make do, the four of them, couldn't they? There were crocuses and tulips and daffodils shooting up in people's flower beds, Piper went on to relate, and the days were distinctly longer. For all that, alas, she was lonesome when she wasn't teaching. She'd been briefly engaged, but the fellow had turned out to be a rascal and a rounder, and there didn't seem to be any likely prospects on the horizon.

Dara Rose read the whole letter and then immediately read it again. Besides Edrina and Harriet, Piper was the only blood relation she had left in all the world, and Dara Rose missed her sorely. Holding the letter, seeing the familiar handwriting spanning the pages, was the next best thing to having her cousin right there, in the flesh, sitting across the table from her.

But what must Piper think of her? Dara Rose fretted, after a third reading. She'd written this letter so long ago, and sent such a generous gift of money, only to receive silence in return.

The lantern guttered out.

Dara Rose sighed, folded the letter carefully and tucked it back into its envelope. She took the ten-dollar bill with her to the bedroom, where the girls were sound asleep, and placed it carefully between the pages in her Bible for safekeeping.

She undressed quickly, since the little room was cold, and donned her flannel nightgown, returned to the kitchen carrying a lighted candle stuck to a jar lid and dipped water from the stove reservoir to wash her face. When that was done, she brushed her teeth at the sink and steeled herself to make the trek to the outhouse, through the snowy cold.

When she got back, she locked the door, used the candle to light her way back to the bedroom, blew out the flame and climbed into bed with her daughters.

She was tired, but too excited to fall asleep right away.

She had ten precious dollars.

The Wildflower Salve Company had offered her honest work.

She'd as good as—well, *almost* as good as—spent an evening with her cousin and dearest friend, Piper.

And Marshal Clay McKettrick had the bluest eyes she'd ever seen.

THE JAILHOUSE, CLAY SOON discovered, was a lonely place at night.

He'd already had supper over at the hotel dining room—

chicken and dumplings almost as good as his ma's—and he'd paid a visit to Outlaw, over at the livery stable, too. He'd even sent a telegram north to Indian Rock, to let his family know he'd arrived and was settling in nicely.

That done, Clay had filled the water bucket and set up the coffeepot for morning, then filled the wood box next to the potbellied stove. There being no place to hang up his clothes, he left them folded in his travel trunk, there in the back room, where the bed was. Most of his books hadn't arrived yet—he had a passel of them and they had to be shipped down from Indian Rock in crates—and he couldn't seem to settle down to read the one favorite he'd brought along on the train, Jules Verne's *Around the World in Eighty Days.* He must have read that book a dozen times over the years, and he never got tired of it, but that night, it failed to hold his interest.

He kept thinking about Dara Rose Nolan, the gold of her hair and the fiery blue spirit in her eyes. He thought about her shapely breasts and small waist and smooth skin and that flash of pride that was so easy to arouse in her.

And the same old question plagued him: Why in the devil would a man with a wife like that squander his time in a whorehouse, the way her husband had done?

Nobody could help dying, of course, but they had at least some choice about *where* they died, didn't they? It was simple common sense—folks didn't turn up their toes in places they hadn't ventured into in the first place.

Knowing he wouldn't sleep, anyhow, Clay strapped on his gun belt, shrugged into his duster and reached for his hat.

He was the marshal, after all.

He'd just take a little stroll up and down Main Street and make sure any visiting cowpokes or drifters were minding their manners. If anybody needed arresting, he'd throw them in the hoosegow and start up a conversation.

What he really needed, he supposed, stepping out onto the dark sidewalk, was a woman. Someone like Dara Rose Nolan.

Maybe he'd get himself a dog—that would provide some companionship. He'd have to do all the talking, of course, but he liked critters. He'd grown up with all manner of them on the ranch.

Yes, sir, he needed a dog.

He hadn't even reached the corner when he heard the first yelp.

He frowned, stopped to pinpoint the direction.

"Dutch, you kick that dog again," he heard a male voice say, "and I'll shoot *you,* 'stead of him!"

Clay, having located the disturbance, pushed his coat back to uncover the handle of his .45 and stepped into the alley.

It was dark, and the snow veiled the moon, but light struggled through the filthy windows of the buildings on either side, and he could make out two men, one holding a pistol, standing over a shivering form huddled close to the ground.

"Hold it right there," Clay said, in deadly earnest, when the man with the pistol raised it to shoot. "What's going on here?"

The dog whimpered.

"Nothin', Marshal," one of the men answered, in a drunken whine. "The poor mutt's half-starved, just a bag of bones. We figured on putting it out of its misery, that's all. Meant it as a kindness."

"Get the hell out of here," Clay said. He could not abide a bully.

The two men responded by turning on their heels and running in the other direction.

Clay waited until they were out of sight before he put the .45 back in its holster and approached the dog. "You in a bad way there, fella?" he asked, crouching to offer a hand.

The animal sniffed cautiously at his fingers and whimpered again.

"Where'd you come from?" Clay asked, gently examining the critter for broken bones or open wounds. He seemed to be all right, though his ribs protruded and his belly was concave and he stunk like all get-out.

The dog whined, though this time there was less sorrow in the sound.

"You know," Clay told the animal companionably, "I was just thinking to myself that what I need is a dog to keep me company. Now, here you are. How'd you like to help me keep the peace in this sorry excuse for a town?"

The dog seemed amenable to the idea, and raised himself slowly, teetering a little, to his four fur-covered feet. He had burrs stuck in his coat, that poor cuss, and there was no telling what color he was, or if he leaned toward any particular breed.

"You come on with me, if you can walk," Clay said. "I brought home what was left of my supper, and it seems to me you could use a decent meal."

With that, he turned to head back toward the sidewalk. The dog limped after him, pausing every few moments, as though afraid he'd committed some transgression without knowing about it.

Back at the jailhouse, Clay got a better look at the dog, after lighting a lantern to see by, but seeing didn't help much. The creature was neither big nor little, and he had floppy ears, but that was the extent of what Clay could make out.

Glad to have something to do, not to mention some companionship, Clay poured the remains of his chicken and dumplings onto the one tin plate he possessed and set it on the floor, near the stove.

The dog sniffed at the food, looked up at Clay with the kind of uncertainty that breaks a decent person's heart and waited.

"You go ahead and have supper," Clay said gently. "I imagine you could use some water, too."

Slowly, cautiously, the dog lowered his muzzle and began to eat.

Clay walked softly, approaching the water bucket, and ladled up a dipperful.

The dog lapped thirstily from the well of the dipper, then returned to his supper, clearly ravenous, licking the plate clean as a whistle.

Clay carried in more water from the pump out back, heated it bucket by bucket on the potbellied stove and finally filled the washtub he'd found in one of the cells. He eased the dog into the warm water and sluiced him down before lathering his hide with his own bar of soap.

The animal didn't raise any fuss, he simply stood there, shivering and looking like nothing so much as a half-drowned rat. Gradually, it became clear that his coat was brown and white, speckled like a pinto horse.

Clay dried him off with one of the two towels he'd purchased earlier, over at the mercantile, hefted him out of the tub and set him gently on his feet, near the stove.

The dog looked up at him curiously, head tilted to one side.

Clay chuckled. "Now, then," he said. "You look a lot more presentable than you did before."

The dog gave a single, tentative *woof,* obviously unsure how the remark would be received in present company.

Clay leaned to pat the animal's damp head. "What you are," he said, "is a coincidence. Like I told you, I was thinking about how much I'd like to have a dog, and then you and I made our acquaintance. But since 'coincidence' would be too much trouble for a name, I figure I'll call you Chester."

"Woof," said Chester, with more confidence than before.

Clay laughed. "Chester it is, then," he agreed.

Using a rough blanket from the cot in the jail cell, Clay fashioned a bed for the dog, close to the stove. Chester sniffed the cloth, stepped gingerly onto it, made a circle and settled down with a sigh.

"Night," Clay said.

Chester closed his eyes, sighed again and slept.

THE HENS HAD ONLY LAID three eggs between the lot of them, Dara Rose discovered the next morning, when she visited the chicken coop, but she wasn't as disappointed by this as she normally would have been.

She had ten dollars tucked between the leaves of her Bible—a fortune.

And she had a future, a bright one, as Blue River, Texas's sole distributor of Wildflower Salve. All she had to do was fill out the coupon and mail it in, and before the New Year, she'd be in business.

Granted, there weren't a lot of people in Blue River, but there were plenty of surrounding farms and ranches, and those isolated women would be thrilled to purchase salve in a pretty tin, especially after she explained the benefits of regular use.

Not that she knew exactly what those benefits *were,* but the Wildflower Salve people had promised to send a training guide along with her first shipment.

As soon as she'd gotten Edrina off to school, she intended to write a long letter to Piper, explaining that *her* letter had been accidentally misplaced all this time, and she'd only received it the day before, and that was why her answer was so late in coming. Of course she'd thank her cousin profusely for the generous gift of ten dollars, and bring Piper up-to-date where she and the girls were concerned.

Her mind bumbled back and forth between the planned letter and her impending career in merchandising like a bee trapped inside a jar while she prepared oatmeal for breakfast, toasted bread in the oven and officiated over a debate between Edrina and Harriet, concerning whose turn it was to sleep in the middle of the bed that night.

Neither one wanted to, and Dara Rose finally said *she'd* take the middle, for heaven's sake, and what had she done to deserve two such argumentative daughters?

After breakfast, Dara Rose and Harriet bundled up to walk Edrina to school. Normally, Edrina managed the distance on her own, but today, Dara Rose wanted a word with Miss Krenshaw.

"I'm *already* being punished," Edrina fussed, as the three of them hurried along a road hoary with frost and hardened snow. "I *told you* I have to stay after and wash the blackboard. So why do you need to talk to Miss Krenshaw, when you know all that?"

Dara Rose hid a smile. She was holding Harriet's hand, and trying to pace herself to the child's much shorter strides. "I merely want to inquire about the Christmas pageant," she replied. There was always some sort of program at the schoolhouse, whether it was carol singing, a Nativity play or an evening of recitals, and everyone attended.

"Oh," said Edrina, still sounding not only mystified, but apparently a little nervous, too.

Dara Rose wondered if there was something her daughter should have told her, but hadn't.

"Do you think it will snow again, Mama?" Harriet asked, tilting her head way back to look up at the glowering sky. "Christmas is less than two weeks away, and St. Nicholas will need a lot of snow, since he travels in a sleigh."

"Goose," Edrina said, nudging her sister with one elbow. "There *isn't* any St. Nicholas, remember?"

"Edrina," Dara Rose interceded gently.

"I'm *pretending,* that's all," Harriet said, with a toss of her head. "You can't *stop* me, either."

"Pretending is *stupid,*" Edrina said. "It's for babies."

Dara Rose stopped, and both her children had to stop, too, since she was holding Harriet's hand at the time and it was easy to catch Edrina by the shoulder and halt her progress.

"Enough," Dara Rose said firmly.

They began to walk again.

THE SKY WAS HEAVY and gray that morning when Clay left Chester to digest the leftovers from his hotel dining room breakfast within the warm radius of the jailhouse stove and headed over to the livery stable to fetch Outlaw.

It was cold and getting colder, so Clay raised the collar of his duster as he led the saddled gelding out into the road. There had been snow during the night, leaving a hard crust on the ground, and there would be more, judging by the weighted clouds brooding overhead, but the ride was a short one and he'd be back in Blue River before any serious weather had a chance to set in.

Raised in the high country, where a soft, slow, feathery snowfall could turn into a raging blizzard within a span of ten minutes, he had a sense of what signs he ought to look out for, as well as those he could safely ignore.

Today, all the indications—the direction of wind, the foul promise of the darkening sky, the way the cold bit through the heavy canvas of his duster—inclined a man toward caution.

He let Outlaw have his head once they were out of town, let the horse run for the sheer joy of it, and they soon reached their destination, the flat acres where Clay intended to erect a house and a barn.

There, he dismounted and left Outlaw to catch his breath and graze on the scant remains of last summer's grass, paced off the perimeters of the house and marked the corners with piles of small rocks. He did the same for the barn, then stood a while, the wind slicing clear to his marrow, and imagined the place, finished.

The house, a kit he'd sent away to Sears, Roebuck and Company for, amounted to a sensible rectangle, the kind he could easily add on to as the years went by, with windows on all sides, white clapboard walls and a shingled roof. He'd have to hire some help to put the thing together, of course, but he planned to do a lot of the work with his own hands, and that included everything from laying floorboards to gathering rock for the fireplace and then mortaring the stones together.

With the McKettrick family expanding the way it had been for some years, Clay had helped build several houses, and put up additions, too. The kit wouldn't arrive until late April, but he'd need to have the foundation ready, and the well dug, too.

Of course, a lot depended on what kind of winter they were in for—Blue River was in the Hill Country, and therefore the climate wasn't as temperate as it was in some parts of Texas—but he could already feel the heft of a shovel in his hands, the steady strain in his muscles, and he was heartened.

Next year at this time, he promised himself, he'd be ranching, right here on this land. He'd have a wife and, if possible, a baby on the way. Christmas would be getting close, and he'd go out and cut a tree and bring it into the house to be hung with ornaments and paper garlands, and there would be a fire crackling on the hearth—

But that was next year, and this was now, Clay reminded himself, with a sigh. He assessed the sky again, then whistled, low, for Outlaw.

The horse trotted over, reins dangling, and Clay gathered them and swung up into the saddle.

"We've got our work cut out for us," he told the animal.

The snow began coming down, slowly at first and then in earnest, when they were still about a mile outside of town, and by the time he and Outlaw reached the livery, it was hard to see farther than a dozen feet in any direction.

Zeb Dooley, the old man who ran the stable and adjoining blacksmith's shop, came out to meet him. Taking Outlaw's reins as soon as Clay had stepped down from the saddle, Zeb shouted to be heard over the rising screech of the wind. "Best head on over to the jailhouse or the Bitter Gulch, Marshal, because this blow is bound to get worse before it gets better!"

Clay took the reins back. "I want to look in over at the

schoolhouse," he called in reply. "Make sure the children are all right."

Zeb, clad for the cold in dungarees and a heavy coat, shook his balding head. "Miss Krenshaw will keep them there 'til it's safe to leave. The town makes sure there's always a stash of firewood and grub, in case they need it."

Clay's worries were only partially allayed by Zeb's reassurance. A storm like this sure as hell meant trouble for *somebody,* and he didn't feel right about heading for the jailhouse to hunker down with Chester and wait it out, not just yet, anyway.

Clay turned away, mounted up again, bent low over Outlaw's neck to speak to him and started for the far edge of town.

He rode slowly, Outlaw stalwartly shouldering his way through the thickening snow, up one street and down another, until he'd covered all of them. Nobody called out to him as he passed, and lantern light glowed in most of the windows so, after half an hour, he and the horse felt their way back to the livery.

There was no sign of Zeb, and the big double doors of the stables were latched and rattling under the assault of the wind.

Clay opened them, led Outlaw inside and into his stall, gave him hay and made sure his water trough was full. Then he retraced his steps, latched the doors again and walked, wind-battered, toward the jailhouse.

Chapter 5

‹ ୧୧୫୬ ›

DARA ROSE RUBBED THE GLASS in the door of the mercantile with one gloved hand, clearing a circle to look through and seeing nothing but dizzying flurries of angry white. She'd come here to mail her letter to Piper and send off the coupon to the Wildflower Salve Company, and now she wished she hadn't been in such a hurry to leave home.

Mr. Bickham doubled as Blue River's postmaster. Being in a position to know who wrote to whom, and who received letters from whom, he tended to mind everybody's business but his own.

"You might just as well sit down here by the stove as try to see any farther than the end of your nose in weather like this," Philo counseled, from behind his long counter. "That's about the tenth time you wiped off that window, and it just keeps fogging up again."

Dara Rose bit her lower lip, still fretful. She and Harriet were safe and warm, but what about Edrina? Suppose she tried to walk home from school in this storm? Miss Krenshaw could be depended upon to keep her students inside, of course, but Edrina was, as recent history proved, well able to get past her teacher when she chose.

Harriet, who considered the whole thing a marvelous lark, sat on top of a pickle barrel and gazed raptly at the exquisite doll in the display window. Dara Rose, noting this, felt another pinch to the heart.

She had the ten dollars Piper had sent; she could buy the doll for Harriet and several books for Edrina, set it all out for them after they went to bed on Christmas Eve, to find in the morning and rejoice over. But both children still needed warm coats, and sturdy shoes that fit properly, and for all the vegetables she'd stored in the root cellar and the chickens producing fresh eggs right along—until this morning, that was—there was barely enough food to see them through the winter.

This year, with Parnell gone and even the roof over their heads a precarious blessing, there would be no store-bought presents, no brightly decorated tree, no goose or turkey for Christmas dinner.

"I could let you have that doll for two dollars even," Philo whispered, suddenly standing beside Dara Rose and startling her half out of her skin. Because of the thick layers of sawdust covering the floor, she hadn't heard him approach. "Put a dollar down, and you can pay the rest over time, out of the egg money."

Dara Rose looked at him sharply, momentarily distracted from her worry over Edrina, who might at any moment take it into her head to strike out for home, blizzard or no blizzard, perhaps concerned about her mother and sister and the chickens.

That would be like Edrina.

"No, Mr. Bickham," Dara Rose whispered back, while

Harriet paid neither one of them a whit of notice, "I will not be purchasing the doll, and that's final."

"But look at your little girl," the storekeeper cajoled. "She wants that pretty thing in the worst way."

Dara Rose's cheeks throbbed, and her throat thickened. It was only by the sternest exercise of self-control that she did not burst into tears. "I can barely afford to give my children what they *need,*" she told him pointedly, though in a very quiet voice. "What they *want* is out of the question just now. Please do not press the matter further."

Philo gave a deep sigh and, at the same moment, the door Dara Rose had been standing next to only moments before burst open on a gust of wind.

Snow blew in, along with a swift and bitter chill, and then Clay McKettrick stepped over the threshold, accompanied by a medium-size dog, coated in white. Even for a strong man like he was, shutting that door again was an effort.

Dara Rose stood looking at the marshal and the dog, feeling oddly stricken, a state this man seemed to inflict upon her at every encounter. *She* might have been the one braving the frigid weather outside, instead of Clay, the way her breath stalled in the back of her throat.

With a smile, Clay took off his hat, dusting off the snow with his other hand, and nodded. "Afternoon, Mrs. Nolan," he said.

His voice was deep and quiet, his manner unhurried.

Dara Rose didn't answer, merely inclined her head briefly in response.

Harriet, meanwhile, forgot the doll she'd been so fascinated by until now, leaped nimbly off the pickle barrel and slowly approached the newcomers.

"Does that dog bite?" she asked forthrightly, studying

the animal closely before tilting her head back to look up at Clay.

"I can't rightly say, one way or the other," Clay replied honestly. "He and I just took up with each other last night, so we're not all that well acquainted yet. Offhand, though, I'd say you oughtn't to pet old Chester until we know a little more about his nature."

Harriet smiled, enchanted. "Hullo, Chester," she said.

Chester looked her over, but stayed close to Clay's side.

"I don't normally allow dogs in my store," Philo said. Then, with a smile and a genial spreading of his hands, "But I'll make an exception for you, Marshal."

"I'm obliged," Clay said. "It's a fair hike back to the jailhouse and I'd rather not leave him alone there, anyhow."

Dara Rose opened her mouth, closed it again. When it came to Clay McKettrick, she was as bad as Harriet with the doll, prone to ogle and be struck dumb with awe.

As if to prove himself a gentleman, Chester ambled away from Clay to nestle down in the warm sawdust in front of the stove. With a sigh of grateful contentment, the dog closed his eyes and went to sleep.

Harriet giggled. "He must be tired," she said.

"I reckon he is at that," Clay agreed. "I think old Chester traveled a hard road before he found his way to me."

Dara Rose had never envied a dog before, but she did in that moment. She'd traveled a hard road, too, she and the girls, but it hadn't led to a handsome, steady-minded man who was probably able to handle just about anything.

She cleared her throat, fixing to make another attempt at speaking, but before a word came to her, Harriet had reached out and taken Clay's hand, tugging him in the direction of the display window.

"Look," she said reverently, pointing at the doll.

Dara Rose finally found her voice, but it didn't hold up for long. "Harriet—"

Clay lifted the child easily, holding her in one arm, so she was at eye level with the splendid toy.

"Isn't she pretty?" Harriet murmured, wonderstruck again.

"Not as pretty as you are," Clay told her. His gaze sought Dara Rose, found her, and brought yet another embarrassing blush to her cheeks. His expression was solemn, as if he wanted to ask some question but knew it would be improper to do so.

"If I sold my hair for two dollars and fifty cents," Harriet prattled on, wide-eyed, seemingly as at home in Clay's arms as she would have been in Parnell's, "I could take her home with me for good. Do you know of a place where folks buy hair?"

Dara Rose closed her eyes briefly, mortified.

"Can't say as I do," Clay replied affably. He was still looking at Dara Rose, though; she could feel it.

She opened her eyes, watched, tongue-tied with misery, as he gently set Harriet back on her feet.

"I'd name her Florence," Harriet continued. "Don't you think that's a pretty name? Florence?"

Clay allowed as how it was a very nice name.

Dara Rose realized she was staring and looked quickly away, only to have her gaze collide with Mr. Bickham's. A benevolent smirk wreathed the storekeeper's round face.

"Looks like the snow's letting up a little," Bickham said, with a glance at the window. "Maybe the marshal and his dog here could see you and little Harriet home safe while there's a lull."

Dara Rose needed to get back to her place, in case Edrina was there or on her way, but it wouldn't be wise for her and Harriet to attempt the journey, however short, on their own. So she swallowed her pride and turned back to Clay. "Would you mind?" she asked.

Clay cleared his throat before answering, but his words still came out sounding husky. "No, ma'am," he said, almost shyly. "I wouldn't mind."

So Dara Rose bundled Harriet up as warmly as she could, and then herself, and Clay lifted Harriet up again, simultaneously whistling for the dog.

Chester got up immediately, ready to go.

"You give some thought to what I said, Miz Nolan," Philo shouted after her, as she followed Clay out into the waning snowstorm. "Ain't no shame in buying on credit!"

Dara Rose ignored him.

The snow, having fallen hard and fast all morning, was nearly knee-deep and powdery. Clay and the dog seemed to navigate it with relative ease, Chester moving in a hopping way that might have been comical under more ordinary circumstances, and Dara Rose picked her way along in the tracks of the marshal's boots.

Harriet, snug against Clay's chest, with the front of his coat around her, looked back over his shoulder at Dara Rose, her eyes merry with adventure. The child was clearly reveling in *Mr. McKettrick's* attention—it was imprudent to think of him as "Clay," Dara Rose had decided—and no doubt pretending she had a papa again.

The thought made Dara Rose's throat ache like one big bruise, and her eyes scalded. She was glad Mr. McKettrick couldn't see her face.

They trooped on, Clay forging a way for all of them when the dog grew tired, and the snow was thickening again by the time they reached the house. The respite, it seemed, was nearly over.

The air was shiver-cold, and Chester needed to rest. Even though Dara Rose was mildly alarmed by the thought of the new marshal filling her house with his purely masculine presence, she had no choice but to ask him in.

There was no sign of Edrina, which was both a relief and a worry to Dara Rose. Once she had her elder daughter at home, safe and sound, she'd move on to the other concerns—how the chickens were faring, for a start, and the state of the woodpile stacked against the back of the house. Thanks to the town council, there was a good supply of firewood, but some of it would need drying out before it could be burned.

Clay—*Mr. McKettrick* suddenly seemed too unwieldy even in her thoughts—walked straight through to the kitchen, set Harriet on her feet and went about building up the dwindling fire in the cookstove.

Chester practically collapsed on the rug in front of the sink.

"I'll go on to the schoolhouse," Clay told Dara Rose, when he'd finished at the stove, "and see about bringing Edrina home. It would be a favor to me, Mrs. Nolan, if you'd let my dog stay here while I'm gone, since he's probably too tuckered out to go much farther."

This time, Dara Rose welcomed the heat that surged through her, pulsing in her face. They weren't without their blessings, she and the children. "Of course," she said awkwardly. "Harriet and I will look after Chester. And I don't mind admitting I'm worried that Edrina might try to make her way home on her own."

Clay nodded, grinned a little. "She might, at that," he said.

That grin *did* something to Dara Rose. She told herself

it was simple thankfulness. She needed help, and someone was there to give it and that was that.

"What about the other children?" she asked, as Clay started for the back door.

"If any of them are stranded at the schoolhouse," he answered, his hand on the knob, "I'll make sure they get where they're supposed to go—after I bring your girl home, that is." He turned toward Harriet, who was now on her knees next to Chester, all concern for his temperament evidently past, drying off his coat with a flour-sack dish towel, and tugged at the brim of his hat. "Thank you for minding my friend, there," he told the child. "Looks as though he likes you."

Harriet beamed. "I *knew* he wouldn't bite me," she said.

Clay smiled briefly then, opened the door, leaned into the wind that rushed to meet him and stepped outside. The door closed behind him.

CLAY FOUND HIS WAY to the schoolhouse more from memory than by use of his eyesight, and Miss Krenshaw met him at the door, took him firmly by the arm and pulled him inside, out of the cold and the wind and the blinding assault of the snow.

Except for Edrina, who was huddled close to the stove and bundled inside a faded quilt, the schoolmarm was alone. Evidently, the other kids had already been collected by kinfolks and taken home.

Edrina smiled at him. "I knew you'd come to fetch me, if Mama didn't," she said, with a certainty that warmed his heart.

"Sit down, Marshal," Miss Krenshaw all but commanded, indicating her desk chair, which was the only one in the schoolroom big enough for an adult. "I've got some coffee brewing in back."

Clay didn't plan to tarry long, since the storm was more likely to get worse than it was to get better, and he wanted to get Edrina back to her mother and sister while the getting was good. But hot coffee sounded mighty nice to him just then, and he wouldn't mind sitting for a few minutes, either. He was still a young man, and fit, but that cold made his bones ache.

"Thank you," he said, and took the offered chair.

Miss Krenshaw disappeared into the back, where she probably had private quarters, and returned promptly with the promised coffee.

"Thanks," Clay repeated, taking the steaming mug from her hand.

Not one to be idle, it would seem, Miss Alvira got busy erasing the day's lessons off the blackboard.

"You'll be all right here, on your own?" Clay asked presently, restored by the tasty brew. Miss Alvira had laced it with whiskey, which raised her a notch in his already high estimation. Too bad he couldn't work up an interest in courting the lady.

"I'll be just fine," Miss Alvira said, still busy. She sounded a mite affronted by the question, in fact. "I have everything I need, right here."

Edrina, still seated by the stove, took in the conversation, but offered no comment. She did look somewhat pensive, though, and Clay wondered briefly what was going through that busy little brain of hers.

He finished the coffee, got to his feet, glanced at one of the windows.

There was no letup to the snow, as far as he could tell.

Miss Alvira marched into the cloakroom, came out with

Edrina's coat and bonnet and briskly prepared the child for the journey home. For good measure, she wrapped the quilt around Edrina again, too.

"There," she said, with a slight smile.

Clay put his hat back on—he'd left it on a peg next to the door, coming in—and hoisted Edrina, quilt and all, into his arms. As he'd done with Harriet, leaving the mercantile, he tried to cover her with his coat, as well.

"You're sure there's nowhere you'd like to go?" he asked Miss Alvira, before opening the door. "To the hotel, maybe? There're bound to be some folks around, and I could walk you over—"

The schoolmarm gave a little sniff and hiked up her chin again. "Marshal," she said, putting a point on the word, "as I've already told you, I am quite capable of looking after myself, and besides, I wouldn't think of spending good money on a hotel room."

"All right, then," Clay said, with a slight smile and a nod of farewell.

He followed his own quickly disappearing boot prints back to Dara Rose's front door, shoulders braced against the wind, his arms tight around the little girl tucked in the folds of that old quilt.

A lamp burned in the center of Dara Rose's kitchen table, and the house was not only blessedly warm, but there was something savory simmering on the stove.

Her face lit up at their return, and even though Clay knew most of that joy was for Edrina, he basked in the welcome, anyway. And Chester was just about beside himself, he was so happy to see Clay.

"You'll stay for supper," Dara Rose informed Clay briskly, once he'd set Edrina down, and then she commenced to unwinding that now-damp quilt from around the little girl.

Clay just stood there for a long moment, in his snowy duster and his wet hat, waiting for his bones and sinews to thaw and just enjoying the sight of her. Dara Rose's aquamarine eyes were bright and her cheeks flushed, probably from the heat of the stove and happiness because Edrina was home.

"All right," he said, finally realizing that her statement called for some kind of response, however mundane. "Whatever you're cooking, it smells good."

She smiled at him, briefly, distractedly, and all but set him back on his heels by the doing of it.

"Edrina, you go in and change into dry clothes," she told the child.

Edrina hesitated, then left the room. Harriet, after trying in vain to get Chester to come along on the jaunt, followed her sister, chattering about the walk home from the mercantile.

It was a heady thing, being alone with Dara Rose in that steamy little room.

And Clay, a quiet man but not a shy one, couldn't come up with a single thing to say.

Dara Rose tightened the bands on her apron, a reachback motion that made her shapely bosom rise and jut out a little. "If the chickens survive this," she said, with an anxious glance toward the room's one opaque window, "it will be a miracle, and I sure hope some of the men in town give a thought to the O'Reillys, like they generally do at times like this...."

Her voice fell away, and she gnawed fretfully at her lower lip, likely pondering the fate of the poultry, the family she'd just mentioned, or both.

"The O'Reillys?" Clay croaked out, grabbing hold of the rapidly sinking conversational lifeline with the first thing that jumped off his tongue.

Dara Rose sighed again, turned away from him to stir whatever was cooking in that pot. The scent of it made his stomach rumble, and it came to him that, except for Miss Krenshaw's whiskeyed-up coffee, he hadn't had anything since breakfast.

"Peg O'Reilly's no-good excuse for a husband," she said quietly, after a glance in the direction of the doorway the little girls had hurried through earlier, "ran off with some…some…*woman* he met at the Bitter Gulch Saloon, and left a wife and three children behind to fend for themselves!"

For a moment, Clay was taken aback—not by the story, which unfortunately was not an uncommon one, especially with the war in Europe picking up momentum—but by Dara Rose's apparent failure to draw any correlation between Mrs. O'Reilly's situation and her own. Except for one obvious variable—Parnell had had the bad fortune to die, while the long-gone Mr. O'Reilly was presumably still alive—the two women had essentially been dealt the same bad hand of cards.

Dara Rose seemed to sense that he was looking at her, and she turned to meet his gaze, colored up again and looked quickly away. The girls returned to the kitchen just then, before anything more could be said, Harriet going on about that doll she meant to name Florence, and Edrina replying in lofty, big-sister fashion that Harriet ought to wish in one hand and spit in the other and see which one got full faster.

Clay went to the sink, rolled up his shirtsleeves and commenced to washing his hands with the harsh yellow soap Dara Rose kept in an old saucer wedged behind the pump handle.

He felt a combination of things while he was at it, but mainly, he realized, he was glad. Glad just to be where he was, right there in that kitchen, out of the cold wind, with a lovely woman, two kids and a dog for company.

For the first time since he'd left Arizona, Clay didn't have to fight down a hankering for home, didn't second-guess his decision to strike out on his own instead of making a life on the ever-expanding Triple M with the rest of the family.

Be sure you're leaving because it's what you really want to do, Clay, his pa had counseled him, *and not because Annabel Carson broke your heart.*

It made Clay smile a little to remember that conversation, and others like it, with various members of the home outfit, and he reckoned now that Annabel hadn't broken his heart at all—she'd just sprained it a little.

The stuff in the pot on the stove turned out to be some kind of mixture of canned venison and leftover vegetable preserves, and it was better, in Clay's opinion, than a big steak at Delmonico's.

"Miss Krenshaw keeps a picture of a soldier in her top desk drawer," Edrina chimed, in the middle of the meal, pretty much out of nowhere.

Snow rasped at the windows and the small cookstove seemed to strain to put out more heat.

"And how would you know a thing like that, Edrina Nolan?" Dara Rose asked, arching one eyebrow, her spoon poised halfway between her mouth and the bowl of soup sitting in front of her.

"She takes it out and looks at it, when she thinks no-body's looking," Edrina explained nonchalantly. "Sometimes, she gets tears in her eyes, and her lips move like she's talking to somebody."

Clay's gaze connected with Dara Rose's.

"Are you going to fight in the war, Mr. McKettrick?" Edrina asked, without missing a beat.

"No," Clay answered. The armed forces would need beef, and plenty of it, and like his granddad said, somebody had to raise the critters. "But my cousin Gabriel thinks he might join up, if things don't simmer down some over the next year or two."

A sad expression flickered across Dara Rose's expressive face; he figured the war was a subject she tried not to think about, since there was nothing she could do to change it.

After supper, Edrina and Harriet cleared the table and set the dishes in the sink, without being told.

Dara Rose crossed the room to take her cloak and bonnet down from their peg near the door. She clearly dreaded whatever she was about to do, and Clay found himself beside her before he'd made a conscious decision to move, reaching for his hat and duster.

Dara Rose looked up at him, and he caught the briefest glimpse into the shimmering vastness of her heart and mind and spirit. There was so much more to her than just her flesh-and-blood person, he realized, with a start akin to waking up suddenly after a long, deep sleep.

"The chickens—" she began, and then went silent.

"I'll see to them," Clay said, very quietly. "You stay here, with the girls."

She considered the idea briefly, then shook her head no. She meant to go out to that chicken coop and that was that. He'd be wasting his breath to argue.

"I'll heat water to wash the dishes when I get back,"

she told the children. "Don't get too close to the stove, and no scuffling."

"Oh, Mama," Edrina said, with a roll of her eyes. "You've told us that a *thousand times* already."

A smile quirked at one corner of Dara Rose's mouth. Like the rest of her, visible and invisible, that mouth fascinated Clay out of all good sense and reason. "Well," she said, "now it's a thousand and *one*."

After a glance at Clay's face, she opened the door and stepped right out into that blizzard.

Clay followed, and the wind was so strong that it buffeted her back a step, so they collided, her back to his torso. He put his arms out to steady her, and a powerful jolt of... *something*...shot through him.

Since it was too cold to dally, they recovered quickly and advanced toward the rickety coop.

The chickens had taken refuge inside and, with the exception of the rooster, who squawked indignantly as he paced the floor of that shed, as though fussing over the pure injustice of a snowstorm, the birds huddled close to one another on the length of wood that served as a roost.

There was a visible easing in Dara Rose as she looked around. "At least none of them have frozen to death," she said, and she might have been addressing herself, not him, trundling over to lift the lid off a wooden bend and lean inside to scoop out feed. Judging by how *far* she had to lean—Lordy, she had a shapely backside—the supply was starting to run low.

Like a lot of other things in her life, probably.

Clay watched, offering no comment, as Dara Rose filled a shallow pan with feed and set it out for the hens to peck at. That done, she picked up a second pan, went to the doorway and shoveled up some snow. The stuff was already melting around the edges, cold as that chicken coop was, when Dara Rose waded back into the center of the noisy flock to set the second pan down beside the first.

They fought their way back to the house, side by side, heads down, shoulders braced. Clay wanted to put an arm around Dara Rose's waist, so she wouldn't fall or blow away, but every instinct warned against it.

The woman had a right to her pride, probably needed it just to press on from one day to the next.

By the time they got back inside the house, the girls had left the kitchen for the front room.

Their voices carried, a happy sound, like the chiming of bells somewhere off in the muffled distance.

Dara Rose moved to untie her bonnet laces, but Clay closed his hands over hers. "You've done a fine job raising those girls of yours," he said, though he hadn't actually planned the words ahead of time.

Those wonderful eyes of hers searched his face, almost warily. Then she smiled and went on to take off her bonnet, Clay's hands falling away from hers and back to his sides.

"Thank you, Mr. McKettrick," she said, stepping back to shed her snow-speckled cloak.

"Clay," he said, knowing she wanted him to step aside so she could get on with whatever it was she planned to do next but stubbornly holding his ground. "I don't generally answer to 'Mr. McKettrick,' as it happens. Usually, when folks use that moniker, they're talking to my granddad."

She blushed, but her eyes flashed. "When I say it," she told him, "I'm addressing *you*. We haven't known each other long enough to use first names."

He chuckled at that. Curved his finger sideways under her chin and lifted. "Have it your way...Dara Rose," he said, partly to get under her hide and partly because he just liked saying her name.

Still wearing his coat and hat, he summoned the dog with a soft whistle.

Edrina and Harriet immediately appeared in the inside doorway, squashed together as though there was barely enough room in the gap to contain both of them. Their eyes were wide with curiosity and something else—maybe worry.

"You're going?" Edrina asked.

"And taking Chester?" Harriet added.

Clay touched the brim of his hat, momentarily ignoring Dara Rose, who was probably still prickly over his impertinent use of her Christian name. "Yep," he said. "Chester and I ought to be getting over to the jailhouse, in case somebody comes looking for us."

"But it's getting dark," Edrina protested.

"And it's still snowing *really hard,*" Harriet said. "What if you and Chester get lost?"

"We'll find our way," Clay promised, his voice a little huskier than normal. "Don't you worry about us."

Dara Rose surprised him by laying a hand on his arm. "Take the lantern," she said.

Clay was moved by the offer, but he didn't let it show, of course. He just shook his head and smiled a little. "It wouldn't do much good, hard as the wind's blowing," he said. "But I thank you kindly, just the same. And thanks for supper, too, and a right pleasant evening."

Dara Rose opened her mouth, closed it again and then sighed. "Be careful," she said.

"I will certainly do that, ma'am," he answered.

The winter night bit into him like teeth when he moved out into it, Chester struggling along at his side.

Before they got as far as the gate, the dog was practically sinking out of sight with every cautious step, so Clay picked him up, carrying him in the curve of his right arm.

With his free hand, Clay pulled his hat brim down low over his eyes and blinked a couple of times, until he could see. If it weren't for thin snatches of lamplight, spilling from various windows along the way, he and Chester might have been in some trouble.

As it was, Clay was half-frozen by the time he fumbled with the latch on his office door, stepped over the threshold and set the dog down to feel along the wall for the metal box that held the matches for the stove and the lanterns.

Chester gave a low growl as Clay struck the match.

There was a shuffling clatter over by the desk, followed by the sound of boot soles striking the plank floor and a grumbled curse.

"Damn it, Clay," growled his cousin Sawyer, "you oughtn't to sneak up on a man like that, especially when he's sleeping."

Chapter 6

"I THOUGHT IT DIDN'T SNOW in Texas," Sawyer said, after stretching and letting go with a lusty yawn.

Clay patted the dog, reassured him with a few quiet words and lit one of the two lanterns he had on hand. "What are you doing here, Sawyer?" he countered gruffly.

"I *was* catching up on my shut-eye," Sawyer replied affably, grinning that cocky grin that sometimes made Clay want to backhand his cousin, "until you came banging through the door and disturbed me."

Clay lit the other lantern, the one that stood on the bookcase, and then went to the stove to build up the fire. The last time he'd seen his cousin and one-time best friend, they'd had words, not just about Annabel, but about a few other things, too.

"You're a long way from home, cousin," Clay finally remarked.

"So are you," Sawyer answered, perching on the edge of Clay's desk now, with his arms folded. The youngest son of Clay's uncle Kade, and aunt Mandy, Sawyer had the fair hair and dark blue eyes that ran in intergenerational streaks through the McKettrick bloodline.

Clay shut the stove door with a clang and rustled up some leftovers for Chester, who seemed to have decided that the surprise visitor made acceptable company.

Which just went to show what a dog knew about anything, Clay thought glumly. Most of them liked everybody, and Chester was no exception.

"I'm going to ask you once more," Clay said evenly, "*just once,* what you're doing here, and if I don't get a clear answer, I swear I'll toss you behind bars on a trespassing charge."

Sawyer chuckled. "I'm just passing through," he said. "Since I was in your neck of the woods, I decided to board my horse in San Antonio and take the train to Blue River, see how you're faring and all."

"I'm faring just fine," Clay responded, "so you can get on tomorrow's train, if it makes it through, and go right back to San Antonio."

Sawyer strolled to the window, in no evident hurry to get there. He had the born horseman's rolling, easy stride. "Good thing I didn't bring the horse," he said, as though Clay hadn't as good as told him, straight out, that he wasn't welcome. "We'd probably be out there in the blizzard someplace, freezing to death." A visible shudder moved through his lean, agile form, but he didn't turn around. "Like I said, nothing anybody ever told me about Texas prepared me for ass-deep snow."

Clay ladled water into the coffeepot, a dented metal receptacle coated with blue enamel, and set it on top of the potbellied stove. Then he commenced to spoon ground coffee beans into it, along with a pinch of salt to make the grounds settle after the stuff brewed. "That's the thing about weather," he said, at considerable length. "It's unpredictable."

Sawyer finally turned around, but he lingered at the window, frost-coated and all but opaque behind him. "Annabel Carson got married soon after you left," he said, gruffly and with care.

"Not to you, it appears," Clay said, turning his back to the stove and absorbing the heat.

Sawyer made a sound that might have been a chuckle, though it contained no noticeable amusement. "Not to me," he confirmed. "She got hitched to Whit Taggard, over near Stone Creek. You know, that banker in his fifties, with more money than one man ever ought to have? She swears it's a love match."

"You came all the way to Blue River to tell me that?" Clay asked, strangely unmoved by news that probably would have devastated him not so long ago. Chester had finished his meal of leftovers from the hotel dining room and gone to curl up on his blanket. The wind howled and hissed under the eaves, as if it were fixing to raise the roof right off that old jailhouse and carry it next door, if not farther.

"No," Sawyer said. "I came all the way to Blue River because your mama's been worried about you, and I love my aunt Chloe."

Clay sighed. "I already sent Ma and Pa a wire," he said, mildly exasperated. "They know I'm fine."

"Your saying it and their knowing it for sure are two different things, Clay," Sawyer went on, his tone reasonable and quiet, as if he were calming a jittery horse or a cow mired in deep mud and struggling against the ropes meant to pull it onto dry ground. "It's not every day a man picks up and leaves the place and the people he's known all his life."

Clay had no answer for that, had already done all the explaining he ever intended to do, where the decision to put home behind him for good—at least as far as living there—was concerned, anyhow. Much as he loved his granddad and his pa and his uncles, he didn't want to spend the rest of his life taking orders from them. He wanted to build and run his own outfit, marry and have sons and daughters, grandchildren and great-grandchildren.

"You hungry?" Clay asked, hoping to get the conversation going in another direction.

"I had fried chicken over at the hotel, soon as I'd checked in and stowed my gear," Sawyer answered, with a shake of his head. He looked around at the humble quarters Clay presently called home, sighed. "Nobody can accuse you of living high on the hog, I reckon," he finished, sounding weary now.

Clay shoved a hand through his hair, recalling the difficult trek back from Dara Rose's place. It had taken him and Chester the better part of half an hour to cover the five hundred yards or so between the jail and that snug little house.

Once he'd warmed up, had some coffee and put on long johns and an extra layer of clothes, he meant to venture out again, track down that family Dara Rose had mentioned—the O'Reillys—and see for himself that they were warm and had something to eat. He figured it was his duty, as marshal, to see that folks made it through when there was an emergency like that snowstorm, especially women and children.

"Finding your way back to the hotel in this blizzard

might be tricky," Clay told his cousin, in his own good time. "You can bunk in the cell there if you want."

One side of Sawyer's mouth quirked upward in a grin. "And give you a prime opportunity to lock me up, soon as I shut my eyes, and then drop the key down a deep well? Not likely, cousin."

"You sorely overestimate my ability to tolerate your company," Clay responded dryly. "The sooner you're on your way, the happier I'm going to be."

Sawyer didn't reply right away, which was a telling thing, because he was usually quick to shoot off his mouth. There *was* a whole other side to Sawyer, though—one nobody, including Clay, really knew much about.

"You must know I never laid a hand on your girl, Clay," Sawyer said, as a chunk of wood crackled and splintered to embers inside the stove. "So what exactly is it about me that sticks in your craw? We used to be as close as brothers."

Too warm now that he'd been standing near the stove for a while, Clay moved on to his desk, reclaimed the creaky wooden chair, sat back in it with his hands cupped behind his head. Chester, lying nearby on his blanket pile, gave a single, chortling snore, and another piece of wood collapsed in the fire, with a series of sharp snaps.

"You come here," Clay answered presently, "uninvited, I might add, and let on that I'm a grief to the family, like some prodigal son off squandering his birthright in a far country, and then you have the gall to ask what sticks in my craw? It's the hypocrisy of it. *You're a gunslinger,* Sawyer, a hired gun. Little better than an outlaw, most likely. It might even be that if I went through all these wanted posters on my desk, I'd come across a fair likeness of your face."

"I'm not an outlaw," Sawyer said flatly. "You know that."

"Do I?" Clay asked. "You blow through the Triple M every few years like a breeze—just long enough last time to turn my girl's head—and then, one fine day, a telegram comes in, and you're gone again, without a word to anybody. Like you know somebody's picked up your trail so you'd better be moving on, pronto."

Sawyer sighed again, and it came out raspy. "I don't reckon anything I say is going to get through that inchthick layer of bone you call a skull," he said. "You made up your mind about me a long time ago, didn't you, cousin?"

There was no denying that. "I reckon I did," Clay replied quietly, feeling wrung out. "You can tell Ma and the rest of the family that you've seen me and I'm fine. Seems to me that your business here is finished."

Even as he spoke those words, Clay wondered what the *real* reason for Sawyer's visit might be. Blue River was too far out of his cousin's way for this to be about Annabel, or a favor to Clay's ma and pa.

Sawyer crossed to the door, took his hat and canvas duster down from their pegs and put them on. Then he hesitated, one hand on the old-fashioned iron latch. "You're right," he said, with more sadness than Clay had heard in his voice since they were ten years old and Sawyer's dog took sick and died. "I guess there's no getting back on your good side. I'll be on tomorrow's train, if it gets here, and you can get on with whatever the hell it is you think you're doing."

With that, Sawyer opened the door and went out, letting in a blast of snow-speckled cold that reached into the deepest parts of Clay and held on.

He almost relented, almost called Sawyer back—but in the end, he figured it was best to let him go.

THE SNOW LAY LIKE A THICK, glittering mantle over the countryside when Dara Rose went out to feed the chickens, carrying the egg basket and a jug to refill their water pan, but the sky was the purest blue, cloudless and benign. As quickly as it had arisen, the storm was over; water dripped rhythmically from the edges of the roof, and the path to the henhouse was slushy under the soles of her high-button shoes.

Hope stirred, springlike, in Dara Rose's heart, as she crossed the yard. She could hear the chickens clucking away in the coop, wanting their breakfast and their liberty from a long night of confinement.

Using the side of her foot, Dara Rose cleared a patch of ground for the birds and let them out while she ducked inside to fetch the water pan. Pleased to see that every member of her little flock had survived, she scattered their feed and then went on to collect the eggs.

There were six—a better count than the day before, though still less than she'd hoped for—and Dara Rose set each one carefully in the basket and returned to the house.

Edrina and Harriet were up and dressed, Edrina full of glee because she didn't have to go to school that day, and Harriet equally happy to have a playmate.

Dara Rose took off her bonnet and cloak, hung them up, washed her hands at the pump in the sink and put a pot of water on to boil, for oatmeal.

In the middle of the meal, a knock sounded at the front door.

Frowning, wondering who would be out and about so early, with the snow still deep enough to make traveling through it a trial, she pushed back her chair, told the children to finish eating and behave themselves and hurried through the small parlor. On some level, she realized, she'd hoped to find Clay McKettrick standing on her tiny porch, but this only came to her when she saw Mayor Wilson Ponder there instead.

Through the glass oval in the door, the older man's face looked purposeful, and a little grim.

Dara Rose opened the door. "Mayor Ponder," she said, not bothering to hide her surprise. He'd arrived, she saw now, looking past him to the street, in a sleigh drawn by two sturdy mules. "Come in."

"I won't tarry," Ponder said gravely, with a distracted tug at the brim of his bowler hat. He remained where he was, forcing Dara Rose to stand in the bright cold of the doorway and wait to hear what business he had with her. "I know this isn't a convenient time, what with the blizzard and all, but frankly, I'm not comfortable putting the task off any longer." He reddened slightly, though that might have been because of the weather, and not any sense of chagrin, and his muttonchop whiskers wobbled as he prepared to go on. "The town purchased this house for the use of the marshal, Mrs. Nolan, and if Clay McKettrick doesn't mean to use the place, well, we—the town council, that is—would prefer to sell it."

Dara Rose felt the floor shift under her feet, but she kept her shoulders squared and even managed not to shiver at the cold, and the news the mayor had just delivered.

"Oh," she said, hugging herself and wishing for her cloak, wishing for summer and better times. "Do you have a prospective buyer?"

"Ezra Maddox wants the property," Mayor Ponder said, after more whisker-wriggling. "He's offering two hundred and fifty dollars cash money and, what with bringing in electricity, the town could use the funds."

Ezra Maddox owned a farm, Dara Rose thought, dazed and frustrated and quite cornered. What did the man want with a run-down house miles from his crops and his dairy cows?

By now, everyone knew Clay had decided to live over at the jailhouse. Could it be that Mr. Maddox was simply trying to force her hand by buying the house out from under her? Was he hoping she would give in and accept his offer of a so-called housekeeping job, possibly followed by marriage, and send her children away in the bargain?

Dara Rose seethed, even as cold terror overtook her. "How long until we have to move?" she asked, amazed at how calm she sounded.

Mayor Ponder hesitated before he answered, perhaps ashamed of that morning's mission. On the other hand, he'd gone to all the bother of hitching mules to a sleigh to get there bright and early, which did not indicate any real degree of reluctance on his part. "Ezra's mighty anxious to take possession of the place," he finally said. "But since Christmas is just two weeks away, well, he's—*we're*— willing to let you stay until the first of the year."

Dara Rose gripped the door frame with one hand, thinking she might actually swoon. Behind her, in the kitchen, the girls' voices rang like chimes as they conducted some merry disagreement, laced with giggles.

"Well, then," Dara Rose managed, meeting the mayor's gaze, seeing both sympathy and resolve there, "that's that, isn't it? Thank you for letting me know."

With that, she shut the door in his face.

And stood trembling, there in the small parlor, until she heard his footsteps retreating on the porch.

"Mama?" Harriet, light-footed as ever and half again too perceptive for a five-year-old, was standing directly behind her. "Can we get a dog? Edrina says we don't need another mouth to feed, but a puppy wouldn't eat very much, would it?"

All of Dara Rose's considerable strength gave way then, like a dam under the strain of rising water. She uttered a small, choked sob, shook her head and fled to the bedroom.

Dara Rose seldom cried—even at Parnell's funeral service, she'd been dry-eyed—but she was only human, after all.

And she'd come to the end of her resources, at least for the moment.

So she sat on the edge of the bed she shared with her daughters—Parnell had slept on the settee in the parlor—covered her face with both hands and wept softly into her palms.

CLAY WAS HAVING BREAKFAST over at the hotel dining room—bacon and eggs and hotcakes, with plenty of hot, fresh coffee—when Sawyer wandered in, looking well-rested and clean-shaven, his manner at once affable and distant.

"Mind if I join you?" he said, pulling back a chair opposite Clay and sitting down before Clay could answer. He picked up the menu and studied it with the same grave concentration their illustrious granddad reserved for government beef contracts.

Politicians and pencil pushers, Angus had been known to remark, on the occasions he did business with such officials. *A man would have to be simpleminded to trust a one of them.*

"Make yourself at home," Clay said, dryly and long

after the fact. He hadn't slept much the night before, thanks to Dara Rose and Sawyer's unexpected presence and the long slog through the snow to the O'Reilly place.

He'd found them huddled around a poor fire like characters in a Dickens novel, wrapped in thin blankets. They'd had fried eggs for supper, Mrs. O'Reilly had told him, and those were all gone, and he was welcome to what was left of yesterday's pinto beans if he was hungry.

Clay had thanked her kindly and said he'd already had supper, which happened to be the truth, though he would have lied without a qualm if it hadn't been, and then he'd carried in most of their dwindling wood supply to dry beside the homemade stove. Before coming to the hotel for breakfast that morning, he'd stopped by the mercantile, pounded at the front door until the storekeeper let him in, and purchased a sackful of dried beans, along with flour, sugar, a pound of coffee and assorted canned goods for the O'Reillys. He'd paid extra to have the food delivered before the store was open for business.

Now, sitting across from his pensive cousin in a warm, clean, well-lighted place where good food could be had in plenty, he felt vaguely ashamed of his own prosperity. While the McKettricks didn't live grandly, they didn't lack for money, either. Clay had never missed a meal in his life, never had to go without shoes or wear clothes that had belonged to somebody else first. Unlike the O'Reilly children, and too many others like them, he'd had a strong, committed father, backed up by three uncles and a granddad.

The cook, a round-bellied man who doubled as a waiter, came over to the table to greet Sawyer and take his order.

Sawyer simply pointed toward Clay's plate and said, "That looks good."

The cook nodded and went away.

Sawyer sat there, easy in his hide, dressed like a prosperous gambler. Instead of his usual plain shirt and even plainer denim trousers, he sported a suit, complete with a white shirt, a string tie and a brocade vest. "You look miserable this morning, cousin," he said cheerfully, "but something tells me it isn't remorse over the uncharitable welcome you offered last night."

Clay gave a raw chuckle, void of mirth. His appetite was gone, all of a sudden, and he set down his knife and fork, pushed his plate away. "It definitely isn't remorse," he said.

Sawyer helped himself to a slice of toasted bread and bit into it, chewed appreciatively. Though his eyes twinkled, his voice was serious when he replied, "You could still go back to the Triple M, you know. They'd welcome you back into the fold with open arms and shouts of 'hurrah.'"

"I'll pay them a visit one of these days," he said. "There aren't any hard feelings on my side."

"Nor theirs, either." Sawyer shoved a hand through his unruly dark-gold hair, which was always a little too long. "You're lucky, Clay," he said, his gaze moving to the window next to their table. "Pa and Granddad can't seem to make up their minds whether to kill the fatted calf in my honor or take a horsewhip to me." He frowned, squinted at the foggy glass. "I think somebody's trying to get your attention," he observed.

Clay looked, and there, on the other side of that steamed-up window, was Edrina, practically pressing her nose to the glass. She waved one unmittened hand and retreated a step.

"I'll be damned," Clay muttered, gesturing for the child to come inside.

"Who's the kid?" Sawyer wanted to know.

"Friend of mine," Clay answered, as Edrina scampered toward the entrance to the dining room.

She hurried over to the table, face flushed with cold and purpose, and stood there like a little soldier.

"Mama's crying," she said. "Mama *never* cries."

Clay scraped back his chair, took Edrina's small hands into his own, trying to chafe some warmth into them. "Where's your bonnet?" he fussed, trying to process the idea of Dara Rose in tears. "You aren't wearing any mittens, and your coat is unbuttoned—"

"I was in a *hurry,*" Edrina told him, with a little sigh of impatience. She spared Sawyer the briefest glance, then looked back at Clay with a proud plea in her eyes. "You'll come home with me, won't you? Right now? Because Mama is crying and Mama never, *ever* cries."

"Go on," Sawyer said to Clay. "I'll settle up for your breakfast."

Clay got up, retrieved his duster from the back of the chair beside his and his hat from the seat and put them on. "What's the matter with her?" he asked, more worried than he could ever remember being before. "Is she sick?"

Gravely, Edrina took his hand, tugged him in the direction of the door. "I don't know," she said fretfully. "Maybe. But she was fine while we were having our oatmeal. Then Mr. Ponder stopped by, and they talked, and when Harriet asked Mama if we could please get a dog, Mama commenced to blubbering and ran right out of the room."

Outside, the snow was melting under a steadily warming sky, but it was still deep. Clay curved an arm around Edrina's waist, much as he had done with Chester the night before, and set off for Dara Rose's place with long strides.

DARA ROSE MARCHED herself out into the kitchen, pumped cold water into the basin she kept on hand and splashed her face repeatedly while Harriet watched her solemnly from the doorway.

"Are you through crying, Mama?" the child asked, very softly.

Dara Rose felt ashamed. Now she'd upset Edrina and Harriet, and for what? A few moments of self-pity?

"I'm quite through," she said, drying her still-puffy face with a dish towel. "And I haven't the slightest idea what came over me." She hugged Harriet, then frowned, looking around. "Where is Edrina?"

Harriet bit her lower lip, clearly reluctant to answer.

"Harriet?" Dara Rose said, taking her little girl gently but firmly by the shoulders. *"Where is your sister?"*

Harriet's eyes were huge and luminous. "She went to fetch Mr. McKettrick," she finally replied.

Alarm rushed through Dara Rose, and not just because a glance at the row of hooks beside the back door revealed that Edrina had gone off through the deep snow without her bonnet or her mittens. She was just reaching for her own cloak when she heard footsteps on the front porch—boots, stomping off snow.

Clay knocked, but then he came right in, carrying Edrina. His gaze locked with Dara Rose's as he set the little girl down and pulled the door closed behind him.

She'd never seen a man look so worried before, not even when Parnell came to that settlement house in Bangor, Maine, to claim her and the children. They'd been mere babies then, Edrina and Harriet, and memories of their real father, Parnell's younger brother, Luke, soon faded.

"Are you sick?" Clay demanded, in the same tone he

might have employed to confront a drunk with disorderly conduct.

Dara Rose wasn't sick, except with mortification. "I'm quite all right," she said, but she didn't sound very convincing, even to herself. She shifted her attention to her elder daughter, letting her know with a look that she was in big trouble. "I apologize for any inconvenience—"

Clay's neck reddened, and his eyes narrowed. "I'd be obliged if you girls would wait in the kitchen," he said, though he never looked away from Dara Rose's face.

Edrina and Harriet, always ready with a protest when *she* made such a request, fled the room like rabbits with a fox on their trail.

"That little girl," Clay said, in a furious whisper, one index finger jabbing in the general direction of the kitchen a few times, "was so worried about you that she braved all that snow to find me and bring me here. So don't think for one minute that you're going to put me off with an apology for any *inconvenience*."

Dara Rose stared at him. "Why are you so angry?" she finally asked. *And why does it thrill me to see you like this?*

"I'm not angry," Clay rasped out, wrenching off his Wyatt Earp–style hat and flinging it so that it landed on the settee, teetered there and dropped to the floor. "Damn it, Dara Rose, whatever went on here this morning scared your daughter half to death, and since Edrina is the most courageous kid I've ever come across, *I* got scared, too."

The thrill didn't subside, and Dara Rose prayed her feelings didn't show. "I lost my composure for a moment," she confessed, as stiffly proud as a Puritan even as her heart raced and her breath threatened to catch in the back of her throat and never come loose. "Believe me, I regret it. I certainly didn't mean to frighten the children—"

"Well," Clay said, in earnest, "you *did*. And I'm not leaving here until you tell me what Ponder said to you that made you go to pieces the way you did."

Dara Rose swallowed, looked down at the floor. Right or wrong, Clay meant what he said—that much was obvious from his tone and his countenance. He wouldn't be going anywhere until she answered him.

"Dara Rose?" He was standing close to her now, his hands resting lightly on her shoulders. He smelled of fresh air, snow and something woodsy. "Tell me."

She knew she ought to pull away from him, ought to look anywhere but up into his face, but she couldn't manage either response. "Mayor Ponder stopped by to tell me that, since you don't want this house, the town council plans to sell it to Ezra Maddox for two hundred and fifty dollars," she said. It was remarkable how calm she sounded, she thought, when her insides were buzzing like a swarm of bees smoked out of their hive. "We have to be out by the first of the year."

"That son of a—" Clay ground out, before catching himself.

Dara Rose felt tears burning behind her eyes again, and she was determined not to disgrace herself by shedding them. "I have ten dollars," she said, like someone talking in their sleep. "And I've saved some of the egg money. It won't take us far, but it's enough to leave town."

"Where would you go?" Clay immediately asked.

"I don't know," Dara Rose replied honestly. "Somewhere."

"The town isn't going to sell this house," Clay said.

"Of course they are," Dara Rose argued, though not with any spirit.

"I'm the marshal," Clay told her, "and under the terms

of our agreement, I'm entitled to living quarters. It just so happens that I've decided I'd rather live here than in the jailhouse."

Dara Rose's jaw dropped, and it took her a moment to recover. A *long* moment. "But we couldn't… Where would the children and I—?"

Clay hooked a finger under her chin. "Right here," he said. "You and Edrina and Harriet could live right here, with me—if you and I were married."

Dara Rose nearly choked. *"Married?"*

"It wouldn't do for us to live under the same roof otherwise," Clay said reasonably.

"But we're nearly total strangers—"

"For now," Clay went on, when her words fell away, "it would be a private arrangement. All business. I won't press you to bed down with me, Dara Rose. This place is too small for such shenanigans, anyhow, with the girls around."

Dara Rose couldn't believe what she was hearing. It was Parnell, all over again. Clay was offering a marriage that *wasn't* a marriage, offering shelter and safety and respectability. But unless she wanted to send her children away and move in with Ezra Maddox, she couldn't afford to refuse.

"Why?" she asked, barely breathing the word. "Why would you want to do this, Clay McKettrick?"

He smiled at her. Tucked a tendril of hair behind her right ear, where it had escaped its pins. "I want a wife," he said, as though that explained everything, instead of raising dozens, if not hundreds, of new questions.

"But you said the marriage wouldn't be real."

"It won't be, at first," Clay told her. Where did he get all that certainty, all that confidence? All that *audacity?* "But maybe, with time…"

"What if nothing changes?" Dara Rose broke in, feeling

almost as though she needed to shout to be heard over the thrumming of her heartbeat, though of course she *didn't* shout, because the children would have heard.

"Then there'll be no harm done," Clay said. "We'll have the marriage annulled, I'll set you and the girls up in decent circumstances somewhere far from Blue River, and we'll go our separate ways."

No harm done? He spoke so blithely.

Was the man insane?

Possibly, Dara Rose decided. But he was also an infinitely better bet than Ezra Maddox.

Chapter 7

⁘

BY THE FOLLOWING MORNING, Sawyer was long gone and the snow had turned to mud so deep that folks had had to lay weathered boards and old doors in the street, just to get from one side to the other without sinking to their knees in the muck. Hardly anybody rode a horse or drove a wagon through town or along the side roads, either, but the sun shone like the herald of an early spring, and the breezes were almost balmy.

Clay considered all this as he stood in his small room at the jailhouse, stooping a little to peer at himself in the cracked shaving mirror fixed to the wall. He'd washed up and shaved, and then shaken out and put on the only suit he'd brought to Blue River—the getup consisted of a black woolen coat fitted at the waist, matching trousers, his best white shirt, starched and pressed for him at the Chinese laundry before he left Indian Rock, a brown brocade vest and a string tie.

He hated ties.

Hated starched shirts, too, for that matter.

He'd worn this suit exactly three times since he bought

it—to one wedding and two funerals. Today, it was a wedding—his own—and even though it was his choice to get married, the occasion had its somber aspects, as well.

Up home, the ceremony would have been a community event, like a circus or a tent revival or the Independence Day fireworks, drawing crowds from miles around and working the womenfolk up into a frenzy of sewing and cooking and marking their calendars so they'd know how long the first baby took to show up. The men would complain about having to wear their Sunday duds, sip moonshine from a shared fruit jar out in the orchard behind the church after the "I do's" had been said and lament that another unwitting member of their sex had been roped in and hog-tied.

Clay smiled to think of all that nuptial chaos and was glad he'd managed to escape it, though he felt a twinge of nostalgia, too. He and Dara Rose would be married quietly and sensibly, in a civil ceremony performed by Mayor Ponder at her place, with Edrina and Harriet the only guests. There would be no cake, no photographs, no rings and no wedding night, let alone a honeymoon, because this was an arrangement, a transaction—not a love match.

Which wasn't to say that Clay didn't fully expect to bed Dara Rose when the time came, and if they got a baby started right away, too, so much the better. He figured the actual consummation of their union would probably have to wait until spring, though, when the ranch house was finished and he and Dara Rose had a room to themselves.

Fine as the weather was, spring seemed a long way off when he thought of it in terms of making love to his wife.

Resigned, and leaving his hat behind because it didn't look right with the suit, Clay bid his dog a temporary farewell—Chester had taken to curling up on the cot inside the jail's one cell whenever he wanted to sleep, which was often—and set out for Dara Rose's little house, following the sidewalk as far as he could and then crossing the street by way of the peculiar system of planks and discarded doors and the beds of old wagons.

Mayor Ponder arrived by the same means, followed single file by a thin woman in very prim garb and one of the town council members—they'd come along to serve as witnesses, Clay supposed. Clutching a copy of the Good Book and a rolled sheet of paper as he minced his way over the swamplike road, Ponder looked none too pleased at the prospect of joining the new marshal and the pretty widow in holy matrimony.

Clay disliked the mayor, mainly because of the remark Ponder had made about not minding if Dara Rose wound up working upstairs at the Bitter Gulch Saloon, but he could tolerate the man long enough to get hitched. The rest of the time, Wilson Ponder was fairly easy to ignore.

"There's still time to change your mind," Ponder boomed out, as if he wanted the whole town to hear, when he and Clay met at Dara Rose's front gate. "Charity is charity, but I think you might be taking it a little too far in this instance."

Charity is charity.

The front door of the house was open, probably to admit as much fresh air as possible before the winter weather returned, and Clay had to unlock his jawbones by an act of will. What if Dara Rose had heard what Ponder said? Or the children?

He didn't respond, but simply glowered at Ponder until the other man cleared his throat and muttered, "Well, let's get on with it, then."

Edrina and Harriet appeared in the doorway, beaming. They had ribbons in their hair, and they were wearing summer dresses, very nearly outgrown and obviously their best.

"Mama looks so pretty in her wedding dress!" Edrina enthused, as Clay moved ahead of the others, stepped onto the porch and immediately swept both children off their feet, one in the curve of each arm.

They giggled at that, and the sound heartened Clay. Reminded him that he'd put on that itchy suit because he was going to a *wedding,* not a funeral.

Behind him, the female witness made a sighlike sound, long-suffering and full of righteous indignation.

Once again, Clay tamped down his temper. He wanted to pin that old biddy's ears back, verbally, anyhow—he'd never struck a woman, a child or an animal, and never intended to, though he'd landed plenty of punches in the faces of his boy cousins growing up—but today was neither the time nor the place to hold forth on what he thought of nasty-natured gossips.

For one thing, he didn't want to spoil the day for Edrina and Harriet. They were clearly overjoyed at the prospect of a wedding, though with Edrina, it was partly about being allowed to miss a few hours of school.

"I'll bet your mama *does* look pretty," Clay agreed, in belated reply to Edrina's statement. "Almost as pretty as the pair of you, maybe."

That got them both giggling again, and Clay smiled as he set them on their feet.

And then nearly tripped over them when Dara Rose appeared, wearing an ivory silk gown with puffed-out sleeves and lace trim at the cuffs. Her cheeks were pink, her eyes bright with a combination of nervousness and hope, her hair done up in a soft knot at her nape and billowing cloud-like around her face.

The sight of her knocked the wind out of Clay as surely as if he'd been thrown from a horse and landed spread-eagle on hard ground.

Ponder cleared his throat again, and the wedding party assembled itself, with surprising grace, in the middle of that cramped front room.

Dara Rose's trim shoulder bumped Clay's arm as she took her place beside him, and he felt a jolt of sweet fire at her touch.

Ponder opened the book, and then his mouth, but before he could get a word said, a ruckus erupted out in the road.

Looking down at Dara Rose, Clay saw her shut her eyes, felt her stiffen next to him.

Outside, a mule brayed, and a drunken voice bellowed.

Clay took Dara Rose's hand and squeezed it lightly before turning to head for the doorway.

Edrina and Harriet were already there, staring out.

"Mama's not going to marry you, Ezra Maddox!" Edrina shouted to the stumbling man trying to free his feet from the deep mud. "She's taken, so you'd better just get your sorry self out of here before there's trouble!"

Clay had to choke back a laugh. He rested one hand on the top of Edrina's head and one on Harriet's, and said quietly, "Go stand with your mama. I'll handle this."

Maddox was a big man, broad-shouldered and clad in work clothes, and his hair and beard were grizzled, wiry. Once he'd gotten loose from the mud, he practically tore the gate off its rusty hinges, getting it open, and stormed in Clay's direction like a locomotive.

Clay stepped out onto the porch, waited.

Behind him, Ponder said, "Now, Ezra, don't be a sore

loser. You're out of the running where Dara Rose is concerned, and making a damn fool of yourself won't change that."

Ezra came to a shambling stop in the middle of the path, not because he'd taken Mayor Ponder's sage advice to heart, Clay reckoned, but because he was used to folks clearing the way between him and whatever it was he aimed to have.

Clay didn't move.

The two men studied each other, at a distance of a dozen yards or so, and Maddox swayed slightly, ran the back of one arm across his mouth. His gaze narrowed.

"Did you get to the part where the justice of the peace inquires as to whether or not anybody has reason to object to this marriage?" Maddox ranted. "Because that's when I mean to say my piece."

"Let's hear it," Clay said, in an affable drawl. He hoped the situation wouldn't disintegrate into a howling brawl in the mud, with him and Maddox rolling back and forth with their hands on each other's throats, because he didn't want that to be what Dara Rose, Edrina and Harriet remembered when they looked back on this day.

Another part of him relished the idea of a knock-down-drag-out fisticuff.

Maddox straightened, swayed again and spoke with alacrity. "I have already offered for you, Dara Rose Nolan, and you belong to me," he said, as she stepped up beside Clay and put her hand on his arm.

A thrill of something rushed through Clay, though he'd hoped Dara Rose would stay inside, out of harm's way, until he and Maddox had settled their differences.

"You belong to me," Maddox reiterated.

"I belong to myself," Dara Rose informed him. "And

no one else, except for my children. I want nothing to do with you, Mr. Maddox, and I'll count it as a favor if you leave, right now."

"All right," Maddox erupted, flinging his beefy arms out from his sides with such force that he nearly fell over sideways, "you can bring the girls along, and I'll marry you straight off—today, if that's what you want."

"You are too late, Mr. Maddox," Dara Rose said, in a clear and steady voice. "Please be on your way so we can get on with the wedding."

Clay wondered distractedly if Dara Rose had ever seriously considered taking up with a lug like Maddox. He couldn't imagine her parting with her children.

Maddox just stood there, evidently weighing his options, which were few, and broke the ensuing silence by spitting violently and barking out, "This feller might have a badge, Dara Rose, but he ain't Parnell come back to life."

He turned partially, as if to walk away, but he jabbed a finger in Dara Rose's direction and went right on running off at the mouth. "I'll tell you what he is, this man you're so dead set on marryin'—he's a *stranger,* a lying drifter, for all you know—and when he moves on, leavin' you with another babe in your belly and no way to feed your brood, don't you come cryin' to me!"

Clay's restraint snapped then, but before he could take more than a single step in Maddox's direction, Dara Rose tightened her grip on his arm and stopped him.

Maddox spat again, but then he whirled around and headed for the gate and the waiting mule, every step he took making a sucking sound because of the mud.

Dara Rose let go of Clay's arm and walked, with high-chinned dignity, back into the house, leaving Clay and Mayor Ponder standing on the porch.

Ponder's gaze followed Maddox as he mounted the mule to ride away. "I'd watch my back if I were you, Marshal," he said thoughtfully. "Ezra's the kind to hold a grudge, and he's got a sneaky side to him."

Inside, Dara Rose was shaken, but she made sure it didn't show.

Mayor Ponder's wife, Heliotrope, was a scandalmonger with nothing better to do than spread gossip, heavily laced with her own interpretation of any given person or situation, of course, and thanks to Ezra Maddox's unexpected visit, she'd have plenty of fodder as it was.

Dara Rose wasn't about to give her more to work with.

Besides, the children were watching her, and they'd follow whatever example she set. She wanted them to see strength in their mother, and courage, and dignity.

So she straightened her spine, lifted her chin and once again took her place at Clay McKettrick's side.

Mayor Ponder opened his book again and began to read out the words that would bind her to this tall man standing next to her.

The mayor's voice turned to a drone, and the very atmosphere seemed to pulse and buzz around Dara Rose, making her light-headed.

She spoke when spoken to, answered by rote.

After three weddings, she could have gotten married in her sleep.

Questions plagued her, swooped down on her like raucous birds. *What if Ezra had been right? Suppose Clay was a liar and a drifter—or worse? Was she marrying him because some deluded part of her had him confused with Parnell?*

"I now pronounce you man and wife," Mayor Ponder

said, slamming the book closed between his pawlike hands. "Mr. McKettrick, you may kiss the bride."

Clay looked down at her, one eyebrow slightly raised, and a grin crooked at a corner of his mouth.

On impulse, and to get it over with, Dara Rose stood on tiptoe and kissed that mouth, very lightly, very quickly and very briefly.

"There," she said. "It's done."

Clay merely chuckled.

She could still back out, Dara Rose reminded herself fitfully. She could refuse to sign the marriage certificate, ask Mayor Ponder to reverse the declaration that they were now man and wife.

Was that legal?

For a moment, Dara Rose thought she might swoon, just faint dead away right there in her own front parlor. But Clay slipped a strong arm around her waist, effectively holding her up until she signaled, with a furtive glance his way, that she could stand without help.

Thoughts still clamored through her mind, though, and her hand shook slightly when she signed "Dara Rose Mc-Kettrick" on the line reserved for the bride.

What had she *done?*

Suppose Clay was really a rascal and a drunk, instead of the solid man he seemed to be? Suppose he already *had* a wife tucked away somewhere, and he'd just made them both bigamists? And what if this stranger had spoken falsely when he promised not to exercise his rights as a husband unless and until she declared herself ready and willing?

The room felt hot, even with a chinook breeze sweeping in through the open door.

Edrina tugged at Dara Rose's hand, bringing her back

into the present moment. "Now you're Mrs. McKettrick," the little girl crowed. "Can Harriet and I be McKettricks, too?"

Dara Rose had no idea how to answer.

Clay, who had clearly overheard, judging by that little smile resting on his mouth as he bent to scrawl his name on the marriage certificate, said nothing. He waited while Mayor Ponder and both witnesses added their signatures where appropriate. Then money changed hands, and the ordeal was over.

The official part of it, at least.

Mayor Ponder and his companions took their leave, and Dara Rose was alone with her new husband and her delighted children.

"We want to be McKettricks, too," Edrina insisted.

"You're Nolans," Dara Rose reasoned. "What would your papa think if you changed your names?"

"*You* changed *yours*," Edrina pointed out. "And, anyhow, Papa's dead."

Harriet's eyes rounded. "Papa's dead?"

"Of course he is, dolt," Edrina snapped. "Why do you suppose we put flowers on a grave with his name on it?"

"Edrina," Dara Rose reprimanded. "Stop it."

"I can't read," Harriet lamented, looking up at Dara Rose now, with tears welling in her eyes. "You said Papa was *gone*—"

Dara Rose exchanged glances with a somber-faced Clay and then bent her knees so she was crouching before her daughter, in the dress she'd worn to marry Luke, and then Parnell, and now Clay.

"Sweetheart," she said softly, "that's what 'gone' means sometimes. I know it's hard for you to understand, but you have to try."

Harriet turned, much to Dara Rose's surprise, and buried her face in one side of Clay's fancy suit coat, wailing in despair. This was unusual behavior, especially for even-tempered Harriet, but Dara Rose put it down to all the excitement of a front-room wedding.

"There, now," Clay said gruffly, as Dara Rose straightened, hoisting Harriet up into his arms. "You go right ahead and cry 'til you feel like stopping."

Dara Rose sank onto the settee, close to tears herself.

She was *married,* and there was so much she didn't know about Clay.

So much he didn't know about her.

Harriet bawled like a banshee—Dara Rose realized the child was going for effect now—her face hidden in Clay's shoulder.

"Here's what I think we ought to do," Clay said, to all of them. "We ought to go out to my ranch—I'll rent a buckboard and a couple of stout mules—and find ourselves a Christmas tree."

Harriet immediately stopped wailing.

Edrina lit up like a lightbulb wired to a power pole.

"A Christmas tree?" Dara Rose repeated, confounded.

"The roads are pretty muddy," Edrina speculated, but she was obviously warming to the idea, and so was Harriet, who had reared back to look at Clay in wet-eyed wonder.

"That's why we need mules," Clay replied.

"Do you believe in St. Nicholas?" Harriet asked him, in a hushed voice.

Clay looked directly at Dara Rose, silently dared her to say otherwise and replied, "I do indeed. One Christmas Eve, when my cousin Sawyer and I were about your age, we caught a glimpse of him flying over the roof of our granddad's barn in that sleigh of his, with eight reindeer harnessed to the rig."

Edrina blinked, swallowed. *"Really?"* she breathed, wanting so much to believe, even at the advanced age of six, that she'd been wrong to think there was no magic in the world.

Dara Rose's heart ached.

"Can't think what else it could have been," Clay answered, as serious in tone and expression as a man bearing witness in a court of law, under oath. "A sleigh pulled by eight reindeer is a fairly distinctive sight."

"Thunderation," Edrina exclaimed softly, while Harriet favored her older sister with a smug I-told-you-so look.

Dara Rose glared up at her bridegroom. "Mr. McKettrick," she began, but he cut her off before she could go on.

"Call me Clay," he said mildly. "I'm your husband now, remember?"

Dara Rose got to her feet. *"Clay,* then," she said dangerously. "I will have you know—"

Again he interrupted, setting Harriet on her feet and saying, "You two go on and change your clothes. Get your bonnets and your coats, too."

Edrina and Harriet rushed to obey.

Dara Rose stood there in her sorry-luck wedding dress, trembling with frustration. "How dare you get their hopes up like that?" she whispered furiously, flushed and near tears again. "How *dare* you encourage them to believe in things that aren't even real?"

"Whoa," Clay said, cupping her chin gently in one hand. "Are you saying that St. Nicholas *isn't real?"*

"Of *course* that's what I'm saying," Dara Rose retorted, under her breath but with plenty of bluster. "He *isn't."*

Clay gave a long, low whistle of surprise, though his too-blue eyes danced with delighted mischief. "I got here just in time," he said.

Dara Rose was brought up short. *"What?"* she managed, with more effort than a single word should have required.

Clay shook his head, as though he couldn't believe another human being could be so deluded as Dara Rose clearly was. "They're only going to be little girls once," he said, "and for a very short time. If I hadn't shown up when I did, you might have ruined one of the best things about being a kid—believing."

Dara Rose's mouth fell open. Clay closed it for her by levering up on her chin with that work-roughened and yet extraordinarily gentle hand of his.

"Now," he went on decisively, "Edrina and Harriet and I are going out to find a Christmas tree. You can either come with us, Mrs. McKettrick, or you can stay right here with the chickens. Which is it going to be?"

Dara Rose wasn't about to send her children out into the countryside in a mule-drawn buckboard with a stranger, but neither did she have the heart to insist that they forget the whole crazy plan.

"Edrina and Harriet are *my* children," she said, hearing the girls laugh and scuffle in the small bedroom as they went about exchanging their wedding garb for warmer things, "and I will not have them misled."

"Fair enough," Clay said, letting his eyes drop. "Shouldn't you get out of that fancy dress before we head out?"

THE MUD WAS DEEP, but the mules that came with the hired buckboard were strong and sure-footed. Once Clay had arranged the transaction, changed his clothes and collected Chester from the jailhouse, they made the short journey to the ranch with no trouble at all—in fact, it seemed to Clay that those mules knew how to avoid the worst of the muck and plant their hooves on solid ground.

He pulled back on the brake lever and simultaneously reined in the mules right where the kit-house would go up, come spring.

He jumped down, smiling as Edrina and Harriet piled eagerly out of the back of the buckboard, Chester leaping after them and barking fit to split a man's eardrums, and went around to reach up a hand to Dara Rose.

She hadn't said two words to him since they'd left town, and her color was high, but she let Clay lift her down.

Gasped when he made sure their bodies collided in the process.

He laughed, though she'd roused an ache inside him.

She blushed and straightened her bonnet with both hands, which made her bosom rise in that tantalizing way he so enjoyed.

"You gave your word," she whispered, narrow-eyed.

"And I'll keep it," Clay assured her. This was what he got for putting his mouth in motion before his head was in gear, he figured. A wife to contradict everything he said and no wedding night to make up for the inevitable difficulties of an intimate alliance.

If Sawyer had been there, he'd surely have called Clay crazy, denying himself the pleasures of matrimony, especially when he was married to a woman like Dara Rose.

And Clay would have had to admit his cousin was right.

He *was* crazy.

But a promise was a promise.

"Let's go," he said, reaching into the wagon-bed for the

short-handled ax he'd borrowed when he rented the team and buckboard over at the livery stable. "It'll be dark in a few hours, and there's no telling when the snow will start up again, so we'd better get started."

Edrina and Harriet were practically beside themselves with excitement, and Chester trotted around them all in big, swoopy circles, livelier than Clay had yet seen him.

The "tree" they finally settled upon looked more like a tumbleweed to Clay, who was used to the lush, fragrant firs that grew in northern Arizona, but Edrina and Harriet were enchanted. So Clay chopped down that waist-high scrub pine and carried it in one hand back to the wagon.

Dara Rose bore silent witness to all this, cautiously enjoying her daughters' delight.

Edrina had noticed the stone markers Clay had set in place the last time he was there, and she squatted on her haunches to peer at one of them. Harriet and Chester stood nearby.

"What *is* this?" Edrina asked.

Clay smiled, tossed the tree into the bed of the wagon and walked back to stand over the little girl. He was aware of Dara Rose on the periphery of things, but he didn't look in her direction.

"This is where I plan to put up my—*our*—house, once it arrives, that is."

Edrina looked up at him, brow crinkling a little. "Houses don't *arrive*," she said.

"This one will," Clay replied, enjoying the exchange. "It's coming by rail, from Sears, Roebuck and Company, all the way out in Chicago, Illinois."

"A *house* can't ride on a train!" Harriet proclaimed gleefully. "Houses are too *big* to fit!"

Clay laughed, crouched between the two girls, to put

himself at eye level with them. Chester nuzzled his arm and then, quick as can be, licked Clay's face.

"I guess you'd say this house is kind of like a jigsaw puzzle," Clay told the children. "It's broken down into parts and packed in crates. When it gets here, I'll have to put it together."

Edrina frowned, absorbing his words. Then she whistled, through her teeth, and said, *"Thunderation and spit."*

"Speak in a ladylike fashion, Edrina Nolan," Dara Rose interceded coolly, "or do not speak at all."

Clay tossed a look in his wife's direction and stood tall again, resting one hand on each bonneted head. "I reckon we'll head back to town now," he said. "I don't like the looks of that cloud bank over there on the horizon."

The wind was beginning to pick up a little, too.

Dara Rose shooed the girls toward the hired buckboard, but they didn't need anybody's help to climb inside. They shinnied up the rear wheels, agile as a pair of monkeys, and planted themselves on either side of the scrub pine.

Clay hoisted Chester aboard and fastened the tailgate, but before he could get to Dara Rose and offer her a hand up, she was already in the front of the wagon, perched on the seat and looking straight ahead.

"Will there be room for us in your new house?" Harriet asked, just as Clay settled in to take the reins.

Clay looked down at Dara Rose, who didn't acknowledge him in any visible way. "Yes," he said. "You and Edrina will have to share a room at first, most likely, but after a year or two, I'll be building on, and you'll each have one of your own."

"Then where will Mama be?" Harriet wanted to know. "In my room, or in Edrina's?"

"Neither," Clay said.

A flush bloomed into Dara Rose's cheeks and, even though she hastened to adjust her bonnet, Clay had already seen. "Harriet," Dara Rose said, "please sit down immediately."

Harriet sat.

Clay bit the inside of his lip, so he wouldn't smile, turned the team and wagon in a wide semicircle and headed toward town.

The girls chattered behind him and Dara Rose, in the bed of the buckboard, Chester no doubt hanging on every word. The wagon wheels, in need of greasing, squealed as the mules pulled the rig overland, puffing clouds of white fog from their nostrils, and the harnesses creaked.

For all that, Clay would remember that trip home as a silent one, because, once again, Dara Rose didn't say a word.

When they drove on along Main Street, passing the road that fronted the house without turning in, Dara Rose nudged him lightly with one elbow but still didn't speak.

"Where are we going?" Edrina called, from the back.

"We're having supper at the hotel tonight," Clay said, with a sidelong glance at Dara Rose. "Call it a celebration," he added dryly.

"Don't be silly," Dara Rose muttered in protest, but the girls were cheering by then, causing Chester to bark, and all of those noises combined to drown her out.

What with all the planks and doors in the road, Clay had to weave the team and wagon in and out half the length of Main Street, but he finally reined in, in front of the Texas Arms Hotel and Dining Room, and set the brake.

"This is extravagant," Dara Rose whispered to Clay, when everybody except Chester was standing on the board sidewalk. "We have food at home...."

"Tonight is special," Clay replied, before shifting his

attention to Chester. "You stay put, dog, and I'll bring you out some supper."

Chester seemed to understand; he settled down next to the Christmas tree, resting his muzzle on his outstretched front legs, sighed once and closed his eyes.

Edrina and Harriet raced, giggling, toward the main entrance to the hotel.

Dara Rose hesitated, though, and took a light but firm hold on Clay's arm. "You mustn't spoil my children," she said. "I don't want Edrina and Harriet getting used to luxuries I cannot hope to provide for them myself."

Clay suppressed a sigh. "Food," he said reasonably, "is not a luxury."

"It is when it's paid for, and someone else cooked and served it," Dara Rose insisted.

Clay smiled down at his bride. "Try to enjoy it just the same," he advised, taking her elbow and gently steering her across the sidewalk.

Chapter 8

⌒৩৩⌒

THE SMALL RUSTIC DINING establishment serving the Texas Arms Hotel was full of savory smells, causing Dara Rose's stomach to rumble.

Someone had hung a wreath made of holly sprigs behind the cash register, and limp tinsel garlands drooped from the edges of a long counter lined with stools.

Only one of the six tables was in use. A man, a woman and a little girl, probably a year or two older than Edrina, dined in companionable silence, their clothes exceedingly fine, their manners impeccable. Since Dara Rose had never laid eyes on them before, she knew they must have arrived on the afternoon train.

She wondered if they were just passing through, or if they'd come to Blue River to spend Christmas with friends or family.

Clay nodded a taciturn greeting to the man and the man nodded back.

Edrina and Harriet, stealing glances at the little girl, scrambled onto chairs at a table in front of the window, sitting side by side and swinging their feet. It had been an exciting day for them—first, the wedding, then the expedition to find a Christmas tree, and now a restaurant meal.

By the time they tumbled into bed that night, Dara Rose thought fondly, her daughters would be so deliciously exhausted, so saturated with fresh air, that they'd sleep like stones settling deep into the silt of a quiet pond.

Clay was just pulling back a chair for Dara Rose when the cook-waiter appeared, smiling a welcome. "I hear this is a wedding supper!" the man thundered. "Congratulations, Marshal."

It wouldn't have been proper to congratulate Dara Rose, since there would inevitably be an implication that she'd somehow *captured* her new husband, rounded him up like a rogue steer, and not by pure feminine allure. While she appreciated the courtesy, she did wish the man hadn't spoken so loudly, because the woman at the other table turned in their direction, her expression impassive, her gaze flickering briefly over Dara Rose's faded cloak, with its frayed, mud-splattered hem.

"Thanks, Roy," Clay responded, addressing the cook, with whom he was obviously acquainted, and the two men shook hands.

Dara Rose was not a person to compare herself to others, but as Clay pulled back a chair for her and she sat down, she couldn't help thinking how shabby she and the children must seem, in the eyes of that elegantly dressed woman and her little girl.

"What's it going to be, ladies?" Clay asked the children, while Dara Rose perused the menu, nearly overwhelmed by all the choices. "I can definitely recommend the fried chicken dinner, and the meat loaf is good, too."

"What's meat loaf?" Harriet wanted to know.

"You'll have the chicken dinner," Dara Rose said, without looking away from the menu. "One will be plenty for both of you."

She thought she might have felt Clay stiffen beside her, but then, as though she hadn't spoken at all, he simply answered Harriet's inquiry about the nature of meat loaf.

"I want that," Harriet said, when he'd finished. "Please."

"And I'll have stew with dumplings," Edrina added, sounding like a small adult, "if I may, please."

"You may," Clay said, without looking at Dara Rose, though she *did* see his mouth quirk briefly at one corner. "This is a very special occasion," he added, after clearing his throat quietly. "And, anyhow, Chester will be pleased to accept any leftovers. He's still building up his strength, you know."

Dara Rose's cheeks flamed. She loved animals. Her rooster and hens all had names, and she went out of her way to take good care of them. But she'd been so poor for so long—since she'd "married" Luke Nolan, a few months before Edrina was born—that the idea of giving a dog restaurant food just wouldn't fit into any of the compartments in her mind.

"There are *people* in this town who could put anything extra to good use," she said, sounding way more prim than she'd intended.

"Like the O'Reillys," Edrina said, with a sigh.

"Among others," Dara Rose agreed.

Clay was watching her so directly, and with such intensity, that she was forced to meet his gaze. "Shall we just scrape it all into a pan," he began, "and set it on the floor of their shanty, the way we'd do with Chester?"

Dara Rose blushed even harder. If they hadn't been in a public place, and if she'd been given to violence, she'd have slapped him across the face.

Before she could speak, Clay summoned Roy, the cook, back to their table with a polite gesture of one hand.

The man hurried over, eager to please.

Clay placed everyone's order—except for Dara Rose's—and then asked the cook to pack up enough fried chicken, meat loaf and trimmings to feed four people. He'd pay for and collect the extra food at the end of the meal, he said, and then looked pointedly at Dara Rose.

Confounded, and a little stung, she asked for chicken.

Edrina and Harriet were watching Clay raptly—they might have expected a laurel wreath or a winged helmet to appear on his head, from their expressions—and, not surprisingly, it was Edrina who broke the pulsing silence.

"Are we taking supper to the O'Reillys?" she asked.

"Yes," Clay said.

"Harriet and I are planning to visit Addie tomorrow," Edrina said. She turned a vaguely challenging glance in Dara Rose's direction. "Mama said we could."

Dara Rose, still feeling as though she'd been put smartly in her place and none too happy about it, thank you very much, returned Edrina's look in spades. "I said *you* could visit," she reminded her child, "since you'd already promised. I did *not* give permission for Harriet to accompany you."

"What's the harm?" Clay asked mildly, though his eyes contained a challenge, just as Edrina's had before. "That little girl looked to me as though she could use some company. Especially somebody close to her own age."

"She has romantic fever," Edrina said solemnly.

"That's not catching," Clay replied, and though his tone was serious, there was a twinkle in his eyes now. "In fact, I'd say your mother is immune to it."

"Other things *are* catching," Dara Rose felt compelled

to say, though she knew there was some kind of battle being waged here, and she was losing ground. Fast.

"It's probably too cold for lice and fleas at this time of year," Clay said.

Dara Rose didn't get a chance to respond. The food arrived, heaped on steaming plates, the children's first, and then Clay's and Dara Rose's.

The family of strangers, meanwhile, had finished their meal, and the man was settling the bill. The mother and the child rose from their chairs, and then the little girl walked right over to Edrina and Harriet and put out one tiny, porcelain-white hand.

"My name is Madeline Howard," she said. With her long, shining brown hair, deep green eyes and fitted emerald velvet dress, she bore a striking resemblance to the doll in the mercantile window. "What's yours?"

"I'm Edrina," answered Dara Rose's elder daughter, barely able to see over the mountain of food before her. "And this is my sister, Harriet."

"We're going to live in Blue River from now on," Madeline said. "Mama and Papa and me, I mean. Papa's going to build an office, and we'll have rooms upstairs."

The woman approached, laid a hand on Madeline's shoulder, offered a pained smile to everyone in general and no one in particular. "You mustn't bother people when they're eating, darling," she said.

Clay stood, put out his hand, and the woman shook it, after the briefest hesitation. "Clay McKettrick," he said. "This is my wife, Dara Rose."

This is my wife, Dara Rose.

No words could have sounded stranger to Dara Rose, and she had to swallow a ridiculous urge to explain, all in a rush, that theirs was a marriage of convenience, not a real one.

She merely nodded, though, and the woman nodded back. Like her daughter, she wore velvet, though her gown and short cape were a rich shade of brown instead of green. Not only that, but the pile on that fabric was plush, not worn away in places like most of the velvet one saw in Blue River, Texas.

The man had reached the table by then, and smiled as he and Clay shook hands. "Glad to meet you, Marshal," he said. "I'm Jim Howard, and my wife is Eloise."

Another stiff smile from Eloise. "My husband is a dentist," she said. "Most people address him as 'Dr. Howard,' of course."

Dara Rose, who had been trying to decide whether or not good manners required that she stand, like Clay, decided to stay seated.

"We could use a dentist around here," Clay said, with a grin dancing in his eyes but not quite reaching his mouth.

Madeline smiled broadly at Edrina and Harriet. "You both have very good teeth," she said admiringly. Her own were like small, square pearls, perfectly strung.

Jim Howard—*Dr.* Howard—chuckled at that. "We'll let you finish your meal in peace," he said, steering his womenfolk gently away, toward the hotel's modest lobby and then the stairs beyond.

Clay sat down. "Nice people," he said.

Madeline, Dara Rose noticed, kept looking back, her expression one of friendly longing, as though she would have liked to stay and chat with Edrina and Harriet.

"The lady is snooty," Edrina announced, holding a dinner roll daintily between a thumb and index finger. "But I like Madeline, and her papa, too."

Dara Rose was keenly aware, in that moment, that Edrina was following her lead. Hadn't she disliked Mrs. Howard almost immediately, and returned coolness for coolness instead of making an effort to be neighborly, offer a welcome to the newcomers?

It was tremendously difficult sometimes, she thought glumly, to be the sort of person she wanted her *daughters* to be, when they grew up. And she'd fallen far short of that standard tonight.

Unexpectedly, Clay reached over and gently squeezed her hand, just once and very briefly, but the gesture raised Dara Rose's flagging spirits.

It also sent something sharp and hot racing through her, a fiery ache she had to work very hard to ignore.

"Perhaps when we get to know Mrs. Howard better," she told Edrina, somehow managing a normal tone of voice, "we'll discover that she's a very nice person."

"Perhaps," Edrina agreed doubtfully.

The girls were practically nodding off in their chairs by the time the meal ended.

Clay took the leftovers out to Chester on a borrowed plate, while Roy packed the O'Reillys' supper into a large wooden crate, carefully covered with a dish towel. The bill was paid—the cost of it would have kept Dara Rose and the girls in groceries for the better part of a month—and Clay carried the crate out to the wagon, stowed it under the seat, where Chester couldn't get at it, and returned with the empty plate.

By then, Dara Rose had put on her cloak, Edrina was wearing her outdoor garb and, together, they maneuvered a sleepy Harriet into her coat and bonnet. Clay whisked the child up into his arms and carried her to the wagon.

A light snowfall was just beginning, and the wind was

picking up, so Clay took Dara Rose, the children and Chester back to the house first, saw them inside, and announced quietly that he'd return as soon as he'd dropped off the food at the O'Reilly place and turned in the mules and wagon at the livery.

Dara Rose moved by rote, helping the girls prepare for bed, tucking them in, hearing their prayers.

Harriet asked for the doll again.

Edrina said she was glad to have a new papa, then promised not to forget the old one.

Dara Rose was glad she'd turned down the wick in the kerosene lantern, leaving the room mostly in shadow, because there were tears in her eyes as she told her children good-night and kissed their foreheads.

THE SETTEE IN DARA Rose's parlor was about a foot shorter than he was, by Clay's estimation, but he'd slept in less comfortable places in his time, just the same. And Dara Rose *had* been considerate enough to set out a blanket and a pillow for him.

He smiled just imagining the joshing he'd get if Sawyer and the rest of his McKettrick cousins knew he was spending his wedding night alone, with his feet hanging over one end of a short sofa. He'd be lucky if he didn't wake up with his spine in the shape of a horseshoe and his toes numb from lack of circulation.

Chester, who'd settled himself nearby on the blanket Clay had brought over from the jailhouse, watched as he sat down on the settee to kick off his boots.

"Believe it or not," he told the dog, low-voiced, "I got married today."

Chester offered no comment.

The tumbleweed Christmas tree stood undecorated in

a corner of the room, stuck in a bucket of water and looking about as festive as Clay felt, but it had a nice pine scent that reminded him of home.

Because the house was small and he was mindful of the children, Clay decided to sleep in his clothes. He was about to extinguish the lantern and stretch out, as best he could, on that blasted settee, when Dara Rose stepped out of the bedroom.

Her hair was down, tumbling well past her waist, and she wore a long nightgown, covered with a plain flannel wrapper, cinched tight at her middle.

Clay's heart skipped a couple of beats, though he knew full well she wasn't there to render an annulment legally and morally impossible.

She stopped, glanced over at the hopeful tumbleweed and then stood a little straighter. This raised her to her full and unremarkable height, but whatever her errand, she sure enough looked like she meant business.

"Either you are an irresponsible man," Dara Rose said, making it clear how Edrina came by her bold certainty about everything, "or you have more money than you let on. Which is it?"

Clay stood, though he suddenly felt bone-tired, because there was a lady in the room. "I never said I was broke, Mrs. McKettrick," he replied dryly.

"Don't call me 'Mrs. McKettrick'!" Dara Rose immediately responded. "We made an agreement. This is a marriage in name only."

"Oh, I'm well aware of that," Clay responded, thinking he'd wait forever for this woman, if that was what he had to do. "But you are legally my wife, and that makes you Mrs. McKettrick."

She pulled so tight on the cinches of her wrapper then

that it was a wonder she didn't split right in two, like one of those showgirls in a magician's act. "Why do you keep pointing out that we are married in the eyes of the law?"

Clay was enjoying her discomfort a lot more than was gentlemanly. "Aren't we?" he asked, raising one eyebrow.

"Yes," she retorted, setting her hands down hard on her hips now and jutting out her elbows, "but it was a matter of expediency on my part, and nothing more."

"Gosh," Clay said, playing the rube. "Thanks."

"I would do anything for my daughters!" she blurted out. "Including marry a virtual stranger. I agreed to this arrangement *because* of them, not out of any desire to be your...your wife...." She stammered to a halt and turned a glorious shade of primrose-pink.

Clay waited a few moments before he spoke again. "That was quite a scene Maddox made today."

Dara Rose hesitated, trembled once and hugged herself as if she thought she might suddenly scatter in every direction, and it was all Clay could do not to cross the room and take her into his arms. "I suppose he believed he had call to object to—to our getting married," she continued, after a few moments of miserable struggle, "and it's true enough that he proposed—sort of."

"Sort of?" He'd known about the situation between Dara Rose and Maddox from Ponder and the others, but he wanted to hear it directly from her.

It was a long time before she answered. "I was supposed to work as his housekeeper for a year, so he could be sure I'd make a suitable wife. Then, if I passed muster, he'd put a ring on my finger."

Clay felt a fresh surge of rage rise up within him, and he waited for it to subside before he said anything. "Where did Edrina and Harriet fit into all this?"

He knew the answer to that question, too, at least indirectly but, again, he wanted the first-hand truth from Dara Rose herself.

Her eyes welled, but she looked so proud and so vulnerable that Clay continued to keep his distance. He figured she *might* actually shatter into bits if he touched her.

"They didn't," she said, at long last. Then, speaking so softly that Clay barely heard her, she went on. "He wanted me to put my children in an orphanage, or send them out to work for their board and room."

That was when Clay took a chance. He held his arms out to her.

Dara Rose paused briefly, considering, and then moved slowly into his embrace.

Clay rested his chin on top of her head. "No matter how things turn out between you and me, Dara Rose," he told her, "you will never have to send your girls away, I promise you that."

She looked up at him, her eyes moist, though she still wouldn't allow tears to fall. "How can you make a promise like that, Clay?" she whispered brokenly. "How?"

At least she hadn't called him "Mr. McKettrick." Wasn't that progress?

"I just *did* make a promise like that," he replied, wanting to kiss her more than he'd ever wanted to kiss a woman before, and still unwilling to take the chance, "and you'll find that I'm a man of my word."

She blinked. "There's so much you don't know about me," she said.

He grinned, holding her loosely, with his hands clasped behind the small of her back. "There are, as it happens, a few things you don't know about me," he replied. "I didn't come to Blue River to work as the town marshal for the rest

of my life, for one. I mean to be a rancher, Dara Rose—
I come from a family of them. That's why I bought two
thousand acres of good grazing land, and that's why I plan
to build a house on the site we visited today."

"And that's why you wanted a wife," she said, almost
forlornly.

"Not just any wife," he pointed out.

"Parnell and I—" She looked at the large likeness on
the wall. And suddenly, she choked up again. Couldn't
seem to go on.

"It's all right, Dara Rose," Clay said, kissing her lightly
on her crown, where her silken hair parted. She smelled
sweetly of rainwater and flowery soap. "We've both got
stories to tell, but it doesn't have to happen tonight."

She sniffled, smiled bravely, but otherwise she gave
no response.

"Exactly why did you come out here in the first place?"
Clay asked.

Dara Rose looked flustered. "I forgot to feed the chickens," she said. "And I was hoping you'd be asleep so I
could sneak past."

Clay chuckled. "Well, I have to admit, that's something
of a disappointment."

"I *never* forget to feed the chickens," Dara Rose fretted, chagrined. "The poor things—"

"I fed them, Dara Rose," Clay said.

"When?"

"Before we went to find the Christmas tree," he said,
with a nod toward the tumbleweed.

She seemed to realize then that he was still holding her,
and she stepped back suddenly, as though startled. "About
Christmas," she began.

"What about Christmas?"

"I'd really rather you didn't encourage Edrina and Harriet to entertain fanciful notions."

"Such as?" Clay asked, feigning innocence.

Dara Rose bristled up again.

He loved it when she did that.

"Well," she huffed, "there *was* that tall tale about seeing St. Nicholas flying past your grandfather's barn roof in a sleigh drawn by reindeer—"

He smiled. "Why, Mrs. McKettrick—are you calling me a liar?"

"You and your cousin must have been inebriated."

"We were eight," Clay said.

"Then you were dreaming."

"The same dream, at the same time? Sawyer and I are blood kin, but we don't share a brain."

Dara Rose sighed again. It was plain that she didn't know what to say next, or what to do, either.

Both were encouraging signs, Clay figured.

"Get some sleep," he told her. "You've had a long day."

She glanced at the settee, then took his measure with her eyes. Drew the obvious conclusion. "You are in for an uncomfortable night," she said, without any discernible concern.

For more reasons than one, Clay thought. But what he said was, "I'll be just fine. See you in the morning."

Dara Rose nodded, turned around and went back into the bedroom.

Clay watched her go, rubbing his chin with one hand, calculating the number of settee nights he'd have to put in between now and spring, when the house would be ready.

In the end, he slept on the floor, next to Chester.

At least that way, he could stretch out.

WHEN HE OPENED HIS EYES again, it was morning, and Edrina and Harriet were standing over him, looking worried.

"We thought you might be dead," Edrina said, with a relieved and somewhat wobbly smile.

"But you're not," Harriet added emphatically.

"No," Clay said, with a laugh, as he sat up. "I do believe I'm still among the living."

Both children were dressed for daytime, with their curly hair brushed and held back at the sides of their heads by small combs. Their faces were rosy from a recent scrubbing and their eyes shone.

"Mama is taking us over to the O'Reillys' place to visit Addie," Edrina said, "as soon as she's finished feeding the chickens and gathering the eggs and making breakfast."

Clay yawned expansively and got to his feet. "Where's Chester?"

"He's outside with Mama," Harriet replied. "She said he needed to do his business."

"What time is it?" Clay wondered aloud. He owned a pocket watch but seldom carried it; there had been no real need for that, back on the Triple M. There, where there was always a full day's work to do, you started at sunrise and finished when you finished, whatever time it was.

Before either child replied, he caught sight of the timepiece hanging prominently on the wall. Eight o'clock.

"When we get back from the O'Reillys'," Harriet piped up, "can we decorate the Christmas tree?"

Clay hesitated to answer, realizing that he didn't even know if Dara Rose *owned* any decorations, or whether she'd take kindly to his buying some for her, over at the mercantile.

Reckon you should have thought about that before you

cut down that sorry sprig of sagebrush you're calling a Christmas tree, he told himself silently.

"That's up to your mama," he finally said.

Both children looked deflated.

"She'll just say it's a whole week 'til Christmas and St. Nicholas isn't coming, anyhow, so what do we need with a silly tree," Edrina said, in a rush of words.

Inwardly, Clay sighed. These were Dara Rose's children, and she had a perfect right to raise them as she saw fit, but he hoped she'd ease up on that rigid personal code of hers a little, and let them be kids while they could.

In the near distance, the back door opened, and Clay felt the rush of cool air where he stood. Dara Rose called out, "Girls? You're not bothering Mr. McKettrick, are you?"

Chester trotted through the inside doorway, came over to greet him.

Clay smiled and ruffled the dog's ears.

"We don't want to call you 'Mr. McKettrick,'" Edrina told Clay.

"We want to call you 'Papa,'" Harriet said.

The backs of Clay's eyes stung a little. "I'd like that," he said quietly, "but that's another thing that's got to be left up to your mama."

"What's to be left up to me?" Dara Rose asked, standing in the doorway. Her hair was pinned up, unlike last night, and like the girls', her cheeks were pink with well-being.

"Whether or not we can call Mr. McKettrick 'Papa,'" Harriet answered.

"And if we can put baubles on the Christmas tree," Edrina added.

Both of them stared expectantly at their mother.

"Oh," she finally said, shifting the handle of the egg basket from one wrist to the other. Her gaze flicked to

Clay's face and then back to the girls. "It's too soon to address Mr. McKettrick in such a familiar fashion," she said. "But I don't see why we couldn't get out the Christmas things."

So she *had* Christmas things, Clay thought. That was something, anyway.

Edrina and Harriet swapped glances and made what would seem to be a tacit agreement to take what they could get.

"Breakfast will be ready in a few minutes," Dara Rose said. "And there are plenty of eggs this morning. We can each have one—Mr. McKettrick may have two, if he wishes—and there will still be enough left to sell over at the mercantile."

"One egg will suit me fine," Clay said, gruff-voiced. Soon as he'd put in a few hours over at the jailhouse and walked through the town once or twice to make sure there wasn't any trouble brewing, he'd head over to the mercantile and stock up on foodstuffs. See if old Philo would agree to deliver what he bought.

Dara Rose wouldn't like it, he supposed, when the storekeeper turned up with sugar and coffee beans and a wagonload of other goods, but he already had an argument ready. He didn't expect her to feed him and Chester; therefore, he wanted to contribute to the grubstake.

Plus, he had to have coffee in the morning, to get himself going.

So they ate their simple breakfast, the girls so excited, between the promised outing and the tree waiting to be festooned with geegaws, that they could barely sit still.

Dara Rose cleared the table while Clay donned his duster and his hat and summoned the dog. He'd left his gun belt and pistol over at the jailhouse, because of Edrina and Harriet, but he'd strap on the long-barreled .45 before he set out on his rounds. It wasn't that he expected to need a firearm, but he wanted any potential troublemakers to know the new marshal was serious about upholding his duties.

"Thanks for breakfast," Clay said, with a tug at his hat brim.

Dara Rose nodded, then looked away.

THE VISIT TO LITTLE Addie O'Reilly was necessarily brief since the child was bedridden. Last night's snow hadn't stuck, thank heaven, but there was still a bitter chill in the air, and Addie's two younger brothers sat on the bare floor near the odd, cobbled-together stove, playing with half a dozen marbles.

Peg tried to put a good face on things, but Dara Rose could tell she was embarrassed. There was no place to sit, except on one of the two beds or an upended crate—undoubtedly the same one that had contained last night's donated supper.

The girls, meanwhile, chatted with Addie.

"Somebody left a box of hot food at my doorstep," Peg said, following Dara Rose's gaze to the crate. Four clean plates, plus utensils, were stacked beside it. "We sure did have ourselves a fine feast, and there's enough left to get us through today, too."

"That's...wonderful," Dara Rose said.

"I figure it had to come from the dining room over to the hotel," Peg went on, wiping her hands down the skirt of her calico dress. "I mean to take the plates and silverware back later."

Dara Rose merely nodded. Clay must have wanted to

keep his part in the enterprise a secret, so she didn't say anything.

Fortunately, neither did Edrina or Harriet. They were busy telling Addie all about the little girl, Madeline, whose papa was a dentist.

"You'll never guess who stopped by here yesterday," Peg said, taking Dara Rose by surprise.

"Who?" Dara Rose asked, simply to make conversation.

"Ezra Maddox," Peg said. "He's offered me housekeeping work, Mrs. Nolan. The job doesn't pay much, but at least there'll be plenty of good farm food for these kids, and if things work out, Mr. Maddox and me will be married come the spring." She paused. "You don't mind, do you? Now that you've married the marshal and all?"

Dara Rose smiled. "I don't mind," she was quick to say. Then, cautiously, afraid Peg O'Reilly might have misunderstood Maddox's offer, she asked, "He didn't object to your bringing the children along?"

"He did," Peg confided, in a whisper, "but I told him I wouldn't be parted from my little ones for anything or anybody, and he finally agreed to take them in."

The boys were still busy with their game of marbles, and Edrina was telling Addie that there wasn't going to be a Christmas program over at the schoolhouse this year because that last snowstorm threw everything out of whack.

"What about—?"

"My husband?" Peg asked. "Ezra knows about him, of course. Says we'll look into getting me a divorce if it comes to that."

Dara Rose's heart ached for Peg O'Reilly. "This is what you want to do?" she asked, very quietly.

"It's the answer to a prayer," Peg replied, looking a little surprised by Dara Rose's question.

Ezra Maddox, the answer to a prayer?

It just went to show, Dara Rose thought, that one woman's idea of hell was *another* woman's idea of heaven.

Chapter 9

FULL OF CONSTERNATION, Dara Rose studied the Closed sign on the door at the mercantile, the handle of the egg basket looped over one wrist, and wondered what on earth could have prompted Mr. Bickham to close his establishment at midmorning. Edrina and Harriet, meanwhile, climbed onto the bench in front of the store and peered in through the display window.

"Mama!" Harriet suddenly cried, so startling Dara Rose that she almost dropped the egg basket. "She's gone! *Florence is gone!*"

Dara Rose caught her breath, the fingers of her free hand splayed across her breastbone to keep her heart from jumping right out of her chest.

Florence?

Harriet let out a despairing wail.

"Hush!" Edrina told her sister, speaking sternly but slipping an arm around the child's shoulders just the same. The two of them looked so small, standing there on the seat of that bench, like a pair of beautiful urchins.

The doll, Dara Rose realized belatedly.

Of course. Florence was the doll Harriet had been admiring—yearning after—ever since it first appeared in the mercantile window, the day after Thanksgiving. And now the doll was gone.

It would be set out for some other child to find on Christmas morning.

Although Dara Rose had never for one moment believed she could buy that doll for her little girl, Harriet's disappointment grieved her sorely. Like any mother, she longed to give her children nice things, but that was a pleasure she couldn't afford; they needed practical things, and some small measure of security, be it the egg money she squirreled away a penny at a time, or the ten dollars resting between the pages of her Bible.

Hurting as much as her child was—maybe more—and doing her best to hide it, Dara Rose set the egg basket down carefully and gathered Harriet into her arms, lifting her off the bench and holding her tightly. "There, now," she whispered, her throat so thick she could barely speak. Not that there was a great deal to say at a moment like that, anyway. "There, now."

"I should have sold my hair!" Harriet sobbed. "Then I would have had the money to buy Florence!"

Once again, Dara Rose thought of Piper's gift, safe at home, and ached.

Edrina jumped down from the bench, tomboylike, and tugged at Harriet's dangling foot. "Stop carrying on, goose," she commanded, but there was a slight quaver in her voice. "You'll have the whole town staring at us."

Harriet shuddered and buried her wet face in Dara Rose's neck. "I—really—thought—I—could—have—Florence—for—my—very—own," she said, punctuating her words with small but violent hiccups.

"Shh," Dara Rose said gently, still holding the child. "Everything will be all right, sweetheart. We'll go home now. Edrina, bring the egg basket."

By the time the three of them reached the end of Main Street and turned toward the house, Harriet had settled down to the occasional quivering sniffle.

A buckboard stood near Dara Rose's front gate, with two mules hitched to it.

Philo Bickham sat in the wagon box, reins in hand, beaming at Dara Rose as she approached with the children.

"I was just about to unload all this merchandise and leave it on the porch," he said. "The marshal said he'd be here to accept delivery, but there's been no sign of him so far."

Dara Rose frowned, at once wary and intrigued.

Edrina bolted forward and scrambled right up the side of that buckboard, skillful as a monkey, using the wheel spokes as footholds. "Thunderation!" she whooped.

Mr. Bickham jumped to the ground, nimble for a man of his age and bulk. He strode around to the back of the wagon and lowered the tailgate. "He darned near bought the place out, your new husband," the storekeeper crowed, no doubt pleased to make such a sale. Blue River was not a wealthy community, which meant the owner of the mercantile scraped by like most everyone else.

"Mama," Edrina spouted, "there's a tin of tea...and a big ham...and *peaches*...and all sorts of things wrapped in brown paper—"

"Edrina Nolan," Dara Rose said, setting Harriet on her feet, "get down from there this instant."

"Don't go poking around in those packages," Mr. Bickham said good-naturedly, shaking a finger at Edrina and then Harriet. "The marshal made himself mighty clear on that score. After all, it's almost Christmas, and there's a secret or two afoot."

Dara Rose was still trying to think what to say when Clay rode around the corner on Outlaw, Chester trotting in their wake.

Mr. Bickham hailed him, and Dara Rose sent the girls inside, over their protests.

"Sorry if I held you up any, Philo," Clay told Mr. Bickham, barely glancing at Dara Rose as he swung down from the saddle. "A telegram came in from Sears, Roebuck and Company. They've shipped the makings of my house out by rail, and the whole works will be arriving here in about ten days."

"You'd better get that foundation dug and that well put in, then," Mr. Bickham said, giving Clay a congratulatory slap on one shoulder. "Reckon you can round up some hired help down at the Bitter Gulch, and if this weather holds, since you've got a put-together house coming, you'll be out there on your own place in no time."

Clay nodded and, once again, his gaze touched on Dara Rose's face.

"What is all this?" she asked evenly, as soon as Mr. Bickham had hoisted the first box from the back of the wagon and started toward the house with it.

Clay gave her a wry look and lifted out a second box. "Chester and I," he said, with a twinkle, "don't believe in freeloading. We always pay our own way."

Dara Rose opened her mouth, closed it again. "But all those packages, and the tea, and that enormous ham—"

"You like tea, don't you?" Clay teased, starting toward the house.

Dara Rose scurried to keep up with his long strides. "Of

course I like tea," she said, flustered, "but it's a luxury, and we don't need it—"

"Sure you do," Clay replied, climbing the porch steps now. "What do you plan on serving all the ladies of Blue River when they start dropping by to see for themselves just what kind of mischief we're up to over here?"

Harriet and Edrina, huddled in the doorway, scattered to let them through.

Mr. Bickham was coming from the other direction, and Clay sidestepped him.

"Mr. McKettrick," Dara Rose persisted, when the two of them were alone in the kitchen, "I do have my pride."

"Yes, Mrs. McKettrick," Clay agreed. "I have taken note of that fact." He took a large tin from the box he'd carried in. "Would you mind putting some coffee on to brew while Bickham and I finish unloading that wagon? I've got a hankering for the stuff, and I like it strong and black."

Dara Rose couldn't seem to untangle her tongue.

"You do own a coffeepot, don't you?" Clay asked offhandedly.

"Yes," she managed, blushing. "Parnell drank coffee every morning."

Clay merely nodded, as though she'd confirmed something he already knew, and went out again.

Dara Rose got out Parnell's coffeepot, rinsed it at the sink and pumped fresh water into it. Then she had to ferret out the grinder, with its black wrought-iron handle.

She was wiping the dust out of the contraption with one corner of a flour-sack dish towel when Clay and Mr. Bickham came in again, both of them carrying boxes.

Edrina and Harriet were, of course, consumed with curiosity.

Harriet, though puffy-eyed, had long since stopped crying.

"Sugar," Edrina cataloged, joyfully examining each item. "And flour. And lard. And *raisins*. Mama, you could bake a pie."

"Perhaps," Dara Rose agreed, afraid to say too much because she wasn't sure she could control all the contradictory emotions welling up inside her. Her pride stung like a snakebite, but in some ways, she was as jubilant as the children.

Tea. Sugar. Flour.

A whole ham, big enough to feed half the town of Blue River.

They'd been doing without such things for so long that it was impossible not to rejoice, at least inwardly.

Firmly, Dara Rose brought herself up short. She squared her shoulders and poured coffee beans into the grinder and began turning the handle, enjoying the rich aroma. "Mr. McKettrick has been very generous," she said, not looking at Edrina and Harriet. "But we mustn't come to expect such things—"

"Why not?" The voice was Clay's.

Dara Rose kept her back to him, spooning freshly ground coffee beans into the well of her dented pot, setting it on to boil. "Because we mustn't, that's all," she said. She bent and opened the stove door and pitched in more wood. Jabbed at the embers with the poker.

"There's some stuff for the Christmas tree in the box I left on the settee," Clay said quietly, sending the girls scampering with chimelike hurrahs into the front room.

Dara Rose, thinking Mr. Bickham must be within earshot, taking it all in, turned to look for him. He was as big a gossip as Heliotrope Ponder and, running the only general store in town, he got plenty of chances to tell everything he knew and then some.

But there was only Clay, filling the doorway, watching her. Philo Bickham must have been outside, fetching another box from the buckboard.

"It's almost Christmas," Clay said gruffly. "Just this once, Dara Rose, let yourself be happy. Let your *daughters* be happy."

Her face burned, and she couldn't help remembering all the times Parnell had splurged on some little treat for the girls, running up an account at the mercantile that had taken her months to pay off.

"Did you go into debt for all this?" she asked, keeping her voice down so the girls and Mr. Bickham wouldn't hear. Nobody knew better than she did how little the marshal of Blue River actually earned.

Clay smiled, though his eyes remained solemn, and then he shook his head, not in reply, but in disbelief. "I paid cash money," he said, turning to walk away.

By the time the coffee was ready, the kitchen and part of the front room were jammed with boxes and crates and brown parcels, tied shut with twine.

"Where's Mr. Bickham?" Dara Rose asked, when Clay returned to the kitchen, squeezed past her to wash his hands at the sink pump. "I thought he'd stay for coffee."

"He has a store to run," Clay said quietly.

In the next room, the girls giggled and Chester barked and the noise was pleasant to hear, even though Dara Rose was uncommon jittery.

She put away the cup she'd set out for Mr. Bickham and filled the remaining one, returned the pot to the stove.

"Mr. McKettrick?"

"What, Mrs. McKettrick?" Clay countered wearily, as

he drew back a chair, sat down and reached for the steaming cup of coffee.

Dara Rose brought out the sugar bowl, long unused, filled it from the newly purchased bag and set it on the table, along with a teaspoon.

"Thank you," she said meekly, not looking at him. "For all these groceries, I mean—"

That was when he pulled her onto his lap. His thighs felt hard as a wagon seat under her backside, and *that* realization started all sorts of untoward things rioting inside her.

"You're welcome," he said, in a throaty drawl.

Dara Rose's heart pounded, and she felt dizzy. "Clay— the *children*—"

He sighed. "They're busy squeezing parcels," he said.

Dara Rose sat very still, afraid to move.

Clay watched her mouth for a few moments, and managed to leave Dara Rose as breathless as if he'd actually kissed her, and soundly. Then he said, very quietly, "Just so we understand each other, Mrs. McKettrick, I do mean to bed you, right and proper, one day soon."

Dara Rose gulped, knowing she ought to pull free and get back on her own two feet but strangely unable to do so. "But you said—"

He rested an index finger on her mouth, and a hot shiver went through her. "I know what I said, Dara Rose, and I'll keep my word. But it's only fair to tell you that I'm fixing to do everything I can to bring you around to my way of thinking."

Dara Rose absolutely could not speak. She was full of indignation and longing and searing heat.

That was when he kissed her—softly at first, and then in a deep way that made everything inside her melt, including her very bones.

When their mouths finally parted, it was Clay's doing, not Dara Rose's.

She'd have been content to let that kiss go on forever, it felt so good.

"I believe I'm making progress," he said, with a certain satisfaction.

He was indeed, Dara Rose thought. If Edrina and Harriet hadn't been in the house, never mind the very next room, she might have taken Marshal Clay McKettrick by the hand and led him straight to her bed. She sighed wistfully.

It had been so long since she'd been held in a strong man's arms, reveled in the sweet responses lovemaking roused in her.

She glanced at the doorway, but her children were still in the front room, playing some game with the dog, filling that little house with barks and giggles. "Parnell and I—we weren't…we didn't…"

Clay simply listened, looking thoughtful.

"What I mean is, we were never…*intimate*," Dara Rose confessed. Even saying that much—telling such a small part of her story—was a tremendous relief. "He married me to give my children a name."

"Go on," Clay said.

Dara Rose checked the doorway again. "I was married—or I *thought* I was married—to Parnell's younger brother, Luke." She swallowed hard. "Edrina was born, and then Harriet, and then—"

Clay didn't prompt her. He was a patient man.

"And then Luke was thrown from a horse and killed, and I learned—I learned that he'd had another wife all along. A *real* wife, and several children. I'd been a—a kept woman from the first, without even knowing it, and our—*my*—children had been born out of wedlock."

Something moved in Clay's handsome face.

Pain? Fury? Pity, perhaps? She couldn't tell.

Afraid she'd lose her courage if she didn't finish the story right now, Dara Rose went on. "I had no money, and no place to go, and after his brother's funeral, Parnell came to me and offered marriage. He was such a good man, Clay." She realized she was crying. When had the tears begun? "When he died upstairs at the Bitter Gulch, everyone felt so sorry for the children and me, and there was this huge scandal, and I couldn't—I couldn't explain that I wasn't a true wife to him. He must have been so lonely...."

When she didn't go on, Clay set her on her feet, and try though she did, Dara Rose couldn't read his expression.

He got up from his chair, his coffee forgotten on the table, and whistled for his dog.

Chester came to him eagerly, without hesitation, as Clay was putting on his duster and his distinctive round-brimmed hat.

"This calls for some thinking about, Dara Rose," he said. "And I need to get Outlaw back to the livery stable, see that he's put up proper for the night."

With that, Clay opened the back door, and he and Chester went out.

Edrina and Harriet appeared in the inside doorway the instant he'd closed the door behind him.

"Aren't we going to decorate the Christmas tree?" Edrina asked plaintively.

Dara Rose didn't answer. She hurried across the kitchen and through the front room to watch through the window as Clay rounded a corner of the house, passed through the gate, gathered his horse's reins and mounted up.

"What about the Christmas tree?" Harriet trilled, from somewhere behind Dara Rose.

"After supper," she heard herself say, as her heart climbed into her throat. "We'll tend to it after supper."

And Clay McKettrick rode away, Chester following, leaving Dara Rose to wonder if he meant to come back.

WHEN HE REACHED the jailhouse, Clay let himself in, started a fire in the potbellied stove and nearly fell over the large crate waiting by his desk.

He approached the box, apparently delivered while he was away, peering down at the return address: *The Triple M. Indian Rock, Arizona.*

He felt a twinge of homesickness, but it passed quickly.

Much as he loved the ranch, and his family, the Triple M wasn't home anymore. Home, for better or for worse, was wherever Dara Rose happened to be.

When had he fallen in love with her?

He wasn't sure. It might have been today, when she sat on his lap in her tiny kitchen and poured out her heart to him.

Or it might have been when he first laid eyes on her, just a few days before.

All he could say for sure was that it felt a lot like being kicked in the belly by a mule, this falling in love.

He was exultant.

He was crushed.

Dara Rose had loved another man, and that man had betrayed her, and if Luke Nolan hadn't already been dead, Clay would have cheerfully killed him.

His deepest regret? That he hadn't been there to step in and make things right for her and for the kids, as illogical as that was. Parnell had been the one to rescue her, give his two-timing brother's family a legal right to the Nolan name.

Clay McKettrick was jealous of a dead man and, at the same time, he knew he could never have settled for the kind of empty marriage Dara Rose and Parnell had had together. He was a young man, and red-blooded, and he needed more.

He wanted everything—wanted Dara Rose's heart, as well as her body. Wanted to adopt Edrina and Harriet, change their last name for good, raise them as McKettricks.

And he surely wanted to make more babies with Dara Rose.

Oh, yes, he wanted it all.

He drew in a deep breath. *Slow down, cowboy,* he thought. *Get a grip.*

There was no telling what Dara Rose thought when he'd walked out on her that way, but he needed to sort things through, needed to *think*.

That was the kind of man he was.

He fetched a knife, pried up the lid on the crate his mother had sent from the Triple M. She must have paid a hefty freight charge to get it there before Christmas, even by train.

Inside, carefully nestled in straw, he found a dozen succulent oranges, a tin full of exotic nuts and a number of his favorite books, some of which he'd owned since he first learned to read. There was more, but Clay's eyes were so blurred by then that he was lucky to be able to read his mother's letter and, even then, he only got this word and that.

"Sawyer wired that you're married…two stepdaughters…bring them home when you can…we're all so anxious to welcome your wife and your children to the family—"

Clay closed his eyes, drew a deep breath. That was Chloe McKettrick for you. If he loved a woman, and that woman's children, then his mother was ready to enfold them in the warmth of her heart, receive them as her own.

It was the McKettrick way. Babies were born into the family, or they arrived by marriage, and it made no difference either way. Once a McKettrick, always a McKettrick.

No matter what happened between him and Dara Rose, Edrina and Harriet were part of the fold, now and forever. If he died tomorrow, or Dara Rose did, his pa and ma, his aunts and uncles and sisters and brothers and cousins— even old Angus and his wife, Concepcion—would take them in and love them like their own flesh and blood.

The knowledge made Clay's throat tighten and his eyes scald.

He wanted to go back to Dara Rose right then, wanted that more than anything, but he didn't give in to the desire.

Yes, she was his wife.

And yes, it was a safe bet that she wanted him as much as he wanted her, after that episode in her kitchen.

But what mattered now was the children.

And that was why Clay McKettrick decided to spend his second night as a married man in the spare room behind the jailhouse. If he'd gone back to Dara Rose's place, he wasn't at all sure he could have resisted her.

He needed her.

He *loved* her.

And that was precisely why he couldn't go home to that little house, with its tiny rooms and its thin walls.

Clay McKettrick knew his limits.

And, where Dara Rose was concerned, he'd reached them.

DARA ROSE LISTENED for Clay's footstep on the back porch as she peeled potatoes to fry up for supper with some of the salt pork he'd bought at the store. When the meal was over and the dishes had been washed and put away and he still wasn't back, she declared that it was time to decorate the Christmas tree.

"We'd rather wait for Mr. McKettrick," Edrina said, looking glum.

"Where did he go?" Harriet asked.

Dara Rose sighed. She'd been a fool to go against her own better judgment and marry Clay McKettrick. Men couldn't be depended upon to stick around. They lied and cheated and got themselves thrown from horses and killed, they died in the arms of prostitutes above some saloon or, like Mr. O'Reilly, they simply decided they'd rather be elsewhere and took to their heels.

Devil take the hindmost.

"To the livery stable, I think," Dara Rose finally replied.

"He left a long time ago," Edrina reasoned. "It's getting dark outside."

Harriet's lower lip wobbled. "Maybe he's not coming back," she said.

Dara Rose pretended not to hear. "I'll fetch the Christmas box from the cedar chest," she told the children, marching into the front room. "And then we'll see what we can do with this tree."

The girls didn't speak, so she turned her head to look at them.

They stood side by side, arms folded, expressions recalcitrant.

"That wouldn't be right," Edrina said staunchly. "Mr. McKettrick cut that tree down himself. We wouldn't even have it if it weren't for him."

Harriet nodded in grim agreement.

Dara Rose thought fast. "Wouldn't it be a nice surprise, though, if he came home to find it all sparkling and merry?"

Edrina, self-appointed spokeswoman for her little sister as well as for herself, stood her ground. "We'd rather wait," she reiterated.

Dara Rose shook her head, proceeded into the bedroom to give the children a chance to change their minds and lifted the lid of the cedar chest at the foot of the bed. She kept the few simple ornaments they owned, most of them homemade, tucked away there, inside an old boot box of Parnell's.

There was a shining paper chain, made of salvaged foils of all sorts.

There were stars, cut from tin, with the sharp edges hammered down to a child-safe smoothness, and ribbons, and Parnell's broken pocket watch.

And there were two tiny angels, sewn up from scraps of calico and embroidered with Edrina's and Harriet's names, their wings improvised out of layers of old newspapers, cut out and pasted together.

Dara Rose had always treasured these humble decorations, as had the girls, but now, in the dim light of the rising moon, falling softly through the window, they looked humble indeed. Nearly pitiful, in fact.

She swallowed, straightened her spine, and returned to the front room with the dog-eared carton, only to find Edrina and Harriet busy with the one Clay had spoken of earlier.

There's some stuff for the Christmas tree in the box I left on the settee, he'd said.

The children looked wonder-struck as they lifted one

glistening item after another out of the box—a porcelain angel, with feathers for wings and a golden halo fashioned of thin wire; shimmering baubles of blown glass, in bright shades of red and blue and gold and silver; a package of glittering tinsel that flashed in the lamplight like a tiny waterfall.

Dara Rose spoke in a normal tone, but it was a struggle. "Shall we decorate the tree after all, then?" she asked.

But Edrina and Harriet shook their heads.

Slowly, carefully, they put all the exquisite ornaments Clay had purchased back into the box from the mercantile.

"We'll wait," Edrina said.

And that was that.

The girls went off to get ready for bed, without being told.

Dara Rose, not quite sure *what* she was feeling exactly, put on her cloak and went outside to make sure the chickens were safe in their coop, with their feed and water pans full.

When that was done, she tarried, looking up at the silvery stars popping out all over the black-velvet sky, hoping Clay would step through the backyard gate.

He didn't, of course.

So Dara Rose went back into the house, to her children, to oversee the washing of faces and the brushing of teeth and the saying of prayers.

Edrina, hands clenched together and one eye slightly open, asked God to make sure Mr. McKettrick and Chester found their way back home, please, and soon.

Harriet said she hoped whatever little girl had Florence would take good care of her and not lose the doll's shoes or break her head.

Dara Rose offered no comment on either prayer.

She simply kissed her precocious children good-night, tucked them in and left the room.

In the kitchen, she brewed tea, and sat savoring it at the table, with the kerosene lantern burning low on the narrow counter.

After Luke, and again after Parnell, Dara Rose had solemnly promised herself she would never wait up for another man as long as she lived.

And here she was, waiting for Clay McKettrick.

HAVING MADE HIS DECISION, Clay locked up the street door and banked the dwindling fire, and he collapsed onto the bed in the back room of the jailhouse, not expecting to sleep.

He must have been more tired than he thought, because he awakened with sunlight streaming into his face through the one grimy window, and Chester snoring away in the nearby cell.

Clay got up, made his way into the office, made a fire in the stove and put on a pot of coffee. He let Chester out the rear door and stood on what passed for a porch, studying the sky.

It was bluer than blue, that sky, and the day promised to be unseasonably warm.

Even with half his mind down the road, following Dara Rose around that little house of hers, there was room in Clay's brain for all the things that needed to be done before the kit-house arrived.

He heated water on the stove top, once the coffee had come to a good boil, and washed up as best he could, but his shaving gear and his spare clothes were stashed behind the settee at Dara Rose's.

In the near distance, church bells rang, and Clay realized it was Sunday.

The good folks of the town would be settling themselves in pews right about now, waiting for the sermon to start—and then waiting for it to end.

The ones who wouldn't mind working on the Sabbath Day, on the other hand, were probably gathered down at the Bitter Gulch Saloon, defiant in their state of sin.

Since he needed a well dug, and a foundation, too, Clay figured he'd better get to the latter bunch before they got a real good start on the day's drinking.

An hour later, Chester stuck to his heels the whole time, he'd hired seven men, roused a blinking and grimacing Philo Bickham to open the mercantile and sell him picks and shovels, a pair of trousers and a plain shirt, and rented two mules and a wagon from the livery to haul the workers and the tools out to the ranch.

For a pack of habitual drunks, those men got a lot of digging done.

Clay worked right alongside them, while Chester roamed the range, probably hunting for rabbits. He'd make a fine cattle-dog when there was a herd to tend.

At noon, Clay drove the team and wagon back to town, Chester along for the ride, bought food enough for an army at the hotel dining room and returned to the work site and his hungry crew.

He'd felt a pang passing the turn to Dara Rose's place, having finally remembered that he'd promised Edrina and Harriet that they'd decorate the Christmas tree the night before, but he'd make that up to them later.

Somehow.

Just about supper time, Clay called a halt to the work, satisfied that the foundation was dug and they'd made good progress on the well. The crew climbed into the back of the wagon, as did Chester, and the marshal of Blue River, Texas, turned the mules townward.

He paid the men generously, turned the team and wagon in at the livery and took his time tending to Outlaw, lest the horse feel neglected after being left to stand idle in his stall all day.

Too tired to bother with supper, and too dirty to stand himself for much longer, Clay returned to the lonely jailhouse, lit a lantern, fed Chester some leftovers from the midday meal and commenced carrying and heating water to fill the round washtub he'd found hanging from a nail just outside the back door.

The new clothes he'd bought that morning were stiff with newness and smelled of starch.

Once there was enough hot water in the washtub to suit him, Clay stripped off his filthy clothes, climbed in and sat down, cross-legged like an Apache at a campfire, sighing as the strain eased out of his muscles. He was no stranger to hard physical work, coming from a family of ranchers, but it had been a while since he'd swung a pick or wielded a shovel.

He was sore.

As the water cooled, Clay scoured off a couple of layers of grime and sweat and planned what he'd say to Dara Rose, later tonight, when he intended to knock at her kitchen door and ask if he and Chester could bunk in her front room again. In the morning, they could talk things through.

Only it didn't happen that way.

Clay was just coming to grips with the fact that he didn't have a towel handy when the jailhouse door flew open and

Dara Rose stormed in, wearing her cloak but no bonnet and, temper-wise, loaded for bear.

Seeing Clay sitting there in the washtub in the altogether, she stopped in her tracks and gasped.

"You're just in time, Mrs. McKettrick," he said. "It seems I'm in something of a predicament here."

Dara Rose blinked and looked quickly away, keeping her head turned and not asking what the predicament might happen to be.

"My children," she said, "refuse to decorate the Christmas tree unless you're there."

"If you'll fetch me a towel, Mrs. McKettrick," Clay drawled, enjoying her discomfort more than he'd enjoyed much of anything since yesterday's kiss at her kitchen table, "I'll make myself decent, and we'll attend to that Christmas tree."

Dara Rose kept her face averted. "Where...?"

"The towel? It's hanging from a hook next to my shaving mirror, in the back room."

"I meant to say," Dara Rose sputtered, still not looking in his direction, "*where have you been* since last night?" She gave him a wide berth as she went in search of the towel.

"I'm glad you asked," Clay said, smiling to himself as he waited for her to come back, so he could dry off and get dressed in his new duds. "It shows you care."

She returned, flung the towel at him and turned her back. "Nonsense," she said. "Edrina and Harriet were very disappointed when you left—that's the only reason I'm here."

Clay rose out of the tub, the towel around his middle, and sloshed his way into the spare room, where he hastily wiped himself dry and put on the other set of clothes.

Dara Rose had her eyes covered with both hands when he came back. "Are you dressed?" she asked pettishly.

"Yes, Mrs. McKettrick," he said easily. "I am properly attired."

She lowered her hands, looked at him with enough female fury to sear off some of his hide and repeated her original question, dead set on an answer.

"Where *were* you, Clay McKettrick?"

Chapter 10

WHERE WERE YOU, Clay McKettrick? Clay crossed to Dara Rose, laid his hands gently on her shoulders and felt a tremor go through her slight but sumptuous body. "First," he began, his voice low, "I'll tell you where I *wasn't,* Mrs. McKettrick. I wasn't with a secret wife, and I wasn't upstairs at the Bitter Gulch Saloon, enjoying the favors of a dance-hall girl. I'm not Luke, and I'm not Parnell. I'm *Clay McKettrick,* and it would behoove you to get that straight in your mind. As for where I was, I slept right here last night, and this morning I hired a crew and went out to the ranch to start digging a foundation and a well. The makings of our house will be here right after the first of the year, as I told Philo Bickham yesterday, in your presence and hearing. And as long as the weather cooperates, I plan to spend as much time as I can out there, making the necessary preparations, because the sooner we can move into a place of our own, the better."

She looked up at him, confused and probably startled by the uncommon length of the speech he'd just given. He could see that she was still afraid to hope, afraid to trust, when it came to any personal dealings with a man. She bit down on her lower lip but didn't speak.

Clay smiled, kissed the top of her head. She wasn't wearing her bonnet, and her hair was coming loose from the knot at her nape, tendrils falling around her cheeks and across her forehead.

I love you, he thought. He was ready to say it right out loud, but he wasn't sure Dara Rose was ready to *hear* it, so he put the declaration by for later.

"I think we'd better get over to the house and decorate the Christmas tree," Clay drawled, enjoying the soft, pliant warmth of her, standing there in his arms, innately uncertain and, at the same time, one of the strongest women he'd ever encountered. "You see, Mrs. McKettrick, if we stay here much longer, I'm liable to seduce you, and I surely do not want our first time together to happen in a jailhouse."

She pinkened in that delightful way that only made him ache to see the rest of her, bare of all that calico, and mischief danced in her upturned eyes. Every signal she was sending out, however subtle, said she was a woman who enjoyed the intimate attentions of a man, who wasn't afraid or ashamed to uncover herself, body, mind and spirit, and then lose herself in the pleasures of making love.

Glory be.

"You seem to have a great deal of confidence in your powers of seduction, *Mr.* McKettrick," she remarked, after twinkling up at him for a few spicy moments. "What makes you think you could persuade me to give in?"

He cupped her chin in his hand, bent to nibble briefly at her mouth. Another shiver went through her at his touch. "Trust me," he said gruffly, after drawing back. "I am a persuasive man."

She sighed. "Yes," she admitted. "I believe you are."

He steered her in the direction of the door, whistled for Chester, took his hat and coat from their pegs. "For instance," he teased, as they stepped out onto the blustery sidewalk, the dog following, "I talked you into marrying me, when we'd only known each other for a few days. And I didn't even ask you to work as my housekeeper for a year before I decided whether to keep you or throw you back."

Dara Rose elbowed him, walked a little faster. "I agreed to your proposal," she whispered, though there was no one on the street to overhear, "*only* because I was desperate to keep my family together, with a roof over our heads."

"Speaking of your children," Clay drawled, "did you leave them home alone to come over here to the jail and hector me?"

She stopped, right there on the sidewalk, with Clay between her and the empty street. "Of *course* not," she said, as indignant as a little hen with her feathers ruffled. "Alvira Krenshaw is with them."

"The schoolmarm?"

Dara Rose nodded pertly. "The woman you probably considered courting before you turned your charms on me," she said.

Clay slipped an arm around Dara Rose's small waist and got her moving again, in the direction of the house where he'd be spending another night on the front room floor, with his dog. "Miss Krenshaw," he said, "was never in the running. And how did you manage to wrangle a woman who herds kids for a living into looking after those two little Apaches of yours?"

"Alvira dropped by with a book she wanted to lend to Edrina. A thick one, with lots of pictures, likely to keep that child busy until school takes up again, after New Year's. Anyhow, I made tea." Dara Rose continued to walk, but she'd turned thoughtful. "Alvira sat down to talk and, well, there's something *about* tea, it seems, that causes a person to drop her guard, at least a little. The whole story—most of it, anyway—just poured out of me."

Clay suppressed a chuckle, knowing it would not be well-received. *Remind me to dose you up with tea first chance I get,* he thought. But, "Go on," was what he said, as they started across the street, his hand resting lightly at the small of her back now, barely touching, but still protective.

"I didn't tell Alvira about Luke, or even how it really was between Parnell and me," Dara Rose confided. "But I *did* say that you and I had had a disagreement and I couldn't stop thinking about where you might be or what you might be doing."

Even in the near darkness, Clay saw her blush. It had cost her, pride-wise, to make that admission, even to a good friend, and it was costing her still.

"I see," he said.

They'd rounded the corner now, and Dara Rose's house was just ahead, so she hastened to finish. "Alvira said I'd better come and find you, then, to settle my mind, while she looked after Edrina and Harriet."

"Is it?" Clay asked.

"Is *what?*" Dara Rose retorted, sounding a mite testy.

"Is your mind settled, where I'm concerned?"

They stood in front of her gate by then, light spilling out of the windows into the darkened yard. The apple tree was a spare shadow, etched into the night.

"Where you are concerned, Mr. McKettrick," Dara Rose finally replied, "*nothing* is settled. I don't know what to think, what to believe—"

He kissed her then, deeply, the way he would have done

if they'd had the whole world to themselves. Adam and Eve, in Texas instead of the Garden.

"Believe *that,*" he said, when he'd caught his breath. "And the rest will take care of itself."

Dara Rose just stood there, looking dazed. Even in the poor light, he could see that her lips were swollen, still moist from his kiss.

Calmly, Clay opened the gate, held it for her and shut it after they'd gone through, Dara Rose and Chester and, finally, himself.

At the base of the porch steps, Dara Rose stopped and sort of bristled, about to make some delayed response to being kissed, Clay supposed, but she didn't get the chance, because the front door sprang open and Edrina and Harriet burst out, barely able to contain their glee.

"*Now* can we decorate the Christmas tree?" Harriet demanded.

Miss Krenshaw stood, smiling, on the threshold behind them, already buttoning her practical woolen coat, ready to leave.

"Yes," Dara Rose confirmed, fondly weary in her tone. "We can decorate the Christmas tree." Her gaze shifted to Miss Krenshaw. "You're not leaving, are you?"

"I have a few letters to write, back at the teacherage," Miss Krenshaw replied, sparing a polite nod of greeting for Clay. And with that, she was past them, down the steps, striding along the walk toward the gate. There, she turned back. "Don't forget about the party at the schoolhouse," she called, most likely addressing Dara Rose.

"WHAT PARTY AT THE schoolhouse?" Clay asked, as Edrina and Harriet beset him with hugs, in their joy at his return. Without missing a beat, he scooped them up, one in each arm, and the sight struck a deep and resonant chord inside Dara Rose.

She led the way into the kitchen, where she'd stowed a plate of supper in the warming oven, in hopes that Clay would be around to eat it.

"After the blizzard," Dara Rose explained, wadding up a dish towel to use as a pot holder and taking Clay's meal from the heat, "Miss Krenshaw decided to call off the Christmas program at school. Now, with all this spring-like weather and Pastor Jacobs called away because of an illness in his family, so there won't be a church service, she's had second thoughts. There's no time for the children to memorize recitations and the like, but we can still have some sort of informal gathering on Christmas Day, for the community—sing a few hymns and carols...."

She paused, glanced back at him, felt a thrill as he set the girls down, then removed and hung up his hat and coat. His movements were easy and deliberate, and he looked from her face to the plate in her hands and back again.

"You must be hungry, after a hard day's work at the ranch," she said, suddenly and desperately shy.

"I am indeed hungry, Mrs. McKettrick," he said, in a throaty voice, letting his eyes move over her once before heading to the sink to wash his hands. Everything about him was so masculine—his stance, the movement of his powerful shoulders, the back of his head where his dark hair curled against the neck band of his collarless shirt. He turned, damp and handsome, his sleeves rolled up to his elbows, water spiking his eyelashes. "I am indeed."

"Eat fast!" Edrina urged Clay, as he sat down at the table. "We've been waiting *forever* to decorate the Christmas tree!"

"*Forever,*" Harriet testified.

"For that," he said, "I do apologize." Clay looked down at the simple but plentiful meal Dara Rose had prepared—boiled potatoes, the last of the preserved venison and green beans she had grown in her own garden the summer before and subsequently put up in jars for the winter. He favored her with a slight, appreciative smile, and then spoke again to the children, who were fairly electrified with energy. "Settle down now," he said quietly. "We'll get to that tree, I promise."

They subsided, dragged themselves melodramatically out of the kitchen, portraying despondency, Chester tagging along, his ears perked up in anticipation of some new and wonderful game the three of them might play.

Clay ate at his own pace, the way he did everything, and seemed to savor the food Dara Rose had put aside for him, with no real conviction that he'd be around to eat it.

Once he'd finished, Dara Rose offered coffee, but Clay shook his head, said, "No thank you," and started for the front room. When Dara Rose lingered to clear the table, Clay shook his head a second time and beckoned politely for her to follow.

Edrina and Harriet had been busy, Dara Rose discovered. They'd taken every single ornament out of the boxes and laid them in neat rows on the settee.

Later, out in the woodshed behind the house, working by lantern light and supervised by two very lively little girls and an eager dog—Dara Rose spent the time fussing over her chickens—Clay cobbled together a stand to support the small tree and they all went back inside.

To Dara Rose, the thing looked more like a shrub than a tree, but both Edrina's and Harriet's eyes glowed with awe as one decoration after another was reverently added to this bough or that one. The homemade ornaments held their own against the store-bought ones, in Dara Rose's opinion, and she had to admit that, when finished, the effect was very nearly magical—especially when the porcelain angel with the wire halo and the feather wings seemed to hover over the whole of it, offering a blessing.

"Thunderation," Edrina breathed, reflected light from the colorful blown-glass ornaments shining on her face.

"It's bee-you-tee-ful," Harriet pronounced.

Even Chester, sitting between the children and gazing at the shining display, seemed spellbound.

"It's enough to make a person believe in St. Nicholas," Clay said quietly, for Dara Rose alone to hear. "Isn't it?"

"No," she said promptly, but without her usual conviction.

Only days ago, Dara Rose reflected dizzily, she'd been alone in the world, with two children to support, winter coming on and the threat of eviction hanging over her head. She might well have lost Edrina and Harriet forever, the way things were going.

But then Clay McKettrick had arrived by train, with his handsome horse, and pinned on the marshal's badge, and turned her entire life upside down.

The man had even managed to turn a scrub pine into a more-than-respectable Christmas tree.

It was hard, under such circumstances, *not* to believe in magic.

Christmas Eve

THE CLOCK ON THE FRONT room wall chimed ten times, and the lantern light wavered as Clay came out of the bedroom, shaking his head.

"Not yet," he said to Dara Rose, who was waiting to fill

the pair of small stockings she'd allowed the girls to hang from the knobs on the side table. She'd sent him in to see if Edrina and Harriet were really asleep, or just pretending. "Those two are playing possum, for sure."

Dara Rose had an orange to drop into the toe of each stocking, thanks to the box from Clay's people up north, along with a bright copper penny and the new mittens she'd bought at the mercantile a few days before.

These things alone would delight the children, she knew, but there was so much more; she'd splurged on shoes and ready-made coats for her daughters, and Clay's packages—still wrapped in their brown paper and tucked beneath the lowest boughs of the tree—contained numerous mysteries.

They retreated into the kitchen, Clay drinking luke-warm coffee left over from supper, and Dara Rose sipping tea. She'd felt downright reckless, spending Piper's ten dollars so freely, and it still made her breath lurch to think how she'd spent some of it.

Idly, Clay took a small package from the pocket of his shirt, and set it down next to Dara Rose's teacup.

She looked up at him, but she didn't—couldn't—speak.

"Open it," he urged, with that crooked grin tilting his mouth upward at one side, in the way she'd come to love.

Dara Rose hesitated, drew a folded sheet of paper from her skirt pocket and handed it to Clay. "This is for you," she said, so softly that he cocked his head slightly in her direction to catch the words.

"You go first," he said, holding the paper between fingers calloused from working practically every spare moment to prepare for the arrival of the Sears, Roebuck and Company house, all while tending to his duties as town marshal.

Dara Rose's fingers trembled as she opened the little packet, folding back its edges.

A golden wedding band gleamed inside, sturdy and full of promise.

"Will you wear my wedding band, Dara Rose?" Clay asked.

In some ways, it would always seem to both of them that *that* was the moment they were truly married, there at the kitchen table, in the light of a single lantern, on Christmas Eve.

She nodded, murmured, "Yes," all the while blinking back tears, and allowed him to slip the ring onto her finger. It was a perfect fit.

Clay sat watching her for a few moments, his gaze like a caress, and then, very slowly, he opened the sheet of paper she'd given him.

His eyebrows rose slightly as he read, and then a grin spread across his face, lighting him up from within.

She'd given him a receipt for a night's lodging at the Texas Arms Hotel—for two.

"Does this mean what I hope it does?" Clay asked.

Dara Rose had been blushing a lot since she met Clay McKettrick, but at that moment, she outdid herself. Her whole face caught fire as she nodded.

Clay still didn't seem convinced. "You're giving me a wedding night for a Christmas gift?"

She blushed even harder. As her legal husband, he was *entitled* to a wedding night, their bargain notwithstanding. Maybe she should have waited, given him socks or a book or perhaps a fishing pole....

Meanwhile, his golden band gleamed on her left ring finger, simple but heavy.

"Yes," she forced herself to say.

"Hallelujah!" Clay replied, and then he got up from his chair and pulled her into his arms—clear off her feet, in fact—and kissed her so thoroughly that she was gasping when he let her go.

Dara Rose dashed out of the kitchen, afraid of her own scandalous tendencies, and went to look in on the children.

Certain that Edrina and Harriet were at last asleep, she returned to the front room just in time to see Clay set the exquisite doll from the mercantile window squarely in front of the Christmas tree, next to a stack of storybooks that must have been meant for Edrina.

Dara Rose drew in her breath.

"Oh, Clay," she whispered. She hadn't dared think, or hope, that he'd been the one to buy Florence.

But he had.

He waggled an index finger at her and spoke gruffly. "Don't you dare tell me I shouldn't have done this, Mrs. McKettrick. I might not be Edrina and Harriet's real father, but I couldn't love them more if I were, and besides, after all they've been through in their short lives, they deserve a special Christmas."

Dara Rose was fresh out of arguments. She simply went to Clay, slipped her arms around his lean waist and let her head rest against his chest. She could feel his steady, regular heartbeat under her cheekbone.

"I love you, Clay McKettrick," she heard herself say.

Clay drew back just far enough to tilt her face upward with one curved finger. "Do you mean it, Dara Rose?"

"I never say anything I don't mean," she replied, quite truthfully.

He grinned. "I meant to be the first one to say 'I love you,'" he told her, "and darned if you didn't beat me to it."

"Hold me," Dara Rose said. "Hold me tightly, so I know this isn't a dream."

"It isn't a dream," he told her. His breath was warm in her hair. "I love you, Dara Rose. I think I have since I first laid eyes on you that first day, when I brought Edrina home on Outlaw and you were so riled up, you were practically standing next to yourself."

She clung to him, with both arms, and her body ached to receive his, but that would have to wait.

Still, it was Christmas Eve, and Clay was holding her, and in a few weeks, they'd be settled in their new house, with a room to themselves and all the privacy a married couple could want.

She'd waited a long time for Clay McKettrick, and she could wait a little longer.

ON CHRISTMAS DAY, in the early afternoon, members of the community began arriving at Blue River's one-room schoolhouse, some on foot, some on horseback, others riding in wagons or buggies.

Miss Alvira Krenshaw had done a fine job decorating the place with paper chains and the like, and everyone who could afford to brought food to share with their neighbors. Clay carefully carried in the huge ham, arranged on a scrubbed slab of wood and draped in clean dish towels, and set it on top of one of the bookcases, with the mounds of fried chicken and the beef roasts and various other dishes already provided by earlier arrivals.

Edrina, preening a little in her new coat and shoes, carried another of her gifts, a game of checkers in a sturdy wooden box, under one arm, hoping, Dara Rose supposed, to find some unsuspecting child to challenge to a game.

Harriet, also sporting a new coat and lace-up shoes—

the first pair she'd ever owned that hadn't belonged to Edrina first—held Florence tightly against her side. The doll came with a small wardrobe, neatly folded inside a travel trunk, and Harriet had changed its clothes three times before they left home.

Everyone was there, including Dr. Howard, his wife, Eloise, and little Madeline, the newcomers.

People laughed and talked, often-lonely country folks crowded together in small quarters, and eventually Miss Krenshaw sat down at the out-of-tune piano and launched into a lively version of "God Rest Ye Merry Gentlemen."

Just about everybody sang along; though, of course, some voices were better than others. Some hearty, some thin and wavering.

"Hark, the Herald Angels Sing" followed, and then "Silent Night."

Snow began drifting past the windows, and Ezra Maddox showed up, along with Peg O'Reilly, her two boys and little Addie, bundled warmly in a quilt.

Holding the child in his strong farmer's arms, Mr. Maddox looked around at the assemblage, as though daring anyone to question his presence.

"Come in, come in," Miss Krenshaw sang out, from the piano seat, "we're just about to start supper."

Dara Rose immediately approached Peg, though she gave Mr. Maddox a wide berth, and hugged her friend warmly. Peg had obviously made an effort to dress up, and the children looked clean and eager to share in festivities.

"Happy Christmas, Peg," Dara Rose said, smiling.

"Ezra didn't say we ought to bring food," Peg whispered, looking fretful, as though she might be poised to flee.

"Never mind that," Dara Rose assured the other woman.

"There's plenty to go around. In fact, I wouldn't be surprised if we wound up with as many leftovers as the Lord's disciples gathered up after the feast of the loaves and fishes."

Peg managed a tentative smile. "Addie shouldn't be out—she's been running a fever. But the little ones were so pleased to have some kind of Christmas…"

Dara Rose couldn't help seeing some of herself in Peg O'Reilly. After her husband's desertion, and all the struggles to keep body and soul together, for her children and herself, Peg barely believed in good fortune anymore, or human generosity. If, indeed, she'd *ever* believed.

Putting a hand on the small of Peg's bony back, she steered her friend toward the part of the schoolhouse where the food awaited, helped her to fill plates for Addie and the little boys and find places for them to sit.

After that, everyone sort of stampeded forward, and there was much merriment and laughter as the people of Blue River, Texas, shared a simple Christmas.

Although she made sure Edrina and Harriet had supper, Dara Rose barely saw her husband for the rest of the evening. He was always on the other side of the crowded schoolhouse, it seemed, but each time she found him with her eyes, he smiled and winked and made her blush.

They finally converged at the cloakroom—Clay and Dara Rose, Edrina and Harriet—and the girls, probably exhausted, seemed unusually reticent.

Harriet tugged at Dara Rose's skirt and said, "Mama, bend down so I can speak to you."

Smiling, Dara Rose leaned to look directly into her youngest daughter's face.

"We have lots of presents at home," Harriet said, with

a rueful glance at her lovely doll, which was now looking a bit rumpled from being clenched so tightly in her arms.

"And the O'Reillys didn't get anything at all," Edrina added, shifting her checkers game from one arm to the other. "They didn't even have a *tree*."

Clay had joined them by then, and he'd managed to collect their coats from the conglomeration in the cloakroom, but he didn't say anything.

"Do you think St. Nicholas would be sad if I gave Florence to Addie?" Harriet asked, her eyes luminous as she searched Dara Rose's face.

"And her brothers would probably like this checkers game," Edrina added.

Dara Rose's vision blurred.

She looked helplessly up at Clay.

He laid a hand on Edrina's shoulder, smiled down at Harriet. "I think a thing like that would make St. Nicholas mighty happy," he said.

Both girls shifted their gazes to Dara Rose.

She could only nod, since her throat had tightened around any words she might have said, cinching them inside her.

Edrina and Harriet raced off, beaming, to give away their Christmas presents.

Epilogue

～⁕～

December 26, 1914

CLAY GAVE DARA ROSE PLENTY of time to settle into their room at the Texas Arms Hotel that evening, making his usual rounds as marshal, tending to Outlaw in his stall at the livery stable and the chickens in the backyard at home. The children were spending the night with Miss Krenshaw, in the teacher's quarters behind the schoolhouse, and the thought made her smile every time it came to her. After all the times Edrina had played hooky, it was ironic, her being so pleased by the idea of sleeping there.

At her leisure, Dara Rose unpacked her tattered carpetbag, took a long, luxurious bath in the gleaming copper tub carried in, set down in front of the room's simple fireplace, the hearth blazing with a crackling and fragrant fire, and filled with steaming, fragrant water. She soaked and scrubbed and dreamed, and when she heard Clay's light knock at the door, she started.

She'd lost track of time. Meant to be properly clad in the lovely lace-trimmed nightgown and wrapper Clay had given her for a private Christmas gift, presented when the children were asleep and they were alone. Instead, though, here she was, stark naked, her skin slick with moisture, her hair still pinned up in a knot at the back of her neck. She stood, trembling, not with fear, but with anticipation, and reached for her towel.

"It's me, Mrs. McKettrick," Clay said, from the other side of the door. "May I come in?"

Dara Rose gulped hard. "Yes," she said.

His key turned in the lock, and the door opened, and Clay stepped inside. His eyes drank her in even as he shut the door again. Slowly, he took off his hat and then his coat, with its star-shaped badge, unbuckled the ominous gun belt he wore when he was working, set it aside.

"Do you really need that towel?" he asked, with a hint of mischief in his eyes, as he ran a hand through his dark hair.

Dara Rose, feeling deliciously reckless, let the towel drop.

Clay looked at her frankly, his gaze touching her bare breasts, rousing her nipples to peaks, gliding like reverent hands down the sides of her waist and over her hips and even to the silk thatch at the juncture of her thighs.

He swallowed visibly. "Mrs. McKettrick," he said, in a rumbling drawl, "you are unreasonably beautiful."

What did one say to that? Dara Rose didn't know, didn't try.

She simply waited to be touched.

Clay approached her then, lifted her out of the tub by her waist and set her in front of him. Kissed her until she felt drunk with the sensation of his mouth on hers, the radiant heat and hard substance of his body promising so much to her soft one.

"You have me at a disadvantage, Mr. McKettrick," Dara

Rose managed, free to be the temptress she was at long last, and exulting in that.

"How's that?" he asked, arching one dark eyebrow and running his hands lightly up and down, along her ribs.

"You, sir," she replied, breathless at his touch, wanting more, so much more, "are fully dressed, while I am quite naked."

"Indeed you are," he agreed huskily, using one hand to loosen her chignon and send her heavy hair spilling down her back.

In the next moment, Clay lifted her again and, secret vixen that she was, Dara Rose locked her bare legs around his hips, tilted her head back with a slight groan when she felt the length of his shaft against her. That made him chuckle, and find her mouth with his, and kiss her into another, even deeper daze of jubilant need.

Suddenly, she landed, with a soft but decisive bounce, on the hotel bed, looked up at Clay as he unbuttoned his shirt, tossed it aside. Instead of stretching out beside her, though, he knelt at the side of the bed, gently parted her legs and kissed his way, very lightly, up the inside of her right thigh.

She gasped and arched her back when he conquered that most intimate place, and took her fully into his mouth.

Suckled, lightly at first, and then with increasing hunger.

Dara Rose, twice married, had never been so deliciously ravished, never felt so beautiful or so womanly, never known such a wild and frantic greed for pleasure.

Instinctively, she arched her back, and Clay slipped his hands under her buttocks, now quivering with the strain of making an offering of her entire self, and feasted on her until her body buckled and undulated in fierce spasms of celebration and she cried out.

The sound was low and long and husky, part howl and full of triumph that must have sounded, instead, like agony.

"That—" Clay chuckled against her still-tingling flesh "—is why we need our own bedroom, Mrs. McKettrick. One with thick walls."

Dara Rose laughed, or sobbed, or both. She couldn't tell which, didn't care.

All that mattered, for the moment, was that she loved this man, and he loved her, and she could, at last, abandon herself completely to this one someone, leave behind her practicality and her fears and simply *be*.

How odd, she thought, that there could be such freedom in surrender.

Still soaring from that first shattering release, Dara Rose was only dimly aware of Clay rising, removing the rest of his clothes. But when he lay down with her, on the turned-back sheets, the deepest satisfaction she'd ever known instantly gave way to the deepest *need*.

It was primitive, urgent, that need. It rocked her.

Desperate, she tried to pull Clay on top of her, feverish to take him inside her. Hold him there, to please him and be pleased *by* him.

Her body, one with his.

Her soul, one with his.

But Clay was as deliberate about making love as he was about everything else he did. He moved with slow confidence, every kiss, every caress, backed with certainty.

He enjoyed her breasts freely, and for a long time.

She moaned, her nipples pebble-hard and wet from his tongue, his lips.

He teased her. He whispered in her ears, and nibbled at

her lobes, and traced the length of her neck with the tip of his tongue, leaving a line of sweet fire behind.

And when he finally lay down flat on the bed, his hands strong, he set her astraddle of his mouth and devoured her all over again, until she was rocking on him, clenching the rails in the headboard of the bed, damp with perspiration, her head tipped back in a low, guttural cry of relief as he finally allowed her to crest the pinnacle and let go.

As she descended, he told her quietly that he had not yet begun to make love to her, that they'd be at it for a lifetime.

He told her all the places he would have her, all the times and ways. She reveled in the knowledge.

"Suppose someone hears?" she fretted, when Clay laid her down again and, at last, poised himself above her.

"Suppose they do?" Clay countered hoarsely, with a grin. And then, in one long, fiery thrust, he was finally inside her, deep, deep inside her.

Part of her.

And all the flexing and needing and carrying on started all over again.

Just as Dara Rose's *life* had started all over again, with the arrival of this man, with his quiet, steady ways and his strength, so at home in his own skin.

It was the beginning of forever, for both of them.

And a fine forever it would be.

* * * * *

DARING MOVES

For Melba. Your friendship was a gift from H.P.

Chapter 1

⟆✧⟅

THE LINE OF PEOPLE WAITING for an autograph reached from the bookstore down the length of the mall to the specialty luggage shop. With a sigh, Amanda Scott bought a cup of coffee from a nearby French bakery, bravely forgoing the delicate, flaky pastries inside the glass counter, and took her place behind a man in an expensive tweed overcoat.

Distractedly he turned and glanced at her, as though somehow finding her to blame for the delay. Then he pushed up his sleeve and consulted a slim gold watch. He was a couple of inches taller than Amanda, with brown hair that was only slightly too long and hazel eyes flecked with green, and he needed a shave.

Never one to pass the time in silence if an excuse to chat presented itself, Amanda took a steadying sip of her coffee and announced, "I'm buying Dr. Marshall's book for my sister, Eunice. She's going through a nasty divorce." The runaway bestseller was called *Gathering Up the Pieces,* and it was meant for people who had suffered some personal loss or setback.

The stranger turned to look back at her. The pleasantly mingled scents of new snow and English Leather seemed to surround him. "Are you talking to me?" he inquired, drawing his brows together in puzzlement.

Amanda fortified herself with another sip of coffee. She hadn't meant to flirt; it was just that waiting could be so tedious. "Actually, I was," she admitted.

He surprised her with a brief but brilliant smile that practically set her back on the heels of her snow boots. In the next second his expression turned grave, but he extended a gloved hand.

"Jordan Richards," he said formally.

Gulping down the mouthful of coffee she'd just taken, Amanda returned the gesture. "Amanda Scott," she managed. "I don't usually strike up conversations with strange men in shopping malls, you understand. It's just that I was bored."

Again that blinding grin, as bright as sunlight on water.

"I see," said Jordan Richards.

The line moved a little, and they both stepped forward. Amanda suddenly felt shy, and wished she hadn't gotten off the bus at the mall. Maybe she should have gone straight home to her cozy apartment and her cat.

She reminded herself that Eunice would benefit by reading the book and that, with this purchase, her Christmas shopping would be finished. After today she could hide in her work, like a soldier crouching in a foxhole, until the holidays and all their painful associations were past.

"Too bad about Eunice," Jordan Richards remarked.

"I'll give her your condolences," Amanda promised, a smile lighting her aquamarine eyes.

The line advanced, and so did Amanda and Jordan.

"Good," he said.

Amanda finished her coffee, crumpled the cup and tossed it into a nearby trash bin. Beside the bin there was a sign that read Is Therapy For You? Attend A Free Minisession With Dr. Marshall After The Book Signing. Beneath was a diagram of the mall, with the public auditorium colored in.

"So," she ventured, "are you buying *Gathering Up the Pieces* for yourself or somebody else?"

"I'm sending it to my grandmother," Jordan answered, consulting his watch again.

Amanda wondered if he had to be somewhere else later, or if he was just an impatient person.

"What happened to her?" she asked sympathetically.

Jordan looked reluctant, but after a few moments and another step forward as the line progressed, he said, "She had some pretty heavy-duty surgery a while back."

"Oh," Amanda said, and without thinking, she reached out and patted his arm so as not to let the mention of the unknown grandmother's misfortune pass without some response from her.

Something softened in Jordan Richards's manner at the small demonstration. "Are you attending the 'free minisession'?" he asked, gesturing toward the sign. The expression in his eyes said he fully expected her to answer no.

Amanda smiled and lifted one shoulder in a shrug. "Why not? I've got the rest of the afternoon to blow, and I could learn something."

Jordan looked thoughtful. "I suppose nobody has to talk if they don't want to."

"Of course not," Amanda replied confidently, even though she had no idea what would be required. Some of the self-help groups could get pretty wild; she'd heard of people walking across burning coals in their bare feet, or letting themselves be dunked in hot tubs.

"I'll go if you'll sit beside me," Jordan said.

Amanda considered the suggestion only briefly. The mall was a well-lit place, crowded with Christmas shoppers. If Jordan Richards were some kind of weirdo—and that seemed unlikely, unless crackpots were dressing like models in *Gentlemen's Quarterly* these days—she would be perfectly safe. "Okay," she said with another shrug.

After the decision was made, they lapsed into a companionable silence. Nearly fifteen minutes had passed by the time Jordan reached the author's table.

Dr. Eugene Marshall, the famous psychology guru, signed his name in a confident scrawl and handed Jordan a book. Amanda had her volume autographed and followed her new acquaintance to the cash register.

Once they'd both paid, they left the store together.

There was already a mob gathered at the double doors of the mall's community auditorium, and according to a sign on an easel, the minisession would start in another ten minutes.

Jordan glanced at the line of fast-food places across the concourse. "Would you like some coffee or something?"

Amanda shook her head, then reached up to pull her light, shoulder-length hair from under the collar of her coat. "No, thanks. What kind of work do you do, Mr. Richards?"

"Jordan," he corrected. He took off his overcoat and draped it over one arm, then loosened his tie and collar slightly. "What kind of work do you think I do?"

Amanda assessed him, narrowing her blue eyes. Jordan looked fit, and he even had a bit of a suntan, but she doubted he worked with his hands. His clothes marked him as an upper-management type, and so did that gold watch he kept checking. "You're a stockbroker," she guessed.

He chuckled. "Close. I'm a partner in an investment firm. What do you do?"

People were starting to move into the auditorium and take seats, and Amanda and Jordan moved along with them. With a half smile, she answered, "Guess."

He considered her thoughtfully. "You're a flight attendant for a major airline," he decided after several moments had passed.

Amanda took his conjecture as a compliment, even though it was wrong. "I'm the assistant manager of the Evergreen Hotel." They found seats near the middle of the auditorium, and Jordan took the one on the aisle. Amanda was just daring to hope she was making a favorable impression, when her stomach rumbled.

"And you haven't had lunch yet," Jordan stated with another of those lethal, quicksilver grins. "It just so happens that I'm a little hungry myself. How about something from that Chinese fast-food place I saw out there—after we're done with the minisession, I mean?"

Again Amanda smiled. She seemed to be smiling a lot, which was odd, because she hadn't felt truly happy since before James Brockman had swept into her life, turned it upside down and swept out again. "I'd like that," she heard herself say.

Just then Dr. Marshall walked out onto the auditorium stage. At his appearance, Jordan became noticeably uncomfortable, shifting in his seat and drawing one Italian-leather-shod foot up to rest on the opposite knee.

The famous author introduced himself, just in case someone who had never watched a TV talk show might have wandered in, and announced that he wanted the audience to break up into groups of twelve.

Jordan looked even more discomfited, and probably wouldn't have participated if a group hadn't formed around him and Amanda. To make things even more interesting, at least to Amanda's way of thinking, the handsome, silver-haired Dr. Marshall chose their group to work with, while his assistants took the others.

"All right, people," he began in a tone of pleasant authority, "let's get started." His knowing gray eyes swept the small gathering. "Why does everybody look so worried? This will be relatively painless—all we're going to do is talk about ourselves a little." He looked at Amanda. "What's your name?" he asked directly. "And what's the worst thing that's happened to you in the past year?"

She swallowed. "Amanda Scott. And—the worst thing?"

Dr. Marshall nodded with kindly amusement.

All of the sudden Amanda wished she'd gone to a matinee or stayed home to clean her apartment. She didn't want to talk about James, especially not in front of strangers, but she was basically an honest person and *James* was the worst thing that had happened to her in a very long time. Not looking at Jordan, she answered, "I fell in love with a man and he turned out to be married."

"What did you do when you found out?" the doctor asked reasonably.

"I cried a lot," Amanda answered, forgetting for the moment that there were twelve other people listening in, including Jordan.

"Did you break off the relationship?" Dr. Marshall pressed.

Amanda still felt the pain and humiliation she'd known when James's wife had stormed into her office and made a scene. Before that, Amanda hadn't even suspected the terrible truth. "Yes," she replied softly with a miserable nod.

"Is this experience still affecting your life?"

Amanda wished she dared to glance at Jordan to see how he was reacting, but she didn't have the courage. She lowered her eyes. "I guess it is."

"Did you stop trusting men?"

Considering all the dates she'd refused in the months since she'd disentangled herself from James, Amanda supposed she had stopped trusting men. Even worse, she'd stopped trusting her own instincts. "Yes," she answered very softly.

Dr. Marshall reached out to touch her shoulder. "I'm not going to pretend you can solve your problems just by sitting in on a minisession, or even by reading my book, but I think it's time for you to stop hiding and take some risks. Agreed?"

Amanda was surprised at the man's insight. "Agreed," she said, and right then and there she made up her mind to read Eunice's copy of *Gathering Up the Pieces* before she wrapped it.

The doctor's attention shifted to the man sitting on Amanda's left. He said he'd lost his job, and the fact that Christmas was coming up made things harder. A woman in the row behind Amanda talked about her child's serious illness. Finally, after about twenty minutes had passed, everyone had spoken except Jordan.

He rubbed his chin, which was already showing a five o'clock shadow, and cleared his throat. Amanda, feeling his tension and reluctance as though they were her own, laid her hand gently on his arm.

"The worst thing that ever happened to me," he said in a low, almost inaudible voice, "was losing my wife."

"How did it happen?" the doctor asked.

Jordan looked as though he wanted to bolt out of his chair and stride up the aisle to the doors, but he answered the question. "A motorcycle accident."

"Were you driving?" Dr. Marshall's expression was sympathetic.

"Yes," Jordan replied after a long silence.

"And you're still not ready to talk about it," the doctor deduced.

"That's right," Jordan said. And he got up and walked slowly up the aisle and out of the auditorium.

Amanda followed, catching up just outside. She didn't quite dare to touch his arm again, yet he slowed down at the sound of her footsteps. "How about that Chinese food you promised me?" she asked gently.

Jordan met her eyes, and for just a moment, she saw straight through to his soul. What pain he'd suffered.

"Sure," he replied, and his voice was hoarse.

"I'm all through with my Christmas shopping," Amanda announced once they were seated at a table, Number Three Regulars in front of them from the Chinese fast-food place. "How about you?"

"My secretary does mine," Jordan responded. He looked relieved at her choice of topic.

"That's above and beyond the call of duty," Amanda remarked lightly. "I hope you're giving her something terrific."

Jordan smiled at that. "She gets a sizable bonus."

"Good."

It was obvious Jordan was feeling better. His eyes twinkled, and some of the strain had left his face.

"I'm glad company policy meets with your approval."

It was surprising, considering her unfortunate and all-too-recent experiences with James, but it wasn't until that moment that Amanda realized that she hadn't checked Jordan's hand for a wedding band. She glanced at the appropriate finger, even though she knew it would be bare, and saw a white strip where the ring had been.

"Like I said, I'm a widower," he told her with a slight smile, obviously having read her glance accurately.

"I'm sorry," Amanda told him.

He speared a piece of sweet-and-sour chicken. "It's been three years."

It seemed to Amanda that the white space on his ring finger should have filled in after three years. "That's quite a while," she said, wondering if she should just get up from her chair, collect her book and her coat and leave. In the end she didn't, because a glance at her watch told her it was still forty minutes until the next bus left. Besides, she was hungry.

Jordan sighed. "Sometimes it seems like three centuries."

Amanda bit her lower lip, then burst out, "You aren't one of those creeps who goes around saying he doesn't have a wife when he really does, are you? I mean, you could have remarried."

He looked very tired all of a sudden, and pale beneath his tan. Amanda wondered why he hadn't gotten around to shaving.

"No," he said. "I'm not married."

Amanda dropped her eyes to her food, ashamed that she'd asked the question, even though she wouldn't have taken it back. The experience with James had taught her that a woman couldn't be too careful about such things.

"Amanda?"

She lifted her gaze to see him studying her. "What?"

"What was his name?"

"What was whose name?"

"The guy who told you he wasn't married."

Amanda cleared her throat and shifted nervously in her chair. The thought of James didn't cause her pain anymore, but she didn't know Jordan Richards well enough to tell him just how badly she'd been hoodwinked. A sudden, crazy panic seized her. "Gosh, look at the time," she said, pulling back her sleeve to check her watch a split second after she'd spoken. "I'd better get home." She bolted out of her chair and put her coat back on, then reached for her purse and the bag from the bookstore. She laid a five-dollar bill on the table to pay for her dinner. "It was nice meeting you."

Jordan frowned and slowly pushed back his chair, then stood. "Wait a minute, Amanda. You're not playing fair."

He was right. Jordan hadn't run away, however much he had probably wanted to, and she wouldn't, either.

She sank back into her seat, all too aware that people at surrounding tables were looking on with interest.

"You're not ready to talk about him," Jordan said, sitting down again, "and I'm not ready to talk about her. Deal?"

"Deal," Amanda said.

They discussed the Seattle Seahawks after that, and the Chinese artifacts on display at one of the museums. Then Jordan walked with her to the nearest corner and waited until the bus pulled up.

"Goodbye, Amanda," he said as she climbed the steps.

She dropped her change into the slot and smiled over one shoulder. "Thanks for the company."

He waved as the bus pulled away, and Amanda ached with a bittersweet loneliness she'd never known before, not even in the awful days after her breakup with James.

When Amanda arrived at her apartment building on Seattle's Queen Anne Hill, she was still thinking about Jordan. He'd wanted to offer to drive her home, she knew, but he'd had the good grace not to, and Amanda liked him for that.

In her mailbox she found a sheaf of bills waiting for her. "I'll never save enough to start a bed and breakfast at this rate," she complained to her black-and-white long-haired cat, Gershwin, when he met her at the door.

Gershwin was unsympathetic. As usual, he was interested only in his dinner.

After flipping on the lights, dropping her purse and the

book onto the hall table and hanging her coat on the brass-plated tree that was really too large for that little space, Amanda went into the kitchenette.

Gershwin purred and wound himself around her ankles as she opened a can of cat food, but when she scraped it out onto his dish, he abandoned her without compunction.

While Gershwin gobbled, Amanda went back to the mail she'd picked up in the lobby and flipped through it again. Three bills, a you-may-have-already-won and a letter from Eunice.

Amanda set the other envelopes down and opened the crisp blue one with her sister's return address printed in italics in one corner. She was disappointed when she realized that the letter was just another litany of Eunice's soon-to-be-ex-husband's sins, and she set it aside to finish later.

In the bathroom she started water running into her huge claw-footed tub, then stripped off the skirt and sweater she'd worn to the mall. After disposing of her underthings and panty hose, Amanda climbed into the soothing water.

Gershwin pushed the door open in that officious way cats have and bounded up to stand on the tub's edge with perfect balance. Like a tightrope walker, he strolled back and forth along the chipped porcelain, telling Amanda about his day in a series of companionable meows.

Amanda listened politely as she bathed, but her mind was wandering. She was thinking about Jordan Richards and that recently removed wedding band of his.

She sighed. All her instincts told her he was telling the truth about his marital status, but those same instincts had once insisted that James was all right, too.

AMANDA WAS WAITING when the bus pulled up at her corner the next morning. The weather was a little warmer, and the snow, so unusual in Seattle, was already melting.

Fifteen minutes later Amanda walked through the huge revolving door of the Evergreen Hotel. Its lush Oriental carpets were soft beneath the soles of her shoes, and crystal chandeliers winked overhead, their multicolored reflections blazing in the floor-to-ceiling mirrors.

Amanda took the elevator to the third floor, where the hotel's business offices were. As she was passing through the small reception area, Mindy Simmons hailed her from her desk.

"Mr. Mansfield is sick today," she said in an undertone. Mindy was small and pretty, with long brown hair and expressive green eyes. "Your desk is buried in messages."

Amanda went into her office and started dealing with problems. The plumbing in the presidential suite was on the fritz, so she called to make sure Maintenance was on top of the situation. A Mrs. Edman in 1203 suspected one of the maids of stealing her pearl earring, and some-one had mixed up some dates at the reception desk—two couples were expecting to occupy the bridal suite on the same night.

It was noon when Amanda finished straightening everything out—Mrs. Edman's pearl earring had fallen behind the television set, the plumbing in the presidential suite was back in working order and each of the newlywed couples would have rooms to themselves. At Mindy's suggestion, she and Amanda went to the busy Westlake Mall for lunch, buying salads at one of the fast-food restaurants and taking a table near a window.

"Two more weeks and I start my vacation," Mindy stated enthusiastically, pouring dressing from a little carton over her salad. "Christmas at Big Mountain. I can hardly wait."

Amanda would just as soon have skipped Christmas altogether if she could have gotten the rest of the world to go along with the idea, but of course she didn't say that. "You and Pete will have a great time at the ski resort."

Mindy was chewing, and she swallowed before answering. "It's just great of his parents to take us along—we could never have afforded it on our own."

With a nod, Amanda poked her fork into a cherry tomato.

"What are you doing over the holidays?" Mindy asked.

Amanda forced a smile. "I'm going to be working," she reminded her friend.

"I know that, but what about a tree and presents and a turkey?"

"I'll have all those things at my mom and stepdad's place."

Mindy, who knew about James and all the dashed hopes he'd left in his wake, looked sympathetic. "You need to meet a new man."

Amanda bristled a little. "It just so happens that a woman can have a perfectly happy life without a man hanging around."

Mindy looked doubtful. "Sure," she said.

"Besides, I met someone just yesterday."

"Who?"

Amanda concentrated on her salad for several long moments. "His name is Jordan Richards, and—"

"Jordan Richards?" Mindy interrupted excitedly. "Wow! How did you ever manage to meet him?"

A little insulted that Mindy seemed to think Jordan was so far out of her orbit that even meeting him was a feat to get excited about, Amanda frowned. "We were in line together at a bookstore. Do you know him?"

"Not exactly," Mindy admitted, subsiding a little. "But my father-in-law does. Jordan Richards practically doubled his retirement fund for him, and they're always writing about him in the financial section of the Sunday paper."

"I didn't know you read that section," Amanda remarked.

"I don't," Mindy admitted readily, unwrapping a bread stick. "But we have dinner with my in-laws practically every Sunday, and that's all Pete and his dad ever talk about. Did he ask you out?"

"Who?"

"Jordan Richards, silly."

Amanda shook her head. "No, we just had Chinese food together and talked a little." She deliberately left out the part about how they'd gone to the minitherapy session and the way she'd reacted when Jordan had asked her about James.

Mindy looked disappointed. "Well, he did ask for your number, didn't he?"

"No. But he knows where I work. If he wants to call, I suppose he will."

A delighted smile lit Mindy's face. Positive thinking was an art form with her. "He'll call. I just know it."

Amanda grinned. "If he does, I won't be able to accept the glory—I owe it all to an article I read in *Cosmo*. I think it was called 'Big Girls Should Talk to Strangers,' or something like that."

Mindy lifted her diet cola in a rousing roast. "Here's to Jordan Richards and a red-hot romance!"

With a chuckle, Amanda touched her cup to Mindy's and drank a toast to something that would probably never happen.

Back at the hotel more crises were waiting to be solved, and there was a message on Amanda's desk, scrawled by the typist who'd filled in for Mindy during lunch. Jordan Richards had called.

A peculiar tightness constricted Amanda's throat, and a flutter started in the pit of her stomach. Mindy's toast echoed in her ears: *"Here's to Jordan Richards and a red-hot romance."*

Amanda laid down the message, telling herself she didn't have time to return the call, then picked it up again. Before she knew it, her finger was punching out the numbers.

"Striner, Striner and Richards," sang a receptionist's voice at the other end of the line.

Amanda drew a deep breath, squared her shoulders and exhaled. "This is Amanda Scott," she said in her most professional voice. "I'm returning a call from Jordan Richards."

"One moment, please."

After a series of clicks and buzzes another female voice came on the line. "Jordan Richards's office. May I help you?"

Again Amanda gave her name. And again she was careful to say she was returning a call that had originated with Jordan.

There was another buzz, then Jordan's deep, crisp voice saying, "Richards."

Amanda hadn't expected a simple thing like the man saying his name to affect her the way it did. It was the strangest sensation to feel dizzy over something like that. She dropped into the swivel chair behind her desk. "Hi. It's Amanda."

"Amanda."

Coming from him, her own name had the same strange impact as his had had.

"How are you?" he asked.

Amanda swallowed. She was a professional with a very responsible job. It was ridiculous to be overwhelmed by something so simple and ordinary as the timbre of a man's voice. "I'm fine," she answered. Nothing more imaginative came to her, and she sat there behind her broad desk, blushing like an eighth-grade schoolgirl trying to work up the courage to ask a boy to a sock hop.

His low, masculine chuckle came over the wire to surround her like a mystical caress. "If I promise not to ask any more questions about you know who, will you go out with me? Some friends of mine are having an informal dinner tonight on their houseboat."

Amanda still felt foolish for talking about James in the therapy session, then practically bolting when Jordan brought him up again over Chinese food. Lately she just seemed to be a mass of contradictions, feeling one way one minute, another the next. What it all came down to was the fact that Dr. Marshall was right—she needed to start taking chances again. "Sounds like fun," she said after drawing a deep breath.

"Pick you up at seven?"

"Yes." And she gave him her address. A little thrill went through her as she laid the receiver back on its cradle, but there was no more time to think about Jordan. The telephone immediately rang again.

"Amanda Scott."

The chef's assistant was calling. A pipe had broken, and the kitchen was flooding fast.

"Just another manic day," Amanda muttered as she hurried off to investigate.

Chapter 2

It was ten minutes after six when Amanda got off the bus in front of her apartment building and dashed inside. After collecting her mail, she hurried up the stairs and jammed her key into the lock. Jordan was picking her up in less than an hour, and she had a hundred things to do to get ready.

Since he'd told her the evening would be a casual one, she selected gray woolen slacks and a cobalt-blue blouse. After a hasty shower, she put on fresh makeup and quickly wove her hair into a French braid.

Gershwin stood on the back of the toilet the whole time she was getting ready, lamenting the treatment of house cats in contemporary America. She had just given him his dinner when a knock sounded at the door.

Amanda's heart lurched like a dizzy ballet dancer, and she wondered why she was being such a ninny. Jordan Richards was just a man, nothing more. And so what if he was successful? She met a lot of men like him in her line of work.

She opened the door and knew a moment of pure exaltation at the look of approval in Jordan's eyes.

"Hi," he said. He wore jeans and a sport shirt, and his

hands rested comfortably in the pockets of his brown leather jacket. "You look fantastic."

Amanda thought he looked pretty fantastic himself, but she didn't say so because she'd used up that week's quota of bold moves by talking about James in front of people she didn't know. "Thanks," she said, stepping back to admit him.

Gershwin did a couple of turns around Jordan's ankles and meowed his approval. With a chuckle, Jordan bent to pick him up. "Look at the size of this guy. Is he on steroids or what?"

Amanda laughed. "No, but I suspect him of throwing wild parties and sending out for pizza when I'm not around."

After scratching the cat once behind the ears, Jordan set him down again with a chuckle, but his eyes were serious when he looked at Amanda.

Something in his expression made her breasts grow heavy and her nipples tighten beneath the smooth silk of her blouse. "I suppose we'd better go," she said, sounding somewhat lame even to her own ears.

"Right," Jordan agreed. His voice had the same effect on Amanda it had had earlier. She felt the starch go out of her knees and she was breathless, as though she'd accidentally stepped onto a runaway skateboard.

She took her blue cloth coat from the coat tree, and Jordan helped her into it. She felt his fingertips brush her nape as he lifted her braid from beneath the collar, and hoped he didn't notice that she trembled ever so slightly at his touch.

His car, a sleek black Porsche—Amanda decided then and there that he didn't have kids of his own—was parked at the curb. Jordan opened the passenger door and walked around to get behind the wheel after Amanda was settled.

Soon they were streaking toward Lake Union. It was

only when he switched on the windshield wipers that Amanda realized it was raining.

"Have you lived in Seattle long?" she asked, uncomfortable with a silence Jordan hadn't seemed to mind.

"I live on Vashon Island now—I've been somewhere in the vicinity all my life," he answered. "What about you?"

"Seattle's home," Amanda replied.

"Have you ever wanted to live anywhere else?"

She smiled. "Sure. Paris, London, Rome. But after I graduated from college, I was hired to work at the Evergreen, so I settled down here."

"You know what they say—life is what happens while we're making other plans. I always intended to work on Wall Street myself."

"Do you regret staying here?"

Amanda had expected a quick, light denial. Instead she received a sober glance and a low, "Sometimes, yes. Things might have been very different if I'd gone to New York."

For some reason Amanda's gaze was drawn to the pale line across Jordan's left-hand ring finger. Although the windows were closed and the heater was going, Amanda suppressed a shiver. She didn't say anything until Lake Union, with its diamondlike trim of lit houseboats, came into sight. Since the holidays were approaching, the place was even more of a spectacle than usual.

"It looks like a tangle of Christmas tree lights."

Jordan surprised her with one of his fleeting, devastating grins.

"You have a colorful way of putting things, Amanda Scott."

She smiled. "Do your friends like living on a houseboat?"

"I think so," he answered, "but they're planning to move in the spring. They're expecting a baby."

Although lots of children were growing up on Lake Union, Amanda could understand why Jordan's friends would want to bring their little one up on dry land. Her thoughts turned bittersweet as she wondered whether she would ever have a child of her own. She was already twenty-eight—time was running out.

As he pulled the car into a parking lot near the wharves and shut the engine off, she sat up a little straighter, realizing that she'd left his remark dangling. "I'm sorry...I... How nice for them that they're having a baby."

Unexpectedly Jordan reached out and closed his hand over Amanda's. "Did I say something wrong?" he asked with a gentleness that almost brought tears to her eyes.

Amanda shook her head. "Of course not. Let's go in— I'm anxious to meet your friends."

David and Claudia Chamberlin were an attractive couple in their early thirties, he with dark hair and eyes, she with very fair coloring and green eyes. They were both architects, and framed drawings and photographs of their work graced the walls of the small but elegantly furnished houseboat.

Amanda thought of her own humble apartment with Gershwin as its outstanding feature, and wondered if Jordan thought she was dull.

Claudia seemed genuinely interested in her, though, and her greeting was warm. "It's good to see Jordan back in circulation—finally," she confided in a whisper when she and Amanda were alone beside the table where an array of wonderful food was being set out by the caterer's helpers.

Amanda didn't reply to the comment right away, but her gaze strayed to Jordan, who was standing only a few feet away, talking with David. "I guess it's been pretty hard for him," she ventured, pretending to know more than she did.

"The worst," Claudia agreed. She pulled Amanda a little distance farther from the men. "We thought he'd never get over losing Becky."

Uneasily Amanda recalled the pale stripe Jordan's wedding band had left on his finger. Perhaps, she reflected warily, there was a corresponding mark on his soul.

Later, when Amanda had met everyone in the room and mingled accordingly, Jordan laid her coat gently over her shoulders. "How about going out on deck with me for a few minutes?" he asked quietly. "I need some air."

Once again Amanda felt that peculiar lurching sensation deep inside. "Sure," she said with a wary glance at the rain-beaded windows.

"The rain stopped a little while ago," Jordan assured her with a slight grin.

The way he seemed to know what she was thinking was disconcerting.

They left the main cabin through a door on the side, and because the deck was slippery, Jordan put a strong arm around Amanda's waist. She was fully independent, but she still liked the feeling of being looked after.

The lights of the harbor twinkled on the dark waters of the lake, and Jordan studied them for a while before asking, "So, what do you think of Claudia and David?"

Amanda smiled. "They're pretty interesting," she replied. "I suppose you know they were married in India when they were there with the Peace Corps."

Jordan propped an elbow on the railing and nodded. "David and Claudia are nothing if not unconventional. That's one of the reasons I like them so much."

Amanda was slightly deflated, though she tried hard not to reveal the fact. With her ordinary job, cat and apartment, she knew she must seem prosaic compared to the Chamberlins. Perhaps it was the strange sense of hopelessness she felt that made her reckless enough to ask, "What about your wife? Was she unconventional?"

He turned away from her to stare out at the water, and for a long moment she was sure he didn't intend to answer. Finally, however, he said in a low voice, "She had a degree in marine biology, but she didn't work after the kids were born."

It was the first mention he'd made of any children—Amanda had been convinced, in fact, that he had none. "Kids?" she asked in a small and puzzled voice.

Jordan looked at her in a way that was almost, but not quite, defensive. "There are two—Jessica's five and Lisa's four."

Amanda knew a peculiar joy, as though she'd stumbled upon an unexpected treasure. She couldn't help the quick, eager smile that curved her lips. "I thought—well, when you were driving a Porsche—"

He smiled back at her in an oddly somber way. "Jessie and Lisa live with my sister over in Port Townsend."

Amanda's jubilation deflated. "They live with your sister? I don't understand."

Jordan sighed. "Becky died two weeks after the accident, and I was in the hospital for close to three months. Karen—my sister—and her husband, Paul, took the kids. By the time I got back on my feet, the four of them had become a family. I couldn't see breaking it up."

An overwhelming sadness caused Amanda to grip the railing for a moment to keep from being swept away by the sheer power of the emotion.

Reading her expression, Jordan gently touched the tip of her nose. "Ready to call it a night? You look tired."

Amanda nodded, too close to tears to speak. She had

a tendency to empathize with other people's joys and sorrows, and she was momentarily crushed by the weight of what Jordan had been through.

"I see my daughters often," he assured her, tenderness glinting in his eyes. He kissed her lightly on the mouth, then took her elbow and escorted her back inside the cabin.

They said their goodbyes to David and Claudia Chamberlin, then walked up the wharf to Jordan's car. He was a perfect gentleman, opening the door for Amanda, and she settled wearily into the suede passenger seat.

Back at Amanda's building, Jordan again helped her out of the car, and he walked her to her door. Amanda waited until the last possible second to decide whether she was going to invite him in, breaking her own suspense by blurting out, "Would you like a cup of coffee or something?"

Jordan's hazel eyes twinkled as he placed one hand on either side of the doorjamb, effectively trapping Amanda between his arms. "Not tonight," he said softly.

Amanda's blue eyes widened in confusion. "Don't look now," she replied in a burst of daring cowardice, "but you're sending out conflicting messages."

He chuckled, and his lips touched hers, very tenderly.

Amanda felt a jolt of spiritual electricity spark through her system, burning away every memory of James's touch. Surprise made her draw back from Jordan so suddenly that her head bumped hard against the door.

Jordan lowered one hand to caress her crown, and she felt the French braid coming undone beneath his fingers.

"Careful," he murmured, and then he kissed her again.

This time there was hunger in his touch, and a sweet, frightening power that made Amanda's knees unsteady.

She laid her hands lightly on his chest, trying to ground this second mystical shock, but he interpreted the contact differently and drew back.

"Good night, Amanda," he said quietly. He waited until she'd unlocked her door with a trembling hand, and then he walked away.

Inside the apartment Amanda flipped on the living room light, crossed to the sofa and sagged onto it. She felt as though she were leaning over the edge of a great canyon and the rocks were slipping away beneath her feet.

Gershwin hurled himself into her lap with a loud meow, and she ran one hand distractedly along his silky back. Dr. Marshall had said it was time she started taking chances, and she had an awful feeling she was on the brink of the biggest risk of her life.

THE MASSIVE REDWOOD-AND-GLASS house overlooking Puget Sound was dark and unwelcoming that night when Jordan pulled into the driveway and reached for the small remote control device lying on his dashboard. He'd barely made the last ferry to the island, and he was tired.

As the garage door rolled upward, he thought of Amanda, and shifted uncomfortably on the seat. He would have given half his stock portfolio to have her sitting beside him now, to talk with her over coffee in the kitchen or wine in front of the fireplace...

To take her to his bed.

Jordan got out of the car and slammed the door behind him. The garage was dark, but he didn't flip on a light until he reached the kitchen. Becky had always said he had the night vision of a vampire.

Becky. He clung to the memory of her smile, her laughter, her perfume. She'd been tiny and spirited, with dark hair and eyes, and it seemed to Jordan that she'd never been far from his side, even after her death. He'd loved her to an excruciating degree, but for the past few months she'd been steadily receding from his mind and heart. Now, with the coming of Amanda, her image seemed to be growing more indistinct with every passing moment.

Jordan glanced into the laundry room, needing something real and mundane to focus on. A pile of jeans, sweatshirts and towels lay on the floor, so he crammed as much as he could into the washing machine, then added soap and turned the dial. A comforting, ordinary sound resulted.

Returning to the kitchen, Jordan shrugged out of his leather jacket and laid it over one of the bar stools at the counter. He opened the refrigerator, studied its contents without actually focusing on a single item, then closed it again. He wasn't hungry for anything except Amanda, and it was too soon for that.

Too soon, he reflected with a rueful grin as he walked through the dining room to the front entryway and the stairs. He hadn't bothered with such niceties as timing with the women he'd dated over the past two years—in truth, their feelings just hadn't mattered much to him, though he'd never been deliberately unkind.

He trailed his hand over the top of the polished oak banister as he climbed the stairs. With Amanda, things were different. Timing was crucial, and so were her feelings.

The empty house yawned around Jordan as he opened his bedroom door and went inside. In the adjoining bathroom he took off his clothes and dropped them neatly into the hamper, then stepped into the shower.

Thinking of Amanda again, he turned on the cold water and endured its biting chill until some of the intolerable heat had abated. But while he was brushing his teeth, Amanda sneaked back into his mind.

He saw her standing on the deck of the Chamberlins' boat, looking up at him with that curious vulnerability showing in her blue-green eyes. It was as though she didn't know how beautiful she was, or how strong, and yet she had to, because she was out there making a life for herself.

Rubbing his now-stubbled chin, Jordan wandered into the bedroom, threw back the covers and slid between the sheets. He felt the first stirrings of rage as he thought about the mysterious James and the damage he'd done to Amanda's soul. Jordan had seen the bruises in her eyes every time she'd looked at him, and the memory made him want to find the bastard who'd hurt her and systematically tear him apart.

Jordan turned onto his stomach and tried to put the scattered images of the past two days out of his thoughts. This time, just before he dropped off to sleep, was reserved for thoughts of Becky, as always.

He waited, but his late wife's face didn't form in his mind. He could only see Amanda, with her wide, trusting blue eyes, her soft, spun-honey hair, her shapely and inviting body. He wanted her with a desperation that made his loins ache.

Furious, Jordan slammed one fist into the mattress and flipped onto his back, training all his considerable energy on remembering Becky's face.

He couldn't.

After several minutes of concentrated effort, all of it fruitless, panic seized him, and he bolted upright, switched on the lamp and reached for the picture on his nightstand.

Becky smiled back at him from the photograph as if to say, *Don't worry, sweetheart. Everything will be okay.*

With a raspy sigh, Jordan set the picture back on the table and turned out the light. Becky's favorite reassurance didn't work that night. Maybe things would be okay in the long run, but there was a lot of emotional white water between him and any kind of happy ending.

IT WAS SATURDAY morning, and Amanda luxuriated in the fact that she didn't have to put on makeup, style her hair, or even get dressed if she didn't want to. She really tried to be lazy, but she felt strangely ambitious, and there was no getting around it.

She climbed out of bed and padded barefoot into the kitchen, where she got the coffee maker going and fed Gershwin. Then she had a quick shower and dressed in battered jeans, a Seahawks T-shirt and sneakers.

She was industriously vacuuming the living room rug, when the telephone rang.

The sound was certainly nothing unusual, but it fairly stopped Amanda's heart. She kicked the switch on the vacuum cleaner with her toe and lunged for the telephone, hoping to hear Jordan's voice since she hadn't seen or heard from him in nearly a week.

Instead it was her mother. "Hello, darling," said Marion Whitfield. "You sound breathless. Were you just coming in from the store or something?"

Amanda sank onto the couch. "No, I was only doing housework," she replied, feeling deflated even though she loved and admired this woman who had made a life for herself and both her daughters after the man of the house had walked out on them all.

"That's nice," Marion commented, for she was a great believer in positive reinforcement. "Listen, I called to ask if you'd like to go Christmas shopping with me. We could have lunch, too, and maybe even take in a movie."

Amanda sighed. She still didn't feel great about Christmas, and the stores and restaurants would be jam-packed. The theaters, of course, would be full of screaming children left there by harried mothers trying to complete their shopping. "I think I'll just stay home, if you don't mind."

She stated the refusal in a kindly tone, not wanting to hurt her mother's feelings.

"Is everything all right?"

Amanda caught one fingernail between her teeth for a moment before answering, "Mostly, yes."

"It's time you put that nasty experience with James Brockman behind you," Marion said forthrightly.

The two women were friends, as well as mother and daughter, and Amanda was not normally secretive with Marion. However, the thing with Jordan was too new and too fragile to be discussed; after all, he might never call again. "I'm trying, Mom," she replied.

"Well, Bob and I want you to come over for dinner soon. Like tomorrow, for instance."

"I'll let you know," Amanda promised quickly as the doorbell made its irritating buzz. "And stop worrying about me, okay?"

"Okay," Marion answered without conviction just before Amanda hung up.

Amanda expected one of the neighbor children, or maybe the postman with a package, so when she opened the door and found Jordan standing in the hallway, she felt as though she'd just run into a wall at full tilt.

For his part, Jordan looked a little bewildered, as though he might be surprised to find himself at Amanda's door. "I should have called," he said.

Amanda recovered herself. "Come in," she replied with a smile.

He hesitated for a moment, then stepped into the apartment, his hands tucked into the pockets of his jacket. He was wearing jeans and a green turtleneck, and his brown hair was damp from the Seattle drizzle. "I was wondering if you'd like to go out to lunch or something."

Amanda glanced at the clock on the mantel and was

amazed to see that it was nearly noon. The morning had flown by in a flurry of housecleaning. "Sure," she said. "I'll just clean up a little—"

He reached out and caught hold of her hand when she would have disappeared into her bedroom. "You look fine," he told her, and his voice was very low, like the rumble of an earthquake deep down in the ground.

By sheer force of will, Amanda shored up her knees, only to have him pull her close and lock his hands lightly behind the small of her back. A hot flush made her cheeks ache, and she had to force herself to meet his eyes.

Jordan chuckled. "Do I really scare you so much?" he asked.

Amanda wet her lips with the tip of her tongue in an unconscious display of nervousness. "Yes."

"Why?"

The question was reasonable, but Amanda didn't know the answer. "I'm not sure."

He grinned. "Where would you like to go for lunch?"

She would have been content not to go out at all, preferring just to stand there in his arms all afternoon, breathing in his scent and enjoying the lean, hard feel of his body against hers. She gave herself an inward shake. "You know, I just refused a similar invitation from my mother, and she would have thrown in a movie."

Jordan laughed and smoothed Amanda's bangs back from her forehead. "All right, so will I."

But Amanda shook her head. "Too many munchkins screaming and throwing popcorn."

His expression changed almost imperceptibly. "Don't you like kids?"

"I love them," Amanda answered, "except when they're traveling in herds."

Jordan chuckled again and gave her another light kiss.

"Okay, we'll go to something R-rated. Nobody under seventeen admitted without a parent."

"You've got a deal," Amanda replied.

Just as he was helping her get into her coat, the telephone rang. Praying there wasn't a disaster at the Evergreen to be taken care of, Amanda answered, "Hello?"

"Hello, Amanda." She hadn't heard that voice in six long months, and the sound of it stunned her. It was James.

Grimacing at Jordan, she spoke into the receiver. "I don't want to talk to you, now or ever."

"Please don't hang up," James said quickly.

Amanda bit down on her lip and lowered her eyes. "What is it?"

"Madge is divorcing me."

She drew a deep breath and let it out again. "Congratulations, James," she said, not with cruelty but with resignation. After all, it was no great surprise, and she had no idea why he felt compelled to share the news with her.

"I'd like for you and me to get back together," he said in that familiar tone that had once rendered her pliant and gullible.

"There's absolutely no chance of that," Amanda replied, forcing herself to meet Jordan's gaze again. He was standing at the door, his hand on the knob, watching her with concern but not condemnation. "Goodbye, James." With that, she placed the receiver back in its cradle.

Jordan remained where he was for a long moment, then he crossed the room to where Amanda stood, bundled in her coat, and gently lifted her hair out from under her collar. "Still want to go out?" he asked quietly.

Amanda was oddly shaken, but she nodded, and they left the apartment together. The phone began ringing again when they reached the top of the stairs, but this time Amanda made no effort to answer it.

"I guess I can't blame him for being persistent," Jordan remarked when they were seated in the Porsche. "You're a beautiful woman, Amanda."

She sighed, ignoring the compliment because it didn't register. "I'll never forgive James for lying to me the way he did," she got out. Tears stung her eyes as she remembered the blinding pain of his deceit.

Jordan pulled out into the rainy-day traffic and kept his eyes on the road. "He wants you back," he guessed.

Amanda noticed that his hands tensed slightly around the steering wheel.

"That's what he said," she confessed, staring out at the decorated streets but not really seeing them.

"Do you believe him?"

Amanda shrugged. "It doesn't matter whether I do or not. I've made my decision and I'm not going to change my mind." She found some tissue in her purse and resolutely dried her eyes, trying in vain to convince herself that Jordan hadn't noticed she was crying.

He drove to a pizza joint across the street from a mall north of the city. "This okay?" he asked, bringing the sleek car to a stop in one of the few parking spaces available. "We could order takeout if you'd rather not go in."

Amanda drew a deep breath, composing herself. The time with James was behind her, and she wanted to keep it there, to enjoy the here and now with Jordan. Christmas crowds or none. "Let's eat here," she said.

He favored her with a half grin and came around to open her door for her. As she stood, she accidentally brushed against him, and felt that familiar twisting ache deep inside herself. She was going to end up making love with Jordan Richards, she just knew it. It was inevitable.

The realization that he was reading her thoughts once more made Amanda blush, and she drew back when he took her hand. His grip only became firmer, however, and she didn't try to pull away again. She was in the mood to follow where Jordan might lead—which, to Amanda's way of thinking, made it a darned good thing they were approaching the door of a pizza parlor instead of a bedroom.

Chapter 3

⟨⟨෧⟩⟩

THE PIZZA WAS UNCOMMONLY good, it seemed to Amanda, but memories of the R-rated movie they saw afterward made her fidget in the passenger seat of Jordan's Porsche. "I've never heard of anybody doing that with an ice cube," she remarked with a slight frown.

Jordan laughed. "That was interesting, all right."

"Do you think it was symbolic?"

He was still grinning. "No. It was definitely hormones, pure and simple."

Amanda finally relaxed a little and managed to smile. "You're probably right."

Since there were a lot of cars parked in front of Amanda's building, a sleek silver Mercedes among them, Jordan parked almost a block away. It seemed natural to hold hands as they walked back to the entrance.

Amanda was stunned to see James sitting on the bottom step of the stairway leading up to the second floor. He was wearing his usual three-piece tailor-made suit, a necessity for a corporate chief executive officer like himself, and his silver gray hair looked as dashing as ever. His tanned face showed signs of strain, however, and the once-over he gave Jordan was one of cordial contempt.

Amanda's first instinct was to let go of Jordan's hand, but he tightened his grip when she tried.

Meanwhile James had risen from his seat on the stairs. "We have to talk," he said to Amanda.

She shook her head, grateful now for Jordan's presence and his grasp on her hand. "There's nothing to say."

The man she had once loved arched an eyebrow. "Isn't there? You could start by introducing me to the new man in your life."

It was Jordan who spoke. "Jordan Richards," he said evenly, without offering his hand.

James studied him with new interest flickering in his shrewd eyes. "Brockman," he answered. "James Brockman."

A glance at Jordan revealed that he recognized the name—anyone active in the business world would have— but he clearly wasn't the least bit intimidated. He simply nodded an acknowledgment.

Amanda ran her tongue over her lips. "Let us pass, James," she said. She'd never spoken so authoritatively to him before, but she took no pleasure in the achievement because she knew she wouldn't have managed it if Jordan hadn't been there.

James did not look at Amanda, but at Jordan. Some challenge passed between them, and the air was charged with static electricity for several moments. Then James stepped aside to lean against the banister, leaving barely enough room for Jordan and Amanda to walk by.

"Richards."

Jordan stopped, still holding Amanda's hand, and looked back at James over one shoulder in inquiry.

"I'll call your office Monday morning. I'd be interested

to know what we have in common—where investments are concerned, naturally."

Amanda felt her face heat. Again she tried to pull away from Jordan; again he restrained her. "Naturally," Jordan responded coldly, and then he continued up the stairway, bringing Amanda with him.

"I'm sorry," she said the moment they were alone in her apartment. She was leaning against the closed door.

"Why?" Jordan asked, reaching out to unbutton her coat. He helped her out of it, then hung it on the brass tree. Amanda watched him with injury in her eyes as he removed his jacket and put it with her coat.

She had been leaning against the door again, and she thrust herself away. "Because of James, of course."

"It wasn't your fault he came here."

She sighed and stopped in the tiny entryway, her back to Jordan, the fingers of one hand pressed to her right temple. She knew he was right, but she was slightly nauseous all the same. "That remark he made about what the two of you might have in common..."

Jordan reached out and took her shoulders in his hands, turning her gently to face him. "Your past is your own business, Amanda. I'm interested in the woman you are now, not the woman you were six months or six years ago."

Amanda blinked, then bit her upper lip for a moment. "But he meant—"

He touched her lip with an index finger. "I know what he meant," he said with hoarse gentleness. "When and if it happens for us, Amanda, you won't be the first woman I've been with. I'm not going to condemn you because I'm not the first man."

With that, the subject of that aspect of Amanda's relationship with James was closed forever. In fact, it was almost as though the subject hadn't been broached. "Would you like some coffee or something?" she asked, feeling better.

Jordan grinned. "Sure."

When Amanda came out of the kitchenette minutes later, carrying two mugs of instant coffee, Jordan was studying the blue-and-white patchwork quilt hanging on the wall behind her couch. Gershwin seemed to have become an appendage to his right ankle.

"Did you make this?"

Amanda nodded proudly. "I designed it, too."

Jordan looked impressed. "So there's more to you than the mild-mannered assistant hotel manager who gets her Christmas shopping done early," he teased.

She smiled. "A little, yes." She extended one mug of coffee and he took it, lifting it to his lips. "I had a good time today, Jordan."

When Amanda sat down on the couch, Jordan did, too. His nearness brought images from the movie they'd seen back to her mind. "So did I," he answered, putting his coffee down on the rickety cocktail table.

Damn that guy with the ice cube, Amanda fretted to herself as Jordan put his hands on her shoulders again and slowly drew her close. It seemed to her that a small eternity passed before their lips touched, igniting the soft suspense Amanda felt into a flame of awareness.

The tip of his tongue encircled her lips, and when they parted at his silent bidding, he took immediate advantage. Somehow Amanda found herself lying down on the sofa instead of sitting up, and when Jordan finally pulled away from her mouth, she arched her neck. He kissed the pulse point at the base of her throat, then progressed to the one beneath her right ear. In the meantime, Amanda could feel her T-shirt being worked slowly up her rib cage.

When he unsnapped her bra and laid it aside, revealing

her ripe breasts, Amanda closed her eyes and lifted her back slightly in a silent offering.

He encircled one taut nipple with feather-light kisses, and Amanda moaned softly when he captured the morsel between his lips and began to suckle. She entangled her hands in his hair and spread her legs, one foot high on the sofa back, the other on the floor, to accommodate him.

The eloquent pressure of his desire made Amanda ache to be taken, but she was too breathless to speak, too swept up in the gentle incursion to ask for conquering. When she felt the snap on her jeans give way, followed soon after by the zipper, she only lifted her hips so the jeans could be peeled away. They vanished, along with her panties and her sneakers, and Jordan began to caress her intimately with one hand while he enjoyed her other breast.

The ordinary light in the living room turned colors and made strange patterns in front of Amanda's eyes as Jordan kissed his way down over her satiny, quivering belly to her thighs.

She whimpered when he burrowed into her deepest secret, gave a lusty cry when he plundered that secret with his mouth. Her hips shot upward, and Jordan cupped his hands beneath her bottom, holding her in his hands as he would sparkling water from a stream. "Jordan," she gasped, turning her head from side to side in a fever of passion when he showed her absolutely no mercy.

He flung her over the savage brink, leaving her to convulse repeatedly at the top of an invisible geyser. When the last trace of response had been wrung from her, he lowered her gently back to the sofa.

She lay there watching him, the back of one hand resting against her mouth, her body covered in a fine mist of perspiration. Jordan was sitting up, one of her bare legs draped across his lap, his eyes gentle as he laid a hand on Amanda's trembling belly as if to soothe it.

"I want you," she said brazenly when she could speak.

Jordan smiled and traced the outline of her jaw with one finger, then the circumferences of both her nipples. "Not this time, Mandy," he answered, his voice hardly more than a ragged whisper.

Amanda was both surprised and insulted. "What the hell do you mean, 'not this time'? Were you just trying to prove—"

Jordan interrupted her tirade by bending to kiss her lips. "I wasn't trying to prove anything. I just don't want you hating my guts when you wake up tomorrow."

Amanda's body, so long untouched by a man, was primed for a loving it wasn't going to receive. "You're too late," she spat, bolting to an upright position and righting her bra and T-shirt. "I *already* hate your guts!"

Jordan obligingly fetched her jeans and panties from the floor where he'd tossed them earlier. "Probably, but you'll forgive me when the time is right."

She squirmed back into the rest of her clothes, then stood looking down at Jordan, one finger waggling. "No, I won't!" she argued hotly.

He clasped her hips in his hands and brought her forward, then softly nipped the place he'd just pillaged so sweetly. Even through her jeans, Amanda felt a piercing response to the contact; a shock went through her, and she gave a soft cry of mingled protest and surrender.

Jordan drew back and gave her a swat on the bottom. "See? You'll forgive me."

Amanda would have whirled away then, but Jordan caught her by the hand and wrenched her onto his lap. When she would have risen, he restricted her by catching hold of her hands and imprisoning them behind her back.

With his free hand, he pushed her T-shirt up in front again, then boldly cupped a lace-covered breast that throbbed to be bared to him once more. "It's going to be very good when we make love," he said firmly, "but that isn't going to happen yet."

Amanda squirmed, infuriated and confused. "Then why don't you let me go?" she breathed.

He chuckled. "Because I want to make damn sure you don't forget that preview of how it's going to be."

"Of all the arrogance—"

Jordan pulled down one side of her bra, causing the breast to spring triumphantly to freedom. "I've got plenty of that," he breathed against a peak that strained toward him.

Amanda moaned despite herself when he took her into his mouth again.

"Umm," he murmured, blatant in his enjoyment.

Utter and complete surprise possessed Amanda when she realized she was being propelled to another release, with Jordan merely gripping her hands behind her and feasting on her breast. She didn't want him to know, and yet her body was already betraying her with feverish jerks and twists.

She bit down hard on her lower lip and tried to keep herself still, but she couldn't. She was moving at lightning speed toward a collision with a comet.

Jordan lifted his mouth from her breast just long enough to mutter, "So it's like that, is it?" before driving her hard up against her own nature as a woman.

She surrendered in a burst of surprised gasps and sagged against Jordan, resting her head on his shoulder when it was finally over. "H-how did that happen?"

Still caressing her breast, Jordan spoke against her ear.

"No idea," he answered, "but it damned near made me change my mind about waiting."

Amanda lay against his chest until she'd recovered the ability to stand and to breathe properly, then she rose from his lap, snapped her bra and pulled down her T-shirt. In a vain effort to regain her dignity, she squared her shoulders and plunged the splayed fingers of both hands through her hair. "You don't find me attractive—that's it, isn't it?"

"That's the most ridiculous question I've ever been asked," Jordan answered, rising a little awkwardly— and painfully, it seemed to Amanda—from the sofa. "I wouldn't have done the things I just did if I didn't."

"Then why don't you want me?"

"Believe me, I do want you. Too badly to risk lousing things up so soon."

Amanda wasn't satisfied with that answer, so she turned on one heel and fled into the bathroom, where she splashed cold water on her face and brushed her love-tousled hair. When she came out, half fearing that Jordan would be gone, she found him standing at the window, gazing out at the city.

Calmer, she stood behind him, slipped her arms around his lean waist and kissed his nape. "Stay for supper?"

He turned in her embrace to smile down into her eyes. "That depends on what's on the menu."

Amanda was mildly affronted, remembering his rejection. "It isn't me," she stated with a small pout, "so you can relax."

He laughed and gave her another playful swat on the bottom. "Take it from me, Mandy—I'm not relaxed."

She grinned, glad to know he was suffering justly, and kissed his chin, which was already darkening with the shadow of a beard. "Nobody has called me 'Mandy' since first grade," she said.

"Good."

"Why is that good?" Amanda inquired, snuggling close.

"Because it saves me the trouble of thinking up some cutesy nickname like 'babycakes' or 'buttercup.'"

She laughed. "I can't imagine you calling me 'buttercup' with a straight face."

"I don't think I could," he replied, bending his head to kiss her thoroughly. Amanda's knees were weak when he finally drew back.

"You delight in tormenting me," she protested.

His eyes twinkled. "What's for supper?"

"Grilled cheese sandwiches, unless we go to the market," Amanda answered.

"The market it is," Jordan replied. Once again, in the entryway he helped Amanda into her coat.

"You have good manners for a rascal," Amanda remarked quite seriously.

Jordan laughed. "Thank you—I think."

They walked to a small store on the corner, where food was overpriced but fresh and plentiful. Amanda selected two steaks, vegetables for a salad and potatoes for baking.

"Does your fireplace work?" Jordan asked, lingering in front of a display of synthetic logs.

Amanda nodded, wondering if she could stand the romance of a crackling fire when Jordan was so determined not to make love to her. "Are you trying to drive me crazy, or what?" she countered, her eyes snapping with irritation.

He gave her one of his nuclear grins, then picked up two of the logs and carried them to the checkout counter, where he threw down a twenty-dollar bill. He would have paid for the food, too, except that Amanda wouldn't let him.

She did permit him to carry everything back to the apartment, however, thinking it might drain off some of his excess energy.

When they were back in Amanda's apartment, he moved the screen from in front of the fireplace as Gershwin meowed curiously at his elbow. After opening the damper, he laid one of the logs he'd bought in the grate. Amanda glanced at the label on the other log and saw it was meant to last a full three hours.

She grinned as she got her favorite skillet out of the drawer underneath the stove. Two logs totaled six hours. Maybe Jordan would change his mind about waiting before that much time slipped past.

Dusting his hands together, he came into the kitchenette, and Amanda could see the flicker of the fire reflected on the shiny front of her refrigerator door. Without being asked, he took the vegetables out of the bag and began washing them at the sink.

Amanda went to his side, handing him both the potatoes. "You're pretty handy in a kitchen, fella," she remarked in a teasing, sultry voice.

Jordan's eyes danced when he looked at her, and his expression said he was pretty handy in a few other rooms, too. "Thanks." He scrubbed the potatoes and handed them back to Amanda, who put a little swing in her hips as she walked away because she knew he was watching.

He laughed. "You need a spanking."

Amanda poked the potatoes with a fork and set them in the tiny microwave oven her mother and stepfather had given her the Christmas before. "Very kinky, Mr. Richards."

Jordan chuckled as he went back to chopping vegetables, and Amanda found the wooden salad bowl she'd bought in Hawaii and set it on the counter beside him.

They ate at the glass table in Amanda's living room, the fire dancing on the hearth and casting its image on their wineglasses. Darkness had long since settled over the city, and Amanda wondered why she hadn't noticed when the daylight fled.

"Tell me about your daughters," she said when the meal was nearly over.

Jordan pushed his plate away and took a sip of his wine before replying. "They're normal kids, I guess. They like to watch *Sesame Street,* have me read the funny papers to them, things like that."

Amanda felt sad, but if someone had asked, she would have had to admit she wasn't thinking about Jordan's children at all. She was remembering how it felt when her dad had gone away that long-ago Christmas Day, swearing never to come back. And he hadn't. "Do you miss them?" she asked.

"Yes," he admitted frankly. "But I know they're better off with Karen and Paul."

"Why?" Amanda dared to ask.

Jordan lifted his shoulders in a slight shrug. "I told you—my sister and her husband took them in when I was in the hospital. I'm more like an uncle to them than a father. They wouldn't understand if I uprooted them now."

Amanda wasn't so sure, but she didn't say that because she knew she'd already overstepped her bounds in some ways. If Jordan didn't want to raise his own children, that was his business, but it made Amanda wonder what would happen if the two of them were ever married and had babies. If she died, would he just send the kids to live with someone else?

She refilled her wineglass and took a healthy sip.

There was a look of quiet understanding in Jordan's eyes as he watched her. "What have I done now?" he asked.

"Nothing," Amanda lied, setting her glass down and jumping up to begin clearing the table.

Jordan rose from his chair and elbowed her aside. "Go and sit by the fire. I'll take care of this."

Apparently giving orders had become a habit with Jordan over the course of his successful career. "I'll help," she insisted, following him into the kitchen with the salad bowl in her hands.

Jordan scraped and rinsed the plates, and Amanda put them, along with the silverware and glasses, into the dishwasher.

"Somebody trained you rather well," she commented grudgingly.

He gave her a meltdown grin. "Thanks for noticing," he said with a slight leer.

Amanda's face turned pink. "I was talking about cooking and doing dishes!"

Jordan smiled at her discomfiture. "Oh," he said, but he sounded patently unconvinced.

Amanda put what remained of the salad in a smaller bowl, covered that tightly with plastic wrap, then stuck it into the refrigerator. She longed to ask him what kind of wife Becky had been, but she didn't dare. She knew he'd say she'd been wonderful, and Amanda wasn't feeling grown-up enough to deal with that.

He was leaning against the sink, watching her, his arms folded in front of his chest. "James is a lot older than you are," he said.

The remark was so out of left field that Amanda was momentarily stunned by it. "I know," she finally managed, standing in the doorway that led to the living room.

"Where did you meet him?"

Amanda couldn't think why she was answering, since they had agreed not to talk about James, but answer she did. "At the hotel," she replied with a sigh. "He taught a management seminar there a year and a half ago."

"And you went?"

She couldn't read Jordan's mood either in his eyes or his voice, and she was unsettled by the question. "Yes. He asked me out to dinner the first night, and after that I saw him whenever he was in Seattle on business."

Jordan crossed the room and enfolded Amanda in his arms, and the relief she felt was totally out of proportion to the circumstances.

"I have to know one thing, Mandy. Do you love him?"

She shook her head. "No." She tasted wine on Jordan's lips when he kissed her. And she tasted wanting. *Do you still love Becky?* she longed to ask, but she was too afraid of the answer to voice the question.

Slipping his arm around her waist, Jordan ushered Amanda into the living room, where they sat on a hooked rug in front of the fireplace. He gripped her hand and stared into the flames in the silence for a long time, then he turned, looked into her fire-lit eyes and said, "I'm sorry, Mandy. I didn't have any right to ask about James."

She let her head rest against the place where his arm and shoulder met. "It's okay. I made a fool of myself, and I can admit that now."

Jordan caught her chin in his hand and wouldn't let her look away. "Let's get one thing straight here," he said in gentle reproach. "The only mistake you made was trusting the bastard. He's the fool."

Amanda sighed. "That's a refreshing opinion. Most people either say or imply that I should have known better."

"Not this people," Jordan answered, tasting her lips.

Although it seemed impossible, Amanda wanted Jordan more now than she had on the couch earlier when he'd brought her face-to-face with her own womanhood. She longed to take him by the hand and lead him to her bed, but the thought of a second rebuff stopped her. In fact, she sup-

posed it was about time she started taking the advice her
mother had given her in ninth grade and play hard to get.

She moved a little apart from Jordan, stiffened her
shoulders and raised her chin. "Maybe you should go,"
she said.

Jordan showed no signs of leaving. Instead he put his
hands on Amanda's shoulders and lowered her to the
hooked rug, stretching out beside her and laying one hand
brazenly on her breast. The nipple tightened obediently
beneath his palm.

Amanda moved to rise, but Jordan pressed her back
down again, this time with a consuming kiss. "Don't you
dare start anything you don't intend to finish," she ordered
in a raspy whisper when at last he'd drawn away from her
mouth. Having obtained the response he wanted from her
right breast, he was now working on her left.

"I'll finish it," he vowed in a husky murmur, "when
the time is right."

He lowered his hand to her belly, covering it with
splayed fingers, and Amanda's heart pounded beneath
her T-shirt. She pulled on his nape until his mouth again
joined with hers, and the punishment for this audacious
act was the unsnapping of her jeans.

"Damn it, Jordan, I don't like being teased."

He pulled at the zipper, and then his hand was in between her jeans and her panties, just resting there, soaking
up her warmth, making her grow moist. That part of her
body was like an exotic orchid flowering in a hothouse.

"Tough," he replied with a cocky grin just before he
bent and scraped one hidden nipple lightly with his teeth,
causing it to leap to attention.

Amanda's formidable pride was almost gone, and she
had to grasp the rug and bite down on her lower lip to keep
from begging him to make love to her.

"This night is just for you," he told her, his hand making a fiery circle at the junction of her thighs. "Why can't you accept that?"

"Because it isn't normal, that's why," Amanda gasped, trying to hold her hips still but finding it impossible. "You're a man. You're supposed to have just one thing on your mind. You're supposed to be trying to jump my bones."

He laughed at that. "What a chauvinistic thing to say."

Amanda groaned as he continued his sweet devilment. "I've never seen anything in *Cosmopolitan* that told what to d-do when this happens," she complained.

Again Jordan laughed. "I can tell you what to do," he said when he'd recovered himself a little. "Enjoy it."

Amanda was beginning to breathe hard. "Damn you, Jordan—I'll make you pay for this!"

"I'm counting on that," he said against her mouth.

Moments later Amanda was soaring again. She dug her fingers into Jordan's shoulders while she plunged her heels into the rug, and everyone in the apartment building would have known how well he'd loved her if he hadn't clamped his mouth over hers and swallowed her cries.

"IF THIS IS some kind of power game," Amanda sputtered five minutes later when she could manage to speak, fastening her jeans and sitting up again, "I don't want to play."

"You could have fooled me," Jordan responded.

Amanda gave a strangled cry of frustration and anger. "I can't imagine why I keep letting you get away with this."

"I can," he replied. "It feels good, and it's been a long time. Right?"

Amanda let her forehead rest against his shoulder, embarrassed. "Yes," she confessed.

He kissed the top of her head. "I should have dessert before dinner more often," he teased.

Amanda groaned, unable to look at him, and he chuckled and lifted her chin for a light kiss. "You're impossible," she murmured.

"And I'm leaving," he added with a glance at his watch. "It's time you were in bed."

Bleakness filled Amanda at the thought of climbing into bed alone, and she was just about to protest, when Jordan laid a finger to her nose and asked, "Will you go Christmas shopping with me tomorrow?"

Amanda would have gone to Zanzibar. "Yes," she answered like a hypnotized person.

Jordan kissed her again, leaving her lips warm and slightly swollen. "Good night," he said. And then, after a backward look and a wave, he was gone.

Chapter 4

෨෴ණ

THE TELEPHONE JANGLED JUST as Amanda finished with her makeup the next morning. She'd managed to camouflage the shadows under her eyes—the result of sleeping only a few hours—with a cover stick.

"Hello?" she blurted into the receiver of her bedside telephone, hoping Jordan wasn't calling to back out of their shopping trip.

"If I remember correctly," her mother began dryly without returning the customary greeting, "you were supposed to call last night and let us know whether you were coming over for supper."

Amanda stretched the phone cord as far as her closet, where she took out black wool slacks. "Sorry, Mom," she answered contritely. "I forgot, but you'll be glad to know it was because of a man." She went to the dresser for her pink cashmere sweater while waiting for her mother to digest her last remark.

"A man?" Marion echoed, unable to hide the pleasure in her voice.

"And James was here yesterday," Amanda went on after pulling the sweater on over her head.

Marion drew in her breath. "Don't tell me you're seeing him again—"

"Of course not, Mom," Amanda scolded, propping the receiver between her shoulder and her ear while she wriggled into the sleek black pants.

"You're deliberately confusing me," Marion accused.

Amanda sighed. "Listen, I'll tell you everything tomorrow, okay? I'll stop by after work and catch you up on all the latest developments."

"So there is somebody besides James?" Marion pressed, sounding pleased.

"Yep," Amanda answered just as the door buzzer sounded. "Gotta go—he's here."

"Bye," Marion said cooperatively, and promptly hung up.

Amanda was brushing her hair as she hurried through the apartment to open the door. She was smiling, since she expected Jordan, but she found a delivery man from one of the more posh department stores in the hallway, instead. He was holding two silver gift boxes, one large and one fairly small. "Ms. A. Scott?" he asked.

Amanda nodded, mystified.

"These are for you—special express delivery," the man said, holding on to the packages while he shoved a clipboard at Amanda. "Sign on line twenty-seven."

She found the appropriate line and scrawled her name there, and the man gave her the packages in return for the clipboard.

After depositing the boxes on the couch and rummaging through her purse for a tip, she closed the door and lifted the lid off the smaller box. A skimpy aqua bikini lay inside, but there was no card or note to explain.

She opened the large box and gasped, faced with the rich, unmistakable splendor of sable. A small envelope lay on top, but Amanda didn't need to read it to know the gifts were from James.

As a matter of curiosity, she looked at the card: "Honeymoon in Hawaii, then on to Copenhagen? Call me. James."

With a sigh, Amanda tossed down the card. She was just about to call the store and ask to return the two boxes, when there was a knock at the door.

She rushed to open it and found Jordan standing in the hallway, looking spectacular in blue jeans, a lightweight yellow sweater and a tweed sport jacket.

"Hi," he said, his bright hazel eyes registering approval as he looked at her.

"Come in," Amanda replied, stepping back and holding the door open wide. "I'm just about finished with my hair. Pour yourself a cup of coffee and I'll be right out."

He stopped her when she would have turned away from him, and lightly entangled the fingers of one hand in her hair. "Don't change it," he said hoarsely. "It looks great."

Amanda's heart was beating a little faster just because he was close and because he was touching her. Since she didn't know what to say, she didn't speak.

Jordan kissed her lightly on the lips. "Good morning, Mandy," he said, and his voice was still husky. Amanda had a vision of him carrying her off to bed, and heat flooded her entire body, a blush rising in her cheeks.

"Good morning," she replied, her voice barely more than a squeak. "How about that coffee?"

His gaze had shifted to the boxes on the couch. "What's this?" There was a teasing reproach in his eyes when they returned to her face. "Opening your presents before Christmas, Mandy? For shame."

Amanda had completely forgotten the unwanted gifts, and the reminder deflated her spirits a little. "I'm sending them back," she said, hoping Jordan wouldn't pursue the subject.

His expression sobered. "James?"

Amanda licked her lips, then nodded nervously. She wasn't entirely displeased to see a muscle in Jordan's cheek grow taut, then relax again.

"Persistent, isn't he?"

"Yes," Amanda admitted. "He is." And after that there seemed to be nothing more to say—about James, anyway.

"Let's go," Jordan told her, kissing her forehead. "We'll get some breakfast on the way."

Amanda disappeared into the bedroom to put on her shoes, and when she came out, Jordan was studying the quilt over her couch again, his hands in his hip pockets.

"You know, you have a real talent for this," he said.

Amanda smiled. James had always been impatient with her quilting, saying she ought to save the needlework for when she was old and had nothing better to do. "Thanks."

Jordan followed her out of the apartment and waited patiently while she locked the door. He held her elbow lightly as they went down the stairs, once again giving her the wonderful sensation of being protected.

The sun was shining, which was cause for rejoicing in Seattle at that time of year, and Amanda felt happy as Jordan closed the car door after her.

When he slid behind the wheel, he just sat there for a few minutes and looked at her. Then he put a hand in her hair again. "Excuse me, lady," he said, his voice low, "but has anybody told you this morning that you're beautiful?"

Amanda flushed, but her eyes were sparkling. "No, sir," she answered, playing the game. "They haven't."

He leaned toward her and gave her a lingering kiss that made a sweet languor blossom inside her.

"There's an oversight that needs correcting," he murmured afterward. "You're beautiful."

Amanda was trembling when he finally turned to start the ignition, fasten his seat belt and steer the car out into the light Sunday morning traffic. Something was terribly wrong in this relationship, she reflected. It was supposed to be the man who wanted to head straight for the bedroom, while the woman held out for knowing each other better.

And yet it was all Amanda could do not to drag Jordan out of the car and back up the stairs to her apartment.

"What's the matter?" Jordan asked, tossing a mischievous glance her way that said he well knew the answer to that question.

Amanda folded her arms and looked straight ahead as they sped up a freeway ramp. The familiar green-and-white signs slipped by overhead. "Nothing," she said.

He sighed. "I hate it when women do that. You ask them what's wrong and they say 'nothing,' and all the while you know they're ready to burst into tears or clout you with the nearest blunt object."

Amanda turned in her seat and studied his profile for a few moments, one fingernail caught between her teeth. "I wasn't about to do either of those things," she finally said. She didn't quite have the fortitude to go the rest of the way and admit she was wondering why he didn't seem to want her.

Jordan reached out and laid a hand gently on her knee, once again sending all her vital organs into a state of alarm.

"What's the problem, then?"

She drew in a deep breath for courage and let it out slowly. "If we sleep together, you'll be the second man I've ever been with in my life, so it's not like I'm hot to trot or anything. But I usually have to fight guys off, not wait for them to decide the time is right."

He was clearly suppressing a smile, which didn't help.

"'Hot to trot'? I didn't think anybody said that anymore."

"Jordan."

He favored her with a high-potency grin. "Believe me, Mandy, I'm a normal man and I want you. But you're going to have to wait, because I've got no intention of—forgive me—screwing this up."

Amanda sighed and folded her arms. "Exactly what is it you're waiting for?"

His wonderful eyes were crinkled with laughter, even though his mouth was unsmiling.

"Exactly what is it you want me to do?" he countered. "Pull the car over to the side of the freeway and, as you put it last night, 'jump your bones'?"

Amanda blushed. "You make me sound like some kind of loose woman," she accused.

He took her hand and squeezed it reassuringly. "I can't even imagine that," he said in a soothing voice. "Now what do you say we change the subject for a while?"

That seemed like the only solution. "Okay," Amanda agreed. "Remember how you admired the quilt I made?"

Jordan nodded, switching lanes to be in position for an upcoming exit. "It's great."

"Well, I've been designing and making quilts for years. Someday I hope to open a bed and breakfast somewhere, with a little craft shop on the premises."

He grinned as he took the exit. "I'm surprised. Given your job and the fact that you live in the city, I thought you were inclined toward more sophisticated dreams."

"I was," Amanda said, recalling some of the glamorous, exciting adventures she had had with James. "But life changes a person. And I've always liked making quilts. I've been selling them at craft shows for a long time, and saving as much money as I could for the bed and breakfast."

Jordan was undoubtedly thinking of her humble apartment when he said, "You must have a pretty solid nest egg."

Amanda sighed, feeling discouraged all over again. "Not really. The real estate market is hot around here, what with so many people moving up from California, and the prices are high."

They had left the freeway, and Jordan pulled the car into the parking lot of a family-style restaurant near the mall. "Working capital is one of my specialties, Mandy. Maybe I can help you."

Amanda surprised even herself when she shook her head so fast. She guessed it was partly pride that made her do that, and partly disappointment that he wasn't trying to talk her out of establishing a business in favor of something else. Like getting married and starting a family.

"Did we just hit another tricky subject?" Jordan asked good-naturedly, when he and Amanda were walking toward the restaurant.

She shrugged. "I want the bed and breakfast to be all my own."

Jordan opened the door for her. "What if you decide to get married or something?"

Amanda felt a little thrill, even though she knew Jordan wasn't on the verge of proposing. She would have refused even if he had. "I guess I'll cross that bridge when I come to it."

A few minutes later they were seated at a small table and given menus. They made their selections and sipped the coffee the waitress had brought while they waited for the food.

"Who are we shopping for today?" Amanda asked, to get the conversation going again. Jordan was sitting across from her, systematically making love to her with his eyes, and she was desperate to distract him.

"Jessie and Lisa mostly, though I still need to get something for Karen and Paul."

Something made Amanda ask, "What about your parents?"

Sadness flickered in the depths of Jordan's eyes, but only for a moment. "They were killed in a car accident when I was in college," he replied.

Amanda reached out on impulse and took his hand. It seemed to her that Jordan had had more than his share of tragedy in his life, and she suddenly wanted to share her mother and stepfather with him. "I'm sorry."

He changed the subject so abruptly his remark was almost a rebuff. "What do you think Karen would like?"

Amanda was annoyed and a little hurt. "How would I know? I've never even met the woman."

The waitress returned with their breakfast, setting bacon and eggs in front of Jordan and giving Amanda wheat toast and a fruit compote. When they were alone again, Jordan replied, "Karen's thirty-five, a little on the chubby side—and totally devoted to Paul and the girls."

Amanda tried to picture the woman and failed. "Do she and Paul have children of their own?"

Jordan was mashing his eggs into his hash browns. "No."

She speared a melon ball and chewed it distractedly. "That's sad," she said after swallowing.

"These things happen," Jordan replied.

Amanda looked straight into his eyes. "I guess Karen would be pretty upset if she ever had to give Jessica and Lisa back to you," she ventured to say.

He returned her bold, assessing stare. "I wouldn't do

that to her or to the girls," he said, and there was no hint of mischief about him this time. He was completely serious.

Things were a little strained between them throughout the rest of the meal, but as soon as they reached the toy store at the mall, they were both caught up in the spirit of the season. They bought games for the girls, and dolls, and little china tea sets.

Amanda couldn't remember the last time she'd had so much fun, and her eyes were sparkling as they stuffed everything into the back of the Porsche.

From the toy store they headed to a big-name department store where, after great deliberation, they chose expensive perfume and bath powder for Karen and a sweater for her husband.

They had lunch in a fast-food hamburger place jammed to the rafters with excited kids, and by the time they returned to Amanda's apartment, she was exhausted.

"Coming in?" she asked at the door because, in spite of everything he'd said about waiting, she'd been entertaining a discreet fantasy all morning.

Jordan shook his head. "Not today," he said. "I've got to drive up to Port Townsend and look in on the kids."

Amanda was hurt that he didn't want to take her along, but she hid it well. After all, she didn't have the right to any injured feelings. "Say hello for me," she said softly.

He kissed her, lightly at first, then with an authority that brought the fantasy to the forefront of her mind. Amanda surreptitiously gripped the doorknob to keep from sliding to the floor.

"I'll be out of town most of next week," he said when the kiss was over. "Is it okay if I call?"

Is it okay? She would be shattered if he didn't. "Sure," she answered in a tone that said it wouldn't matter one way or the other because she'd be busy with her glamorous, sophisticated life.

Jordan waited until she'd unlocked the door and stepped safely inside, then she heard him walking away.

She tossed aside her purse, kicked off her shoes and hung up her coat. The coming week yawned before her like an abyss.

Ignoring the boxes still sitting on her couch, she bent distractedly to pet a meowing Gershwin, then stumbled into her bedroom, stripped off her clothes and crawled back into the unmade bed. All those hours she hadn't slept the night before were catching up with her.

Later she awoke to full darkness, the weight of Gershwin curled up on her stomach and the ringing of the phone.

Groping with one hand, she found the receiver, brought it to her ear and yawned, "Hello?"

"It's Mom," Marion announced. "How are you, dear?"

Amanda yawned again. "Tired. And hungry."

"Perfect," Marion responded with her customary good cheer and indefatigable energy. "Drag yourself over here, and I'll serve you a home-cooked meal that will put hair on your chest."

Amanda giggled, rubbing her eyes and stretching. The movement made Gershwin jump down from her stomach and land with a solid *thump* on the floor. "There's one flaw in your proposal, Mom. Who needs hair on their chest?"

Marion laughed. "Just get in your car and drive over here. Or should I send Bob, so you don't have to go wandering around in that dark parking lot behind your building?"

"There's an attendant," Amanda said, sitting up. "I'll drive over as soon as I've had a quick shower to revive myself."

Marion agreed, and the conversation came to an amicable end.

With her hair pulled back into a ponytail, Amanda was wearing jeans, a football jersey and sneakers when she arrived at her parents' house in another part of the city. And she was making a determined effort not to think about Jordan and the fact that he hadn't asked her to go to Port Townsend with him.

Her mother, a slender, attractive woman with shoulder-length hennaed hair and skillfully applied makeup, met her at the front door. Marion looked wonderful in her trim green jumpsuit, and her smile and hug were both warm.

"Bob's in the living room, cussing that string of Christmas tree lights that always goes on the blink," the older woman confided in a merry whisper.

Amanda laughed and wandered into the front room. There were cards everywhere—they lined the top of the piano, the mantel and were arranged into the shape of a Christmas tree on one wall. Amanda had been putting hers in a desk drawer that year.

"Hi, Bob," she said, giving her stepfather a hug. He was a tall man, with thinning blond hair and kindly blue eyes, and he'd been very good to Marion. Amanda loved him for that reason, if for no other.

He was standing beside a fresh-smelling, undecorated pine tree, which was, as usual, set up in front of the bay window facing the street. The infamous string of lights was in his hands. "I don't know why she won't let me throw these darned things out and buy new ones," he fussed in a conspiratorial whisper. "It's not as if we couldn't afford to."

Amanda chuckled. "Mom's sentimental about those lights," she reminded him. "They've been on the tree since Eunice and I were babies."

"Speaking of your sister," Marion remarked from the

kitchen doorway, wiping her hands on her white apron, "we had a call from her today. She's coming home for Christmas."

Amanda was pleased. This was a hard time in Eunice's life; she needed to get away from the wreckage of her marriage, if only for a week or two. "What about her job at the university?"

Marion shrugged. "I guess she's taking time off. Bob and I are picking her up at the airport late next Friday night."

Amanda left Bob to his Christmas tree light quandary and followed her mother into the bright, fragrant kitchen, where they had had so many talks before. "Seattle will be a shock to Eunice after Southern California," she remarked.

Marion gave her a playful flick with a dish towel. "Forget the harmless chitchat," she said with a grin. "What's going on in your life these days? Who's the new man, and what the devil was James doing, dropping by?"

Drawing up a battered metal stool, Amanda sat down at the breakfast counter Bob had built when he remodeled the kitchen, and started cutting up the salad vegetables her mother indicated. "James is getting divorced," she said, avoiding Marion's gaze. "Evidently he has some idea that we can get back together."

"I presume you set him straight on that."

"I did." Amanda sighed. "But I'm not sure he's getting the message. He sent me a sable jacket and a silk bikini today, along with an invitation to Hawaii and Copenhagen."

The oven door slammed a touch too hard after Marion pulled a pan of fragrant lasagna from it. "You'd never guess he was such a scumbag, would you?"

Amanda grinned and tossed a handful of chopped celery into the salad bowl. "You've got to stop watching all those cop shows, Mom. It's affecting your vocabulary."

"No way," replied Marion, who had a minor crush on Don Johnson. "So, who's the other guy?"

"Did I say there was another guy?"

"I think so," Marion replied airily, "but you wouldn't have had to. There's a sparkle in your eyes and your cheeks are pink."

"His name is Jordan Richards," Amanda said. Personally she attributed any sparkle in her eyes or color in her cheeks to the nap she'd taken.

Marion stopped slicing the lasagna to look directly at her daughter. "And?"

"And he makes me crazy, that's what."

Marion beamed. "That's a good sign."

Amanda wondered if her mother would still be of the same opinion if she knew just how hard her daughter had fallen. And how bold she'd been. "I guess so."

"What does he do for a living?" Bob asked from the kitchen doorway. Since it was a classic parental question, Amanda didn't take offense.

"He's a partner in an investment firm—Striner, Striner and Richards."

Bob whistled and tucked his hands in his pockets. "That's the big time, all right."

"Amanda doesn't care how much money he makes," Marion said with mock haughtiness. "She just wants his body."

At this, both Amanda and Bob laughed.

"Mom!" Amanda protested.

"It's true," Marion insisted. "I'd know that look anywhere. Now let's all sit down and eat."

They trooped into the dining room, where Marion had set a festive table using the special Christmas dishes that always came out of storage, along with the nativity set, on the first of December. Despite the good food and the conversation, Amanda's mind was on Jordan.

"About those presents James sent you," Marion began when she and Amanda were alone in the kitchen again, washing dishes while Bob fought it out with the Christmas tree lights. "You are sending them back, aren't you?"

Amanda favored her mother with a rueful smile. "Of course I am. First thing tomorrow."

"Some women would have their heads turned, you know, by such expensive things."

"Expensive is right. All James wants in return for his presents is my soul. What a bargain."

Marion finished washing the last pot, drained the sink and washed her hands. "I'm glad you're wise enough to see that."

Amanda shrugged. "I don't know how smart I am," she replied. "The only reason I'm so sure about everything where James is concerned is that I don't love him anymore. I'm not sure what I'd do if I still cared."

"I am," Marion said confidently. "You've always had a good head on your shoulders. That's why I think this new man must really be something."

Amanda indulged in a smile as she shook out the dish towel and hung it on the rack to dry. "He is." But her smile faded as she thought of those two little girls living far away from their father with an aunt and uncle, and of Becky, cut down before she'd even had a chance to live.

"What is it?" Marion wanted to know. She had already poured two cups full of coffee, and she carried them to the kitchen table while waiting for Amanda to answer.

Amanda sank dejectedly into one of the chairs and cupped her hands around a steaming mug. "He's a widower, and I think—well, I think he might have some problems with commitment."

"Don't they all?" Marion asked, stirring artificial sweetener into her coffee.

"Bob didn't," Amanda pointed out, her voice solemn. "He loved you enough to marry you, even though he knew you had two teenage daughters and a pile of debts."

Marion looked thoughtful. "How long have you known this man?"

"Not very long," Amanda confessed. "About ten days, I guess."

Marion chuckled and shook her head. "And you're already bandying words like 'commitment' about?"

"No. I'm only *thinking* words like 'commitment.'"

"I see. Well, this is serious. Why do you think he wouldn't want to settle down?"

Amanda ran the tip of her index finger around the rim of her coffee mug. "He has two little girls, and they don't live with him—his sister and brother-in-law are raising them. He sort of bristled when I asked him about it."

Marion laid a hand on her daughter's arm. "You're a little gun-shy, dear, and that's natural after what happened with James. Just give yourself some time."

Time. Jordan was asking the same thing of her. Didn't anyone act on impulse anymore?

Marion smiled at her daughter's frustrated expression. "Just take life one day at a time, Amanda, and everything will work out."

Amanda nodded, and after chatting briefly with her mother about Eunice's upcoming visit, she put on her coat, kissed both her parents goodbye and went out to her nondescript car.

"You be careful to park where the attendant can see

you," Bob instructed her just before she pulled away from the curb.

The attendant was on duty, and Amanda parked where there was plenty of light.

It turned out, however, that it was the inside of her building that she should have looked out for, not the parking lot.

James was sitting on the stairs again, and this time she didn't have Jordan along to act as a buffer.

"I'm glad you're here," Amanda said in a cold voice. "You can take back the fur and the bikini."

James's handsome, distinguished face fell. "You still haven't forgiven me, have you?" he asked in a pained voice, spreading his hands wide for emphasis. "Baby, how many times do I have to tell you? Madge and I haven't been in love for years."

Amanda ached as she remembered Madge Brockman's raging agony during the confrontation. "Maybe *you* haven't been," she muttered sadly.

James either didn't hear the remark or chose to ignore it. "Just let me talk to you. Please."

Having summoned up the courage she needed, Amanda passed him on the narrow stairway. "Nothing you can say will change my mind, James." She reached her door and unlocked it as he made to follow her. "So just take your presents and give them to some other fool."

Suddenly James caught her elbow in a hard grasp and wrenched her around to face him. "You're in love with Richards, aren't you? The boy wonder! You think he's pretty hot stuff, I'll bet! Well, let me tell you something— I could buy and sell him ten times over!"

Amanda pulled free of James, stormed over to the couch, picked up the boxes and shoved them at him. "Take these and get out!"

He stared at her as though she'd lost her mind.

"And while you're at it, you can just take everything *else* you've ever given me, too!"

With that, she strode into the bedroom and yanked open her jewelry box, intending to return the gold bracelet and pearl earrings she'd forgotten about. She only became aware that James had followed her when he cried out.

Turning, Amanda saw him clasp his chest with one hand and topple to the floor.

Chapter 5

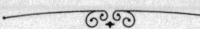

James's face was contorted with pain, and he was only partially conscious. "Help—me—" he groaned.

Amanda lunged for the phone on her bedside table, punched 911 and barked out her address when someone came on the line. She followed that with a brief description of the problem.

"Someone will be there in a few minutes," the woman on the telephone assured her. "Is the patient conscious?"

James was clearly in agony, but he was awake. "Yes."

"Then just cover him up and make him as comfortable as you can—and try to reassure him. The paramedics will take care of everything else when they get there."

Amanda hung up and draped James with a quilt dragged from her bed. When it was in place, she knelt beside him and grasped his hand.

"It's going to be okay, James," she said, her eyes stinging with tears. "Everything is going to be okay."

His free hand was clenched against his chest. "Hurts— so much…crushing…"

"I know," Amanda whispered, holding his knuckles to

her lips. She could hear sirens in the distance. "Help will be here soon."

A loud knock sounded at the door just a few minutes later.

"In here!" Amanda called, and soon two paramedics burst into the bedroom, bringing a stretcher and some other equipment. She scrambled out of the way and perched on the end of her bed, still unmade from her nap earlier, watching as James was examined, loaded onto the stretcher and given oxygen and an IV.

"Any history of heart disease?" one of the men asked Amanda as he and his partner lifted the stretcher.

"I—I don't know," Amanda whispered.

"We'll be taking him to Harborview Hospital, if you'd like to come along," the other volunteered.

Amanda only sat there, gripping the edge of the mattress and shaking her head, unable to tell them she wasn't James's wife.

When the telephone rang a full hour later, she was still sitting in the exact same place.

"H-hello?"

Jordan's voice was warm and low. "Hello, Mandy. Is something wrong?"

Amanda dragged her forearm across her face, wiping away tears that had long since dried. *James had a heart attack in my bedroom,* she imagined herself answering.

She couldn't explain the situation to Jordan over the phone, she decided, sinking her teeth into her lower lip.

"Mandy?" Jordan prompted when the silence had stretched on too long.

"I thought you were in Port Townsend," she managed in a small voice that was hoarse from crying.

"I just got back," he answered. "As a matter of fact, I'm

spending the night in a hotel out by the airport, since my plane leaves so early tomorrow."

Amanda swallowed hard and did her best to sound ordinary. There would be time enough to tell Jordan what had happened when he got back from his business trip. "Wh-where are you going?"

"Chicago. Mandy, what's the matter?"

She closed her eyes. "We can talk about it when you get home."

There was a long pause while he digested that. "Is this something I should know about?"

Amanda nodded, even though he wasn't there to see her. "Yes," she admitted, "but I can't talk about it like this. I have to be with you."

"I could get in the car and be there in half an hour."

Amanda would have given anything short of her very soul to have Jordan there in the room with her, to be held and comforted by him. But she'd only known him a little while, and she had no right to make demands. "I'll be okay," she said softly.

After that, there didn't seem to be much to say. Jordan promised to phone her from Chicago the first chance he got and Amanda wished him well, then the call was over.

Amanda had barely replaced the receiver, when the bell jangled again, startling her. If it had been Jordan she would have relented and asked him to come over, but the voice on the other end of the line was a woman's.

"Well, I must say, I half expected you to be at the hospital, clutching James's hand and swearing your undying love."

Amanda closed her eyes again, feeling as though she'd been struck. The caller was Madge Brockman, James's estranged wife. "Mrs. Brockman, I—"

"Don't lie to me, please. I just spoke to someone on the

hospital staff, and they told me James had suffered a heart attack 'at the home of a friend.' It didn't take a genius to figure out just who that 'friend' might be."

Deciding to let the innuendos pass unchallenged, Amanda asked, "Is James going to be all right?"

"He's in critical condition. I'm flying in tonight to sit with him."

It was a relief to know James wouldn't be going through this difficult time alone. "Mrs. Brockman, I'm very sorry—for everything."

The woman hung up with a slam, leaving Amanda holding the receiver in one trembling hand and listening to a dial tone. Slowly she put down the phone, then crouched to unplug it from the outlet. After disconnecting the living room phone, as well, she took a long, hot shower and crawled into bed.

The sound of her alarm and faceful of bright sunshine woke her early the next morning. The memory of James lying on her bedroom floor in terrible pain was still all too fresh in her mind.

But Amanda had a job, so, even though she would have preferred to stay in bed with her face turned to the wall, she fed the cat, showered, dressed and put on makeup. Once she'd pinned her hair up in a businesslike chignon, she reconnected the telephones and called the hospital.

James was in stable condition.

Longing for Jordan, who might have been able to put the situation into some kind of perspective, Amanda pulled on her coat and gloves and left her apartment.

Late that afternoon, just as she was preparing to go home for the day, Jordan called. He was getting ready to have dinner with some clients, and there was something clipped about his voice. Something distant.

"Feeling better?" he asked.

Amanda heard a whole glacier of emotion shifting beneath the tip of the iceberg. "Not a whole lot," she admitted, "but it's nothing for you to worry about."

She could almost see him hooking his cuff links. "I read about James in the afternoon edition of the paper, Amanda."

So he knew about the heart attack, and she was no longer 'Mandy.' "Word gets around," she managed, propping one elbow on her desk and sinking her forehead into her palm.

"Is that what you didn't want to talk about last night?"

There was no point in trying to evade the question further. "Yes. It happened in my bedroom, Jordan."

He was quiet for a long time. Much too long.

"Jordan?"

"I'm here. What was he doing in your bedroom, or don't I have the right to ask?"

Tears were brimming in Amanda's eyes, and she prayed no one would step into her office and catch her displaying such unprofessional emotions. "Of course you have the right. He came over because he wanted to persuade me to start seeing him again. I told him to take back the things he gave me, and then I remembered some jewelry he'd given me a long time ago. I went to get them, and he followed me." She drew in a shaky breath, then let it out again. "He got very angry, and he was yelling at me. He just—just fell to the floor."

"My God," Jordan rasped. "What kind of shape is he in now?"

"When I called the hospital this morning, he was stable."

Jordan's voice was husky. "Mandy, I'm sorry."

Amanda didn't know whether he meant he was sorry

for doubting her, or he was sorry about James's misfortune. "I wish you were here," she said, testing the water. Everything would ride on his reply.

"So do I," he answered.

Relief flooded over Amanda. "You're not angry?"

He sighed. "No. I guess I just lost my head for a little while there. Do you want me to come back tonight, Mandy? There's a flight at midnight."

"No." She shook her head. "Stay there and set the financial world on its ear. I'll be okay."

"Promise?"

For the first time since before James's collapse, Amanda smiled. "I promise."

"In that case, I'll be back sometime on Friday night. How about penciling me into your busy schedule, Ms. Scott?"

Amanda chuckled. "Consider yourself penciled."

"In fact," he went on, "have a bag packed. I'll stop and pick you up on my way home from the airport."

"Have a bag packed?" Amanda echoed. "Wait a minute, Jordan. What are you proposing here?"

He hesitated only a moment before answering, "I want you to spend the weekend at my place."

Amanda's throat tightened. "Is this the Jordan I know—the one who insists on taking things slow and easy?"

"The same," Jordan replied, his words husky. "I need to have you under the same roof with me, Mandy. Whether we sleep together is entirely up to you."

She plucked some tissue from the box on her desk and began wiping away the mascara stains on her cheeks. "That's mighty mannerly of you, Mr. Richards," she drawled.

"See you Friday," he replied.

And after just a few more words, Amanda hung up.

It was some time before she got out of her chair, though. She'd had some violent ups and downs in the past twenty-four hours, and her emotional equilibrium was not what it might have been.

After taking a few minutes to sit with her head resting on her folded arms, Amanda finished up a report she'd been working on, then slipped into the ladies' room to repair her makeup. Leaving the elevator on the first floor of the hotel, she encountered Madge Brockman.

Mrs. Brockman was a slender, attractive brunette, expensively dressed and clearly well educated. There were huge shadows under her eyes.

"Hello, Amanda," she said.

At first Amanda thought it was just extraordinarily bad luck that she'd run into Mrs. Brockman, but moments later she realized the woman had been waiting in the lobby for her. "Hello, Mrs. Brockman. How is James?"

James's wife reached for Amanda's arm, then let her hand fall back to her side. "I was wondering if you wouldn't have a drink with me or something," she said awkwardly. "So we could talk."

Amanda took a deep breath. "If there's going to be a scene—"

Madge shook her head quickly. "There won't be, I promise."

Hoping Mrs. Brockman meant what she'd said, Amanda followed her into the cocktail lounge, where they took a quiet table in a corner. When the waiter came, Amanda asked for a diet cola and Mrs. Brockman ordered a gin and tonic.

"The doctor tells me James is going to live," Mrs. Brockman said when the drinks had arrived and the waiter was gone again.

Amanda dared a slight smile. "That's wonderful."

Madge looked at her with tormented eyes. "James admitted he went to your apartment on his own last night, and not because you'd invited him. He—he's a proud man, my James, so it wasn't easy for him to say that you'd rejected him."

Not knowing what to say, Amanda simply waited, her hands folded in her lap, her diet cola untouched.

"He's agreed to come back home to California with me when he gets out of the hospital," Mrs. Brockman went on. "I don't know if that's a new start or what, but I do know this much—I love James. If there's any way we can begin again, well, I want a fighting chance."

"It's over between James and me," Amanda said gently. "It has been for months and months."

Mrs. Brockman's eyes held a flicker of hope. "You were telling the truth six months ago when I confronted you in your office, weren't you? You honestly didn't know James was married."

Amanda sighed. "That's right. As soon as I found out, I broke it off."

"But you loved him, didn't you?"

Amanda felt a twinge of the pain that time and hard work and Jordan had finally healed. "Yes."

"Then why didn't you hold on? Why didn't you fight for him?"

"If he'd been my husband instead of yours, I would have," Amanda answered, reaching for her purse. She wasn't going to be able to choke down so much as a sip of that cola. "I'm not cut out to be the Other Woman, Mrs. Brockman. I want a man I don't have to share."

Madge Brockman smiled sadly as Amanda stood up. "Have you found one?"

"I hope so," Amanda answered. Then she laid a hand lightly on Mrs. Brockman's shoulder, just for a moment, before walking away.

JORDAN ARRIVED AT seven o'clock on Friday night, looking slightly wan, his expensive suit wrinkled from the trip. "Hi, Mandy," he said, reaching out to gather her close.

Dressed for the island in blue jeans, walking boots and a heavy beige cable-knit sweater, Amanda went into his arms without hesitation. "Hi," she answered, tilting her head back for his kiss.

He tasted her mouth before moving on to possess it entirely. "I don't suppose you're going to be merciful enough to tell me what you've decided," he said, sounding a little breathless, when the long kiss was over.

"About what?" Amanda asked with feigned innocence, and kissed the beard-stubbled underside of his chin. Of course she knew he wanted to know what the sleeping arrangements would be on the island that night.

Jordan laughed hoarsely and gave her a swat. "You know damn well 'about what'!" he lectured.

Despite the weariness she felt, Amanda grinned at him. "If you guess right, I'll tell you," she teased.

He studied her with tired, laughing, hungry eyes. "Okay, here's my guess. You're going to say you want to sleep in the guest room."

Amanda rocked back on her heels, resting against his hands, which were interwoven behind her, and said nothing.

"Well?" Jordan prodded.

"You guessed wrong," Amanda told him.

"Thank God," he groaned.

Amanda laughed. "Let's go—we'll miss the ferry."

Jordan's lips, warm and moist, touched hers. "We could just stay here—"

"No way, Mr. Richards," Amanda protested, pulling back. "You invited me to go away for the weekend and I want to *go away*."

"What about the cat?" Jordan reasoned as Gershwin jumped onto the back of an easy chair and meowed plaintively.

"My landlady is going to take care of him," Amanda said, pulling out of Jordan's embrace and picking up her suitcase and overnight case. "Here," she said, shoving the suitcase at him.

"I like a subtle woman," Jordan muttered, accepting it.

Soon they were leaving the heart of the city behind for West Seattle, where they caught the Southworth ferry. Once they were on board the enormous white boat, however, they remained in the car instead of going upstairs to the snack bar with most of the other passengers.

"I've missed you," Jordan said, leaning back in the seat, resting his hand on Amanda's upper thigh and gripping her fingers.

"And I've missed you," Amanda answered. They'd already run through all the small talk; Jordan had told her about his business trip and she'd detailed her hectic week. By tacit agreement, they hadn't discussed James's heart attack.

Jordan splayed the fingers of his left hand and ran them through his rumpled hair, then gave a heavy sigh. He moved his thumb soothingly over Amanda's knuckles. "Do you have any idea how much I want you?"

She lifted his hand to her mouth and kissed it. "How much?"

He chuckled. "Enough to wish this were a van instead of a sports car." Jordan turned in the seat and cupped Amanda's chin in his hand. "You're sure you're ready for this?" he asked gently.

Amanda nodded. "I'm sure. How about you?"

Jordan grinned. "I've been ready since I turned around and saw you standing in line behind me."

"You have not."

"Okay," he admitted, "it started after that, when you threw five bucks on the table to pay for your Chinese food. For just a moment, when you thought I was going to refuse it, you had blue fire in your eyes."

"And?"

"And I had this fantasy about the whole mall being deserted—except for us, of course. I made love to you right there on the table."

Amanda felt a hot shiver go through her. "Jordan?"

His lips were moving against hers. "Yes?"

"We're fogging up the windows. People will notice that."

He chuckled and drew back. "Maybe we should go upstairs and have some coffee or something, then."

She felt the rough texture of his cheek against her palm. "Then what kind of fantasies would you be having?"

"I'd probably start imagining that we were right here, alone in a dark car, with nobody around." Slowly he unbuttoned the front of her coat. "I suppose I'd picture myself touching you like this." He curved his fingers around her breast.

Even through the weight of her sweater and the lacy barrier of her bra, Amanda could feel his caress in every nerve. "Jordan."

He moved his hand beneath the sweater and then, to the accompaniment of a little gasp of surprised pleasure from Amanda, beneath the bra. Cupping her warm breast, he

rolled the nipple gently between his fingers. "I'd be thinking about doing this, no doubt."

Amanda was squirming a little, and her breath was
quickening. "Damn it, Jordan—this isn't funny. Someone could walk by!"

"Not likely," he murmured, touching his mouth to hers
as he continued to fondle her.

Although she knew she should, Amanda couldn't bring
herself to push his hand away. What he was doing felt too
good. "S-someone might see—they'd think…"

Jordan bent his head to kiss the pulse point at the base
of her throat. "They'd think we were necking. And they'd
be right." Satisfied that he'd set one nipple to throbbing,
he proceeded to attend the other. "Ummm. Where were
you on prom night, lady?"

"Out with somebody like you," Amanda gasped breathlessly.

Jordan chuckled and continued nibbling at her throat.
She felt the snap on her jeans pop, heard the faint whisper
of the zipper. "Did he do this?"

The windows were definitely fogging up. "No…"
Amanda moaned as he slid his fingers down her warm
abdomen to find what they sought.

"Lift up your sweater," Jordan said. "I want to taste
you."

Amanda whimpered a halfhearted protest even as she
obeyed, but when she felt his mouth close over a distended
nipple, she groaned out loud and entangled her fingers in
his hair. In the meantime he continued the other delicious
mischief, causing Amanda to fidget on the seat.

She ran her hands down his back, then up to his hair
again in a frantic search for a place to touch him and make
him feel what she was feeling. His name fell repeatedly
from her lips in a breathless, senseless litany of passion.

Just as the ferry horn sounded, Amanda arched her back and cried out in release. Her body buckled over and over again against Jordan's hand before she sagged into the seat, temporarily soothed. Gradually her breathing steadied.

"Rat," she said when her good sense returned. She righted her bra and pulled her sweater down while Jordan zipped and snapped her jeans. Not two seconds after that, the first of the passengers returning from the upper deck walked past the car and waved.

Amanda's cheeks glowed as Jordan drove off the ferry minutes later.

"Relax, Mandy," he said, shoving a tape into the slot on the dashboard. The car filled with soft music. "I'm on your side, remember?"

She ran her tongue over her lips and turned in the seat to look at him. Her body was still quivering like a resonating string on some exotic instrument. "I'm not angry— just surprised. Nobody's ever been able to make me forget where I was."

"Good," Jordan replied, turning the Porsche onto a paved road lined with towering pine trees. "I'd be something less than thrilled if that was a regular thing with you."

Amanda gazed out the window for a moment, then looked back at Jordan. "Is it a regular thing with you?" she asked, almost in a whisper.

He looked at her, but she couldn't read his expression in the darkness. "There have been women since Becky, if that's what you mean. But if it'll make you feel better, none of them has ever had quite the same effect on me that you do. And I've never taken any of them to the island."

Amanda didn't know whether she felt better or not. She peered at his towering house as they pulled into the driveway, but all she could see was a shadowy shape and a lot of dark windows.

The garage door opened at the push of a button, and Jordan pulled in and got out, then turned on the lights before coming around to open Amanda's door for her. Gripping the handle of her suitcase in one hand, the other hand pressed to the small of her back, he escorted her through a side door and into a spacious, well-designed kitchen.

Amanda stopped when he set the suitcase down on the floor. "Did you live here with Becky?" she blurted. She'd known she wouldn't have the courage to ask if she waited too long.

"No," Jordan answered, taking the overnight case from her hand and setting it on the counter.

She shrugged out of her coat, avoiding his eyes. "Oh."

"Are you hungry or anything?" Jordan asked, glancing around the kitchen as though he expected it to be changed somehow from the last time he'd seen it.

"I could use a cup of coffee," Amanda admitted. "Maybe with a little brandy in it."

Jordan chuckled and disappeared with her coat. When he came back, he was minus his suit jacket and one hand was at his throat, loosening his tie. "The coffee maker's there on the counter," he said, pointing. "The other stuff is in the cupboard above it. Why don't you start the coffee brewing while I bring my stuff in from the car?"

It sounded like a reasonable idea to Amanda, and she was thankful for something to occupy her. What she and Jordan were about to do was as old as time, but she felt like the first virgin ever to be deflowered. She nodded and busily set about making coffee.

Jordan made one trip to the garage and then went upstairs. When he returned, he stood behind Amanda and put his arms around her. "Are you sure you want coffee? It's late, and that's the regular stuff."

His lips moved against her nape, and she couldn't help the tremor that went through her. "I guess not," she managed to say.

Without another word, Jordan lifted her into his arms and carried her through the dark house and up a set of stairs. The light was on in his spacious bedroom, and Amanda murmured an exclamation at the low-key luxury of the place.

The bed was enormous, and it faced a big-screen TV equipped with a VCR and heaven-only-knows-what other kinds of high-tech electronic equipment. One wall was made entirely of windows, while another was lined with mirrors, and the gray carpet was deep and plush.

Amanda glanced nervously at the mirrors and saw her own wide eyes looking back at her.

Jordan kicked off his shoes, flung his tie aside and vanished into the bathroom, whistling and unbuttoning his shirt as he went. A few moments later Amanda heard the sound of a shower running.

Quickly she scrambled off the bed and found her suitcase, still feeling like a shy virgin. Suddenly the skimpy black nightgown she'd brought along didn't look sturdy enough, so she helped herself to a heavy terry-cloth robe from Jordan's closet. After hastily stripping, she wrapped herself in the robe and tied the belt with a double knot.

When Jordan came out sometime later, he was wearing nothing but a towel around his waist. His hair was blow-dried and combed back from his face, and his eyes twinkled at Amanda when he saw her sitting fitfully on the edge of the chair farthest from the bed.

"Scared?" he asked, approaching her and pulling her gently to her feet.

"Of course not," Amanda lied. The truth was, she was terrified.

Jordan undid the double knot at her waist as though it were nothing. "I guess I should have invited you to share my shower," he said, his voice a leisurely rumble.

"I had one at home," Amanda was quick to point out.

He opened the robe, laid it aside and looked at her, slowly and thoroughly, before meeting her eyes again. His lips quirked. "You're awfully nervous, considering how mad you were when I wouldn't make love to you last week."

Amanda moved to close the robe, but Jordan grasped her wrists and stopped her. He subjected her to another lingering assessment before pushing the garment off her shoulders with warm, gentle hands. It fell silently to the floor.

"We—we could turn the light out," she dared to suggest as Jordan lifted her again and carried her back to the bed.

"We could," he agreed, stretching out beside her, "but we're not going to."

He'd shaved, and his face was smooth and fragrant. He took her mouth and mastered it skillfully, leaving Amanda dizzy and disoriented when he drew away.

Tenderly he turned Amanda's head so that she was facing the mirrors, and a moan lodged in her throat when she saw him move his hand toward her breast.

"Jordan," she whispered.

"Shhh," he murmured against the tingling flesh of her neck, and Amanda was quiet, her eyes widening as she watched her conquering begin.

Chapter 6

ᏬᏬᏬ

THE DARK BLUE VELOUR bedspread felt incredibly soft against Amanda's bare skin, and she forgot the mirrored wall and even the lights as Jordan kissed and caressed her. Although she tried, she couldn't hold back the soft moans that escaped her, or the whispered pleas for release.

But Jordan would not be hurried. "All in good time, Mandy," he assured her, his mouth at her throat. "All in good time. Just relax."

"Relax?" Amanda gave a rueful semihysterical chuckle at the word. "Now? Are you crazy?"

He trailed his lips down over her collarbone, over the plump rounding of one breast. "Ummm-hmm," he said just before he took her nipple into his mouth. In the meantime he was stroking the tender skin on the insides of Amanda's thighs.

"Stop teasing me," she whimpered, moving her hands through his hair and over the muscular sleekness of his back.

"Never," he paused long enough to say. He left off tormenting Amanda to reach for a pillow, which he deftly tucked underneath her bottom. And then he caressed her in earnest.

Amanda was frantic. Jordan had been subjecting her to various kinds of foreplay for a week, and she simply couldn't wait any longer for gratification. Her body demanded it.

"Jordan," she pleaded, half-blind with the need of him, "*now*. Oh, please—"

She felt him part her legs, then come to rest between them. "Mandy," he rasped like a man being consumed by invisible fire. In one fierce, beautiful thrust, he was a part of her, but then he lay very still. "Mandy, open your eyes and look at me."

She obeyed, but she could barely focus on his features because she was caught up in a whirlwind of sensation. The pillow raised her to him like a pagan offering, and her body was still reacting to the single stroke he'd allowed her. "Jordan," she pleaded, and all her desperation, all her need, echoed in the name.

He kissed her thoroughly, his tongue staking the same claim that the other part of his body was making on her. Finally he began to move upon her, slowly at first, making her ask for every motion of his powerful hips, but as Amanda's passion heated, so did his own. Soon they were parting and coming together again in a wild, primitive rhythm.

Amanda was the first to scale the peak, and the splintering explosion in her senses was everything she'd hoped it would be. Her body arched like a bow with the string drawn tight, and her cries of surrender echoed off the walls.

Jordan was more restrained, but Amanda saw a panorama of emotions cross his face as he gave himself up to her in a series of short, frenzied thrusts.

They lay on their sides, facing each other, legs still entwined, for long minutes after their lovemaking had ended.

Jordan gave a raspy chuckle.

"What's funny?" Amanda asked softly, winding a tendril of his rich brown hair around one finger.

"I was just thinking of the first time I saw you. You were bored with waiting in line, so you struck up a conversation. I wondered if you were a member of some weird religious sect."

Amanda gave him a playful punch in the chest.

He laughed and leaned over to kiss her. "Let's go down to the kitchen," he said when it was over. "I'm starving."

Jordan rose off the bed and retrieved the yellow bathrobe from the floor, tossing it to Amanda. He took a hooded one of striped silk from the closet and put that on. Together, they went downstairs.

Jordan plundered the cupboards, while Amanda perched on a stool, watching him and sipping a cup of the coffee she'd made earlier. He finally decided on popcorn and thrust a bag into the microwave.

"This is a great house," Amanda said as the oven's motor began to whir. "What I've seen of it, anyway."

Jordan was busy digging through another cupboard for a serving bowl that suited him. "Thanks."

"And it's pretty big." Saying those words gave Amanda the same sense of breathless anticipation she would have felt if she'd walked outside with the intention of plunging a toe into the frigid sound.

He set a red bowl on the counter with a thump, and the grin he gave her was tinged with exasperation. "Big enough for a couple of kids, I suppose," he said.

Amanda shrugged and lifted her eyebrows. "Seems like you could fit Jessica and Lisa in here somewhere."

The popcorn was snapping like muted gunfire inside

its colorful paper bag. For just a moment, Jordan's eyes snapped, too. "We've been over that, Amanda," he said.

She took another sip of her coffee. "Okay. I was just wondering why you'd want a house like this when you live all alone."

The bell on the microwave chimed, and Jordan took the popcorn out, carefully opened the bag and dumped the contents into the bowl. The fragrance filled the kitchen, causing Amanda to decide she was hungry, after all.

"Jordan?" she prompted when he didn't reply.

He picked up a kernel and tossed it at her. "How about cooling it with the questions I can't answer?"

Amanda sighed and wriggled off the stool. "I'm sorry," she said. "Your living arrangements are none of my business, anyway."

Jordan didn't counter that statement. He simply took up the bowl and started back through the house and up the stairs. Amanda had no choice but to follow.

Returning to the bed, they settled themselves under the covers, with pillows at their backs, the popcorn between them, and Jordan switched on the gigantic TV screen.

The news was on. "I'm not in the mood to be depressed," Jordan said, working the remote control device with his thumb until a cable channel came on.

Amanda settled against his shoulder and crunched thoughtfully on a mouthful of popcorn. "I've seen this movie before," she said. "It's good."

Jordan slipped an arm around her and plunged the opposite hand into the bowl. "I'll take your word for it."

Images flickered across the screen, the popcorn diminished until there were only yellow kernels in the bottom of the bowl and the moon rose high and beautiful beyond the wall of windows. Amanda sighed and closed her eyes, feeling warm and contented.

THE NEXT THING she knew, it was morning, and Jordan was lying beside her, propped up on one elbow, smiling. "Hi," he said. He'd showered, and his breath smelled of mint toothpaste.

Amanda was well aware she hadn't and hers didn't. "Hi," she responded, speaking into the covers.

Jordan laughed and kissed her forehead. "Breakfast in twenty minutes," he said, and then he rose off the bed and walked away, wearing only a pair of jeans.

The moment he was gone, Amanda dashed to the bathroom. When he returned in the prescribed twenty minutes, he was carrying a tray and Amanda was sitting cross-legged in the middle of the bed. She'd exchanged Jordan's robe for a short nightgown of turquoise silk, and she grinned when she saw the tray in his hands.

"Room service! I'm impressed, Mr. Richards."

He set the food tray carefully in her lap, and Amanda's stomach rumbled in anticipation as she looked under various lids, finding sliced banana, toast, orange juice and two slices of crisp bacon. "Our services are *très* expensive, *madame*," he teased in a very good French accent.

"Put it on my credit card," Amanda bantered back, and picked up a slice of bacon and bit into it.

Jordan chuckled, still playing the Frenchman. "Oh, but *madame*, this we cannot do." He reached out to touch the tip of her right breast with his index finger, making the nipple turn button-hard beneath its covering of silk. "Zee policy is strictly cash and carry."

Amanda's eyes were sparkling as she widened them in mock horror. "We have a terrible problem then, *monsieur*, for I haven't a franc to my name. Not a single, solitary one!"

"This is a true pity," Jordan continued, laying a light, exploratory finger to Amanda's knee and drawing it slowly down to her ankle. "I am afraid you cannot leave this room until you have made proper restitution."

Amanda ate in silence for a time, while Jordan lingered, watching her with mischievous expectancy in his eyes. "Aren't you going to eat?" she asked, forgetting the game for a moment, and she went red the instant the words were out of her mouth.

Jordan chuckled, took the tray from her lap and set it aside. "About the price of your room, *madame*. Some agreement must be reached."

Recovered from her earlier embarrassment, Amanda slipped her arms around Jordan's neck and kissed him softly on the lips. "I'm sure we can work out something to our mutual satisfaction, *monsieur*."

He drew the silk nightgown gently over her head and tossed it away. *"Oui,"* he answered, laying a hand to her bare thigh even as he pressed her back onto the pillows.

Amanda groaned as he moved his hand from her thigh to her stomach, and when instinct caused her to draw up her knees, he claimed her with a finger in a sudden motion of his hand.

The sensation was exquisite, and Amanda arched her neck, her eyes drifting closed as Jordan choreographed a dance for her eager body. She groaned as Jordan's tongue tamed a pulsing nipple.

"Of course," he told her in that same accented English, "the customer, she must always have satisfaction first."

Only moments later, Amanda was caught in the throes of a climax that caused her to thrash on the bed and call Jordan's name even as she clutched blindly at his shoulders.

"Easy," he told her, moving his warm lips against her neck. "Nice and easy."

Amanda sagged back to the mattress, her breath coming in fevered gasps, her eyes smoldering as she watched

Jordan slip out of his jeans and poise himself above her. "No more waiting," she said. "I want you, Jordan."

He gave her only a portion of his magnificence at first, but then, when she traced the circumference of each of his nipples with a fingertip, he gave a low growl and plunged into her in earnest. And the whole splendid rite began all over again.

"A CHRISTMAS TREE?" Amanda echoed, standing in the middle of Jordan's living room with its high, beamed ceilings and breathtaking view of the mountains and Puget Sound. She was wearing jeans, sneakers and a sweatshirt, like Jordan, and there was a cozy fire snapping on the raised hearth.

"Is that so strange?" Jordan asked. "After all, it is December."

Amanda assessed the towering tinted glass window that let in the view. "It would be a shame to cover that up," she said.

Jordan pinched her cheek. "Thank you, Ebenezer Scrooge," he teased. Then he widened his eyes at her. "What is it with you and Christmas, anyway?"

With a sigh, Amanda collapsed into a cushy chair upholstered in dark blue brushed cotton, her arms folded. "I guess I'd like to let it just sort of slip past unnoticed."

"Fat chance," Jordan replied, perching on the arm of her chair. "It's everywhere."

"Yeah," Amanda said, lowering her eyes.

He put a finger under her chin and lifted. "What is it, Mandy?"

She tried to smile. "My dad left at Christmas," she admitted, her voice small as she momentarily became a little girl again.

"Ouch," Jordan whispered, pulling her to her feet. Then

he sank into the chair and drew Amanda onto his lap. "That was a dirty trick."

"You don't know the half of it," Amanda reflected, staring out at mountains she didn't really see. "We never heard another word from him, ever. He didn't even take his presents."

Jordan pressed Amanda's head against his shoulder. "Know what?" he asked softly. "Hating Christmas isn't going to change what happened."

She lifted her head so that she could look into Jordan's eyes. "It's the hardest time of the year when you've lost somebody you loved."

He kissed her forehead. "Believe me, Mandy, I know that. The first year after Becky died, Jessie asked me to write a letter to Santa Claus for her. She wanted him to bring her mother back."

Amanda smoothed the hair at Jordan's temple, even though it wasn't rumpled. "What did you do?"

"My first impulse was to get falling-down drunk and stay that way until spring." He sighed. "I didn't, of course. With some help from my sister, I explained to Jessie that even Santa couldn't pull off anything that big. It was tough, but we all got through it."

"Don't you miss them?" Amanda dared to ask, her voice barely more than a breath. "Jessica and Lisa, I mean?"

"Every day of my life," Jordan replied, "but I've got to think about what's best for them." His tone said the conversation was over, and so did his action. He got out of the chair, propelling Amanda to her feet in the process. "Let's go cut a Christmas tree."

Amanda smiled. "I haven't done that since I was still at home. My stepdad used to take my sister and me along every year—we drove all the way to Issaquah."

"So," Jordan teased with a light in his eyes, "your memories of Christmas aren't all bad."

Recalling how hard Bob had tried to make up not only for Marion's loss, but the girls', as well, Amanda had a warm feeling. "You're right," she admitted.

Jordan squinted at her and twisted the end of an imaginary mustache. This time his accent was Viennese, and he was, according to Amanda's best guess, Sigmund Freud. "Absolutely of course I am right," he said.

And then he pulled Amanda close and kissed her soundly, and she found herself wanting to go back upstairs.

That wasn't in the cards, however. Jordan had decided to cut down a Christmas tree, and his purpose was evidently unshakable. They put on coats, climbed into the small, late-model pickup truck parked beside the Porsche and sped off toward the tree farm.

Slogging up and down the rows of Christmas trees while the attendant walked behind them with a chain saw at the ready, Amanda actually felt festive. The piney smell was pungent, the air crisp, the sky painfully blue.

"How about this one?" Jordan said, pausing to inspect a twelve-footer.

Amanda looked at him in bewilderment. "What about it?"

Jordan gave her a wry glance. "Do you like it?" he asked patiently.

Amanda couldn't think why it mattered whether she liked the tree or not, but she nodded. "It's beautiful."

"We'll take this one," Jordan told the attendant.

They stood back while the man in the plaid woolen coat and blue overalls felled the tree, and followed when he dragged it off toward the truck.

By the time the tree had been paid for and tied down

in the back of Jordan's truck, it was noon and Amanda was famished.

Jordan favored her with a sidelong grin when they were seated in the cab. "Hungry?"

"How do you always know?" Amanda demanded, half surprised and half exasperated. A person couldn't have a private thought around this man.

"I'm psychic," Jordan teased, starting the engine. "Of course, the fact that you haven't eaten in four hours and your stomach is rumbling helped me come to the conclusion. How does seafood sound?"

"Wonderful," Amanda replied. The scent of the tree was on her clothes and Jordan's, and she loved its pungency.

They drove to a café overlooking the water and took a table next to a window, where they could see a ferry passing, along with the occasional intrepid sailboat and a number of other small vessels. Jordan flirted with the middle-aged waitress, who obviously knew him and gave Amanda a kindly assessment with heavily made-up eyes.

"So, Jordan Richards," the older woman teased, "you've been stepping out on me."

Jordan grinned. "Sorry, Wanda."

Wanda swatted him on the shoulder with a plastic-covered menu. "I'm always the last to know," she said. Her eyes came back to Amanda again. "Since Jordan doesn't have enough manners to introduce us, we'll just have to handle the job ourselves. My name's Wanda Carson."

Amanda smiled and held out her hand. "Amanda Scott," she replied.

After shaking Amanda's hand, Wanda laid the menus down and said, "We got a real good special today. It's baked chicken with rice."

Jordan ordered the special, perhaps to atone for "stepping out on" Wanda, but Amanda had her heart set on sea-food, so she ordered deep-fried prawns and French fries.

Amanda couldn't remember ever enjoying a meal more than she did that one, but honesty would have forced her to admit it was not the food but the company that made it special.

On the way back to Jordan's house, they stopped at a variety store, which was crowded with shopping carts and people, and bought an enormous tree stand, strings of lights, colorful glass ornaments and tinsel. "I gave away the stuff Becky and I had," he admitted offhandedly while they waited in line to pay.

A bittersweet pang squeezed Amanda's heart at the thought, but she only smiled.

They spent a good hour just dragging the massive tree inside the house and setting it up. It fell over repeatedly, and Jordan finally had to put hooks in the wall and tie it in place. It towered to the ceiling, every needle of its fresh, green branches filling the room with perfume.

"It's beautiful," Amanda vowed, resting her hands on her hips.

Jordan was bringing a high stepladder in from the garage. "So are you," he told her, setting the ladder up beside the tree. "In fact, why don't you come over here?"

Amanda laughed and shook her head. "No thanks. This fly knows a spider when she sees one."

Assuming a pretend glower, Jordan stomped over to Amanda, put his fingers against her ribs and tickled her until she toppled onto the couch, shrieking with laughter.

Then he pinned her down with his body and stretched her arms far above her head. "Hello, fly," he said, his eyes twinkling as he placed his mouth on hers.

"Hello, spider," Amanda responded, her lips touching

his. Just as the piney scent of the tree pervaded the house, Jordan's closeness permeated her senses.

Things might have progressed from there if the telephone hadn't rung, but it did, and Jordan reached over Amanda's head to grasp the receiver. There was a note of impatience in his voice when he answered, but his expression changed completely when the caller spoke.

He sat up on the edge of the couch, Amanda apparently forgotten. "Hi, Jessie. I'm fine, honey. How are you?"

Amanda suddenly felt like an eavesdropper. She got up from the couch and tiptoed out of the living room and up the stairs. She was pacing back and forth across the bedroom, when she noticed an overturned photograph on the bedside table.

An ache twisted in the pit of her stomach as she walked over, grasped the photograph and set it upright. A beautiful dark-haired woman smiled at her from the picture, her eyes full of love and laughter.

"Hello, Becky," Amanda whispered sadly, recalling the white stripe on Jordan's finger where his wedding band had been.

Becky seemed to regard her with kind understanding.

Amanda set the photo carefully back on the bedside table and stood up. A fathomless sorrow filled her; she felt as though she'd made love to another woman's husband. But this time she'd known what she was doing.

Turning her back on the picture, Amanda found her suitcase and her overnighter and packed them both. She was just snapping the catches on the suitcase, when the door opened and Jordan came in.

His gaze shifted from Amanda to the photograph and back again. "Is this about the picture?" he asked quietly.

Amanda lowered her head. "I'm not sure."

"Not good enough, Mandy." Jordan's voice was husky. "Until ten minutes ago when my daughters called, everything was okay. Then you came up here and saw the picture, and you packed your clothes."

She made herself look at him, and it hurt that he lingered in the doorway instead of crossing the room to take her into his arms. "I guess I feel like this is her house and you're her husband. It's kind of like being the other woman all over again."

"That's crazy."

Amanda shook her head. "No, it isn't. Look at your left hand, Jordan. You can still see where the wedding band was. When did you take it off? Two weeks ago? Last month?"

Jordan folded his arms. "What does it matter when I took it off? The point is, I'm not wearing it anymore. And as for the picture, I just forgot to put it away, that's all."

"The night we had dinner at my place, you told me I wasn't ready for a relationship. I think maybe *you're* the one who isn't ready, Jordan."

He sprang away from the door frame, strode across the room and took the suitcase and overnighter from Amanda's hands, tossing them aside with a clatter. "Remember me? I'm the guy whose mind you blew in that bed over there," he bit out. "Damn it, have you forgotten the way it was with us?"

"That isn't the issue!" Amanda cried, frustrated and confused.

"Isn't it?" Jordan asked, clasping her wrists in his hands and wrenching her close to him. "You're scared, Amanda, so you're looking for an excuse to make a quick exit. That way you won't have to face what's really happening here."

Amanda swallowed hard. "What *is* happening here?" she asked miserably.

Jordan withdrew from her, albeit reluctantly, except for the grip he'd taken on her hand. "I don't know exactly," he confessed, calmer now. "But I think we'd damn well better find out, don't you?"

At Amanda's nod, he led her out of the bedroom and down the stairs again. She sank despondently into an easy chair while he built up the fire on the hearth.

"I don't want to be the other woman, Jordan," she said when he turned to face her.

He crossed the room, knelt in front of her and placed one of her blue-jeaned legs over each arm of the chair, setting her afire all over again as he stroked the insides of her thighs. "You're the *only* woman," he answered, and he nipped at one of her nipples through the bra and sweatshirt that covered it. "Show me your breasts, Mandy."

It was a measure of her obsession with him that she pulled up her sweatshirt and unfastened the front catch on her bra so that she spilled out into full view. He grasped her knees, holding them up on the arms of the chair as he leaned forward to tease one nipple with his tongue.

Amanda remembered that there was somebody else in Jordan's life, but she couldn't remember a face or a name. Perspiration glowed on her upper lip as Jordan took his pleasure at her breasts, moving his right hand from one knee to the other, slowly following an erotic path.

Finally, when Amanda was half-delirious with wanting, he kissed his way down over her belly and lightly bit her through the denim at the crossroads of her thighs.

Amanda moaned helplessly and moved to close her legs, and Jordan allowed that, but only long enough to unsnap her jeans and dispose of them, along with her panties and shoes. Then he put her knees back into their original position, opened his own jeans and took her in a powerful, possessive thrust so pleasurable that she nearly fainted.

She longed to embrace Jordan with her legs, as well as her arms, but he didn't permit it. It was a battle of sorts, but Amanda couldn't be sure who was the loser, since every lunge Jordan made wrung a cry of delight from her throat.

Her climax made her give a long, low scream as she pressed her head into the chair's back. Jordan, both hands still holding her knees, uttered a desolate groan as his body convulsed and he spilled himself into Amanda.

Once the gasping aftermath was over and Amanda's breathing and heart rate had gone back to normal, she was angry. Jordan hadn't forced her, but he had turned her own body against her, and that was a power no one had ever had over Amanda before.

She moved to fasten her bra, but Jordan, still breathing hard, his eyes flashing with challenge, interrupted the action and took her tingling breasts gently but firmly into his hands. "We're not through, Amanda," he ground out.

"The hell we aren't!" she sputtered.

Keeping his hands where they were, he turned his head and lightly kissed the back of her knee.

Amanda trembled. "Damn it, Jordan..."

He moved his lips along her inner thigh, leaving a trail of fire behind them, and slid one of his hands down to rest on her lower abdomen, finding the hidden plum and making a small circle around it with the pad of his thumb. "Yes?" he answered at his leisure.

A whimper escaped Amanda, and Jordan chuckled at the sound, still working his lethal magic. "You were saying?" he prompted huskily.

Amanda reached backward to grasp the top of the chair, fearing she would fly away like a rocket if she didn't. "We're n-not through," she concluded.

Her reward was another baptism in sweet fire, and it made a believer out of her through and through.

THE NEXT DAY was cold and pristinely beautiful, and Jordan and Amanda decided to leave the tree undecorated and take a drive around the island. That was when Amanda saw the house.

It stood between Jordan's place and the ferry terminal, and she couldn't imagine why she hadn't noticed it before. It was white with green shutters, and very Victorian, and there was even a lighthouse within walking distance. Best of all a For Sale sign stood in the yard, swinging slowly in the salty breeze.

"Jordan, stop!" Amanda cried, barely able to restrain herself from reaching out and grasping the steering wheel.

After giving her one half-amused, half-bewildered look, Jordan steered the truck onto the rocky, rutted driveway leading past a tumbledown mailbox and a few discarded tires and empty rabbit pens.

Amanda was out of the truck a moment after they came to a jolting halt.

Chapter 7

———— ⟶⟨◦⟩⟵ ————

THE GRASS IN THE YARD was overgrown, and the outside of the building needed paint, but neither of these facts dampened Amanda's enthusiasm. She hurried around the back of the house and found a screened porch that ran the full length of the place. On the upper floor there were lots of windows, providing an unobstructed view of the water and the mountains.

It was the perfect place for a bed and breakfast, and Amanda felt a thrill of excitement race through her blood.

A moment later, though, as Jordan caught up to her, her spirits plummeted. The place had obviously been neglected for a long time and would cost far more than she had to spend. People were willing to pay a premium price for waterfront property.

"I could help you," Jordan suggested, reading her mind.

Amanda quickly shook her head. A personal loan could poison their relationship if things went wrong later on, and besides, she wanted the accomplishment to be her own.

After they'd walked around the house and looked into the windows, Amanda wrote down the name of the real estate company and the phone number, tucking the information into her purse.

She could hardly wait to get to a telephone, and Jordan, discerning this, headed straight for the café where Wanda worked. While he chatted with the waitress and ordered clubhouse sandwiches, Amanda dialed the real estate agency's number and got an answering machine. She left her name and her numbers for home and work in Seattle and returned to the table.

"No luck?" Jordan asked as she sat down across from him in the booth and reached for the cup of coffee he'd ordered for her.

"They'll get in touch," Amanda answered with a little shrug. "I don't know why I'm so excited. I probably won't be able to afford the place, anyway."

Jordan's eyes twinkled as he looked at her. "That was a negative thing to say," he scolded. "You're not going to get anywhere in life if you don't believe in yourself."

"Thank you, Norman Vincent Peale," Amanda said somewhat irritably as she wriggled out of her coat and set it aside. "Just because you could probably write a check for the place on the spot doesn't mean I'd be able to."

The clubhouse sandwiches arrived, and Jordan picked up a potato chip and crunched it between his teeth. "Okay, so I have a knack with money. I should have—it's my business. And I don't understand why you won't let me help."

"I have my reasons, Jordan."

"Like what?"

Amanda shrugged. "Suppose in two days or two weeks we decide we don't want to see each other anymore. If I owed you a big chunk of money, things could get pretty sticky."

Jordan shook his head. "That's just an excuse, Mandy.

People borrow money to start businesses every day of the week."

In the short time they'd known each other, Amanda had to admit that Jordan had learned to read her well. "I want it to be mine," she confessed. "Is that too much to ask?"

"Nope," Jordan replied good-naturedly, and after that they dropped the subject and talked of other things.

They spent the rest of the afternoon exploring the beach fronting the property Amanda wanted to buy, and the time sped by. Too soon the weekend was over and Jordan was putting her suitcase and overnighter in the back of the Porsche.

Even the prospect of separation was difficult for Amanda. "How about having dinner at my place before you come back?" she asked somewhat shyly as Jordan pushed the button to turn on the answering machine in his study.

He smiled at her. "Smooth talker," he teased.

Amanda barely stopped herself from suggesting that he bring fresh clothes and a toothbrush, as well. All her life she'd been a patient, methodical person, but where this man was concerned, she had a dangerous tendency to be impulsive. She trembled a little when Jordan kissed her, and devoutly hoped he hadn't noticed.

During the ferry ride back to Seattle, they drank coffee in the snack bar, and when they reached the city, Amanda asked Jordan to stop at a supermarket. She bought chicken, fresh corn and potatoes.

Gershwin greeted them with a mournful meow when they entered Amanda's apartment. Appeasing his pique was easy, though; Jordan simply opened a can of cat food and set it on the floor for him.

Amanda was busy cutting up the chicken and washing the corn, so Jordan wandered back into the living room and used the log left from his last visit to start a fire on the hearth.

"We forgot to decorate your tree," Amanda said when he returned to the kitchenette to lean against the counter, watching her put floured chicken pieces into a hot skillet.

"It'll keep," Jordan answered. When she'd finished putting the chicken on to brown, he took her into his arms. "Mandy, Karen's bringing the girls to Seattle Friday night. They're going to spend two weeks with me."

Amanda was pleased, but a little puzzled that he'd waited until now to mention it. "That's great. I guess you found that out when the kids called."

He nodded.

"Why didn't you tell me?"

Jordan shrugged. "If you recall, we were a little busy after that phone call," he pointed out. "And then I was trying to work out how to ask you to spend next weekend on the island with us."

Amanda broke away long enough to turn the chicken pieces and put the corn on to boil. "I don't think that would be a very good idea, Jordan," she finally said, looking back at him over her shoulder. "After all, we aren't married, and we don't want to confuse the kids."

"How could we confuse them? They're not teenagers, Amanda. They're too small to understand about sex."

Amanda shook her head. "Kids know something is going on, whether they understand what it is or not. They sense emotional undercurrents, Jordan, and I don't want to get off on the wrong foot with them." She turned down the heat under the chicken and covered it with a lid. "Now how about a glass of wine?"

Jordan nodded his assent, but he looked distracted. After uncorking the bottle and pouring a glass for himself and for Amanda, he wandered into the living room.

Amanda followed, perching on the arm of the sofa while he stood at the window, watching the city lights.

"Come on, Jordan," she urged gently. "'Fess up. You're scared, aren't you? When was the last time you were responsible for your kids for two weeks straight?"

There was a hint of anger in his eyes when he turned to look at her. "I've been 'responsible' for them since they were born, Amanda."

"Maybe so," she retorted quietly, "but somebody else did the nitty-gritty stuff—first Becky, then your sister. You don't have any idea how to really take care of your daughters, do you?"

Jordan was offended initially, but then his ire gave way to a sort of indignant resignation. "Okay," he admitted, "you've got me. I wanted you to spend next weekend with us because I need moral support."

Amanda went back to the kitchen for plates and silverware, then began to set the small, round table in the living room. "You know my phone number," she said. "If you want moral support, you can call me. But you don't need somebody else in the way when you're bonding with your kids, Jordan."

"Bonding? Hell, you've been reading too many pop psychology books."

"You have a right to your opinion," Amanda responded, "but I'm not going to be there to act as a buffer. You're on your own with this one, buddy."

Jordan gave her an irate look, but then his expression softened and he took her in his arms. "Maybe I can't change your mind," he told her huskily, "but I can sure as hell let you know what you'll be missing."

Amanda pushed him away. "The chicken will burn."

Jordan chuckled. "Okay, Mandy, you win. For now."

Twenty minutes later they sat down to a dinner of fried

chicken, corn on the cob, mashed potatoes and gravy. Amanda's portable TV set was turned to the evening news, and the ambience of the evening was quietly domestic.

When they were through eating, Amanda began clearing the table, only to have Jordan stop her by slipping his arms around her waist from behind. "Aren't you forgetting something?" he asked, his voice a low rumble as he bent his head to kiss her nape and sent a jagged thrill swirling through her system.

"W-what?" Amanda asked, already a little breathless.

Jordan slid his hands up beneath her shirt to cup the undersides of her breasts. "Dessert," he answered.

Amanda was trembling. "Jordan, the food—"

"The food will still be here when we're through."

"No, it won't," Amanda argued, following her protest with a little moan as Jordan unfastened her bra and rubbed her nipples to attention with the sides of his thumbs. "G-Gershwin will eat it."

His lips were on her nape again. "Who cares?"

Amanda realized that she didn't. She turned in Jordan's embrace and tilted her head back for his kiss.

While taming her mouth, he grasped her hips in his hands and pressed her close, making her feel his size and power.

She was dazed when he drew back, pliant when he steered her toward the bedroom and closed the door behind them.

The small room was shadowy, the bed neatly made. Jordan set Amanda on the edge of the mattress and knelt to slowly untie her shoes and roll down her socks. For a time he caressed her feet, one by one, and Amanda was surprised at the sensual pleasure such a simple act could evoke.

When she was tingling from head to foot, he rose and

pulled her shirt off over her head, then smoothed away the bra he'd already opened. He pressed Amanda onto her back to unsnap her jeans and remove them and her panties, and she didn't make a move to stop him. All she could do was sigh.

After the last of her garments was tossed away, Jordan began removing his own clothes. They joined Amanda's in a pile on the floor.

"Jordan," Amanda whispered, entwining her fingers in his hair as he stretched out beside her, "don't make me wait. Please."

He gave her a nibbling kiss. "So impatient," he scolded sleepily, trailing his lips down over her chin to her neck. "Lovemaking takes time, Mandy. Especially if it's good."

Amanda remembered their session in Jordan's living room the day before. It had been fast and ferocious, and if it had been any better, it would have killed her. She moaned as Jordan made a slow, silken circle on her belly with his hand. "I can only stand so much pleasure!" she whimpered in a lame protest.

Jordan chuckled. "We're going to have to raise your tolerance," he said.

Two hours later, when both Jordan and Amanda were showered and dressed and the table had been cleared, he reached for his jacket and shrugged into it. Amanda had to fight back tears when he kissed her, as well as pleas for him to spend the night. On a practical, rational level, she knew they both needed to let things cool down a little so they could get some perspective.

But when she'd closed the door behind Jordan, Amanda rested her forehead against it for a long moment and bit down hard on her lower lip. It was all she could do not to run out into the hallway and call him back.

Slowly she turned from the door and went about her usual Sunday night routine, choosing the outfits she would wear to work during the coming week, manicuring her nails and watching a mystery program on TV.

The bed was rumpled, and it still smelled of Jordan's cologne and their fevered lovemaking. Forlornly Amanda remade it and crawled under the covers, the small TV she kept in her room turned to her favorite show.

Two minutes after that week's victim had been done in, the telephone rang. Hoping for a call from the real estate agent or from Jordan, Amanda reached for the receiver on her bedside table and answered on the second ring.

"Amanda?"

The voice was Eunice's, and she sounded as though she'd been crying for a week.

Amanda spoke gently to her sister, because they'd always been close. "Hi, kid," she said, for she was the older of the two and Eunice had been "kid" since she was born. "What's the problem?"

"It's Jim," Eunice sobbed.

Now there's a real surprise, Amanda thought ruefully while she waited for her sister to recover herself.

"There's been someone else the whole time," Eunice wept, making a valiant, sniffling attempt to get a hold on herself.

Amanda was painfully reminded of what Madge Brockman had gone through because of her. "Are you sure?" she asked gently.

"She called this afternoon," Eunice said. "She said if Jim wouldn't tell me, she would. He's moved in with her!"

For a moment Amanda knew a pure, white-hot rage entirely directed at her soon-to-be ex-brother-in-law. Since her anger wouldn't help Eunice in any way, she counted to herself until the worst of it had passed. "Honey, this doesn't look like something you can change. And that means you have to accept it."

Eunice was quiet for almost a minute. "I guess you're right," she admitted softly. "I'll try, Amanda."

"I know you will," Amanda replied, wishing she could be nearer to her sister to lend moral support.

"Mom tells me you've met a guy." Eunice snuffled. "That's really great, Mand. What's he like?"

Amanda remembered making love with Jordan on the very bed she was lying in, and a wave of heat rolled over her. She also remembered the photograph of Becky and the white strip of skin on Jordan's left hand ring finger. "He's moderately terrific," she answered demurely.

Eunice laughed, and it was a good sound to hear. "Maybe I can meet him when I come home next week."

"I'd like that," Amanda replied. "And I'm glad you're coming home. How long can you stay?"

"Perhaps forever," Eunice replied, sounding blue again. "Everywhere I turn here, there's another reminder of Jim staring me in the face."

Amanda spoke gently. "Don't misunderstand me, sis, because I'd love for you to live in Seattle again, but I hope you realize you can't run away from your problems. You'll still have to find a way to work them out."

"That might be easier with you and Mom and Bob nearby," Eunice said quietly.

"You know we'll help in any way we can," Amanda assured her.

"Yeah, I know. It means the world to know you're there for me, Mand—you and Mom and Daddy Bob. But listen, I'll get off the line now because I know you're probably trying to watch that murder show you like so much. See you next week."

Amanda smiled. "You just try and avoid it, kid."

After that, the two sisters said their goodbyes and hung up. Amanda, having lost track of her TV show, switched off the set and the lamp on her bedside table and wriggled down between the covers.

How empty the bed seemed without Jordan sprawled out beside her, taking more than his share of the space.

Two DAYS PASSED before Amanda saw Jordan again; they met for lunch in a hotel restaurant.

"Did you ever hear from the real estate agent?" Jordan asked, drawing back Amanda's chair for her.

She sank into it, inordinately relieved just to be with him again. She wondered, with a chill, if she wasn't letting herself in for a major bruise to the soul somewhere down the line. "She called me at work yesterday. The down payment is five times what I have in the bank."

Jordan sat down across from her and reached out for her hand, which she willingly gave. "Mandy, I can lend you the money with no problem."

"You must be loaded," Amanda teased, having no intention of accepting, "if you can make an offer like that without even knowing how much is involved."

He grinned one of his melting grins. "I confess—I called the agency and asked."

Amanda shook out her napkin and placed it neatly on her lap. It was time to change the subject. "Who's going to take care of the kids while you're working?" she asked.

"Much to the consternation of Striner and Striner," said Jordan, "I'm taking two weeks off. I figure I'm going to need all my wits about me."

Amanda laughed. "No doubt about that."

Jordan leaned forward in his chair with a look of mock reprimand on his face. "I'll thank you to extend a little sympathy, here, Ms. Scott. You're looking at a man who has no idea how to take care of two little girls."

"They need to eat three times a day, Jordan," Amanda pointed out with teasing patience, "and it's a good idea if they have a bath at night, followed by about eight hours of sleep. Beyond that, they mainly just need to know they're loved."

Jordan was turning his table knife from end to end. "You're sure you won't come out for the weekend?"

"My sister is arriving on Friday night—in pieces, from the sounds of things."

"Ah," Jordan answered as a waiter brought menus and filled their water glasses. "The recipient of *Gathering Up the Pieces,* the pop psychology book of the decade. I'm sorry to hear things haven't improved for her."

Amanda sighed. "They've gone from bad to worse, actually," she replied. "But there's hope. Eunice is intelligent, and she's attractive, too. She'll work through this."

"Maybe she could work through the first part of it—say next Saturday and Sunday—without you?"

Amanda shook her head as she opened her menu. "Don't you ever give up?"

"Never," Jordan replied. "It's my credo—keep bugging them until they give in to shut you up."

Amanda laughed. "Such sage advice."

They made their selections and placed their orders before the conversation continued. Jordan reached out and took Amanda's hand again when the waiter was gone.

"I've missed you a whole lot."

"Then how come you didn't call?"

"I've been in meetings day and night, Amanda. Besides, I figured if I heard your voice, I wouldn't be able to stop myself from walking into your office and taking you on your desk."

Amanda's cheeks burned, but she knew her eyes were sparkling. "Jordan," she protested in a whisper, "this is a public place."

"That's why you're not lying on the table with your skirt up around your waist," Jordan answered with a perfectly straight face.

"You have to be the most arrogant man I've ever met," Amanda told him, but a smile hovered around her mouth. She couldn't very well deny that Jordan could make her do extraordinary things.

The waiter returned with their seafood salads, sparing Jordan from having to answer. His reply probably would have been cocky, anyway, Amanda figured.

The conversation had turned to more conventional subjects, when Madge Brockman suddenly appeared beside the table. There was a look of infinite strain in her face as she assessed Amanda, then Jordan.

Amanda braced herself, having no idea whether to expect a civil greeting or violent recriminations. "Hello, Mrs. Brockman," she said as Jordan pushed back his chair to stand. "I'd like you to meet Jordan Richards."

"Do sit down," Madge Brockman said when she and Jordan had shaken hands.

Jordan remained standing. "How is your husband?" he asked, knowing Amanda wouldn't dare ask.

"He's recovering," Madge replied with a sigh. "And he's adamant about wanting a divorce."

"I'm sorry," Amanda said softly.

The older woman managed a faulty smile. "I'll get over it, I guess. Well, if you'll excuse me, I'm supposed to meet my attorney, and I see him sitting right over there."

Jordan dropped back into his chair when Mrs. Brockman had walked away. "Are you okay?" he asked.

Amanda pushed her salad away. Even though she'd done

it inadvertently, she was partly responsible for destroying Mrs. Brockman's marriage, and the knowledge was shattering. "No," she answered. "I'm not okay."

"It wasn't your fault, Amanda."

There it was again, that strange clairvoyance of his.

"Yes, it was—part of it, at least. I didn't even bother to ask if James was married. And now look what's happening."

Jordan gave a ragged sigh. Apparently his appetite had fled, too, for he set down his fork and sank back in his chair, one hand to his chin.

"The man's marital status wouldn't have made a difference to a lot of women, you know," he remarked. "For instance, you're the first one I've dated who's asked me whether I was married."

"Okay, so infidelity is widespread. So is cocaine addiction. That doesn't make either of them right."

Jordan raised his eyebrows. "I wasn't saying it did, Mandy. My point is, you're being too damn hard on yourself. So you made a mistake. Welcome to the human race."

Amanda met Jordan's gaze. "Were you faithful to Becky?" she asked, having no idea why it was suddenly so important to know. But it was.

"That's none of your damn business," Jordan retorted politely, making a steeple under his chin with his hands, "but I'll answer, anyway. I was true to my wife, and she was true to me."

Amanda had known, in some corner of her heart, that Jordan was a man of his word, and she believed him. "Were you ever tempted?"

"About a thousand times," he replied. "But there's a difference between thinking about something and doing it, Mandy. Now, do you want to ask me about my bank balance or my tax return? Or maybe how I voted in the last election?"

Amanda smiled. "You've made your point, Mr. Richards. I'm being nosy. But I'm glad you were faithful to Becky."

"So am I," Jordan said, as by tacit agreement they rose to go. "When am I going to see you again, Mandy?"

Amanda held off answering until the bill was paid and they were walking down the sidewalk, wending their way through hordes of Christmas shoppers. "When do you want to see me?"

"As soon as possible."

"You could come to dinner tonight."

"Amanda Scott, you have a silver tongue. I'll bring the wine and the food, so don't cook."

Amanda's smile was born deep inside her, and it took its time reaching her mouth. "Seven?"

"Eight," Jordan said as they stopped in front of the Evergreen Hotel. "I have a meeting, and it might run late."

She stood on tiptoe to kiss him briefly. "I'll be waiting, Mr. Richards."

He grinned as he rubbed a tendril of her hair between his fingers. "Good," he answered.

His voice made Amanda's knees quiver beneath her green suede skirt.

WHEN AMANDA REACHED her desk, there was a message waiting for her. In a flash, work—and Jordan—fled her uppermost thoughts. The hospital had called about James, and the matter was urgent.

Amanda's fingers trembled as she reached for the panel of buttons on her telephone. She punched out the numbers written on the message slip and, when an operator answered, asked for the designated extension.

"Intensive Care," a sunny voice said when the call was put through. "This is Betsy Andrews."

Amanda sank into her desk chair, a terrible headache throbbing beneath her temples. "My name is Amanda Scott," she said in a voice that sounded surprisingly crisp and professional. "I received a message asking me to call about Mr. Brockman."

There was a short silence while the nurse checked her records. "Yes. Mr. Brockman isn't doing very well, Ms. Scott. And he's constantly asking for you."

Amanda closed her eyes and rubbed one temple with her fingertips. She'd broken up with James long ago, and had refused his gifts and his requests for a reconciliation. When was it going to be over? "I see."

"His wife has explained the—er—situation to us," the nurse went on, "but Mr. Brockman still insists on seeing you."

"What is his doctor's recommendation?"

"It was his idea that we call you. We all feel that, well, maybe Mr. Brockman would calm down if he could just have a short visit from you."

Amanda glanced at her watch. Her headache was so intense that the numbers blurred. "I could stop by briefly after work." James had won this round. Under the circumstances, there was no way she could refuse to visit him. "That would be about six o'clock."

Betsy Andrews sounded relieved. "I'll be off duty then, but I'll make a note in the record and tell Mr. Brockman you'll be coming in."

"Thank you," Amanda said with a defeated sigh. Once she'd hung up, she reached for the phone again, planning to call Jordan, but her hand fell back to the desk. She was a grown woman, and this was her problem, not Jordan's.

She couldn't go running to him every time some difficulty came up.

Pulling open her desk drawer, Amanda took out a bottle of aspirin, shook two tablets into her palm and swallowed them with water from the tap in her bathroom. Then she rolled up her sleeves and did her best to concentrate on her work.

At six-fifteen she approached James's door in the Intensive Care Unit, having gotten directions from a nurse.

He was lying in a room banked with flowers. Tubes led into his nose and the veins in both his hands. He seemed to sense Amanda's arrival and turned to look at her.

She approached the bed. "Hello, James," she said.

"You came," he managed, his voice hoarse and broken.

She nodded, unable for the moment to speak. And not knowing what to say.

"I'm going to die," he told her.

Amanda shook her head, her eyes filling with tears. She didn't love James anymore, but she had once, and it was hard to see him suffer. "No."

His eyes half-closed, he pleaded with her, "Just tell me there's a chance for us, and I'll have a reason not to give up."

Amanda started to tell him there was someone else, that there could never be anything between the two of them again, but something stopped her in the last instant. Some instinct that he really meant to die if she didn't give him hope, and she couldn't just abandon him to death. She bit down on her lower lip, then whispered, "All right, James. Maybe we could—start again."

Chapter 8

<hr/>

JORDAN WAS DUE TO ARRIVE a little more than twenty minutes after Amanda reached her apartment. Gershwin was hungry and petulant, and the boxes containing the fur jacket and the skimpy bikini James had sent were still sitting on the hallway table. Amanda had intended to return them to the department store and ask the clerk to credit James's account, but she hadn't gotten around to it.

Now, without stopping to analyze her motives—certainly she meant to tell Jordan about her promise to James—she stuffed the boxes into the back of her bedroom closet and hastily changed into a silky beige jumpsuit. She had just misted herself with cologne, when the door buzzer sounded.

After drawing a deep breath to steady herself, Amanda dashed through the apartment and opened the door. Jordan was standing in the hallway, a tired grin on his face, a bottle of wine and several bags from a Chinese take-out place in his arms.

Looking at him, Amanda thought of how it would be to have him walk out of her life forever, and promptly lost her courage. She told herself it wasn't the right time to tell him about James.

Smiling shakily, she took the wine and fragrant bags from him and stood on tiptoe to kiss his cheek.

He shrugged out of his overcoat and hung it on the coat tree while Amanda carried the food to the table. She hadn't put out place settings yet, so she hurried back to the kitchenette for plates, silverware, wineglasses and a cork screw.

Jordan looked at her strangely when she returned. "Is something wrong, Mandy?"

Amanda swallowed. *Tell him,* ordered the voice of reason. *Just come right out and tell him you're planning to visit James in the hospital until he's out of danger.* "Wr-wrong?" she echoed.

"You seem nervous."

Amanda imagined the scenario: herself telling Jordan that she meant to pretend she was still in love with James just until he was stronger, Jordan saying the idea was stupid, getting angry, walking out. Maybe forever. "I'm okay," she lied.

Jordan popped the cork on the wine bottle. "If you say so," he said with a sigh, and they both sat down at the table to consume prawns, fried noodles and chow mein. Their conversation, usually so free and easy, was guarded.

When they were through with dinner, Jordan made Amanda stay at the table, nursing a second glass of wine, while he cleared away the debris of their meal. Returning, he put gentle hands on Amanda's shoulders and began massaging her tense muscles.

"Will you stay tonight?" she asked, holding her breath after the words were out. She needed Jordan desperately, but at the same time she knew guilt would prevent her from enjoying their lovemaking.

Jordan sighed. "You've been through a lot lately, Mandy. I think it would be better if we let things cool off a little."

She turned to look up at him with worried eyes. "Is this the brush-off, Mr. Richards?"

He smiled and bent to kiss her forehead. "No. I just think you need some extra rest." With that, he turned and crossed the room to the entryway. He reached for his overcoat and put it on.

Amanda stood up quickly and went to him. Even though Jordan didn't know what was going on, he sensed something, and he was already distancing himself from her. She had to tell him. "Jordan—"

He interrupted her with a kiss. "Good night, Mandy. I'll talk to you tomorrow."

Amanda tried to call out to him, but the words stopped in her throat. In the end she simply closed the door, locked it and stood there leaning against the panel, wondering how she'd gotten herself into such a mess.

TRUE TO HIS word, Jordan called her the next morning at work, but their conversation was brief because he was busy and so was Amanda. She threw her mind into her job in order to distract herself from the fact that she had, in effect, lied to him. And a chilling instinct told her that deceit was one thing Jordan wouldn't tolerate.

At six-thirty that evening, Amanda walked into James's room in Intensive Care, after first making sure Madge wasn't there. She was wearing jeans and a sweater, and was carrying a bouquet of flowers from the gift shop downstairs.

He smiled thinly when he saw her and extended one hand. "Hello, Amanda."

She took his hand and bent to kiss his forehead. "Hi. How are you feeling today?"

"They're moving me out of the ICU tomorrow," he answered.

But he looked very sick to Amanda. He was gaunt, and his skin still had a ghastly pallor to it.

"That's good."

"You look wonderful."

Amanda averted her eyes for a moment, feeling like a highly paid call girl. What she was doing was all wrong, but how could she turn her back on another human being, allowing him to give up and die? That would be heartless. "Thanks."

James's grip on her hand was remarkably firm. "You're better off without that Richards character," he confided. "He might have made his mark in the business world, but he's really nothing more than an overgrown kid. Killed his own wife with his recklessness, you know."

Amanda was willing to go only so far with this charade, and listening to James bad-mouth Jordan was beyond the boundary. Somewhat abruptly she changed the subject. "Is there anything you'd like me to bring you? Magazines or books?"

He shook his head. "All I want is to know I'm going to get well and see you wear—and not wear—that blue bikini."

Feeling slightly ill, Amanda nonetheless managed a smile. "You shouldn't be thinking thoughts like that," she scolded. She had to get out of that room or soon she'd be smothered. "Listen, the nurses made me promise not to stay too long, so I'm going now. But I'll be back after work tomorrow."

When she would have walked away, James held her fast by the hand. "I want a kiss first," he said, a shrewd expression in his eyes.

Amanda shook her head, unable to grant his request.

She smiled brittlely and said in a too-bright voice, "You're too ill for that." Ignoring his obvious disappointment, she squeezed his hand once and then dashed out of the room, calling a hasty farewell over her shoulder.

Only when Amanda was outside in the crisp December air was she able to breathe properly again. She went home, flung her coat onto the couch and took a long, scalding hot shower. No matter how she tried, though, she couldn't wash away the awful feeling that she was selling herself.

In an effort to escape, Amanda telephoned the real estate agency on Vashon Island the next morning to see if the Victorian house had been sold. It hadn't, and even though she had no means of buying it herself, the news lifted her flagging spirits.

She visited James that night, and the next, and he seemed to be improving steadily. He told her repeatedly that she was his only reason for holding on.

By Friday, when Eunice was due to arrive, Amanda was practically a wreck. She had been avoiding Jordan's calls for several days, and she could barely concentrate on her job.

Marion noticed her elder daughter's general dishevelment when they met at the airport in front of the gate assigned to Eunice's flight. "What on earth is the matter with you?" she demanded. "You have bags under your eyes and you must have lost five pounds since I saw you last week!"

Amanda would have given anything to be able to confide in her mother, but she didn't want to spoil Eunice's homecoming—her sister would need all of Marion's and Bob's support. She shrugged and managed a halfhearted smile. "You know how it is. Falling in love takes a lot out of a person."

Marion's gaze was slightly narrowed and alarmingly shrewd. "You're not fooling me, you know," she said. "But just because I don't have time to drag it out of you now doesn't mean I won't."

Bob was just returning from parking the car, and he smiled and gave Amanda a hug. "You're looking a little peaky," he pointed out good-naturedly.

"She's up to something," Marion informed him just before the passengers from Eunice's flight began pouring out of the gate.

Amanda was the first to reach her brown-eyed, dark-haired sister, and they embraced. Tears stung both their eyes.

After the usual hassles of getting the luggage from the baggage carousel and fighting the traffic out of the airport, they drove back to the family home. Eunice chattered the whole time about how glad she was to be in Seattle again, how miserable she'd been in California, how she wished she'd never met Jim, let alone married him. By the time they reached the quiet residential area where Bob and Marion lived, Eunice had exhausted herself.

She stumbled into the room she and Amanda had once shared and collapsed on one of the twin beds.

Amanda took a seat on the other one. "I'm glad you're back," she said.

Her sister sat up on the bed and began unbuttoning her coat. "I didn't exactly return in triumph, like I thought I would," Eunice observed sadly. "Oh, Amanda, my life is a disaster area."

"I know what you mean," Amanda answered sadly, thinking of the deception she hadn't had the courage to straighten out.

Eunice yawned. "Maybe tomorrow we can put our heads together and figure out how to get ourselves back on track."

With a smile, Amanda opened her sister's suitcase and

found a nightgown for her. "Here," she said, tossing the billow of pink chiffon into Eunice's lap. "Get some sleep."

When Eunice had disappeared into the adjoining bathroom, Amanda returned to the kitchen. Her mother was sitting at the table, sipping decaffeinated coffee, and Bob was in the living room, listening to the news.

"How's Eunice?" Marion asked.

Amanda wedged her hands into the front pockets of her worn brown corduroy pants. "She'll be okay once she gets a perspective on things."

"And what about you?"

"I'm in a fix, Mom," Amanda admitted, staring at the darkened window over the kitchen sink. "And I don't know how to get out of it."

Marion went to the counter, poured a cup of coffee from the percolator and brought it back to the table for Amanda. "Sit down and tell me about it."

Amanda sank into the chair. "Some very good things have been happening between Jordan and me," she said, closing her fingers around the cup to warm them. "I never thought I'd meet anybody like him."

Marion smiled. "I feel the same way about Bob."

Amanda touched her mother's hand fondly. "I know."

"So what's the problem?"

"About a week ago," Amanda began reluctantly, "someone from the hospital called and said James was asking for me. He was in the ICU at the time, so I didn't feel I could ignore the whole thing. I went to see him, and while I was there, he told me he'd given up, that he was going to die."

Marion's lips thinned in irritation, but she seemed to know how hard it was for Amanda to keep up her momentum, so she didn't interrupt.

"Essentially, he said I was the only reason he had to go on living, and if I didn't want him, he was just going to give up. So I've been visiting him and pretending we'll be getting back together again once he's well."

Marion sighed heavily. "Amanda."

"I know it sounds crazy, but I feel guilty enough without being the reason somebody died!"

Marion reached out and covered Amanda's hand with her own. "I suppose you haven't told Jordan any of this."

"I'm afraid to. Maybe it would have been all right if I'd mentioned it that very first night after I spoke to James, when Jordan and I were together for dinner, but I couldn't bring myself to do it. I was too afraid he'd make me choose between him and James."

"I didn't think there was any question of a choice," Marion said. "You're in love with Jordan Richards, whether you know it or not."

Amanda bit her lower lip for a moment. "I guess I am."

"Tell him the truth, Amanda," Marion urged. "Don't put it off for another second. March right over to that phone and call him."

"I can't," Amanda said with a shake of her head. "It's not something I can say over the telephone, and besides, his little girls will be there. This is their first night together, and I don't want to spoil it."

"You're going to regret it if you don't straighten this out," Marion warned.

"I think it might already be too late," Amanda said brokenly, and then she rose from her chair, emptied her coffee into the sink and set the cup down. "You just concentrate on Eunice, Mom, and don't worry about me."

Marion shook her head as she got up to see her daughter to the door. "Talk to Jordan," she insisted as Amanda put on her coat and wrapped a colorful knitted scarf around her neck.

Amanda nodded and hurried through the cold night to her car.

The light on her answering machine was blinking when she arrived home, and after brewing herself a cup of tea, she pushed the Play button and sat down at the little table in her living room to listen.

The first call was from James. He'd missed her that night and hoped she'd come to visit in the morning.

Amanda closed her eyes against the prospect, though she knew she would have to do as he asked. Maybe if she used Eunice's visit as an excuse, she could get away after only a half hour or so.

The next message nearly made her spill her tea. "This is Madge Brockman," an angry female voice said, "and I just wanted to tell you that you're not going to get away with this. You took my husband, and I'm going to take something from you." After those bitter words, the woman had hung up with a crash.

Amanda was struggling to compose herself, when yet another voice came on. "Mandy, this is Jordan. I've survived supper, and the kids' baths and story time. I have a new respect for mothers. Call me, will you?" There was a click, and then the machine rewound itself.

Despite the fact that Madge Brockman's call had shaken her to her soul, Amanda reached for the phone and dialed Jordan's number at the island house.

He answered on the second ring.

"Hi, Jordan. It's Amanda."

"Thank God," he replied with a lilt to his voice.

"How are the girls?" She dabbed at her eyes with her sleeve and resisted an impulse to sniffle.

"They're fine. Mandy, are you all right?"

"I—I need to see you. Could I c-come out there?"

Jordan hesitated, then said, "Sure. If you hurry, you can still make the last ferry. Mandy—"

"I'll be there as soon as I can," Amanda broke in, and then she hung up the phone and dashed into her bedroom. She pulled her suitcase out from under the bed and tossed in two pairs of jeans, two sets of clean underwear and two sweaters. Then, after snatching up her toothbrush and makeup bag, she made sure Gershwin had plenty of food and water and hurried out of the apartment.

Several times on the way to West Seattle Amanda's eyes were so full of tears that she nearly had to pull over to the side of the road. But finally she drove on board the ferry and parked.

Safe in the bottom of the enormous boat, she let her forehead rest against the steering wheel and sobbed.

By the time she'd reached Vashon Island and driven to Jordan's house, however, she was beginning to feel a little foolish. She wasn't a child, she told herself sternly, and she couldn't expect Jordan to solve her problems. She might have backed out of the driveway and raced back to the ferry dock if Jordan hadn't come outside to greet her.

He was wearing sneakers, jeans and a Seahawks sweatshirt, and he looked so good to Amanda that she nearly burst into tears again.

Without a word, he opened the door and helped her out, then fetched her suitcase and overnighter from the backseat. Amanda preceded him into the house, wondering what she was going to say.

There was a fire snapping on the hearth, and after setting her luggage down in the entryway, Jordan helped Amanda out of her coat. "Sit down and I'll get you some brandy," he said hoarsely after kissing her on the cheek.

Amanda took a seat on the raised stone hearth of the

fireplace, hoping the warmth would take the numb chill out of her soul.

When Jordan sat down next to her and handed her a crystal snifter with brandy glowing golden in the bottom, her heart turned over. She knew she'd waited too long to explain things; she was going to lose him.

"Talk to me, Mandy," he said when she was silent, studying him with miserable eyes.

"I can't," she replied, setting the brandy aside untouched. "Will you just hold me, Jordan? Just for a few minutes?"

Gently he pulled her into his arms and pressed her head to his shoulder. He moved his hand soothingly up and down her back, but he didn't ask any questions or make any demands, and Amanda loved him more than ever for that.

Amanda had just about worked up her courage to tell him about her promise to James, when a small, curious voice asked, "Who's that, Daddy?"

Amanda started in Jordan's arms, but he held her fast. She turned her head and saw a little dark-haired girl standing a few feet away. She was wearing a pink quilted robe and tiny fluffy slippers to match.

"This is Amanda, Jess. Amanda, my daughter, Jessica."

"Hi," Amanda managed.

"How come you're hugging her?" Jessica wanted to know. "Did she fall down and hurt herself?"

"Sort of," Jordan answered. "Why don't you go back to bed now, honey? You can get to know Amanda better in the morning."

Jessica's smile was so like Becky's that Amanda was shaken by it. "Okay. Good night, Daddy. Good night, Amanda."

When the little girl was gone, Amanda sat there in Jordan's arms, sorely wishing she hadn't intruded. She didn't belong here.

"I shouldn't have come," she said, bolting to her feet.

Jordan pulled her back so that she landed on his lap. "You've missed the last ferry, Mandy," he pointed out. "Besides, I'm not letting you go anywhere in the shape you're in."

Amanda swallowed hard. "I can't sleep with you—not with your daughters in the house."

"I understand that," Jordan replied. "I have a guest room."

Why did he have to be so damned reasonable? Amanda fretted. She didn't deserve his patience or his kindness. "Okay," she said lamely, reaching for her brandy and downing the whole thing practically in one gulp. Maybe that would give her the courage to say what she needed to say.

But it only made her woozy and very nauseous. Jordan lifted her into his arms and carried her to the guest room, where he undressed her like a weary child, put her into one of his pajama tops because she'd forgotten to bring a nightgown and tucked her in.

"Jordan, I made a terrible mistake."

He kissed her forehead. "We'll talk tomorrow," he said. "Go to sleep."

Exhaustion immediately conquered Amanda, and when she awakened, it was morning. Jordan had brought her things to her room. There was a small bathroom adjoining, so she showered, brushed her teeth and put on make-up. When she arrived in the kitchen, wearing jeans and a blue sweater, she felt a hundred percent better than she had the night before.

Jordan was making pancakes on an electric griddle and cooking bacon in the microwave, while his daughters sat at the table, drinking their orange juice and watching him with amusing consternation. While Jessica resembled Becky, the smaller child, Lisa, looked like Jordan. She had his maple-brown hair and hazel eyes, and she smiled broadly when she saw Amanda.

Again, despite her improved mood, Amanda felt like an imposter shoving herself in where she didn't belong. She would have fled to her car if she hadn't known it would only compound her problems.

"Hungry?" Jordan asked, his eyes gentle as he studied Amanda's face.

She nodded, and, seeing that there were four places set at the table, took a chair beside Lisa.

"That's Daddy's chair," Jessica pointed out.

Amanda started to move, but Jordan slapped his hand down on her shoulder and pushed her back.

"It doesn't matter where Amanda sits," he said.

Jessica didn't take offense at the correction, and Amanda reached for the orange juice carton with a trembling hand. She was more than ready to tell Jordan the truth now, but it didn't look as though she was going to get the opportunity. After all, she couldn't just drop an emotional bombshell in front of his daughters.

Jordan's cooking was good, and Amanda managed to put away three pancakes and a couple of strips of bacon even though she couldn't remember the last time she'd been so nervous.

"I think it's about time we decorated that Christmas tree, don't you?" Jordan asked when the meal was over.

The girls gave a rousing cheer and bounded out of their chairs and into the living room.

"You'll have to get dressed first," Jordan called after them. Despite his lack of experience, he seemed to be picking up the fundamentals of active fatherhood rather easily.

"Lisa can't tie her shoes," Jessica confided from the kitchen doorway.

"Then you can do it for her," Jordan replied, beginning to clear the table.

Amanda insisted on helping, and the moment Jordan heard the kids' feet pounding up the stairway, he took her into his arms and gave her a thorough kiss. She melted against him, overpowered, as always, by his strange magic.

"It's very good to have you here, lady," he said in a rumbling whisper. "I just wish I could take you upstairs and spend about two hours making love to you."

Amanda shivered at the prospect. She wished that, too, with all her heart, but once she told Jordan about her visits to James's hospital room and her pretense of rekindling their affair, he probably wouldn't ever want to touch her again.

The idea of never lying in Jordan's arms another night, never feeling the weight of his body or going crazy under the touch of his hands or his mouth, made a hard lump form in her throat.

"Still not ready to talk?" he asked, touching the tip of her nose with a gentle finger.

Amanda shook her head.

"There's time," Jordan said, and he kissed her again, making her throw her arms around his neck in an instinctive plea for more.

"Daddy!" a little voice shouted from upstairs. "I can't find my red shoes!"

Amanda pushed away from Jordan as though he'd struck her, and lifted the back of one hand to her mouth when he turned away to go and help his daughter.

While he was gone, Amanda's bravery completely deserted her. She found her purse and dashed for her car, leaving her luggage behind in Jordan's guest room. He ran outside just as she pulled out of the driveway, but Amanda didn't stop. She put her foot down hard on the accelerator and drove away.

A glance at her watch told her the ferry wouldn't leave for another twenty minutes, and Amanda was half-afraid Jordan would toss the kids in the car and come chasing after her. Since she couldn't face him, she drove to the café where they'd eaten on a couple of occasions.

After parking her car behind a delivery truck, Amanda went into the restaurant, took a chair as far from the front door as she could and hid behind her menu until Wanda arrived.

"Well, hello there," the pleasant woman boomed. "Where's Jordan?"

"He's—busy. Could I get a cup of coffee?"

Wanda arched one artfully plucked eyebrow, but she didn't ask any more questions. She just brought a cup to Amanda's table and filled it from the pot in her other hand.

"Thanks," Amanda said, wishing she didn't have to give up the menu.

Jordan didn't show up, and Amanda was half disappointed and half relieved. She finished her coffee and went back to the ferry terminal just in time to board the boat.

Because she hoped there would be a message on the answering machine from Jordan and feared there would not, she went to the hospital first, instead of her apartment.

"You're late," James fussed when she walked into his room.

"I'm sorry—" Amanda began.

She'd forgotten what a master James was of the quicksilver change, and the brightness of his smile stunned her. "That's okay," he said generously. "I'm just glad you're here."

Amanda lowered her eyes. She would have given anything to be with Jordan and his children at that moment, helping to decorate the Christmas tree or even listening to a lecture. She regretted giving in to her impulse and running away. "Me, too," she lied.

"Tell me you love me," James said.

Amanda's heart stopped beating. She would have choked on the words if she'd tried to utter them.

For better or worse, Madge Brockman spared her the trouble. "Isn't this sweet?" she asked, sweeping like a storm into the room in a black full-length mink with a matching hat. Her eyes, full of poison, swung to Amanda. "To think I believed you when you said you and James were through."

"Amanda and I are going to be married," James protested, and he raised one hand to his chest.

Amanda was terrified.

"You idiot," Madge growled at him, gesturing wildly with one mink-swathed arm. "She's two-timing you with Jordan Richards!"

"That's a lie!" James shouted.

A nurse burst into the room. "Mr. Brockman, you must be calm!"

Terrified, Amanda backed blindly out into the hallway and ran to the elevator. It seemed to be her day for running away, she thought to herself as she got into her car and sped out of the parking lot.

For a time she just drove around Seattle, following an aimless path, trying to gather her composure. She considered visiting her mother, or one of her friends, but she couldn't, because she knew she'd break down and cry if she tried to explain things to anyone.

Finally Amanda drove back to her apartment building and went in through the rear entrance.

In the bathroom she splashed cold water on her face,

washing away the tearstains, but her eyes were still puffy afterward, and her nose was an unglamorous red. It was no real surprise when the door buzzer sounded.

"Jordan or the tiger?" she asked herself with a sort of wounded fancy as she made her way determinedly across the living room and reached for the doorknob.

Chapter 9

⟨∘⟩∘⟨∘⟩

JORDAN STOOD IN THE HALLWAY, holding Amanda's suitcase. He was alone, and his expression was quietly contemptuous.

For the moment Amanda couldn't speak, so she stepped back to let him pass. He set the luggage down with a clatter just inside the entryway and jammed his hands into the pockets of his leather jacket.

"Why the hell did you run off like that?" he demanded.

For a second or so, Amanda swung wildly between relief and dread. She turned away from Jordan, walked to the sofa and sank onto it. "You haven't had a call from Mrs. Brockman?" she asked in a small voice.

Without bothering to take off his jacket—he obviously didn't intend to stay long—Jordan perched on the arm of an easy chair. "James's wife? Why would she call me?"

Amanda swallowed. "I've been visiting James in the hospital," she blurted out. "I told him we could t-take up where we left off."

The color drained from Jordan's face. "What?"

"He said he was going to give up and die—that I was

all he had to live for. So I decided to pretend I still loved him, just until he was strong enough to go on his own."

"And you believed that?" His voice was low, lethal.

"Of course I believed it!" Amanda flared.

"Well, you've been had," Jordan replied coldly.

Amanda stared at him, wounded, her worst suspicions confirmed. "I knew you wouldn't understand, Jordan," she said. "That's why I was afraid to tell you."

"Damn it," he rasped, "don't make excuses. A lie is a lie, Amanda, and there's no room in my life for games like this!"

"It wasn't a game! You didn't see him, hear him…"

Jordan was on his feet again, his hands back in his pockets. "I didn't have to." He walked to the door and stood there for a moment with his back to Amanda. "I could understand your wanting to help," he said in parting. "But I'll never understand why you didn't tell me about it." With that, he opened the door and walked out.

Amanda jumped off the couch and raced to the entryway—she couldn't lose him, she *couldn't*—but at the door she stopped. Jordan had judged her and found her guilty, and he wasn't going to change his mind.

It was over.

Slowly Amanda closed the door. With a concerned meow, Gershwin circled her ankles. "He's gone," she said to the cat, and then she went into the bedroom, found the fur jacket and the skimpy bikini, and returned to her car.

With every mile she drove, Amanda became more certain that Jordan had been right: James had used emotional blackmail to get her to come back to him. She could see now that he'd given a performance every time she'd visited his room; she recalled the shrewd expression in his eyes, the things he'd said about Jordan.

"Fool!" Amanda muttered to herself, flipping on her windshield wipers as a light rain began to fall.

When she reached the hospital, Amanda marched inside, carrying the fur coat over her arm and the bikini in her purse. Some of her resolution faded as she got into the elevator, though. James had a serious heart condition, and for a time he'd been in real danger. Suppose what she meant to say caused him to suffer another attack? Suppose he died and it was her fault?

Amanda approached James's room reluctantly, then stopped when she heard him laughing. "Face it, Richards," he said. "You lose. In another week or two I'll be out of this place. And believe me, Amanda will be more than happy to fly off to Hawaii with me and make sure I recuperate properly."

Her first instinct was to flee, but Amanda couldn't move. She stood frozen in the hallway, resting one hand against the wall.

Jordan said something in response, but Amanda didn't hear what it was—maybe because the thundering of her heart drowned it out.

The scraping of a chair broke Amanda's spell, and she didn't know whether to stay and face Jordan or dodge into the little nook across the hall where a coffee machine stood. In the end she decided she'd done enough running away for a lifetime, and stayed where she was.

When Jordan walked out of James's room, he stopped cold for a moment, but then a weary expression of resignation came over his face.

"I'm going to tell him the truth," she said, her voice hardly more than a whisper.

Jordan shrugged. "It's a little late for that, isn't it?" His eyes dropped to the rich sable jacket draped over her arm. "Merry Christmas, Amanda."

Amanda saw all her hopes going down the drain, and something inside drove her to fight to save them. "Jordan, be reasonable. You know I never meant for things to turn out this way!"

He looked at her for a moment, then walked around her, as he would something objectionable lying on the sidewalk, and strode off down the hall.

Amanda watched him go into the elevator. He looked straight through her as the doors closed.

It was a few moments before she could bring herself to walk into James's room and face him. She no longer feared that her news would cause him another heart attack; now it was her anger she struggled to control.

Finally she was able to force herself through the doorway. She laid the coat at the foot of James's bed without meeting his eyes, then took the bikini from her purse and put it with the coat. When she thought she could manage it without hysterics, she turned to him and said, "You had no right to manipulate me that way."

"Amanda." His voice was a scolding drawl, and he stretched out his hand to her.

She evaded his grasp. "It's over, James. I can't see you anymore."

Surprisingly James smiled at her and let his hand fall to his side. "You might as well come back to me, baby. It's plain enough that Richards is through with you."

Hot rage made Amanda's backbone ramrod straight, but she didn't allow her anger to erupt in a flow of nasty retorts. Clinging to the last of her dignity, she whispered, "Maybe the time I had with Jordan will have to last me a lifetime. But he's the only man I'll ever love." With that, she turned and walked out.

"You'll be back!" James shouted after her. "You'll come

begging for my forgiveness! Damn it, Amanda, nobody walks out on me...."

While a nurse rushed into James's room, Amanda went straight on until she got to the elevator. She pushed the button and waited circumspectly for a ride to the main floor, even though her emotions were howling in her spirit like a storm. She wanted to be anywhere but there, anybody besides herself.

She'd hoped Jordan might be lingering somewhere downstairs, or maybe in her section of the parking lot, but there was no sign of him.

Beyond tears, she climbed behind the wheel of her car and started toward the house where she and Eunice had grown up.

She knocked at the door and called out "It's me!" and her mother instantly replied with a cheerful "Come in!"

Bob, it turned out, was putting in some overtime at the aircraft plant where he worked, but Marion and Eunice were wrapping festive presents on the dining room table. Eunice looked a little tired, but other than that she seemed to be in good spirits. Marion was taking her usual delight in the yuletide season, but her face fell when she got a look at her elder daughter.

"Merciful heavens," she sputtered, rushing over and forcing Amanda into a chair. "You're as pale as Marley's ghost! What on earth is the matter?"

Just minutes before, Amanda had been convinced she had no tears left to cry, but now a despondent wail escaped her and tears streamed down her face.

Eunice immediately rushed to her side. "Sis, what is it?" she whispered, near tears herself. She had always cried whenever Amanda did, even if she didn't know what was bothering her sister.

"It's Jordan!" Amanda sobbed. "He's gone—he never wants to see me again...."

"Get her a glass of water," Marion said to Eunice. She rested her hands on Amanda's shoulders, much as Jordan once had, trying to soothe away the terrible tension.

Eunice reappeared moments later, looking stricken, a glass of water in one hand.

"You told him," Marion said as Amanda sipped the cold water.

Eunice dragged up a chair beside her. "Told him what?"

Setting the water down with a thump, Amanda blurted out the whole story—how she'd fallen hopelessly in love with Jordan, how James had hoodwinked her into ruining everything. She ended with an account of the scene in James's hospital room when she'd given back his gifts once and for all.

"What kind of lunkhead is this Jordan," Eunice demanded, "that he doesn't understand something so simple?"

Amanda dragged her sleeve across her eyes, feeling like a five-year-old with both knees skinned raw. Only it was her heart that was hurting. "He's angry because I didn't tell him about it from the first." She paused to sniffle, and her mother produced a handful of tissues in that magical way mothers have. "I tried, I honestly did, but I was so scared of losing him."

"Men," muttered Eunice. "Who needs them?"

"I do," chorused Amanda and Marion. And at that, all three women laughed.

Eunice patted Amanda's shoulder. "Don't worry. After he thinks about it for a while, he'll forgive you."

Amanda shook her head, dabbing at her puffy eyes with a wad of damp tissue. "You don't know Jordan. He's probably never told a lie in his life. He just flat out doesn't understand deception."

"Maybe he's never lied," Marion said briskly, "but he's made mistakes, just like the rest of us. When he calms down, Amanda, he'll call."

Amanda prayed her mother was right, but the hollow feeling in the center of her heart made that seem unlikely.

An hour later, when Amanda announced that she was going home, Eunice grabbed her coat and insisted on riding along. She'd make supper, she said, and the two of them could just hang around the way they had in high school.

"I wasn't planning to stick my head in the oven or anything, if that's what you're worried about," Amanda said with a sad smile as she backed her car out of her parents' driveway.

Eunice grinned. "And singe those gorgeous, golden tresses? I should hope not."

Amanda laughed at the image. "You know what, kid? It's good to have you back."

Her younger sister patted her arm. "I'll be around awhile, I think," she replied. "There's an opening for a computer programmer at the university. I have an interview the day after Christmas."

"There's really no hope of getting back together with Jim, then?" Amanda asked as they wended their way through rainy streets, the windshield wipers beating out a rhythmic accompaniment to their conversation.

Eunice shook her head. "Not when there's somebody else involved," she said.

Amanda nodded. Just the idea of Jordan seeing another woman was more than she could tolerate, even with the relationship in ruins.

After parking the car, Amanda and Eunice dashed through the rain to the store on the corner and bought popcorn, a log for the fireplace, a pound of fresh shrimp and the makings for a salad.

Back at Amanda's apartment, Eunice prepared and cooked the succulent shrimp while Amanda washed and cut up the vegetables.

"You don't even have a Christmas tree," Eunice complained later when she was kneeling on the hearth, lighting the paper-wrapped log.

Amanda shrugged. "I was just planning to skip the whole holiday," she said.

"Knowing Jordan didn't change that?"

"When I was with him, he was all I thought about," Amanda explained. "Same thing when I wasn't with him."

Eunice grinned and got to her feet, dusting her hands off on the legs of her jeans as if she'd just carried wood in from the wilderness like a pioneer. "You could always throw yourself at his feet and beg for forgiveness."

Amanda lifted her chin stubbornly and went to the living room window. "I explained everything to him, and he wouldn't listen."

Rain pattered at the glass and made the people on the sidewalks below hurry along under their colorful umbrellas. Amanda wondered how many of them were happy and how many had broken hearts.

"You shouldn't give up if you really care about the guy," Eunice said softly.

Amanda sighed. "I didn't give up, Eunice," she said. "He did."

At that, the two sisters dropped the subject of Jordan and talked about other Christmases.

JORDAN HAD HIS own reasons for welcoming the rain, and after he drove on board the ferry to Vashon Island, he stayed in the car, staring bleakly at the empty van ahead of him. He felt hollow and numb, as though all his vitals had shriveled up and disappeared, but he knew the pain would come eventually, and he dreaded it.

After losing Becky, Jordan had made up his mind never to really care about another woman again. That way, he'd reasoned in his naïveté, he'd never have to suffer the way he had after his wife's death.

The trouble was, he'd reckoned without Amanda Scott.

He'd fallen hard for her without ever really being aware of what was happening. Had he told her that he loved her? He couldn't remember.

Maybe things would have been different if he had.

Jordan shook his head. He was being stupid. Telling her he cared wouldn't have prevented her from deceiving him. He drifted into a restless sleep, haunted by dreams of things that might have been, and when the ferry's horn blasted, he was startled. He hadn't been aware of the passing time.

Once the boat docked and his turn came, Jordan drove down the ramp, just as he had a million times before. Rain danced on the pavement, and wet gulls hid out beneath the picnic tables in the park he passed. The world was the same, and yet it was different.

He was alone again.

When he entered the kitchen through the garage door minutes later, he heard the stereo blasting. Taking off his jacket and running a hand through his rumpled hair, he went into the living room.

Jessie and Lisa had dragged their presents out from under the mammoth Christmas tree he and Amanda had chosen together, and piled them up in two teetering stacks. The babysitter, a teenage girl from down the road, was curled up on the couch, chattering into the telephone receiver.

Sighting Jordan, his daughters flung themselves at him with shrieks of glee, and he lifted one in each arm, making the growling sound they loved and pretending to be bent on chewing off their ears.

The babysitter, a plain little thing with thick glasses, hung up the telephone and tiptoed over to the stereo to turn it off.

Jordan let the girls down to the floor, took out his wallet and paid the sitter. The moment she was gone, Jessie folded her arms and announced, "Lisa has more presents than I do."

Jordan pretended to be horrified. "No!"

"Count them for yourself," Jessie challenged.

He knelt and began to count. The red-and-silver striped package on the top of Lisa's stack turned out to be the culprit. "This one is for both of you," Jordan said, tapping at the gift tag with his finger. "See? It says 'Lisa *and* Jessie.'"

Jessie examined the tag studiously and was then satisfied that it was still a just world. "Where did Amanda go?" she asked, looking at him with Becky's eyes. "Why did she run away?"

Jordan had no idea how to explain Amanda's abrupt disappearance. He still didn't understand it completely himself. "She's at her apartment, I guess," he finally answered.

"But why did she runned away?" Lisa asked, rubbing her eye with the back of one dimpled hand.

"She probably went to heaven, like Mommy," Jessie said importantly.

Her innocent words went through Jordan like a lance. Young as they were, these kids were developing a strategy for being left—Mommy went to heaven; Daddy doesn't have time for us; Amanda was just passing through.

Jordan kissed both his girls resoundingly on the forehead. "Amanda's not in heaven," he said, sounding hoarse even to himself. "She's in Seattle. Now put these presents back under the tree before Santa finds out you've been messing around with them and fills your stockings with clam shells."

The telephone rang just as Jordan was rising to his feet, but he didn't lunge for it, even though that was his first instinct. He answered in a leisurely, offhand way, but his heart was pounding.

"Hi, little brother. It's Karen," his sister said warmly. "How are the monkeys getting along?"

Jordan forced himself to chuckle; he felt like weeping with disappointment. So it wasn't Amanda. What would he have said to her if it had been? "Do they always pile their presents in the middle of the living room?" he countered, trying to sound lighthearted.

Karen laughed. "No, that's a new one," she said. "How are you doing, Jord?"

He ran a hand through his hair. "Me? I'm doing great." *For somebody who's just had his insides torn out, that is.*

"No problems with memories?"

Jordan sighed and watched his children as they put their colorful gifts back underneath the tree. It seemed hard to believe there had ever been a time when he found it difficult even to look at them because they reminded him so much of Becky. "I guess I'm over that," he said huskily.

"Sounds to me like things are a little rocky."

Karen had always been perceptive. "It's something else," he said. The pain he'd been expecting was just starting to set in. "Listen, Karen, you and Paul and I have to have a talk about the girls. I want to spend more time with them."

"Took you long enough," Karen responded, her voice gentle.

Jordan remembered how she'd helped him through those dark days after Becky had died; she'd been there for him while he was in the hospital, and later, too. If she'd been in his living room instead of miles away on the peninsula, he'd have told her about Amanda.

"Better late than never," he finally replied.

"Paul and I will be down on Christmas Eve, as planned," Karen went on, probably sensing that Jordan wasn't going to confide anything important over the phone. "Save some room under that tree, because we're bringing a carload of loot, and Becky's parents will send boxes of stuff."

Jordan chuckled and shook his head. "Just what they need," he said, watching the greedy munchkins playing tug-of-war with a box wrapped in shiny blue paper. "See you Christmas Eve, sis."

Karen said a few more words, then hung up.

"I'm hungry," said Lisa as a stain spread slowly through the fabric of her plaid jeans.

"She peed her pants," Jessie pointed out quite unnecessarily.

With a grin, Jordan swept his younger daughter up in his arms and carried her off to the bathroom.

'TWAS THE NIGHT before Christmas, and Amanda Scott was feeling sorry for herself. She sat with her feet up in front of the fire while her mother, stepfather and sister bundled up to go to the midnight service at church.

"No fair peeking in the stockings while we're gone," said Bob with a smile and a shake of his finger.

Marion and Eunice were less understanding. They both looked as though they wanted to shake her.

"Moping around this house won't change anything," Marion scolded.

"Yeah," Eunice agreed, gesturing. "Put on your coat and come with us."

"I'm wearing jeans and a sweatshirt, in case you haven't noticed," Amanda pointed out archly. Bob had on his best suit, and Marion and Eunice were both in new dresses.

"Nobody's going to notice," Marion fussed, and she looked so hopeful that Amanda would change her mind that Amanda relented and pushed herself out of the chair.

Soon, she was settled beside Eunice in the backseat of her parents' car. It was so much like the old days that for a while Amanda was able to pretend her life wasn't in ruins.

"Maybe a little angel will whisper in Jordan's ear and he'll call you," Eunice said in a low voice as Marion and Bob sang carols exuberantly in the front seat.

Amanda gave her sister a look. "And maybe Saint Nicholas will land on our roof tonight in a sleigh drawn by eight tiny reindeer."

"Okay, then," Eunice responded, bristling, "why don't you call him?"

The truth was that Amanda had dialed Jordan's number a hundred times since they'd parted. Once she'd even waited to hear him say hello before hanging up. "Gee, why don't I?" she retorted. "Or better yet, I could plunge head-first off an overpass. I just *love* pain."

Eunice folded her arms. "Don't be such a poop, Amanda. I'm only trying to help."

"It isn't working," Amanda responded, turning her head to look out at the festive lights trimming roofs and windows and shrubbery.

The church service was soothing, as family traditions often are, and Amanda was feeling a little better when they drove back home. They all sat around the tree, sipping eggnog and listening to carols, and when Bob and

Marion finally retired for the night, Eunice dug a package out from under a mountain of gifts and extended it.

Amanda accepted the present, but refused to open it until she had found her gift to Eunice. It was another tradition; as girls, the sisters had always made their exchange just before going to bed.

When Amanda opened her gift, she laughed. It was a copy of *Gathering Up the Pieces,* the same book she'd bought for Eunice.

Eunice was amazed when she opened her package. "I don't believe this," she whispered, a wide smile on her face. She turned back the flyleaf. "And it's autographed. Wow."

"I waited in line for hours to get it signed," Amanda exaggerated. She was remembering meeting Jordan that day, and feeling all the resultant pain.

"Let's go to bed and read ourselves to sleep," Eunice suggested, standing up and switching off the Christmas tree. Its veil of tinsel seemed to whisper a silvery song in the darkness.

"Good idea," Amanda answered.

She was all the way up to chapter three before she finally closed her eyes.

THE KIDS WERE asleep and so, as far as Jordan knew, were Paul and Karen. He sat up in bed, switched on the lamp and reached for the telephone on the nightstand. The picture of Becky had been moved to a shelf in his study, but he looked at the place where it had stood and said, "Know what, Becky? I've got it bad."

A glance at his watch told him it was after two in the morning. If he called Amanda now, he would be sure to wake her up, but he didn't care. Whatever happened, he had to hear her voice and wish her a merry Christmas.

He punched out the number and waited, nervous as

a high school kid. While the call went through, a number of scenarios came to mind—such as James answering with a sleepy "Hello." Or Amanda telling him to go straight to hell.

Instead he got a recorded voice. "Hi. This is Amanda Scott, and I can't come to the phone right now...."

Jordan hung up without leaving a message, switched off the light and lay back on his pillows. She was probably at her parents' place, he told himself.

Or maybe she was in Hawaii, helping James recuperate.

Jordan turned onto his stomach and slammed one fist into the pillow. He knew the lush plains and contours of Amanda's body, and he begrudged them to every other man on earth. They were his to touch, and no one else's.

His groin knotted as he recalled how it was to bury himself in Amanda's depths, to feel her hands moving on his back and the insides of her thighs against his hips. She'd lain beneath him like a temptress, her eyes smoldering, her body rising to meet his, stroke for stroke, her hands curled on the sides of the pillow.

But then, as release approached, she would bite down hard on her lower lip and roll her eyes back, focusing dreamily on nothing at all. A low, keening whimper would escape her as she surrendered completely, breaking past her clamped teeth to become a shameless groan...

Jordan sat bolt upright in bed and switched on the lamp again. He couldn't quite face the prospect of a cold shower, but he was too uncomfortable to stay where he was. He tossed back the covers, reached for his robe and tied it tightly around his waist. The cloth stood out like canvas stretched over a tent pole.

Feeling reasonably certain he wouldn't meet anybody, Jordan slipped out of his room and down the darkened stairs. In the kitchen he poured himself a glass of chocolate milk and carried it back to the living room. There he sat, staring at the silent glimmer of the dark Christmas tree, the bulging shapes of the stockings. The thin light of a winter moon poured in through the smoked-glass windows, making everything look unfamiliar.

"Jordan?" It was Karen's voice, and seconds before she switched on the lights, he grabbed a sofa pillow and laid it on his lap. His plump, pretty sister, bundled in her practical blue chenille robe, looked at him with concern. "Are you all right?"

"No," Jordan answered, tossing back the last of his chocolate milk as though it could give him the same solace as brandy or good whiskey. Since it was safe to set aside the pillow, he did. "Don't ever let anybody tell you it's 'better to have loved and lost, than never to have loved at all,'" he advised, sounding for all the world like a melancholy drunk. "I've done it twice, and I wish to God I'd joined the foreign legion, instead."

Karen sat down next to him. "So you're just going to give up, huh?"

"Yeah," Jordan answered obstinately. He had to change the subject, or risk being smothered in images of Amanda lying in somebody else's bed. "About the kids—"

"You want them back," Karen guessed with a gentle smile.

Jordan nodded.

Chapter 10

━━━━━━━━ ᕙᓕᕗ ━━━━━━━━

AMANDA SAT STARING AT THE bank draft in amazement that dreary Saturday morning in February while a gray rain drizzled at the kitchen windows. "I don't understand," she muttered, glancing from Marion's smiling face to Bob's to Eunice's. "What's this for?"

Bob reached across the table to cover her hand with his. "I guess you could say it's an investment. You've been walking around here for two months looking as though you've lost your last friend, so your mother and I decided you needed a lift. It's enough for the down payment on that old house you wanted, isn't it?"

Amanda swallowed, reading the numbers on the check in disbelief. It was five times the down payment the owner demanded—Amanda still called once a week to see if the house had sold, and had gone to see it twice—and must have represented a major chunk of her parents' savings account. "I can't take this," she said. "You've worked so hard and budgeted so carefully...."

But Bob and Marion presented a united front, and they were backed up by a beaming Eunice, who was now working full-time at the university and living in her own apartment.

"You have to accept it," Marion said firmly. "We won't take no for an answer."

"But suppose I fail?" Since the breakup with Jordan, Amanda's confidence had taken a decided dip, and everything was more difficult than it should have been.

"You won't," Bob said with certainty. "Now call that real estate woman and make an offer before the place is snapped up by some doctor or lawyer looking for a summer house."

Amanda hesitated only a moment. Hope was fluttering in her heart like a bird rising skyward; for the first time in two months she could see herself as a happy woman. With a shriek of delight, she bolted out of her chair and dashed for the telephone, and Bob and Marion laughed until they had tears in their eyes.

The real estate agent was delighted at Amanda's offer, and offered to bring the papers over to Seattle for her to sign. They agreed to meet Monday morning at Amanda's office in the Evergreen Hotel.

When Amanda was off the phone, she turned to her parents. "I can't believe you're doing this for me—taking such a chance—"

"A person can't expect to win in life if they're afraid to take a risk," Bob said quietly.

Amanda went back to the table and bent to hug each of her parents. "You'll be proud of me," she promised.

"We already are," Marion assured her.

On Monday morning Amanda arrived at work with a carefully typed letter of resignation tucked into her briefcase. In another two weeks she would be rolling up her sleeves and making a start on her dream—or, at least, part of it.

She flipped through the messages on her desk, sorting them in order of importance, and at the same time looked into the future. The house she was buying was hardly more than a mile from Jordan's place. She was bound to meet him on the highway or run into him in the supermarket, and she wondered if she could deal with that.

Even after two months Amanda ached every time she thought of Jordan. Actually encountering him face-to-face might really set her back.

There was a rap at the door, and Mindy stepped in, smiling. "You look pretty cheerful today. What's going on? Did you and Jordan get back together or something?"

Amanda opened her briefcase and took out the letter of resignation, keeping her eyes down to hide the sudden pain the mention of Jordan had caused her. "No," she answered, "but I'll be leaving the Evergreen in a couple of weeks— I'm buying that house I wanted on Vashon Island."

"Wow," Mindy responded. "That's great!"

Amanda lifted her eyes to meet her friend's gaze. "Thanks, Mindy."

Mindy's brow puckered in a frown. "I'll miss you a lot, though."

"And I'll miss you." At that moment the intercom on Amanda's telephone buzzed, and she picked up the receiver as Mindy left the office. "Amanda Scott."

"Ms. Scott, this is Betty Prestwood, Prestwood Real Estate. I'm afraid I've been delayed, so I won't be arriving in the city until around noon. Could we possibly meet at Ivar's for lunch at twelve-fifteen? I'll have the proper papers with me, of course."

Amanda automatically glanced at her calendar, even though she already knew she was free for lunch that day. She probably would have eaten yogurt in her office or gone to the mall with Mindy for fast food. "That will be fine."

After ending that phone call, Amanda went to the executive manager's office suite and handed in her resignation. Mr. Mansfield, a middle-aged man with a bald head and an ulcer, was not pleased that his trusty assistant manager was leaving.

He instructed her to start preliminary interviews for a replacement as soon as possible.

Amanda spent the rest of the morning on the telephone with various employment agencies in the city, and when it came time to meet Mrs. Prestwood for lunch, she was relieved. It wasn't the food that attracted her, but the prospect of a break.

After exchanging her high heels for sneakers, Amanda walked the six blocks from the hotel to the seafood restaurant on the waterfront. The sun was shining, and the harbor was its usual noisy, busy self.

Mrs. Prestwood, a small, trim woman with carefully coiffed blond hair and tasteful makeup, was waiting by the reservations desk.

She and Amanda shook hands, then followed the hostess to a table by a window.

Just as Amanda was sitting down, she spotted Jordan—it was as though her eyes were magnetized to him. He looked very Wall Street in his three-piece suit as he lunched with two other men and a woman.

Evidently he'd sensed Amanda's stare, for his eyes shifted to her almost instantly.

For a moment the whole restaurant seemed to fall into eerie silence for Amanda; she had the odd sensation of standing on the bottom of the ocean. It was only with enormous effort that she surfaced and forced her gaze to the menu the waitress had handed her. *Don't let him come over here,* she prayed silently. *If he does, I'll fall apart right in front of everybody.*

"Is something wrong?" Betty Prestwood asked pleasantly.

Amanda swallowed and shook her head, but out of the corner of her eye she was watching Jordan.

He had turned his attention back to his companions, especially the woman, who was attractive, in a tweedy sort of way, with her trim suit and her dark hair pulled back into a French twist. She was laughing at something Jordan had said.

Amanda made herself study the menu, even though she couldn't have eaten if her life depended on it. She finally decided on the spinach salad and iced tea, just for show.

Mrs. Prestwood brought out the contracts as soon as the waitress had taken their orders, and Amanda read them through carefully. Lunch had arrived by the time she was done, and in a glance she saw that Jordan and his party were leaving. He was resting his hand lightly on the small of the woman's back, and Amanda felt for all the world like a betrayed wife.

Forcing her eyes back to the contracts, she signed them and handed Mrs. Prestwood a check. Since the owner was financing the sale himself, it was now just a matter of waiting for closing. Amanda could rent the house in the interim if she wished.

She wrote another check, then stabbed a leaf of spinach with her fork. Try as she might, she couldn't lift it to her mouth. Her stomach was roiling angrily, unwilling to accept anything.

She laid the fork down.

"Is everything all right?" Mrs. Prestwood asked, seeming genuinely concerned.

Amanda lied by nodding her head.

"You don't seem very hungry."

Amanda managed a smile. Was Jordan sleeping with

that woman? Did she visit him on the island on weekends? "I'm just getting over the flu," she said, which was at least a partial truth. She was probably coming down with it, not getting over it.

Mrs. Prestwood accepted that excuse and finished her lunch in good time. The two women parted outside the restaurant with another handshake, then Amanda started back up the hill to the hotel. By the time she arrived, her head was pounding and there were two people waiting to be interviewed for her job.

She talked to both of them and didn't pass either application on to Mr. Mansfield for his consideration. One had obviously considered herself too good for such a menial position, and the other had an offensive personal manner.

Amanda's headache got progressively worse as the afternoon passed, but she was too busy interviewing to go home to bed, and besides, she couldn't be sure the malady wasn't psychosomatic. She hadn't started feeling really sick until after she'd seen Jordan with that woman in the dress-for-success clothes.

At the end of the day Amanda dragged herself home, fed Gershwin, made herself a bowl of chicken noodle soup and watched the evening news in her favorite bathrobe. By the time she'd been apprised of all the shootings, rapes, drug deals and political scandals of the day, she was thoroughly depressed. She put her empty soup bowl in the sink, took two aspirin and fell into bed.

The next morning she felt really terrible. Her head seemed thick and heavy as a medicine ball, and her chest ached.

Reluctantly she called in sick, took more aspirin and went back to sleep.

A loud knocking at the door awakened her around eleven-thirty, and Amanda rolled out of bed, stumbled into the living room with one hand pressed to her aching head and called, "Who is it?"

"It's me," a feminine voice replied. "Mindy. Let me in—I come bearing gifts."

With a sigh, Amanda undid the chains, twisted the lock and opened the door. "You're taking your life in your hands, coming in here," she warned in a thick voice. "This place is infested with germs."

Mindy's pretty hair was sprinkled with raindrops, and her smile was warm. "I'll risk it," she said, stepping past Amanda with a stack of magazines and a box of something that smelled good. She grimaced as she assessed Amanda's rumpled nightgown and unbrushed hair. "You look like the victim in a horror movie," she observed cheerfully. "Sit down before you fall down."

Amanda dropped into a chair. "What's going on at the office?"

"It's bedlam," Mindy answered, setting the magazines and food down on the table to shrug out of her coat. "Mr. Mansfield is finding out just how valuable you really are." Her voice trailed back from the kitchenette, where she was opening cupboards and drawers. "He's been interviewing all morning, and he's such a bear today, he'll be lucky if anybody wants to work for him."

Amanda sighed. "I should be there."

Mindy returned from the kitchenette and handed Amanda a plate of the fried Chinese noodles she knew she loved. "And spread bubonic plague among your friends and coworkers? Bad idea. Eat this, Amanda."

Amanda took the plate of noodles and dug in with a fork. Although she still had no appetite, she knew her body needed food to recover, and she hadn't had anything to eat since last night's chicken soup. "Thanks."

Mindy glanced at the blank TV screen in amazement.

"Do you mean to tell me you have a chance to catch up on all the soaps and you aren't even watching?"

"I'm sick, not on vacation," Amanda pointed out.

Mindy rushed to turn on the set and tune in her favorite. "Lord, will you look at him?" she asked, pointing to a shirtless hero soulfully telling a woman she was the only one for him.

"Don't listen to him," Amanda muttered. "As soon as you make one wrong move, he'll dump you."

"You *have* been watching this show!" Mindy accused.

Amanda shook her head glumly. "I was speaking from the perspective of real life," she said, chewing.

Mindy sighed. "I knew that rascal would be fooling around with Lorinda the minute Jennifer turned her back," she fretted, shaking her finger at the screen.

Amanda chuckled, even though she would have had to feel better just to die, and took another bite of the noodles Mindy had brought. "How do you know so much about the story line when you work every day?"

"I tape it," Mindy answered. Then, somewhat reluctantly, she snapped off the set and turned back to her mission of mercy. "Is there anything you want me to do at the office, Amanda? Or I could shop for you—"

Amanda interrupted with a shake of her head. "It's enough that you came over. That was really nice of you."

Mindy rose from the couch and put her hands on her slim hips. "I know. I'll make a bed for you on the couch so you can watch TV. Mom always did that for me when I was sick, and it never failed to cheer me up."

With that, Mindy disappeared into the bedroom, returning soon afterward with sheets, blankets and pillows. True to her word, she made a place for Amanda on the couch and all but tucked her in when she was settled with her magazines and the controls for the TV.

Before going back to work, she made Amanda a cup of hot tea, put the phone within reach and forced her to take more aspirin.

When Mindy was gone, Amanda got up to lock the door behind her, then padded back to the bed. She was comfortably settled when the telephone rang. A queer feeling quivered in the pit of her stomach as she remembered seeing Jordan in the restaurant the day before, felt again the electricity that passed between them when their eyes met. "Hello?" she said hopefully.

"Hello, Amanda."

The voice didn't belong to Jordan, but to Mrs. Prestwood. Amanda could pick up the keys to her house at the real estate office whenever she was ready.

Amanda promised to be there within the week, and asked Mrs. Prestwood to have telephone service hooked up at the house, along with electricity. Then she hung up and flipped slowly through the magazines, seeing none of the glossy photographs and enticing article titles. She was going to be living on the same island with Jordan, and that was all she could think about.

BY THE TIME Amanda recovered enough to return to work, half her notice was up and Mr. Mansfield had selected a replacement. Handing her her final paycheck, which was sizable because there was vacation pay added in, he wished her well. On her last day, he and Mindy and the others held a going away party for her in the hotel's elegant lounge, and Bob, Marion and Eunice attended, too.

That Friday evening, Amanda filled her car with boxes, one of which contained Gershwin, leaving the rest of her things behind for the movers to bring, and boarded the ferry for Vashon Island.

Since it was cold and dark in the bottom of the ship, she decided to venture upstairs to the snack bar for a cup of hot coffee. Just as she arrived, however, she spotted Jordan again. This time he was with his daughters, and the three of them were eating French fries while both girls talked at once.

Amanda's first instinct was to approach them and say hello, but in the end she lost her courage and slipped back out of the snack bar and down the stairs to her car. She sat hunched behind the wheel, waiting for the whistle announcing their arrival at Vashon Island to blast, and feeling miserable. What kind of life was she going to have in her new community if she had to worry about avoiding Jordan?

In those moments Amanda felt terribly alone, and the enormity of the things she'd done—giving up her job and apartment and borrowing such a staggering sum of money from her parents—oppressed her.

Finally the ferry came into port, and Amanda drove her car down the ramp, wondering if Jordan and the girls were in one of the cars ahead, or one behind. She didn't get a glimpse of them, which wasn't surprising, considering how dark it was.

When Amanda arrived at her new old house, the lights were on and Mrs. Prestwood was waiting in the kitchen to present the key, since Amanda had not had a chance to pick it up at the office. The old oil furnace was rumbling beneath the floor, filling the spacious rooms with warmth.

Amanda wandered through the rooms, sipping coffee from the percolator Betty Prestwood had thoughtfully loaned her and dreaming of the things she meant to do. There would be winter parties around the huge fireplace in the front parlor—she would serve mulled wine and spice cake with whipped cream. And in summer, guests could sleep on the screened sun porch if they wanted to, and be lulled into slumber by the quiet rhythm of the tide and the salty whisper of the breezes.

There were seven bedrooms upstairs, but only one bathroom. Amanda made a mental note to call in a plumbing contractor for estimates the next morning. She would have to add at least one more.

Amanda's private room, a small one off the kitchen, looked especially inviting after the long day she'd had. While Gershwin continued to explore the farthest reaches of his new home, she went out to the car to get the cot and sleeping bag she'd borrowed from her stepdad. After a bath upstairs, she crawled onto the cot with a book.

She hadn't read more than a page, when Gershwin suddenly landed in the middle of her stomach with a plop and meow.

Amanda let her book rest against her chin and stroked his silky fur. "Don't worry, Big Guy. We're both going to like it here." The instant the words were out of her mouth, though, she thought of the jolt that seeing Jordan and the girls had caused her, and her throat tightened painfully. "You'd think I'd be over him by now, wouldn't you?" she said when she could speak, her vision so blurred that there seemed to be two Gershwins lying on her stomach instead of one.

"Reoww," Gershwin agreed, before bending his head to lick one of his paws.

"Love is hell," Amanda went on with a sniffle. "Be glad you're neutered."

Gershwin made no comment on that, so Amanda dried her eyes and focused determinedly on her book again.

THE NEXT MORNING brought a storm in off Puget Sound. It slashed at the windows and howled around the corners of the house, and Gershwin kept himself within six inches of Amanda's feet. She left him only to carry in the boxes from the car and drive to the supermarket for food.

Since she'd prepared herself to encounter Jordan, Amanda was both relieved and disappointed when there was no sign of him. She filled her cart with groceries, taking care to buy a can of Gershwin's favorite food to make up for leaving him, and drove back over rain-slickened roads to the house.

The tempest raged all day, but Amanda was fascinated by it, rather than frightened. While Gershwin was sleeping off the feast Amanda had brought him, she put on her slicker and a pair of rubber boots she'd found in the basement and walked down to the beach.

Lightning cracked the sky like a mirror dropped on a hard floor, and the water lashed furiously at the rocky shoreline. Amanda stood with her hands in the pockets of her slicker, watching the spectacle in awe.

When she returned to the house half an hour later, her jeans were wet to her knees despite the rain garb she wore, and her hair was dripping. She felt strangely comforted, though, and when she saw Betty Prestwood's car splashing up the puddle-riddled driveway, she smiled and waved.

The two women dashed onto the enclosed porch together, laughing. Betty was only a few years older than Amanda, and they were getting to be good friends.

"There's an estate sale scheduled for today," Betty said breathlessly when they were in the kitchen and Amanda had handed her a cup of steaming coffee. "I thought you might like to go, since you need so much furniture. It's just on the other side of the island, and we could have lunch out."

Amanda was pleased that Betty had thought of her. Even though she had a surplus of funds, thanks to her own savings and the loan from Bob and Marion, it was going to cost a lot of money to get the bed and breakfast into operation. She needed to furnish the place attractively for a reasonable price. "Sounds great," Amanda said, ruefully comparing her soggy jeans and crumpled flannel shirt to Betty's stylish pink suit. "Just give me a few minutes, and I'll change."

Betty smiled. "Fine. Do you mind if I use the phone? I like to check in with the office periodically."

Amanda gestured toward the wall phone between the sink and stove. "Help yourself. And have some more coffee if you want it. I won't be long."

After finding a pair of black woolen slacks and a burgundy sweater, along with clean underthings and a towel and washcloth, Amanda dashed upstairs and took a quick, hot shower. When she was dressed, with her hair blow-dried and a light application of makeup highlighting her features, she hurried downstairs.

Betty was leaning against one of the kitchen counters, sipping coffee. "When are the movers coming?"

"Monday," Amanda answered, pulling on a pair of shoes that would probably be ruined the instant she wore them outside. "But even when all my stuff is here, the place is still going to echo like a cavern."

Betty laughed. "Maybe we can fix that this afternoon."

After saying goodbye to Gershwin, who still hadn't recovered from his stupor, Amanda pulled the ugly rubber boots she'd worn earlier on over her shoes, put on her slicker and followed Betty to her car.

Since the auction was scheduled for one o'clock, they had time for a leisurely lunch. Mercifully Betty suggested a small soup-and-sandwich place in town, rather than the roadside café Amanda knew Jordan frequented.

She ordered a turkey sandwich with bean sprouts, along with a bowl of minestrone, and ate with enthusiasm. She wasn't over Jordan, and she was still weak with lingering traces of the flu, but her appetite was back.

After lunch, she and Betty drove to a secluded house on the opposite side of the island, where folding chairs had been set up under huge pink-and-white striped canopies. Amanda's heart sank when she saw how many people had braved the nasty weather in search of a bargain, but Betty seemed to be taking a positive attitude, so she tried to follow suit.

The articles available for sale were scattered throughout the house—there were pianos and bedroom sets, tea services and bureaus, sets of china boasting imprints like Limoges and Haviland. Embroidered linens were offered, too, along with exquisite lace curtains and grandfather clocks, and wonderful old books that smelled of age and refinement.

Amanda's excitement built, and she crossed her fingers as she and Betty took their places in the horde of metal chairs.

A beautiful old sleigh bed with a matching bureau and armoire came up for sale first, and Amanda, thinking of her seven empty bedrooms, held up her bid card when the auctioneer asked for a modest amount to start the sale rolling.

A man in the back row bid against her, and it was nip and tuck, but Amanda finally won the skirmish with fairly minimal damage to her bank balance.

After that she bought linens, one of the grandfather clocks and a set of English bone china, while Betty purchased a full-length mirror in a cherrywood stand and an old jewelry box. At the end of the sale, Amanda made arrangements for the auction company to deliver her purchases, then wrote out a check.

It was midafternoon by then, and her soup and sandwich were beginning to wear off. Having lost sight of Betty in the crowd, she bought a hot dog with mustard and relish and a diet cola, then sat quietly in one of the folding chairs to eat.

She nearly choked when Jordan walked up, turned the chair in front of hers around and straddled it, his arms draped across the back. His expression was every bit as remote as it had been the last time she'd seen him, and Amanda prayed he couldn't hear her heart thudding against her rib cage.

"What are you doing here?" he asked, his voice insinuating that she was probably up to no good.

Amanda was instantly offended. She swallowed a chunk of her hot dog in a painful lump and replied, "I thought I'd try to steal some of the silverware, or maybe palm an antique broach or two."

He grinned, though the expression didn't quite reach his eyes. "You bought a bedroom set, a grandfather clock and some dishes. Getting married, Ms. Scott, now that Mrs. Brockman is out of the picture?"

It was all Amanda could do not to poke him in the eye with the rest of her hot dog. Obviously he didn't know she'd bought the Victorian house, and she wasn't about to tell him. "It'll be a June wedding," she said evenly. "Would you like to come?"

"I'm busy for the rest of the decade," Jordan answered in a taut voice, his hazel eyes snapping as he rose from the chair and put it back into line with the others. "See you around."

As abruptly as that, he was gone, and Amanda was

left to sit there wondering why she'd let him walk away. When Betty returned, bringing along two of her friends to be introduced, Amanda was staring glumly at her unfinished hot dog.

BECAUSE JESSIE AND Lisa were staying with Becky's parents in Bellevue that weekend, Jordan was driving the Porsche. He strode back to it, oblivious to the rain saturating his hair and his shirt, and threw himself behind the wheel, slamming the door behind him.

Damn it all to hell, if Amanda was going to go on as if nothing had happened between them, couldn't she at least stay on her own turf? It drove him crazy, catching glimpses of her in restaurants, and in the midst of crowds waiting to cross streets, and in the next aisle at bookstores.

After slamming his palms against the steering wheel once, he turned the key in the ignition, and the powerful engine surged to life. The decision had been made by the time the conglomeration of striped canopies had disappeared from the rearview mirror; he would go home, change his clothes and spend the rest of the day in Seattle, working.

The plan seemed to be falling into place until an hour later, when he was passing by that Victorian place Amanda had liked so much. The lights were on, and there was a familiar car parked in the driveway.

He met Betty Prestwood's pink Cadillac midway between the highway and the house. She smiled and waved, and Jordan waved back distractedly, noticing for the first time that the For Sale sign was gone from the yard.

He braked the car to a stop and sprinted through the rain to the door, feeling a peculiar mixture of elation and outrage as he hammered at it with one fist.

Chapter 11

AMANDA HAD JUST CHANGED back into her jeans and a T-shirt when the thunderous knock sounded at the door. Expecting an enthusiastic salesperson, she was taken aback to find Jordan standing on her porch, dripping rainwater and indignation.

"Aren't you going to ask me in?" he demanded.

Amanda stepped back without a word, watching with round eyes as Jordan stomped into the warm kitchen, scowling at her.

"Well?" he prompted, putting his hands on his hips.

He seemed to have a particular scenario in mind, but Amanda couldn't think for the life of her what it would be.

She left him standing there while she went into her bathroom for a dry towel. Handing it to him upon her return, she asked, "Well, what?"

"What are you doing in this house? For that matter, what are you doing on this *island*?" He was drying his hair all the while he spoke, a grudging expression on his face.

Amanda hooked her thumbs in the waistband of her jeans and tilted her head to one side. "I own this house," she replied. "As for why I'm on the island, well—" she paused to shrug and spread her hands "—I guess I just didn't know I was supposed to get your approval before I stepped off the ferry."

Jordan flung the towel across the room, and it caught on the handle of the old-fashioned refrigerator. "Are you married to James?"

She went to the percolator and filled two cups with coffee, one for her and one for Jordan. "No," she answered, turning her head to look back at him over her shoulder. "I explained the situation to you. I was only trying to help James in my own misguided way. Where did you get the idea I meant to marry him?"

Jordan sighed and shoved his hand through damp, tangled hair. "Okay, so my imagination ran away with me. I tried to call you on Christmas Eve, and you weren't home. I had all these pictures in my mind of you lying on some secluded beach in Hawaii, helping James recuperate."

Although she was delighted, even jubilant, to know Jordan had tried to call her, she wasn't about to let on. She brought the coffee cup to him and held it out until he took it. "How would my lying on a secluded beach help James recuperate?"

"With you for a visual aid, a corpse would recuperate," he replied with a sheepish grin. His eyes remained serious. "I've missed you, Mandy."

She felt tears rising in her eyes and lowered her head while she struggled to hold them back. She didn't trust herself to speak.

Jordan took her coffee and set it, with his own, on the counter. "Don't you have any chairs in this place?"

Amanda made herself meet his eyes as she shook her head. "Not yet. The movers will be here on Monday."

He approached her, hooked his index fingers through the belt loops on her jeans and pulled her close. So close that every intimacy they'd ever shared came surging back to her memory at the contact, making her feel light-headed.

"I may have neglected to mention this before," he said in a voice like summer thunder rumbling far in the distance, "but I'm in love with you, and I have a feeling it's a lifetime thing."

Amanda linked her hands behind his neck, reveling in her closeness to Jordan and the priceless words he'd just said. "Actually, you did neglect to mention that, Mr. Richards."

He tasted her lips, sending a thrill careening through her system. "I apologize abjectly, even though you're guilty of the same oversight."

"Only too true," Amanda whispered, her mouth against his. "I love you, Jordan."

He ran his hands up and down her back, strong and sure and full of the power to set her senses aflame. He pressed his lips to her neck and answered with a teasing growl.

Amanda called upon all her self-control to lean back in his arms. "Jordan, we have things to talk about—things to work out. We can't just take up where we left off."

His fingers were hooked in her belt loops again. "I'll grant you that we have a lot to work through, and it's going to take some time. Why don't we go over to my place and talk?"

With considerable effort, Amanda willed her heart to slow down to a normal beat. She knew what was going to happen—it was inevitable—but she wanted to be sure they were on solid ground first. "We can talk here," she said, and she led him into the giant, empty parlor with its view of the sound. They sat together on a window seat with no cushion, their hands clasped. "I was wrong not to tell you I was seeing James again, Jordan, and I'm sorry."

He touched her lips with an index finger. Outside, beyond the rain-dappled glass, the storm raged on. "Looking back, I guess I wouldn't have been very receptive, anyway. I was feeling pretty possessive."

Amanda rested her head against his damp shoulder, unable to resist his warmth any longer, trembling as he traced a tingling pattern on her nape. "I thought I was going to die when I saw you at Ivar's with that corporation chick."

Jordan laughed and curved his fingers under her chin. "'Corporation chick'? That was Clarissa Robbins. She works in the legal department and is married to one of my best friends."

Amanda felt foolish, but she was also relieved, and she guessed that showed in her face, because Jordan was grinning at her. "You have your girls back," she said. "I saw you on the ferry last night."

Jordan nodded. "They didn't actually move in until a month ago. After all, they were used to living with Paul and Karen, so we just did weekends at first. And they're staying with Becky's parents until tomorrow night."

She tried to lower her head again, but Jordan wouldn't allow it.

"Think you could fall for a guy with two kids, Mandy?" he asked.

"I already have," she answered softly.

Jordan's mouth descended to hers, gentle at first, and then possessive and commanding. By the time he withdrew, Amanda was dazed.

"Show me the bridal suite," he said, rising to his feet and pulling Amanda after him.

She swallowed. "There's no bed in there, Jordan," she explained timidly.

"Where do you sleep?"

His voice was downright hypnotic. In fact, if he'd started undressing her right there in the middle of the parlor, she wouldn't have been able to raise an objection. "In a little room off the kitchen, but—"

"Show me," Jordan interrupted, and she led him back to where she slept.

"That'll never hold up," he said, eyeing the cot Amanda had spent the night on. With an inspired grin, he grabbed up the sleeping bag and pillow. "Now," he went on, grasping her hand again, "let's break in the bridal suite."

Amanda felt color rise in her cheeks, and she averted her eyes before leading the way around to the front of the house and up the stairs.

The best room faced the water and boasted its own fireplace, but it was unfurnished except for a large hooked rug centered in the middle of the floor.

Jordan spread the sleeping bag out on the rug and tossed the pillow carelessly on top of it, then stood watching Amanda with a mingling of humor and hunger in his eyes. "Come here, Mandy," he said with gentle authority.

She approached him shyly, because in some ways everything was new between them.

He slipped his hands beneath her T-shirt, resting them lightly on the sides of her waist; his hands were surprisingly warm.

"I love you, Amanda Scott," he told her firmly. "And in a month or a year or whenever you're ready, I'm going to make you my wife. Any objections?"

Amanda's lips were dry, and she wet them with her tongue. "None at all," she answered, and she drew in a sharp breath and closed her eyes as Jordan slid his hands up her sides to her breasts. With his thumbs he stroked her long-neglected nipples through the lacy fabric of her bra. When they stood erect, he pulled Amanda's T-shirt off over her head and tossed it aside.

"Let me look at you," he said, standing back a little.

Slowly, a little awkwardly, Amanda unhooked her bra and let it drop, revealing her full breasts. She let her hand fall back in ecstatic surrender as Jordan boldly closed his hands over her. When he bent his head and began to suckle at one pulsing nipple, she gave a little cry and entangled her hands in his hair.

He drew on both her breasts, one after the other, until she was half-delirious, and then he dropped to his knees on the sleeping bag and gently took Amanda's shoes from her feet. She started to sink down, needing union with him, but he grasped her hips and held her upright.

She bit down on her lower lip as she felt his finger beneath the waistband of her jeans. The snap gave way, and then the zipper, and then Amanda was bared to him, except for her panties and socks.

Her knees bent of their own accord, and her pelvis shifted forward as Jordan nipped at the hidden mound, all the time rolling one of her socks down. When her feet were bare, he pulled her panties down very slowly, and she kicked them aside impatiently, sure that Jordan would appease her now.

But he wasn't through tormenting her. He massaged the insides of her thighs, carefully avoiding the place that most needed his attention, and then lifted one of her knees and placed it over his shoulder.

Amanda was forced to link her hands behind his neck to keep from falling. "Oh," she whimpered as she realized what a vulnerable position she was in. "Jordan—"

He parted her with his fingers. "What?"

Her answer was cut off, and forced forever into the recesses of her mind when Jordan suddenly took her fully, greedily, into his mouth. She thrust her head back with the proud abandon of a tigress and gave a primitive groan that echoed in the empty room.

Jordan raised one hand to fondle her breast as he consumed her, and the two sensations combined to drive her to the very edge of sanity. She began to plead with him, and tug at the back of his shirt in a fruitless effort to strip him and feel his nakedness under her hands.

He lay back on the floor, bringing Amanda with him, and she rocked wildly in a shameless search for release while he moved his hands in gentle circles on her quivering belly. When he caught both her nipples between his fingers, Amanda's quest ended in a spectacular explosion that wrung a series of hoarse cries from her throat.

She sagged to the floor when it was over, only half-conscious, and Jordan arranged her on the sleeping bag before slowly removing his clothes. When he was naked, he tucked the pillow under her bottom and parted her knees, kneeling between them to tease her.

The back of one hand resting against her mouth, Amanda gave a soft moan. "Jordan—"

"Umm?" He gave her barely an inch of himself, but that was enough to arouse her all over again, to stir the fires he'd just banked. At the same time, he bent to sip at one of her nipples in a leisurely fashion.

Amanda groaned.

"What was that?" Jordan teased, barely pausing in his enjoyment of her breast.

"I want—oh, God, Jordan, please—I need you so much.…"

He drew in a ragged breath, and she felt him tremble against the insides of her thighs as he gave her another inch.

She clutched at his arms, trying to pull him to her. "Jordan!" she wailed suddenly in utter desperation, and he gave her just a little more of himself.

Amanda couldn't wait any longer. She'd had release

once, it was true, but her every instinct drove her toward complete fulfillment. She needed Jordan's weight, his substance, his force, and she needed it immediately.

With a fierce cry, she thrust her hips upward, taking him all the way inside her, and at that point Jordan's awesome control snapped.

Amanda watched through a haze of passion as he surrendered. Bracing his hands on the rug and arching his back, he withdrew and lunged into her again in a long, violent stroke, leaving no doubt as to the extent of his claim on her.

Triumph came at the peak of a sweet frenzy that tore a rasping shout from Jordan's throat and set Amanda's spirit to spiraling within her. For a few dizzying moments she was sure it would escape and soar off into the cosmos, leaving her body behind forever. The feeling passed, like a fever, and when Jordan fell to her, she was there to receive him.

He kissed her bare shoulder between gasps for air, and finally whispered, "Don't mind me. I'll be fine in a year or two."

Amanda's breath had just returned, and she laughed, moving her hands over his back in a gesture meant both to soothe and to claim. But her eyes were solemn when Jordan lifted his head to study her face a few moments later.

"Do you think it will take a long time for us to get things ironed out, Jordan?"

He kissed her forehead. "Judging by what just happened here, I'd say no."

"Good," she answered.

He traced the outline of her mouth with the tip of one finger. "Will you give me a baby, Mandy?" he asked huskily.

Her heart warmed within her, and seemed to grow larger. "Probably sooner than you think," she replied.

Jordan chuckled and drew her close to him, and they lay together for a long time, recovering. Remembering. Finally, he bent to kiss her once more before rising from her to reach for his clothes. He gave her a long look as she sat up and wrapped her arms around her knees, then sighed. "We've got a lot of talking to do," he said. "Now that there's some chance of concentrating, let's go over to my place and get started."

Amanda nodded and grabbed her jeans and panties. Because her things were scattered all over the rug, she wasn't able to dress as fast as Jordan, and he was brazen enough to watch her put on every garment.

Fifteen minutes later they pulled into his garage. When a blaze was snapping in the living room fireplace, they sat side by side on the floor in front of it, cross-legged and sipping wine.

Amanda started the conversation with a blunt but necessary question. "Are you still in love with Becky?"

Jordan considered her words solemnly and for a long time. "Not in the way you mean," he finally said, his eyes caressing Amanda he watched her reactions. "But I'll always care about her. It's just that I feel a different kind of love for her now. Sort of mellow and quiet and nostalgic."

Amanda nodded, then let her head rest against his shoulder. "In a way, she lives on in Jessie and Lisa."

Jordan sighed, watching the fire. He told her about the accident then, about feeling Becky's arms tighten around his waist in fear just before impact, about the pain, about being in the hospital when her funeral was held. "I felt responsible for her death for a long time," he said, "but I finally realized I was just using that as an excuse to go on mourning forever. Deep down inside, I knew it was really an accident."

Amanda gave him a hug.

"Thanks, Mandy," he said hoarsely.

She sat up straight to look at him. "For what?"

"For coming along when you did, and for being who you are. Until I met you, I didn't think love was an option for me."

The rain began to slacken in its seemingly incessant chatter on the roof and against the windows, and Amanda thought she saw a hint of sunshine glimmering at the edge of a distant cloud. She linked her arm through Jordan's and laid her temple to his shoulder, content just to be close to him.

Jordan intertwined his fingers with Amanda's, and his grip was strong and tight. With his other hand he tapped his wineglass against hers. "Here's to taking chances," he said softly.

THE MOVERS ARRIVED on Monday, and so did the furniture Amanda had bought at the estate sale. She called in several plumbers for estimates on extra bathrooms, and that night she and Jordan and the girls sat around her kitchen table, eating chicken from a red-and-white striped bucket.

"I'm glad you didn't go to heaven," Jessie told Amanda, her dark eyes round and earnest.

"Me, too," Lisa put in, nibbling on a drumstick.

Amanda's gaze linked with Jordan's. "I could have sworn I visited there once," she said mysteriously.

Jordan gave her a look. "Dirty pool, lady," he accused.

"Uh-uh, Daddy," Jessie argued. "Amanda doesn't even *have* a pool."

"I stand corrected," Jordan told his daughter, but his eyes were on Amanda.

Tossing a denuded chicken bone onto her plate, Amanda stood up and bent to give greasy, top-of-the-head kisses to both Jessie and Lisa. "Thanks for being glad I'm around, gang," she told the girls in a conspiratorial whisper.

"You're welcome," Jessie replied.

Lisa was busy tilting the bucket to see if there was another drumstick inside.

Jordan watched Amanda with mischievous eyes as she dropped her plate into the trash and then leaned back against the sink with her arms folded.

"I suppose you people think I can't cook," she said.

No one offered a comment except for Gershwin, who came strolling into the kitchen with a cordial meow. The girls were delighted, and instantly abandoned what remained of their dinners to pet him.

When he realized he wasn't going to get any chicken, the cat wandered out of the room again. Jessie and Lisa were right behind him.

"Come here," Jordan said with just the hint of a grin.

"I've got no willpower at all where you're concerned," Amanda answered, allowing herself to be pulled onto his lap.

"Good. Will you marry me, Mandy?"

She tilted her head to one side. "Yes. But we agreed to wait, give things time—"

"We've had enough time. I love you, and that's never going to change."

Amanda kissed him. "If it's never going to change, then it won't matter if we wait."

He let his forehead fall against her breasts, pretending to be forlorn. "Do you know what it's going to do to me to go home tonight and leave you here?" he muttered.

She rested her chin on the top of his head. "You'll survive," she assured him. "I need a few months to get the business going, Jordan."

He sighed heavily. "Okay," he said with such a tone of martyrdom that Amanda laughed out loud.

Jordan repaid her by sliding a hand up under her shirt and cupping her breast.

Amanda squirmed and uttered a protest, but the steady strokes of his thumb across her nipple raised a fever in her. "We'll just have to be—flexible," she acquiesced with a sigh of supreme longing.

"We're not going to have much time alone together," Jordan warned, continuing his quiet campaign to drive her crazy. "Of course, if we were married, it would be perfectly natural for us to sleep together every night." He'd lifted one side of Amanda's bra so that her bare breast nestled in his hand.

"Jordan," Amanda whispered. "Stop it."

In the parlor, Amanda's television set came on, and the theme song of the girls' favorite sitcom filled the air. "A nuclear war wouldn't distract them from that show," Jordan said sleepily, lifting Amanda's T-shirt and closing his lips brazenly around her nipple.

She knew she should twist away, but the truth was, the most she could manage was to turn on Jordan's lap so that she could see the parlor doorway clearly. The position provided Jordan with better access to her breast, which he enjoyed without a hint of self-consciousness.

When he'd had enough, he righted her bra, pulled her shirt down and swatted her lightly on the bottom. "Well," he said with an exaggerated yawn, "it's a school night. I'd better take the girls home."

Amanda was indignant. "Jordan Richards, you deliberately got me worked up...."

He grinned and lifted her off his lap. "Yep," he confessed, rising from his chair and wandering idly in the direction of the parlor.

Flushed, Amanda flounced back and forth between the table and the trash can, disposing of the remains of dinner. After that, she wiped the table off in furious motions, and when she carried the dishcloth back to the sink, she realized Jordan was watching her with a twinkle in his eyes.

"In three days we could have a license," he said.

In the parlor, Jessie and Lisa laughed at some event in their favorite program, and the sound lifted Amanda's heart. The children would always be Becky and Jordan's, but she loved them already, and she wanted to be a part of their lives almost as much as she wanted to be a part of their father's.

She walked slowly over to the man she loved and put her arms around his waist. "Okay, Jordan, you win. I want to be with you and the kids too much to wait any longer. But you'll have to be patient with me, because getting a new business off the ground takes a lot of time and energy."

His eyes danced with delight as he lifted one hand for a solemn oath. "I'll be patient if you will," he said.

Amanda bit down on her lower lip, worried. "I don't want to fail at this, Jordan."

He kissed her forehead. "We'll have to work at marriage, Mandy—just like everybody else does. But it'll last, I promise you."

"How can you be so sure?" she asked, watching his face for some sign of reservation or caution.

She saw only confidence and love. "The odds are in our favor," he answered, "and I'm taking the rest on faith."

IT WAS SEPTEMBER, and the maples and elms scattered between the evergreens across the road were turning to bright gold. They matched the lumbering yellow school bus that ground to a halt beside the sign that read Amanda's Place.

The bus door opened and Jessie bounded down the steps and leaped to the ground, then turned to catch hold of Lisa's hand and patiently help her down.

Amanda smiled and placed one hand on her distended stomach, watching as her stepdaughters raced toward the house, their school papers fluttering in the autumn breeze.

"I made a house!" Lisa shouted, breathless with excitement as she raced ahead of her sister to meet Amanda on the step.

Amanda bent to properly examine the drawing Lisa had done in the afternoon kindergarten session. A crude square with windows represented the house, and there were four stick figures in front. "Here's me," Lisa said with a sniffle, pointing a pudgy little finger at the smallest form in the picture, "and here's Jessie and Daddy and you. I didn't draw the baby 'cause I don't know what he looks like."

Amanda kissed the child soundly on the forehead. "That's such a good picture that I'm going to put it up in the shop so everybody who comes in can admire it."

Lisa beamed at the prospect, sniffled again and toddled past Amanda and into the warm kitchen.

"How about you?" she asked Jessie, who had waited patiently on the bottom step for her turn. "Did you draw a picture, too?"

"I'm too big for that," Jessie said importantly. "I wrote the whole alphabet."

Putting an arm on the little girl's back, Amanda gently steered her into the kitchen. "Let's see," she said.

Jessie proudly extended the paper. "I already know enough to be in second grade," she said.

Amanda assessed the neatly printed letters marching

smartly across Jessie's paper. "This is certainly one of the nicest papers I've ever seen," she said.

Jessie eyed her shrewdly. "Good enough to be in the shop like Lisa's picture?"

"Absolutely," Amanda replied. To prove her assertion, she strode through the big dining room, now completely furnished, and the large parlor, where Lisa was plunking on the piano, into the shop. Several of her quilts were displayed there, along with the work of many local craftspeople.

Her live-in manager, Millie Delano, was behind the cash register. It had been a slow day, but there were guests scheduled for the weekend, and the quilts and other items had sold extremely well over the summer. Amanda was making a go of her bed and breakfast, although it would be a long time before she got rich.

She held up both Lisa's picture and Jessie's printing for Millie's inspection. The pleasant middle-aged woman smiled broadly as Amanda made places for the papers on the bulletin board behind the counter and pinned them into place.

Jessie, who sometimes worried that her fondness for Amanda made her disloyal to her mother, beamed with pride.

The girls were settled in the kitchen, drinking milk and eating bananas, when Jordan arrived from the city. "Is my family ready to go home?" he asked, poking his head around the door.

Jessie and Lisa, who were always delighted to see him, whether he'd been away five minutes, five hours or five days, flung themselves at him with shrieks of welcome. Amanda, her hands resting on her protruding stomach, stood back, watching. Her eyes brimmed with tears as she

thought how lucky she was to have the three of them filling her life with love and confusion and laughter.

After gently freeing himself from his daughters, Jordan
walked over to Amanda and laid his hands on either side
of her face. With his thumbs he brushed away her tears.
"Hi, pregnant lady," he said. A quiet pride made Amanda's heart swell.

"Hi," she replied with a soft smile.

He gave her a leisurely kiss, then steered her toward
the door. Her coat was hanging on a wooden peg nearby,
and he helped her into it before handing Jessie and Lisa
their jackets.

Amanda was struck again by the depth of her love for
him when, in his tailored suit, he dropped to one knee to
help Lisa with a jammed zipper. She couldn't have asked
for a better father for her child than Jordan Richards.

When the hectic family project of preparing dinner was
behind them, and Lisa and Jessie had had their baths, their
stories and their good-night kisses, Jordan led Amanda into
the living room. They sat on the sofa in front of a snapping
fire, with their heads touching.

Jordan brought his hand to rest on Amanda's stomach,
and when the baby kicked, his eyes were as bright as the
flames on the hearth. Amanda couldn't help smiling.

He smoothed back a lock of her hair. "Tired?" he asked.

"Yes." Amanda sighed. "How about you?"

"Beat," Jordan replied. "Personally, I don't see that we
have any choice but to go straight to bed."

Amanda laughed and thrust herself off the couch. "Last
one there is a rotten egg!" she cried, waddling toward the
stairs.

* * * * *

BESTSELLING AUTHOR COLLECTION

CLASSIC ROMANCES IN COLLECTIBLE VOLUMES

New York Times **Bestselling Author**

LINDA LAEL MILLER

Rue Claridge never dreamed she'd find herself more than
one hundred years in the past...and in jail courtesy of
Marshal Farley Haynes. Fascinated by the rugged marshal, Rue
dreams of a lifetime with him in her modern world—but would he
choose her over everything he's ever known?

HERE AND THEN

Available November 13 wherever books are sold!

Plus, enjoy the bonus story *Dalton's Undoing*
by *USA TODAY* bestselling author RaeAnne Thayne,
included in this 2-in-1 volume!

New York Times bestselling author

SUSAN MALLERY

**brings you home for the holidays
with a timeless collection featuring
romances that will warm your heart!**

Only Us: A Fool's Gold Holiday

Pet groomer Carina Fiore wants nothing more than to confess her feelings to the man she loves. She's drawn to veterinarian Cameron McKenzie's good looks, caring nature and especially his devotion to his young daughter. There's just one problem—he's her boss. But when a kiss under the mistletoe unlocks the simmering passion between them, Rina and Cameron may just find love for the holidays after all....

The Sheik and The Christmas Bride

When Prince As'ad of El Deharia agrees to adopt three orphaned American girls, he does so on one condition—that their beautiful teacher, Kayleen James, become their nanny. His plan is to leave her to deal with the children as he continues his life undisturbed. But all that changes when Kayleen and the girls invade the palace—and As'ad's heart—and change it for the better.

A Christmas Bride

Available now.

REQUEST YOUR FREE BOOKS!

2 FREE NOVELS
FROM THE ROMANCE COLLECTION
PLUS 2 FREE GIFTS!

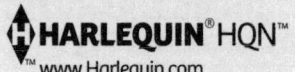

LINDA LAEL MILLER

77661	BIG SKY MOUNTAIN	___ $7.99 U.S.	___	$9.99 CAN.
77681	McKETTRICK'S HEART	___ $7.99 U.S.	___	$9.99 CAN.
77677	McKETTRICK'S PRIDE	___ $7.99 U.S.	___	$9.99 CAN.
77643	BIG SKY COUNTRY	___ $7.99 U.S.	___	$9.99 CAN.
77642	McKETTRICK'S LUCK	___ $7.99 U.S.	___	$9.99 CAN.
77623	THE McKETTRICK LEGEND	___ $7.99 U.S.	___	$9.99 CAN.
77606	HOLIDAY IN STONE CREEK	___ $7.99 U.S.	___	$9.99 CAN.
77600	THE CREED LEGACY	___ $7.99 U.S.	___	$9.99 CAN.
77580	CREED'S HONOR	___ $7.99 U.S.	___	$9.99 CAN.
77561	MONTANA CREEDS: LOGAN	___ $7.99 U.S.	___	$9.99 CAN.
77555	A CREED IN STONE CREEK	___ $7.99 U.S.	___	$9.99 CAN.
77502	THE CHRISTMAS BRIDES	___ $7.99 U.S.	___	$9.99 CAN.
77492	McKETTRICK'S CHOICE	___ $7.99 U.S.	___	$9.99 CAN.
77446	McKETTRICKS OF TEXAS: AUSTIN	___ $7.99 U.S.	___	$9.99 CAN.
77441	McKETTRICKS OF TEXAS: GARRETT	___ $7.99 U.S.	___	$9.99 CAN.
77436	McKETTRICKS OF TEXAS: TATE	___ $7.99 U.S.	___	$9.99 CAN.
77388	THE BRIDEGROOM	___ $7.99 U.S.	___	$8.99 CAN.
77364	MONTANA CREEDS: TYLER	___ $7.99 U.S.	___	$7.99 CAN.
77358	MONTANA CREEDS: DYLAN	___ $7.99 U.S.	___	$7.99 CAN.
77330	THE RUSTLER	___ $7.99 U.S.	___	$7.99 CAN.
77296	A WANTED MAN	___ $7.99 U.S.	___	$7.99 CAN.
77200	DEADLY GAMBLE	___ $7.99 U.S.	___	$9.50 CAN.
77198	THE MAN FROM STONE CREEK	___ $7.99 U.S.	___	$9.50 CAN.

(limited quantities available)

TOTAL AMOUNT	$	_____
POSTAGE & HANDLING	$	_____
($1.00 FOR 1 BOOK, 50¢ for each additional)		
APPLICABLE TAXES*	$	_____
TOTAL PAYABLE	$	_____

(check or money order—please do not send cash)

To order, complete this form and send it, along with a check or money order for the total above, payable to Harlequin HQN, to: **In the U.S.:** 3010 Walden Avenue, P.O. Box 9077, Buffalo, NY 14269-9077; **In Canada:** P.O. Box 636, Fort Erie, Ontario, L2A 5X3.

Name: _____

Address: _____ City: _____

State/Prov.: _____ Zip/Postal Code: _____

Account Number (if applicable): _____

075 CSAS

*New York residents remit applicable sales taxes.
*Canadian residents remit applicable GST and provincial taxes.

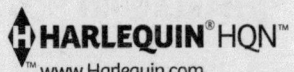

HARLEQUIN®HQN™
www.Harlequin.com

PHLLM1112BL

The Author

MARGARET LAURENCE was born in Neepawa, Manitoba, in 1926. Upon graduation from Winnipeg's United College in 1947, she took a job as a reporter for the *Winnipeg Citizen*.

From 1950 until 1957 Laurence lived in Africa, the first two years in Somalia, the next five in Ghana, where her husband, a civil engineer, was working. She translated Somali poetry and prose during this time, and began her career as a fiction writer with stories set in Africa.

When Laurence returned to Canada in 1957, she settled in Vancouver, where she devoted herself to fiction with a Ghanaian setting: in her first novel, *This Side Jordan*, and in her first collection of short fiction, *The Tomorrow-Tamer*. Her two years in Somalia were the subject of her memoir, *The Prophet's Camel Bell*.

Separating from her husband in 1962, Laurence moved to England, which became her home for a decade, the time she devoted to the creation of five books about the fictional town of Manawaka, patterned after her birthplace, and its people: *The Stone Angel*, *A Jest of God*, *The Fire-Dwellers*, *A Bird in the House*, and *The Diviners*.

Laurence settled in Lakefield, Ontario, in 1974. She complemented her fiction with essays, book reviews, and four children's books. Her many honours include two Governor General's Awards for Fiction and more than a dozen honorary degrees.

Margaret Laurence died in Lakefield, Ontario, in 1987.

MARGARET LAURENCE

The Fire-Dwellers

With an Afterword by Sylvia Fraser

M&S

Canadian Cataloguing in Publication Data

Laurence, Margaret, 1926-1987
The fire-dwellers

(New Canadian Library)

ISBN 0-7710-9987-8

I. Title   II. Series
PS8523.A86F57 1988   C813'.54   C88-094198-7
PR9199.3.L39F57 1988

McClelland & Stewart Inc.
The Canadian Publishers
481 University Avenue
Toronto, Ontario
M5G 2E9

Printed and bound in Canada
Typesetting by Pickwick

If I pass the burial spot of Nero
I shall say to the wind, "Well, well" –
I who have fiddled in a world on fire,
I who have done so many stunts not worth doing.

CARL SANDBURG, *Losers*

One

Ladybird, ladybird,
Fly away home;
Your house is on fire,
Your children are gone.

CRAZY RHYME. Got it on the brain this morning. That's from trying to teach Jen a few human words yesterday. Why anybody would want to teach a kid a thing like that, I wouldn't know. Half those nursery rhymes are gruesome, when you come to think of it. Here is a candle to light you to bed, and here comes a chopper to chop off your head. Just the thing to make the sprouts sleep soundly, especially if followed by that prayer about if I should die before I wake. Maybe it's okay, though. Prepares them for what they can expect. Stacey, you sure are joyful first thing in the morning. First thing, hell. It's a quarter to nine, and here's me not dressed yet.

The full-length mirror is on the bedroom door. Stacey sees images reflected there, distanced by the glass like humans on TV, less real than real and yet more sharply focused because isolated and limited by a frame. The double bed is unmade, and on a chair rests a jumble of her clothes, carelessly shed stockings like round nylon puddles, roll-on girdle in the shape of a tire where she has rolled it off. On another chair, Mac's dirty shirt is neatly folded. Two books reside on the bedside table – *The Golden Bough* and *Investments and You*, Hers and His, both unread. On the dressing table, amid the nonmagic jars and lipsticks are scattered photographs of Katie, Ian, Duncan and Jen at various ages. Hung above the bed is a wedding picture, Stacey twenty-three, almost beautiful although not knowing it then, and Mac twenty-seven, hopeful confident lean, Agamemnon king of men or the equivalent, at least to her. Sitting on the bed, Stacey sees mirrored her own self in the present flesh, insufficiently concealed by a short mauve nylon nightgown with the ribbon now gone from the neckline and one shoulder frill yanked off by some kid or other.

— God knows how old this damn nightie is. I've got to get some new ones. One, anyway. We're not all that broke any more. I'll get two, today, both fancy as hell. What difference will that make? None. Look at that Christly book – why do I keep it on the bedside table? I'll never get around to reading it. *Essential background*, the guy kept saying. He had probably read it a thousand times. If I wanted to take yet another evening course, why did I have to pick Mythology and Modern Man? Sounded classy, that's why. I went twice. Fees wasted.

Stacey looks at her underwear on the chair but makes no move toward it. Her eyes are drawn back to the mirror.

— Everything would be all right if only I was better educated. I mean, if I were. Or if I were beautiful. Okay, that's asking too much. Let's say if I took off ten or so pounds. Listen, Stacey, at thirty-nine, after four kids, you can't expect to look like a sylph. Maybe not, but for hips like mine there's no excuse. I wish I lived in some country where broad-beamed women were fashionable. Everything will be all right when the kids are older. I'll be more free. Free for what? What in hell is the matter with you, anyway? Everything *is* all right. *Everything is all right.* Come on, fat slob, get up off your ass and get going. There's a sale on downtown, remember? Singing ad on local station – *Dollar Forty-nine Day plink plink*. Funny thing, I never swear in front of my kids. This makes me feel I'm being a good example to them. Example of what? All the things I hate. Hate, but perpetuate.

Stacey gets dressed and takes Jen, two, over to Tess Fogler's, next door. Tess is still in her housecoat, but being tall and slender looks as though ready to receive the Peruvian ambassador. Tess's hair is honey-blond and even this early in the day is done in a flawless French roll. Stacey, who is shorter than she would like to be, is wearing her pale-blue last year's spring coat and, because her dark unruly hair needs doing, a small white veil-enfolded straw hat which she dislikes.

— My God I look awful   how does she always look so
    Tess, it's terribly kind of you.
    Heavens no, I'm always glad to
    Well I certainly appreciate
    Jen's no bother, are you honey?
    Mumble mumble squawk
    My, she's determined not to communicate, isn't she?
— That's right, rub it in. If you had kids, you'd know it's not such a laugh.
    I guess the other kids wait on her too much.
    Come on, honey, want a cookie?
    She's just had breakfast.
— Don't feed the animals. I know your cookies. Short-bread. Last time she threw up when I got her home. God, I'm ungrateful.
    Tess, thanks a million – I'm really grateful.
    It's nothing. Now you run right along now.
    What cat noises go on in her head? Maybe none. Maybe only me. Stacey, you rotten old bitch.
— Tess, Katie will pick up Jen on the way back from school at lunchtime if I'm not back, okay?
    Sure, okay.
    Stacey walks to the corner of Bluejay Crescent and gets the bus downtown. But she does not go to the sale. She gets off near the waterfront and starts walking. She is

not cracking up. It is just that she has lived in this city, jewel of the Pacific Northwest, for going on twenty years, and she does not know anything about it. Inexplicably and suddenly, she feels it is time she learned. She knows she will not learn this way.

The pigeons are shitting all over the granite ceno-taph, she is glad to see. Stacey stops and reads the inscription. *Their Names Shall Live Forevermore.* And on another side, *Does It Mean Nothing to You.* No question mark. Along the steps at the base, three old men sit in the feeble sunlight, coughing and spitting, clenching their arms across their skinny chests, murmuring something to one another, memories, perhaps, or curses against now.

— I guess they feel at home here. It was their war, my father's war. He spoke of it once, just once. Mother was out one evening, and Rachel was seven and asleep. He told me about a boy of eighteen – hand grenade went off near him and the blast caught the kid between the legs. My dad cried when he told it, because the kid didn't die. My dad was drunk, but then he wouldn't have spoken of it if he hadn't been. Mac never talks about his war, never has, not that he talks much about anything any more. Ian was ten this year and Duncan seven. Well, even if I'd had four girls, so what?

The streets are just beginning to waken. They keep late hours at night in this part of town. A few men in windbreakers and jeans are hanging around café doors. At Ben's Economy Mart, the windows are full of little penned cards – *Get a Load of This Bargain Only $10.95, How About This at $4.75? We're Cheating Ourselves at $9.95* – and other pieces of folk literature, propped against suit-cases, kitbags, lumberjacks' boots, bush knives, thermos flasks and shiny double-bitted axes. In the lobby of the Princess Regal Hotel, some yawning yellow-toothed fish-wife, fleshwife, sagging guttily in a print dress sad with poppies, is sweeping up last night – heel-squashed ciga-rette butts, Kleenex blown into or bawled into, and ashes.

Old men are sitting there, too, sitting in the red plastic-covered chairs, waiting for the beer parlor to open, so somebody can stand them a drink and they can accept haughtily, their scorn some kind of sop to their pride.

— What is it like, really? How would I know? People live in those rooms above the stores, people who go to the cafés and bars at night, who prowl these streets that are their territory. Men down from the forests or off the fish boats. Faithless loggers clobbering their faithless women. Kids gaming with LSD – *look at me, Polly, I'm Batman – zoom* from sixth floor window into the warm red embrace of a cement death. Ancient mariners tottering around in search of lifeblood, a gallon of Calona Royal Red. Whores too old or sick-riddled to work any classier streets. Granite-eyed youngsters looking for a fix, trying to hold their desperation down. Is it like that? All I know is what I read in the papers. "Seventeen-Year-Old on Drug Charge." "Girl Kills Self, Lover." "Homeless Population Growing, Says Survey." "Car Smash Decapitates Indian Bride, Groom." "Man Sets Room Ablaze, Perishes." All sorts of cheery stuff. What do I know of it? I see the dead faces in a mocking procession, looking at me, looking again, shrugging, saying *There's stability for you.* Do I deserve this? Yes, and yet goddammit, *not* yes. Nearly twenty years here, and I don't know the place at all or feel at home. Maybe I wouldn't have, in any city. I never like to say so to anybody. I always think they might think it's obvious I'm from a small town.

Stacey Cameron, nearly nineteen, expert typist, having shaken the dust of Manawaka off herself at last. Stacey, five foot three, breasts like apples as it says in the Song of Solomon. Stacey in scarlet dressmaker suit, fussy lace blouse. Good-bye to the town undertaker, her father, capable only of dressing the dead in between bouts with his own special embalming fluid. (Dad? I'm sorry. But I had to go.) Good-bye to her long-suffering mother. (Now

I'm not sure any longer what lay behind your whining eyes.) Good-bye to Stacey's sister, always so clever. (When I think you're still there, I can't bear it.) Good-bye, prairies. On the train, a Newfoundland woman with six kids, going to join her husband in an army camp in Chilliwack. None of them had ever seen a train before. One of the kids vomited in the Ladies', and Stacey started to help her wipe it up. Then the porter came in and said he'd do it. He was brown and big and he looked at Stacey with amusement. It hadn't occurred to her that on a train you weren't expected to clean up as you were at home. The lady left with her bleak brat, and the porter said *Where you going?* Stacey told him Vancouver, and he asked if she had a place to stay. She said, chirpy as a sparrow now, out of pure need, I thought I'd look around. *Don't look around, sweetheart,* he said. *Go to the YWCA. That's what I tell all the prairie girls.* So she did that. Small-town girl.

Stacey's children will need to know this city. At present, the boys' domain is only the back yards, the white-flowering dogwood trees for climbing, the alleys where garbage tins teeter and lean castaway cats scrounge, the garages empty in daytime and littered with planks and tins of nails and stiffened paintbrushes – the places where children plot their secret revolutions.

— Maybe the best thing would be to bring them up in the very veins of the city, toss them into it like into a lake and say swim or else. But I couldn't bring myself to do that. Mac would think I was off my rocker even to think of it, if I ever mentioned it to him, which of course I wouldn't.

Stacey walks more quickly and uneasily. Then she finds she is beside the harbor. The gulls are spinning high, freewheeling. Wings like white arcs of light crescenting above the waterfront. Voices mocking piratically at the city's edges. But the city is doing too much shrieking itself to hear the gulls.

— If they're prophets in bird form, they might as well save their breath. They aren't prophets, though. They only look it, angelic presences and voices like gravel out of a grave. Birds in prophet form. They couldn't care less. They scavenge from the city, that's all, and from those black rusty freighters doing their imitations of monolithic ghosts, clanking and groaning out there. If this city were gone, the wings would skim unmourningly away, off to deride and suck up to some other city, if there were any. Even if there weren't, the gulls wouldn't be too upset. Change of diet, that's all. No more sea-sodden bread crusts and waterlogged orange peel.

> At the beach, once. Stacey watching a gull repeat-edly dropping a closed clamshell from a great height. Finally the shell cracked on a rock, and the bird landed and calmly fed. Stacey had to admire such a simple knowledge of survival.

— I don't want to look any more. Why did I come here? I want to go home. The kids will be back from school for lunch. What'll they think if I'm not there? Katie will make the sandwiches for the others. That's no excuse. Mustn't rely on her like that. She's only fourteen. It's not fair to her. Ian won't be worried, but Duncan will. *Where's Mum?* He always thinks I've been run over or something. Who made him that way? Where's the bus stop? Here. Come on, blasted bus – I've got to get home, right now. *Ladybird, ladybird, fly away home* – now, stop it, Stacey. Just cut it out. They are perfectly all right. Everything is all right. Tomorrow I will go on the banana diet. With luck, I should be able to lose seven pounds in seven days. Will Mac ever be surprised. Yeh, you do that, Stacey, doll. You just do that, eh?

Stacey sits very quietly on the bus, looking out the window in the belief that if she does not look at other people, they will not look at her. It is her matronly coat, hat and gloves which make her self-conscious. She feels more at home in slacks, but cannot wear them downtown in case it should embarrass her children to know she had done so.

— Must've been off my head, wandering around the harbor so long. Didn't even get the nightgowns. Are the kids okay? Damn, I wish I didn't always have to be home at the right time. At the Day of Judgment, God will say *Stacey MacAindra, what have you done with your life?* And I'll say, *Well, let's see, Sir, I think I loved my kids.* And He'll say, *Are you certain of that?* And I'll say, *God, I'm not certain about anything any more.* So He'll say, *To hell with you, then. We're all positive thinkers up here.* Then again, maybe He wouldn't. Maybe He'd say, *Don't worry, Stacey, I'm not all that certain, either. Sometimes I wonder if I even exist.* And I'd say, *I know what you mean, Lord. I have the same trouble with myself.*

The bus crawls. The traffic is like two shoals of great metallic fish, frantic to get back to the spawning grounds, but not moving with the fine silence of fishes. Hooting and honking. Grinding of gears. Starting and stopping. And people yelling. The noise strikes at Stacey.

— I'm getting so I can't stand uproar any more. I never used to be this way. Now one of the kids shrieks and I pounce, snarling. It's unnatural. I used to have very steady nerves. Sometimes I look through the living-room window at the snow mountains, far off, and I wish I could go there, just for a while, with no one else around and hardly any sounds at all, the wind muttering, maybe, and the snow in weird sculptures and caverns, quiet. I said some of this to Jake Fogler once and he said I had a death wish. So now I don't think I've got a right to think that about the mountains. How can you win? On the other hand, since when is Jake a psychiatrist?

The buildings at the heart of the city are brash, flashing with colors, solid and self-confident. Stacey is reassured by them, until she looks again and sees them charred, open to the impersonal winds, glass and steel broken like vulnerable live bones, shadows of people frog-splayed on the stone like in that other city.

— Lunatic. Mac says *Less danger now than ten years ago*. I guess he's right. I always say *I guess you're right*. More fool me, for agreeing so easily, but is it worth the upset not to? I ask myself. *Pre-mourning*. Such a brainy female she was – which evening course was that? Oh yeh, Aspects of Contemporary Thought. I asked her if she didn't worry. I'd worried for twenty years and couldn't seem to stop. And she said in that aloof crystalline voice, *Pre-mourning is a form of self-indulgence*. What should I do? Make a sign and hang it up in my kitchen?

A girl gets on the bus and sits beside Stacey. She has clear skin, unpimpled and unpowdered, and long straight blond hair which looks as though she has ironed it. Stacey smiles a little, being reminded of Katie. Then her smile is lost in self-awareness.

— What's she seeing? Housewife, mother of four, this slightly too short and too amply rumped woman with coat of yesteryear, hemlines all the wrong length as Katie is always telling me, lipstick wrong color, and crowning comic touch, the hat. *Man, how antediluvian can you get?* Is that what she's thinking? I don't know. But I still have this sense of some monstrous injustice. I want to explain. *Under this chapeau lurks a mermaid, a whore, a tigress.* She'd call a cop and I'd be put in a mental ward.

> Stacey Cameron, seventeen. Flamingo Dance Hall every Saturday night, jitterbugging. Knowing by instinct how to move, loving the boy's closeness, whoever he was, loving the male smell of him. Stacey spinning like light, like all the painted singing tops of all the spinning world, whirling laughter across a polished floor. Five minutes ago. *Is* time? How?

Stacey gets off the bus at Bluejay Crescent. Then the sound she always dreads to hear. *Scree-ee!* Brakes. The white Buick shudders to a stop and the man climbs out. Very very slowly, as though he were moving underwater.

He is terrified to look at the boy lying on the road. Stacey cannot see the boy's face. Only the blue jeans. He could be seven years old, or ten. He is not making a sound. No cry. Nothing.

Stacey does not go over to look, because she cannot. Instead, she begins running. Along the sidewalk, heels snagging on the cement, running crazily, until she reaches the big dark-green frame house with gabled roof and screened front porch.

Katie!

Yeh? What?

Where are the boys?

How should I know? They were here a minute ago. Where you been?

Stacey runs through the house and out the back door. Ian and Duncan are playing in the back yard. The two auburn heads are bent over the wheels of the bug Ian is making. They look up and see her.

Hi. Where *you* been, all this time?

Sorry. I – I missed the bus. I'll get your lunch right now.

Katie comes downstairs and looks curiously at Stacey, who is now sitting in the kitchen with her hands over her face.

Mum? You okay? Hey, what's the matter?

I'm okay. I thought for a second – there was this boy – an accident – white Buick – just at the corner. I didn't know –

Oh Mum. That's awful. Please, don't cry. Here – have a Kleenex.

Katie stands there, awkwardly, inexperienced at consoling, looking at Stacey from wide grey eyes. She is wearing a dress the startling color of unripe apples, and her long straight auburn hair looks as though she has ironed it, which she has. No lipstick, but green eye make-up. For an instant Stacey catches hold of her hand and holds it.

— It's supposed to be the other way around. What a rock of Gibraltar I turned out to be. Katie, you're so goddam beautiful. Sometimes I feel like a beat-up old bitch.

Katie, I feel about a hundred.

Well, you don't look so hot, either. Just at the moment, I mean. Want me to bring Jen downstairs. She's playing in her room. I fetched her from the Foglers'.

Thanks, honey.

Normality is re-established, and Stacey takes off her coat and hat and starts making sandwiches.

> Stacey in hospital, holding Katherine Elizabeth, age twenty-four hours. Katie with eyes shut tightly, walnut-sized fists clenched, look of utter composure. *I did it. She's here. She's alive. Who'd believe I could have borne a kid this beautiful?* (Or any kind of kid, for that matter.)

You have to keep quiet about all that. Restraint. Some wise guy is always telling you how you're sapping the national strength. Overprotective. Or else, you don't really care about them – you're just compensating because you're guilty on account of the fact that in your core you're trying to possess them, like hypnosis. Or something. Article in magazine at hairdresser's. "Nine Ways the Modern Mum May Be Ruining Her Daughter." I should never read them, but I always do, and then I check in my mind to see how many ways I'm ruining Katie. But how can you tell? I can see the doll who wrote that one. Jazzy office stuffed with plastic plants and never a daughter in sight.

The boys come in. Stacey does not hug them. She restricts herself to putting a hand on their hair and mentioning the need for haircuts. Ian's hair is the exact color of Mac's, dark red, and Duncan's is a little lighter, red-gold.

At quarter to one, Katie and the boys go back to school. Stacey watches them go. Ian walks ahead, as usual, slim and wiry, tall for ten, impatient, moving with a quick grace, perfectly in command of his muscles. Duncan rarely hurries, and is largely unaware of other people. Yet he will tell Stacey what he is thinking, sometimes. Ian guards himself at every turn.

— What did I do to make him that way? It's the confusion that bothers me. Everything happens all at once, never one thing at a time, so how in hell do you know what effect anything is having on them? That other article, last week. "Are You Castrating Your Son?" God, Sir, how do I know? It's getting so I'm suspicious of my slightest word or act. Maybe I shouldn't have ruffled Ian's hair just now.

Stacey picks up Jen, who is robust enough but who seems fragile. Picking her up is like holding a kitten, when the first thing that is noticeable is not the softness of it but the fact that all its bones can be felt.

Come on, flower. Time for a sleep.

Babble babble

Come on, honey, *talk*. It's easy when you try.

— Maybe she's got ESP, like those sickening kids in that SF movie, whose eyes glowed like lighthouses when they were communicating by mental telepathy with one another. She's probably chatting away silently this very moment with some mutated kid in Samarkand or Omsk. Oh God, it's not all that funny. What if there really is something wrong? Should I be doing something about it? What I should be doing right now is finding out who that boy is, and how badly hurt. I can't. It's all I can do to cope with what goes on inside these four walls. This fortress, which I'd like to believe strong.

After school, Ian and Duncan are in the back yard. The bug consists of wheels, planks, steering apparatus, nails, pieces of wire with some essential purpose. Ian works dartingly, knowing which hammer or screwdriver to use. Duncan has no mechanical know-how, but is trying hard to please Ian. Then wham. Chaos. Yells. Imprecations, threats, denials. Poundingly, they are both in the kitchen.

Mum, tell Duncan to leave my bug alone!

You said I could help. You *said!*

I didn't say you could wreck it, dumb idiot.

I wasn't. I never.

You can't just nail on the wheels, you moron. How do
you think they'll turn?

You think you're so

You keep your hands off it

I won't – it's not fair

You better, or I'll

Fighting, Ian holds himself back a little, using his
brains to plan attack. Duncan fights with the flailing recklessness of the one who knows he cannot possibly win.
The fury rises until at last Stacey is unable to bear their
battle and their noise. Cain and his brother must have
started their hatred like this.

Cut it out! Both of you! You hear?

Slam. Only when she has done it does Stacey realize
she has grabbed their shoulders and flung them both to
the floor with as much force as she could muster. Ian does
not cry. His pride sometimes permits him stomach
cramps, but never tears. His bony face is bleached with
anger. He rises and rushes outside, seizes the uncompleted
vehicle and throws it down the outside cement steps which
lead into the basement.

The hell with it then! I don't give a damn!

The wheels come off and tumble across the basement
floor. The cracking sound is the nailed boards coming
apart. Duncan, listening, looks blank with bewilderment.

He *can't*. He can't go and break it, Mum.

Duncan does not ever destroy the work he has done.
He draws pictures of the shark-shaped rocket which will
one day take him to Mars or Saturn, and of the scarlet
forests he will walk there, under the glare of innumerable
purple suns. He puts them away, and sometimes digs one
out and looks at it with amusement as the product of an
earlier self. But he never destroys them.

Ian looks at the shambles for an instant, his face
desolated. Then he turns and runs to the garage, to the
loft, full of tent poles and torn canvas chairs and sparrows'
nests, where once Stacey found a scribbler half full of

writing, headed "Captain Ian MacAindra His Direy of How We Beat Enimy." And she had wondered where he was bound for.

Stacey puts her arms around Duncan for a minute. Then he goes outside and glances up at the loft, as though wanting to go there but not daring. He stands on the lawn, looking as though he cannot figure out what to do.

— If Mac knew, he would think I was unbalanced. He never hits the kids in anger. No, maybe not, but that icy calm of his is worse. Okay, so I'm trying to justify myself. Earlier, I was worried sick in case that kid was one of mine. Now, look. Why? What if I hit one of them too hard sometime, without meaning to? Am I a monster? They nourish me and yet they devour me, too. God, how can I make all this better as if it hadn't happened? No answer. No illumination from on high. As if I expected any. If I could only talk about it. But who wants to know, and anyway, could I say? I can't forget that piece in the paper. Young mother killed her two-month-old infant by smothering it. I wondered how that sort of thing could ever happen. But maybe it was only that the baby was crying and crying, and she didn't know what to do, and was maybe frantic about other things entirely, and suddenly she found she had stopped the noise. I cannot think this way. I must not.

Stacey pours herself a massive gin and tonic, and gets dinner. Mac is away on the road and will not be home until late tonight. The kids eat, do homework, look at TV. At eleven, even Katie is stashed away in bed and Stacey is off duty. She takes the current glass of gin and tonic up to the bedroom. She locks the door, temporarily, in case a kid wakens, strips and looks at herself in the full-length mirror.

> Every time Stacey ran down the stairs from the apartment above Cameron's Funeral Home, which was home, she paused in flight like a hummingbird or helicopter and sneaked a glance into the mirror halfway down, circular and heavy, gilded in coy

cherubs with bunches of grapes draped over their private parts. *Stacey, Stacey, vanity isn't becoming.* The soft persistent mew from upstairs, the voice that never tired of saying how others ought to be and never were. And Stacey would be off, to laugh and talk so loudly in the jukebox-loud café that no one would guess she cared about her ugliness.

She actually believed it was vanity, Mother did. *It's not how you look, it's what you are that counts*, she used to say – admirably, I guess, but brother, that was one of the finest lies anyone ever spun me. Do I know that little about Katie now? That old album – and when I saw a snapshot of myself, years ago, I thought *My heavens, I was actually pretty – why didn't I know it then?*

Stacey drinks the gin and tonic slowly, trying to make it last. She brushes her hair and makes up her face and puts on perfume. Then she looks in the mirror again. No change.

— Oh Cleopatra. You old swayback. Four kids have altered me. The stretch marks look like little silver worms in parallel processions across my belly and thighs. My breasts aren't bad, and at least my ankles aren't thick. Mac said once he liked the color of my eyes, greenish-grey. But there used to be a slight hollow on the side of my buttocks, a little concave place that showed when I wore a tight skirt, and he liked that, too, and it isn't there any more. Filled in with the slow accumulation of flesh. Not flesh. Fat. F.A.T. I can make the hollow be there again momentarily if I tense my muscles. But who is going to go through life remembering to hold their tight muscles in, just so they'll have an attractive ass?

Stacey slops on some more perfume. The gin is gone. She puts on her housecoat and tiptoes downstairs to refill the glass. She returns, sits on the bedroom chair, smoking, no longer looking in the mirror.

— Why doesn't he get home? I want him. Right now, this minute. No, I don't. I want some other man, someone

I've never been with. Only Mac for sixteen years. What are other men like? It's just as bad for him, maybe worse. He looks at the girls on the street, all the young secretaries stepping lightly, the slim fillies of all the summers, and his face grows inheld and bitter. I want to comfort him, but can't, any more than he can comfort me, for neither of us is supposed to feel this way. Except that I know he does. I wonder if he knows I do? Sometimes I think I'd like to hold an entire army between my legs. I think of all the men I'll never make love with, and I regret it as though it were the approach of my own death. I'm not monogamous by nature. And yet I am. I can't imagine myself as anyone else's woman, for keeps. What does Mac do when he's on the road? He doesn't sell vanilla essence every evening, that's for sure. God, I'm unfair. Are the small-town whores so glamorous? And anyway, it's only my conditioned reflex. I don't worry that much, whatever he does out there. It doesn't seem all that earth-shattering. It's jealousy, baby, admit it. He can and you can't. So okay. But apart from that angle, I'd like to be on the road. Not for anything but just to be going somewhere.

Mac on the road, soaring along as though the old Chev were a winged chariot, through the mountains and the turquoise air, into the valley where the rivers run with names like silkenly flowing water, Similkameen, Tulameen, Coquihalla, the names on maps, clear brown water over the shifting green stones, where the pine and tamarack and the thin spruce trees stand a little way off, blue-green and black-green needles dry in the dry gold air, where the tall barbed grasses are never touched or cut but remain eternally high with their pale seedheads like oats bent in the light wind that blows always, where it is sun all the way in the fields of purple fireweed where only the bees make their furred music.

Stacey knows it is not like that for him. He does door-to-door. Nights, it is motels on the fringes of towns, gaudy dusty shacks with names like Rainbow and River-view and small neon signs announcing *Eats* and *Vacancy*, where drowsy Alsatian dogs sprawl on the gravel drive-ways and the proprietor's kids throw stones at one another, and the cars rocket past – *ching! ching! ching!* – like a roaring clock recording the minutes, and the rooms are scantily clad in imitation furniture, the table covered with burn scars and wet beer bottle circles, the floor buck-ling linoleum, and the shower that dribbles lukewarm water unpredictably. Days, and it is all doors, knocking and waiting, and flint-faced females who imagine their unappetizing virtue to be in peril, so *slam*.

— He never talks of it. He won't. He refuses. Last week a man knocked at my door, a young man with amber eyes pale and circular behind magnifying glasses. He held out a pamphlet in half-apologetic offering. *Safety in Time of War*. Ragged crimson letters like rising flames. I did a double take and saw the smaller letters underneath. *God's War of the Last Day*. Oh, that war. He was a Redeemer's Advocate. I nearly closed the door quickly. But then I didn't. He was in the living room for an hour and a half and I thought he'd never go. It can't be good, to have a door slammed in your face.

Drabble's, as well as being a purveyor of vanilla, lemon and orange essence, peppermint and raspberry extract and maple-type flavoring, also handles a wide se-lection of sprays – Forest Petal House Freshener, Silk Brocade Hair Spray, Pink Cross Athlete's Foot Spray, Angel-Breath Mouth Freshener, Honey Blossom Garbage Tin Spray, and others. Mac has been doing the circuit for Drabble's for seven years. He took it on immediately after he stopped selling encyclopedias.

— He was doing okay, in encyclopedias. He never lost his job. He quit. He kicked himself for it afterwards. Listen, Mac, you did right. He's never mentioned it since, but I've never forgotten the night he told me what hap-pened.

Mac, in a one-room flat above a store, near the docks. Going through the spiel. You, too, can travel to London, England, or Paris, France, or the frangipani-perfumed South Seas, through these spectacularly scenic pictures in *Once-Over World*, given free with every contract for a full set of encyclopedias, agreeable monthly or weekly terms. And the guy who was picking up the pen to sign was a pensioner, old retired logger, who wanted to see the picture of Piccadilly, London, where he'd once gone on leave in 1917 from the trenches. Mac suddenly grabbed the contract and tore it up, telling the old guy he needed encyclopedias like he needed a hole in the head, and there was a public library only a few blocks away. The old guy was furious, cheated. So much for gesture. But Mac went back to the office and quit, anyway.

— At that precise moment, didn't I have to go and get pregnant? I shouldn't have. It was my fault. We were both a little stoned the night it happened. I thought I'd put the damn equipment in, but next morning there it was on the floor beside the bed. After I was certain, Mac didn't say a word. He went to work for Drabble's, which was the first job that came along. Was it then he started to go underground, living in his own caves? If I mentioned the possibility of trying something else, looking around for another job, he'd only say *I'm not complaining, am I?* I couldn't very well say *Yes*, but it seemed he was, in some way. I kept saying I was sorry, which must have got pretty boring for him. I *was* sorry, and yet I wasn't, too. I feel the exact same now. How can I regret Duncan, who isn't like any other person on this earth? When Duncan was born, Mac came to see me, and didn't ask about the baby at all, simply said *You okay?* I guess it was terrible for him. It *was* terrible. But it was his kid, too. It wasn't immaculate conception. Well, he took on the responsibilities, Stacey. What more do you want? After a while business picked up in the spray and flavor trade, and Jen was born, planned.

Stacey in yet another hospital. Mac, handing her two dozen yellow chrysanthemums. *Hey, a girl, eh? You did well.* Stacey taking the flowers, smiling at him, suddenly knowing how late it was, unable to care at all what he said or thought about the new child. They're beautiful, Mac, the flowers. *Glad you like them.* Yes, they're lovely – thanks a million. *That's all right.* Everything was all right. Certainly. Of course. She held Jen in her arms and thought of Duncan.

— Well past midnight, Mac gets home. Stacey wakens and hears his key in the door. He climbs the stairs slowly, his footsteps sounding to her like those of her father, like Matthew's footsteps on the front steps on Sundays, seventy-four years old.

— Mac, for Christ's sake, you're forty-three.

But when he switches on the light in the bedroom, and stands in the doorway, Stacey cannot see that he has changed all that much in sixteen years. He is still as lean as ever, and although his auburn hair has darkened, he has lost none of it. He is still handsome to her. The main change is in the webbed lines around his eyes and on his forehead.

— Worrying about how to support us? If I could only go away and leave him alone, take the sword off his neck. Would he want me to? No good saying he chose me and the kids. He didn't know what he was getting himself into, just as I didn't. Mac – let me explain. Let me tell you how it's been with me. Can't we ever say anything to one another to make up for the lies, the trivialities, the tiredness we never knew about until it had taken up permanent residence inside our arteries?

Hi. You're late, Mac.

My God. Is that my fault? I had to finish up before I started home.

I didn't mean it that way.

Well, that's how it sounded to me.

I'm sorry. I only meant you're late and isn't that too bad. For *you*, for heaven's sake, I meant.

Okay, okay, it doesn't matter.

Doesn't matter! That you misunderstand every single word I utter.

Oh Stacey, for God's sake. I'm tired. Quit exaggerating.

Okay, so I'm exaggerating. It would just be nice if you knew what I meant.

— Why am I doing it like this? If I knew what you meant, as well. Oh Mac. Talk. Please.

I'm sorry. I'm obtuse – okay? But I'm bloody tired and I don't feel like starting one of these

I'm sorry. I didn't mean *that*

All right, all right. Let's forget it, eh? Let's just forget it. I've had about enough for one day.

— And he has. He has. Let's forget it, then. When we're both dead, we'll forget it.

Mac undresses and climbs into bed beside her.

Christ, am I ever beat.

You better get to sleep right away, then.

I've got to.

It's okay, I know.

Well, I'm sorry

You don't have to be sorry

Yeh, but you've been alone all week

It's okay – I'm used to it

Look, are you sure you don't mind?

I don't mind. It's not that. Look, it's okay. Everything is all right – okay?

Yeh, I guess so. God, the traffic was terrible tonight, coming back in. Kids okay?

Yes, everything's fine here. How was it this time?

Oh – could've been worse.

Tell me about it.

Nothing to tell. Same as usual.

What's usual?

Oh, I don't know. Same old crap. Look, are you sure you're okay?

Yes, I'm okay

Good night, then.

Good night.

Stacey Cameron, twelve, visiting for a week with a remote cousin who lived on a farm fifty miles from Manawaka, hating every minute of it, knotted with strangeness and loneliness, scared of cows and coyote-like dogs, sickened by unfamiliar food, potatoes and apple pie at breakfast, thinking of home where she didn't want to be, either, the tomb silences between Niall Cameron and his wife. Stacey, writing her letter home. *How are you? I am fine.*

Beside her, Mac moans a little in his sleep, turns over and is quiet. Stacey is not able to sleep.

— Damn him, snoring away so unconcernedly. I feel like giving him a sharp kick, so he'll wake up and at least we'll both be suffering. All right, God, don't tell me, let me guess. I'm a mean old bitch. I know it. But I ask you, Sir, is it fair that Mac should be systematically restoring his physical and mental energy through sleep while I lie here like a bloody board? What's that you say? You are suggesting that if I am expecting justice I am a bird-brain? You have a point there, Lord. I will have to mull that one over.

One of them cries. The games vanish. Stacey sits up in bed. Mac half wakens.

— Which one? Duncan.

What in hell is the matter now, Stacey?

Duncan. I think he's having a bad dream.

Leave him. You're going to ruin that kid, Stacey. Boy of his age shouldn't have his mother tearing in to see what's the matter every time he wakes up.

The crying increases, thin, attenuated, frightened.

I can't just leave him, Mac.

Go ahead, then. What a man he's going to grow up to be.

Stacey stumbles out of bed and down the long hall, through the darkness, no light needed, every hillock of carpet known to her bare feet. It has been this way always with the boys. Ian used to have nightmares, and now Duncan does.

— It's the one thought Mac can't bear, the insufficient masculinity of one of his sons. He wonders what will happen when they leave home, what unnatural flowering. He tortures himself (or so I think) with the idea, and then he turns on them and does his sergeant-major act, the toughening process, or so he believes. Sometimes I see it his way, and I think *How can I ever make up for what I've done to them? How can I ever answer or atone for it?* And yet I keep going to them when they waken and cry out. It's as though I'm compelled. What I cannot bear is the thought that one of them is trapped in his nightmare, alone in there. Then I think that lots worse things could happen to them than to be queer, and that when they're away and on their own, in some ways it wouldn't matter to me at all who they held as long as there was someone and they could bring themselves to cry out. If Katie grew up bent, would I feel the same? The question could never arise with Katie. Oh? There you are, doll – confusion again.

Duncan is partly awake, rubbing his eyes and trying to come back to the world.

Mum?

It's okay, honey. I think you just had a bad dream.

There was all these spikes coming up through my bed.

It's okay – you're awake now.

It was a dream, wasn't it, Mum?

Yeh. Just a dream. Can you go back to sleep now?

Guess so

Duncan rolls over and is asleep once more.

— Has the trap released him? It was of my making, wasn't it? What I did this afternoon to stop the noise.

Stacey kissed his forehead, touching his sweat-damp hair. Then she turns to go. There is a stirring from the other bed, across the room.

Mum?

Ian? You awake? Did Duncan waken you? That's too bad.

It doesn't matter. Good night.

Ian reaches out a hand. For him, this is extraordinary. Stacey holds his hand briefly, trying to interpret, then folds his blankets in around him.

Good night, honey. Sleep well.

Good night, Mum.

— Has he forgiven me? Or does he only need my reassurance, at any price?

When she gets back to the bedroom, Mac is sitting up, smoking.

If you want a pansy for a son, Stacey, you're going the right way about it.

I don't think so.

I know so.

Didn't your mother ever get up in the night when you had a bad dream?

I didn't have any bad dreams that I can think of.

I don't believe it. You've forgotten.

I'm not in the habit of forgetting. Duncan would damn soon get over having bad dreams if he once realized you weren't going to trot in to him every time.

He doesn't do it on purpose. He was scared.

I'll bet. He quieted down soon enough once you traipsed in there.

Mac – don't be angry

I'm not angry

You are

Stacey, I am not angry. I am merely trying to point out that you are babying that boy and it isn't doing him any good. Can't you understand even that?

— Even that. Among all the other incomprehensions? No, I can't understand even that. But if he's right, where does that leave me? Kid-ruiner. Also, his unadmitted fury. But the kids find mine the same. *Mum, don't be mad.* I'm not mad, I tell them. Spoken with deathly intent.

I don't mean to baby him. I'll try not to. Honestly, Mac, I will.

Well, really you should, honey. For his own good.

I will. Honestly.

— I will. I will anything. I will turn myself inside out. I will dance on the head of a pin. I will yodel from the top of the nearest dogwood tree. I will promise anything, for peace. Then I'll curse myself for it, and I'll curse you, too. Oh Mac.

Honestly, Stacey, it's only because I

Yes, I know.

She gets back into bed. Then Mac is not too tired, just when she is. He draws her between his legs, and she touches him sirenly so he will not know. When he is inside her, he puts his hands on her neck, as he sometimes does unpredictably. He presses down deeply on her collarbone.

Mac   please

That can't hurt you   not that much   that's not much Say it doesn't hurt.

It hurts.

It can't. Not even this much. Say it doesn't hurt.

It doesn't hurt.

He comes, then, and goes to sleep. The edges of the day are blurring in Stacey's head now.

— God, Sir, do I know why? Okay, I've aged this man. I've foisted my kids upon him. I yak away at him and he gets fed up, and he finds his exit where I can't follow and don't understand. There are too many people involved in this situation, Lord, you know that? You don't know. Well, Stacey, for heaven's sake get some sleep. Tomorrow everything will look better. Or at least different. Optimist.

The hillside is burning. Who dropped a lighted cigarette? Did she? Evergreen catches fire with terrible ease. In case of forest fire, all the men around have to go and fight it. That is the law of the land. Everyone has to obey the law of the land. But only the men are forced to go. The children have no business to be there. Only one way to get to them. A black fallen tree across the pit. A suspension bridge across the jagged rock canyon. Tree bridge. The ravine is so deep no one has ever dared look down. She will be all right, if only she does not look down. Come on, Stacey, only a little way. The hands. She is holding the hands of one. Which? She will not be allowed to return. Only this one can she take with her, away from the crackling smoke, back to the green world. She must not look to see which one. She must never look, never again, to see which one. She must never know who was left behind. She has to know. No. Not to be borne. Not to be born would be not to have to die. But that would be useless. Philosophy, my dear, is useless under certain circumstances. Their voices? Oh yes – no mistaking them. She would know their voices anywhere. She has to count the voices. But she must not. They know she can hear their voices. They do not know why she cannot come to them. Can she explain, while there is still a moment of time? No time

    BR R R RING

— Where's the damn alarm clock? Oh here. Shut up, you. That's better. Bloody morning once again.

Two

THE MACAINDRA residence on Bluejay Crescent is not classy, but it is not rundown either. Mac and Stacey have lived for twelve years within this large square structure with its high-gabled grey shingled roof, its evergreen-painted cedar-shake-covered walls and its only slightly sagging screened veranda. Stacey is attached to it, partly because she fears new houses and partly because her own veins and skin cells seem connected with this one.

— Mac hates it more every year because it's so dowdy and reflects on him, or so he thinks. Or so I think he thinks. One of these days he'll manage a switch, and we'll move to a pricey new split-level on the west side, furnished with that kind of sleek teak which will make me feel inferior to my own coffee table.

Jen is scrabbling around on the veranda floor. The afternoon has the feverish damp warmth of early summer and Stacey is swinging in the brown-and-white-striped hammock, with tasseled edges, which Mac refers to as The Anachronism. She is studying the front door, which is a lilac color.

— What a fool I was. "Want To Be a Little Off-Beat?" Here's ten ways, the article said. A lilac door was one. So off I tripped to the nearest hardware store to assert my unique individuality with the same tin of paint as two million other dimwits. Conned into idiocy. My mind is full of trivialities. At lunch Ian said *Duncan's piece of cake is miles bigger than mine – it's not fair*, and I roared that they should quit bothering me with trivialities. So when they're at school, do I settle down with the plays of Sophocles? I do not. I think about the color of my front door. That's being unfair to myself. I took that course, Ancient Greek Drama, last winter. Yeh, I took it all right.

Young academic generously giving up his Thursday evenings in the cause of adult education. *Mrs. MacAindra, I don't think you've got quite the right slant on Clytemnestra.* Why not? The king sacrificed their youngest daughter for success in war – what's the queen supposed to do, shout for joy? *That's not quite the point we're discussing, is it? She murdered her husband, Mrs. MacAindra,* (Oh God, don't you think I know that? The poor bitch.) Yeh well I guess you must know, Dr. Thorne. Sorry. *Oh, that's fine – I always try to encourage people to express themselves.*

— Young twerp. Let somebody try killing one of his daughters. But still, he had his Ph.D. What do I have? Grade Eleven. My own fault. I couldn't wait to be on my own and out of Manawaka. Those damn freight trains – I can still hear them, the way they used to wail away far off at night on the prairies, through all the suffocating nights of summer when the air smelled hotly of lilacs, and in winter when the silence was so cold-brittle you thought any sound would crack it like a sheet of thin ice, and all the trains ever said was *Get on your way, somewhere, just so something will happen, get up and get out of this town.* So I did. Business course in Winnipeg, then saving every nickel to come out here. And look at me. Self-educated, but zanily. No wonder I bore Mac. Do I bore him? How do I know? The slightest effort at speech seems too much for him lately, too debilitating. What's he want? I'm not a complete dope. He wouldn't be any better off with someone like Tess Fogler, gorgeous though she may be. Would he? She had a sign made for their house – *Three Five Seven* in scrolled numerals and a bluejay perched on a

crescent moon. *Get it, Stacey? Bluejay Crescent. Cute, eh?*
And I said, *Gee that's really cute, Tess.* These lies will be
the death of me sooner than later, if they haven't already
been. What goes on inside isn't ever the same as what goes
on outside. It's a disease I've picked up somewhere.

*Everything drifts. Everything is slowly swirling, phil-
osophies tangled with the grocery lists, unreal-real anxieties like rose thorns waiting to tear the uncertain flesh,
nonentities of thoughts floating like plankton, green and
orange particles, seaweed – lots of that, dark purple and
waving, sharks with fins like cutlasses, herself held underwater by her hair, snared around auburn-rusted anchor
chains*

Hey! You asleep?

Mac's voice. Stacey leaps out of the hammock, di-
shevelled in pink Bermuda shorts, and looks around for
Jen. What negligence. Asleep on duty. Jen is playing
quietly with her blue plastic tea set on the floor. Relief.

What on earth are you doing home at this time of
day, Mac?

Mac does not reply at once. He stands there, looking
pleased, the lines around his eyes easing a little. Then he
points to a new teal-blue Buick parked in front of the
house.

I've got a new job.

— A new job. He's got a new job. And suddenly I've got
a weird feeling. As though I'd been forgiven after all.

Oh honey that's wonderful. That's terrific. What
doing?

No more door-to-door. Getting orders from drugstores, mainly.

What *is* it?

Richalife. I guess you've heard of *them*.

— I've heard all right. Full-page ads in newspapers.
*Richalife – Not Just Vitamins – A New Concept – A New
Way of Life.* With testimonials. *Both Spirit and Flesh
Altered. Richness Is a Quality of Living.* Singing ads on

local stations, blond angelic trilling. Rallies. Gimmicks falling like the golden shower of stars from fireworks. Oh Jesus lover of my soul

Gosh, Mac, that's – why, that's wonderful.

Whatsamatter? You don't like it?

Sure I like it. Of course. I said so, didn't I? It's marvelous.

Well, I certainly *hope* you think so. Considering it's the best opportunity I've had in

I like it. I think it's great. I'm really delighted, Mac. Tell me.

It's go-ahead, that's all. None of this business of refusing to spend a dime to make a quarter of a million. National firm – headquarters in the east, but they really give the branches their head and let them decide how to handle the local campaign Thor Thorlakson – he's the provincial manager – well, he's a young guy, but exceptional. Really exceptional. If you get a young guy who's good, he's in touch – you know. Thor's got everything going for him. He's quite a guy. You'll have to meet him soon.

I'd love to.

— Yeh, I can hardly wait. Dr. Spender, here I come for forty billion tranquilizers.

He wants to meet all the wives. He likes to find out what a guy's home atmosphere is like.

— Oh he does, does he? I'll turn up in long black tights, a green wig, and a feather boa, mouthing obscenities.

Why is that any of his business, Mac? I mean

All those things affect the way a man does his job. Surely you can see that.

Oh sure. I guess so. The Buick's lovely, Mac.

Yeh, and when I think Drabble's didn't even supply a car. I'm not going to sell the old Chev, Stacey. You need a car.

Me? Oh Mac – honestly?

Sure. You pleased?

Am I!

Stacey kisses him and he holds her unexpectedly closely for an instant. She feels his tremor – not sex, something else.

— Mac, what is it? Are you nervous about taking on a new job? You're only forty-three, for heaven's sake. Or what is it? Why don't you say?

Mac – you're happy about it, aren't you?

I'm bloody delighted. Why ask? Can't you see?

Yeh, sure. The – product – it's okay, you think?

What do you mean? Of course it's okay. Listen, I'll bring the Chev home tonight, eh?

Gosh, Mac, thanks a million. It'll be a lifesaver it'll be absolutely terrific shopping taking the kids to the beach all the hundreds of

That's okay. I'm glad you're pleased.

Then Stacey realizes why he looks different and why she has been puzzling about it at the edges of her mind. He has a crew cut. His dark auburn hair is like a soft brush. Crew cut, fashion of his college days. He sees her looking and he reaches up a hand and touches his head.

Think it looks all right?

I *wondered* why you looked different. It looks great. Really great.

— How many times has he protected me from the sight of myself? *Sure, Stacey, you look really good in that dress*, he said when I bought the green and gold last month. It was only later I knew it was Katie's dress, although wrong size for her. Mac, you're only forty-three. Last time I thought that, I meant how relatively young. Now I mean how relatively not-young.

The evening they go to see Thorlakson, both Mac and Stacey are edgy. Stacey in their bedroom tussles with her hair, while Mac repeatedly clears his throat.

Hem hem hem hem

— Stop it, for heaven's sake, Mac, can't you? It's getting worse, and that awful cough at the end of the throat-clearing – *Whoop! Whoop!* The rosy-fingered dawn in this house sounds like its playing bongo drums. But he keeps on smoking nonstop and gets mad as blazes if I say anything. It worries me, but it revolts me, too, to hear him hoicking up phlegm from his inner recesses. It disgusts him that I pluck out handfuls of my eyebrows with my fingers without knowing it. No one ought to have repulsive mannerisms. We all ought to be physically perfect. I need a state of unblemishment more as the years go by, but I have it less.

Do I look all right, Mac?

Stacey is wearing her black sheath dress, supposedly slenderizing. She tugs at the waist, trying to straighten the wrinkles in the material, but her hips are against her. Mac is looking at his watch and does not glance in her direction.

Fine fine fine you look fine. Aren't you ready *yet?*

Right this minute. C'mon then. *Katie!* No later than ten for you, and don't forget to put Jen before you go to bed, eh? Ian – Duncan – you're to go to bed when Katie tells you, you hear? And no fighting.

A chorus of *Yeh, yeh, okay* comes from various corners of the house.

For Christ's sake, Stacey, they're all *right*. Can't you just leave them?

Sorry sorry sorry

— He's right. I fuss. Mother-hen type. All a load of nonsense. All unnecessary. Another nervous tic. How can I break habits I've acquired so gradually I'm not even aware of them until I see they drive Mac out of his mind?

Timber Lake, sixteen years ago, had hardly any cottages. Jungles of blackberry bushes and salmonberry. Spruce trees darkly still in the sun, and the water so unsullied that you could see the grey-gold minnows flickering. You know something,

Mac? *What?* I like everything about you. *That's good, honey. I like everything about you, too.*

— Why should I think it unbalanced to want to mourn? Why shouldn't I wail like the widows of Ashur if I feel like it? I have cause. Come, come, Stacey. Act your age. That's precisely what I'm doing, God, if you really want to know. Too much mental baggage. Too damn much, at this point. More more more than I want. Things keep spilling out of the suitcases, taking me by surprise, bewildering me as I stand on the platform.

Whatever else you do, Stacey, for God's sake don't get into an argument, will you?

I won't   I won't   do you have to tell me?

I'm only thinking of the time you told Crimpton you were going to join the Redeemer's Advocates – that's all I'm thinking of.

Well, I *was* considering it, Mac. Serenity, I thought. I was going to give it a whirl. But I couldn't. Maybe it was the thought of your dad that stopped me even from going to a meeting. You know, having been a United Church minister and that. I thought he'd have a fit.

He wouldn't have been the only one. C'mon, we're here.

Thor's apartment is in one of the high-risers near the bay. There is a mirror in the elevator, and Stacey spends the up-flight in patting distractedly at her hair. Down a thickly carpeted hall, and then at the gentle bell buzz the door opens and a massive figure fills the doorway.

He*llo* there. Great to see you, Mac. And this

Thor turns to Stacey, gazes down at her, sizes her up, frowns a trace, then gives her an oblique and uninterpretable smile. Mac steps in.

Thor, I'd like you to meet my wife, Stacey.

Now Thor's smile broadens and widens, grows relaxed, genuine, sincere.

Well, *hi* there, Stacey. I've really been looking forward to meeting you.

Mutter mutter me to

Well, come on *in*.

Thor Thorlakson is not actually taller than Mac, but he carries himself carefully straight as though he practices every morning in front of a full-length mirror. His suit is a costly blue-grey, giving the impression of a luminous uniform, a doorman in heaven or perhaps a mace bearer behind the celestial throne. His features have clearly been sculptured by an expert, and his hair is silver. Above the out-jutting jaw and the young face, the silver hair forestedly flourishes, a lion's share of it which he tosses imperially back as they walk along a slippery hall.

— How do you like that? How has he achieved that crowning glory? No peroxide in the kitchen sink for him, you can be quite sure. No damn crew cut, either. He looks vaguely familiar. I think I must've seen him in a magazine or newspaper. It would be funny if he'd ever been a male model. He looks as though he just stepped out of *The Venusian Warlock*, that SF movie I rushed off and saw once when everything got too much. I thought warlock was something like deadlock, but no, and when I saw the movie I thought brother things have come to a fine pass if I can learn from a piece of garbage like this. Thor's the wizard.

Thor motions Stacey to a royal blue canvas-looking chair shaped like an upside-down tent. She sinks down nervously. On the floor, a black-and-white fur rug looks as though it had been made from the skins of stillborn monkeys, softly eerie. The coffee table top is grey-veined marble. Voluminous white drapes are like the heavy fine linens of ancient Rome. On the walls, two abstract paintings in selected shades of orange, black and white. On a sideboard, a sharply orange vessel like a misshapen triangle in thin glass. The place is both ascetic and voluptuous.

I've gone off booze ha-ha. Never was a heavy drinker but used to enjoy a martini before dinner. That was in the B.R. days – before Richalife. Same with caffeine and nicotine – you could say the shackles have been lifted. Once upon a time I could barely face the morning without three cups of coffee and as many cigarettes. Then I started reaching for a Richalife instead. I think we've all got to remember that we're not just selling vitamin pills – we're selling ourselves. I mean ha-ha that sounded a little ambiguous but what I was meaning to say was we stand as living examples. What program you got the family on, Mac?

Well, I haven't quite had time to get it worked out for all of them yet, but I plan to start them the beginning of the week.

— You do, eh? Over my dead body.

Mac, you never said

Then Stacey's jaw clamps shut as her brain receives the signal from Mac's red-flare-sending eyes. His voice goes on without a pause.

I'm on 35-ADDB myself, Thor.

— Another unknown. What has he been doing? Slogging down pills secretly in the bathroom? Now he won't look at me.

Oh yes – let's see now – 35-ADDB – that's age thirty-five to forty, height medium to tall, temperament fair to medium calm, slight tendency to anxiety. Right?

Right. Can you remember them all, Thor?

Most of them. I couldn't have, at one time, of course, but I find now my memory potential was hardly being tapped at all, before. Alertness-wise, the change has been really gratifying. I always had a good memory, mind you, but not what you would call really excellent. Now I think I can honestly and truthfully say it's reached the excellent mark. Have you noticed much change in yourself, Mac?

I sleep better I think

— He *sleeps* better? Better than what? Mac, who's never lain awake one single night in his life that I know of? Has he suffered insomnia in country motels I never knew? Counting cockroaches marching in procession across the floor or patterned petunias parading across the wallpaper?

That's splendid. Takes a little time for the changes in depth, you know. Even Richalife can't reach the deep cells of the mind instantly. I'm on 25-Triple A myself, that's twenty-five to thirty, height tall, temperament outgoing, slight tendency to variable depression. I remember when I began, just over a year ago now, it took – oh, I should say about three or four weeks, approximately, before the depth changes were really well established. These very slight depression feelings I used to get – they were alleviated almost right straight off, definitely alleviated, but it must have been more or less a month or so before they totally disappeared. Cut down any on smoking?

Mac, who has been reaching into his pocket for a cigarette, withdraws his hand.

Some

Well, I feel confident there'll be a marked drop. Let me know how you're getting on caffeine-wise, too, won't you?

Oh certainly of course

Stacey leans forward as far as the chair shape permits.

How do you decide who's to have which   uh course of tablets?

Mac fixes her with a stone idol's eye.

I explained to you, honey. *You* remember. It's done by the Richalife Quiz.

— Did he explain? He did a certain amount of yakking last night, and I was thinking all the time of how it could be that Duncan keeps getting such awful marks in arithmetic. I'm always wanting him to talk, and when he does, I'm absent. Sad defection of duty. Goddam, though, I'm not convinced that he *did* explain.

Oh sure. Yeh. I recall it now. It just slipped my mind for a second, there.

Thor smiles again and rises to his feet. Standing beside a grey-veined marble fireplace he looks almost as striking as he presumably intends.

Time your program was designed for you, Stacey. I'll bet you make lists so you won't forget things – come on, now, don't you?

Stacey nods dumbly. Thor's voice continues slow and dreamily, intimate.

Think of the moment when you can throw away your lists. That'll be a red-letter day. Not to mention energy. Are you satisfied with your present level of energy?

Well

Mothers very often aren't, I do know that. Kids can take a lot out of you, can't they? I know. I'll bet some days you feel just pretty beat and exhausted, don't you? It's certainly not a very pleasant feeling. I don't know from personal experience – never having been a mother ha-ha – but I surely can sympathize.

— Come on, little fish, there it is. Boy, if Mac ever came home one evening and said *Honey, I'll bet you're beat*, I'd fall into his arms. Well, nuts. I'm not rising to this. No dice.

Thor looks at Stacey, and she looks into his blue eyes, blue as the copper sulphate that used to be put in the near-shore water of Diamond Lake to clear it of the snails that caused itch. Still blue eyes without any gleam or flicker of themselves in them, no fathoming of them possible. Then he glances towards the hallway.

Well, it's been just great talking to you two. I don't mean to hustle you good people off, but Mickey Jameson's bringing his wife in to meet me in another few minutes, and I've got Stewart Essex coming in after that with his fiancée. I think it's always more personal if you talk to people by themselves. Of course I enjoy parties as well. We're going to have to see about an office party soon. Small celebration. Because I just have this feeling that we're going places together. I think the Head Office is really going to sit up and take notice of the fact that in this province we're *moving* and we're not moving slow. Am I right?

Sure – you sure are.

Good-bye   good-bye

So glad to have met you

Thanks so much

A pleasure
Blabber blabber
Click.

The Buick zooms lightly over the bridge, and Stacey, looking back, can see the lights of the city, rearing neons in lightning strokes of color, jagged scarlet, blue like the crested heart of a flame. She puts down the car window on her side, and can smell the sea, salt warmth and decaying seaweed, like the presence of some rank stinking turbulent primeval creature which has not yet realized the fact of its own passing.

What was that bit about the quiz, Mac?

Just answering some questions. There's nothing to it.

What sort of questions?

Oh – about your personality, and what worries you, stuff like that.

I won't.

Don't be ridiculous, Stacey. Of course you will.

We'll see about that.

Oh God, Stacey, why do you always have to make everything so difficult?

I don't mean to

Well you *do*

I'm sorry. I *mean* it. I'm sorry. What about the kids?

I can answer for them. That's allowed.

Mac

What now for God's sake

What do you think, I mean, in yourself?

What do you mean what do I think in myself?

Just what do you *think*?

What do you *mean*, what do I think? Like what?

Well, I mean

Just what *do* you mean, Stacey?

I guess the product's pretty good, eh?

I told you.

What about – I mean, what do you think of Thor?

I think he's a guy with drive.

I think he's bat-winged Mephistopheles.

You must be out of your mind.

Are you leveling with me, Mac?

For heaven's sake. What is there to level *about*?

Why don't you say what you mean, just once? Why not? Look, I *know*

You do, eh? You really think you do?

Stacey looks at him, at his face in the half-light of the car, his face bitter and real.

> Cameron's Funeral Home in the prairie town, and Stacey, seventeen, coming in late from a dance, stepping behind the Caragana hedge to avoid encountering her mother, who had come downstairs and outside in her dressing gown and was trying to open the mortuary door, which was locked. *Niall – you come upstairs and quit drinking. I know what you're doing in there. I know you.* And the low gentle terrifying voice in reply – *You do? You really think you do?*

No. I don't know, Mac. Okay, I don't know. Isn't it strange? I thought it couldn't happen to me.

What're you talking about? What couldn't happen?

The silences

Oh God. What gimmick are we in for now?

Nothing. Look – nothing. It's okay. Everything's okay. I'll do the quiz.

— I've just remembered. The pill parade Mac's on is for age thirty-five to forty. Exactly how young did he tell Thor he was? Well, whatever the game happens to be, it's a form of solitaire for Mac. He's decided on that.

Stacey, look – you know I don't want to be unreasonable, but

Yeh, I know. It's okay. I wish I knew more.

About what?

I don't know.

Six o'clock, the dinner ready, the kids groaning about their emptiness, and no sign of Mac. Stacey pours herself a large gin and tonic and raises her glass.

— Here's to the god of thunder. He's right. If I spent my life pouring myself full of vitamins and tomato juice instead of gin, coffee and smoke, maybe I would be a better person. I would be slim, calm, good-tempered, efficient, sexy and wise.

Also beautiful. Beautiful and intelligent.

What did you say, Mum?

Katie has snaked in around the kitchen door.

Nothing. Just talking to myself, I guess.

When's dinner? Marnie and I are going to the show.

Who said? The local, you mean? What's on?

Just this experimental film.

Which one?

Oh, you know. *Psychedelic Sidewalk.*

You can't. It's an A.

Katie drapes herself slenderly across the kitchen chair. She is wearing a turquoise dress with canary-colored plastic earrings.

So what else is new?

I'm just telling you, you won't be allowed in, that's all.

Jingle-jangle. Coinage. Ever heard of it, mini-mind? You can get in anywhere if you've got the price of admission.

Well, that's pretty cynical, I must say. Anyway, what makes you think I'll let you go?

You said I could go tonight. You *did* say.

I didn't say you could go to that one.

— What difference does it make? Why are we going on like this? Do I really believe it's going to alter her out of all recognition? No. I feel it's my duty to appear to be doing my duty, that's all. A farce.

Katie flies up from the chair like a rust-feathered pheasant from cover.

You said I could go and I'm going. I just simply am.
That's all.

— Such rudeness. I never spoke to my mother that way,
at her age.

> Stacey Cameron, fourteen, dark hair set rigidly in
> rolls on top of the head, transference from movie
> star queens to a million clumsy-fingered small-
> town girls. Stacey with tomato-colored mouth, re-
> garded by mother more in sorrow than anger. *You
> are certainly not going to a public dance hall, dear.
> You wouldn't want to be the sort of girl people
> wouldn't respect, would you?* It's a dance, Mother,
> for heaven's sake, not an orgy. Mother sniffling
> into lace-edged hanky. *I never thought a daughter
> of mine would speak to me like that. Your father's
> going to have to deal* – (But he was down among
> the dead men, bottles and flesh, and didn't hear
> when she called.)

— I stand in relation to my life both as child and as
parent, never quite finished with the old battles, never able
to arbitrate properly the new, able to look both ways, but
whichever way I look, God, it looks pretty confusing to
me.

Katie   listen, I'm sorry   try to be reasonable

Why don't *you* try being reasonable for a change?
You give with one hand and take away with the other,
that's your standard pattern. It's not only inconsistent –
it's – it's immoral.

— Lord assist me not to laugh. If the worst thing on my
conscience were refusing to let her see *Psychedelic Sidewalk*, I would be a happy happy lady. Yet from where she
stands I look unreasonable, inconsistent and immoral.
And I'm not certain I'm not.

> Katie gives Stacey a look filled with something
> deeply her own. Scorn? Pity? Then her turquoise
> shoulders slope a little and her long loose hair falls across
> her face. She turns and walks upstairs. Stacey can hear

her sliding the bolt across her bedroom door. Stacey reaches for the gin and tonic and drinks it as though she has just stumbled in from the Sahara.

— Katie? Listen. Just let me explain. I can explain everything. Sure, Explainer of the Year, that's me. How can I explain anything? How can I tell you what you should be doing? I don't know what I should be doing. But I think if I don't tell you, it'll look bad. If I could level with you, would we be further ahead? Do you really want to know what I'm like? I can't believe it.

Stacey rounds up Jen and feeds her. The boys are playing in the back yard, and the fighting is at present suppressed and undeclared. Stacey peers into saucepans, turns the stove elements lower, and pours another gin and tonic.

— Where in hell is he? Knocking himself out for Thorlakson. He's working too hard. Yeh, but doing well, you have to admit. Sure, doing splendid. On his way to a heart attack. If he'd finished university, everything would be all right. He'd have a profession. How come he could only stick to it for two years after the war? It was more fun to go out drinking with Buckle. I can't imagine Mac ever being like that. Damn you, Buckle Fennick, you ruined my husband's life. What nonsense. Things don't happen that way. It was Mac himself who had to quit university. Because his dad was a minister? Because Matthew was upright to the point of unbearability? If only Mac were a doctor, say, or a lawyer. Yeh, that would solve everything. Last month in this city two lawyers and one doctor killed themselves. The lawyers used the exhaust pipes on their cars, the doctor simply swallowed the appropriate pills. Come on, Stacey, let me freshen your drink. That's what Tess says. Yes, she does. She is a very dainty type. Freshen, indeed. Let me give you another slug of this drug – she doesn't say that. She is also wont to say, in such places as the City Hall or the Hudson's Bay Company, that she wonders where the

Little Girls' Room is, making the john sound like a council hall for countless nymphets. I shouldn't talk. Katie is always saying how outdated my slang is. Gosh. Gee. Twerp. Heavenly days.

Clump-clump-clump. A man's footsteps, but not Mac's. Stacey thrusts her glass into the deep concealing blue bowl of the Mixmaster on the kitchen cabinet, and goes to the door.

— Mac's father?

But it is not Mac's father. It is Buckle Fennick. He stands there on the front porch, grinning. For Buckle, to swagger does not mean to walk boastfully, or not necessarily. Buckle can swagger while standing still. He wears a sleazily shiny sports shirt, cerise and silver, and jeans.

— Man of his age, I ask you. His jeans are always too tight and they bulge where his sex is, and it embarrasses me and infuriates me that it does, yet I always look, as he damn well knows and laughs at, one of the many unspoken small malices between us in our years of competition for Mac. No – that's unfair to all of us. I didn't mean it. Oh?

Buckle is only slightly taller than Stacey, but he is stocky with muscular hair-flecked arms. He has a face like an Iroquois, angular, and faintly slanted dark eyes. His hair is night-black and straight. He never loses the tan on his face and arms, not even in the winter, and on the occasions when he goes to the beach with Mac and Stacey and the kids it surprises Stacey to see how pale his legs are under the black hairs.

— Okay, so he's sexy. It's an optical illusion. How many men do I see? You could count them on one hand, and most of those like Jake Fogler, about three feet tall with heavy-rimmed glasses and semi-collapsed chests, talking earnestly about media or some damn thing. Buckle's just around here half the time, that's all. Mac's dear old buddy from during the war. I detest him. I try to be nice to him for Mac's sake, but sometimes I don't try hard enough and make some private remark to Mac, very restrained, like *Why does that slob always drop in at dinnertime?* and then Mac is furious. He doesn't know that Buckle scares me. It's ridiculous. It's untrue. That article – "I'm Almost Ready for an Affair," which turned out to mean she wasn't at all, ending in an old-fashioned sunburst of joy, Epithalamium Twenty Years After, virtuous while conveying the impression that dozens of virile men would be eager to oblige if she weren't. She was probably like me – the only guys she knew were her husband's friends.

Hi, gorgeous.

— Buckle, when are you going to stop talking like that? Where do you get your lines? Old B-grade movies? Oh God, I should criticize. Here's me, dressed in none-too-clean slacks and a blouse which Katie discarded when indelible red ink got spilled on it, so I look like I'm bleeding severely from a chest wound. Thrice hell.

Oh hi, Buckle. Come on in. I'm just getting dinner. Mac's not home yet, but he should be here any minute.

— My good-wife-and-mother voice. I can't seem to talk to Buckle in any other way. I always sound so prim. Sometimes I wonder what kind of person he imagines I must be.

I just got back from a haul north, so I'm off for a couple days. Thought I'd drop in and see how the guy's getting on with the new job.

Mac's getting on fine.

You don't sound too pleased.

Sorry – I'm tired. End-of-day bit. Want to stay for dinner?

Twist my arm.

— Will I, hell. Your arm needs less twisting than anybody's I know, you cheap bastard. Don't you ever have a meal at home?

Sure, do stay. There's plenty. Let me get you a drink. Gin and tonic?

Don't mind if I do.

— Buckle, can't you vary the response from time to time? I once said this – *Don't mind if I do* – and Mac told me later it was vulgar. I didn't tell him it had been a take-off. I was too overcome with shame at my spiritual acidity.

Jen is playing with her plastic tea set on the kitchen floor. Buckle picks her up and swings her around above his head. Stacey, preparing one drink, having adroitly lifted her own out of the Mixmaster bowl, gazes in the hope that Jen will scream bloody murder. But no. Jen chortles for more.

Hey, how's my girl friend, eh? How's the champion pisser of the neighborhood?

— Just once. Only, for heaven's sake, *once* did Jen wet on him when she was a very young baby. He still thinks this is the wittiest remark going. Take your hands off my kid, you ape.

Here's your drink, Buckle.

He sets Jen down and picks up the glass.

Here's looking at you.

How was the trip, Buckle?

Buckle is a trucker. He drives a diesel dinosaur, a steel monster, innumerable great tires, heavy as a mountain, roaringly full of crazy power. Buckle loves it. It is his portable fortress, his movable furnace. It is his lover and himself all in one. He mainly goes north, up the Cariboo Highway and the Alaska Highway, up to the Peace River country where the forests grasp the ancient moss-covered rocks, to the last little towns raw in the mud of new clearings.

Same old shit. Bananas this time. Had to unload along the way, but the last of them had to get to Fort St. John before they rotted black. So what happens?

What?

Ten miles out of Williams Lake the steering goes. She's supposed to be serviced before each haul. Those buggers of mechanics at Ace don't know a spanner from their own cocks. Lucky it was me driving. Slightest thing happens, Harvey's nerves go on the blink. I'd slowed to light a cigarette, and that was lucky, too. My luck's still in – I make good and sure of that. If ever I go, it's not gonna be that way, some dumb thing like the steering going. *Doing!* I brake. Hard, but not too hard, see? She shudders and skids and finally comes to a standstill. Oncoming car nearly swerves right off the road. Terrified tourist climbs out and screams *What d'you think you're doing? Listen, bud,* I tell him, very calm, *it's a lucky thing for you my reaction time's pretty good and this crate decided to go for the verge and not for you, or you'd be strummin' your motherfuckin' harp this very second, and don't you forget it, eh?* Harvey's sleeping in the back all the time. I swear that guy's made out of plasticine. Six and a half hours we're held up.

What about the bananas?

They got there okay. I never lost a load of anything yet. Harvey keeps peeking away at them, like he's a hen with unhatched eggs or something. I tell him, *Relax, I'll take the night shift and we can make time.*

I bet that pleased him no end.

He's no good any more. Too slow. He's getting on, and he gets jittery. I'm trying to work a change. I'd like to go by myself, if they'll let me.

You never get jittery, I suppose.

Look, Stacey, I've told you. Nothing can happen to me while my luck's in. See?

No.

No what?

I don't see.

Well, like I know every inch of that goddamn highway, and I know my vehicle, see? I know how she responds, and what she'll do and won't do. She'll do what I want because I *know.* Anyway, it's always Russian roulette to some extent. That's not bad. That's just the way it is. You know that before you start out.

— He's never consistent. He contradicts himself all the time, and there are things he only hints at, or else mentions as though you were bound to know all about them – as though they were commonplace. His luck – something apart from him and yet within his control, like the steering wheel, although with the possibility of abrupt change. His head must be full of unnamed gods meshing like a whole set of complicated gears. He's as superstitious as a caveman, but he always denies having any superstitions.

Anyway, Stacey, I don't aim to get taken by some bonehead mechanic's mistake, not if I can help it – I mean, not even something I did, or another driver.

What do you mean – another driver?

When I say another driver, I mean another *driver*, see? Not some jerk of a farmer or tourist. I don't include Mac in that. He drives a car, sure, but he's as near to a driver as you could get.

— Maybe Buckle has a recurring nightmare about being smashed by a Volkswagen. Fate worse than death. Well, so what? All he wants is a jury of his peers.

How do you keep your luck? Praying?

You kidding? None of that crap for me. Reilly keeps a St. Christopher medal strung up there in front so he can see it all the time. Lots of guys do. Everything from kewpie dolls to saints. I know a guy keeps his wife's picture up there, framed with doodads and plastic flowers. All a lot of bullshit. I'm not superstitious.

Yeh, so you've said.

— His shrines are invisible. I wonder what they look like, and what fetishes and offerings lurk on those altars? Yeh, doll, that evening course Man and His Gods. Great authority, you. What do you know of it? Don't be silly. Don't think of it. It always seems unbelievable that I met Mac through Buckle, in a way.

> Stacey Cameron walking out of the brown-wainscotted office at five, wondering if she wouldn't be better off working for T. Eaton's or almost anyone rather than Janus Importers. *Stacey, well for the*

Lord's sake, is it really you? Julie, a girl from Ma-nawaka. Gosh, Julie, what you been doing? *I should only tell you, kiddo. Everything from fruit-picker to hairdresser. Married now. Yep. True. Mrs. Fennick, that's me. Real swell guy, a little on the nutty side but what a dancer. What about you?* Oh, I been working for these importers, but my boss makes horoscopes for people – I think it's some kind of a racket – think I oughta quit? Stacey went home for supper with Julie, to talk it over, and one of Buckle's friends was there. Clifford MacAindra. Six months later she thought how fortunate, to have her whole life settled once and for all, so ideally, at twenty-three.

Whatsamatter, Stacey?

Oh – nothing. Want another drink?

Twist my arm.

— Julie left him four years later, when their boy was two. The last couple of years we saw very little of them. When she left, she never said why, not to me, anyway. She just lit out. Buckle blamed it all on her, how she complained about his long-distance driving and that, and wanted him to change, and he wasn't having any of that crap, et cetera. Only a long time later I began to hear in his talk just how often he claimed somebody was trying to force him somewhere he didn't want to be. I never knew how it was, for her.

How's your mother, Buckle?

Buckle's face takes on further concealment. He has lived with his mother in an apartment over a store on Grenoble Street ever since Julie left him. He has never asked Mac and Stacey there, so they have never seen the old lady.

Oh great. Always great, she is. She's only got one tune.

What tune is that?

Be careful on them dangerous roads, she keeps telling

me. She couldn't care less about me, you understand. She just wonders what'd become of her if I went. I don't blame her.

— Maybe he can't stand anyone to go to his place because she probably calls him Arbuckle, which is his name and which he hates even more than Mac hates his name, Clifford.

Click, Slam. Mac at last. Stacey now realizes that she has not gone upstairs to fix her hair or put on a decent dress.

Hi, Stacey.

Hi. Everything okay?

Mm. Everything's fine. You?

Fine. Buckle's here.

That's good.

— The automatic kiss bit. Does he actually not see me when he kisses me like that, or is it really the opposite – out of the corner of his day-beleaguered eyes he sees his life's partner, slacks and scruffy blouse, sagging in all directions and doing damn-all about it, and he shuts off the sight like you shut off the street noises because if you didn't, one day you might run amok and that wouldn't do?

Mac picks up Jen.

Hi, princess.

Jen laughs straight from her belly, the deep delighted laughter of a child loved.

— He's crazy about her. If ever I suggest maybe I should take her to the doctor and see about why she doesn't talk, he nearly has a fit. *Don't be ridiculous*, he says. It's because he can't bear to think anything might be wrong with her. Not with Jen.

Katie refuses to come down for dinner, and Mac inquires what the hell could possibly upset the kid like that. Stacey refuses to answer. Buckle goes into his steering story again. He is interrupted by Ian and Duncan, who argue over the relative size of each other's dessert, both claiming that the other has the larger portion, until

Stacey suggests that they trade, which both refuse to do.

— Spoiled brats. What have I done to them? Fighting over a square inch of frozen artificial cream. Not dying of hunger. Not even aware of the possibility. Squabbling over nil. Who made them so? What will happen when the horsemen of the Apocalypse ride through this town? Oh Stacey, enough.

Mac finally cannot bear the uproar.

Shut up, for God's sake, can't you? Stacey, can't you keep these kids quiet for one minute? Here, you two – neither of you will get any ice cream, if that's the way you're going to carry on. Just you leave the table right now. You don't know how damn lucky you are. When I was a kid, ice cream was a treat.

— I was thinking the exact same. Yet when it's spoken, it doesn't sound convincing. It sounds corny.

— Mac – leave them. Please. They'll simmer down. C'mon, kids.

— My placating voice. Running interference again, never knowing if rightly or wrongly, or whose side I'm on or why I should be on anybody's side. Am I undermining Mac? "Are You Emasculating Your Husband?" I swear those articles are written by male anarchists, delighting in the tapeworms of doubt which they sound out to squirm through my guts. How do I know if I'm emasculating him or not? Every time I disagree with him I feel I'm knocking him down. So I agree with him profusely and then it's me who's doing the disappearing act. Now he's on the point of real anger. Action, quick.

Ian! Duncan! You heard what your dad said. Eat your ice cream right now and then leave the table and no more horsing around, eh?

This is not what Mac has said, but maybe he will let it pass. Stacey's voice sounds to her own ears like some harpy of the mountains, the cold shrill of the north wind. And yet, after dinner, Ian approaches Mac with no apparent qualms and it works.

Hey, Dad, you wanna see something?

What?

My bug. I got it finished today.

Yeh? How'd it turn out?

Not bad. You should see the steering – it's really neat, how I got it rigged up. C'mon – it's in the back yard.

Okay. Want to come, Buckle? Big deal, here.

Sure, okay. I'll come along. You know what you're gonna be, Ian? A long-distance driver like me. You got the feel for a vehicle, eh?

Naw, I'm gonna be an inventor.

Great, boy. You can support me in my old age. The hell with driving, like your Uncle Buckle and I do. You invent a new-type rocket, see?

— It's good when it's like that. Why can't it be all the time? Ian needs it so much. He doesn't give a damn for my approval. He knows he's got it anyway. It's Mac's he needs. And yet they turn around and knife each other with words, both suspicious. I should be able to prevent it, but I don't know how.

The gin has completely worn off now. Stacey clears the table and perceives that Duncan is standing by himself near the kitchen door. She puts an arm around him, asking him to help with the dishes because he is so talented in this way, and he consents to the deception for the sake of belonging somewhere. Stacey takes a bowl of stew and one of ice cream upstairs and leaves them outside Katie's door where Katie's dignity may permit her to claim them in due course. Then Stacey bathes Jen, puts her to bed, calls the boys, gets them stowed away after a one-hour exchange of repartee, and finally changes her own clothes, from slacks to bronze linen sheath with ersatz gold pendant.

— Pour on the Chanel Number Five. Drench yourself in it, woman. Go On. Mac and Buckle will spring to their feet. *Gad!* they will exclaim. *Who is this apparition of delight? Who is this refugee queen from The Perfumed Garden?* In a pig's eye, they will.

Mac and Buckle are not in the dining room or the kitchen or the living room. They are down in the basement, in the darkened TV room. Buckle is lighting two cigarettes, holding them both in his mouth at once. He hands one to Mac, who takes it without a word.

— I'd like to knock that damn cigarette to the floor and stamp on it hard. Yeh, that would be splendid. Mac would have me certified.

Stacey says nothing. She sits down and lights a cigarette for herself, crossing her legs so that her ankles, still slender, show. Or would have done if the room had been lighted and anyone had been looking.

— The Ever-Open Eye. Western serial. Sing yippee for the days of the mad frontier. Boys were sure men in those days all right and men were sure giants. How could they miss? Not with them dandy six shooters. *Tak! Tak! Splat!* Instant power. Who needs women?

The program ends, and then the News. This time the bodies that fall stay fallen. *Flicker-flicker-flicker.* From one dimension to another. Stacey does not know whether Ian and Duncan, when they look, know the difference.

— Everything is happening on TV. Everything is equally unreal. Except that it isn't. Do the kids know? How to tell them? I can't. Maybe they know more than I do. Or maybe they know nothing. I can't know.

It's depressing.

Don't look then, honey. Want a beer, Buckle?

Don't mind if I do. They oughta drop an H-bomb on them bastards.

You'd like that, wouldn't you?

What d'you mean, Stacey? It would settle them. It would settle a lot of things.

Yeh, so would slitting your own throat.

Stacey, would you kindly go and get a couple of beers for Buckle and me, if it's not asking too much?

I was only

I cannot stand these pointless arguments over nothing.

Nothing!

There isn't any use in talking. It doesn't change anything.

— True. And he really can't stand it when I argue with Buckle. God, Mac's terrible need for quiet, and my denial of it.

I'm sorry. I'll get the beer.

— Anyway, I probably exaggerate. Do I? *Doom everywhere* is the message I get. A person ought not to be affected, maybe. I've got an accumulation of years, and a fat lot of good it does me. I wish I could chuck it all away.

The Eye, shining, newly acquired, five or so years back. *Interviewer:* Now, tell me, Mrs. Frenfield, what effect has this new – uh – shelter in your basement had upon your peace of mind? *Mrs. Frenfield* (smiling anxiously, never thought she'd ever be on TV): Well, I used to have these very disturbed dreams, see, like I mean nightmares they were, actually. Now we got the shelter, I definitely got more peace of mind, like. I mean, it stands to reason. *Interviewer:* Yes, I see. Well, now, in an – um – emergency, what would you do if one of your neighbors who didn't have a shelter tried to – *Mrs. Frenfield:* Boy, let them try, that's all I can say, just let them try. My husband's got an old army rifle, and he – *Interviewer:* Well, thanks very much, Mrs. Frenfield. It's been been very interesting talking to you, and – uh – sweet dreams, eh?

— Around that time I used to figure out how we would get away if need be. We would all pile into the old Chev and rocket on up to the great north woods. Ignoring traffic jams, that is. I used to visualize us taking some little-known road which we would cleverly discover on the spur of the moment. Armed with radish seeds, we would conquer that muskeg, the rock and the green-black silences of the timberlands. We would hack out our village, grub up slugs for the soup pot, spear deer, and teach the kids all we remembered of Shakespeare. Only one or two snags. Neither Mac nor I could have mustered more than about two lines of Shakespeare, and neither of us would last more than twenty-four hours in the great north woods. Also, who would the kids marry? Incest was out. So I gave up on that one. It wasn't such a hot sedative.

Here's your beer.

Oh, thanks, honey. Listen, Buckle, I'm sorry, but I'm going to have to go up and do some work. Got to finish a report on sales. Seeing Thor tomorrow. You'd hardly believe it, but that guy keeps all the sales figures for each area in his head. Not just city, either – all over the province. See you around, boy, eh?

Sure. So long.

Buckle and Stacey remain looking at the screen. Buckle, who normally drinks a bottle of beer in four gulps, now sits holding it without drinking.

Guess Mac thinks this Thorlakson guy is okay, eh, Stacey?

Yeh. I guess so.

Sounds like quite a guy.

Yeh.

I noticed his picture in the paper few days ago. You see it? In connection with some kinda rally he's putting on. Pretty well-educated guy, would you say, Stacey?

— I never before in my life felt sorry for Buckle Fennick and I don't want to now. It disorients me.

I don't know. Yeh, I guess Thor is pretty well educated.

Funny name – Thor. Sounds made up.

Icelandic, I guess. Used to be lots of Icelanders in the prairies, around Gimli.

— I wonder if I ever saw Thor in Winnipeg or somewhere? Imagine Buckle feeling like that. I think I'm badly off with Grade Eleven. I bet he's got about Grade Five.

After Buckle has gone, and even Katie is now reluctantly in bed, Mac emerges from the study, which is his

retreat, the place where he can shut himself away, amid
his business files and racing car magazines and *Playboy*,
away from the yammering of his wife and young.

Thought you'd gone to bed, Stacey.

Sorry. I didn't know you wanted the house to yourself.

— Oh hell. Again. Grabbed for a rapier even before I
found out whether a duel was intended.

Christ, I can't say anything right, can I?

— He does feel like that. Of course. How is it we can
both feel that way, simultaneously?

Mac, I'm sorry. I didn't mean

Skip it. I only wanted you to fill in this quiz. I
should've asked you before, only Buckle was here.

Stacey reaches for the paper.

BLOCK CAPITALS PLEASE.

Name   *Address*

Year of Birth   *Month*   *Day*

Weight   *Height*

Any Illness in Childhood

Any Illness in Childhood

Any Illness Since Age Eighteen (Specify Year and Severity)

Deficiencies I Feel in Myself

My Best Qualities Are

Qualities I Would Like to Have

My Energy Is: (a) consistently high

(b) variable

(c) low

Anxieties: (1)

             (2)

             (3)

Guilt Feelings: (1)

             (2)

             (3)

My Relationships With My Family Are:

                    (a) richly rewarding

                    (b) satisfactory

                    (c) less than
                        satisfactory

My Goals Are (Specify Briefly):

             (1)

             (2)

             (3)

— Two more pages in the same vein. I have the feeling I've seen this form before. "Is Your Marriage Happy? Answer These Ten Questions." "How Do You Rate As Mother/Mother-In-Law/Auntie/Fairy Godmother?"

What's the trouble, for heaven's sake?

I don't want to fill it in, Mac.

Look, Stacey, it's late and I don't feel like standing around arguing.

Okay okay okay. Lies are permitted, I take it?

All right. If you're going to get all worked up about it, let's forget the whole thing. It was only a thought. Pardon me for ever suggesting it.

Do we have to do it?

We have been asked to do it. I thought I had made that fairly plain.

I'll do it, Mac. Please. Honestly.

Yeh, like you did with that form for Ian, I suppose.

>Ian MacAindra, seven, Grade Two. *You got to fill
>in this form for me, Mum.* Civil Defense. Name of
>Child. Name and Address of parents. Home tele-
>phone. Name, address and phone of person who
>could be contacted in National Emergency if par-
>ents not available. To the final question, Stacey
>had written: *Name:* God. *Address:* Heaven. Ian,
>stark-faced with fury, had stormed to Mac. Look
>what she's written! I'm not taking that to school!
>Why embarrass Ian, Mac said, quite rightly. So
>she wrote instead: Matthew MacAindra (grand-
>father), Apartment 21, 704 Ballantyne Road.

That was three years ago, Mac. Can't you forget it?

Well, if you're all teed up for a wisecrack, you don't
need to bother.

I get the message. You can even dictate the answers if
you want. Here gimme the bloody thing   gimme it

Stacey

What?

If I were like Buckle, on my own, without anyone
really around me, do you think I'd give a damn?

Stacey stares at him.

— It's real. His acceptance of the responsibilities he
took on long ago when he never suspected what they
might mean. He doesn't intend it to be a gun at my head.
Or if he does, in some crevice of his mind, he doesn't
know. Just as my acting up isn't consciously intended to
hurt him. My motives aren't any better or any clearer.
Impasse.

Mac   I know   or I don't know. If we could talk
about

It's late.

You're right. It sure as hell is.

What now? Sardonic implications again?

Let's go to bed, Mac. Let's just go to bed.

Yeh. Okay.

Three

S TACEY, my dear. How are you this lovely morning?
  Matthew never knocks. He always walks straight in.
This has irked Stacey for many years, although she is not
convinced that she has a right to be irked by it.

— After all, he's Mac's dad and we're all the family he's
got. It's mean of me, but I can't help it. I mentioned it to
Mac once, and he said *He's got a right to walk in.* So that
settled that.

Oh – hello. I'm just fine. How're you? Yes, what a
lovely day.

— Burble-burble. I always talk to Matthew this way. I
dread an uneasy lull or anything fringing on what I'm
thinking about. I'm always afraid he'll guess. And yet I
long to tell him I don't see life his way – gentle Jesus meek
and mild and God's in his heaven all's right with the
world. But I can't. Mac would be furious. Anyway, why
do it? So I should be relieved of habitual fib-telling? It
wouldn't be worth the commotion. Or is this just my excuse for being a goddam coward? God knows why I chat
to you, God – it's not that I believe in you. Or I do and I
don't, like echoes in my head. It's somebody to talk to. Is
that all? I don't know. How would I like to be only an
echo in somebody's head? Sorry, God. But then you're
not dependent upon me, or let's hope not.

Where's Clifford?

Stacey turns her glance away so that Mac's father will not see her icicle eyes. Matthew is the only person who ever calls Mac by the name of Clifford, never apparently having realized that Mac discarded it deliberately.

Out washing the car.

Oh yes. His Sunday ritual. I forgot. For a moment I thought he might have gone to church.

— What in hell do you mean? You know perfectly well that Mac never goes to church. He was made to go, as a kid, to listen to you. Let up on him, can't you? He placates you in every possible way except that one.

Well no. He's washing the car, like I said. Ian and Duncan are at Sunday school.

Not Katherine?

Katie had a headache.

— This reason has been used too often lately. I'll have to find another.

Stacey moves into the kitchen and Matthew follows her. This is his custom. The instant she moves into the dining room, even momentarily, he will follow her there. Irritation flares in her like a struck match, but goes out as quickly. She looks at him, not knowing what could be done about him at no personal inconvenience to herself. Matthew does not have enough people to talk to these days, and practically nothing ever happens to him. He still attends the church where he once used to preach, but the people he knew there are getting fewer. The young minister is painstakingly cordial, but cannot think of anything Matthew could usefully do, and Matthew himself is afraid of getting in the way.

Matthew is a tall man, almost as tall as Mac, and he is careful to carry himself straight, a fact which only emphasizes his gauntness and assailability. His hair must once have been the MacAindra auburn, but now it is yellowish-white. The skin of his face stretches tightly over his big bones so that it appears exaggeratedly pale, almost transparent, lightly purple-etched with veins. He keeps himself scrupulously clean and neat, and his dark suits are never in need of dry cleaning. But he still wears shirts with detachable collars, and today he has put on a light-green collar with a blue shirt.

— If only none of the kids point it out. I'll clobber them if they do.

We had a guest preacher this morning.

That's nice. Was he good?

I think he promises extremely well. His theme was Christian humility, and although he might have chosen some of his texts more tellingly, he spoke quite well. He's young David Brownlee – I knew his father years ago. Dead now.

How've you been, yourself, this week?

Stacey can never address Matthew by any name. In sixteen years she has been unable to discover what to call her father-in-law. She cannot bring herself to call him Dad, for this still to her means Niall Cameron, long dead. Mr. MacAindra is out of the question, and only in her mind can she refer to him as Matthew. If the children are present, she calls him Granddad. If not, she cannot call him anything.

Oh, all right. My digestion's never very reliable, but it's no worse than usual. I eat very simply, as you know, but I fear I shall never get the hang of cooking. The apartment is very close these warm days.

Mac's mother died eighteen years ago and remains a mystery to Stacey, who knows about her only through Matthew's remarks, which tend to semi-canonize her, and the occasional remark from Mac – *She always went by what he said; she wanted me to learn to play the piano, but I wasn't very good at it.* Since her death, Matthew has lived alone. As long as he was preaching, he had a housekeeper. When he retired and moved into the small apartment, he began making his own meals. Mac's sister is married and now lives half a continent away.

— I know we ought to have him here. Don't tell me, God. I know. But when I think of it, I think – *mental hospital, here I come.* Following me around from room to room, desperate to make talking sounds, someone else who'd have to be told everything is all right.

I'll be taking the kids to the beach on Saturdays now that the weather's getting warmer. Why don't you come along?

— Madwoman.

Thanks, but I don't think I would be much of an addition, Stacey. The children think I fuss.

No, they don't. You must come.

We'll see.

His voice is quite gentle, and Stacey feels deservedly rebuked. Then Mac comes in from the back yard.

Hello, Dad.

Hello, Clifford. How are you liking the new job?

Fine. Just fine.

Well, that's wonderful. I always did feel that Drabble's wasn't really worthy of your abilities.

Yeh well

It's too bad you couldn't get something on the administration side with the new firm, though, Clifford. I've always thought that would be a better type of work for you, and it must be hard on Stacey to be on her own so much here when you're away. Perhaps in time you'll

Well, administration's not actually so much my line, Dad. I'm a salesman from way back.

It's too bad you never finished university, Clifford.

Yeh, well – that's water under the bridge. Lunch nearly ready, Stacey?

Just about. Only waiting for the boys to get home.

Mac lights a cigarette, draws on it and immediately begins coughing, at first politely – *hem hem hem* – then in deep chest-wracking spasms.

You shouldn't smoke so much, Clifford.

Yeh – *hack! hack!* – well, I've cut down.

You ought to give it up entirely. It's what I've always said. Even before these discoveries about how dangerous it is, I was always certain it was harmful. I always said so, if you remember.

Yeh. I recall your having mentioned it.

— That's the closest Mac ever allows himself to get to irony, with Matthew.

Katie sweeps in. Pastel-orange lipstick. Green-pearl nail polish. Eyeshadow like all the greenish-blue sea fern that ever flourished full fathom five. Burnt-orange earrings. Ocean-green dress. Long clean straight auburn hair.

— Katie, baby, how can you be so gorgeous? I love you for it, but it makes me feel about a thousand.

When's lunch? I'm starving. Hi, Granddad. How's tricks?

Mac frowns and Matthew tries not to look offended.

— Matthew thinks it's flippancy. But she's only trying to please, using slang which isn't hers and which belongs to some vague past. She's easy on him, but he doesn't see that. Everybody should stop from time to time and explain what they mean. But none of us in this house do.

Ian steams in, followed some dawdling moments later by Duncan. Ian has learned how to evade Matthew's Sabbath quiz. He begins talking about cars to Mac. Duncan, slower on the uptake, squirms at what he appears to feel inevitable. Matthew turns attention on him.

Well, Duncan, nice to see you. What did you learn at Sunday school?

Duncan, trapped, looks into the middle distance.

God loves birds.

Pardon?

Birds. Like sparrows and that.

You mean – "God sees the little sparrow fall"? Did you sing that hymn?

Yeh.

That's a fine hymn, especially when you really think about its meaning. It used to be your dad's favorite hymn, when he was your age. Did you know that?

Gee.

What else did you learn?

I got my paper. It's right here somewhere.

Duncan reaches into his pocket, then withdraws his hand hastily, as though he has remembered something just in time.

Guess I lost it, Granddad.

Stacey quickly picks up Jen and heads for the dining room.

Everybody to the table. C'mon.

Later, Stacey finds the Sunday-school paper where Duncan has crumpled it small and put it into his wastepaper basket upstairs. There is a rainbow-tinted picture of a sweetly innocuous and vacant-faced St. Francis surrounded by feathered companions. Around the edges, where there was a little blank paper, Duncan has put cramped and secretive pencil drawings – the various stages in the launching of a spaceship, its journey past moons and constellations, its arrival on a planet beyond our stars, where twining trees twist octopus-like and the stickmen are met by starfishmen.

— Not the Stations of the Cross. Not any more. Whose fault? Mine? Or is it maybe better this way? I haven't done well by them. I've failed them by failing to believe, myself. I pretend to it, but they are not deceived. Yet I am the one who wakens them on Sunday mornings and shoves them off churchwards. One more strand in the tapestry of phoniness. I want to tell them. What? That I mourn my disbelief? I don't tell them, though. I go along with the game. It's easier that way.

> *Ye holy angels bright*
> *Who wait at God's right hand*
> *Or through the realms of light*
> *Fly at your Lord's command,*
> *Assist our song,*
> *Or else the theme too high doth seem*
> *For mortal tongue.*

My God, Stacey, what's happened to you, warbling hymns all of a sudden?

Nothing. It just came into my head. Used to sing it when I was a kid.

You should tell Dad that. He'd be pleased to think you even remembered. Hey – what's up, honey? You're not crying, are you?

No. Eyelash in my eye.

— So why complain about Mac being guarded?

Morning, and the sky is like the light water-color blue from a paintbox. Warm-cool, the air smells of grass and last night's rain. On Bluejay Crescent the laburnum branches bend a little with the yellow wind-swaying burden of blossoms, and the leaves of the big chestnuts are green outspread tree-hands. Kids under school age are out already, whizzing up and down the sidewalks with wagons and tricycles. In the distance, the mountains form the city's walls and boundaries, some of them snow mountains even now, as though this place belonged to two worlds, two simultaneous seasons.

C'mon, flower. We're going shopping.

Jen replies unintelligibly, then begins to sing, not loudly, but recognizably the tune of a song Duncan once brought home from school.

Hey, that's marvelous. That's lovely. What about trying the words?

— I can see it all now. Jennifer MacAindra, The World's One and Only Nontalking Opera Star. Very funny, Stacey. In the meantime, have you taken her to Dr. Spender, just to check? You have not. He's so busy and I hate to pester him unless it's a real crisis. Mac thinks I'm nuts to worry, and probably I am. The truth is I'm scared to take her.

Stacey puts Jen in the Chev and they drive to the supermarket.

— Nobody could help feeling some lift on a day like this. I don't get out enough. My boundaries are four walls. Whose fault? Okay, mine. By the time the day ends, I'm too beat to seek rich cultural experiences, whatever that may mean. That babe in *Varying Views of Urban Life.*

That's what she said. *What we must seek is rich cultural experiences.* I thought she probably meant she didn't get laid often enough. But I sat there nodding and smiling and agreeing with her. I swear I'll never take another of those damn evening courses. What's left of me? Where have I gone? I've brought it on myself, without realizing it. How to stop telling lies? How to get out? This madness. I'm not trapped. I've got everything I always wanted.

Hang on, doll, and don't lean out the window, eh?

Down on the streets near the beaches where Stacey often takes the children, there are rows of high old shaky timber houses, no proper fire escapes. Dwelt in by whom? Sandaled artists courting immortality and trying to scrape by in this life? Extravagant-voiced poets preaching themselves? Semi-prophets with shoulder-length hair, baubled in strings of colored seeds or glass, pseudo gemmery, maybe not pseudo for their purposes? Languid long-legged girls who speak a new tongue and make love when they feel like it, with whoever, and no regrets or recriminations?

— It changes too rapidly for me to keep track. What do I know of it? Only what I read in the papers. What do they think about? Impossible for me to know? What do they think about me? "Love-In Held in Park." Newspaper couple of years ago. "We Aim to Love, Not Hassle, Says Leader." "Love who?" reporter asked. "Everybody" was the brave if reckless reply. Why did I have the persistent nasty suspicion that that generality and generosity would most likely stop just short of me? I wanted to explain myself. I still do. Wait, you! Let me tell you. I'm not what I may appear to be. Or if I am, it's happened imperceptibly, like eating what the kids leave on their plates and discovering ten years later the solid roll of lard now oddly living there under your own skin. I didn't used to be. Once I was different.

Stacey, traveling light, unfearful in the sun, swimming outward as though the sea were shallow and known, drinking without indignity, making spendthrift love in the days when flesh and love were indestructible.

Here we are, flower. Let's hope it's not too crowded.
— What'll it be like, when Jen is at school? I'll have to be careful, then, or I'll find myself speaking aloud one day when I'm alone among the Zoomy Puffs and the Choco-Corn Bleeps, and the young mums (damn them – they get younger every year, it seems to me) pushing carts full of groceries and babies will smile in embarrassment and pretend not to notice.

The long aisles of the temple. Side chapels with the silver-flash of chrome where the dead fish lie among the icy strawberries. The mounds of offerings, yellow planets of grapefruit, jungles of lettuce, tentacles of green onions, Arctic effluvia flavored raspberry and orange, a thousand bear-faced mouse-legended space-crafted plastic-gifted strangely transformed sproutings of oat and wheat fields. Music hymning from invisible choirs.

I'll be seeing you
In all the old familiar places –

Diamond Lake, fifty miles north of Manawaka. At night the spruce trees held themselves intensely still, dark and immutable as old Indian gods, holding up the star-heavy sky. The path of the moon lighted the black lake. The fishes danced and the night birds dipped and pirouetted in obeisance towards the fallen light, the shreds of heaven. And Stacey Cameron, under the green-purple neon starlight of the Wapakata Dancehall, danced with the airman from Montreal. He held her close, his sex pressed against hers. Then miles along the beach, the sand still day-warm under their bare feet, until they reached the leaf-blanketed hillside. Feeling the tacit agreement of the forest for their unspoken plans. Stacey afraid, but wanting too much to let go. Unexpectedly rising to him, not having known before that it was to be like this, everything focused in the crux where they met and joined. They both cried out, and then they half slept and wakened tender and it was nearly morning there on the curled yellow-green moss of the spruce-screened slope with the lapping of the lake in their heads.

— Whatever happened to him? How did he get on? Dead over Germany? The local paper only ever printed the lists of provincial casualties. Running a shoe store in Montreal? A bar in Antigonish? A ranch in the Cariboo? The unanswered questions.

Stacey suddenly realizes what is happening. Last week it was pop music, and the week before that. New manager now, maybe, someone who knows what age the women are who do most of the spending here.

— Conned again. Conned into memory. Now I'm not even certain that this music hasn't been going on for weeks or months. How long have I been remembering without knowing it? Al, was it really more than twenty years ago? Al Duschesne, half French, half English, claiming he was doubly outcast. Belonging once for half a night in me. I remember everything about you. The way the hair was gold on your belly and forearms in the almost-morning. Your sex. Everything. I wish I could see you. No, I don't. I wouldn't want you to see me, not now, not in my present shape. Of course, you'll have changed, too. But not as much. Women may live longer but they age faster. God has a sick sense of humor, if you ask me.

Jen, sitting at the front of the grocery cart and dangling her short legs, begins to sing, a wordless humming but tuneful. Her narrow fine-boned face seeks Stacey's, and her eyes are watchful, hesistant with hope. Stacey smiles quickly.

Hey, you're improving, flower. That's great.

— Stacey, how dare you complain about even one single solitary thing? Listen, God, I didn't mean it. Just don't let anything terrible happen to any of them, will you? I've had everything I always wanted. I married a guy I loved, and I had my kids. I *know* everything is all right. I wasn't meaning to complain. I never will again. I promise.

> Duncan and Ian last summer at the beach, wrestling and wisecracking, brown skinny legs and arms, the shaggy flames of their hair, their skin smelling of sand and salt-water. Sea-children, as though they should have been crowned with fronds of kelp and ridden dolphins.

— Please. Let them be okay, all their lives, all four of them. Let me die before they do. Only not before they grow up, or what would happen to them?

When Mac comes in that evening, he hands Stacey five small boxes and five rolled-up scrolls. Gingerly, she unfolds one of the scrolls. It tells her that Duncan Cameron MacAindra is seven years old and has been enrolled in the Richa Younglife Program. He is ABBD (Junior), and he promises to record on the following chart the zoom ratings of his energy up-go and his memory snap-up. Stacey opens one of the boxes. Each pill occupies its own nest. There are seven colors – pink, purple, peacock blue, tangerine, canary, green and crimson. Stacey touches them lightly.

Pretty. They'd make a nice necklace.

The kids better take them at breakfast, so they won't forget. A color for every day, see, so it's quite simple. Only don't get the boxes mixed up. Each one's got a different combination, depending on which program the particular person is on.

Mac?

What?

When you worked for Drabble's, we didn't go around spraying them with Angel-Breath Mouth Freshener.

Thor goes through the charts personally every month, for all members of staff and their families.

He's got a nerve.

You can't mount a real campaign unless you've got a hard core of support. If somebody can't even be bothered to give them to his own family, well

Okay. Okay okay okay. Give 'em here. Let's round everybody up.

You are making things damn difficult, Stacey. I hope you're enjoying it.

I don't mean to. Honestly. Honestly, Mac. Mac?

What?

I'm sorry.

Yeh, so you say. Look, I don't want you to be *sorry*. Only quit bugging me, eh? Haven't you seen the Richalife displays in the drugstore down the street?

Yes.

Well, it's like that all over. Big displays. It's catching on. I suppose you don't want the kids to go to university?

Oh Mac. Of course I do. You know that.

Well, then. Get off my neck. I'm earning more than I ever have.

You're working too hard.

Stacey, I am not working any harder than I have to. Now, please.

Okay, honey. Really.

By seven in the evening, Mac is closeted in his study, as he has been every evening this week. Stacey knocks and enters. Mac is sitting at his desk. In front of him are many colored brochures, a map of the province, sales charts, and several Xeroxed memo pages – *Let's Talk Richness, A Quality of Living* and *Getting Across the Message Audiovisually.* Mac looks up, frowning.

Whatsamatter?

Nothing's the matter. I have to go over to Tess's tonight. I promised. What does he mean, A Quality of Living?

Stacey, I'm busy. Can't you see?

Okay, I'm just going. What did Thor say about my quiz?

He said he never heard of anybody feeling guilty because they couldn't bake bread. I told you you shouldn't have put that.

You laughed at the time. Don't deny it. What did he expect me to do? Put down what I feel guilty about or something?

Ha bloody ha.

You never showed me what you put down.

It wasn't spectacular. Listen, Stacey, I'm busy.

Doing what? Yoga?

Everybody has to present their idea for totally new types of sales campaigns.

That's not fair. What's he trying to do?

How should I know? I guess he doesn't want any dead wood.

Mac – why did you say that?

A joke.

Yeh. Ha bloody ha. Mac?

Mm?

Are you afraid?

Me? What of? You must be kidding.

You're only forty-three. You're a damn good salesman. There have never been any complaints about you, that I know of. You've been working like a dog since you joined Richalife. You don't need to be afraid.

Stacey, for Christ's sake. I am not afraid. I am busy at the moment trying to work out ideas. Now will you please leave me alone?

You're really not – well let's say nervous – about Thor? He scares me. Something about him. I don't know.

Stacey, everything is okay. How many times do I have to say it? Can't you please for heaven's sake quit yakking about my work?

I'm sorry. But you won't talk. You won't ever say.

There is nothing to say.

Oh well in that case

Look, what do you *want* me to say?

I don't *want* you to say anything

Then why do you keep on
I'm sorry   it's just that
Well, everything is all right, see?
Yeh. Well, okay. I feel very strange sometimes.
What do you mean, strange?
Like as though everything is receding
Receding?
As though I'm out of touch with everything. Everybody, I mean. And vice-versa. If you see what I mean.
Maybe you need to see the doctor. Do you feel sick?
At heart
What?
Nothing. I don't know what I'm talking about. I'm sorry. It was – I don't know. Do you want some more coffee before I go?
No thanks. Are you okay, Stacey?
Sure. I'm fine. You're sure *you* are?
Yes, yes. Quite sure. Have fun at Tess's.
Thanks. I won't be late.
I may turn in early.
Okay. Well good-bye.
Good-bye.

Stacey goes upstairs to dress. No use in trying to compete with Tess, who would look splendid even if she were wearing an old potato sack tied with bindertwine. Stacey puts on her blue-silk suit. This is the first time she has worn it this spring, and the zipper on the skirt will hardly do up.

— Hell. I can't have put on that much. Oh heavens – look at me. Feast your eyes on those hips. Tomorrow – I swear it – the banana diet. I will buy half a ton of bananas and eat nothing else. I'll stick to it. So help me, I will. What did Mac mean, nothing to talk about? He probably isn't worried in the slightest. I'm making him nervous. "Are You Increasing Your Husband's Tensions?" More than likely. Why should I think he's worried? It's only me that's worried – only I who am worried. Compared with mothers of fifteen kids who are swallowing only air in India or somewhere, have I got troubles? No. God, to tell you the truth, it's getting so I feel guilty about worrying. I know I have no right to it, but it keeps creeping up on me. I'm surrounded by voices all the time but none of them seem to be saying anything, including mine. This gives me the feeling that we may all be one-dimensional.

Very far away, in a galaxy countless light-years from this planet, a scorpion-tailed flower-faced film buff sits watching a nothing-shaped undulating screen. He decides he's seen enough. He switches off the pictures which humans always believed were themselves, and the imaginary planet known as Earth vanishes.

— You're losing your mind, Stacey girl. Well, I may be, but I'm sure as hell not losing these hips.

Stacey is the first to arrive at the Foglers'. Tess is wearing an oatmeal-colored dress, straight and unadorned, with an Italian leather belt, costly in appearance, draped around almost nonexistent hips.

— How's she got such good taste in clothes and such awful taste in furnishings? Those drapes – demented turquoise trees and crimson-jacketed hunting gents on puffing black horses, and the entire scene shot through with simulated gold threads at regular intervals. Cut it out, Stacey. I'm getting worse. I used to be nicer. If I live to be ninety, I'll be positively venomous. My grandchildren will flee from me in terror.

Am I early, Tess? Gosh, I love your dress.

Not a bit. It's only Bertha and you coming. Glad you like it – I just got it this week. I think it's kind of fun, myself. Listen, I must show you what I got at Twiller's sale today.

— Don't tell me. Let me guess. Ten cuckoo clocks, forty-seven TV tables with puce-and-orange ballerinas prinking on them, two hundred packets of bath salts done up to look like dinosaurs and labeled *Hers* and *His*, five thousand hankies embroidered with pink tuberous-rooted begonias, and a partridge in a plastic pear tree.

Yeh, I'd love to see.

Tess brings out two salt and pepper sets shaped like harlequins and colored lavishly. The salt or pepper comes out of the hats.

Oh, they're sweet, Tess.

I thought they were kind of cute, myself. We don't really need them, I guess, but I can put them away for Christmas or shower gifts. Jake isn't crazy about them, but then, he's kind of hard to suit, I guess, in a way.

Jake Fogler is a radio actor who is fond of talking about the breakdown of verbal communications and the problems of semantics in mass media. Stacey cannot imagine either of them needing any salt or pepper shakers whatsoever. Tess lives on pineapple and cottage cheese salads, and Jake, if Tess is to be believed, exists mainly on brandy and raw eggs. He has a talented voice, but he does not stand a look-in with TV. Sometimes he retires to the spare bedroom and broods, and then Tess goes over to Stacey's and says in her high light voice, *Jake's ulcer is acting up.*

The doorbell chimes softly in four notes, and Tess opens the door to Bertha Garvey, whose voice rasps anxiously.

I'm not late, am I?

Why no. Only Stacey's here. The Polyglam lady hasn't even got here yet. I hope she hasn't got the date wrong.

Bertha comes into the living room. Pressing sixty, corseted to the point of shallow breathing, grey hair with slightly too true-blue rinse and done in a profusion of springy curls, hands big and capable – telling what her life work has been – eyes always a little worried behind up-curled green-framed glasses.

I would've been here sooner, Tess, but you know what Julian's like. Any time I'm going out – and goodness knows that's not often – he thinks of all kinds of things to delay me. Tonight nothing would do but I should get his navy suit laid out ready for him to take to the dry cleaners in the morning. Mercy, I could do it with no trouble at all before breakfast, I told him. But that wouldn't do. Oh no. Had to have it all ready in a shopping bag right that minute. I guess it's not his fault, really. He's getting on. And it's hard for him to be retired – he's never got used to it. You girls just wait. You'll see. Although I'm not saying it'll hit your hubbies that same way.

Julian Garvey is twelve years older than Bertha. He used to be an accountant. Now he putters around the house or does a little gardening, which he dislikes. He is small and dignified, meticulous-mannered with everyone else, but crabby with Bertha.

Bertha Garvey, one New Year's Eve, brought up a Baptist, only taking a drink on high days and holidays, as she said, and being quickly affected. Strapping efficient Bertha in Stacey's kitchen, shedding absurd cartoon tears (until Stacey looked again and saw them) into her Bloody Mary. *Hardly anyone knows, but I was born and raised in a lumber camp.* Stacey saying in amazement, good heavens, what's so awful about that? *Well it was the schooling I missed. My mother wanted me to go and live with my aunt and go to high school but Dad wouldn't hear of it. He was a high-rigger, my dad was, and when he got too heavy for it, he still went on, and then one day he lopped the top off a Douglas fir and lopped himself off with it.* Bertha had sworn not to marry a lumberman, so she had married Julian when he was a pay clerk in camp. *Julian was my fate, Stacey, but he can't forget I never went beyond grade school.*

The doorbell croons, and Tess patters excitedly into the front hall.

Oh – she's here, girls!

The plastic lady is petite and emaciated, high frothed-up hair metallic blonde, high thin teetery heels supporting bird-bone ankles, face gay-gay-gay with its haggardness fairly well masked by tan make-up and the scarlet gash of a lipstick smile. Her sleeveless silver dress shimmers like the scanty robe of some new oracle, and on the right breast it bears the iridescent ice-blue letters *Polyglam*.

Hello, Mrs. Fogler. Hello, girls. My, it's a real pleasure to meet you. Now, if I can just find a table.

Quick as a slickly sleight-of-handing magician, she hauls boxes in from her car and sets up shop in the Foglers' dining room. The company gathers. Stacey chain-smokes. Bertha knots her hands together, cat's cradles of broad fingers, and smiles hopefully. Tess sits wide-eyed like a child about to behold marvels. The marvels are there, arranged in heaps and rows on the table, plastic vessels gleaming softly, pearl-pink, mauve, green like the pale underthighs of a mermaid, blue as pastel as angel veins.

Picnic plates. Beakers. Sandwich cases. Pie containers. Cookie jars. Breadboxes. Buckets and dishpans. Dogs' feeding bowls. Infants' cereal bowls. Mixing bowls giant human and elfin. Ice-cube trays. Vats suitable for making wine or drowning enemies. Beach pails. Juice holders. Jugs all sizes from cream to martini. Tumblers and eggcups, plant pots and kid pots. To name only a few. The Polyglam lady takes her stance in front of the display.

Now, girls, just to get acquainted, we're going to play a little game. I think you'll all really enjoy it. All my clients say it's the nicest fun thing ever. It's a simple little word game – not *too* simple, mind you – that wouldn't do for you bright girls, eh? I'm going to give you each this full-colored Polyglam booklet, and on the first page you'll see the words *Polyglam Superware*. See? That's it. Now, see those blank spaces? I'm going to give you each a pencil, and I want you to see how many words you can make using only the letters in *Polyglam Superware*. We've got ten minutes. Ready? *Go!*

— My mind has gone blank. There's old Bertha scribbling away as though her entire future is at stake. Tess looks like Katie did once at about ten, when she had measles and wrote her exams at home – chewing her pencil, trying terribly hard.

Stacey after several minutes writes down *Mug*. She looks at the word for awhile, contemplating its inner truth. Then she writes *Pee*. She crosses this out and writes *Woe* instead. By this time the ten minutes are up.

Now let's just count them up, shall we, girls? Ho ho Mrs. Uh MacAindra, you haven't got very many, have you? Not to worry. It's only a game, isn't it? Mrs. Garvey, ten for you – that's fine. Mrs. Fogler, let's see now – *Glam, Spam, Lam, Pew, Sew, Are* – oh this is very good. Very good. Mrs. Fogler's got twelve words, girls! Isn't that nice? Now, Mrs. Fogler, it gives me real pleasure to present you with a little prize – this set of six Polyglam Juicicles. Yes, you can make your very own juice popsicles any flavor you wish. The kiddies can't get enough of them.
— Pure tact. She might have found out whether Tess had kids or not. I still wonder if it's by accident or design that she and Jake never have. Tess has never said.

Look – look at this, Bertha. Aren't they the cutest?

Real nice, Tess. Real handy. Really handy, that is to say.

Now if you'll just take your pencils again, girls, I'm going to let you in on a recipe which our Polyglam kitchens have just dreamed up – and is it ever a dream! It's the yummiest dessert you've ever tasted. We call it Tropical Paradise. I made it only yesterday for my own youngsters, and every single one of them polished their plates and asked for more. I'm positive your toddlers and teens will all be saying – *Mm – this is sure a tummy treat, Mum*. Okay? Ready? One cup maraschino cherries, chopped very fine. One cup melted marshmallows. One cup diced pineapple. Two cups whipped cream. A teaspoon of

Stacey writes *Safe in the Arms of Jesus*. Then she writes *Lost in the Arms of Morpheus*, followed by *Yummy Yummy Says My Tummy*. After that, she has time for one quick game of X's and O's.

— Without realizing it, that woman may actually be suffering severely from myopia. I'm only thinking of Bertha's toddlers.

Everybody got it all down? You, Mrs. MacAindra?

Yes, thanks.

Good. Now, then, I'd just like to point out a few features of this lovely Polyglam Superware – features you may not have noticed. For instance, would you ever guess just how durable Polyglam is? Oh sure, we all know it won't break, but the average person may not realize just *how* strong this unique material is.

Three lake-water blue dishpans, upturned, become the Polyglam lady's platform. She jumps up and down, tap dances, stomps with stiletto heels, leaps from one to another.

— My God, what if she falls? I can see her skimming down, slamming her pointed chin on the grey Chinese carpet, unable to rise out of sheer mortification. Am I *willing* this to happen? Stop it, Stacey, for heaven's sake – you may not realize your own tremendous mental powers. Yeh, a likely thought.

The Polyglam lady does not slip. She does a ballet-like zigzag in the air and comes down in a proficient landing on two dishpans, legs outspread but not vulgarly so.

Now, I don't want any of you girls to feel you have to, but if you'd like to look at the various pieces of Polyglam

These sandwich cases are just perfectly

What adorable eggcups

It's this cookie jar that I think is so

— If I get out of here for less than ten bucks it will be a bloody miracle. Two weeks ago it was copper-bottomed stoveware at Bertha's, and I bought a Dutch oven, which I needed slightly less than I need a Dutch uncle. I'm weak-minded, that's my trouble. Anything to look agreeable. Don't rock the boat. Why can't I? Why am I unable to? Help me. Who? How strange if Bertha and Tess were thinking the exact same thing. We could unite. This could start an underground movement. The Bluejay Crescent

Irregulars. I can see it all now. We're too damn complacent. No – we're not complacent one bit. We're just scared. Of what? Making a scene? Finding out we're alone after all – better not to test it out? How do I know what Tess and Bertha think? Am I going to risk offending Tess by asking? I have to live next door to her. She frequently minds Jen for me. Oh Katie, you're dead right about me, baby. I'm corrupt. Or was it immoral you said? Jesus, if I'm going to be immoral, I should scout around for some slightly jazzier way of being it.

Two and a half decades back, to the Dragon Lady of Terry and the Pirates. Wearing Stacey's face and a slinky black velvet ensemble that clings to her gifted breasts and friendly thighs. What was it you wanted to know, McNab? She is addressing the customs officer. Did you say smuggled opium? But McNab (about thirty, muscles like wire rope) can only stand and drool, overcome by his impossible desire. (Switch here from Saturday colored funnies page to elsewhere.) This way, McNab – nothing is impossible. Will it be the bed or the deck?

— I am either suffering from delayed adolescence or premature menopausal symptoms, most likely both.

When the purchases have been made, Tess serves coffee, two kinds of sandwiches, shortbread and layer cake with three-inch mocha icing.

— Shut up, God. I feel too lousy not to eat. Bananas tomorrow.

The Polyglam lady makes the first move to go.

It's been such a pleasure meeting you ladies, and thanks a million, Mrs. Fogler, and now I really must

Thank *you* for coming. We certainly all had a wonderful

I must be getting along now, too, Tess. Thanks loads

Lovely evening thanks   thanks

Thanks a million

Well, good night

G'night – watch the step, Bertha

Well, thanks again

A pleasure   thanks for coming

Well, good night

G'night, then, see you real soon

Yeh   sure thing   well good night

Good night

On the doorstep, as Bertha and Stacey are finally sidling out, Jake Fogler appears. His enormous glasses and slightly worn face give him the look of an aging owl-like boy caught in some moment of nefariousness.

— How long has he been standing here waiting for us to go?

Hello, Jake.

Evening, all. Tess has foisted all the gimcrackery on you, I see. Christ, Bertha, you can hardly stagger under the weight of all that crap.

Oh *Jake* – don't talk like that to Bertha. Don't be an old

Sorry, dear. Do I spoil all your fun? Coming back in for a drink, Stacey?

Thanks, no. Got to get home. 'Night, Tess.

Good night, Stacey.

Tess's small puzzled voice is at complete variance with her impressively packaged exterior. She waves uncertainly, then follows Jake into the house.

Stacey, entering home, takes off her shoes in the hall, goes to the kitchen and pours a gargantuan gin and tonic. Mac is in bed and none of the upstairs lights are on. Stacey flicks on a small lamp in the living room and curls up on the chesterfield, the Polyglam booklet in one hand. Along with the Superware, families are shown on each page. Kids beam peacefully and undisturbedly. Mothers with young untired faces flow contentedly. Fathers with young untired faces smile proudly and successfully. Grandmothers with young untired faces gaze graciously and untroubledly.

— Shit.

The booklet skids and lies still under the coffee table. Stacey turns off the lamp and stands near the window, drinking and looking at the lights of the city out there. They flash and shift like the prairie northern lights in the winter sky, here captured and bound.

The thin panthers are stalking the streets of the city, their claws unretracted after the cages of time and time again. The Roman legions are marching – listen to the hate-thudding of their boot leather. Strange things are happening, and the skeletal horsemen ride, ride, ride with all the winds of the world at their backs. There is nowhere to go this time

— Today I saw a girl walking up the street towards me, a plain girl unfashionably dressed, and from a distance I thought it was myself coming back to meet me with a wiser chance. But it wasn't.

No other facet to the city-face? There must be. There has to be.

Out there in unknown houses are people who live without lies, and who touch each other. One day she will discover them, pierce through to them. Then everything will be all right, and she will live in the light of the morning.

Four

COME ON, you kids. Aren't you ever coming for breakfast?

THIS IS THE EIGHT-O'CLOCK NEWS BOMBING RAIDS LAST NIGHT DESTROYED FOUR VILLAGES IN

Mum! Where's my social studies scribbler?
I don't know, Ian. Have you looked for it?
It's gone. I gotta take it to school this morning
Well, *look*. Katie, have you seen Ian's social studies scribbler?
No, and I'm not looking for it, either. If he wasn't so
Stacey, the party starts at eight tonight. Be ready, eh?
Sure, yes yes of course. Duncan, eat your cereal.
I hate this kind. Why do you always buy it?
You say that about every kind I buy. C'mon.

WORD FROM OUR SPONSOR IF YOU HAVEN'T SEEN TOOLEY'S NEW SHOWROOM YOU'RE IN FOR A REAL COOL SURPRISE

Chatter buzz wail
Okay, Jen, I'll be up in a sec. Are you finished? Don't try to get off by yourself – I'm coming.
You going to get your hair done, Stacey?
Yes, of course, whaddya think?
I only asked, for heaven's sake. No need to

I'm sorry, Mac. Yes, I'm getting it done this morning. Want an egg?

Please.

Mum, it's not here, and Mr. Gaines will be mad as fury. I got to find

Okay, Ian, one minute and I'll look. Where have you looked?

Everywhere.

ROAD DEATHS UP TEN PER CENT MAKING THIS MONTH THE WORST IN

I got to take fifty cents, Mum.

Duncan! What for?

Cripples or something

What?

It tells about it right here, in this piece of paper they gave us

Why didn't you show me this last night?

I forgot

So long, Stacey. So long, kids.

'Bye, Dad.

Oh good-bye, honey. Wait – you didn't have your egg. It's just done now

Can't. Said I'd be in by eight thirty. You eat it.

I hate eggs.

Miss Walsh said earn it if we can but I dunno how to earn fifty cents

WHEN QUESTIONED THE BOY SAID HE HAD SEEN THE GIRL TAKING THE PILLS BUT HE HAD NOT KNOWN THEY WERE

Scream

Okay, Jen – I'm coming right now

Mother, what have you done with my orange earrings?

I never touched them, Katie, and anyway you can't wear them to

Who says I can't?

Mum, I've looked in the desk and everywhere and my social studies scribbler just isn't

YANCY'S FANCIES ARE THE BEST TASTE TREAT OF THE GOLDEN WEST

Maybe you could advance me fifty cents on my allowance and I could

Mr. Gaines will have hysterics I mean it boy you don't know him

They were on my dresser yesterday with my green earrings and now they're both

BRR-RING

Katie, answer the phone, will you?

I can't I'm in the bathroom doing my hair

Well, take Jen off, then, while you're there

Man, who was your servant last year?

Oh shut up and do as you're told

BRR-RING

Hello?

Oh, hello. Stacey?

Yeh. Hello, Tess.

Got time for coffee this morning?

Well, I have to get my hair done. Maybe a quick one.

Leave Jen with me, why don't you?

Oh gosh, Tess, I can't ever pay you back. No, she'll be okay with me.

I don't mind having her a single speck, Stacey. Really and truly

Well, that's certainly nice of you we'll see look I gotta run now see you eh?

Sure, okay. G'bye.

G'bye. Come on, you kids! Ian, for the Lord's sake whatsamatter with your eyes? Your scribbler's under the cushion on the chesterfield. Here, Duncan, and please the next time let me know when you come home from school instead of springing things on me like this. You can earn it by clipping the edges on the lawn. Katie! You find your earrings?

Yeh. They were on the floor behind my dresser.

Well, next time don't be so

AND NOW THE PINK BALLOONS SINGING WELL WELL WELL WELL

Okay, you guys, everybody out of here. Got everything?

You missed your calling, Mother. You should've been in the army. You would've made a great sergeant-major.

Nuts to you. So long, Katie. 'Bye, kids.

'Bye.

Slam.

Okay, flower. Here's your cereal.

— Quick, coffee, or I faint.

EIGHT-THIRTY NEWS BOMBERS LAST NIGHT CLAIMED A DECISIVE VICTORY FOUR VILLAGES TOTALLY DESTROYED AND A NUMBER OF OTHERS SET ABLAZE

Stacey stirs her coffee and lights a cigarette. Then she switches off the radio.

— I can't listen. It's too much too much too much. What can you do, anyhow? Nothing. Just agonize. Useless. All useless. Me included. Listen, God, I know it's a worthwhile job to bring up four kids. You don't need to propagandize me; I'm converted. But how is it I can feel as well that I'm spending my life in one unbroken series of trivialities? The kids don't belong to me. They belong to themselves. It would be nice to have something of my own, that's all. I can't go anywhere as myself. Only as Mac's wife or the kids' mother. And yet I'm getting now so that I actually prefer to have either Mac or one of the kids along. Even to the hairdresser, I'd rather take Jen. It's easier to face the world with one of them along. Then I know who I'm supposed to be.

> *What's your name, little girl?* Stacey Cameron. *That's a funny name – Stacey.* It is not! It is not! It's my name and don't you say anything about it, see? *Stacey, don't be rude – this is Reverend McPhail, our new minister. Say you're sorry.* I will not. *Go to your room, then.* (In the bedroom, an oval mirror, and she put her face very close to it, so she could see deeply into her own eyes – Anastasia, princess of all the Russias; Anastasia, queen of the Hebrides, soon to inherit the ancestral castle in the craggy isles.)

Come on, opera star. Let's go and see Aunt Tess. We better put a few presentable clothes on first. Gosh, I wish I had a skin like yours, flower. Not a blemish. All the other kids have got a certain amount of freckles, but you're like milk. Too pale, maybe. Yeh, you could stand with a little more color. C'mon, this is where you're supposed to say nuts to you, Mum, I'm absolutely gorgeous the way I am. Okay – you've convinced me.

> Newspaper photograph. Some new kind of napalm just invented, a substance which, when it alights burning onto skin, cannot be removed. It adheres. The woman was holding a child about eighteen months old and she was trying to pluck something away from the scorch-spreading area on the child's face.

Come on, Jen, let's get dressed and get out of here.

Tess is waiting for them with the coffee cups out.

> Gee, that's a cute outfit, Stacey.
>
> Like it? I got it for her last summer.

No, I meant your dress.

What, mine? Oh – well, thanks, Tess. I can hardly squeeze into it.

You haven't put on any weight, surely?

That's what you think. I'm on a diet this week.

Oh? What kind?

Well, I tried the banana diet, but I get so fed up with bananas that I'm not fit to live with. This one's high protein, no carbohydrates.

How do you find it?

It's hell. It's the bread I miss. I've got no willpower, that's my trouble.

Oh Stacey, you? I always think you've got terrific willpower.

Who, me?

I mean to say, all those kids and running the house and all.

That's not willpower. That's just elbow grease.

Well, my heavens, I know I couldn't do it. I tire so quickly. Sometimes it's like I can hardly lift a finger without getting all played out. I saw the doctor again about my blood pressure.

Oh? What did he say?

The usual. Take it easy. Keep up the pills. Salt-free diet. I didn't tell Jake I went.

Why not?

I don't know, Stacey. He doesn't like people not feeling well.

It's not your fault.

I know, but then again – well, I don't know. You know what men are like.

No, but I sure wish I did.

I wish I had your way of laughing at everything, Stacey.

I don't really

Sure you do. It's a real gift. My dad used to say, *Tess, when God gave out the sense of humor, he missed you.* I've never forgotten that. I guess it's true. Of course, I mean, I like laughing. But I can never remember jokes and that. Did I show you the goldfish?

No. You got goldfish?

Yeh. Jake bought them for me. For company, he said. See, here they are. I like the little wee castle at the bottom of the bowl, there, don't you? And all those pink and blue pebbles. Kind of sweet, I thought. See, there's the big goldfish hiding behind that fern or whatever it is. Where's the smaller one got to? Don't tell me – no, there it is. There were three when Jake brought them home.

Did the other one die?

Well, not exactly. The big one ate it.

What?

Apparently it's a quite common thing among goldfish. Some just do. I saw it happen. It was kind of peculiar. The big goldfish bit it on the back of the neck, sort of, and it had this convulsion, like, and then the big one took it to the bottom of the bowl and just ate it. I saw the whole thing happen. It didn't even take very long.

That's gruesome.

Yes. It looked really peculiar, like I said. I am keeping my eye on this other one now. To see what happens

Can't you take it out? Or do something

Well, it's their natural way isn't it after all

What'll you do if it *does*

Jake said he would bring home another one tonight just in case

Expensive fish food

Oh, they don't cost very much

— Dog eat dog and fish eat fish. Don't tell me any more because I don't want to know.

Thanks for the coffee, Tess. My appointment's for ten. I must get going

You'll leave Jen?

Well, I don't think I should

Sure. Leave her, Stacey.

Okay, if you're sure it's no

Oh, positive. She's as good as gold. You're as good as a little goldfish, aren't you, sweetie? No trouble

— Jen? You okay, flower? I want to take you along with me, but I don't know how to say it politely.

The hair dryer purrs whirringly like a metallic tiger. Stacey turns the magazine page. The article is entitled "Pruning Down with Prunes – New Concept in Dieting." She sighs, closes the magazine and looks around. The dryer prevents any other sound from reaching her, so everything in front of her eyes is taking place in silence, as though she were observing it through some thick and isolating glass barrier or like TV with the voices turned off.

The priestesses are clad in pale mauve smocks. They glide and dart, the movements perfectly assured and smooth, no wasted effort. A heavy woman with heavy grey hair sinks down into a chair in front of the grape-fruit-yellow basin. With a visible sigh of pleasure, tweed-covered bosom lifting like hills in a minor earthquake, she leans back her head to receive the benediction of the shampoo. The priestess's plastic-sheathed hands adminis-ter to her scalp, the fingers updrawn like yellow talonless claws. In a chair facing the wall-to-wall mirror, a young woman laughs soundlessly up at her priestess, who is twirling the strands of black hair rapidly around yellow rollers. An ammonia whiff and a conglomeration of humid perfumes come to Stacey's nostrils.

Not Earth. Somewhere else. Quite a small planet, but with a very advanced technology. The whole process is absolutely painless, here on Zabyul. The silver mechanism is simply fitted over the head, creating an impression of gentle warmth. Soon she will emerge from the Chrysalis. That is what the mechanism is called. One of the butterfly priestesses comes over, checks the controls. All set – the transformation is complete. She steps out. The entire room is made of a substance which reflects softly. She stares. Her? This very young woman has her features, but altered, made finer, the shape of the bones incredibly beautiful under the cream-textured skin. Quick – Jartek will be waiting. And there he is, strong and supple, his sex discernible under the sleek tight-fitting uniform of a galactic pilot. Then they are in one of the life-domes. He is a senior pilot, so naturally his life-dome is a relatively spacious gracious one, furnished with golden-foam couches that grow organically out of the walls at a flick of the Environator on his steady-boned yet now trembling wrist. He puts his hands on her breasts, then slides his finger down to her willing sex. Now   quickly.

Okay, Mrs. MacAindra? If you'd like to come over here, Lenore will comb you out.

Thanks.

— No wonder I'm afraid of having an anaesthetic or undergoing hypnosis. What if I talked? I'm a freak. Or maybe I'm not, but how can you tell? There is only one thing you have to remember, Stacey, doll. Tonight, drink tomato juice.

Outside the door of the hotel banqueting room, Mac touches Stacey's arm. Half surprised, she glances at him and finds that he is smiling.

Now just don't worry, Stacey. It'll be all right.

Gosh, I hope so. I'm kind of nervous.

There's nothing to be nervous *about*. Just don't argue or

I won't   I swear it.

The room is large, old-fashioned, plush, velvet-draped, and full of people. Stacey straightens her black cocktail dress with perspiring hands. At one end of the room there is a long bar, behind which three waiters are being kept busy. Stacey pats at her hair. In the middle of the room is a bandstand, from which members of a small and bored-looking orchestra are dispensing waltzes and slow foxtrots. Stacey resists the desire to look behind her and make sure her waist-slip has not edged disastrously downwards. Across the room, corner to corner, stretches a white banner with one word in cerise, gold-edged.

RICHALIFE

Standing with a group of laughing girls, all lissome and blonde with good teeth and no waists, is Thor, dressed in midnight-blue evening suit and drinking tomato juice. His silver hair glimmers phosphorescently. Stacey checks by running one finger along her outer thighs to make sure her panties have not by any chance suddenly lost their elasticity and begun to descend. Thor waves and grins, and Mac lifts a hand in a return salute. Stacey unobtrusively puts one hand behind her and touches a thumb to the small of her back in case her bra has become unhooked. The orchestra goes into the droning circles of a Viennese waltz, and before Stacey and Mac can reach Thor, he is dancing with one of the girls.

C'mon, then. Let's get a drink, eh?

You think we should, Mac?

Don't be ridiculous, Stacey. He's not intolerant. He doesn't try to foist his opinions on other people.

Not much, he doesn't.

Well, if you're going to take that line, you better stick to Coke.

No – I'm not. I mean I won't.

— Resolutions, where have you gone? All night on Coke and I will be a raving lunatic. Two, though. Only two. Then stop. Spirits of my dead forefathers, strengthen me. They should strengthen you, nitwit? They probably all died of whiskey. Mac, don't leave me. I can't cope with this crew.

Stacey, this is Mickey Jameson. Mick, I'd like you to meet my wife.

Pleased to meetcha.

Hello – glad to meet you

And this is my wife, Priscilla – dear, this is Mac Mac-Aindra and Stacey.

Hello there

Glad to meet you

What'll it be, Stacey?

Oh – Scotch and water, please, with lots of ice.

— Maybe gin and tonic would be better? Mother's ruin. No, that's for home. Mac prefers gin. Scotch for the crises. Up, the clans.

Mickey Jameson is short, young, blue-eyed, pink-faced. His wife is similar in feminine version. Stacey contemplates the girl, wondering if she really is not perspiring or is only pretending not to. The girl's dress is short and white but not virginal, and her make-up is a work of abstract art. The long false eyelashes glow diamondly with a touch of what appears to be the instant-snow spray that Stacey associates with Christmas trees.

— Can't be. Must be some other gloop. Must ask Katie. If I would only read articles on make-up instead of those epistles telling me all the harm I'm doing, then I'd know. I can't read them. I look at them from the edge of one eye, at a distance, but they always scare me off. It looks so complicated. Things used to be a hell of a lot simpler, in my day. Cream, lipstick and powder. Finish. *In my day.* Lovely phrase, that.

Been with Richalife long?

Who, Mac? Oh, not so very long. What about your husband?

Just a month or so. But he loves it. It's the greatest, isn't it?

Yeh. It's fine.

Mickey says he was just marking time, before. Just simply marking time. He was in house paints. What was your hubby in, before?

He was in essence – I mean to say, the essence of his work was kind of educational. Encyclopedias, like.

Oh, say. Well, think of that, now. What made him switch?

Oh you know   go-ahead firm and that

Yeh   well   that's just exactly what Mickey said, too.

Mac and Mickey are standing shoulder to shoulder. Stouthearted men.

Yeh, well, like I said, Mick, I used to do the Okanagan – up and down the whole valley – with my previous firm, so that's why I wanted to keep the area for the time being. I know it like the palm of my hand.

Sure, boy, I can see that all right. I would've figured you for the city, though.

You could be right, there. Maybe it's time I changed territory.

A change is as good as a rest, I always say.

Well, you could be right.

At this point, Thor saunters up and joins the group, or rather, the group re-forms around him.

Hi, Mac. Hi, Mickey. Good to see you. Well, hel*lo* there, Priscilla. You don't mind if I call you Priscilla, do you?

Why, certainly not. I'd just love you to, Mr. Thorlakson.

Thor's the name sweetheart. Just Thor. And who have we here? Stacey, isn't it? Well, and how are *you*, Stacey?

Just fine, thanks.

I'm glad to hear it. Have you got all those nice kids of yours on the Younglife Program yet? Oh yes, you have. I remember the charts now. And if I remember correctly, they're doing just dandy, too. Just great. Well, that's splendid, Stacey. You have any trouble getting the whole brood to line up for the Program every morning, Mac?

Nope. None whatsoever.

— Like fun. He leaves it to me, and sometimes I give them one and mostly I forget, or forget on purpose, thinking the stuff is probably subtly addictive, or will ultimately be found to contain traces of arsenic, and then I flush the baubles down the john when no one's around, and probably Katie will rat on me one of these days. I don't know when Mac takes his. It is not a subject which is discussed between us.

Well, that's great. Say, you know, Mickey, this guy's got four children. Brave fellow, eh? You going to try for a baseball team, Mac?

Not yet a while

Well, let me know when you think of trying, and we'll give you an extra ration of Richalife. How about that? Only save enough energy to get the product across, won't you, Mac? If possible, that is.

— What's going on? What are you getting at, you slimy bastard?

Four kids aren't many these days

What's that? Oh – yes, you're perfectly right there, Stacey. Yes, indeed. Large families are coming back in, all right. Personally, I've got nothing against large families. Provided people can look after them and educate them adequately. No, not adequately – properly. I would say *properly*.

We aim to.

Of course you do, Stacey. I'd never doubt that for an instant. Well, if you good people will excuse me, I see one of the office girls over there and I think I really must go and dance with her.

Thor skims shiningly off. Stacey goes to the bar and gets another Scotch by herself.

Mac?

Yeh?

What was all that?

What was all what?

Oh for heaven's sake, *you* know. He was needling

He was kidding. Can't you take a joke *yet*, Stacey?

Nope. No sense of humor. Me, Tess and Queen Victoria.

Look, I gotta go and see Stewart Essex for a minute. He mentioned he'd like a country circuit. I think it's time I got onto a city run. You okay here?

Sure. You go ahead. I'll find somebody to talk to.

The evening grinds along. Stacey discovers several other aimless wives whose husbands are in essential conference together.

Hello. Mind if I join you?

Oh, do. I'm Clare Gallagher and this is Joanie Storey.

Hi. Glad to meet you. I'm Stacey MacAindra.

Your old man's talking shop, too, I suppose?

What else?

Boy, I really love it. I was saying to Joanie, here, they take you out about once a month and then what do they do? Dance with you? Not on your sweet Nelly they don't. You got kids?

Yeh. Four.

Yeh? How old?

Daughter fourteen, son ten, son seven, daughter two. You?

I got only the two, but believe me, that's plenty. My little boy just turned five, and my girl is eighteen months. They're sure a handful.

I know, but they get easier. It makes a lotta difference when they're at school.

I suppose. But then again, I think the house'll seem awfully empty.

Well, I guess so. My youngest isn't at school yet, of course, so I don't know.

— How to get out of this? They're thinking the same, maybe. Funny thing – when I'm with those know-everythings in some evening class or other, I think the hell with intellectual pursuits and all I feel like doing is gabbing about my kids. But when I'm with women who are gabbing about kids, I think the hell with it. Powder room – that's it.

In the course of the next hour, Stacey visits the Ladies' twice, on each occasion slipping a small cake of the provided pink soap into her evening bag. She repairs her make-up, stares gloomily at herself in the antiseptic-looking mirror, smiles stiffly at the other women who clank in and out of the toilet cubicles. She then goes back to the bar and obtains another double Scotch. She dances once with a corpulent youngish man who pumps her hand up and down and maneuvers her around the corners by swiveling her on his belly. After that, nobody asks her. She decides to stay within easy reach of the bar.

— Who would want to dance to that dreary music, anyway? Not me. I used to love dancing. I used to be a good dancer. I said to Katie and Ian once, *You may not believe it, but I used to be a good dancer.* What kind of music in those days, they wanted to know. *Boogie-woogie,* I foolishly said. They damn near killed themselves laughing. They went around for days saying it – *Boo-oo-gie-woo-oo-gie* – and collapsing in mirth. Ha bloody ha.

Double Scotch, please.

— Come on, doll, be sociable. Don't want to be sociable. Don't know anybody. What did Thor mean, needling Mac like that? He was needling him. And saying like that, *Who have we here?* Like I was something that just crawled out from under a stone. The bastard. Who does he think he is? How dare he talk to Mac like that? Listen, you thunder god, you, you double-dyed snake-in-the-grass, you refugee from the discards of Lucifer's army. Let me tell you one simple thing. Just one. Do you want to know why Mac didn't reply? Do you want to know why he didn't wipe the floor verbally with you? I'll tell you. I'll tell you straight. Because he is a gentleman, that's why. Because he cannot be bothered to stoop to your paltry jesting, you sick clown, that's why. Believe me, I'd say it to your face.

Thor's face. Immediately in front of her and somewhat above. His height. Very tall man. Surrounded by a circle of anonymous others. Stacey sees only Thor – the white opalescent skin, the eyes like turquoises, opaque blue, the silver mane. She realizes she has walked all around the room in search of him, and now she has found him.

Excuse me.

Why, hi there, Stacey. You enjoying the party?

Yes. Yes, thanks. There was only one thing I wanted to ask you about.

Go right ahead. What is it? It isn't – ah – private?

Oh hell no it's not private it's only about that quiz

Quiz?

Quiz. Why'd you do it?

You mean the Richalife Quiz? I don't think I quite see

I said why'd you do it? What can you gain? Who's gonna tell you anything on a thing like that?

You don't think so?

Hell I know so. I mean if I feel guilty or anxious, like let's say I stabbed my dear old grandmother in the back for her money or I find I got stigmata on both palms and I gotta wear gloves everywhere I go, you think I'm gonna *say*?

Titters of general laughter. Thor reaches out and takes Stacey's hands.

Here – let me see. No, you're all clear, Stacey, I'm glad to say. You didn't strike me like the type. Well, about the quiz, now.

— I got to stop. Stacey, girl, shut your trap. Change subject. Now. Essential. Get a grip on yourself. Think of Mac.

No, it's only that it's an intrusion or do I mean infringement? I mean infrusion, that's what I mean but I guess I shouldn't have brought it up.

One of the circle, a slender man in glasses, puts a hand on her rump.

As long as that's all you bring up

Hey the party's getting rough

We've all got good manners here

Stacey lets the talk flow away from her. She glances around to find Mac, knowing she must focus on him. Finally she sees him. He is standing near a window, his face turned away from her. He is talking with a tall brown-haired girl whose face is a medieval tomb carving, elongated, drawn in subtle lines of earnestness and prayer. Stacey quickly looks away.

— Don't be ridiculous. He's only talking to her. Yeh, but that look on her face. What is she *saying*? None of your business, Stacey. None of your damn business. She looks so much more sensitive and that, than I look. What about one for the road? Stacey, kid, you're stoned. I am not stoned. All right, so even if I am, so what? I don't give a fuck.

She spins around to face Thor again, and in doing so, her evening bag spills open and two pink soaps slither down onto the polished floor. Stacey looks at them as though she has never seen them before. There is a small moment of silence and uncertainty. Then someone laughs, a high fluting. Stacey discovers with some astonishment that it is herself.

I always take them home for the kids. I do it with those wrapped sugar lumps too

Thor picks them up for her.

Think nothing of it. I know I used to like things like that, as a kid.

Yeh? Well, I'm certainly glad to hear it. Were you – were you always called Thor?

Except when I was called late for supper   ha-ha. Yes, it's an Icelandic name.

That's what I figured. Lots of people of Icelandic descent where I came from. Not exactly where I *came* from, but same province. Manitoba. Prairie girl, that's me.

Really? How interesting.

He looks bored almost to the limit of endurance, and she recalls too late that she told him once before where she came from, as though compelled to flaunt her small-town background.

Yeh, and you know what? The only joke I can ever remember is about Thor.

Well, in that case, it must be a pretty good joke.

It's so-so. The great god Thor comes to earth once, see? And I guess this would likely be in some Scandinavian country, eh? Anyway, he meets this lovely country girl. So he – he – persuades her. You know, he persuades her. To go into a hayfield with him. Well, he seduces her, see? But later on, he feels kind of bad, being as he had an advantage. I mean, he is – like – a god, see, so who could resist him? You know? So he says to her, *Look, there's something I oughta tell you. I'm Thor. And she says, Tho am I, but it wath worth it, wathn't it*?

Laughter. Ripples, extending outwards. Thor's uninterpretable face. The young henchmen, simpering in spectacles. Women's shrill braying giggles. Men's deep-voiced guffaws. Then Mac's arm on her elbow, pressing hard enough to bruise.

C'mon, Stacey. We promised the kids we'd be home by twelve.

Did we? I don't remember

Goodnight, Thor.

Thor is talking to someone else.

Oh – good night, Mac. Good night, Stacey.

G'night

The car is flying, and out in a blackness of sky, when the city lights have gone away, the moon is also flying, descending the hollow hill of night, climbing again to the center of everything, in trails of moonstone light. Stacey, leaning her head against the back of the car seat, can see it happening.

You know what they called the moon in the Highlands, Mac?

(No reply)

Mac, you know what they used to call the moon, there? They used to call it MacFarlane's lantern. You know that? And you know something else? That was because the MacFarlanes were a pretty sneaky lot, see, buncha thieves, actually, and they used to go around on these raids, see? Banditti. That's what they were, the MacFarlanes. Buncha banditti. So that moon was their lantern.

And you know something else? The MacAindras belong to the MacFarlane clan. How d'you like that? That's you, kid. Banditti. MacFarlane's lantern. Only that isn't you, is it, Mac? That isn't you at all. *Au contraire*, as we say in Quebec.

Dry up, Stacey. You've said enough tonight.

Dry up, Stacey. Shut up and simmer down, Stacey. Do this do that. I would like to live on a desert island. What would you like?

Don't ask me. I might tell you. No use in your condition.

What d'you mean, in my condition? You make it sound like I'm pregnant.

C'mon. We're home.

Home Sweet Home. Oh boy.

C'mon. Stacey. Just get to bed.

Okay okay okay okay

She is lying on a magic carpet. Must be a magic carpet, what else? It is moving very rapidly, in upward and downward swooshes. Each swirl leaves a color in its path   jet-trails of color smoke   one for each day of the week   pink   purple   peacock   blue   tangerine   green leaves   greensleeves   bird-feather   yellow   raspberry no not raspberry   that's an essence   the essence of the whole matter is is is

Blackness.

— Help. Water. Water. I'm dying of thirst. Bathroom. Oh man, that's one degree better at least. What time is it? Half past seven. Morning. Can't be. Is. Oh perdition. Am I going to throw up? Nothing to throw except two glasses of water. Back to bed. No. Got to get up. Impossible. Not impossible. Got to.

Stacey goes back to the bedroom. Mac is almost dressed. He looks at her silently. Then she remembers.

Stacey, tottering over to Thor's court. Stacey, arguing in a loud harridan voice, her hair disarranged, her make-up long since vanished. *It's a-a-inf-infrusion, tha's what it is, so there, see?* Oh God. Two pink soap tablets tumbling out of her handbag. The gusts and shrieks of pointing laughter. Thief, thief – takes the soap from the ladies' john. Stacey, regaling the company with corny slightly low joke about – what? Joke about Thor. Oh God. Stacey, believing they were laughing *with* her.

— Oh no. It couldn't have been. It was. Was it that bad? Am I exaggerating? No. No, I'm not. It was probably far worse than that, even.

Mac – oh Mac, was it awful?

Look, Stacey, there's no point in discussing it.

It *was* awful. I can remember everything. Every word. Oh Mac, I'm sorry.

Yeh. Well.

I don't know what got *into* me.

Allow me to tell you, then. What got into you was Scotch.

Mac   please don't look like that

Oh Christ. Like what?

Grim. Like ice. I can't stand it

Look, Stacey, it's nearly eight o'clock. Can we just get breakfast?

Mac, I'm sorry. Honestly, I'm terribly terribly sorry.

Yeh. So you said.

I was kind of nervous anyway, and then you left me on my own.

Great. So now it's my fault.

I didn't say that.

Stacey, there is absolutely no use in talking. I got to get to work. I don't want to discuss it.

I think we should. I think we should discuss everything

Oh God. Look, Stacey, I'm not asking much. I'm only suggesting that breakfast would be a good idea. Is that asking too much?

Okay okay okay I'm going downstairs right this minute. Mac, do you think you should tell Thor I'm sorry?

If he doesn't mention it, I most certainly will not bring up the subject. Now if you don't mind

Okay okay I'm on my way

Clutching her housecoat around her, Stacey rushes down to the kitchen. The motions of getting breakfast are automatic. The minutes are eternal, the voices piercing.

— Hush. Please. Just be quiet for once. I tell you, my eardrums will crack. How'd you like to have a mother with cracked eardrums?

She says as little as possible. At last they are all out of the house, and Stacey is alone with Jen. She pours her coffee and begins to sip at it cautiously.

— Oh my guts. When this coffee hits them, they will rebel into convulsions. Slowly, that's it. There. That's a bit better. Why did I do it? I'll never live it down. Mac will never forgive me. I'll never forgive myself. It isn't as though it's never happened before. No, Stacey, girl, don't think of the other times. Not that many. No, but all dreadful. Don't *think* – I command you. You do, eh? Who're you? One of your other selves. Help, I'm schizophrenic. Oh God, why did I do it? I was so damn scared of not doing well, and then I didn't do well. Maybe if I hadn't been so scared – don't make excuses, Stacey. *Mea culpa.* It must be wonderful to be a Catholic. Pour it all out. Somebody listens. Not me. I'm stuck with it, all of it, every goddam awful detail, for the rest of my natural or unnatural life. Mac scares me when he's like he was this morning. Why can't he ever say? Maybe if he ever did, he'd throttle me. I wouldn't blame him. My God, maybe he *will* throttle me one of these days. "Salesman Strangles Wife" – it could happen to anybody. Nobody is an exception. What would happen to the kids if that happened? Oh my guts, churning around like a covey of serpents. Covey? Nest? Medusa does in summer wear a nest of serpents in her hair. Joyce Kilmer. I can't seem to focus on anything. Whatsamatter with my eyeballs? When I close my eyes, something flickers across them. Jangled nerves. Feels like that tropical worm in that article – lives under people's eyelids and crawls over the eyes when so inclined. Charming. I'm sick. I'm ill. Have I ruined Mac's job? Was it as awful as I remember?

> Stacey, face distorted into a swollen mask like the face of a woman drowned, the features blurred. The lunatic laughter, hers.

— I am exaggerating. I must be. Am I? I can't tell. It seems worse every time I think of it.

NINE-O'CLOCK NEWS PELLET BOMBS CAUSED THE DEATH OF A HUNDRED AND TWENTY-FIVE CIVILIANS MAINLY WOMEN AND CHILDREN IN

C'mon, flower. The least we can do is clean this house.

Duncan can play alone, for when he feels the world's aloofness he goes inward to more satisfactory countries. After school, he is not to be seen and Stacey finally discovers him in the basement, not in the playroom but standing beside the automatic washer, spinning the dials.

Duncan – what you are doing? Don't you dare

It's okay, Mum. It's not switched on.

Well, all right. What is it? A spaceship?

Duncan looks at her, half surprised and half pleased, a short stocky figure in jeans and striped T shirt.

Yeh. Sort of. I'm taking it to Venus. That's a neat planet, you know, Mum? It's very bright, all surrounded by these gases that they don't know what they are. Miss Walsh said.

How you going to get through all the gases, then?

This ship has a built-in-gas-goer-througher.

Well, that's great. But shouldn't you be outside, nice day like this?

I don't want to.

Why not?

Ian just tells me to scram.

Well, it's your yard, too. Come on, I'll speak to Ian.

I don't want to, Mum.

Oh, okay, but you ought to be out in the sun.

Stacey goes upstairs to the kitchen to begin dinner. Ian is standing beside the long low window, breaking small pieces of leaf off the potted plants.

Hey, my African violets! Cut it out, Ian. What's the matter?

There's nothing to do around here.

Why don't you play with your bug?

It's no fun. The wheels keep coming off.

Why don't you find somebody to play with, then?

Ron's gone with his mum to see his aunt. Terry's playing with Robert and they don't want me.

What about TV, then? Not that you should, this early.

Nothing on I want to see.

Well, what about going to see if Peter can play? He doesn't live that far. You could go on your bike.

Ian swings around slowly to face her.

Who?

Peter. Peter Challoner. You haven't played with him for quite a while.

Ian's grey eyes turn hard, hooded almost, and Stacey can see the small vein along his throat pulsing, as it does sometimes when he is more than usually tense.

What is it, Ian?

Peter's dead. I thought you knew.

Stacey looks at him, unbelieving. Ian's face prohibits questions, but she has to speak.

He can't be. What – what happened?

He got run over. It was that day you came home late for lunch.

Oh Ian – I didn't know – I must've missed it in the paper

> The *scree-ee* of brakes. A white Buick. The driver getting out slowly, as though unable to look. The slight quiet figure under the front wheels. Stacey,

running along the sidewalk towards home, heels
snagging on the cement.

You didn't tell me, Ian. I didn't know. Oh honey.
Why didn't you tell me?

Ian's face is pinched and rigid with its control, its go-
away quality.

What would've been the use? What could you have
done?

I could've

— I don't know. For you, maybe nothing.

Stacey makes a tentative move towards him, one
hand out to his shoulder. Ian breaks away, his thin
strength arrowing past her, and reaches the back door.
Then he turns upon her, a flame-furred young fox cornered, snarling, self-protective.

Can't you just shut up about it? He was dumb, see?
Nobody but a moron would run out into the avenue after
a football. It doesn't happen that easy unless guys are
pretty dumb.

Ian, wait

But he is gone, out to his lair, the loft of the garage.

— What's he been having nightmares about these past
weeks? Why can't he ever say? How did he get to be that
way, or was it born in him? God, how should I know? He
gets further and further away. I can't reach him at all. Was
he always that way, only I never noticed so much when he
was younger?

Ian MacAindra, age four, marching around and
around the kitchen table, to the martial music on
the radio. Stacey, amused. Aren't you tired,
honey? *Yes.* Why don't you stop then? *I can't stop
till the music stops.* So she turned off the radio
when she saw he wasn't joking.

Mac has just come in, when there is a wail from the
basement, and pounding footsteps. Duncan runs up the
stairs into the kitchen, one hand bloodily scarlet. Stacey
goes to him.

What happened?

Duncan's voice is barely discernible through his fear-sobbing.

Nail sticking out of the wall – didn't see it – it was rusty too will I die Mum? Ian says you die if it's rusty

No, you won't die. I'll fix it up. It'll soon be better. Don't worry. It'll be all right.

Duncan continues to sob, the tears runneling through the dust on his wide youngly plump face. Mac comes in from the hall, running his fingers distractedly through his brush of hair.

Duncan, for goodness sake shut up and quit making such a fuss about nothing.

Leave him, Mac. He was scared. Ian told him a rusty nail would

Scared, hell. He doesn't need to roar like that. Shut up, Duncan, you hear me?

Duncan nods, gulps down the salt from his eyes and the mucus from his nose. His chest heaves and he continues to cry, but quietly. Mac clamps a hand on his shoulder and spins him around.

Now listen here, Duncan, I'll give you one minute to stop.

Duncan stares with wet slit-eyes into his father's face. Stacey clenches her hands together.

— I could kill you, Mac. I could stab you to the very heart right this minute. But how can I even argue, after last night? My bargaining power is at an all-time low. Damn you. Damn you. Take your hands off my kid. Oh, God, I know, Sir – I know. Mac's probably spent the day placating Thor. And I haven't forgotten pitching Duncan and Ian to the floor either. What right have I got to say anything? But I can't help it. I can't stand this.

Leave him, Mac, can't you? Please just leave him alone.

Listen, Stacey, if he doesn't begin to learn some control now, when is he going to learn? Duncan, you just listen to me. You can't go through life bawling your head off, the slightest thing happens. What a mess you'll be if you go on that way. You'll never get to first base if you can't learn to control yourself. Okay – you're going to get hurt; you're going to get bashed around; that's life. But for heaven's sake try to show a little guts.

— All useless. Everything anybody says to their kids is useless. Kids don't go by that. Or do they? Who is right, Mac or me? Maybe we're both wrong. All I want to do is hold Duncan so he isn't afraid. Is that wrong? What if Mac's dead right? Duncan did make a lot of fuss, I have to admit. How to stop myself ruining him?

Later, when Duncan has gone upstairs, Stacey follows him, first making sure that Mac is watching the news on TV in the basement playroom.

Duncan?

He is sitting on his bed, holding one of his model cars in one hand, turning it over and over without seeing it.

You okay now, Duncan?

He looks up at her, his eyes tearless, almost passive.

I never do anything right.

He didn't mean that, Duncan. He only meant

Well, I *don't*, Mum. I just don't do anything right

— What words? I haven't got any. It isn't mine he wants anyway. It's Mac's and Ian's, and those he won't get. I'm far from him, too. Far even from Duncan. How did it happen like this?

After dinner, Katie is doing her homework in her room. Stacey is bathing Jen. Mac has gone with his briefcase into the study. Duncan is looking at TV, and Ian is prowling. Then Katie's infuriated shrieking voice.

Mother! Tell Ian to get out of here!

— Heaven. She's started calling me Mother instead of Mum. How long? I never noticed before.

Ian! What're you doing?

He barged right into my room without knocking. I can't *stand* people doing that. Scram, you little creep!

Quit shoving me, you, or I'll

Ow! That hurt! Boy, I'll show you

Yeh? Well, how d'you like this then

Crash. Scream. Slam. Stacey flies out of the bathroom, hands soap-slippery, and along the corridor. She pulls Katie and Ian apart and pushes them into their respective bedrooms.

Okay, Ian. Just leave her *alone*, eh?

I was only

All right all right – you know what I told you about knocking before you go into people's bedrooms. And do not throw the hall chair *any more*, see?

Stacey carefully knocks and enters Katie's room. Katie is gathering up the littered textbooks, her long hair trailing on the floor as she stoops.

Katie, I know it was wrong of him. But he's been in a pretty low mood today. Try to be patient with

Patient! What good does that do? He never pays any attention.

Well, try

You try. That's your job.

Yeh, well just wait, sweetheart, till you've got your own kids

I'm not going to have

Oh? Why not?

Because it's for the birds, that's why.

What is?

The whole deal. You saying we get on your nerves all the time. You and Dad yakking away at each other – *Whatsmatter? Nothing's the matter. No need to talk to me in that tone of voice.* Man, not for me.

> Stacey Cameron, sixteen, watching granite-eyed while her mother retreated softly and billowingly into temporary but recurring nerves, meaning the solace of flowing eyes and codeine for the headaches. *I won't argue any more with you, Stacey – it hurts me too much when you're so stubborn, and it isn't as though I could even ask your father. You wait, you just wait until you have your own chil-*

dren. (I'll have them, all right, but it won't ever be
like this, my setup.)

Stacey stands in the doorway, unmoving, staring.

Katie – does it really strike you like that?

Katie does not reply. She cannot, because she is crying. Stacey moves towards her, but Katie turns and faces
the wall, her voice low and muffled.

Go away, can't you?

— It's her age. They're all like that, at about this age. Of
course I know that. Katie – talk to me.

Mac, talk to me.

Oh Christ, Stacey.

I know I know it's late – time for sleep – work tomorrow – but please

It is eleven thirty and they are in bed. The light is out.
Mac has just butted his last cigarette and replaced the
ashtray on the bedside table. He sighs, and Stacey can feel
him edging a little further towards his own side of the bed.

— You'll fall out of bed in a minute, Mac, if you're not
careful. What do you think it would do – pollute you, if
you touched me? And yet if I said that, it would be a
terrible thing to say. Unforgivable. Like what I did last
night at the party. Nothing is ever looked at and torn up
and thrown away like scrap paper. The abrasions just go
on accumulating. What a lot of heavy invisible garbage we
live with.

Mac, about last night

Look, I told you. Let's drop it, eh? No use talking
about it.

Okay. But you don't seem to drop it.

What do you *mean*, I don't seem to drop it? It's you
who

Well, you go around being gloomy and not talking –
naturally I don't expect you to *like* what I did but was it
really so terrible? I'd rather you got mad and yelled at me
and then it would be all over maybe and we could forget it.

If I did yell at you or beat you up, would you really like that any better?

I only meant saying something, to clear the air. I didn't mean beating me up, for heaven's sake. I'd walk out on you if you did that.

— Would I? With four kids? How could you walk out on him, Stacey, whatever he did or was like? You couldn't, sweetheart, and don't you forget it. You haven't got a nickel of your own. This is what they mean by emancipation. I'm lucky he's not more externally violent, that's all. I see it, God, but don't expect me to like it.

Stacey, I don't care to discuss it. Is that clear?

Yessir.

Cut it out, will you?

Cut what out?

That act.

Oh Mac, please

She has turned to him, and put her hands on his shoulders. For a moment he lies still, while she undoes his pajamas and begins slowly touching him where she knows it will have effect. Her hands move across the hair on his chest and down to his sex. He stirs then, and suddenly, abruptly, almost roughly, begins making love to her.

— Strange that the hair under his arms and on his chest is auburn but between his legs dark. Can't see the color but I know it. The mole on his right shoulder. The scar on his thigh – right here – where he got gashed playing hockey when he was a kid. I know every inch of his skin. Mac? You want me? Yes, now he does.

I do too, Mac.

You do what?

Want you

Yeh, I know I know. Now, Stacey?

Yes. Now.

Stacey rises to him, her legs linked around his, and cries out as she always does without knowing it. He comes in pain-pleasure silence as almost always, telling her only through veins and muscles and skin that he is with her.

When it is over, they separate because his weight on her ribs always makes her cough after a few moments, and anyway he always has to get up and go to the bathroom.

— Did I take that christly pill this morning? I was feeling so grim – can't remember. Yes, I did take it. Along with the blue Richalife and four aspirins, with second cup of coffee. All these considerations.

> The apartment was cramped and dingy, and they had hardly any furniture. *It's ours, Stacey – just think of that – fantastic, eh?* And they slept in each other's arms and legs all night, with peace, and wakened whole.

You okay, Stacey?

Oh yes.

Good night, then

Good night

Within minutes she can hear Mac breathing deeply in sleep. Sometimes he moans in his sleep and she always asks him the next day if he had a dream but he can never remember. Tonight he is quiet. Stacey turns over on her right side, and pulls her legs up so she is lying Z-shaped.

— Tonight I'll sleep. Let us be thankful for mercies, whatever.

The rain forest is thick, matted, overgrown with thorned berry bushes, the fallen needles from the pine and tamarack bronzing the earth. Smell of moss, wet branches, mellowly rotten leaves. It is very difficult to walk through. The wild brambles stretch out their fish hooks to tear at exposed skin. The ground is spongy underfoot, for the moss tops centuries of leaf mold. She has to continue, bringing what she is carrying with her. The thing is bleeding from the neck stump, but that cannot be helped. The severed head spills only blood, nothing else. She has tunneled at last through the undergrowth. Now she has the right to look. She holds it up in front of her. How is it that she can see it? What is she seeing it with? That is the question. The head she has been carrying is of course none but hers.

Five

EVER-OPEN EYE   BOUGAINVILLAEA BURGEONING, EDG-
ING STREETS WHERE BEGGARS SQUAT IN DUST. MAN
BURNING. HIS FACE CANNOT BE SEEN. HE LIES STILL, PERHAPS
ALREADY DEAD. FLAMES LEAP AND QUIVER FROM HIS BLACK-
ENED ROBE LIKE EXCITED CHILDREN OF HELL. VOICE: TODAY
ANOTHER BUDDHIST MONK SET FIRE TO HIMSELF IN PROTEST
AGAINST THE WAR IN

Bloody fools. What do they think it'll accomplish?
I know.   But   they believe
Any coffee left, Stacey?
Yeh. I'll heat it up.
Stacey comes back from the kitchen and hands Mac
his cup. He is sitting in the old chintz-covered armchair
which was their second piece of furniture, the first having
been their bed, and which has now been dismissed to the
basement TV room. Mac's legs are stretched out full
length, and the frown lines between his eyes are still there
even after an entire evening of no work.

EVER-OPEN EYE   A HILLSIDE AND SMALL TREES SEEN FROM
HIGH AND FARAWAY. THE SMOKE RISING IN ROLLING
CLOUDS. VOICE: ACCELERATED BOMBING IN THE AREA OF

Mac?
Yeh?

Oh – nothing. I just thought it was kind of flickering for a minute, there.

— Why talk? Mac doesn't like to, and he's right. What good does it do? Can we do one goddam thing? No. And what are my reasons, anyway? I said to Jake one evening two three years ago that I had this feeling like the fall of Rome and he said *you're not afraid it'll happen; you're afraid it won't.* Since then I always wonder. Anything for a little excitement? Goddam you, Jake Fogler. It's a lie. There are still a few things I do know. At least, I think there are. But even those are mixed now. Like laughing amid the desire to puke re: that newspaper interview with that woman somewhere in the States. *He came home on leave and it's like all his reflexes have been changed, sort of. His little sister jumped out at him from behind the door, just for fun, like, and he only just stopped himself in time from karate chopping her.* Little sisters of the world, watch it, eh? Never mind the broken-hearts bit. Broken necks are the concern these days. But I laughed as well. Conditioned into monsterdom, like the soldier. The look on Ian's face that time I pitched them both to the floor. And my eyes, covered with blood that wasn't there, so I couldn't for a moment see anything but rage. *Stop the noise, just stop the noise.* That's what I thought. How can I ever make up for it? What if it happens again? That precise thing won't, but something else may. In God's name, what is *Mac* like, in there, wherever he lives?

EVER-OPEN EYE   THE SON OF ROBIN HOOD IS CANTERING ALONG THROUGH SHERWOOD. LUCKILY THERE HAPPENS TO BE A SIGN ON A ZIGZAG PIECE OF BOARD AS IN NORTH AMERICAN NATIONAL PARKS. NOTTINGHAM 3½ MILES.

Boy, this one's as old as the hills. You ever seen it before, Mac?

Yes, I think so. May as well watch it anyway.

Yeh, may as well.

Ian nineteen, in love with the uniform he is wearing. Jen, eleven, talking by this time, suddenly startling him and yelling as she jumps out from behind a something. Ian's lifted hand caught by himself in mid-strike. His face not his own, and yet his own, belonging totally to the embryonic cougar which has always been there.

— No. No, Stacey. Do that one over again.

Ian nineteen in plain well-cut business suit, having just graduated (early, admittedly, but he is bright) from university, now entering his first job. There is a great future in the sale of nasal contraceptives, tapes of apes and rapes, instant-color chameleon embalming fluid and deep freeze for cancer patients who will be melted and resuscitated when a cure is found. This year a Volkswagen; next year a Jaguar. Like a mighty army moves the unbesodden; brothers we are treading where saints have been introdden.

— Very funny, doll. Try again.

Ian nineteen quitting university. I am a dropout. I opt out. Let the maggots crawl. I believe in peace, love, expanded consciousness and nonviolent violence. Ian, poet, artist, musician, going his own way.

— Nuts. Never Ian. Duncan, maybe. Anyway, what's the use in opting out? Maybe there is, but it's beyond me. I can't reach it. I'm in forevermore, like it or not.

Mac?

Mm?

What shall I put on those charts for Richalife? Where it says energy snap-up and that.

You mean you haven't put anything?

Well, no

Oh for Christ's sake, Stacey. Well, give them all to me, then. I'll do them.

For all of us?

Somebody's got to.

Yeh, well I guess that would be the best thing. Mac, I would've thought you wouldn't have to work quite so hard now you've got a city area.

It's the exact opposite.

I thought maybe I'd ask Tess and Jake in on Thursday. Will you be home?

No. I have to go to a rally.

A what?

Rally. R-A-double L-Y.

Oh for heaven's sake. Well, can I come, too?

You wouldn't find it interesting.

How do you know?

Now look, Stacey

Okay okay. You don't want me to see Thor. You're afraid I'll disgrace you. Well, I wouldn't.

I did not say that. Did I say that?

Not in so many words. But that resigned tone of yours

Good God, Stacey. I can't say anything right, can I? If I have to check on my tone every time I open my mouth

Oh, I know. That's how it sounded. But I didn't mean

What precisely did you mean, then?

I don't know. I've lost it.

This is the first evening I've taken off in weeks, and now you

I'm sorry. Honestly, Mac. I know. I don't know what's the matter with me.

Look, Stacey, are you feeling okay?

I don't know. I've been getting these headaches

— Is that true? Or did I just make it up? I say I am not much in love with the lies, but they don't get less – they get more. How can this be? God forgive me a poor spinner.

Well, you better see the doctor, then.

No – I think I'm exaggerating. It's nothing. It's just from looking at the TV all evening. I'll take a couple of aspirins.

— I haven't got a headache at all. Yes, I have. As a matter of fact, now that I notice it, it's excruciating.

Maybe you need glasses.

Yeh, maybe

EVER-OPEN EYE   THE SON OF ROBIN HOOD STANDS BEHIND
KING JOHN AT RUNNYMEDE, MAKING THE RELUCTANT MON-
ARCH SIGN THE MAGNA CARTA.

— Sometimes a person feels that something else must
have been meant to happen in your own life, or is this all
there's ever going to be, just like this? Until I die. What'll
it be like to die? Not able to breathe? Fighting for air? Or
letting everything slide away, seeing shapes like shadows
that used to be people, nothing real because in a minute
you won't be real any more? Holy Mary, Mother of God,
be with me now and in the hour of my death. If only I
could say that, but no. My father's dead face, looking no
different except the eyes closed, and I thought his face had
been dead for a long time before he died, so what did it
matter, but I didn't believe that. Something should
happen before it's too late. Idiot-child, what more could
happen? What more do you want? You've got – yeh, I
know, God. No need to write me a list. And I'm grateful.
Don't take me seriously. Don't let anything terrible
happen to the kids.
      Click.
      Well, c'mon, Stacey, it's getting late.
      Yeh, so it is

Doctor Spender's waiting room is walled with plants – tall
rubber plants with leaves slickly green as though var-
nished, ferns drooping like miniature willow trees,
needled cacti. They are real, not plastic, and this, ob-
scurely, gives Stacey faith in Doctor Spender's medical
abilities. Stacey is the only person waiting. She riffles
through magazines, looking only at the pictures. She is
wearing her black skirt and a yellow tailored blouse, so it
will be easier to strip to the waist in case he wants to listen
to her lungs.

— Should I tell Mac I've been? I don't think so. If there *is* something wrong, it would only worry him, and if there isn't, he'd think I was neurotic. Boy, he'd sure be right about that. I shouldn't have come. There isn't a darned thing the matter with me. I wish I'd worn my blue suit instead of this skirt. Katie's right – it looks like Victoriana. Does it, hell. Why should it? I only bought it last year. What does Mac think about Thor? What does Mac think about? What are you thinking about, Mac? *Oh, nothing much.* Well, what sort of a nothing? *For heaven's sake, Stacey, what does it matter?*

> Mac recounting, once, something that happened a long time ago. *Don't know why I did it, but when I was a kid I got mad one day and shoved my fist through a pane of glass in the kitchen window.* You did? It doesn't sound like you. What did your dad say? *Oh, he was furious, but he didn't strap me. He said that even if I had lost my self-control, he wasn't going to lose his.* What did he do, then? *Made me pray with him, for self-control. Sounds pretty funny, likely.* Well, not all that funny. *The prayer bit didn't do much good, but he was right about the other.* Yeh, I guess so.

— What really happened? How was it for him?

Mac, about Ian's age, listening to his mother's softly chiding voice. Must remember you are a minister's son, dear, and set a good example. It isn't asking very much dear and of course a BB gun is out of the question and it hurts me so when I hear you using swear words and. Mac, maybe only the once, when it was too much, his face like Ian's face, inheld, bitterly uncommunicative, lashing out, not knowing he was going to smash the window until he had done it. Matthew, towering like Moses, bearing in his eyes the letter of the Law. Kneel down, Clifford, kneel down right here in the study with me, and we will both pray. Mac, longing for any whip rather than this one, knowing this occasion would never arise again, must not,

*looking at his father's clamped-shut eyes, listening to the
flat voice calling upon the lord of all the galaxies to bear
witness to a fragmented square of a brittle substance
called glass by some of the users of it who lived on a small
planet and who must learn not to break, not by not wanting to, but by some other reinforced and steel means.*

— Was it like that? If it was, how come we've got a
window left? But how do I know? Mac, I'm a rotten
guesser.

Okay, Mrs. MacAindra – you can go in now.

Oh – thanks.

Doctor Spender is youngish, overworked, soft-
spoken, perpetually tired-looking. He looks up from the
file card on his desk and smiles.

Hello, Mrs. MacAindra. What seems to be the trouble?

Well, it's these headaches I've been getting. And
there's this place right at the back of my head, and it sort
of goes *kaboom-kaboom* when I'm trying to get to sleep.
Not really an ache – just a dull throbbing, but it bothers
me. Then I get neurotic and start thinking I've got a
tumor of the brain.

— That's right, clown. Make yourself sound like a nut
case. Yes, but what if it *is* a tumor? These things happen.
Oh God, dead at thirty-nine. What kind of a death would
that be? You'd be incoherent long before it happened; the
kids would see you mindless, dribbling, maybe shouting
all the four-letter words you've decorously never said in
front of them. No, I wouldn't let them see me. If I was
incompetent, Mac wouldn't let them see, I hope. What
would happen to the kids? Who'd bring them up? My
sister? But she doesn't know them, what they're like. I
don't want anybody else to bring them up.

We'll see, now. Show me exactly where the throbbing
comes, Mrs. MacAindra. That's fine.

The examination goes on. Heart and lungs. Blood
pressure. Any other symptoms? Finally the doctor looks
at her, mildly inquiring.

Can't find anything wrong, superficially. Not worried about anything, are you?

Oh no. Everything's all right. I mean, at home.

— How can I say anything else, without making it sound foolish? I can't put my finger on it, anyway. Too many threads. I can't say it, and who would believe me if I did? It's like being inside a balloon made out of some kind of glue, and when you try to get out, you only get tangled and stuck.

Well, I think I'll send you for an X ray, just to make sure there's nothing wrong.

I'm sure there isn't. It's probably just my imagination. I probably need to have my head examined.

Doctor Spender smiles.

That's exactly what you're going to have.

The X-ray results are negative. Stacey does not have tumor of the brain. She thanks Doctor Spender and puts down the phone. It is early afternoon, and Jen is asleep. Stacey moves around the house without knowing in advance what she is going to do. She goes upstairs to the bedroom and looks at herself in the full-length mirror. She is wearing a blue-and-pink-print dress, bought on sale last autumn. The pink is in the form of small clocks, all of whose hands indicate five minutes before either noon or midnight. She removes the dress and her slip, and puts on a pair of tight-fitting green velvet slacks and a purple overblouse which has been hanging in the cupboard for some months, as yet unworn. She then rummages at the back of the cupboard, on the floor, and comes up with a pair of high-heeled gold-strapped sandals.

— Okay, so of course I know you shouldn't wear high heels with sandals. But I love high heels. I just do. All right, Mac, I know these are vulgar, especially with slacks. But I like them, see? And I can do with the extra height.

She listens at Jen's door. No sound. Let sleeping kids lie. Stacey in golden high-heel sandals tiptoes downstairs to the kitchen, collects the gin bottle and two bottles of tonic, and goes down to the basement room, leaving the door between the kitchen and basement open in case Jen calls.

— This calls for some slight celebration. Reprieve. I'm not a goner yet. Did I really think I was? Well, it's in the middle of the night I start thinking about it, and then it seems pretty certain. Really, it's only what would happen to the kids. Yeh? It doesn't matter about you, Stacey? Well, It shouldn't matter. Why not? Because I'm thirty-nine and I can't complain. But they haven't begun yet. That's not how you feel about yourself, though. It matters. Okay, but so what? I think of Katie – maybe Ian, now, too – thinking of me like I'm prehistoric, and it bugs me. I'm sorry, but it does. I'm not a good mother. I'm not a good wife. I don't want to be. I'm Stacey Cameron and I still love to dance.

The floor is dark-red linoleum tiles. Stacey kicks aside the numdah scatter rugs with their rough embroidery of magic trees, trees of life flowering unexpectedly into azure birds, green unlikely leaves. She pours a gin and tonic, drinks half of it and tops it up. The records are kept in a mock wrought-iron stand. Stacey shuffles impatiently through them and finally finds what she is looking for. She changes the record player to seventy-eight and puts the old disc on. The needle skids a little, complaining at the scratches on the surface.

Tommy Dorsey Boogie. The clear beat announces itself. Stacey finishes her drink, fixes another one, drinks half of it quickly and sets the glass down on top of the TV. She looks at her gold sandals, her green-velvet thighs. She puts her arms out, stretching them in front of her, her fingers moving slightly, feeling the music as though it were tangibly there to be touched in the air. Slowly, she begins to dance. Then faster and faster.

Stacey Cameron in her yellow dress with pleats all around the full skirt. Knowing by instinct how to move, loving the boy's closeness, whoever he was.

Stacey twirling out onto the floor, flung by the hand that would catch her when she came jazzily flying back. *Tommy Dorsey Boogie*. Stacey spinning like light, whirling laughter across a polished floor. Every muscle knowing what to do by itself. Every bone knowing. Dance hope, girl, dance hurt. Dance the fucking you've never yet done.

— Once it seemed almost violent, this music. Now it seems incredibly gentle. Sentimental, self-indulgent? Yeh, probably. But I love it. It's *my* beat. I can still do it. I can still move without knowing where, beforehand. Yes. Yes. Yes. Like this. Like this. I can. My hips may not be so hot but my ankles are pretty good, and my legs. Damn good in fact. My feet still know what to do without being told. I love to dance. I love it. I love it. It can't be over. I can still do it. I don't do it badly. See? Like this. Like this.

— I love it. The hell with what the kids say. In fifteen years their music will be just as corny. Naturally they don't know that. I love this music. It's mine. Buzz off, you little buggers, you don't understand. No – I didn't mean that. I meant it. I was myself before any of you were born. (Don't listen in, God – this is none of your business.)

The music crests, subsides, crests again, blue-green sound, saltwater with the incoming tide, the blues of the night freight trains across snow deserts, the green beckoning voices, the men still unheld and the children yet unborn, the voices cautioning no caution no caution only dance what happens to come along until

The record player switches off.

— Was I hearing what was there, or what? How many times have I played it? God it's three thirty in the afternoon and I'm stoned. The kids will be home in one hour. Okay, pick up the pieces. Why did I do it? Yours not to reason why, Stacey baby, yours but to go and make nineteen cups of Nescafé before the kids get home. Quickly. Jen? Lord, she must've been awake for hours. Oh Stacey.

The black coffee washes around in her stomach like a

tidal wave. She gets Jen up, murmuring carefully, and then goes to her own bedroom and Mac's and changes into her blue silk suit. She puts on a pair of medium-heel navy-blue shoes. She holds the gold sandals for a moment in her hands, then delves into the clothes cupboard and buries them under a pile of tennis shoes and snow boots. She brushes her hair, back-combing it slightly, then slicking it down into neatness and spraying it so it will hold. She applies lipstick and powder. She examines herself in the full-length mirror.

— Am I okay? No lurching hemlines, protruding slip straps, off-base lipstick or any other sign of disrepair? I think I'm okay, but how's my appraisal power? Shaken, no doubt. Remorse – overdose of same. I'm not fit to be in charge of kids, that's the plain truth. God, accept my apologies herewith. He won't. Would you, in His place? No. Come on, be practical. Dinner. Mac won't be here. Dinner downtown for him, the lucky bastard. When did I last have dinner downtown? Precious lot he cares. Goddam him, some night when he comes bowling in at ten o'clock expecting me to have kept dinner hot in the oven since six, I'm gonna say *Now listen here, sweetheart, want me to tell you something? There isn't any bloody dinner and if you want any, why don't you just go along and scramble yourself an ostrich egg? Why don't you just do that little thing?* Oh Stacey, this is madness. Get a grip on yourself. Yeh, well let's see now – pork chops, cauliflower with cheese sauce, mashed potatoes, and what for dessert? It'll have to be ice cream. Got half a carton in the freezer. Maybe I should make apple Betty. What a slut I am, not a cooked dessert for those kids. No, I can't. I'm incapable of peeling an apple. Sometimes I want to say – *listen, if all of you never had another dessert for the rest of your lives, would that kill you?* Answering chorus of *It sure would*, spoken with conviction. Come on, bitch. Another cup of coffee.

Stacey prepares dinner primly and with caution. When the children arrive home, she talks as little as possible. The meal is finally over and the noise begins to subside. The mist is beginning to clear. Stacey washes the dishes and then bathes Jen, reads two Little Golden Books to her, and puts her to bed. After some considerable time, Duncan and Ian are also in bed. Only Katie remains. Katie has finished her homework and is down in the TV room. Stacey goes down but does not go in. She stands near the doorway, looking, unnoticed.

Katie has put on one of her own records. Something with a strong and simple beat, slow, almost languid, and yet with an excitement underneath, the lyrics deliberately ambiguous.

Katie is dancing. In a green dress Katie MacAindra simple and intricate as grass is dancing by herself. Her auburn hair, long and straight, touches her shoulders and sways a little when she moves. She wears no make-up. Her bones and flesh are thin, plain-moving, unfrenetic, knowing their idiom.

> Stacey MacAindra, thirty-nine, hips ass and face heavier than once, shamrock velvet pants, petunia-purple blouse, cheap gilt sandals high-heeled, prancing squirming jiggling

Stacey turns and goes very quietly up the basement steps and into the living room.

— You won't be dancing alone for long, Katie. It's all going for you. I'm glad. Don't you think I'm glad? Don't you think I know how beautiful you are? Oh Katie love. I'm glad. I swear it. Strike me dead, God, if I don't mean it.

At ten thirty, Katie is in bed at last. Stacey is now off duty. Mac is at a conference and will probably not be home until midnight. Stacey has a scalding bath, puts on a nightgown and housecoat, and goes downstairs again.

— What now? I should go to bed. Okay, Stacey, not more than one gin, eh? Well, all right, if it's going to be only one, let's make it good and strong. Too much has disappeared from this bottle. I'll go to the Liquor Commission tomorrow and get another bottle and pour half of it into this one. So Mac won't think it's odd. The other half strictly to be stashed away for emergencies. Yeh, I can see it all now. Every other minute is an emergency. Does he know? He must. Mac – listen. Just listen. I have something to tell you. No. It's not up to him. It's up to me. Any normal person can cope okay, calmly, soberly. And if you can't, kid, then there's something wrong with you. No there isn't. Everything is okay. Everything is *all right*, see? Only I'm tired tonight and a little tense. Why not try Ovaltine, then? Oh get lost, you.

Stacey takes her drink into the living room and sits on the chesterfield with the lights off, looking out the window at the city which is both close and far away.

> Stacey, naked with Mac three quarters of a year before Katherine Elizabeth was born. The cottage at the lake where they'd gone for the one week holiday they couldn't afford. The pine and spruce harps in the black ground outside, in the dark wind from the lake that never penetrated the narrow-windowed cabin. Their skins slippery with sweat together, slithering as though with some fine and pleasurable oil. Stacey knowing his moment and her own as both separate and unseparable. Oh my love   now

Going into the kitchen, Stacey swings the gin bottle out from the lower cupboard and fills a jug with water from the tap.

— No use wasting tonic water. Of course this will taste like essence of pine needles with a dash of kerosene, but then my mother always used to speak very scornful-like of ladies whose taste was all in their mouths. Couldn't say that about me. Nope. My taste isn't anywhere. Between my legs, maybe. Okay, doll, that's enough. So who wants to know?

Stacey returns to the living room and curls up on the chesterfield once more, her slippered feet underneath her. The big sliding door leads out into the hall and thence up the iron-banistered staircase to the bedrooms. Stacey leans around in the semidarkness to check. The door is closed. Should she put on the radio? She decides against it. If she uses her own voice, she can select the music.

> *There's a gold mine in the sky*
> > *Faraway –*
> *We will go there, you and I,*
> > *Some sweet day,*
> *And we'll say hello to friends who said goodbye,*
> *When we find that long lost gold mine in the sky.*
> > *Faraway, faraw-a-ay –*

— Oh boy. Jen comes by her operatic tendencies naturally. Where did that song come from? Old man Invergordon used to sing it at local concerts in Manawaka when I was a little kid. Nobody knew how to tell him they'd rather he didn't. They weren't so bad, any of them, I now see. How I used to dislike them then, the Ladies' Aid and mother's bridge cronies and all of them, never seeing beyond their own spectacles and what will the neighbors think what will they say? But who here or anywhere, now, would put up with old Invergordon? *Drop dead*, that's what he'd get here and now. He stank all right but he had a lovely baritone. Only difference between Invergordon and Niall Cameron was that my dad was a private drunk and the old guy was a public one. It isn't the fact that there's no gold mine in the sky which bothers me. I mean who wants to say hello to people who are dead even if you happen to be dead yourself? It's the ones who say good-bye before they're dead who bug me. I start thinking – it's Mac. Then I think – hell, no, it's not Mac it's me and then I don't know.

Twelve thirty. Stacey takes the empty bottle into the kitchen and places it behind three bottles of wine and a bottle of vinegar. She takes the frying pan down from its hook and puts it on the stove. She takes the bacon out of the refrigerator and puts two slices in the pan. Cheese. Bread. The fried sandwich is made. She looks at it seriously, considering it. It does not look edible.

— Must eat something absorptive. Can't. Repulsive. Mac, talk to me. Mac? Katie? Ian? Duncan? Where are you or is it just me   I don't know what the hell I'm talking about well what you should be talking about kid is coffee.

Stacey makes herself a cup of instant coffee. She looks again at the congealing sandwich in the frying pan and decides to heat it up. She switches on an element but does not put the frying pan on until the circular coil is red. She reaches for the frying pan, stumbles, puts out a hand to balance herself. The hand lands on the edge of the electrical scarlet circle.

— It hurts it hurts it hurts   what is it

She has without knowing it pulled her hand away. She regards it with curiosity. Two red crescent lines have appeared on the skin of her left palm.

— My brand of stigmata. My western brand. The Double Crescent. It hurts hurts

She takes the frying pan and throws its sandwich into the garbage pail. She switches off the stove, reaches into the cupboard for baking soda, mixes some with water and applies it to her hand. She then applies a light gauze bandage, one which can be removed easily tomorrow morning without anyone noticing. She walks upstairs and gets into bed. Blackness scurries around her in the room but within her head the neon is white and cold like the stars in the prairie winters.

— How to explain this? Anybody can explain anything, if they put their mind to it. It's not difficult. I put the kettle on, and accidentally put my hand over the boiling spout. Mac – I'm scared. Help me. But it goes a long way back. Where to begin? What can I possibly say to you that you will take seriously? What would it need, with you, what possible cataclysm, for you to say anything of yourself to me? What should I do? I'm not sure I really want to go on living at all. I can't cope. I do cope. Not well, though. Not with anyone. Jesus I get tired sometimes. Self-pity. Yeh, I guess. But sometimes I want to abdicate, only that. Quit. Can't. What would it be like for one of the kids to come into the bedroom, say, one evening when Mac isn't home yet, any one of them, maybe waking up in the night and calling and me not answering, and coming in here and finding I'd gone away from them for good, overdose? Maybe they'd think it was their fault. I couldn't come back mysteriously and say *Listen, it wasn't anything to do with you, or not in the way you think, and I love you, see?* Even if I left one of those I'm-getting-off-the-world letters, saying *I care about you*, they wouldn't believe it. And they'd be right. Goddam you, God. I'm stuck with it. But I'm a mess and I'm scared. What if I had burned myself when one of the kids saw? Mac?

Stacey goes into half sleep, where the sounds of occasional cars and the light wind and the way-off ships can be heard but only in a way which needs no response.

Mac comes in at one o'clock.

It's okay, Mac. You can turn on the light.

Hi, I thought you'd be asleep.

Well, I was, sort of. How was it?

Okay.

Mac?

Mm?

I want to tell

Christ, am I ever beat. What?

Oh – nothing

You okay, Stacey?

Yeh, I'm okay

Kids all right?

Yeh, they're all right

Well, good night then.

Good night Mac

Stacey, neatly and matronly dressed, her gloves in hand, adjusts the despised veil on her white straw hat, pulling it down over her forehead and eyebrows as though she intends it to act as a disguise. She hesitates in the doorway of the large chair-filled hall, but the pressure of other people carries her forward and in. She chooses an aisle seat quickly, keeping her head down until she is sitting. But the precaution has been unnecessary. There are too many people around. Mac couldn't possibly have noticed her. When she cranes her neck and peers over head tops, she cannot even see him. The platform at the front is decorated with gilded wicker baskets full of white roses. In between the baskets are tall white shields, each bearing one golden letter to form a word.

RICHALIFE

At the back of the platform there is a white velvet curtain, descending from the ceiling. A small gilt structure, a cross between a podium and a pulpit, stands in the middle of the stage, with microphone attachments.

Then Stacey spots Mac's auburn brush-cut. He is sitting in the third row from the front, with all the other salesmen. Stacey twists and squints, trying to see around the magnolia-covered hat of the woman directly in front of her. Finally she manages to focus on Mac. His tallness is hunched a little, and while she watches, he puts up a hand and runs it over his hair. Stacey turns away, unable to look.

— When he does that, is it like me looking in the mirror to make sure I'm really there? What's he thinking? It may not be any of my business, but I'd like to know anyway. What if he starts coughing? Everyone will look at him. Maybe it would embarrass me more than it would him. Would he be livid if he knew I'd come? Well, come on, fellows, what are we waiting for? Let's get the show on the road, eh?

The audience is mainly middle-aged, half men and half women. They sit quietly, for the most part, not looking at one another.

— Maybe they'd all like to be incognito. I know damn well I would. I'd like to have a woolly muffler or a long trailing length of chiffon wrapped around my pan. If somebody like Bertha Garvey should chance to stroll in, I would crawl under the seat, so help me. Here we are – action at last.

The white velvet curtains part, revealing another section of stage on which six girls are gathered around a microphone. Their costumes are modest to a degree, long loose-fitting white robes, toga-like, with the Greek key design slanting diagonally across each bosom. The girls' hair ranges from white-blonde to honey, all long and straight. The hall grows still, the whispers die, the ticking coughs are subdued, the feet compose themselves. When the audience is ready, the girls begin to sing, not loudly or jazzily, but in clear treble voices like a clutch of meadow larks.

> *Richness is a quality of living,*
> *Richness quells the trouble and the strife,*
> *Richness is the being and the giving,*
> *Anyone can reach a Richalife.*

Stacey surreptitiously slips out of her purse one of the tranquilizers Doctor Spender has given her for her pulsing-head condition, conceals it in her handkerchief and slips it into her mouth under the pretext of blowing her nose.

— Lucky for me I always could swallow pills without water. Well, well. Listen to that. They sure aren't what I would have expected. I thought it would be all zing-twanging and go-go-go. But unless you go to the hangouts of the young, I guess you only find that kind of noisy stuff in churches now. Those little birds aren't even refined. They're refeened. Has Mac got his eye on them? Well, naturally, what do you expect, Stacey? All the same. You bastard, Clifford MacAindra, they're young enough to be your daughters.

The white curtain closes and the girls disappear. The audience sits uncertainly, not knowing whether applause is expected or not. Sporadic and nervous clapping breaks out like acne in isolated and obvious areas, then quickly fades.

Thor walks onto the platform alone and takes his place behind the gilt stand. A sprinkling of female exclamations can be heard, and he smiles a trifle, acknowledging them. This evening he is approximately seven feet tall. His newly laundered mane is accentuated by the spotlight which now comes to rest just above his head. He has abandoned his midnight blue in favor of a suit of silver, some luminous material that has the look of frost sheening on windows and patterning into faint ferns or snow flowers transferred from the farthest reaches of the polestar. But when he talks, his voice is not distant or unapproachable. The reverse. He talks with the people, not at them. His voice is warm, friendly, sincere.

You heard the girls, here, singing about richness. Well, richness is something we all hear a lot about these days, don't we? Yes, we surely do, and sometimes we begin to wonder what it means, don't we? Well, sure do all know it means money in the bank. I guess there isn't one of us who doesn't know that. But that's not *all* it means. No, that definitely is not all it means, friends. It means response, happiness, a healthy mind in a healthy body. Wouldn't you agree? You, sir, right there, would you agree? You would? Well, you're right. Yes, richness means a healthy mind in a healthy body. But just how do we go about getting this? That's what I used to ask myself. That was in the old B.R. days – before Richalife. I'm not asking you to believe a whole lot of printed data. I only want to tell you what happened to me personally. I'm not trying to sell you anything, either. Believe me, the kind of person who feels he's being pressured into anything – We don't want him. We only want people who can believe that the human body and the human spirit can be changed, changed beyond belief, in the short space of one month. Amazing? Certainly it's amazing. But it can happen. I know. Because it happened to me. You know something? Once upon a time I could barely face the morning without three cups of coffee and as many cigarettes. Then I started reaching for a Richalife instead. And that is just what I got – A RICHER LIFE. Take my memory, for instance. My memory potential was hardly being tapped at all, before. Alertness-wise, the change A.R. – after Richalife – was really gratifying. I aways had a good memory, mind you. Good, but not what you would call really excellent. Now I think I can honestly and truthfully say it's reached the excellent mark. I don't claim that the depth changes happened overnight. No, I wouldn't claim that. Even Richalife can't reach the deep cells of the mind instantly. When I began, just over a year ago, it took – oh, I should say about three or four weeks, approximately, before the depth changes were really well established. These very slight depression feelings I used to get – they were alleviated almost right straight off, definitely alleviated, but it must have been more or less a month before they totally disappeared. Yes, totally disappeared. Another thing, now

    Stacey sits sifting her memory. Then it comes back.

        Thor's apartment. Stacey with a thimbleful of sherry, feeling like a savage drinker, her feet slithering silkily on the skins of stillborn monkeys.

        They were alleviated almost right straight off

— Well, I'm buggered. Does he just press his navel and the record switches on? No. Worse. It's the Martians. Must be.

We will begin with one creature, Zuq tells the assembled Council of Spirit Sires. He must of course look as nearly human as possible. He must have a blood-like substance (red, mind, not the proper polka-dotted purple to which we are accustomed), a substance which will flow if he is accidentally cut. The control shaft, in order to escape possible detection in case of severe and unpredictable wounding, must be buried deeply in what would be his left lung if he were an earthman. The first transmitted messages from his – as it were – mouth will be of a simple nature. We will then – I am speaking out of my many years of research and accumulated knowl-

edge – we will then put into effect what I term the lemming syndrome.

Stacey squirms on her chair. The hall is growing sultry. She discovers to her surprise that Thor has stopped talking and is being loudly applauded. The white velvet curtains are sneaking apart, and the girls, with their arms lightly but not pervertedly around each other's shoulders, begin a soft humming which grows into a croon.

> *Peace of mind*
> *Can be combined*
> *With vigor*

> *Peace of mind*
> *Can be combined*
> *With fun*

Beside Stacey, an old man with a red neck like a retired prairie farmer looks hopefully and steadfastly ahead. His expression changes from concealed to open yearning, the yearning for rain in drought. Stacey glances quickly to the stage and sees the reason. The choir has vanished again, and now there is only one girl, a different one, on the stage with Thor. Her white dress is street-length but it bears the same Greek key design along the straight neckline. Her skin is extremely pale, and her features are delicate, severe, withdrawn, a girl from a medieval tomb carving. It is the girl Mac was talking to, or who was talking so earnestly to Mac, the night of the party. Thor takes her by the hand and leads her over to the microphone.

Now, ladies and gentlemen, it gives me real pleasure to introduce this charming young lady to you. Miss Delores Appleton.

He leaves her. The girl stands there, staring out at the upturned faces. Her hand goes up and she touches her visible collarbone. Then quickly she pulls the hand away and it returns limply to her side. A moment of silence. The audience is frightened, frightened for her that she may not be able to speak a word. She looks towards Thor, and he nods. Her face slowly unfreezes. She grasps the mike and begins to talk in a high bell-voice, rapid, tinkling.

Well, really, all I want to tell you is just about my own personal experience. I mean, that's all we can say for sure, isn't it, our own personal experience. I grew up in a small town, like, and when I came to the city I was sort of nervous. I mean I had never lived in the city before and I didn't know what might. I mean you never know who you might and what they might. And then it got so I couldn't sleep very well nights and at the office they started saying why did I look so tired out but it was only because I wasn't sleeping that well and so on. Well things sort of went from bad to worse, like, and then I heard about Mr. Thorlakson and Richalife and I thought why not so I tried it and it worked. I mean, may anxieties and this nervousness I had, well they just were so much alleviated and I went to tell Mr. Thorlakson about it and now I am working in his office and well that's about all I guess

Her voice ends in a small chime of laughter. The audience claps mightily. The girl walks offstage swiftly.

— Supposing that had been Katie? It doesn't bear thinking about. Who is she? What could *her* parents have been like? She can't be more then eighteen or twenty. Somebody ought to do something, but then again, she claims she's fine. Everything is all right for her now.

Stacey looks to see where the girl has gone. For a moment she cannot see, and then she finds the pallid hair and the Greek keys. The girl is sitting beside Mac, and he has one arm around her, not casually but tightly, like a wall against the world.

Dear Mother – Well here it is June and less than a month till summer holidays – horrors! Although I guess Rachel will be glad. Her free season starts when mine finishes. But I have to admit the kids are pretty good generally these days – the boys already making plans for putting up tent in back yard and sleeping there – mighty woodsmen and all that – perfectly safe, Mother, so don't panic –

Stacey puts down her pen and gazes at what she has written.

— I wonder what would happen if just for once I put down what was really happening? Dear Mother – There must be some way of talking to kids but I don't seem usually to find it. Yeh, sometimes, and then I say *There there,* and they're partially restored, whatever was wrong. But Duncan said *I don't do anything right, Mum,* meaning it, and Mac was helping Ian with his arithmetic a day or so ago and bawled him out for carelessness but Ian is the opposite of careless maybe he didn't understand what he was supposed to be doing but then Ian all inclenched came out to the kitchen and said *Dad never makes mistakes,* believing it. I don't know what to do. I worry. I get afraid. I drink too much. I get unreasonably angry. The valleys under my eyes look like permanent blue-black ink even though I get enough sleep, and my hips are nobody's business. I think Mac has fallen for that girl and who could blame him I guess and I really think I wouldn't be so blamed mad about it if I could go and do the the same thing myself with some guy but how and anyway I think this is a despicable reaction. After that evening at the rally I phoned the hairdresser and made an appointment to have my hair dyed. Bleached and then dyed fair, not ash blond, just fair. And when I got there, she said *You sure you really want to, Mrs. MacAindra?* And I looked in the damn mirror and said *Uh – well, I guess maybe not.* Not even the strength of my neuroses, if you would believe it. Please write immediately and let me know what was actually in your mind all those years because I haven't a clue and it's only now that this bothers me, now that I'm not seen either. Love, Stacey. P.S. Did you ever dance? No, that wouldn't be feasible, that kind of letter. She'd say to Rachel, *I can't think what Stacey can possibly mean.* She'd be upset for days.

Stacey picks up her pen again.

Oh, nearly forgot. Jen sings now. At least a step towards speech. Mac loves his new job and is doing awfully well. He's given me the old Chev. Everything is fine. Hope you are okay. Love, Stacey.

She puts the page in an envelope, addresses and stamps it, and goes out to the letterbox at the corner. Julian and Bertha Garvey have driven out for the day to visit Julian's sister and have taken Jen along, ostensibly for the ride but actually because conversation is difficult there and Jen provides some possibility of amused distraction. Stacey is alone and it feels peculiar to her. She is wearing black slacks, a yellow sweater and sandals, and as she reaches the end of Bluejay Crescent, she looks back at it and feels disconnected, younger, separate.

— Hey, it's a nice feeling. Yet I feel I oughtn't to feel glad. When Jen goes to school, though, I could take a job. I used to be quite good. I guess my shorthand is rusty, but I could brush it up.

The chief architect's office is large but not at all flashy. No plastic plants or phony veneer for him. Andrew Delver, of Delver & Plumb, has designed every piece of furniture here, and it is all both functional and beautiful, sleek cool lines. She answers the bell's summons. God, Stacey, what a mess we're in with these contracts. Think you can make sense of my notes and get me four copies by lunchtime? Of course, Mr. Delver. Andrew, Andrew, for God's sake woman – it's about time you called me that – you're a love – I don't know what I'd do without you to cope

The truck hoots and draws up to the curb beside Stacey. She looks up and sees the grinning black-haired driver leaning out of the window. Buckle Fennick.

Hi Stacey

Hi

Where you going?

Just to the letterbox.

Hop in. I'll give you a lift.

It's not that far.

Where's Jen?

Bertha's got her this afternoon.

Hey, got a holiday? Climb in. I gotta take a few things out to Coquitlam. Coming right back. C'mon along, why doncha?

Stacey looks back at Bluejay Crescent, seeing it recede. Then, without thinking or knowing she is going to do it, she climbs into the truck beside Buckle.

Within seconds, it seems to her, they are in a mainstream of traffic and Buckle is manipulating the big truck in and out, weaving in a fast and inexorable pattern of sound and movement, intimidating the vulnerable cars, flying and swinging along the highway.

Haven't seen you for awhile, Buckle.

Naw. Want to know why?

Why?

Buckle increases speed. The highway shivers past, honking, obstacle-laden. Buckle crouches over the wheel, like a jockey.

Well, I thought Mac was kinda busy

He's always glad to see you. You know that.

Yeh?

What's the matter, Buckle?

Mac and me have known each other a long time.

I know.

Since the war.

Yes.

We went all through Italy together.

My God, Buckle, I know that.

— Does that mean Mac's got to live with you on his doorstep for the rest of his life? No, that's mean. Mac wouldn't say that. How many friends has Buckle got? One, maybe. How do I know?

Yeh, well I'm coming from Ace this day, see, on my way out and up north, and I happen to pass near where Mac's office is, see, and he's walking along the street with this Thor guy, so naturally I give him the old sign on the horn – beep beep beep BLAT, V for Victory. He looks up all right. That's all. No *Hi* or wave, nothing like that. He doesn't know me.

Buckle, he didn't mean

Shit, Stacey

Maybe he didn't see

He saw.

Well, I'm sorry. What can I say? Don't take it so hard. His mind was likely on the job. It's never on anything else now. He works all the time, like something was after him.

Stacey hears the vehemence in someone's voice that is coming from her mouth.

— Traitor. How can you speak about Mac to anyone else? It's no one else's business. Not even Buckle's. Especially not Buckle's. Shut up shut up shut up. If you don't, it'll all come out and then

The house is burning. Everything and everyone in it. Nothing can put out the flames. The house wasn't fire-resistant. One match was all it took.

Buckle has momentarily taken his eyes off the road and Stacey sees him sizing her up.

Buckle, for God's sake the road

He laughs and looks again at the wheeling metallic ballet ahead.

Don't worry. I know what I'm doing.

So you say. I've never driven with you before, Buckle, you know that?

You should come on a long haul sometime just for the hell of it.

Yeh, I can see it all now.

The northern highway, uncrowded. Spruce and fir spearing upwards, and the high arched blue silences of the sky. When the truck stops, there are only small earth-close sounds – a few lethargic flies, the grass voices. Sun saturates and warms the moss and fallen bronze pine needles. He is poised above her – hard, ready, taut – and she can hardly wait for him to

— I must be berserk. I don't even like him.

Don't worry, Stacey. I wouldn't play chicken if you were along.

Play chicken? What? Oh yeh. You still do that?

It passes the time.

It'll pass it permanently one of these days.

I've never yet met a guy who didn't give way.

You never give way?

I don't have to. I know the other guy is going to.

That's crazy. You can't know.

Sure I know. I'm prepared to gamble that fraction of a second longer than he is.

You know all the truckers on the road, then? You know them all well enough to be able to tell?

I don't have to know them all. It's something I learned a long time ago.

You can have it.

It's better on the night hauls because then you've only got the other guy's lights to go by. Take a couple of weeks ago. I'm in the Cariboo, few miles past Hundred-Mile House, and it's about three in the morning and I'm getting kinda bored when I see these lights coming. From the spread of the lights it looks like a diesel job, about the same weight as mine and she'll do about the same speed. So I step on the gas just a little and pull out slightly. He does the same. He wants to play. I think it's probably Charlie Norton, Excello Cartage guy, does this run back on a Tuesday and never drives day time. So I think, okay Charlie boy, we'll see. He's told guys in all the truckers' cafés from here to Fort St. John that he's going to take it away from me, see? Because they all know no one's ever beat me. So we're roaring along and he doesn't swerve and I'm starting to sweat a little but then I think Charlie Norton's the kind of guy who'll say he's going to do a thing before he's done it and that is a dead giveaway. So I keep on, see? Well, when we're practically close enough for both of us to see the sweat on each other's foreheads, suddenly he gives a sharp right to the wheel and misses me by no more than a cunt-span if you don't mind the expression. He sort of swivels to a stop, and I pull up too. He gets out and whaddyaknow? It's not Charlie Norton at all. It's some young guy I've never seen before, and he's nearly drowning in his own sweat. We have a cigarette together, and he's leaning against the front tires all the time, holding his own elbow so I won't see his cigarette hand trembling away there.

You of course were perfectly calm.

I wouldn't say that but at least I wasn't shaking like a raped virgin. You can see what I mean about not having to know the guys. I'm okay while my luck's in and it's in because of what I know, see?

— Here we go again.

No I don't see

Well it's simple but if you don't see it you don't see it. Here we are, kid.

Buckle pulls in and halts beside a warehouse. Men who have been expecting this arrival now rush out, opening the back doors of the truck, beginning to unload. One of the men, sloping past, looks up at Stacey and grins knifedly.

— My God. It isn't possible. He looked at me like I'm a whore or something. And I can't say to him, *Listen bud I'm a respectable married woman named thus.* Because here I'm not. They don't know what I am. They only see a woman in slacks and sweater, in the cab of Buckle's truck. My, my. Doesn't that seem strange. Do I mind? Am I offended? Hell, no. I'm delighted.

Buckle climbs back into the truck, waves to cohorts, starts up and they are off, back into the city.

How you doing?

Fine. Buckle, I think I should get home quite soon. I mean, if Bertha and Julian get back with Jen and I'm not there

Relax.

Yeh, well

Relax. How many days off do you get, Stacey? C'mon to my place. We'll have a beer, and you'll be home in lots of time to

I can't.

Why not?

Well, I don't think there's time

There's time.

Well

It's settled, then. I never wanted to ask you and Mac to my place after Julie took off.

Why not?

Well, it's not the same, like, is it?

Don't you have to take the truck back to Ace?

It can wait. They won't say anything. If they do, let them. They don't want to lose me.

Grenoble Street, finally, not far from the docks, and Buckle draws into an alley to park. He climbs out, goes around to the other side, and hands Stacey down. The alley is wet with leftover rain, and littered with chocolate bar wrappers, crumpled newspapers, a few purple paper squares from the discarded paraphernalia of quick love, an eggshell or two dropped from emptied garbage tins and resting fragile on the edge of mud ponds, a grapefruit husk from the beginning of someone's new day.

Okay, Stacey?

Yes.

The apartment is over a store which sells cut-price children's clothes. Honest Ernie's. The plastic raincoats glisten yellowly from the window, and the rows of rubber boots, black white or red, diminish from teen down to doll boots for creatures knee high to a grasshopper, who will plod purposefully through all the puddles of spring. Stacey looks away, reproached.

The stairs are covered with brown linoleum. On the second landing Buckle stops, takes out his key and opens the door. Stacey hesitates, smoothing her sweater down over her hips. Buckle takes her elbow gently, and they are inside.

The room is large. There is probably a bathroom and a bedroom or two elsewhere, but this room is for living and cooking. The window opens onto Grenoble Street, and the whine and wham of traffic curl upward and in. The floor is covered with the same brown linoleum as the stairs. A round oak table stands at one side of the room, covered in a white plastic lace-patterned cloth unrecently wiped over and yellow-flecked with egg yolk from the frying pans of the past. The gas stove stands in a corner, beside a sink which has a calico frill around its lower portions to hide the pipes. A chesterfield, once upholstered in grey, now worn to its cloth bone, stands gawkily in the center of the room. None of this creates more than a momentary flicker on Stacey's eye camera. All she is looking at is the big armchair positioned near the window.

Arbuckle – that you?

Yeh. Who else?

The woman is gigantic, outspread like rising dough gone amok, swelling and undulating over the stiff upholstery of the chair, gaping body covered with tiny-flower-printed dress huge and shroud-shaped, vastly numerous chins trembling eel-like separate but involved, eyes closed, and at the end of the Kodiak arms, contrasting hands neatly made, fine-fingered, encrusted with silver-and-gold-colored rings which might almost have been costly, from the way the hands flairfully wear them.

Beside her, on a low table within easy reach, is a brown teapot and a pink-pearl opalescent glass mug. The hand reaches out.

Stacey makes as if to step forward. Buckle stops her, holding her shoulder.

You don't have to. She doesn't know you're here.

What?

She's blind.

Then Stacey sees that it is true, for the hand

searches for the teapot's handle, finds it, feels skillfully for the mug, and pours, the other hand slipped inside the rim of the mug to judge the rising height of the liquid. Stacey looks at Buckle. He is standing in front of her, her hands on his narrow hard-boned hips, and he is laughing but without sound. His voice is low, but not all that low.

She wasn't always blind. Another broad threw acid at her once. No doubt she deserved it, for whatever it was she did. After that she couldn't work her beat any more, but she was getting beyond it anyhow. It was only then that she put on all the tonnage, though. Don't worry, Stacey. She isn't listening. Did you think it was tea in the pot?

What? I don't know what you

It's port, the cheapest money can buy. She likes it to be in a teapot, that's all. She thinks it looks more respectable. Who sees it, but never mind. You gotta be respectable, maybe, if you're a retired

Buckle. No.

You don't want me to say it? Okay. I won't. Well, now you know why I never asked you here. She moved in the minute Julie left. Hey, I was forgetting. That beer. There's lots in the fridge. We got a fridge, in case you didn't notice. Then I think maybe we're gonna

I can't

Buckle opens two bottles of beer and hands Stacey one. She does not want it, and puts it aside on the table. Buckle's straight black hair falls over his eyes and he brushes it back. His face is brown, sharp, smiling.

You wouldn't have come here if you couldn't. So don't give me that line, eh?

He is wearing his usual jeans which proclaim his sex. His shirt is a black sports shirt, decorated with artificial gold threads, open at the neck. Stacey smells him, the clean sweat smell, the dust, the oil, the smell of man-flesh. She holds herself in hiatus, waiting. Waiting for the clue, the instructions which she will follow. She can feel his shoulder bones under her fingers

although she has not touched him. She can almost feel
his sex in her. In the chair beside the window, the undersea giant woman raises the pearl-pink heavy cup to her
mouth and drinks unspeaking, listening or not listening.

Can she?

No. I told you. It's afternoon. She's away to hell and
gone. So?

Stacey moves slowly towards him, not with the slowness of caution but the opposite. Then, as she is about to
place her hands on him, his acute rasping voice.

Okay   that's it   don't touch me

What he is doing now concerns only himself, his sex
open and erect in his hands. But although he retreats from
her presence, he watches her, needing to see some image in
eyes, some witness to the agony of his pleasure.

You won't get it   Julie didn't like it when I did it this
way   all she ever wanted was to take it   you're not getting it see

Stacey looks at him only for an instant. Then fear
like tides. She turns for the door and finds beside her on
the floor two silver coins, thrown.

There's your bus fare, lady.

She realizes that she has no money on her. She
reaches down to the floor and picks up the silver. Then she
runs. Down the stairs, onto the inhabited street, to the bus
stop.

Saturday, and Mac arrives home midafternoon. Stacey is
ironing a dress for Katie to wear to the school dance this
evening.

You're home early.

Yeh. Where are the kids, Stacey?

Down looking at TV. Why?

Come on into the study for a minute, will you?

What's up?

Just come.

Okay. Wait till I unplug my iron.

She follows him into the study. Mac lights a cigarette and stands looking out the window.

Close the door, Stacey, will you, please?

Hey, what is it? Okay. There.

Mac turns to face her, and she sees in his eyes some nearly unbearable pain. His voice is steady, deliberately contained, exaggeratedly calm.

Buckle phoned me.

The nerves at the base of Stacey's stomach begin crawling.

Oh?

Yes. He told me.

He told you – what?

Everything. How you wouldn't take no for an answer. How he finally took you to bed.

He told you *that?*

Yes. Well? What've you got to say?

Fury floods in adrenalin bursts through Stacey's veins. She hears her voice, raucous.

What d'you mean, what have I got to say? Who're you? God? You don't own me. You believed Buckle, didn't you? It's a lie   I never did any such thing

Then, at last, she hears the outraged virtue in her own voice

— Oh God. No, I didn't do any such thing. But I would've, if Buckle had. No, damn it, I wouldn't. I wouldn't. I don't even like Buckle. Even at that moment I didn't like him. I would've stopped. I would've found I couldn't go through with it. Wouldn't I? I don't know. I think I would have gone to bed with him. Even there. With her there. How could I? Buckle was smart – he found a two-edged sword.

Why would Buckle lie about a thing like that, for Christ's sake, Stacey?

If you don't know, then there's no use me telling you. But you'd take the word of a friend against mine, wouldn't you?

He's no friend of mine, not any more. Stacey – why?

Why would you? Was it true?

No.

You went to his place, though, didn't you?

Yes. I went. I don't know why. I can't explain. You wouldn't believe me. But I went. All right, I went. But that's all. I never   I never   I never

For God's sake keep your voice down. No need to scream

I'm not screaming

You are. Now *cut it out,* see?

All right   I won't say a word   what's the use

Oh Stacey for God's sake don't go on like that. Quit crying. Okay. Okay. I believe you.

Do you?

Mac puts out his cigarette and lights another. His hands are not steady and his face is misshapen with a private grief.

I don't know what the hell to believe. I just don't see why you went to Buckle's place at all, that's all. It doesn't make sense. I would've thought I could've trusted both of you.

It would be the absolute end of the world even if it had happened?

Mac puts one hand on her shoulder and tightens it around the bone.

I won't have anybody else touching you   see

Stacey yanks away and looks at him unbelieving.

— He's really hurt. And I'd like to comfort him but how can I – it's I who've caused it. And yet I hate him for feeling that way about me. I might as well be a car or a toothbrush. Damn him. Damn Buckle. Damn both of them. I want to go away by myself. Right away. Far.

What about the girl, Mac? Thor's secretary. That's different, I suppose. It's okay for you to touch her.

Pain changes to anger in Mac's eyes.

Yes, it *is* different, if you really want to know. It's not what you're obviously thinking.

I bet   I just bet

— We go on this way and the needle jabs become razor strokes and the razors become hunting knives and the knives become swords and how do we stop?

Leave her out of it, Stacey. Just leave her out of it. You don't know a damn thing about it, so shut up about it, eh?

I will shut up. I'll just do that little thing. Don't worry I won't say a word about anything from now on

For God's sake, Stacey, quit acting like a child.

I'm acting like a child? What about you? I suppose if a chance acquaintance told you I'd robbed a bank you'd believe that too

I told you   I don't know what in hell to believe

Well that shows pretty clearly what you *do* believe

Now listen here Stacey

Sh – the kids are coming upstairs.

That night in bed he makes hate with her, his hands clenched around her collarbones and on her throat until she is able to bring herself to speak the release. *It doesn't hurt. You can't hurt me.* But afterwards neither of them can sleep. Finally, separately, they each rise and take a sleeping pill.

The following day Mac's father arrives for Sunday lunch. Matthew is as scrupulously dressed as always, his dark suit clean and well pressed, his fine faintly lemon-colored white hair brushed neatly. But there is one difference. He is carrying a black silver-topped cane.

Hello, Stacey, my dear. How are you?

Oh, just fine, thanks. How're you? The cane is new, isn't it?

Well, not exactly new. My congregation gave it to me some years ago, and do you know, at the time I thought I would never have occasion to use it. But I've found a little bit of difficulty in navigating the steps at the apartment just recently, so I dug this out. It's most useful. Where is Clifford?

Out cleaning the car.

Oh yes, of course. And the children – at Sunday school, I suppose?

Yes. The boys are, at least. Katie got home rather late from the school dance last night, so I thought just this once.

— Katie got home at two in the morning and I was frantic and couldn't sleep despite sleeping pill and she was furious at me for being frantic. What if she gets pregnant? What if some guy is really cruel to her, sometime, ditching her? What if she takes drugs? Whatifwhatifwhatif? Then I think I'm worrying needlessly, just like my mother did, and Katie isn't stupid and she was with a whole group of kids. And I think she's probably a damn sight more principled than I am at this point.

Matthew is looking at her gravely, nodding his head as though with understanding.

Oh, I know Katherine doesn't miss going many Sundays, Stacey. I quite realize that. But a few weeks of not attending can develop into a habit, you know. Not that I'm implying it will, in Katherine's case. I'm sure you and Clifford are much too conscientious parents to allow that.

— I and Clifford as parents you do not have one single solitary notion about. If I ever said that, what would Matthew say? Would he have a stroke? Or would he just be quietly wounded? Nothing ever can come out. I sometimes see us like moles, living in our underground burrows, with eyes that can't stand any light. Once I thought it was only people like Matthew and my mother who had that kind of weak eyes. Now I know it's me, as much. C'mon, Stacey, say something nice, something agreeable.

How was church?

Just fine. The text for the sermon was from Psalms. One I always find particularly – well, you know – particularly fine.

What was it?

Matthew smiles and his voice is even, gentle, the almost toneless drone of one accustomed to reading from the pulpit.

Save me, O God, for the waters are come in unto my soul

Stacey looks at him, but can find no clues anywhere in his apparently untroubled face. She walks out of the kitchen and goes upstairs. She locks the bathroom door and when she has stopped crying she washes her face with cold water.

Six

T HE KIDS are in bed, even Katie. Stacey sits on the chesterfield, turning the pages of a magazine. "Salad Days – Here's How to be Slim in the Swim." Stacey looks frowningly at the mound of edible vegetation in the color photograph, and quickly flicks the page. "Icings with Spicings." Flick. "A Nervous Breakdown Taught Me Life's Meaning." Flick. Finally she hears Mac's key in the door. But he does not come into the living room. He goes straight down to the basement TV room. Stacey follows him. He has turned on the set and is already sitting in the armchair in front of it.

Mac?

I'm looking at the news, Stacey, if you don't mind.

EVER-OPEN EYE   A SMILING MAN READS PRINTED DISASTERS IN A VANILLA-FLAVORED WHIPPED-CREAM VOICE

I *do* mind, as it happens. What about listening to a piece of news from me? I didn't go to bed with Buckle.

So you say.

You still don't believe me, do you?

Mac's voice is cool and steady, appraising the situation like a member of the legal profession.

How can I be sure?

Stacey's anger bursts away like blood from under a torn scab.

All right, okay, you can't be sure. Even if it did happen, is that the only important thing? Is that all that interests you about me? Not me, or even going to bed with me, but just making sure that I don't ever glance in any other direction? Because if that's all

Mac has risen and taken hold of her wrist.

You did go to bed with him, didn't you?

Stacey pulls away.

No I didn't but I damn well wish I had

Go ahead then

Mac – this is crazy. Look, can't we just talk without getting all steamed up?

I'm not steamed up in the very slightest. You're the one that's doing all the shouting.

If we could just talk about everything I mean like everything

Mac looks at her from incomprehensible eyes. His voice begins low, then suddenly rises, becomes almost not his voice at all.

Leave me alone, can't you? Can't you just *leave me alone?*

Stacey stares. Then she turns and runs up the stairs to the hall and up the next flight of stairs to their bedroom. Rapidly, she changes out of her dress and into her dark green slacks. She puts on a green high-neck sweater, grabs her purse and goes quietly down the stairs.

The Chev is parked in front of the house. Stacey turns the key and starts. Before she has driven a block she realizes she is driving too fast but she does not slow down. She looks in the rear-view mirror, half expecting to see Mac's car, but there is nothing behind her at all. She has no idea where she is going. She heads into the city along streets now inhabited only by the eternal flames of the neon forest fires and a few old men with nowhere to go or youngsters with nothing to do. Then through the half-wild park where the giant firs and cedars darken the dark sky, and across the great bridge that spans the harbor, past the shacks dwelt in by the remnants of coast Indians and the apartments and garden-surrounded houses of the well heeled. Along the highway that leads up the Sound, finally and at last away from habitation, where the road clings to the mountain and the evergreens rise tall and gaunt, and the saltwater laps blackly on the narrow shore, and the stars can be seen, away from human lights. Only now does Stacey slow down, not because the road is too winding and hazardous to drive swiftly, although it is, but because she can now bring herself to drive more carefully.

— Does he hate me? If so, how long? Where did it start? Everything goes too far back to be traced. The roots vanish, because they don't end with Matthew, even if it were possible to trace them that far. They go back and back forever. Our father Adam. *Leave me alone.* And maybe Eve thought *Okay, Sahib, if that's the way you want it,* and it was after that she started getting crafty. How did Mac get to be that way? How did I get to be this way? I can't figure it. But God knows we don't ever make much of a stab at figuring it. What's the matter with us that we can't talk? How can anyone know unless people say? How come we feel it's indecent?

> Stacey Cameron, eight or nine, back from playing in the bush at the foot of the hill that led out of Manawaka. There was this gopher on the road, Mother, and somebody had shot it with a twenty-two and all its stomach and that was all out and it wasn't dead yet. *Please, dear, don't talk about it – it isn't nice.* But I saw it and it was trying to breathe only it couldn't and it was. *Sh, it isn't nice.* (I hurt, Mother. I'm scared.) (Sh, it isn't nice.) (I hurt, you hurt, he hurts – Sh.)

Another car has approached and Stacey edges over to the cliff face just in time. It shoots past, but she is shaken. At the next widened pass point she draws in, stops and lights a cigarette.

— Stacey, go easy. What if anything happened? What would happen to the kids? Maybe Mac would marry Delores Appleton. I could almost face the thought, and yet I know he wouldn't. She is too young, too edgy, too somehow battered a long time ago. I don't give a good goddam who he might marry if I got wrecked, but I don't want anybody else bringing up my kids. Yeh, you're such a marvelous mother. Great example to the young, you. A veritable pillar of strength, I don't think. Listen here, God, don't talk to me like that. You have no right. *You* try bringing up four kids. Don't tell me you've brought up countless millions because I don't buy that. We've brought our own selves up and precious little help we've had from you. If you're there. Which probably you aren't, although I'm never convinced totally, one way or another. So next time you send somebody down here, get It born as a her with seven young or a him with a large family and a rotten boss, eh? Then we'll see how the inspirational bit goes. God, pay no attention. I'm nuts. I'm not myself.

Stacey starts up again. The night is getting chilly and she rolls up the window of the car, wishing she had brought along her dufflecoat.

— How could Buckle tell Mac that? Why ask? You know why. Mac wasn't paying enough attention to him. Buckle is like a kid. Oh? None of my kids could conceivably be that vicious. Buckle, how could you? How do I know? I'd have to know everything that ever happened to him. I think I'm a crumby mother at times, but what about his? Yet she kept him and brought him up somehow. I can only guess, fragments here and there. Mac, can't I ever say how it was with me or what happened at all? You don't want to know. You want everything to be all right. *Is everything all right, Stacey?* Yes, everything is all right. Okay. I get the message. If that's the way you want it, that's the way it'll be. From now on, I live alone in a house full of people where everything is always always all right.

Ahead, the road is coming close to the shore of the Sound. Stacey pulls across the road and draws up on a flat stretch of grass. She climbs out, not bothering to lock the car, and looks around. She wants to go to the shore but is uncertain how to get there. A stretch of sparse forest is in front of her, and she can see the dim lights of several shacks or houses. She goes back to the car and gets the flashlight from the glove compartment. When she shines the subdued light, she can see a muddy trail, overhung with grass, leading at right angles from the road and towards the beach.

— Hell. All private property, no doubt. Can I get past those houses? I'm freezing. It can't be mid-June. I'm scared. Where am I and what am I doing here? Okay, take it easy, Stacey. Where is the flask of Scotch you so providentially stuck in your purse? Here. Little tin flask. It was my dad's. Yep. Niall Cameron carried it with him in the First World War. Meant to be a water flask. When I went back for the funeral, it was with his things and she was going to throw it out. *I'll have that,* I said, and she looked at me with rank suspicions, all completely justified. Okay, Dad. Here's looking at you. You couldn't cope, either. I never even felt all that sorry for you, way back when. Nor for her. I only thought people ought to be strong and loving and not make a mess of their lives and they ought to rear kids with whom it would be possible to talk because one would be so goddam comprehending and would win them over like nothing on earth, and I would sure know how to do it all. So I married a guy who was confident and (in those days or so it seemed) outgoing and full of laughs and free of doubts, fond of watching football and telling low jokes and knowing just where he was going, yessir, very different from you, Dad. Now I don't know. Perhaps it isn't that the masks have been put on, one for each year like the circles that tell the age of a tree. Perhaps they've been gradually peeled off, and what's there underneath is the face that's always been there for me, the unspeaking eyes, the mouth for whom words were too difficult. *No. No. No.* I can't take that. I won't. Hush. How to get through, just this minute, to the shore? What if there are dogs? Alsatians. Dobermans. Come on, Stacey. (I'm scared. What am I doing out here alone?)

Her feet squelch in the rain-wet earth of the rutted track. She walks slowly, brushing aside the thorned tendrils of blackberry bushes, past the dwelling half-concealed in the undergrowth, the light glowing uncertainly from one window. She makes her way slippingly to the shore.

The beach is not a proper beach. It is at most three feet wide, and the sand is pebbled over, knotted with rocks and with shells which crisp underfoot. The trees do not come down quite this far, but heavy-leafed bushes bend almost to the water's edge. Driftwood has been washed up, gnarled branches and fragments now seen as sea-bleached dead-bone grey in the glim of the flashlight. A log strayed from a boom is grey-white on the outside rounded edge but on the circular cut-through it is a water-deepened rust color. The log is half as high as Stacey, but she clambers onto it. She is wearing rubber-soled canvas shoes and her feet are wet. The log is only slightly damp on the surface, although sea-soaked at its core. Stacey opens her purse and gets out a cigarette. In front of her, the black water dances lightly, glancingly, towards the shore, sending the little stones skeltering down in thin ridges after each retreating wave. Out deeper, the water is more rough, breaking in wind-stirred crests. No night clouds, and the sky is as black as the water, but shot through with stars which one instant look close, earth-related, lights provided for us, small almost cozy night-lights to keep us from the dark, and the next instant look like themselves and alien, inconceivably far, giant and burning, not even hostile or anything identifiable, only indifferent. Stacey smokes and lets the silence exist around her. The sounds are only the underlying steady ones of the water and wind, and the occasional pierce of water birds.

— How good to hear nothing, no voices. I thought you were the one who was screaming about nobody wanting to talk. Yeh. Well. How good it feels, no voices. Except yours, Stacey. Well, that's my shadow. It won't be switched off until I die. I'm stuck with it, and I get bloody sick of it, I can tell you. Who is this *you*? I don't know. Shut up. I'm trying to be quiet and you won't let me. If only I could get away, by myself, for about three weeks. Joke. Laugh now. The only time I can ever get away is when all the kids are in bed. And this period of rationed time is rapidly diminishing. It's because we had the kids over so many years. Jen's there all day, and so okay she's in bed by seven, but then the boys and Katie are home and Katie doesn't get to bed until halfway through the night now or so it seems. You can't tell a fourteen-year-old to go to bed at seven. I don't have any time to myself. I'm on duty from seven thirty in the morning until ten thirty at night. Well, poor you. Let's all have a good cry. What would you do if you weren't on duty, bitch? Contemplate? Write poetry? Oh shut up. I would sort out and under-stand my life, that is what I would do, if you really want to know. You would, eh? Well, you're alone now. You're off duty. Start sorting, brain child.

A water bird cries, a far eerie ululating.

Diamond Lake, that one year when Niall Cameron managed to take them all there for two weeks in the summer, Stacey ten and Rachel five. Stacey, sturdy-legged, curious, energetic, flashing along the shore day and night, gawking up at the spruces and down at the moss sprouting with wild-pink bells which looked like lilies of the valley but with no leaves only deep-pink stalks and mild-pink waxen flowers. Stacey listening at night on the beach alone, frightened but having to stay, listen-ing to the lunatic voices of the loons, witch birds out there in the night lake, or voices of dead sha-mans, mourning the departed Indian gods, she not thinking of it like that then, only wholly immersed in the unhuman voices, the begone voices that cared nothing for lights or shelter or the known quality of home. But when she went back to Dia-mond Lake, eight years later, the birds had left. When the people came in numbers, the loons went

away, always. She never discovered where they
went, but she thought then, that eighteenth
summer, of where they might be, somewhere so far
north that people would never penetrate to drive
them off again.

— There *isn't* any place that far north, that far anywhere. There must be. That's where I'd like to go, very far
away from all this jazz. If only the kids could be okay.

*The lake is not large, but in the daytime it shines a
deep oil blue. It is somewhere in the Cariboo. The Cariboo country. Up there. Somewhere. The barns are made
of logs (Mac has told her, so she knows; he has been
there). The boat she owns is only a rowboat, but she can
manage it very well, skillfully in fact, and Ian and Duncan
are good with it, too. The house is made of logs, but
tightly chinked so that it is extremely weatherproof. It is
an old converted barn. Two floors. With careful planning,
she has organized five bedrooms. One for each of the kids,
and one for herself. She teaches school. It is a small community, and naturally everyone knows everyone else, but
the farmers and Indians and (? etc.) are glad that at last a
teacher has come who wants to settle here and*

— Doll, let me ask you one simple question. Can you
add more than two and two? Great teacher you'd make.
Ian says *How do they expect me to do these problems
when Mr. Gaines won't explain?* And I say, *Wait until
Daddy gets home from work, and maybe he can help you
with them.* And Mac looks at the damn things and I guess
braces himself and tackles it, because there's nobody else
to shove it off onto and then I have the gall to wonder why
he bawls Ian out. He probably doesn't know how to do
them any more than I do. Teacher. Oh boy. But the lake
the lake the lake and the way the trees looked, spearing up
there into the sky and the loons' voices and everything
mysterious waiting to be discovered

Stacey pulls her sweater sleeves down around her
wrists, and lights another cigarette. The wind is rising and
she is cold. She resists the urge to look at her watch.

— This erstwhile piece of the forest hurts my ass more than any pew in church when I was a kid. Go home, Stacey. You've got to, sometime. That's for sure. Got to be there to get breakfast – the immutable law of something or other. Where's the flask? Here. There. One more swallow and that's it. I don't want to go home. I want to go away. A long way off. I'm bloody sick of trying to cope. I don't want to be a good wife and mother.

> Diamond Lake, and Stacey, eighteen, swimming outward. She was a strong swimmer, and when she reached the place where she could see the one spruce veering out of the rock on the distant point, she always turned back, not really accepting her limits, believing she could have gone on across the lake, but willing to acknowledge this arbitrary place of reference because it was further out than most of her friends could swim. This summer they had come here on their own, at last, without parents. Stacey, swimming back to shore, coming up for air intermittently, knowing with no doubt that she would make it fine, thinking already of the dance she would go to that evening, feeling already the pressure on her lake-covered thighs of the boys

— Okay. I see it, Sir. I didn't see it before, but I see it now. Thanks for nothing. That's the place I want to get away to, eh? The Cariboo? Up north? No. I've never been any of those places. I only think of Mac or else Buckle, on the road, up there somewhere. When I imagine it, it always looks like Diamond Lake. Like, I guess I mean, everything will be just fine when I'm eighteen again. Come on, Stacey. Home.

Hi. Do you mind me asking you what in hell you are doing there?

Crash. Out of the inner and into the outer. Stacey peers through the darkness. At least he is not accompanied by an Alsatian. Presumably this is the occupant of the dimly outlined dwelling she weasled past some time ago.

I'm sorry. Is this your property?

Not exactly. I'm staying up there. It belongs to some friends of mine – they're away at the moment, so I'm caretaking. The beach is supposed to be everybody's property. Only this one being about a quarter of an inch wide and not that accessible, we don't often get people here. Especially around midnight. You contemplating a swim?

Well no

Don't drown yourself, that's all I ask. Guy drowned himself here not long ago and we haven't heard the last of it yet. By all means do it, but not right here, eh?

I didn't intend

Hey, sorry. Want to come up and have some coffee?

I think I should be getting home

Yeh, sure. Well, come and have some coffee first. Aren't you cold?

Well

Stacey's eyes, now accustomed to the darkness, examine him. He is shorter than Mac but not that much shorter, brown indifferent hair slightly too long and with an uncombed look, broad square face with outjutting chin and thick eyebrows, face supposed to be clean shaven but not all that recently, body solid but too young yet to have accumulated any extra fat around the belly or chest, dressed in paint-splashed brown corduroy pants and a brown and off-white Indian sweater in thick wool with Haida or something motifs of outspread eagle wings and bear masks.

— He doesn't look like a murderer. Oh doll. You have a great eye for a sweater or a muscle, but how in hell do you know what a murderer looks like? If it was Katie, going to this guy's shack or whatever, for coffee, what would you think? I'd have a fit, that's what. And yet right this minute I couldn't care less. Maybe he *is* a murderer. "Salesman's Wife Stabbed on Sound." Should I go?

The young man is standing beside the log on which Stacey sits, and his eyes look amused.

You coming or not?

Well, it's very nice of you

C'mon we don't live on manners here if you're coming, come

She follows him up the mud-soft trail to the house. The raw plank steps lead into the kitchen. It is an A-frame, fairly large but as yet unfinished, the boards unpainted, the lumber still yellow-brown and smelling of pinegum. The ceiling of the main room stretches pointedly upwards, and from one rafter is suspended a looped cord from which hangs an exposed bulb, alight. The room is filled with assorted junk – coarse-webbed fishnets in grey piles on the floor, the big smoke-green thick glass bubbles used as weights on nets, suitcases imperfectly closed and half spilling their underwear and shirts, teetering stacks of books in corners, books outspread or dog-eared on a low table made out of a polished pine slab glowing and golden but with roughly tacked-on uneven do-it-yourself wrought-iron legs, somebody having got sick of the job of an artisan. The half-finished greystone fireplace has no mantel and bears deep eyeless cement pits where future hand-selected stones will possibly one day go. Ten-foot-high unhemmed and floor-trailing curtains of moss-green sackcloth veil the huge front window. An open and beautifully illustrated child's ABC rests on a rumpled loose-weave green and grey wool rug, Arabic-patterned.

— Heavens. A semiclassy pad. If people have to safety-pin up the hems of their curtains – well. Okay, so a bourgeois I may be, but that kind of a slob I'm not. Still, all the books. What right have I to say? The hell with that. They're trying to intimidate me with the superiority of unhemmed curtains.

The man points out a black canvas chair, and Stacey tensely sits on the edge. Then, seeing his smile, she slopes back. The stove in the outer region is kerosene – she can smell it. He returns in a little while with two mugs of coffee.

Sugar? Cream?

Well, thanks. Both.

He sits down on a hassock and looks at her. He is still smiling, but when he questions her she feels unprepared.

So, okay. What's the bad news?

Stacey cradles the hot coffee mug between her hands. What?

He grins now, but whether mockingly or not, she cannot tell.

The bad news. What's with you? Why are you here?

I it's nothing I just drove out

Oh. You just drove out? At this time of night? Here? Look, if you don't want to level with me, don't level with me. Go home. But don't sit here and drink my coffee and tell me you were out for a little fresh air. By the way, my name is Luke. Luke Venturi.

Stacey mumbles her own name and he laughs.

Hey, you're really scared, aren't you? Whatsamatter? Think I'm gonna strangle you with one of your own nylons? Come on. Why you here?

Stacey does not look at him.

I didn't want to stay at home any longer. I took off.

Her hand is too unstable to light her own cigarette. Luke takes it from her, lights it, hands it back.

You took off. Well, well. That's all right. Don't worry. Sometimes people do.

She can look at him now, but she feels her own eyes apologizing.

They don't. They don't. Not where I come from.

Luke laughs again, but it does not strike her as cruel, only removed from her, as though he were looking at things from some very different point of view.

Well, maybe not, where you come from. Wouldn't know. You know, once I was up in the Cariboo, hitching, and I stopped off at this farmhouse in the middle of, like, nothing, this goddam broken-down old house, huge actually it was, and the usual pump and cows outside and all I wanted was a meal and only this one kid came out, see, kid about twelve he must've been, and I asked where was his dad and mum, and he said *My dad's out there he'll be back at five. Mum, she took off, two-three months ago.* And you thought, Christ, no wonder she took off. But there he was, though. Hey, Stacey? What did I do? Is that where you live?

She has put her coffee mug on the floor and her head is in her outfolded arms. She does not know where the crying began or when it can end.

I'm sorry I'm sorry

It's okay, Stacey, you don't have to be sorry. It hurts?

Yes.

Well go ahead and bawl. No shame in that. You're not alone.

She lifts her head and looks at him.

That's where you're wrong.

Luke picks up her coffee mug and goes to refill it

No, baby, that's where *you're* wrong.

She takes the coffee mug from him.

You're real? You're not real. I'm imagining.

He smiles.

You're not imagining. But maybe I'm not *that* real, so don't count on it. You drive far?

Not that far. What do you do?

Luke lights another cigarette for her, and takes one himself from her package.

Do? What do I do? Well, that's a good question.

I mean, what work do you do?

Yeh, that's what you have to find out, first thing, eh? Well, I think I'll get on with a fish boat this summer, go north.

You're lucky

Lucky?

I always thought I'd like to go somewhere up there. But I've got four kids.

Now we come to it, eh? Four kids. Well.

Don't you do anything else, the rest of the year?

Sure. Work here and there. Sawmills. Sometimes I sign on as cook, lumber camps. Wouldn't think I'd be a good cook, would you? But I'm not bad, if I do say so myself. Pastry is my downfall, though. I make pastry which is – not to put too fine a point upon it – like porcelain. Well, nobody wins them all. You make good pastry, Stacey?

Not bad.

I thought as much. I said to myself, there is a woman who looks like she makes good pastry.

Stacey has been drawn into his laughter.

It sounds like an insult to me.

What? You give someone a compliment and they interpret it in reverse. It's a semantic problem we have. I do other things, too, sometimes. I write.

Oh? What?

Luke shrugs and bends his head.

Science fiction. SF. Not space opera with sex. Allegory, more, and all happening on this planet. The bug-eyed monster bit is dead. Don't get me wrong. Asimov, Bradbury, Blish and all the old brigade don't have to lie awake nights worrying about competition from me. Not yet, anyhow. I've had precisely one story published. Want my autograph? It's free.

I like SF. I sometimes

Yeh? You sometimes what? You started to say it, then you quit, like I'd think you were way-out for mentioning it. How funny you are, merwoman. Who held you down? Was it for too long?

Stacey examines his face, unable for the moment to believe the easiness of his words.

Maybe. I never thought of it that way. Or – yeh, maybe I did, but I'm not sure any more. I was only going to say I sometimes　you know　like imagine that kind of situation　SF I mean

Luke now cannot withhold his laughter, but it encompasses her as his hand encompasses her wrist.

Like it's the secret of the confessional? Oh baby. You're unbelievable. It's so sensational?

She takes her wrist back and drinks her coffee, saying nothing. Luke accepts it but after a moment comes back again.

I'm sorry. Four kids, eh? What are you trying to be? A good example?

I can't be.

Well, that's good. So why try? Why don't you come out a little?

What?

Come out. From wherever you're hiding yourself. See – if I look very hard, I can just about make you out in there, but miniature, like looking through the wrong end of a telescope.

I can see what you mean, sort of. But it's odd

Everything is odd, merwoman, everything

That's what I think. Only

Only what?

They don't think so

Luke's eyebrows, heavy over the square quizzical face, now lighten purposely.

Well, I'm not them.

Stacey gathers her purse, gets out her car keys.

I have to go home. Thanks for the coffee.

That's okay. And cheer up, eh?

I'll try. Thanks for noticing I wasn't so cheerful.

That's me – perceptive to a degree. It only stood out all over you.

Stacey hesitates in the doorway, not wanting to go, wanting Luke to suggest that she might like to drive out again sometime. But he only smiles at her, so she finally turns.

Well, so long.

So long.

Stacey pulls up the Chev on Bluejay Crescent and goes with extreme quietness into the house. She tiptoes up the stairs. No sound. She creaks the bedroom door open.

Mac is sitting up in bed, smoking. He looks at her.

Great. You've decided to come home? Where in the bloody fucking hell have you been, Stacey? I damn near called the police.

I have been out driving.

Out driving? At this hour?

Yes.

All right. Did you go to Buckle's place?

No.

That's what you say.

If you don't believe me, hire detectives. Who cares? I went out driving, that's all.

If you had stayed out half an hour longer I would have called the

Why?

Because I have some sense of responsibility even if you don't.

Yeh, well maybe you're right. But I'm back in time to make breakfast. I'm not totally lacking in a sense of

Look all right I believe you what else can I do for God's sake get to bed will you please it is two A.M.

Okay right away

Stacey pussyfoots into the bathroom, washes her face, puts on her nightly cold cream and steps back into the silent hall. There, in front of her bedroom door is Katie, in her yellow lace nightie, long red hair along her shoulders, not saying anything, just looking.

Katie –

Katie turns and goes back into her bedroom. Her words are on purpose not loud enough to wake the younger kids.

Just don't ever bawl me out again, eh?

For three days Stacey housecleans compulsively, lugging the vacuum cleaner savagely from room to room, washing and ironing curtains, turfing out boxloads of broken toys from the boys' room, straightening her dresser drawers. In the evenings, she goes to bed even before Katie is in bed, and tries to read. She leaves Mac's dinner in the oven for him, and when she hears his key in the door, about ten, she switches off the light on the bedside table. Their bedroom is at the front of the house and he drives in the back lane to the garage so he cannot see the bedroom light as he approaches. Her eyes are closed by the time he comes upstairs and she does not open them. She listens each night to Mac's daytime breathing turning into sleep. She lies stiffly, far to her own side of the bed, not moving in case she wakens him and speech becomes unavoidable. In the mornings they are protected from each other by the presence of the children.

On the fourth morning, Stacey phones Tess Fogler and asks her over for coffee. The high-pitched girl-voice comes back at her.

Why thanks Stacey I'd just love to

Stacey replaces the receiver and looks at herself in the hall mirror. She is wearing her dark-green slacks and green pullover. The day is too warm for them. It is only now that Stacey realizes she has been wearing them for the past four days as though they were the one contact with what she now does not believe actually took place.

— How can I get out? Evenings are out of the question. If Mac is home it's impossible; if he isn't home it still is impossible. Katie would be okay with the other kids for a few hours in the evening. Sure, but where am I going? Out to see a sick friend? Days. I can't ask Tess to mind Jen again. I've already imposed on her too much. I'm not going to ask her. I simply am not. What you ought to do, Stacey, is ask Tess over more often, no strings. I know, I know. But she never has anything to talk about. Yeh, and you're such a brilliant conversationalist yourself? Oh shut up. I will ask her over more often. I swear it. And I won't ever ask her about Jen again. It would be different if it could be reciprocal, but what can I do for her that would be any use? Let her pour out her woes? She never does. Maybe she hasn't got any, not really to speak of. I look at her, done up like a Christmas present, and I wonder what's actually inside. Maybe nothing. How can you tell unless people say? He didn't mind talking, Luke. He took it for granted. *What's the bad news?* As though it were to be expected, to mention it. Okay, God, say what you like, but I damn well wish I could get away just sometimes by myself. But no. It's a criminal offense, nearly. What makes any of them think they've got the right to tell me own me have me always there not that they notice when I am only when I'm not.

> Katie, four, almost as chunky as Stacey had been as a child, Katie with then-short auburn hair, sitting beside Stacey on the chesterfield, gravely turning the magazine pages, coming to the picture of the ever-alluring Girl in White Lace. *Do ladies wear it then, Mum?* Wear what when? *Their bride dress when they go out to find the husband.* Well, no, not just then. *I'm going to.* Sure, you do that, gorgeous – you'll be a knockout. And they laughed conspiratorially together. Ten years later, Katie in the upstairs hall outside her room, eyes fully aware, unforgiving. *Just don't ever bawl me out again, eh?*

— Katie, wait. Let me explain. No, I guess I can't. And if I did, it might be worse for you than not trying. Katie, I promise – never again. I won't leave even for an hour. I swear it. How could I go out there again, anyway? He didn't ask me to come. What do you imagine he'd do, Stacey? Greet you with a vast shout of joy? Like hell he would. He'd stare at you aloofly, and say *Oh, it's you.* No – he'd smile politely but it would be only that, just politeness, And what would you say, dream girl? *I need to talk to you please please talk touch me even if it's only your hands on my shoulders.* That would go down wonderfully. Have a little pride, Stacey. Why?

Jen is warbling beside Stacey, running up and down the hall with her short arms extended around a multitude of dolls. She drops them and reaches for Stacey's arm.

What is it, flower?

Yatter-yatter

You mean your doll carriage? Okay, let's get it. I'm going to phone Doctor Spender this week and have him have a look at you. No – I'm just impatient, aren't I? You're perfectly okay, aren't you? Daddy's right – I just get worked up over nothing. Don't I?

R-r-ring.

Stacey opens the front door and Tess comes in, fawn-graceful in new dull-orange dress, carrying in her hands a number of swan-necked gilt-headed bottles and portly drum-bellied jars, like a collection of princesses and frogs.

Look, Stacey, my new facial stuff. It's fabulous. Just simply amazing. I've only been using it a few days but I can really notice the difference already. You can't buy it in the drugstores – it's only sold door-to-door. This awfully nice woman came around and I asked her in more out of politeness than anything you know and then we got talking and well I mean I don't usually buy cosmetics door-to-door but this sounded so interesting. They're all natural products.

Tess deposits the bottles and jars on the kitchen table and Stacey picks up a squat translucent jar filled with a green perfumed ointment. The label reads HATSHEPSUT – Avocado Wrinkle Cream.

Natural products?

Yes, I mean, like, they don't contain any animal substances.

Is that good?

Tess nods.

It's much better for your skin. All natural vegetable substances.

What's so unnatural about animals?

Tess laughs trillingly.

Oh Stacey, you're just like Jake. Well, there's nothing I guess what you would exactly call unnatural about animals except they are animals aren't they and creams and that made out of animal fat well there's something sort of *unfresh* about it, isn't there? It never struck me until Mrs.

Clovelly – that's her name – pointed it out and then I could see it right away. You take natural vegetable oils, now, and there's something sort of, well, *nicer* about it, you know? Also, it's much more compassionate. I mean, you don't have to have all those animals killed for their fat.

Yeh. Well, you could be right. What all kinds you got, Tess?

Tess displays them one by one, cuddling them between her long smooth fingers.

Well, this one's *Geranium Leaf Skin Astringent*, for toning up the skin. This is *Pineapple Shampoo*, for restoring the natural oils of the hair. And *Rose and Rhubarb Night Cream* – this pale-pink one – rhubarb may sound a little funny, but it's so refreshing, really, and just smell it – the roses are for the perfume, and the rhubarb juices are for the skin-cell restoring process. And *Violet-Rosemary Hand Cream* – smell – isn't it lovely? And *Strawbery Under-Eye Lotion*, and you've seen the *Avocado Wrinkle Cream*.

— My God, does she apply them or eat them? Sh, doll, don't offend her. Sale on at Eaton's – remember? No. Don't. You're not to ask.

Gosh, they make quite an imposing array, Tess. What does it mean – HATSHEP – whatever it says?

HATSHEPSUT. Pronounced Hat-shep-*soot*. Mrs. Clovelly said. That's the name of the whole line. They're called after an ancient Egyptian queen. Queen Hatshepsut. She was very famous. She ruled as pharaoh in her own right.

Gee. Well. How interesting.

Jake had to look her up, of course, in a book. He came downstairs laughing like crazy and saying she was famous for her cruelty and she dressed as a man and married her stepson or some such relative and he hated her so much he had her name chiseled off all the monuments after she died. But I bet that's not true. Jake gets a big bang out of jokes, I mean. But anyway, I like the name, don't you? I think it's sort of cute to name them after an ancient Egyptian queen.

Yeh it's very

No sugar or cream for me, thanks Stacey. I just have it black.

Oh sorry. Absent-minded. I don't see why *you* diet.

I just feel I mustn't ever let myself go, that's all. How's your diet coming along, Stacey?

Lousy. I haven't got the perseverance of a grasshopper.

Well, you *do* so much. You must burn up a lot of energy.

Yeh, I guess. Things get on top of me every so often. I been doing spring cleaning these past couple of days. Haven't had a minute. I meant to get downtown while the sale's on at Eaton's. If I don't get those kids some new pajamas soon, they'll be going to bed bare.

Why don't you go this afternoon, then? I'll take Jen.

Oh, I couldn't, Tess. You've been so good

It's nothing. I like having her. We get on famously, don't we, sweetie?

Jen, arranging her young in the doll carriage, looks up and nods agreeably.

Well, it's terrifically nice of you, Tess

I don't mind. She may not talk but she talks to me, at least I feel she's talking. You go ahead, Stacey.

Thanks a million. I really am grateful. Listen, if there's ever anything I can do for you, Tess – anything – please let me, eh?

There isn't, honey, but thanks.

I'll tell Katie to pick Jen up after school if I'm not home yet.

Sure. Okay.

After Tess has gone, Stacey begins making the kids' sandwiches for lunch. Then she realizes it is only ten minutes past eleven, and they will not be home for another hour. She leaves Jen playing in the veranda and goes upstairs. She shuffles rapidly through the coat hangers in the clothes cupboard and finally pulls out a cotton dress, slightly shabby, not belonging to any identifiable age group, printed in blue and dark green, like seawater and fir trees.

When Katie and the boys have gone back to school after lunch, Stacey takes Jen over to the Foglers' house. She then gets in the Chev and drives downtown to Eaton's, where she purchases the first pajamas she sees which are the right sizes. Back to the car, and out of the city along the winding road that leads up the Sound.

— He won't be home. Or he'll be home and he won't even recognize me. Or there'll be a girl there – long fair hair, about twenty. Why did I come? I'm off my rocker. It isn't me, it's somebody wearing my appearance, my face, takeover by aliens from out there. My real mind is in the deep freeze in their spaceship. Why would he want to see me again? He wouldn't. Otherwise, he would've asked me to come out. Just for half an hour – that won't take up much of his time. It shouldn't have been so easy, with Tess. All right, don't rub it in. Stacey, you're a monster. Am I? Am I? I don't care if I am. All I know is I have to get out. *I have to get out.*

The A-frame in the daytime looks more obvious than it did at night. Unpainted, the timber a cool light brown, it juts up among the green-needled trees and the welter of bushes like a small strange cathedral with a rubble of trodden timothy grass, paint tins and splinters of kindling wood at its feet. Uncertainly Stacey walks up to the steps and looks at the door, which is open. Luke appears in the doorway. He is still dressed in the thick wool Indian sweater and brown corduroys. He flicks his coarse slightly too-long hair away from his forehead, wipes a hand over his mouth as though he has only just finished eating, and stands looking down at her. He has not shaved, and his jaw is now beard-brown as though he intended it that way. Then, mercifully, he grins.

Hey, how about that? It's the merwoman. I had a hunch you'd come back. It was in the horoscope, more or less.

Stacey walks up the wooden plank steps.

Your horoscope? You don't believe in

Well, it's as certain as anything else, isn't it? I'm Cancer. Cheerful sign to be, eh? The forecasts are always telling me my artistic temperament is due for a surprise, and it never fails to happen. Come on in.

I – thanks. I mustn't stay long

Sure.

I used to work for a guy who did horoscopes. Before I was married, that was. I mean, it was sort of a sideline with him. He was really in the import business. Stuff from Hong Kong, like fried bees and chocolate-covered ants. Tinned, naturally. But maybe the horoscopes were his real business. He used to get me to mimeograph them. He had a big mailing list. I always wondered if it was legal. His name was Janus Uranus, not his real name of course, the one he put on the mimeographed horoscopes. His real name was Curtis W. Forrester. Probably that wasn't his real name, either.

— Was it really me, wondering then if it was legal? Or was it Mac? The first time I met Mac, he definitely stated *It doesn't sound legal to me, Stacey.* What if I'd stayed on with the old guy for a while longer? My whole life would've been different. I might have married – who? (Whom?) A fortune teller, an artist, a master mariner, a prophet. Yeh?

> Stacey, bringing in the supposedly individual horoscopes in job lots for the old man to leaf through. The fifth-floor one-room office heavy with abandoned paperwork, tribes of spiders, decrepit carved-oak desks from a gaudier era. The old guy, short and blue-eyed, bald but sideburned like her imagining of the Wizard of Oz. *We won't disappoint them, Stacey. These must go out tonight –*

think of the people who are waiting for the ineffable Word, Stacey, waiting to be told what life holds and withholds, the inalterable soul movements, stately as orchestral or bowel. Think on it, girl, I implore you. Yes, Mr. Forrester. Call me Janus. What kind of reply are you fobbing me off with, anyway, girl? What is your young brain doing in there? (Thinking you're off your rocker, you mangy old coyote, that's what.)

Luke is laughing and bringing the coffeepot and two pottery mugs into the main room. Stacey sits down on the Arabic-patterned rug and tucks her feet underneath her. He hands her one of the cups.

Janus Uranus? That's a terrific name, Stacey. Why did you ever leave?

He scared me. And embarrassed me. Eccentrics always do. I don't want them to, but they do. It has something to do with the way I was brought up, I guess. Actually, I left to get married, so it wasn't only Janus. I was relieved to get out, though. I don't know how much that had to do with how I felt about Mac. Maybe it did. I never thought of it until now.

Timber Lake sixteen years ago had hardly any cottages. Jungles of blackberry bushes and salmonberry. Spruce trees darkly still in the sun, and the water so clear you could see the grey-gold minnows flickering. You know something, Mac? What? I like everything about you. That's good, honey. I like everything about you, too.

Stacey reaches out and touches the sleeve of Luke's Indian sweater.

Luke – that's not true. Janus didn't have anything to do with the way I felt about Mac.

Mm? Janus, the two-faced god. Uranus, the frozen planet, farthest from our sun. Combined with the recurrence of *anus* in each word. He sounds a great guy. Do you reckon he's still alive?

Stacey withdraws her hand.

— He collects people, maybe? Sure, Stacey – fine collector's piece you'd make. Still, he didn't hear what I said this time. Idiot child, why should he want to discuss Mac? I don't want to, either. That's just who I don't want. So okay – don't, then.

I wouldn't know if he's still there or not. It wasn't quite a century ago.

Luke turns to her in amazement.

Hey – that supersensitivity. It's too much. You waiting for the verbal cracks, or what? It wasn't meant

I'm sorry

Don't be sorry, Stacey. People should never be sorry – it's a waste of time.

Aren't you, ever?

Nope. You keep on communicating your own awfulness to yourself, and nothing changes. You just go on in the same old groove.

How old are you, Luke?

He takes the cigarette packet from her outheld fingers and lights one for each of them. He hands hers to her, and looks at her, directly, as though purposely not evading her eyes.

How old? What's that got to do with anything?

I was just curious

Well, to be precise, I was twenty-nine on my last birthday. But being Cancer I'm due to age another year soon. You seem to be waiting for me to ask you how old you are. Okay. How old are you, Stacey?

I wasn't I didn't mean well, I'm thirty-five, actually.

— My kingdom it extendeth from lie to shining lie. I was the one who nearly flipped when Mac pared off a few years from himself with Thor. Well, I only took off four. Luke's nearly thirty. Nine years younger. So what? I'm only talking to him.

Thirty-five. You make it sound like about eighty. Does it bug you?

No, not really. Only I guess I've changed somehow without realizing it. I worry more. I scare easier.

What scares you, merwoman?

You don't want to be bored with hearing that kind of thing.

Hey, don't be coy, Stacey, or I may just throw you back on the beach. It's okay. Don't worry. If I get bored, I'll let you know. The things that scare people are hardly ever boring. You could be an exception, of course.

It's about the kids mostly, I guess. What'll become of them? How'll they end up? I can't face the thought of anything awful happening to them. But I can't do anything to prevent it happening, either. Everybody's living dangerously – that's how I see it. What if they got hurt, killed even? That seems the one thing I couldn't bear. But everybody feels that way, or nearly everybody, and that doesn't stop it happening. There was this newspaper picture of this boy some city in the States kid about twelve Negro kid you know shot by accident it said by the police in a riot and he was just lying there not dead but lying with his arm cradled up in a dark pool his blood and his eyes were wide open and you wondered what he was seeing. His parents cared about him as much as I do about my kids, no doubt, and worried about what might happen to him, but that didn't stop it happening. You think I'm silly to think about   I can't help it.

Luke refills her coffee mug and comes down from his perch on the canvas chair to sit cross-legged beside her on the rough wool rug.

No. *Silly* isn't the exact word I would have chosen.

A strange thing happened seven years ago – that was the last time I went back home I mean to my home town Manawaka. My mother and sister live there. My sister hasn't got any use for going through all the old rubbish in trunks in the attic, but I kind of get a bang out of it and so does my mother and I never got on well with her when I was a kid but after I had my own kids I felt different I guess I could see more why she used to fuss – it was mainly because she was scared about us. So we went up to the attic this day, my mother and I, and among the junk I found a revolver which used to be my dad's – he died some time before this – and I said to my mother *I'll have this as a souvenir.* She didn't know there were any bullets for it, but there were. When I got back home I mean my home here I hid it in the basement on a little shelf under one of the rafters.

Yeh? What did you plan to do with it? Or rather, whom? Yourself, when the Goths' chariots and the final bill came in, or when some evangelist corporal decided this is the way the world ends not with a whimper but a bang?

I didn't – I wasn't thinking of it exactly like that. I didn't have all that wide a view, to tell you the truth. It was at that time – remember – when people from California and around there were saying they planned to come up here for safety and I had to laugh, living here, because it didn't feel that much better here to me. It sounds crazy, even to me, now. I've never told anyone. I thought – *if anything happened* – that's the way I always thought of it – *if anything happened* – that phrase only, just like my mother could never bring herself to say anyone had died – they had always passed on – anyway, if anything did, and the kids got – you know – damaged or like burned so they couldn't recover and I didn't know where to take them and there was no place to go anyway, then I'd

Luke puts a hand over hers to steady it.

Sh. It's all right. It didn't happen. Hush, Stacey. Have you still got it?

No. I thought about it and thought what it would be like to have to do a thing like that and after a while I realized that I couldn't not even if they were even if I couldn't do anything except wait I'd just have to do that and look at them and hold them whatever they were like or I was like because I couldn't do anything else. Maybe I'd have to keep telling them everything would be all right. We went to Timber Lake that summer with the kids. I took the revolver along and went out one night by myself and threw it in the lake. I never told Mac. He always used to say I shouldn't worry – that it was useless, and of course that was right. Maybe he worried, too, for all I know. But he never said.

That's not good.

No. But it *is* useless to worry. What can you do?

Luke shrugs.

I don't know, baby. I always walk along in the right-intentioned marches, but I don't tell myself that the face of the world is going to be altered that way. My mother believes in the power of corporate prayer. She's still an Italian farmwoman at heart. She was blessed once by the Pope – it was just before she and my dad came over to this country and I was about two months old – she had me when she was fifteen, great for her, eh? Anyway, it was in the big square of St. Peter's, and the Holy Father stood on the balcony and lifted his arms and there was this huge crowd milling around. To hear her tell it, you could feel the radiance as though there were hosts of angels swooping around like so many pigeons. I never bought that, but then again, there could be something in it. So I plod along. It makes as much sense as anything else.

You know something, Luke? The other thing worries me just about as much. I sometimes think in the end it's me who's hurting them the most, after all.

You could be right. You probably are. I'm not much of an authority on the subject.

Stacey eyes him alertly, hearing the faint drawl of boredom only just now in his voice.

— Enough, doll. Enough about the kids. They're not real to him. Why should they be?

Luke – I should be going. Did I interrupt your work?

My work? Well, not exactly. I don't work that hard. I was put off it as a kid by having parents who never quit working.

What do you do when you're not writing?

I putter, sort of. Look

he jumps to his feet and pulls Stacey by the wrist,

taking her to the far side of the room, cluttered with books and pieces of driftwood.

I did these this morning – bookshelves. The old brick and plank method. These friends who own this place won't ever get around to making any for themselves, but they could sure do with some. Other times I go fishing. I'm no hell of a fisherman, but it makes me feel good if I can catch something I can live off. Frustrated pioneer instincts, too well known to be detailed here. We've got a boat. It's a terrible boat – leaks like a senile gent, but we patch it up. Only a rowboat, not one of those fiber-glass speedboat jobs that all the salesmen have.

Not all the salesmen

What?

Not all the salesmen, I said. My husband is a salesman.

Yeh?

He used to sell encyclopedias. Then he sold essences. Now he sells – never mind. He's doing well at it   very well really

Look out there, Stacey, eh? I like going out when the Sound isn't all that quiet, when it's talking to itself, and the water goes slap-crash against this feeble little boat and you wonder who is down there like that prehistoric undersea creature in that story and after ten million years or something it rose up to answer the mating call only sad to tell what it actually heard was the foghorn from a lighthouse

I got married sixteen years ago and I thought he was like Agamemnon King of Men except I'd never heard of Agamemnon then only later when I took all those goddam night courses like in Ancient Greek Drama but that was how I thought of him only of course that view couldn't last all that long how could it if you are with somebody all the time and see how they go to sleep with their mouth open or something and I wouldn't have minded about that except he doesn't talk any more hardly at all can you imagine what it's like to live in the same house with somebody who doesn't talk or who can't or else won't and I don't know which reason it could be.

I go out there in the boat and I don't mind being absolutely and utterly alone in fact I like it that's when I get ideas for whatever it is I'm going to write and when I was kid it was impossible ever to be alone.

Stacey all at once recognizes the parallel lines which if they go on being parallel cannot ever meet.

Why couldn't you be alone when you were a kid, Luke?

Because after me came my five sisters and the house was also always full of cousins and aunts or somebody. Funny thing – I liked them all, and yet I used to wish they'd all get the hell out sometimes so things could be a trifle peaceful. Our house was the noisiest for miles around. Still is. You should've been there the night of my sister Angela's wedding about six months ago. My dad and two of my uncles set up an orchestra in the kitchen – an accordion. a guitar, and my dad on drums, actually a well-chosen selection of frying pans and soup kettles. Everybody dancing all over the house. At about four in the morning, people bawling their eyes out over great classical airs like "Santa Lucia." It was murder. The police finally arrived, and my dad offered them some of his homemade wine. I thought I'd rupture myself laughing.

Stacey gazes at him enviously.

I wish   I wish

What? You wish what, merwoman?

I wish I'd had that kind of family

Luke smiles.

Everything looks both better and worse from the outside, I guess. You think – *How lucky they are or How in hell can they stand it?* Maybe they're not so lucky, but they can stand it. Want some of my dad's wine?

He really makes his own?

Of course. I would not say he was the most skilled winemaker in North Vancouver, but he must be in the top brackets. None of this chemical slop for him, he says. He gets half a truckload of California grapes every year. Then the crusher comes in. You ever seen a grape crusher? You hire it by the hour. Nothing unprofessional for my old man. He puts the brew down in oak barrels in which whiskey has been made. Fermentation – and then you rack it and bottle it and six months later you got a good rough red, like Chianti.

What's he do, your dad?

People always want to know what a guy does. I wonder why is that?

I take it back.

No, don't. He works for a building contractor. He believes you have to work very hard in this life, just to keep your head above water, or to escape whatever it is that's waiting to crush you like a grape. And even then you may lose at any moment. Like *Christ in Concrete*. Only he couldn't visualize himself in a star role. One of the lesser apostles, you might say. I'm not sorry he hasn't got anywhere. Where is there to get, that you would all that much want to be? I'm only sorry he doesn't see it that way. He thinks he's a failure. How much better, I think he tells himself, if he owned four apartment blocks like my mother's brother. Here – try the wine.

It's good.

Not bad, is it? I'll put the bottle between us. Help yourself.

Thanks. I mustn't stay much longer

Sure.

Tell me about your SF stories.

Luke pulls his Indian sweater down around his wrists and leans back, propping himself on an elbow.

I've written mostly short stories, but the one I'm trying to do now is longer, like maybe novel-length. I won't talk about it – it'll go away if I do. Superstition. Sometimes I think it's great – or, well, let's say not bad, anyway. Other times I think it's pure crap. It's called *The Greyfolk*. Takes place some thousand or so years hence, when this continent is all desert and the few remaining people are governed by African administrators who followed the First Expedition which was sent from Africa centuries after the Cataclysm here, when the radiation danger had finally disappeared, to see if there were any survivors. There were. A few small creatures looking almost human crawled out of their hidey holes in the dunes. They'd evolved over the years into wizened grey-scaled folk who lived on sand lizards and water from dew ponds. They'd lost their language and all knowledge of their past, although they had a few dim racial memories and some bizarre quasi-religious cults. The Administration taught them basic Bantu, and after a hundred or so years, the greyfolk are producing some brilliant students, but none of them will do anything except invent gimmicks like the Cacophonoscope, which gives out with lamenting green-songs in color, or the Ululator, which is the sob machine, and you take your pick for whatever variety gives you your kicks. Story really concerns the dilemma of Kwaame Acquaah, the Chief Administrator, who is deeply against Africa having colonies and who wants the greyfolk themselves to discover how to restore their soil et cetera, but who can't think how to overcome the mental block that obviously exists among them. The educated greyfolk have developed the belief that their ancestral culture was harmonious, agrarian and ideal until the disaster, which some believe to have been an act of nature such as multitudinous volcanic eruptions and others believe to have been an outside attack by unnamed destroyers. Acquaah's problem is whether to let them continue in these comforting beliefs or to tell them what really happened. In the end, they have to know, of course. Trouble is, I'm not sure what happens when they find out.

He laughs and turns towards her, refilling both their glasses. Stacey cannot think of anything intelligent to say, but it does not seem to matter. Luke drinks and goes on, and she realizes it is not her opinion he is seeking.

Goddam, Stacey – I've gone and talked about it, haven't I? Not much, though. I could've gone into a lot more detail. I haven't given away much. Anyway, maybe it'll all get changed. I know the basic situation's been done before, but not by me. What kind of remark is that? Egotistical? Or just self-protective? I can't think of any way to end the story, and I guess some sort of ending is required, although sometimes I wonder why. Why not just stop and let the reader make up his own ending? Don't get me wrong. I don't expect you to say. It's my problem. Sometimes I wish

Wish what?

That I had less imagination or more talent. I don't wish that often. Mostly, it's okay just to *be*. Only sometimes you get these delusions of purpose. But we don't have to mean anything.

I'm not convinced.

Aren't you, merwoman?

I don't think you are, either.

Don't you, Stacey?

Stacey puts her fingers on the hairs of his arm. He glances at her, unsmiling. Then, after a moment, he begins to stroke her wrist.

— He seems so damn young. And he wants me to say *Everything's all right*. He, too. Even though he knows I can't. How peculiar. Luke, hold me. Stacey, don't beg. Am I?

Luke's hands are on her shoulders, pulling her inward towards him. Then his tongue is in her mouth. She is surprised by the force of her own response, the intensity and explicitness of her pleasure.

— Stacey, ease up. Not so fast. Now I see what the trouble is. I've grown unaccustomed to the ritual of the preliminaries. I'm out of touch with the rules. I've only gone to bed with one man for a hell of a long time, when the byplay was necessary. Rein in, Stacey, or Luke will think you're a whore. Well, he'll be wrong, then. Whores don't want it that much. Only women like me, who think there may not be that much time left. Luke – Luke? Am I begging? All right, so I'm begging.

Luke withdraws slightly and looks at her, questioningly.

Stacey – if you want to go home, now's the time

No

So okay, eh?

Yes

Her thought processes switch off, and she is momentarily saying nothing inside herself. She reacts as she once did to jazz, taking it as it was told to her unverbally, following the beat. Luke takes her hand and puts it on his sex. The surge in her own sex is so great that she presses herself hard against him, urging him. Luke laughs.

You really want it, don't you?

Yes

But when they are taking their clothes off, thought returns unwelcomely to her.

— I don't want to expose myself to him. I'm not perfect enough. He's too young. I've got on me the stretchmarks of four kids, the lines of dead silver worming across my belly. Will he notice? He'd have to be blind, not to. I can't help it. I'm not twenty any more. The padding of fat on my hips and on the inner reaches of my thighs. Goddam. I never knew it would be like this. It's different with Mac – he's seen me alter so gradually that he hardly notices, or if he does at least it doesn't make him want to throw up. Or so I like to think. Mac knows what I looked like when I was twenty-three, and I didn't look bad then, in fact I looked pretty good. I don't want Luke to see me as I am now. I want him to see me as I was then. He hasn't been knocked about that much yet. Men preserve themselves for longer than women, anyhow. Mac's got life's scribblings under his eyes, and his belly isn't so absolutely taut as it once was, but it is a damn sight tauter than mine, let's face it. Four kids have ruined me. It's not their fault. It would have happened anyway – at least I've got something to show for it. Oh God I wish I looked better. What you need, Stacey girl, is a kaftan with a small zipper. Does he think I look too terrible?

Luke   I'm not twenty

He puts his fingers across her mouth, gently but also reprovingly.

Sh

He is certain, assured, unscarred. The hair on his rib cage is dark brown, almost black, and his thighs are dark-haired, his sex hardsoft long eager to be in her. He puts a cushion under her head on the Arabic-patterned rug, and kneels above her.

Merwoman   you're trembling

Am I? I guess it's because I want

What you want is this

Then she takes his sex in her hands and guides it into her. She comes before he does, but she is still there when he reaches it. She feels him shudder, return to himself. Then he rests on her, and she explores his skin. His voice is barely audible.

Stacey. That was

Yes

You really loved it, didn't you? You wanted it for a long time, didn't you?

Yes

— But that's not true, either. It makes me sound like I was deprived for lo these many years. It wasn't like that at all. It was something else. It's too complicated to explain, and anyway, he doesn't want to know. Maybe it gives him something, to imagine he's like the rain in a dry year? And in a way, he is. But not in quite the way he thinks. What does he think? I'll never know. Was he only being kind? Did he want me? I'll never know. So accept it, doll. I can't. I want to know. But you can't. I know. It might be worse, really to know. I know that, too.

Luke is looking at her in what appears to be astonishment.

Hey. Whatsamatter?

She has drawn up her left arm and is trying to see her watch.

I have to go home. My God, what time is it? I should've gone home long ago.

Luke shuts her eyelids with his fingers. She can feel his relaxation, his sleepiness.

You don't have to go. Stay the night.

Stacey's hands take in his jawbone, his collarbone, the brown hair under his arms.

Luke   I'd like to   but I can't

Why not?

Because   because

You want to sleep with me, all night, so why don't you?

I can't. I can't stay away all night. It's not possible.

You're a strange woman.

That's not being strange. The other would be.

Okay. That's your problem, I guess.

She dresses swiftly, and by the time she has her hair combed Luke is also dressed and standing by the door. He kisses her lightly.

So long, then. Stacey.

— I actually want to thank him. I want to explain myself to him, make myself real to him. I want to say – look, this is what I'm like. It would take too much time, and he's been patient enough.

So long.

The drive home is endless. Stacey hazards quick glances at her watch and each time finds that it is later than she imagined it could possibly be.

— I should've been home two hours ago. Okay, so Mac won't be home, but the kids will have been home for ages. What'll I say? What'll they think? I don't care. I don't give a damn. I do, though. Katie? Ian? Duncan? Jen? What if they think I've had an accident or something? What if they phone the police? They wouldn't – they'd phone Mac. God, just don't let them phone Mac. Okay, Sir, so that's not a proper request – you don't need to remind me. I refuse to feel quilty. Be patient, God. I will, no doubt. Just give a little time. Don't begrudge me a couple of free hours. I feel marvelous, if you really want to know. I feel set up. Luke. His is a little wider than Mac's but not quite so long. Bitch. Only a whore would compare. That's not true. Who could help it? It's not a qualitative difference, anyway. It doesn't matter a damn to me. That's not what is important. Would a guy think of it that way, though? I don't suppose so. They'd see it as a personal assessment or – how do I know what they'd think? Wouldn't it be strange if I could ever stop thinking in terms of *them* and *me*? Luke Venturi. I don't even know who he is. I know he's too young. Nine years – well, okay, nearly ten, then – that's not so much difference. Luke – you did want me. Didn't you? Did you? Well, nobody makes love with someone who absolutely repels them – he couldn't have, if he'd felt that way. He wanted me. He wanted *me*. Do we deceive ourselves by any chance, Stacey, doll? Very well, then, we deceive ourselves. Bugger off, voice. I'm happy as I am, at least momentarily. If only I could get out to see him more often. Luke, I couldn't get enough of you. I'd like to go to bed with you for seven days and seven unbroken nights. I'd like to start again, everything, all of life, start again with someone like you – with you – with everything simpler and clearer. No lies. No recriminations. No unmerry-go-round of pointless words. Just everything plain and good, like today, and making love and not worrying about unimportant things and not trying to change each other.

> Stacey, touching him too urgently – now, now, no time to waste, I haven't got all day. Stacey lacking any merciful robe.

— All right, all right. Don't tell me. I don't want to know. My God, I actually made love with someone other than Mac. *How could I?* I'm not like that. What do you mean – *that?* I feel just fine, to be truthful. I feel like about a million dollars or so. Let us not speak in such crude terms, kid. God, I feel set up like anything. My heavens, it's six fifteen. Faster, Stacey. The kids will be frantic.

Seven

STACEY pulls up in front of the house on Bluejay Crescent and scrambles out of the car, her arms filled with parcels of pajamas. Inside the veranda, Katie is standing, slowly rocking Jen in the old hammock. Jen is nearly asleep. Katie has been crying and has fairly obviously only recently stopped.

— What's the matter? I shouldn't have stayed away so long. It's worried Katie. Or is she just angry? How can I ever make up for it? Is Jen ill? Is that it? God, let Jen be all right. Don't let it be that. Please. I'll never go away again. I swear it.

Katie – what is it?

Katie leaves off swinging the hammock and goes to Stacey, stumblingly, putting her arms around Stacey's neck and her head on Stacey's shoulder.

Oh Mum

What *is* it, Katie? Please, honey, just tell me.

Jen

What about her? Is she all right? She isn't sick? Katie, I'm sorry I'm so late. I stopped in for coffee and then the traffic

— How can I lie to her like this and expect to hear the truth from her? Sure, so tell her the truth – would that make the situation any better? What's *wrong?*

No, she's not sick. She's okay. I think she was just

scared. Let's go into the kitchen, Mum. I don't want to tell you in front of her.

Okay, honey. Hush, Katie, love. Don't cry. Just tell me what happened.

In the kitchen, Katie sits down, her head bent, the flames of her hair covering her shoulders and breasts. She has stopped crying, but her voice is strained and there is a kind of bewilderment in it.

Well, I went over to Mrs. Fogler's to pick up Jen, like you asked me to. The door was open, see, and I was just going to ring when I heard Mrs. Fogler talking to Jen. It seemed kind of strange, what she was saying, so I listened for a minute. She was saying *The little fish doesn't want to get eaten up but she's silly, isn't she? She doesn't run away and hide. So the big fish catches her, see? Watch now – look what he's doing to her. Nasty – he's nasty, isn't he?* Maybe I shouldn't have done it, Mum, but I tore inside the living room without thinking, and Mrs. Fogler was kneeling beside the table where the fishbowl is, and she was holding Jen on a chair, I mean she had her hands on Jen's shoulders and wouldn't let her get down, and Jen was sort of squirming to get away and Mrs. Fogler was making her look. And the big goldfish had killed the other one and it was

Oh Katie

Then Mrs. Fogler looked up and saw me. Mum – she looked sort of – I don't know – frightened. I just grabbed Jen and brought her home and didn't say anything. I couldn't. I didn't know what to say.

Stacey puts her arms around Katie.

There, honey. You did right.

But what *is* it with her, Mum?

I don't know. I don't know. I should never have left Jen with her.

Katie looks up.

No – it wasn't your fault. You didn't know. How could you?

— Yeh, how could I? Maybe I should've, though. If I hadn't wanted so much to go out. Katie doesn't know any of that, or she wouldn't be so sympathetic. What's it done to Jen? Maybe nothing; maybe something I'll never know, something concealed, some unknown fear that'll be part of her mental baggage from now on.

I suppose not, but I'll never forgive myself all the same.

You shouldn't feel that way, Mum. Listen, don't worry, eh? Jen's okay now. I think this trauma thing is exaggerated, anyway.

Well, we won't leave her there again.

No. What do you think we ought to say, though? To Mrs. Fogler.

Gosh, Katie, I don't know. What could be said? Maybe it's better not to say anything. Maybe she'll say something.

Yeh. Maybe.

Stacey recognizes all at once the way in which she and Katie have been talking. *We*. They have never before encountered one another as persons. At the same time, Katie has been unwittingly calling her *Mum* instead of *Mother*.

Katie – thanks

For nothing. I thought I made a mess of it. I just snatched Jen and ran.

I would've done the same.

Really? No, you would've known what to say. You always do. I never do.

I don't always, either. Sometimes I think I hardly ever do.

Really?

Yeh.

Stacey makes the dinner and puts Mac's in the oven for him. She cannot eat, but when the kids have eaten, she takes Jen upstairs for her bath. Jen has wakened up fully by now and insists on having her entire collection of plastic ducks, cups and teapots in the bath with her. Having soaped and rinsed her, Stacey lets her play for a while, and watches while Jen scoops up the bath water and pours it out again. Jen sings to herself, unaware that she is doing so.

— Flower, you're beautiful. Is she really fragile or is it just my imagination? Her arms always look so thin. But Ian wasn't ever plump as a very young kid, either. Katie was, and so was Duncan, but that doesn't mean anything. Probably Jen's okay. Surely she'll talk soon. What's she feeling now? If only she could say. She doesn't look upset. How can you ever tell what's going on in anybody else's head? Maybe it was worse for Katie than for Jen. Or maybe not. Jen was squirming to get away, Katie said. Jen – I'm sorry sorry sorry. I shouldn't have gone out. I shouldn't have stayed away so long. I never will again. Oh? You won't, Stacey? You won't ever go out to Luke's again? Luke – I want you. I want to talk to you. I want to make love with you again – and again and again. I thought at the back of my head somewhere that I could do it only once, and then all demons would be laid to rest, laid in both meanings. I would know just once again the feeling of another man, and I would have done something that belonged only to me, was mine only, related only to me, nothing to do with any of them. Did I want to get back at Mac? Yes, that too. If it hadn't been Luke, it would've been somebody else, sooner or later. But it was Luke, and now I want him again, even now, already. Better to marry than burn, St. Paul said, but he didn't say what to do if you married *and* burned. I can't leave Jen with Tess any more. What is it with Tess? What can I do about it? You can't say to somebody, pardon me but maybe you ought to see a good headshrinker. Should I tell Jake? Probably he knows. He brought the damn things home. Should I tell Mac? Yeh, and have him say I'm making a fuss about nothing. He doesn't want to know anything difficult about me or the kids. Nothing. Okay, and now I don't want to tell him, either, so we're even. I can't ever get away alone now. Bertha, maybe? With Julian on her hands all day long, crabbing away at her, she's got enough to worry about. *I can't go out alone*. That's what it amounts to. Jen, honey, I love you. I love your thin arms and your wide grey eyes and that fine red-gold hair of yours. I love the way you sing without any words that nutty song you learned from Duncan, "I'm Bringing Home a Baby Bumblebee." I love you – and resent you. No, I don't. That's an awful way to feel. It may be, but I feel it all the same. I can't get away by myself because of you. And I have to get away sometimes. I have to. I'm trapped. I have to see Luke. *I have to*. Too many people here, too many crises I don't know how to deal with, too much yakkity-yak from all of us, too few words that tell any of us a damn thing about any of the others. With Luke, everything is simple. He doesn't complicate things. He says what he's thinking. Luke – you make love beautifully. It was lovely. Luke, it was lovely. I can still feel him in me. Goddam Tess. Stacey, that's barbaric of you. I don't care. I don't care. I want to get out of here and I can't and one day I'll forget that Jen was scared and I'll get mad at her for something that isn't her fault, for holding me here. God, Sir, don't let it happen that way. It may though. I have a terrible temper. I always have had. My mother used to say *Stacey, you have a terrible temper – you must learn to bank your fires*. How right she was, not that I saw it then, only thinking she'd never had any fires so couldn't know. But they're not that easy to bank. What if I slap Jen one day, suddenly, hard, without knowing I'm going to do it, just because she's here and young? God, don't let me. Stay my hand. I scare the hell out of myself when I think this way.

Come on, flower. Time to get out of your bath. C'mon – that's it.

> Newspaper story. Young divorced mother found in bathroom in catatonic state beside the body of her three-year-old son. A broken wine bottle had been plunged deeply into the child's chest. Photograph showed girl being led away, her face dull, absent, her hands darkly bloodied up to the wrists.

— She was a hophead, for heaven's sake, Stacey. Yeh. Nothing like that, nothing even remotely like that could happen here. And then again, anything that could happen to anybody could happen to anybody. Anything. When I think that way, my guts turn over. Even if I never lay a hand on Jen in anger, never, what if I become temporarily deranged some day, some day when I'm feeling the trap worst, and yell and scream at her? Just because she isn't yet school age and she needs me. You want to know something, God? Sometimes all I want to do is sit down quietly in a secluded corner and bawl my goddam eyes out. Okay, so you don't want to know. I'm telling you anyway.

Want some pretty-smelling powder, Jen? That's right – you sprinkle it on yourself. Hey, how about that? Now you smell like a flower as well as looking like one.

Stacey hugs Jen tightly and gently, wanting only to be aware of Jen's warmth and perfection. But as she does so, she recalls that *Hey, how about that?* is Luke's phrase.

Mac still is not home. Stacey puts Jen to bed and goes downstairs to round up the boys. Duncan is in the kitchen, his face pressed against the screen of the back door, his shoulders in an attitude of dejection.

Hi, honey. What's the matter?

Ian's upstairs and he won't let me in the room. It's my room, too.

What's the matter with him?

How should I know? He's mad at me. He's always mad at me.

Okay, I'll go and see.

Stacey goes upstairs again and tries the door of the boys' bedroom. It is locked.

Ian?

The voice that reaches her is sullen and suspicious.

Whaddya want?

Why won't you let Duncan in? Come on, open that door right this minute. What's the trouble, anyway?

He's a dumb moron and I don't want him in here.

Why can't I have my own room? I'm sick of sharing with him.

Because there are not enough bedrooms for you to have your own room, that's why. As you very well know.

Jen and Katie have got their own rooms. Why can't they share for change? I *hate* Duncan in here with me. He's always breaking my models and stuff. He hasn't got any brains.

Stacey feels her annoyance beginning, like a nettle sting in the mind.

Now listen here, Ian, you unlock that door, you hear? Duncan has as much right in there as you, and he isn't always breaking your models at all, and it's time for both of you to go to bed. All right. I'm going downstairs and I'll give you ten minutes. You open the door and we won't say any more about it.

Stacey goes back down to the kitchen. Duncan is still looking out into the back yard. Stacey sits down on a kitchen chair and finds to her surprise that she is crying.

— For heaven's sake, what's the matter with me? I don't know I don't know I don't know

Duncan turns and sees her. He looks shocked.

Mum – you're not *crying*, are you?

— Mothers don't cry. Only kids. Pull yourself together, Stacey.

No, not really. I just felt sort of tired for a minute, there. I'm okay now. Everything's all right.

Ian bawled today.

What?

He bawled. He never bawls, does he, Mum? But he did. I saw him. I guess that's why he's mad at me, maybe. He doesn't like people to see him bawling.

Duncan – tell me. What was wrong with him?

He – well, a bunch of us kids were playing out on the Crescent after school, and Ian went out on the road after the football, only he didn't see this car coming, and it just missed him. He said he didn't want to play any more and when I went to look for him, he was in the basement, bawling.

Oh Duncan – why didn't you tell me before? Before I went upstairs. I didn't know he was

Stacey rushes back upstairs.

— I was away away away with Luke making love with Luke and Ian was here and he might have been hurt. He might have been run over. Stacey, don't be a fool. You couldn't have stopped it even if you had been here. Maybe not, but even so even so even so. And Ian cried. Ian. Who never cries. Because of what happened to Peter Challoner and because Ian thinks about death – how much? Some people don't know they're ever going to die until it happens to them, but Ian knows he's going to die. He knows it will happen to him some day. He's ten, and he knows that already. Was it Peter's death that taught it to him? Or has he known for a long time, in ways I don't know anything about? Maybe he thinks of it as I've always thought of it, wondering what form it would take for me, what face it would wear, what moment in my time it would choose for our encounter, imagining it as sudden severed or seared flesh and then again imagining it as something to be fought for in senility when there isn't any strength for even that battle and they keep you going against your will on tubes and oxygen, the total indignity, imagining it in order to defeat it, like a kid I used to imagine the dead men below in the mortuary, conjure them up on purpose so they wouldn't take me by surprise, although in reality I never saw even one of them. I always thought that was why I thought about it, but Ian does too and *his* father deals in rejuvenating vitamins. Have I passed it on, along with the chromosomes and genes?

Ian?

Yeh?

Honey, I'm sorry I was cross. I didn't know – Duncan just told me – about the road – Ian, try not to let it upset you. It's all right now.

And from the bedroom, from behind the locked door, the sudden shrill desperate voice.

Can't you leave me alone? *Can't you just leave me alone?*

— Ian. Mac's words. Ian, don't – I can't bear it. And you can't bear the way I try to know, the way I try to enter your locked room, can you? All your locked rooms.

Stacey goes down to the kitchen without another word.

Duncan – you go to sleep in Daddy's and my bed for now, and I'll move you after a while. Ian's kind of upset.

Mac has just come in and has overheard.

What's the matter with Ian?

Stacey tells him. Mac sets down his briefcase and prepares to go upstairs.

He'll open the door all right. I'm not going to have that kind of temperamental display.

Mac – leave him.

Now listen here, Stacey, it's perfectly ridiculous for Duncan to go to sleep somewhere else just because Ian doesn't choose to open the door. He's got to learn to consider other people.

Yes, but he needs consideration, too.

He's damn well going to learn to show a little responsibility.

— My God, of course it's not Ian he's mad at. It's me. Only maybe he doesn't know it.

Mac starts out of the kitchen, but Stacey takes hold of his arm.

Mac, don't you dare go up there. Just don't. Ian has to be left alone for a while – he *has* to. Can't you see? You, of all people, ought to be able to see that. You got no business knocking Ian for wanting to be left alone occasionally.

Mac removes her hand from his sleeve. He turns and walks into his study.

Okay. Have it your way, Stacey. Do anything you like with them. Ruin them, for all I care.

Stacey looks at Duncan. His eyes are fixed on her face, but she cannot guess at all what he is seeing. Then he trudges upstairs. She hears him knocking very softly at Ian's door and after a few minutes, the door opens. The boys go to bed in silence, without speaking to one another.

— All right. I shouldn't have said that, in front of Duncan. But you shouldn't have, either, Mac. Damn you damn you damn you. Imagine saying *Ruin them, for all I care*. What in hell does he think Duncan's going to make of that? That I'm no good and Mac couldn't careless about any of them? Mac, how could you? Let me tell you one simple fact – whatever you're like, whatever you're thinking, whatever you're going through, I don't want to know, see? I just don't want to know. Not any more. All right, I don't have the guts to say it to you. But there it is. I hate you. I wish to God I'd never laid eyes on you. There it is.

Doorbell. Stacey answers it, and finds Julian Garvey standing inside the veranda. He is a small man, and with old age he has shrunken even more. He has a wispy tonsure of pepper-grey hair, and his seamed red mottled face resembles a surly gnome. With Stacey, he is invariably courteous, even exaggeratedly so. He saves his salvos for Bertha.

Evening, Stacey. I trust this isn't an inconvenient moment? If you're busy, just say so.

No, not at all. Come in, Julian.

Well, actually it was Mac I wanted to see, really. Is he home?

Yes, he's just come in. I'll call him. He's in the study.

Oh – well, maybe I could go in there? I just wanted to have a private word with him. Get his advice, you know. I've been seeing these Richalife pills advertised all over the place, and I sort of wondered

— Oh Lord. Sure. What else? You wondered if they'd restore your virility? Or prolong your life eternally? There's one born every minute. And Mac will sell them to you, too. Never doubt it. He's not the same guy as the one who told the pensioner on Grenoble Street that he needed encyclopedias like he needed a hole in the head. No. Mr. MacAindra has altered more than somewhat. Well, climb on the magic carousel, you stupid old bugger. Who gives a damn?

Sure, Julian. Come right in.

Stacey knocks.

Mac?

What?

It's Julian. He's here to see you.

Oh – okay. C'mon in.

The door opens and Julian goes in. Stacey pours herself a gin and tonic and saunters quietly near the study. Unfortunately the door is thick and the voices are not loud, so she cannot hear anything except a low mumbling. At last Julian emerges. Stacey sees him to the door. His hands are empty.

Mac said he didn't really think   man of my age, you know   well, I just wondered

Oh. Well, good night, Julian.

Good night, Stacey.

The study door is partly open and Stacey looks in. Mac is sitting at his desk with his head leaning against his outstretched hands, his palms covering his eyes.

— Mac? Mac, I'm sorry. You did right – are you wondering if you did, or cursing yourself for it? You're still the same guy at least in some ways and I'm the same too in some ways. I don't hate you. Maybe you don't hate me, either. I'm just sorry sorry sorry. For us both.

For three days Stacey prowls the house, unable to settle to any work. She prepares meals numbly, almost without noticing. She intends to go over and try to talk to Tess, but she does not go. On the fourth morning the doorbell rings and Tess is standing in the veranda. Involuntarily, Stacey glances around. But Jen is playing in the back yard.

Hi, Stacey. Have you got a minute?

Sure. Come in. Have some coffee?

Well, thanks. Don't make it specially.

No, I was just going to have some anyway.

I thought I'd pop over and see if you wanted me to mind Jen. I mean, when you get your hair done.

— Tell her. Say something. I can't. I don't know how. I'm embarrassed.

Oh – well, thanks, Tess. But I'm not getting it done this week.

Are you okay, Stacey? There's nothing wrong, is there?

N-no. I've just been feeling kind of tired these past few days. It's nothing. Everything's okay.

— Coward.

Well, I just wondered, seeing as you usually get it done about this time of week.

No, I'm fine. I'm – getting kind of sick of going to the hairdresser's every week. And she never does it the way I want it, anyway. I'm thinking of growing it and doing it myself.

Well, it's a time-saver if you do. I've always done my own.

Tess?

Mm?

Are you okay? Are you feeling all right? I mean, there's nothing worrying you?

Tess's eyes grow wide with question and alarm.

What makes you say that, Stacey? Do you think I don't look all right?

No, it wasn't that. Well, maybe I thought you looked a little worried or something.

Heavens, everything is all right. I don't know why you should think

— Tell her why. Say it. You've got to. I can't. She doesn't want to talk. She doesn't want to say anything about anything. Maybe she believes everything is all right. Maybe it *is* all right, actually. Maybe it didn't really mean anything, that day. Maybe it happened sort of accidentally, and she didn't give it a second thought.

Well, I'm sorry. I just wondered.

No, everything's fine. The doctor says my blood pressure's much better, and he's given me these new tranquilizers. Not that I really need them, but I'm very highly strung, as you know. I always was, even as a child. My father used to say *Tess, quit jumping around like a flea – you get on my nerves*. He was right. I always had to be doing something. I was always on the go. I'm thinking of taking up tennis again. What do you think?

Good idea. You probably need to get out more.

Oh, I go downtown a lot. I'm a great little bargain hunter.

Yeh.

Jake's got a part in a new six-episode series.

That's good.

Yes. He's playing opposite Fay Faulkner. She's a lovely girl.

So-so, I'd say.

Well, she's got that very dark hair and that absolutely white skin. Jake says she's very intelligent as an actress. He says not many of them are. He's trying out for TV again. It would be wonderful if he got in. They ought to take him on – he's got such an interesting face. He'd be so happy if he could. Not that he's not happy right now, in radio, but I mean he'd be even happier. Oh, I meant to say, Stacey, if you want any of the HATSHEPSUT line of cosmetics, I can give you Mrs. Clovelly's phone number.

Thanks. I'll let you know. I'm sort of overstocked at the moment.

I think they've made a lot of difference to my skin. I really firmly believe they have. Don't you think so?

Yes – I think they probably have. I always thought you had a marvelous skin, anyway, though.

It takes a lot of looking after, believe me. I've got one of those skins that has a tendency to be dry. It needs nourishment. I just have to keep at it.

Yeh, well maybe I should try the night cream.

— Tess. What's the matter with us? Or maybe you really are only talking about the outer skin? I don't know. I can't get through the sound barrier any more than I can with any of them. Is it only me who wants to? (Is it only I who want to?) Goddam. I can only break through with one person. Luke Luke Luke

I should be running along now, Stacey. Thanks for the coffee. You'll give me a ring when you want to leave Jen?

Yes. Sure. Thanks, Tess.

— I won't, though. Not ever again. And I don't know how to explain it. I'll have to quit going to the hairdresser's. I can't suddenly begin to take Jen along with me.

When Tess has gone, Stacey checks to make sure Jen is all right and then goes upstairs. She sits on the bed and looks at herself in the full-length mirror.

— I can't get out. I can't. There's no way. Not now. I've got to. I've got to see him again. I can't help it. It's not a luxury, it's a necessity. Look at that face in the mirror. You're thirty-nine, kid. Well, I don't know. Maybe I'm not so terrible to look at. That's odd – I look better to myself now than I did a week ago. Sure, and guess why. I do look better, though. I'm not a bad-looking woman. I haven't got wrinkles – well, not many, anyway – even though I don't plaster on the *Avocado Wrinkle Cream*. My legs are good, and so are my breasts. All right, I'm no glamour girl, but strong men wouldn't necessarily flinch at the sight of me. Luke thought I was all right. He liked it. He loved it. Oh my God, it was marvelous. I've got to see him again. And talk to him as well. He doesn't need to. Okay, I know it's crazy. I am well aware that it is even ludicrous. If it were the other way around, Luke ten years older, it wouldn't seem peculiar in the slightest, so why should it, this way? It isn't the number of years that count, it's the way people feel about each other. I'm damn well going to see him again. You can't. I'm going to. How? I don't know

– yet. That remains to be seen. Mac has a conference tonight. He won't be home until midnight, more than likely. Oh Stacey. The more you want to level with everybody, the less you do. I know. You don't need to tell me. Ease up on me, God, can't you?

That evening, when Mac has gone out again after dinner, Stacey puts Jen to bed and approaches Katie, who is doing her homework in her bedroom.

Katie – you remember Rosalind Ackerman? I met her at the Ancient Greek Drama course last winter, remember? She was over here a few times. Well, she phoned today and asked me to go over tonight – she's having a few women in for bridge. Would that be okay? You wouldn't mind? I wouldn't be late.

Katie looks up and smiles.

Sure, that's okay. You run along. Can you get the boys in bed first, though?

— Oh Katie, you're stabbing me to the heart.

Yes, of course. I'll get them tucked in before I go. Thanks, honey.

That's okay.

As Stacey is saying good night to Ian, he props himself up in bed on one elbow and looks at her, frowningly.

Mum – I don't feel very well.

Stacey's heart turns over. She puts a hand on his forehead.

Where don't you feel well, Ian? I don't think you've got a fever.

It's my stomach, like. I got this sort of an ache, right here.

— Could it be a reverberation from the car thing, the other day? Yeh, you think psychosomatic, and one day it turns out to be appendix, burst before anybody can do anything. They don't die of it any more. There's antibiotics. But I'm never convinced.

Show me where.

Right here.

Well, that's your stomach all right. It wouldn't be your appendix that high up. Did you eat anything different from anybody else today?

No, I don't think so. Grant and me had some salted peanuts. He bought them with his money.

Maybe that was it. Gee, I don't know, honey. I wonder if I should stay home? It isn't a sharp pain?

More like a dull ache, kind of. But then it comes in twinges, you know, and gets sharper.

— The old question. How serious? I never know.

Well, it doesn't seem all that serious to me, Ian. Listen, if it gets worse, you tell Katie, eh? If it got really bad, she could phone Doctor Spender. I won't be late. You settle down now, and try to sleep.

Okay. G'night, Mum.

Good night, honey.

Stacey calls good-bye to Katie and goes outside and into the Chev. The drive out to Luke's is interminable tonight.

— Blasted traffic. And I've got to be home by eleven at the latest. It isn't fair to put that responsibility on Katie. Would she know when to phone the doctor? It's hard enough even for me to know. But I don't think it was anything much. He didn't have a fever. What if someone's there, at Luke's? What if he isn't there? What if some other woman is there? What'll I say? I'll approach quietly, and if I hear voices, I'll just go away, that's all. If only he had a phone. He's really bushed out there. I guess that's the best way for him to be able to write. I wish I could be there to make meals for him. To sleep with him all night.

Luke is home and alone. He stands in the doorway of the A-frame, still wearing the Indian sweater with the bear mask design, his beard now recognizable as such.

— Too good to be true. Thanks, God. Travel now, pay later. Send me the bill at the end of the month. No – don't. Is he smiling? Or is he only trying to smile? I wish I hadn't come. It was madness. He's never yet asked me to come out. I've just arrived. What a situation to put him in. What can he do, short of ordering me off the premises? Luke, I'm sorry. I couldn't help it.

— Worse. That makes it even worse. How can I humiliate myself and yet not stop doing it? Luke – please – just once more.

Hi, merwoman. How's life?

Life? Oh, not bad, I guess.

Nice dress – bronze, like those chrysanthemums in fall.

That's because I'm at a bridge party.

Luke laughs, but a little wryly.

Yeh. I guess that's necessary. Well, come in.

Thanks. How's your work?

Luke leads here into the main room and shows her a pile of typed pages.

It's coming on. Only I'm beginning to see a lot of flaws in the structure. And I'm not sure the inventions are sharp enough – you know, like the perambulating statues of African statesmen in the Residence garden, in lieu of trees. Well, the hell with it. I wish I could take you out fishing. Would you like to go out in the cockleshell that we jokingly refer to as a boat?

— No. I'd like to go to bed with you, if you really want to know.

I'd love to, but honestly I can't stay very long

Well, let's have some coffee, then.

Luke puts the coffee on the stove, and she goes and stands beside him, putting an arm tentatively around him. He laughs, turns the stove low, and at last holds her tightly, his sex hard against her.

Who wants tea and sympathy? Let's have coffee and sex, Stacey, eh?

They make love on the rough wool rug, as before. Stacey's hands knead his shoulders, his ribs. She reaches a climax almost as soon as he is inside her, and again when he comes. When it is over, he outlines her face with his hands and kisses her eyelids.

Luke

Mm? I'm feeling no pain

Me neither. Or is it – I'm not, either?

Who cares?

I'm illiterate, Luke.

Who cares? You're pretty good, you know?

I didn't know. Tell me again.

You're great. I like it with you.

Oh Luke   I like it with you too   I love it

That's good   the coffee's boiling over

Don't tell me. Let me guess. You're a romantic at heart.

Well, sure. But have you ever wiped up scorched coffee from a stove?

They have the coffee without getting dressed, but the evening has an edge of chill, so Luke drags in a blanket and drapes it over them both. Stacey touches his chin.

Your beard is coming along nicely.

Yeh, well it's only because I'm too lazy to shave, that's all. I won't need to shave where I'm going this summer anyhow.

Where you going?

I was going to sign on with a fish boat, but I think maybe I'll just hitch and see what happens. If I can finish this book for better or worse in a couple of weeks, I'd like to go north again. That's a great country, Stacey. Ever seen it? Up the Skeena River – Kispiox, Kitwanga, crazy names like that. In some parts, nearer the coast, you drive along the edge of a mountain and the trees are like a jungle, only it's mostly evergreen, but all this fantastic growth, bushes and ferns and moss and jack pine, all crowding each other, dark and light greens, northern jungle, rain forest, and the damn road's so narrow you swear any minute you're going to plummet over into some canyon or other.

I've never seen it.

There's this place where there's a ferry. Is it Kit-wanga? Yeh, maybe. Anyway, this beat-up old raft crawls across the Skeena and it's attached to some kind of cable, and you think – man, if that cable goes, that's it – the river is wild as hell. But the old guy who runs it is calm as anything, probably been there forever. Charon. He talks very easy and slow, and you think – maybe it wouldn't be such a bad death, after all. And there's this village near there somewhere, Indian village, a bunch of rundown huts and everything dusty, even the kids and the dogs covered with dust like they were all hundreds of years old which maybe they are and dying which they almost certainly are. And they look at you with these dark slanted eyes they've got, all the people there. They come out and look at you with a sort of inchoate hatred and who could be surprised at it? Because lots of people visit the place every summer, for maybe half an hour. The attraction is the totem poles. And there they are – high, thin, beaked, bleached in the sun, cracking and splintering, the totems of the dead. And of the living dead. If I were one of them, the nominally living, I'd sure as hell hate people like me, coming in from the outside. You want to ask them if they know any longer what the poles mean, or if it's a language which has got lost and now there isn't anything to replace it except silence and sometimes the howling of men who've been separated from themselves for so long that it's only a dim memory, a kind of violent mourning, only a reason to stay as drunk as they can for as long as they can. You don't ask anybody anything. You haven't suffered enough. You don't know what they know. You don't have the right to pry. So you look, and then you go away.

Is it really like that?

Luke turns to her, sharply, unexpectedly.

I don't know. That's the way it looked to me. Why don't you come along and see, Stacey?

What?

Come with me. See what you make of it.

I'd like to, more than I could ever say. but I can't.

Why not, merwoman? You want to get away, don't you? I thought that was the whole point with you.

I've imagined myself getting away more times than I can tell you

Then do it.

Stacey looks at him, appalled and shaken by the suggestion of choice. Then she turns away again.

If I had two lives, I would. You think I don't want to?

I don't know what you want. That's what interests me. What *do* you want? The most, I mean.

I want to go with you.

Okay. Then it's settled.

No. Luke – I can't leave.

What can't you leave.

My kids and and

Luke nods and hands her her clothes. They dress without speaking. Then she lights two cigarettes and gives him one. He puts an arm around her.

It's okay, merwoman. I didn't really think you'd come along.

He withdraws from her, a little, and smiles. His voice has an undercurrent of mockery, but his fingers reassure her shoulder.

> *Ladybird, ladybird,*
> *Fly away home;*
> *Your house is on fire,*
> *Your children are gone.*

Stacey becomes tense, examining his face to discover his meaning, but not discovering it.

Luke – why did you say that?

He shrugs.

I don't know. It just came into my mind. Hey – how about that? I've scared you, haven't I? I'm sorry, Stacey. I didn't mean to.

I have to go home

Right now? You haven't been here long.

It's just that

— It's something I can't tell you. Sure, you level with him, Stacey, you just go ahead and do that little thing. You thought you could.

You don't have to explain, Stacey.

Luke, I want to come out again.

I know, baby. It's a pity that you can't.

How do you know I can't?

My horoscope told me. Or else I've got second sight. That must be it. You wonder if there's a third or fourth sight, and how that'll work out, in a thousand or so years. Merwoman

What?

I'm not twenty-nine. I'm twenty-four.

In Stacey's bones the sword turns with slowness and pain. Her hand circles his wrist, but she does not look at him.

Luke   why

Let it be. Just let it be, eh? Ease up on yourself, merwoman. You going to be okay?

Me? Sure – I guess so. Well

Well

But neither of them can say anything more. Then she goes. The car responds to her tension, and she drives fast, hardly seeing where she is going, her inner automatic pilot having taken over.

Luke, his Indian sweater bulking around him, recounting something. *She was once blessed by the Pope – it was just before she and my dad came to this country, and I was about two months old – she had me when she was fifteen, great for her, eh?*

— I'm not old enough to be every twenty-four-year-old's mother. But I'm old enough to be his mother. She's the same age as I am. I can't bear it. You have to, Stacey. There isn't anything else you can do. And in the end, he said what was so, but I didn't. I didn't say I lied about my age, too, but in the opposite direction. But he knew.

Ladybird, ladybird

— It's all right. He didn't have a fever, Ian. But what if

anything developed? What if it did turn out to be appendix, this time? Would Katie call the doctor or would she just wait, hoping everything would be all right and I'd get home soon? Look, it's all right, Stacey. Don't panic. Why did Luke have to say that idiotic rhyme?

Ladybird, ladybird

— Luke. I can't not see you again. I have to. I didn't even ask you exactly when you were going away. It isn't so easy for me to organize, getting out to your place. Don't you see? Stacey, have you forgotten what he told you? Let me tell you one simple fact, doll. He's only ten years older than Katie. Lots of girls marry men who are ten year older than themselves. Okay, God. That's enough. That's enough for the bill. Aren't you ever satisfied? Ease up on me, eh? Why did he ask me to go north with him? Why? What if I'd said yes? Would he have backed down? He knew I wouldn't say yes.

Bluejay Crescent. Stacey pulls the Chev to a jarring halt and climbs out. Mac is coming down the steps out of the house.

Mac? I thought you

Mac runs one hand through his brush-cut hair. His tall lank frame communicates tiredness and something else which she cannot guess.

Mac? Is everything okay?

He looks at her then, and his voice is drab, drained, dry.

Stacey, he's dead

Stacey crumples, and he grabs for her, pulling her up. Her eyes see nothing, not even Mac's face, and she does not know she is speaking the one mourning word.

Ian Ian Ian

Mac takes her by the shoulders, to steady her, and she suddenly can feel him trembling, trying to control it and not succeeding.

Stacey – it's not Ian. Christ, why should you have thought that? Ian's asleep. He's quite okay. It's Buckle.

Eight

Buckle? It's Buckle?

Stacey cannot take in the reality of Mac's words, or quite believe yet that Ian is safe and she herself essentially unpunished after all. She pulls away from Mac and looks at him as though suspecting she may read in his eyes some insane and subtle deception. But Mac's face reveals only his open hurt.

Yes. They've just phoned me.

They?

The police. They want me to go to the the to identify

— He can't say *morgue*. Oh my God – Buckle is dead. And my first thought was only relief that Ian was okay. Buckle can't be dead. He can't be. But he is. I never cared for him, but I wouldn't have wished him any harm.

> Stacey, seeing Buckle approach her, feeling him already inside her although they were still apart. Stacey wanting him, even there even in that room under the sightless eyes of the she-whale. Then the words he spoke, and the flung coins. Stacey, running down the linoleum-covered stairs, hating hating hating

— He won't be able to tell Mac any more lies about me. That's over. Serves him right. No – I'm not thinking that. I can't. That's terrible. I'm not like that. I'm not like that at all.

Mac, who never touches her in public in case somebody might see, suddenly puts his arms around her again and holds her cruelly tight, blind to the streetlights, blind to Bluejay Crescent, holding her not for her need now but for his own.

Stacey – he had an identification card on him and he had he had put me down as his next of kin.

She can feel his enormous effort not to break down. This one thing, the contrived kinship with its implications, he can bear less, almost, than Buckle's death.

Mac oh Mac I'm sorry

— Now he can't ever settle it with Buckle. They were friends for a long time and then they weren't and that was my fault. I can't bear that. No – yes, I can. I didn't do it all – it was Buckle, too, and for reasons further back than mine. Why did Buckle say that to Mac about me? Now Mac won't ever know, or be able to say he's sorry he told Buckle to go to hell. If he is sorry. He *is* sorry. But he wouldn't have been if Buckle hadn't got killed. Got killed? I don't even know what happened. Yes, I do, though.

Mac – how did it happen? It was on the road?

Oh sure. What else? Head-on collision. Both killed. At least Buckle was driving alone on that run.

Collision with another truck?

Yes.

With another truck like his? One of the big diesels? I mean I mean

I know. Yes. It was one like his.

I guess it would have had to be. He never played chicken except with

> The highway shivering past, honking, obstacle-laden. Buckle riding the truck like a jockey. Buckle, for God's sake, watch the road. His laughter, as he looked at the wheeling metallic ballet ahead. *I've never yet met a guy who didn't give way.*

— I thought it was pure ego, superconfidence, when he said that. But maybe after all it was only disappointment.

Mac turns to go.

I told them I'd be right down.

Mac – why do you have to go tonight? Wouldn't tomorrow be

I'd rather go now and get it over with.

I'm coming with you.

For a moment, she thinks he is going to refuse. Then he nods, and it is almost like a need-admitting sigh.

Okay, Stacey. Would you   would you drive?

Sure. Of course.

They take the Chev instead of the Buick because Stacey is more familiar with it. They drive in silence. Stacey is on the point of speaking, several times, but she is afraid she may say the one wrong or fuselike word which may make something explode in his head or heart and break the control which he will need, which he would never forgive himself for not having in this final encounter.

A grey building, not far from the waterfront, where the cheap-wine and meths drinkers gurgle and cough out intolerable lives. Only one light burning. The courtrooms, coroner's office, all black, shut, nobody home. Only the chapel of the violent dead holding its eternal hours, crash and stab not knowing nine to five. Stacey parks, and Mac puts a hand on her arm.

You stay here, Stacey.

I'll come if you want me to. I mean it.

Yeh. I know. I – thanks. But no.

The car door opens and closes; the door of the building opens and closes. Stacey smokes and waits.

— I couldn't have gone in. Yes, I could have. No, I couldn't. Well, if I'd had to, I would have. And yet I'm curious as well. How do they stash them away? In grey-metal drawers like outsize filing cabinets, chilled for preservation? I don't want to know. And yet I think of it, and what it would be like to be lying there, among them, one of them, not in a hospital with fragmentary hope but there with none, everything broken, drained out, gashed. Don't be ridiculous, Stacey. As if you'd know, if you were. But somehow I always think I would know it, be able to see myself battered and wrecked, extinguished.

Cameron's Funeral Home was never entered into by children. Stacey and her sister were forbidden. After Niall Cameron's funeral, when Stacey was grown and had her own children, she went in, forced herself in, to banish the long-ago cold tenants once and for all, send them back to limbo or even heaven, put them under that dutifully flower-prinked earth where they had lain years. Everything was dusty and jumbled, bottles once booze mixed with the jars and potions of a profession old as the pharaohs. Her mother found her there. *He would never let me clean here, your father wouldn't. He'd never let me tidy up. He said it would be a violation – I've never understood what he could have meant, but then he was always a little well you know.* Yes. And they'd turned and exited, locked up again, and Stacey went to the Liquor Commission and bought a mickey of rye but had to drink it in the bathroom and gargle with mouthwash after, and her mother said *You might consider that someone else might like to have a bath dear.* Sorry. Sorry. Sorry.

— Buckle? Buckle – I'm sorry. I'm sorry. I shouldn't have gone with you that afternoon. It was only because because. I didn't mean. Did it hurt you that Mac's wife would? Naturally it did. What do I do about that? One more piece of baggage to lug along. I wish I could get rid of all of it. I wish I could start all over, with things simpler, really simple, none of this mishmash. Luke? I want to see him again. I can't. I can't want to. But I do. He's not fifteen years younger. He is, though. Even if he weren't, how could I get out? Out of where I am. All I want to do, God, is go away and throw all of this overboard. What about the kids? Yeh. And Mac? I don't know. Whatever he's feeling, I don't want to know. But I do know. And I can't get rid of that.

Mac opens the door and climbs in. He lights a cigarette and does not look at Stacey. She eases the car into motion as though she has to be careful not to have it jolt. They travel home in silence.

— I can't say anything. God, don't let him tell me. I don't want to know.

Once home, they go to bed without yet speaking. Mac turns off the light on the bedside table. Then, almost immediately, he switches it on again and walks very quickly to the bathroom. Stacey, lying stretched straight and stiff as a brass curtain rail, hears him vomiting, flushing the toilet to mask the sound. Mercifully, no child wakens. Mac returns, crawls into bed, turns to her and puts his arms around her. He is crying now, the lung-wrenching spasms of a man to whom crying is forbidden. Shocked and frightened, she can only hold him, stroke his shoulders. Finally it subsides and he gets up and gropes for Kleenex and cigarettes. His voice is rough with self-condemnation.

Sorry.

Mac – you don't have to be

Well. It was just that

He returns to bed and lights cigarettes for both of them, something he has not done in a long time. They sit up in bed with the ashtray between them. Stacey cannot say anything to enable him to speak, because she is afraid of what he will say. But after a while he tries again.

Stacey – you don't mind me saying?

Of course not. How could I?

— I could. I do. But if he doesn't say, it'll be the worst thing that ever happened to him. What I lack is strength. Enough strength. Enough calm. Just give me enough to boggle through this one night, God, and I'll never ask for anything again. Yeh – I know. You've heard all of that before.

Mac speaks in an untoned voice, at least to begin with.

His back was broken, so he looked   twisted sort of and his head was was

Buckle Fennick, prince of the highway, superstitious as a caveman, Buckle who could swagger standing still, now lying stilled once and for all, Buckle with torn eyes unsocketed, blood wiped boredly away by attendants but smears still on the dark skin of his Indian-like face

Sh   sh   it's all right

He hadn't changed the identification card, Stacey. Not even after he phoned me that time. He left it the way it was. Me as his nearest

I know

Why? How could he? I don't get it. You know, I never did that well by him.

You did so. You did.

I always kind of resented how much he came around.

You never said. He didn't know. I didn't, either.

Well, how could I say? It was something that happened a long time ago

It is a time they have seldom spoken about, Stacey and Mac. Their children will learn it from books.

Preceded by pipers, the men of the Queen's Own Cameron Highlanders marched through the streets of Manawaka on their way overseas. Stacey, fifteen, watched them go, the boymen whom she soon might have known, perhaps married one if they had stayed. Nearly all the Manawaka boys of that age joined the same regiment. That was the war, to Stacey. She felt at the time ashamed of her own distance and safety. But after Dieppe, she could never again listen to the pipes playing *The March of the Cameron Men*. Even twenty years later, it remained a pibroch for them. The rough-fibered music forced mourning on her as though it had perpetually happened only the day before.

You mean in the war?

Yes. I didn't understand it very well and I thought maybe I was just imagining things

What was it?

In Italy. Quite near the end. At that point we were cleaning up. You know, sweeping all before us, like. And maybe careless. Anyway, there was this bridge – funny, I can see it right now, a little brick bridge, those Roman arches, been there for centuries, I guess. Buckle and I were on supply transport, truck full of rations, spelled each other off. He was driving, and you know how he drives. Bat outa hell isn't in it with him   and how we got separated from the convoy I'll never know because I hadn't had any sleep the night before and he hadn't either but it didn't seem to affect him so much. I dozed off and when I wakened there we were on this godawful road all by ourselves and he said he had looked at the map and figured a short cut which I thought was lunacy but try to tell him anything. Anyway, there we were at this bridge and I said let's get out and have a look first and he said – God, Stacey, I can hear the way he said it – he said, *Okay, chickadee, you get out and walk because I'm driving across*. I was a kid – only just turned twenty, and I didn't like to be reminded. It made me bloody angry, because he always thought he was so goddam tough and all that, and I guess I thought he was being patronizing, but I wasn't going back on what I'd said, so I did get out. He went bowling on, not waiting for a check and

Go on – say it.

Well

Say it.

The bridge blew. Mined. It went before Buckle got properly onto it, or there wouldn't have been much of him left to pick up, but the truck was thrown and flung half into the river, which wasn't that deep. I hauled him out. He had three broken ribs and concussion – I only learned this later – at the time I thought every bone in his body was broken. He kept bleeding from his mouth and nose. He was unconscious. I thought he'd had it. I thought he'd choke with the blood in his throat, so I – but I didn't really know what the hell to do. After what seemed about a year, I found a farmer with a donkey cart, and finally we got back to the other road and met up with the last of the convoy. I don't know, Stacey – that trek in the cart, it was weird, like it was only being imagined or some such thing. It wasn't that I hadn't seen worse things – nothing like that. But Buckle kept coming to, just for a few seconds at a time, and from the way he looked   it wasn't only because he was in pain   it was something else entirely

Mac – what bugs you?

Mac stubs out his cigarette and lights another. She can now see him, her eyes having adjusted to the dark. His face shows nothing. His voice is so plain as to be almost casual.

I couldn't figure it at the time. But later on I thought maybe it was just that I hadn't done him any favor. I hadn't done anything he wanted me to do.

So then you had to take him on for life? Because

— Who is this guy? Why did I never know?

It sounds crazy I guess.

It doesn't sound crazy. Mac – stop beating yourself. You're not God. You couldn't save him.

That's only too obvious.

Not obvious enough, maybe. Mac?

Yeh?

I never went to bed with him.

Mac reaches out and puts a hand tentatively on one of her breasts.

I believe you now. I wish to Christ I had before. I just felt   I don't know

Look – I might have. I guess I actually might have. But that wasn't what he wanted. I don't guess he was all that interested in women, Mac. That was why Julie left him. He liked it with himself but with somebody looking on.

Oh Jesus

Would it have been better if I hadn't told you?

No. It's better this way. It's   believable

Maybe he wanted you.

Mac involuntarily tenses.

Yeh   maybe

Did it scare you, that?

Christ, Stacey, we're talking a lot of bullshit. We better go to sleep.

Would it have been the end for you if I had gone to bed with him? In a way it wouldn't have mattered.

Maybe not. But you didn't.

No. I didn't.

— But I did with Luke, and you don't know that and I can't tell you because would it do any good to tell you? I don't think so. I want to, but I can't. Maybe it'll come out twenty years from now just like this about Buckle has come out now. In the meantime, we carry our own suit-cases. How was it I never knew how many you were carry-ing? Too busy toting my own.

Stacey?

Yeh?

— What now? Whatever it is, I can't take it.

About Delores

Who?

Delores Appleton. That girl.

Oh yeh. Her. What?

I did.

— What does he expect me to do? Throw a fit? I'm de-lighted. I'm not the only one

Oh?

Only once, though. And only after I thought you'd gone to bed with Buckle.

— Thanks. Heap coals of fire on my head. I'm made of asbestos.

Oh?

Yeh. But it wasn't it wasn't well I could see it wasn't what she needed and what she needed I couldn't

How do you mean?

Well I guess she really needs to be cared about by some guy over a long time

— Oh Mac. Like I have been, by you, come hell or high

water, in some way or other. Go ahead – stab me to the heart. Maybe I'll undergo a change of heart. The new one will be plastic and unbreakable. And yet, goddam it, you did want her before, and couldn't admit it until I'd given you some kind of cause for permission.

Yes. I can see that. I guess she does. Mac – I don't mind   honestly

Don't you?

Well

— Does he *want* me to mind?

Mac – we'd better try to go to sleep   seven o'clock isn't that far off

Yeh   you're right

Good night, Mac.

Good night, Stacey.

After a while, he is asleep but Stacey still is not. Something remains to be done. Gingerly, she edges out of bed, so as not to waken him, partly because he needs to sleep and partly because she could not explain. She goes into the boys' room. Ian is sleeping, on his left side as always, his forehead slightly damp with sweat. Stacey does not touch him. She only listens to hear very definitely his breathing.

EVER-OPEN EYE   TROOPS PARACHUTING INTO ANOTHER COUNTRY   THE COMMENTING VOICE IS BUSINESSLIKE, IN-TERPRETING DEATH AS NUMERALS

How come you never take us to the beach, Mum?

I will, Ian.

Yeh, but summer holidays started one week ago – one whole week – and so far we haven't been down once.

Yeh, that's right, Mum. Ian's right. You *never* take us to the beach. It's not fair.

Okay, okay, Duncan. We'll go tomorrow.

EVER-OPEN EYE   POLICE TURN HOSES ONTO RIOTING NEGROES IN A CITY'S STREETS   CLOSEUP OF A BOY'S FACE

ANGER PAIN RAW THE WATER BLAST HITS HIM WITH
THE FORCE OF WHIPS HE CRIES OUT AND CRUMPLES AND IS
SWEPT ACROSS THE PAVEMENT LIKE A LEAF LIGHTLY DIS-
CARDED FROM SOME TREE

Is that a promise?

Yes. Yes, it is, Ian. I should've taken you before. I
know. I'm sorry. We'll go tomorrow. Jen too.

> Duncan and Ian last summer at the beach, wres-
> tling and wisecracking, brown skinny legs and
> arms, the shaggy flames of their hair, their skin
> smelling of sand and saltwater. Sea-children, as
> though they should have been crowned with fronds
> of kelp and ridden dolphins.

— Luke? I could tell you. I could talk. How can I with
Mac? He's got enough to worry about. I can't upset him
any more. I mustn't. If I could just talk, Luke, nothing
else, just talk

*The totem poles are high, thin, beaked, bleached in
the sun, carvings of monsters that never were, in that far
dusty land of wild grasses, where the rivers speed and
thunder while the ancient-eyed boatman waits. Luke is
walking beside her. Luke, I'm frightened to death of life.
It's okay, baby – you're not alone – I'm with you there.*

> Luke in his Indian sweater, his beard brown and
> beginning to be soft. *Merwoman* – What? *I'm not
> twenty-nine. I'm twenty-four.* Luke, before that,
> sitting cross-legged (was it?) on the Arabic-pat-
> terned rug. *She had me when she was fifteen –
> great for her, eh?*

— I can't see him again. He doesn't want to. He knew
I'd lied about my age. He probably thinks I'm older even
than I am. Okay – big deal, Stacey. You've done what
thousands of other women have done. Don't I know it?
That's what hurts the most, maybe. Shameless shameful
attempt at rejuvenation. Pitiful, really. By Christ, I loathe
that thought. The only blessing is at least I don't have to
worry about being pregnant. Sure, count your blessings,

kid. Go ahead and do that. *I Was Pollyanna's Mum*. A ray of sunshine. Face it – he was only being kind. I asked, and he didn't say no. Was that all? Wasn't he lonely out there? Didn't he need a woman? He probably needed a girl, and that is precisely what he will get and maybe he will tell her about me. *There was this middle-aged old doll, see, and* No. I won't think of it.

Katie's voice shrilling from the kitchen.

Mum! Granddad's here.

Oh – okay, Katie. I'll be right there. The dinner's all ready. Where's Dad?

How should I know?

Stacey flicks off the TV and gathers Ian and Duncan.

Come on, kids. Go and say hello to Granddad.

Duncan eyes her doubtfully.

What'll we tell him about Sunday school? He won't like it.

You don't need to tell him anything. I'll tell him.

What'll you say?

Stacey's voice is sharper than she intended.

Listen in, then, why don't you, if you're so curious?

— That was a hell of a thing to say. I take it out on Duncan, just because he's quite rightly concerned at how Matthew will feel that the kids have quit going. I told them they could quit, because I was sick of that particular sham, and I nearly fainted with surprise when Mac didn't even argue, but now do I feel good about being honest for once in my life? No. I reproach myself and wonder if I'm denying them something for which they'll later reproach me. And I don't know how to tell Matthew, either.

Sorry, Duncan. I didn't mean it to sound like I was mad. I don't know how to tell Granddad, either.

Duncan puts his hand in hers.

Well, you'll think of something.

— Don't bank on it, boy. I wish I had your confidence in me. I'd be a world-beater. Your temporary confidence, that is. Ian's outgrown it, nearly, and Katie lost it long ago. And yet in some ways not. Look at how she was that day with Tess. She thought I would have known what to say.

Matthew is Sunday-dressed, immaculate as always, his eyes a little vaguer to Stacey's view than last week, his straight determined body held that way with a little more difficulty.

Stacey, my dear. How are you?

Just fine, thanks. How're you?

Oh, pretty well. I can't complain. The apartment's very hot these nights and I haven't been sleeping too well, but apart from that, everything's fine.

Why don't you ask Doctor Spender for some sleeping pills?

Matthew shakes his head firmly.

No. I'm sure that it's not a good idea to rely on external props of that nature.

Yeh. Well, you could be right

— Praise God I finished off the triple-strength gin and tonic in the TV room and didn't bring the glass up with me. Well, I haven't been stoned since that time with the stove. I don't guess Matthew would think that sufficient cause for feeling heartened, though. He'd never be able to get over the fact that it happened at all.

I'm sure everyone sleeps as much as they actually require. I don't suppose I require quite so much sleep any more. All the same, it's nice to get away from the apartment. It's much cooler here.

— He doesn't get out enough. I know it, and what do I do about it? Bugger all.

I – I'm taking the kids to the beach tomorrow. Why don't you come along?

Oh no – I couldn't do that. It would be too many for you   the car   too crowded

No it wouldn't. Katie's not coming. She goes with her friends by bus. The boys and you can go in the back seat.

Well, it would be very nice, but

— Look. Either come or don't come but please for mercy's sake don't make me persuade you because I just may not do that little thing.

Oh come on. It'll do you good.

Well, perhaps I will, then. It would be very nice

Good. We'll pick you up about two.

Well, it's very nice of you, Stacey.

— No, it damn well isn't. You don't know. Don't kid yourself – I'll regret it. You'll fuss like fury every time a kid puts a foot in the water, and I'll get silently to screaming pitch. Oh boy. I can hardly wait.

Stacey goes to the study door and knocks.

Mac?

Yeh?

Dinner's ready. Your dad is here.

Okay.

— What's he doing in there? Accounts? Sales reports? Mourning? I don't care, whatever it is. Or I don't want to care. All I want to do is get dinner over with. Why we have to change from Sunday lunch to Sunday dinner, every summer, I do not know. It's supposed to be so we can go out for long relaxing drives in the day. Mac has been in that goddam study since eleven this morning, emerging only for a sandwich at one. Let the kids scream and roar. Let me go out of my mind, nearly. Fat lot he cares. Damn you, Mac, don't you think I might ever like to get away by myself? But no. Oh Stacey – ease up, can't you? Buckle was his best friend. Strange – I told the kids, and they said hardly anything and they haven't mentioned it since. I don't know how they feel, or if they know that Mac is feeling anything at all.

Mac unlocks the bolted door and comes out of the study. He brushes past Stacey without looking at her and goes upstairs to the bathroom. But his face has passed close to her, close enough for her to be able to see that he has been crying.

— Mac   listen   tell me

But it is not the time, and there are too many people

around, so nothing can be said even if it could be said.

The following evening, Mac is home from work earlier than usual. Stacey pours him a drink, expecting him to go down to the TV room. She drinks her own while getting the dinner. Mac stands in the kitchen doorway, glass in hand, propping his height against the doorframe, and now Stacey notices for the first time that his brush-cut is growing out and the auburn of his hair looks almost like itself again. She does not know whether to mention it or not. If she says it is an improvement, he may take it as a criticism of his previous appearance. Alternatively, he may realize that if he intends to keep a brush-cut he ought to have it trimmed. She decides not to say anything.

— He's got something to say to me. What's the bad news now? Oh God, I didn't mean that. The way his face looked yesterday

Stacey?

What?

Thor's giving a party. At his place.

Oh God. When?

Tomorrow.

Tomorrow? My hair's a mess. I went in the water with the kids today. And I can't get it done.

Why not, for heaven's sake? The hairdresser can't be that booked up. If so, find another one.

It's not that. It's

— Doesn't he ever get himself in these fixes? Is it only me? How can I explain? I still don't know what to do about Tess. If she sees me going out, I could say I'm taking Jen downtown for clothes. Yeh, but then later she'll notice I've had my hair done. Hell.

Mac is frowning.

Honestly, Stacey, why you have to make everything so complicated I just do not know.

It's okay it's okay I'll get my hair done don't worry. Do we really have to go?

Naturally we have to go. What do you think? What would Thor think if we didn't?

Search me. What would he think?

He'd think – oh, for Christ's sake, Stacey, why do we have to go on like this? You know damn well what he'd think.

— His voice. Tired. Beat. And I go on and on about nothing. I don't want to go to Thor's. I don't want ever to see that character again.

I'm sorry.

And look – this time please don't

I won't I won't. I won't. I'll drink tomato juice, like him.

Yeh, I can see it all now.

Ease up on me, Mac.

Me ease up on *you?* I was only

Okay. I know. Listen, could you call the kids for dinner?

In the morning, Stacey washes and sets her own hair. When it is dry, she brushes it out, sitting in front of the dressing-table mirror in the bedroom, with Jen on the floor going through the large morocco leather jewellery case which contains Stacey's earrings. Stacey flings down the brush, grabs her comb, re-combs and back-combs, squirts hairspray thickly over the total effect, then angrily runs her hands through, tousling and dishevelling.

What a sight. Why wasn't I born with beautiful fine red hair like you and Katie, flower? Thor will take one look at me and say *Who let her out of the zoo?* Well, I won't go, that's all. How can I? No – the heck with it – I will so go. I'll say *Oh Mr. Thorlakson how do you like my new wig? On sale at Woolworth's.* Yeh. Laugh now. What am I going to do?

Babble babble mutter

Look, sweetie – if you don't want to talk, don't talk. But just don't give me that halfway stuff, eh?

— That's marvelous. Blame it all on her. For a second, there, I really wanted to swat her.

It's okay, honey. Everything's okay. C'mon – I'll have some coffee and you'll have some juice and we'll feel a lot better.

— Everything's okay. Everything's just dandy. Oh Luke. I want to go home, but I can't, because this is home.

By that evening, Stacey has managed to tame and subdue the tangled jungle of her hair. Jen is in bed. Duncan, Ian and Katie are looking at TV. Stacey is wearing her black sheath dress, supposedly slenderizing. She tugs at the waist, trying to straighten the wrinkles in the material, but her hips are against her.

Do I look okay, Mac?

Mac is looking at his watch.

Fine fine you look fine. Aren't you ready *yet?*

Coming coming. Right this minute.

— Still the same. Same drill, same marching tunes whistled by us both.

Thor has not risked his apartment. The party is being held on the roof of the building, an extensive patio-like square, which has been prudently fenced in with chicken wire to a height of some eight feet, for the area is habitually rented for tenants' parties and the management does not wish to be sued by widows whose husbands have been accidentally splattered onto the far-down pavement below. The wire is threaded discreetly with green-leafed vines, placed with just enough gaps to provide one view of the city on each side. On top of the leaves, at regular intervals, small pink plastic flowers have been attached, as being more reliable than the live variety. Round white-painted tables with scrolled white-painted metal legs are sprinkled here and there, and potted rhododendrons still bear the brown corpses of this spring's flowering. At one end is the bar, draped with a purple and gold RICHALIFE banner, and behind the arrayed bottles and siphons stands a worried-looking boy in a white drill jacket.

Most of the salesmen and their wives and the office staff are already here, in knots and clusters, drinking rye and proclaiming in voices which will carry as far as Thor their intentions of alternating each one with plain ginger ale.

Stacey grins and nudges Mac in order to overcome the ice which seems to have become lodged in her stomach.

So much for his tomato juice campaign, eh?

Sh. And for God's sake don't point it out. And don't

Stacey's upsurge of rage wipes out all memory of Mac's pain over Buckle, all memory of his worry about Thor.

Okay. Fine. I get the message. I'll be a campaigning teetotaller if you like. How be if I get an ax and break up the bar?

Christ Christ why do you always   if you're going to start *that*, then we may as well turn around right now and go home

Sh, for heaven's sake. I won't. I promise. Don't talk so loud.

Me talk loud? What about *you?*

Sh sh sh   here comes the angelman

Thor approaches like a mobile tower. He is dressed in a suit of pale pigeon-grey, and his turquoise eyes gleam flatly, exuding cordiality but betraying nothing of himself. His silver hair is ruffled very slightly and attractively by the light night wind.

Stacey   Mac   well, *hi* there. Wonderful to see you. How have you been, Stacey?

Oh just fine thanks

No more stigmata ha-ha?

Oh   yeh   well   ha-ha   no

— Mean bugger.

Now – what'll you have to drink, Stacey?

Mm – Coca-Cola please.

What? Hey, you don't *have* to.

Mumble

Could it be that the Program is reducing your need

for stimulants? How do you find you are, smoke-wise?

Madness seizes Stacey. Her smile glints up into his face.

Oh, I'm tons better. I hardly smoke anything at all now. And caffeine-wise I'm like a new woman. And golly, the kids have got so much energy now that I may have to put them back on to dreary old cod-liver oil, in sheer self-protection ha-ha.

She feels Mac's fingers digging into her elbow. Thor turns the microscope of his eyes upon her.

Well well. You don't say. Well, that's great, isn't it? Now, if you good people will excuse me, I see the Storeys have just come in.

He departs. Mac glowers.

You certainly overdid *that* bit.

Stacey shrugs. She is light-headed, euphoric, adrenalin-laden.

Not to worry. Nobody wins them all.

— I couldn't care less. Less than absolute nothing do I care what Thor thinks of me. Am I deliberately trying to sabotage Mac's job? There's a thought. I don't think so, but I might be. How can you tell? Oh Katie, imagine thinking that I always knew what to say. Well, the hell with it. I will not be intimidated by that white-haired boy, that hybrid offspring of a moronic lion and a lady wrestler. Thor – what a name, anyway. Even if you were christened that, imagine keeping it. If I knew any good hexes, I'd sure put one on him. I will carry off this evening with tremendous dignity and poise if it's the last thing I ever do. I'd give my eyeteeth for just one large Scotch. But I won't. Damned if I will.

Mac has drifted off to talk to Mickey Jameson. Stacey perceives that a small detachment of lone wives is making its frilly way towards her. She recognizes them but is totally unable to remember any of their names.

Hi there, Stacey.

Oh, hi. How *are* you? Nice to see you again.

Yeh. Say, this is some *place*, eh? I was just saying to

Joanie, here, this really is a lovely spot for a party, isn't it?
Yeh   lovely

— Joanie Storey. Praise the Lord. Now get to work on
detecting the others, oh female Saint.

The babble and babel of voices go on, rising to crescendo, to cacophony. Stacey shouts questions and answers. How many kids you got? What grades are they in?
It's been a pretty good summer so far, hasn't it? Yeh, no
rain to speak of.

> The shore of the Sound. The huge water-whitened
> log, and herself perched on it. The black water
> lighted streakily by stars. Luke. The A-frame.
> *What's the bad news? What's with you? I took off.*
> *Well, don't worry. Sometimes people do.* Then,
> later, after what he said about the kid in the Cariboo, the one whose mother took off. *Stacey, you*
> *don't need to be sorry. It hurts?* Yes. *Well, go*
> *ahead and bawl. No shame in that. You're not*
> *alone.*

— I am, though. I am now. Why did it have to happen
like that? Why couldn't it have been different – Luke older
– me unattached? If only I could get out of here. *If only I*
could get out. What if everybody is thinking that, in some
deep half-buried cave of themselves? What an irony that
would be. If that were so, you'd think we ought to be able
to move mountains. But it doesn't happen that way.

Stacey's resolve breaks at eleven thirty and she goes
to the bar for a double Scotch. She drinks half of it in a
mouthful. Then she sees the diversion which is happening
on the other side of the plateau, an entertainment for men.
Somebody has produced a large number of beach balls, in
as many colors as Richalife pills, scarlet jade azure apricot. The men are busily pelting one another. The laughter
is hoarse, explosive.

Here y'are, Mick. Catch!

The ball flies strongly and catches Mickey Jameson
on the shoulder and off guard, nearly knocking him over.
The thrower roars gleefully.

Pow! Gotcha!

Stacey stares as the game gets rougher. A number of other women are also watching. Some of them are clapping and cheering. Some are standing in silence. Then Thor bounds like an outsize faun into the middle of the group. He, too, is laughing. He picks up a beach ball as though it were the world and hovers for a moment with it, searching.

Mac has not been participating. He is standing with a glass in his hands at the extreme edge of the group, looking on. Thor makes as though to throw the ball directly ahead, then abruptly swings around and sends it in the opposite direction. Mac sees it coming too late. It catches him squarely in the face. His neck jerks back, and Stacey's guts turn over. A few men gasp and a few women shriek titteringly. Then the clapping and laughter go on as before. Mac's head rights itself and Stacey can now see the dribble of blood from his nostrils. His fists clench and unclench and clench again. Stacey can see his jagged breathing. Then Thor's voice.

Hey – *sorry*. You oughta been looking *out*, fella.

Mac's voice is low but steady.

Yeh. I'll know better next time.

You're not *hurt*, are you?

No. It's nothing.

The game breaks up and chatter fills the gaps. Somebody puts a record on, and dancing begins. Stacey sees Mac going through the door which leads to the lower regions. She follows him. He is wiping his face with his handkerchief. They go into the elevator without speaking. Then outside and into the car.

Do you want me to drive, Mac?

Yeh. I guess you better. Still a certain amount of stars inside my head.

Goddam him. Goddam him. Goddam him.

Mac's voice is tight and controlled, grating.

Yeh. It would be nice to know why he's got it in for me. One of life's mysteries.

At home, Stacey makes coffee and takes it upstairs. Mac is already in bed, sitting up and smoking.

How is it now, Mac?

Oh, okay. It wasn't anything much. It's what's behind it

I know.

He turns to her, propping himself on an elbow.

You know something, Stacey? I damn near hit him as hard as I could. For a second, there, it was almost like an automatic reflex. I didn't care about anything. I couldn't even look ahead as far as any consequences. I thought afterwards – I wonder if a lot of murders are done that way? Not that I would've been able to do him that much damage – but you know what I mean?

Yes. I know. What stopped you?

Mac shrugs and lights another cigarette from the end of the first.

I don't know, really. You, I guess.

Me? How come?

Well – the kids and you, and me with no job at my age

Mac, you're forty-three. You talk as though you were a hundred. Has it bugged you so much? The possibility of being without a job? You're a damn good salesman. They're in demand.

Yeh, I know all that. It's a hangover from the past, I guess. Also, it isn't so easy to re-establish yourself. I've done better, at least financially, in this job than I ever have. Not that that's saying much.

Stacey is shocked by the bitterness in his voice.

What do you mean? You've done all right, Mac.

I would've liked to do better. You know – something that meant something. I won't, now. I guess that's why I had to convince myself that Richalife was pretty terrific.

Stacey's hands are shaking. She sets the coffee cup down on the bedside table.

— Now is a fine time to tell me. Why didn't he tell me before? Okay, I know why.

Mac – why didn't you say all this before? What do you really think?

About the firm? I think it's a load of crap. I don't suppose the bloody pills actually do anybody any harm, though. But probably I'd sell them even if they did.

Stop it. You've got to. You mustn't be that tough on yourself. Look what all you've done.

Yeh, just look

But why didn't you ever say? Why didn't you level with me?

What good would that have done?

It would've   it would've

Mac's voice is abrasive, bound with ropes of an effort not to let go, an effort which almost doesn't work.

No, it wouldn't. It's my problem. Can't you see? It's got to be.

— I see. Maybe I do begin to see. If he doesn't deal with everything alone, no help, then he thinks he's a total washout. Thanks, Matthew – you passed that one on all right, but at least you had your Heavenly Father to strengthen your right arm or resolve, to put the steel reinforcing in your spine. Mac's got only himself. And if he doesn't speak of it to some extent, one of these days he'll crack up.

Okay, I guess it has to be that way, Mac. If you insist. It would've helped me, though. It would've made me feel you needed me, even just to talk to.

You mean you ever doubted *that*, Stacey?

Yeh. I doubted it all right.

Oh Christ. How could you?

I don't know. But I did.

Mac turns away from her, as though at the moment of turning closer or being forced there by innumerable and to her unknown memories, he still must keep private his face, his eyes.

How could I tell you it scared the hell out of me when Thor needled me? He's been doing it in various ways a lot of the time. That would've made me look pretty useless, wouldn't it, to be bugged that much by a thing like that?

Not to me. Only to yourself. And that's crazy, Mac. You're not made of granite. Nobody is.

Why do you think I've worked like the devil? Just so he couldn't point to anything which would give him a real excuse to get rid of me. What else did you expect me to do? Christ, Stacey, the mortgage company isn't going to wait for the payments, is it? And Katie'll be ready for university in another three years.

— He took us all on at a time when most of us didn't then exist. I guess he wouldn't ever believe he's brave.

I know. I know. I know. I didn't expect you to do anything else. I always blame myself that we've got so many kids. Not that four is all that many but you know what I mean like, Duncan

You blame yourself? But that's insane, Stacey. Anyway, that's all in the past.

The past doesn't seem ever to be over

Mac stubs out his cigarette and she does the same. He leans across and switches out the light.

We've gotta get some sleep, Stacey. It's past one. I got a million things to do tomorrow.

Yes. Mac – are you going to stay? With the firm? Now?

He hesitates before replying. Her eyes, unused to the darkness, cannot discover anything from his face. When he speaks, it is very slowly.

I don't know. I just don't know. I don't see how I can stay and yet I don't see how I can leave, either.

— I know what you mean. I've felt the same myself. What can I say that'll be any use?

Nothing comes to her, so at last she turns over on her side and after a while she falls asleep.

The place is a prison but not totally so. It must be an island, surely, some place where people are free to walk around but nobody can get away. The huts are made of poplar poles chinked with mud and they have flat roofs where the people sleep. There is a ladder leading up to each sleeping plateau, and when she and Mac are safely on top, they pull up the rope ladder after them. The children are not here. They are in another place, grown and free, nothing to worry about for her at this moment. Lying together on the bed of leaves, she and Mac listen to the guards' boots. The legions are marching tonight through the streets and their boot leather strikes hard against the pavements and there is nowhere to go but here

Nine

THE GULLS fly flashingly above the sun-lightened water, then latch on to air currents and glide so slow-motion that they seem to be hovering unmoving in the morning bright air at the city's rim where the long-shoremen shout and the vessels move in ponderously to be unladen like great sea cows swimming in to be milked.

Stacey looks at the harbor, half an eye on her watch. She has not come down here to observe the gulls and ships, but she cannot yet bring herself to walk along Grenoble Street and enter the one door she must enter.

— I've got to. Can't stay away from home much longer. It isn't fair to Katie, to expect her to look after Jen all day. Come on, Stacey. Okay, in a minute when I feel stronger. Just a minute. You haven't got the guts of a grasshopper, that's your trouble. Come on. Not later. Now.

She turns and walks quickly. She reaches Grenoble Street and her footsteps dwindle, dawdle past cafés and the cheap hotels where old men doze in the barely waking lobbies which will blare and brawl when night falls. Stacey finds Honest Ernie's cut-price children's clothes, and enters the doorway at the side. Up the brown linoleum stairs to the second landing. She stops, then, being unable yet to knock.

The gigantic woman, outspread like rising dough

gone amok, swelling and undulating over the stiff upholstery of the chair, gaping body covered with tiny-flower-printed dress huge and shroud-shaped, and beside her on a low table the pink-pearl glass mug and the port-filled teapot. Buckle laughing.

— I can't go in. I can't. My head's spinning. I feel really awful. What if I throw up here? It wouldn't alter the smell of this hallway much, that's for sure. Go on – knock. I should've come before. I should at least have inquired. Maybe nobody found her, and she's dead, and when I open the door there she'll be, decomposing away like sixty in the chair, her head lolling and her eyes just as blind in death as they were in life. It was crazy to come here. I should've phoned the police, the day after Buckle crashed. But I didn't. And now I can't. They'd say *This is a hell of a fine time to be telling us, lady*.

Stacey knocks. There is a flurry of movement inside the room, and Stacey's stomach begins to cramp in apprehension. The door is opened, only a crack, and a face peers out. A girl with long uncombed hair, sharp catlike features breathing suspicion.

Whatcha want?

I – didn't Mrs. Fennick live here?

Who? Oh, you mean the old blind dame? Yeh. But her son got himself wiped out in a crash. He was a trucker. I used to live on the top floor but I moved, see? This place is better. Anything else you want to know? Such as the story of my life, for instance?

What   what happened to her?

Oh, they took her away.

They?

Yeh, Salvation Army or some do-good bunch like that. It was real funny, the way it happened. The way I heard is, they told her about the son and said they was coming back the next day to fetch her off somewheres, one of them homes, like, I guess. Well, she tries to cut her throat, see? Only she can't find the butcher knife. When they come in the morning there she was, still crawling around the floor, feeling everything, but she still hadn't found it. Ever see her? Built like the back of a barn, she was. She must've looked real cute, crawling around on her hands and knees, with her great big tits bumping along on the floor, there.

I see. Well   thanks very much

The girl laughs, and Stacey can hear Buckle's laughter again, the stone-grained quality of laughter long used as both weapon and wall. The girl imitates what she has presumably heard as phony politeness in Stacey's voice.

Oh, don't mention it, I'm sure. Always glad to oblige.

The door slams. Stacey walks down the stairs and out into the street. She walks without noticing the sidewalk, the people, the buildings.

— She may not have been much, but she didn't abort him all that time ago, at least not before his birth. She had him and brought him up. She did that. What could have been in her mind that day I came here with Buckle? Or any of the days, for that matter. But he never turned her out, whatever else he may have said or done. When I think of the number of times I felt like clobbering him for coming around so often to our place, for coming around at all. Buckle – you can't be dead. I can't cry here. What would everybody think, passing by? But I am, damn damn damn. That's right, Stacey – requiem for a truck driver. You really time things well.

Stacey hears, strangely, her name being spoken by a woman's voice, a voice raucous as the gulls'.

Stacey   hey Stacey

She blinks. Coming towards her is a woman whose black hair has been upfrizzed until it resembles the nest of some large wild bird. Her dark eyes and her features are prairie Indian but not entirely. Her skin, or what can be seen of it under the thick crust of make-up, is a pale brown. Her mouth has been lipsticked into a wide bizarre cupid's bow. She is wearing a smeared hem-drooping mauve silkish dress which reveals her body's blunt thickness, the once-high breasts that are dugs now.

It *is* Stacey, ain't it? Stacey Cameron? I dunno your married name.

Yes   that's right   I   I

Valentine Tonnere. Val. Doncha remember me?

Well, for heaven's sake. Well, sure I do. Of course.

The Tonnerre family shack, surrounded by discarded tin cans and old car parts and extending in a series of lean-tos, at the foot of the hill in Manawaka, originally built a long time ago by old Jules Tonnere, who was a boy then, when he stopped off and stayed in the Wachakwa Valley on his way back from the last uprising of his people, on his way back from Batoche and Fish Creek, from the last and failed attempt to save themselves and their land, the last of their hopeless hope which was finished the year Riel was hanged in Regina. After that, the *Bois Brûlés*, the French-Indians, the *Métis*, those who sang Falcon's Song, once the prairie horse lords, would be known as half-breeds and would live the way the Tonneres lived, in ramshackledom, belonging nowhere. And Jules begat Lazarus, and Lazarus begat a multitude. Stacey Cameron at school saw the straggling tribe of kids only as *those Tonnerres*. Their name meant thunder but she did not know until a long time later.

Stacey does not know what to say. She would like to go back in time, to explain that she never meant the town's invisible stabbing, but this is not possible, and it was hers, too, so she cannot edge away from it.

— Valentine. So-named because born on February 14. Her sister once told me when I said it wasn't a girl's name. Val must be three or four years younger than I am. My God, she looks ten years older. Her sister? Her sister? What was it?

You were younger than I, Val. It was your sister who was my age. Piquette. What   I heard something   what was it

Valentine's face, expert at concealment, takes on blankness.

Yeh. You seen it in the *Manawaka Banner*, maybe. They wrote it up there. Maybe you remember she had TB in the bone, one leg. She used to limp quite a lot. Doctor Macleod, there, got it fixed up, after quite a while, when she was a kid. So then she kind of took off, like, soon as she could. She married this guy from Winnipeg, English fella. Bastard walked out on her and the two kids. She went back to the old place. You know, cooked and that for Dad and the boys. Happened in winter. They used to make red biddy down there. If I know Piquette, she was stoned out of her mind, most likely. The others were out. We had one of them big old wood stoves. Place caught fire. She never got out. The kids neither.

    Val   I didn't know

— Or did I just forget, put it from mind?

Yeh well. You feel like a cuppa coffee?

Sure. Gosh, it's nice to see you. I don't often see anybody from Manawaka.

— I'm overdoing it and she will know. I don't want to have coffee with her. Even her presence is a reproach to me, for all I've got now and have been given and still manage to bitch on and on about it. And a reproach for the sins of my fathers, maybe. The debts are inherited and how could the damage ever be undone or forgiven? I don't want to, but I seem to believe in a day of judgment, just like all my Presbyterian forebears did, only I don't think it'll happen in the clouds or elsewhere and I don't think I'll be judged for the same things they thought they'd be. Piquette and her kids, and the snow and fire. Ian and Duncan in a burning house.

Well, c'mon then, Stacey. Here's the Emerald Café, right here. They'll put it on the cuff sometimes. But I don't guess you'd have to be too interested in that.

    Well   sure, let's go in

— And yet I resent her making a crack like that.

They sit down in a booth and order two coffees.

Stacey lights a cigarette and offers one to Valentine, who takes it.

How long you been here, Val?

Oh, going on three years now. Won't be here much longer.

Why? You going somewhere?

Valentine smiles, the ruby creamed mouth now askew.

Yeh. Long trip. The last one.

How do you mean?

Don't ask, Stacey. You don't want to know.

— Heroin? Booze? Sickness? A knife under the ribs? Luke was right. You can't ask. You don't have the right. You haven't lived in that particular cave.

Okay. I'm sorry, Val.

For what? I don't give a fuck. Today tomorrow next week, it's all the same to me. How you been, Stacey? Lived here long?

Yeh. Quite a few years now. I'm okay I guess

You sound pissed off.

Yeh, well. My husband works for a guy who's got it in for him for no reason and there's the four kids and things get kind of

What's he do, your old man?

Salesman. Ever heard of Richalife?

To Stacey's astonishment, Valentine Tonnerre leans back in the booth and laughs, smoking at the same time and then going into a spasm of coughing. She fumbles for the coffee cup, drinks, and then looks at Stacey with uninterpretable eyes.

Yeh. I heard of it. Especially the guy they got there now. I seen his picture in the paper and then I seen him once on the street. God, I laughed so hard I nearly puked. You must've laughed too.

Stacey stares.

Laughed? What at?

You mean you never recognized him? Well, he was younger than you, a few years, so you probably never knew him, to speak of. I knew him, though. Jesus, I often thought of touching him for a few bucks, but then again, I'm not that smart and it might not work. Someday when I'm high maybe I'll do it.

Val – what are you talking about?

Him. Thor Thorlakson or whatever the hell he calls himself. Yeh, sure, he's had his pan all jazzed up by doctors whaddya call it some kinda surgery and I am damn sure he wears built-up shoes. When he took me into the bushes way back when, he was in high school but he sure wasn't that tall, and his name was Vernon Winkler.

Stacey's stunned disbelief alters only gradually, as the recollection filters blurredly back.

> A kid in the graveled schoolgrounds of Manawaka Public School. A kid maybe eight or nine years old, surrounded by a gang of older, fiercer kids, scorn-chanting. *Ver-non Ver-non Ver-non*. A series of hard knees in the crotch until the teacher came along and distractedly said *Boys boys boys*. The kid crying, mucus pouring from his nose. Stacey and Vanessa and Mavis watching from a distance, disgusted and excited

Val   I didn't know   I didn't know

Whatsamatter? You look scared. You scared or something?

Stacey is hardly aware of speaking aloud, or to anyone.

That's why he was down on Mac. Nothing to do with Mac. Only with me. But how could I have known that? And he didn't have to worry. I didn't recognize him. How could I? I never knew him at all, not really. I only ever noticed him that once, as far as I can remember, but I wouldn't have associated *that* kid with Thor, for heaven's sake. Maybe he remembered me, once he knew where I came from, or maybe he was only scared because he didn't know whether I knew all about him or not. My God, he probably thought there was something ominous about it, every time I mentioned the prairies or the name Thor –

but there wasn't. There wasn't. And now he'll find an excuse to fire Mac or else he'll keep on needling until Mac has to quit. Mac can't stand to be without a job   not now

Stacey pulls herself together and looks across the café table. Valentine Tonnerre is leaning on the red arborite surface, her chin in her hands. Her eyes are watchful, unsympathetic, even pleased.

Shit, Stacey, you got worries? Go ahead – make me laugh.

You could be right. Then again, maybe not. I got to get home now, Val. My kids will be wondering where I am.

Yeh. I guess your kids would.

Val   did you ever   you know   have you got any

The known and total stranger sitting opposite shakes her head, laughs her coarse-textured laugh and takes a cigarette out of Stacey's pack on the table.

I got a couple somewhere   I kind of lost track

— The necessary lie. Where? How many? With whom? How much does it hurt? The questions that can't be asked or answered. All I can do is go. Now she wants me to go. Too little can be said, because there is too much to say. And I'm relieved to be going, because I can't cope here.

Val   come over some evening. Phone me. We're in the phone book. MacAindra, Bluejay Crescent. We'll kill a bottle.

— Stacey, you are phony as a three-dollar bill, and she knows it.

Valentine Tonnerre looks at her, unsmiling. Then she reaches under her left breast and scratches, a long slow deliberate gesture.

Yeh well

So long, then.

But Valentine does not appear to have heard, so Stacey rises, dutifully pays and goes.

— God of thunder. Vernon Winkler. I'll bet a nickel to a doughnut hole that he puts vodka in that tomato juice of his. How can I tell Mac, and what will I say? *You've been scared by a strawman*. How could anybody say that? If we're scared, at least there is some dignity in being scared of genuine demons. Aren't there any demons left in hell? How in hell can we live without them?

Bluejay Crescent. Stacey parks the car in front of the house and goes quickly up the steps, inside, through the house and out the back door. Duncan is swinging Jen on the low swing and she is shrieking with laughter and excitement. Ian and assorted friends are constructing a new and larger bug, and the grass around them is littered with wheels, boards, nails, hammers and other essentials. Katie is rubbing her newly washed hair with a towel.

Hi. Everything okay, Katie?

Sure. Why shouldn't it be?

I didn't mean it that way. Sorry I was so long, honey. Do you want to go now?

I can't until my hair's dry. If you'd come back half an hour ago, I could have gone to the beach with Marnie and washed my hair tonight.

Sorry. I was delayed

Seems like you're always delayed when it's me who's looking after Jen. When it was Mrs. Fogler, you used to get home when you said you would.

My heavens, Katie, I've said I'm sorry – what more can I

Okay okay okay

The phone rings. Katie leaps to her feet and sprints towards the house.

I'll get it, Mother. I'm expecting a call.

All right.

— You are, eh? Who from? Why doesn't she say? She's getting very secretive all of a sudden lately. Oh for heaven's sake, Stacey, what do you expect?

In a moment Katie emerges and looks oddly at Stacey.

It wasn't for me. It was for you. It was Mr. Fogler,

but he's rung off now. He sounded kind of strange. He wants you to go over right away. I think Mrs. Fogler must be sick or something.

Stacey goes swiftly. When she reaches the Foglers' doorstep, Jake opens the door before she can ring the bell. It is the first time Stacey has ever seen him without his glasses. He looks younger and less owlish. But then she sees why he has taken his glasses off. He grinds away at his eyes with his palms as though his tears are repugnant and shameful to himself.

Jake – what is it?

It's Tess

But he cannot say anything more. He takes Stacey's hand and draws her into the living room. He motions her to the chesterfield, and then he gropes over to the liquor cabinet, pours two brandies and hands one to Stacey. He drinks his own quickly, pours another and then lowers himself into an armchair. His voice is steadier now, but there is a kind of self-dramatizing hysteria in it which repels Stacey despite herself.

I found her this morning, Stacey. Here. Right here, where I'm sitting now. She'd swallowed Christ knows how many sleeping pills and nearly a whole bottle of rye.

Stacey's hands around the brandy glass begin to shake.

Jake　that's　is she

No. She's not dead.

Thank God

I took here to hospital　Stacey it was terrible　I got her into the car all by myself　I should've phoned for you or Mac　or phoned the ambulance　but I wasn't think-ing straight at all　I just thought I had to get her there right away and she was limp and I couldn't tell whether she was breathing or not　her breathing was so shallow and faint

Jake　I'm sorry

They pumped her out and it was touch-and-go for most of the day and then they said they thought she'd be okay Stacey she has to go to to you know the mental hospital

Listen, Jake, don't feel badly about that. They'll be able to help her.

Now he is not dramatizing. His voice is only pain and bewilderment.

Yes but why? Why would she? What's the matter with her? What did I do wrong? Was it me? What was it?

I don't know

— I don't know and I do know. Dog eat dog and fish eat fish. How many things added up? But I didn't get the message either. Why didn't I? I always envied her for being so glamorous. I couldn't see anything else.

Jake I'm so damn sorry I did know she was upset sometimes and I might have tried but I didn't

You shouldn't think that way, Stacey. It was me. I guess. But what did I do or not do?

Maybe it wasn't you Jake. Everything starts a long time ago.

Do you think so? Do you really think so?

Sure. Of course. It's well known.

— He was the one who used to tell me slickly that I had a death wish because I would have liked from time to time to be on a snow mountain by myself, no voices. Now he clutches at any naive theory that might totally exonerate him. Never mind. Who could blame him for wanting that? *It wasn't me*, the kids say. It is always the other guy who starts the trouble. And I say furiously, *How am I supposed to find out? How can I sift it all?*

Jake pours another brandy for them both.

Maybe I should've agreed years ago for her to have kids, Stacey. But whenever we talked of it, she seemed so damn scared. I thought that was what she *wanted* me to say – that she was enough and that I didn't feel the need of any

Maybe that's what she did want you to say. Or maybe she did and didn't.

Jake puts his head in his hands and once again there is the faintly shrill teetering quality in his voice.

I don't know what the hell she *ever* wanted, to tell you the truth. She was so goddam beautiful it seemed incredible that she would marry me at all

I think she thought she was stupid

Christ, Stacey, surely you realize that if I kidded her sometimes it was only because she was so goddam beautiful and I look like some kind of chimpanzee and I thought she could take the odd crack how did I know

Jake – stop it. This could go on and on. Come to our place for dinner tonight. And for as long as you want or until

Thanks, Stacey. But I couldn't do that. It may be months. I'll come tonight if I can

— He won't, though. He couldn't sit there and talk. He couldn't bear the glances of my kids. He'll have a light delicious dinner of brandy.

He sees her to the door and she walks home slowly, wondering how to tell Katie. The boys don't need to know, but Katie has to be told.

Katie?

What happened to her, Mum? Is she dead?

No she's not

Did she try to kill herself?

Yes. How did you know?

Katie shrugs, throwing back her half-damp hair. Under the flippancy of her voice there seems to be an undertone of something else, perhaps fear.

Oh well, that's the usual gimmick, isn't it?

Not that usual, I'd say.

You never read the papers? Mum – will she be all right?

I hope so. She needs

Yeh, I know. Treatment. Mother

Yes?

You couldn't have done anything. It must've been past that point. So let's not get all worked up, eh?

Oh Katie

Hey don't worry please please just don't cry
Mum *please* you're okay there there you're okay now

Yes. Thanks, Katie.

— One day she will have to take over as the mother, and
she's beginning to sense it. No wonder it frightens her. It
damn near terrifies me, the whole business, even after all
these years. And then I give in like now, and lean on her. I
mustn't.

Mum?

What?

Don't ever pull that stunt like she did will you?

No. I won't.

— I promise you, Katie. I give you my word. But what if
the day ever comes a long time from now when Katie is
worn out and would half or even three quarters wish to
release me from that kind of promise? Shut up, you. We'll
have to deal with that one when the time comes.

Stacey goes next door to tell Bertha Garvey. From
the front porch she can hear Julian's voice ranting in his
accustomed manner at Bertha over some offense real or
imagined. Then when he comes to the door he is calm,
smiling, almost courtly.

Stacey. How nice to see you. Do come in. Bertha's in
the kitchen.

— Where else, you old fraud? She spends her entire life
there.

Bertha is making applesauce. She listens silently and
then she turns and faces Stacey. She does not gasp or
make horrified noises. Her voice is as ordinary as always.

She never ate enough, Tess didn't. She starved herself. No wonder she got so rundown and keyed up. When
she gets home, I'm going to make good and sure she eats.

Stacey cannot help smiling.

Bertha, you're great. You know that?

Bertha motions with the wooden spoon towards
Julian.

Try telling him.

— What does Bertha concoct for her personal theater? The lumberjack she never married, the one who would have loved her with perfect admiration just as she is?

As she is going out, Stacey can hear their voices, Julian's crotchety and yet frightened.

Don't you go letting that Tess give you any fancy notions, Bertha.

And Bertha's voice, plain and solid as a pine board.

Don't you ever worry. I'm too stubborn to die yet for a while.

The march winds its way across the bridge, and Stacey, glancing backward, can see the banners, each carried by two people, the words curving and only partially visible as the marchers pace.

> WE REMEMBER HIROSHIMA
> STOP THE WAR IN
> PEACE IN
> STOP THE
> WE REMEMBER
> PEACE

Beside Stacey, a girl in a green corduroy slacks suit takes long slow measured steps. She has informed Stacey that this style of walking is less tiring. Stacey, however, is not able to take the advice because her own legs are not long enough. Also, she has not had the foresight to wear slacks. She is wearing a blue-and-white-striped cotton dress and sandals, and apart from one or two elderly tweed-clad ladies near the rear of the column, she is the only woman wearing a skirt. She looks around, flinching, trying not to notice, trying not to let it make any difference.

— Something like this is supposed to be serious, and here you are, Stacey, worrying about how you look. I know, I know. But I'd feel easier and less conspicuous if I'd worn my slacks. What if Mac should drive past and see me? He'd have a fit. Why can't I tell him? There's nothing furtive about it, for heaven's sake. In fact, it was with the opposite in mind that I came. *I don't kid myself that it's going to change the world, but I plod along – it makes as much sense as anything else.* That's what Luke said. Why did I think of that? I wish I hadn't. Because now I don't know if I am really plodding along out of conviction or only because it was in the back of my mind that he might be here and I might see him again. I must not want to see him again. I mustn't. But I do. I can help what I do but not what I feel.

Someone starts singing "We Shall Overcome." Most of the marchers are young. Their voices are strong and certain. High on the bridge, with the gulls' mocking bird-voices around them, the marchers sing. Stacey tries to sing, but she cannot. The green corduroy girl gives her a wry look, so she tries again, but no music emerges from her open mouth.

— I see myself tromping along here, this slightly too short woman, slightly too heavy in the hips, no longer young. And all I can feel is embarrassment. I might at least have the decency not to feel embarrassed. Maybe I'd feel differently if I had faith. But I can't seem to manage it.

They have crossed the bridge, and at a street corner a small group is waiting to join the march. One of them is Luke. The same clothes, the same Indian sweater. He still wears his beard, except that now it is thicker and looks as though it belongs. Standing beside him is a girl about twenty, with long fine brown hair, wearing white jeans and sweater, and carrying a sign. PEACE. Luke has his arm around her.

Stacey turns to the green-corduroy girl.

Gosh I'm sorry but I just have to go to the bath-room. I'm going to have to drop out at this corner and find a john somewhere.

Gee, bad luck. Never mind. If you hurry, you can catch us up.

I'll try

Stacey, conscious of disapproving looks which she feels convinced must be aimed at her retreat, darts out of the line of marchers. Quickly, then, into the anonymity and shelter of the nearest doorway, which happens to be a hamburger place. A boy is mopping the counter with a wet and greyish rag.

Yes ma'am?

Oh – coffee please.

She drinks it slowly, to make it last as long as possible, and watches through the window the remainder of the marchers going past. They are singing "Where Have All the Flowers Gone." Their voices reach back to the bridge where the gulls eternally whirl. Perhaps they reach to the city as well, or perhaps not.

When the last marcher is out of sight, Stacey goes out and gets a bus back home.

— I might at least have seen it through. For what, though? It's like church – you think maybe if you go, the faith will be given, but it isn't. It has to be there already in you, I guess. Or maybe you have to persevere. I wish I'd stayed. Despite Luke. Despite embarrassment. Despite no faith. But bravery has never been my specialty. All I know how to do is get by somehow. I'd like to talk to somebody. Somebody who wouldn't refuse really to look at me, whatever I was like. I'd like to talk to my sister. I'd like to write to her. I'd like to tell her how I feel about everything. No. She'd think I was crazy, probably. She's too sensible ever to do this sort of thing, like today, or like with Luke and all that. She'd think I must be mad, not to be perfectly happy, with four healthy kids and a good man. I couldn't write to her. She'd never see. She'd think even worse of me than she already does. Luke? I couldn't let you see me. All right – you showed me where I belonged, when you said *What can't you leave?* I guess I should be grateful. I *am* grateful. Maybe not for that, so much. I guess I knew it anyway. For the way you talked to me and held me for a while – that's why I'm grateful. I said unspokenly *Help* and you didn't turn away. You faced me and touched me. You were gentle. You needn't have been, but you were, and that I won't forget or cease being glad for. Even if you'd been older, or I'd been younger and free, it wouldn't have turned out any simpler with you than it is with Mac. I didn't see that at one time, but I see it now.

The bus pulls to a halt. Stacey gets out and walks down Bluejay Crescent. Katie is in the back yard with Jen. Stacey stands on the back porch.

Hi. Where are the boys?

Over at Weller's. Jim's got a new bike. Are you going to pay me for minding Jen?

I said I would, so I will.

How did it go?

Oh – all right, I guess. I quit before the end.

Never mind. It's quite a walk. Why don't you want Dad to know you went?

I don't know. I guess it doesn't matter one way or another if he knows. Maybe it should've been you who went.

Katie looks up, smiling but not in a way which Stacey finds possible to decipher with any certainty.

You mean – athletic me?

Stacey wants to touch her, to hold fast to her and at the same time to support her. But she expresses none of these, having to be careful, unable to gauge accurately, having to guess only.

Yeh. Athletic you.

Stacey goes back into the kitchen, finds the notebook she uses for shopping lists, tears out a page, writes on it and sticks it up above the sink with Scotch tape.

No Pre-Mourning.

She stands for a while and looks at it.

Newspaper photograph – slash-eyed woman crouched on some temporarily unviolated steps in the far city, skull and bones outstanding under shriveled skin, holding the dead child, she not able to realize it is actually and unhelpably finished and yet knowing this is so. The woman's mouth open wide – a sound of unbearability but rendered in silence by the camera clicking. Only the zero mouth to be seen, noiselessly proclaiming the gone-early child.

Now Stacey cannot recall what it was that might have been meant by *Pre*. Also, she cannot figure out a way of explaining the sign to Ian and Duncan. So she takes it down and puts it into the garbage.

Sunday. They have taken the kids to the beach in the morning. In the afternoon Matthew has arrived and has been pacing the kitchen floor while Stacey prepares dinner. Turning from sink to stove, Stacey nearly bumps into him. They both step aside and once again nearly collide. But Matthew is not aware of Stacey's teeth-grinding fury, so the small gauche ballet continues. Mac is out cleaning the car, assisted by Ian. Jen is playing under the kitchen table. Duncan stands in the doorway. Stacey, angry at Matthew, flies at Duncan.

For heaven's sake, honey, can't you find something to do? Why don't you go and help Dad and Ian with the car?

Duncan mumbles indistinguishable words.

Speak properly, Duncan. What did you say?

His voice is now abnormally loud and high.

I said they don't want me

Stacey stops and looks at him.

Did you ask?

Yeh. He said to buzz off – he was busy.

Duncan   he didn't mean

It's okay. I don't care.

— Not much you don't.

Duncan goes upstairs. A moment later, Matthew also walks up the stairs to the bathroom, and Stacey with relief pours herself a gin and tonic. She has gulped only half of it when she hears a thudding sound, followed by Duncan's frightened voice.

Mum! C'mere – quick!

What is it, Duncan? What's happened?

It's Granddad – he's fallen.

Stacey runs through into the front hall. Matthew is lying at the foot of the stairs, having evidently missed his footing on the bottom steps. He does not seem able to rise, but Stacey can detect no broken bones. More than anything, he is humiliated and apologetic.

Stacey   I'm so sorry   it was so stupid of me

No   no   you mustn't say that. Here, Duncan, give me a hand, will you?

Between them, they manage to get Matthew into an armchair in the living room.

Okay, Duncan. Granddad's okay now.

You sure? Should I call Dad, maybe?

No. It's all right. Would you just go and make sure Jen's all right, though?

Duncan looks once again at Matthew, who is moving one hand across his forehead. Then he looks away, as though he has witnessed something not intended for his eyes. He walks into the kitchen and stays there. Matthew is breathing heavily but making a strained effort to breathe normally.

What happened?

As soon as she has spoken, Stacey realizes that her voice has been more incisive than she meant it to be, more piercing and demanding. Matthew leans his head back against the chair, as though at last having to accept the unacceptable.

Stacey   I'm sorry

You're sorry? What for?

Well, I guess I've got glaucoma. The eyes aren't much good any more. That's why I fell. The doctor told me sometime ago but I didn't want to let you know. I have drops for them but

Stacey looks at him, appalled.

You should have said. You should have told us.

I suppose so. But I didn't want   well   I didn't want you to feel you had to

Dad?

— Dad. I've never called him that before. I might as well begin. I'm going to be seeing a lot of him from now on. Strange – it's only a name now, that, only a way of identifying Matthew. Niall Cameron has been dead a long time. If someone else needs the name, no point in not using it. It doesn't mean anything to me any more. I never knew until now.

Yes? What is it, Stacey?

Wait. I'll be back in a sec.

Stacey flashes into the kitchen and snatches her drink from its cave concealment in the blue Mixmaster bowl.

— Well, Dad, old buddy, you may as well get used to it, because I am certainly not taking to tomato juice with invisible vodka, for you or anyone else. For what I am about to say, I need this.

She returns to the living room and sits on the chester-field. Matthew eyes the glass but says nothing.

Listen, Dad. You can't live there any more. Not now. Not with this. You'll live here. With us.

— Oh Christ, will I ever regret it. I'll regret it every day of my life. It'll be pure bloody murder. We've got enough to deal with, without him. He'll follow me around all day long. Move over, Tess – I'll soon be out to join you. No, I damn well won't. I will not let this get me down. I just damn well will not. Oh heavens – I'll have to take him up and down the stairs to the bathroom. I can't. I can't. Yes, you can. If you think it'll be awful for you, doll, how do you think he'll feel about it? Matthew, who doesn't even like to admit he has any natural functions. Matthew, al-ways so neat and so proud.

Stacey   thank you my dear but I can't impose

No. You mustn't feel like that. That's – unrealistic. We want to have you. Naturally. Of course. There's no question.

— Naturally. Of course. Oh brother. Why did I ever once feel that to tell the truth the whole truth and nothing but the truth would be a relief? It would be dynamite, that's all it would be. It would set the house on fire.

Stacey, I don't know what to say. I would like to come and live here. I can't deny that. But – it's Mac.

How do you mean?

Matthew turns his face away from hers. It is Mac's gesture and Matthew's voice could almost be Mac's voice at the moments of difficult telling.

I didn't do very well by him when he was a boy.

Dad   I don't think he thinks that

He must. It isn't easy for a minister's children. Everyone expects them to be some kind of example. I see now that I expected too much of him. Strange – I could even see the unfairness of it then, from his point of view. But I never told him that. I wanted him to grow up with some strong background of faith. But he didn't. The reason must be that I had so many doubts myself. I must have passed them on even though I never spoke of them.

I never knew you had any doubts at all. I don't think Mac ever knew, either. Maybe it would have been better if he had known.

— And Matthew's despair.

Oh no – that couldn't have been better for him or his sister or anyone. One should be certain. A minister should be. If he isn't, he must at least try not to put anyone else's faith in jeopardy. That always seemed to me to be the least I could do. But with Mac I failed. Perhaps there is something contagious about doubt. He must have known all along about that essential flaw in me.

Dad   you've got it all wrong

I'm afraid not, my dear.

Mac would have been relieved if he'd known you weren't always certain. But he didn't know.

Matthew hears her words but not their meaning. He has to continue in his own groove.

Stacey – I always wanted to talk about it to someone,

but I couldn't. I wish now that I had talked of it. Not to Mac, but perhaps to my wife. But she was – well, I don't think she ever had any doubts about anything, so how could I? It would have weakened me so much in her eyes.

Maybe she wasn't all that sure.

Oh yes, she certainly was. I used to admire her for it. She never needed the things that some people need. Her faith was very strong and

— And she didn't like to be fucked. But not because her faith was very strong. Something else. Poor goddam her. Poor Matthew. Too late now.

Sh. It's all right, Dad. Everything's going to be all right. Listen, you rest here for a minute, until dinner's ready, and I'll go see Mac. Don't worry.

She goes outside and calls Mac. When they are in the study, she hands him a gin and tonic.

Mac

Yeh? What's the matter?

It's your dad. He fell down on the stairs.

Oh Christ, what next?

He's got glaucoma. Mac, we'll have to have him here.

Stacey, we can't. Where's the room?

We'll have to turn the study into a bedroom and build a study for you in the basement.

Great. Wonderful. You got it all figured out, haven't you?

For God's sake, then, what's your suggestion?

Stacey   I don't want him here   I can't

You were the one who always said he had a right to walk in without knocking and that we should send the kids to Sunday school so as not to upset him and all that.

I know I know I know. Lay off, can't you?

I'm sorry. Mac – what is it?

He looks at her as though they have never before met, as though she is the stranger on shipboard to whom he may possibly be able to relate his edited past.

I never bought what he was preaching about, but

still, he was doing something, you have to admit it. He didn't spend his life doing nothing.

— Like you? Is that what you mean? Mac, you can't mean that. It isn't true. What to say that'll do any good?

Mac – he thinks he didn't do well by you.

I'll bet.

He does. He said so.

In the heat of the moment, maybe. Don't kid yourself. He doesn't think that. He thinks the other way around.

What do you think, yourself, about the boys, Mac?

What? What's that got to do with it?

I just wondered. Because they quite often have the notion that they'll never be as smart as you are. Especially Duncan.

They'll learn differently.

Yeh? Thanks for reassuring me.

Mac dredges up a kind of laughter and puts an arm around her shoulders. Suddenly Stacey is filled with the knowledge of what it will mean to have Matthew in the house.

Mac – what'll we do? It'll be impossible. I just can't

Well, as you say, there's nothing else we can do. Hush, honey. It'll be all right. We'll manage. But I'll have to use the TV room as a study until we can get another room built down there. The kids will squawk like hell, I suppose.

Let them squawk. Mac –

They hold on to one another for an unpredicted moment. Then Stacey goes out to the hall and bellows at Ian and Duncan.

C'mon you guys! Is Katie home?

Katie's voice floats down.

I'm here. And I'm not deaf – yet.

Stacey picks up Jen and plonks her onto the cushion-heightened chair in the dining room.

— A few more years of this life, God, and if I'm not

dead or demented, I'll have a hide like a rhinoceros. Odd
– Mac has to pretend he's absolutely strong, and now I see
he doesn't believe a word of it and never has. Yet he's a
whole lot stronger than he thinks he is. Maybe they all
are. Maybe even Duncan is. Maybe even I am.

Ten

STACEY STILL cannot decide whether to tell Mac about Thor or not. Mac has said nothing about the job since the evening of Thor's party. Stacey vacillates inwardly for several days, being careful to keep outwardly busy. She takes the three younger children to the beach, does baking, writes letters, has Bertha in for coffee. She watches Mac covertly but cannot discover anything from his manner. He works just the same, grindingly. But one afternoon he comes home early. Jen and Stacey are in the back yard, Stacey dutifully spread out on the lawn, wearing her bathing suit, trying to gain more tan.

— I must be out of my mind. I don't give the smallest damn whether I've got a tan or not. But every summer I do this, because it's taken for granted that everybody wants a tan.

She looks up and sees Mac standing in the back doorway. His brush-cut has completely grown out now and his russet hair looks like himself once more.

Mac – what're you doing home?

— Has he quit or been fired? Lord, please let it be that he's quit, not the other.

Hi. I came to tell you something. C'mon inside, eh?

Stacey snatches up Jen and carries her, wriggling and protesting, into the house. Jen begins screeching, a piercing enraged voice which proclaims her intention of going on and on until Stacey takes her back to the garden. Stacey shakes her.

— Shut up shut up shut up   you goddam little nuisance.

She has not said a word aloud, but she can feel her own anger mounting in direct proportion to her tension, assaulted eardrums and sense of apprehension about Mac. She pats Jen's shoulders.

Hush, flower. It's okay. Please, honey, please. *Jen*. Listen, if you don't shut up, I'll smack you, see?

— Oh God. Now she'll roar forever. Why why is Mac home?

In the kitchen, Jen suddenly stops screaming, as unreasonably as she began. Mac is in the process of pouring two gin and tonics. Stacey looks at him in surprise.

Hey – what's this in aid of?

He hands a glass to her and raises his own.

Guess what's happened, Stacey.

What?

Thor's been offered a head office job in Montreal and he's decided to take it. They want me to be manager here.

Mac! You don't mean it.

— *Thor* is leaving? Thor is *leaving?* But he was the god here, and he won't be that in head office. Was he really invited to go, or did he ask for a transfer himself, for his own reasons? Val, did you get stoned one night and go to see him? You didn't have any cause to do me a favor, that's for sure. I couldn't even bring myself to ask you around – I didn't want you swearing in front of my kids. Did you say something to Thor? Was it settling an old score, for you? I'll never know. And I'll never find out from you, either, because I'll never find you. No fixed address. Val – I'm sorry. I'm sorry. Too late. *Was* it you?

Mac is smiling.

Yeh, it's true all right. I was pretty taken aback myself. Anyway, I'm going to accept. It's a funny thing – I had just about decided to quit. In fact, I was going to hand in my notice this week.

You didn't say anything.

Yeh, well I was going to tell you

— Thanks.

I can't take it in all at once, Mac. When – when did you hear about Thor?

Just today. And the offer came to me at the same time.

Mac   that's great   it's really wonderful

I thought you'd be pleased. Apparently they decided to offer me the job on account of the fact that I've actually sold more than any of the other guys here. I'm going to change a few things. A lot of the jazz in the campaign was Thor's, not head office's. The charts and quiz and that. We can cut out that crap. It'll be a pretty good job. It's a going firm.

Sure. I know it is. Gee, that's just fine, Mac. It's marvelous.

— Life's games. He knocks himself out because he thinks Thor's got it in for him, and he winds up manager in an outfit he really thinks is a load of phony baloney. Dear Lord and Father of mankind, forgive our foolish ways, as some goon once said. Reclothe us in our rightful mind. And so on. But what if this *is* our rightful mind, or at least the only one we're likely to have? Anyway, it *is* a good job. It's somewhere. It's better than nowhere.

Luke. *I think I'll just hitch and see what happens. I'd like to go north. That's a great country, Stacey. Up the Skeena River – Kispiox, Kitwanga, crazy names like that. Northern jungle, rain forest –*

— Okay, Stacey, simmer down. The fun is over. It's been over for some time, only you didn't see it before. No – you saw it all right but you couldn't take it. You're nearly forty. You got four kids and a mortgage, and in just over three years Katie will be ready for university if she works hard enough, which is dubious. I guess the fun's been over for Mac for quite a while. It would be nice if we were different people but we are not different people. We are ourselves and we are sure as hell not going to undergo some total transformation at this point. That's right, doll. Mrs. C. MacAindra, by an overwhelming majority voted The Most Sensible Woman of the Year. We can save our money. When we've got all four kids through university or launched somewhere, and Mac retires and is so thin you have to look twice to seem him and I'm so portly I can hardly waddle, we can go to Acapulco and do the Mexican hat dance. I can't stand it. I cannot. I can't take it. Yeh, I can, though. By God, I can, if I set my mind to it. And I'm not going to tell him about Thor. It's not actually like lying. It's just refraining from saying. The silences aren't all bad. How do I know how many times Mac has protected me by not saying? He probably noticed the burn on my hand that time.

Mac, I don't know what to say. I think it's just terrific.

Yeh. It's good. We're getting somewhere.

Only one thing

What?

Let's not move, eh? I mean, we'll be able sometime to afford another house – you know, bigger or like that – but I don't want to.

For Christ's sake, Stacey, why not?

I just don't

You can't mean it. Listen, honey, it'll be me who has to have the staff parties and all that. Can you see us having them here? There isn't room to swing a cat, and the kids' stuff is littered all over the place. We need at least a decent-sized living room, and for the boys to have their own bedrooms, and now that Dad is here it would be pretty convenient to have a house that had a downstairs john as well as an upstairs one.

You've got it all figured out, eh? That was quick work.

Now, listen Stacey

I don't want to move. I like this old dump. I'm used to it. It's not you who has to be around the house all day long.

I know. I know. I'm only saying I just don't see how

we can manage here indefinitely. That's all I'm saying. I'm not suggesting we should move tomorrow. I'm only saying that at some point it's going to become

Okay. So we'll move, if you want to so much. But don't be stunned if I bitch about it, eh?

Oh for God's sake what's the matter now?

Nothing   nothing's the matter

The sand of the beach is fine and pale brown, lightly strewn with fringed yellow-green fronds of seafern and bulbous kelp cast up and drying in the late August sun. Stacey and Jen walk barefoot, picking up grey-white coarse clam shells, small purple shells paired and open like moth wings, greenly iridescent shells shaped like miniature coolie hats.

Hey, that's a nice one, angel bud. Shall I put it in my bag?

Jen nods and Stacey gravely takes the cracked shell and stows it away. The tide is low. Some distance out, Ian and Duncan have gone to the retreating sea. Stacey glances up and sees the two auburn heads. Then she looks back to Jen.

C'mon, flower. What've you got? That's a crab claw – you don't really want that, do you? Oh, all right.

Ian's voice, thin and far.

Mum!

Stacey looks up and sees Ian's hair caught by the sun. Not Duncan's. She places her hands briefly on Jen's shoulders.

Stay here, Jen. Don't move. Don't follow me. Understand? I'll be right back.

Then she runs. Through the dry sand and after that the wet heavy sand and the shallow water, until the water is halfway up her thighs. Ian's face is unrecognizable and he is straining, tugging at one of Duncan's arms. By the time she reaches Ian, he has pulled Duncan out of the water, but only part of the way.

Mum – I think his foot is caught under the rock
What happened? Ian – *what happened?*

She is not aware of having spoken. She kneels and manages to dislodge Duncan's foot, hauling him up and out of the now-brown muddied water. Ian's voice comes to her, treble with fright.

He tripped – I don't know how – I guess the seaweed. I looked and he'd gone down and I thought he'd get up right away. It's not even deep, Mum. But the tide's low. So we came out as far as the rocks. Look – he hit his head when he fell. Maybe it sort of stunned him, but it didn't knock him out or anything, because I saw him thrashing around and I thought he was okay. But he must've got his foot hooked under the rock. By the time I got to him, he wasn't thrashing around any more. He was just lying there.

Duncan   Duncan

His head is bleeding and the sea pours from his nostrils. His mouth is open, and his eyes. But he is not seeing anything and he does not seem to be breathing. His seven-year-old body is heavy in Stacey's arms, a dead weight. She flounders through the water and weed-netted mud, back to the damp exposed sand. She puts Duncan down. She cannot think what to do. She cannot seem to think at all.

Ian – get my bag and take the change purse and go phone Dad. You know where the call box is?

Yes. Sure.

Ian runs, sprints, and she does not even know that he is no longer beside her. She places Duncan on his front and presses down on the place where she thinks his lungs are. Seawater trickles yellowly from his mouth. But he remains inert.

— I don't know what to do. I never learned artificial respiration. How could he fall like that? So quickly? I wasn't watching. I should've been watching. Why wasn't I? I thought they were all right. The tide was out. It was shallow, the water. The rocks covered with barnacles. But he knew they were there. He's been there dozens of times. How could it happen like that, so quickly? It couldn't. But it did. Duncan! You've got to be all right.

Duncan! You've got to be all right.

The words have been screamed, and although she does not hear her own voice, she is suddenly aware of the words' total lie. They are rune words, trinket charms to ward off the evil eye, and that is all. There is nothing she can do.

Now several people on the beach are running towards her, two women and a man, but when they get there, they stand talking at her because they do not know what to do, either.

What happened?

What's the matter?

How did it happen?

I saw those two kids out there and they were perfectly okay and then

Stacey does not hear their voices.

— God, let him be all right, and I'll never want to get away again, I promise. If it was anything I did, take it out on me, not on him – that's too much punishment for me.

She wants to hold Duncan in her arms, but some vestigial knowledge tells her this might be harmful. She is still pressing down on Duncan's ribs, on his warm limp back, her hands filled with the fear of their own ignorance. Then she feels herself pushed aside by a pair of unknown hands and a man is kneeling over Duncan, kneading his body until the brackish water gushes again from his mouth. The man is no more than twenty, tanned, wearing a red swimsuit. One of the lifeguards.

Your other boy fetched me. Just keep a little aside, eh?

He turns Duncan over onto his back, and puts his mouth to Duncan's, breathing from one pair of lungs into the other. Stacey, crouched on the sand, is momentarily blinded, her sight extinguished by saltwater not from the sea. Her mind is empty of everything except Duncan's name which repeats itself over and over. When her sight clears, Duncan is half propped up by the man's arm and is vomiting and also struggling to breath, his breath creaking and uncertain. Then he begins to cry, the attenuated wail of a very young child, an infant voice, not his own voice at all. Stacey puts her arms around him. Once again she cannot see him because of her sight-destroying tears, but she can feel him moving even through her own trembling.

Will he be okay? Mum – will he be okay?

Ian. Stacey does not know the answer. She looks at the young man, who nods and replies for her.

Yeh. He'll be okay, I think. Good job you fetched me, though. It wouldn't have been too good for him to have gone that much longer. He swallowed quite a bit of sea.

Ian does not say anything. He turns away because he does not want either Stacey or the university student to see his face. But Stacey sees that his shoulders are shaking with his dry sobbing, which he has to deal with himself. Then she turns again to Duncan.

His head

Yeh. Well, if you'll bring him along, we can patch that up until you can get him to a doctor. He had quite a wallop, but I don't think it's all that deep. Scalp wounds always bleed a lot.

Stacey! Duncan – I got here as soon as I could – is he

Mac is on his knees beside Duncan in the sand, uncaring about the vomited slime in which he is kneeling.

He's okay now. I think. I think he is. Mac – he nearly

I know. Ian said. Is he really okay?

Duncan has almost stopped crying now. His eyes are half closed. The young man, semi-embarrassed, tries to explain, seeing that Stacey cannot.

He'll be okay, I'm pretty sure. Shock – he'll probably go to sleep. If you want to bring him along to the first-aid post, I can mop up that

But Mac somehow replies unequivocally.

No. Thanks. I think we better take him straight to the Emergency. Thanks all the same. What did you do?

Mouth-to-mouth

My God. Not much point saying thanks, is there? But thanks

That's okay

Mac lifts Duncan out of Stacey's arms. For a moment, she protests.

It's okay, Mac. I can take him.

No. Let me. I'll carry him.

She looks at Mac dazedly. His face is under control, but only just. He picks up Duncan carefully, and for an instant, his own head bowed over Duncan's, holds him tightly, almost cradlingly.

— He's never held Duncan before, not ever. Why did I think he didn't care about Duncan? Maybe he didn't, once. But he does now. Why didn't I see how much, before? He never showed it, that's why.

We'll take my car, Stacey, eh?

Yes. But – Mac, I don't think I can drive.

That's okay. I never meant you should. You take him in the back seat.

All right. Mac – I never thought to call the lifeguard. I wasn't thinking straight. It was Ian, on his way to phone you.

Mac puts Duncan in the back seat of the Buick. Stacey and Jen climb in beside him, Jen very quiet. Mac and Ian go into the front seat. Duncan is nearly asleep. Stacey holds him. Mac starts the car and speaks to Ian in a low gruff voice.

Ian?

Yeh?

You did fine.

Stacey looks at the two unbending necks in the front seat.

— That's the most Mac will ever be able to say. They're not like me, either of them. They don't want to say it in full technicolor and intense detail. And that's okay, I guess. Ian gets the message. It's his language, too. I wish it were mine. All I can do is accept that it is a language, and that it works, at least sometimes. And maybe it's mine more than I like to admit. Whatever I think that I think of it, it's the one I most use.

Unbiddenly, then, she remembers what she was thinking out there on the sand when she did not know what to do and when Duncan's still-warm but nearly unhuman body seemed to be going beyond reach.

God, if it was anything I did, take it out on me, not on him – that's too much punishment for me.

— Judgment. All the things I don't like to think I believe in. But at the severe moments, up they rise, the tomb birds, scaring the guts out of me with their vulture wings. Maybe it's as well to know they're there. Maybe knowing might help to keep them at least a little in their place. Or maybe not. I used to think about Buckle that he was as superstitious as a caveman. I didn't know then that I was too.

Duncan sits up in bed and sips ginger ale through a straw.

Dad   I almost

Duncan knows that Mac carried him from the beach. Mac did not tell Duncan. Stacey did, when Mac was not around. Now Mac is sitting on Duncan's bed.

Yeh. Well, lucky for you that you didn't, eh? Next time you better watch out for your footing.

Next time?

This is not something that Duncan has previously considered. Stacey, standing in the doorway, examines his face and wonders if he has taken for granted that the sea and himself will in future no longer be on any kind of terms.

— Mac's right. I know. But at the same time, it's not Mac who has to go through with it. I don't ever want to take that kid to the beach again.

After a week, Duncan is back to himself. It is the last week of the summer holidays, so Ian is agitating to be taken to the beach. Katie has gone with her friends. Mac, entrenched in myriad administrative responsibilities, has gone to work that morning absentmindedly. Matthew roams the house.

Dad – how be we take the kids to the beach?

Well, that would be quite nice, Stacey.

Okay, you guys – c'mon, then, get your swimsuits and let's get going. C'mon, flower – you, too.

Stacey, Jen and Matthew station themselves fairly high up on the beach, equipped with plastic shovels and sandpails. Ian looks at Duncan and then flashes off on his own towards the sea.

— Ian. If Duncan goes to the sea, Ian will keep an eye on him. But he doesn't want to be responsible. I don't blame him. Maybe he only thinks it would be an insult to Duncan, to watch over him.

Ian rushes into the high-tided water alone, plunging outward and then turning and swimming in, as he has been taught to do. Never swim outward, or you'll get too far beyond your depth. One day he will disobey, and that will be right, then.

Duncan plays in the sand by himself, constructing a moated fort, shoring it up with walls of hard-packed sand. Then, after a while, as though it is something he knows has been laid upon him and which he cannot deny, he walks by himself along the wet reaches of the sand down to the sea.

Stacey watches him, but she makes herself not move. Duncan reaches the edge of the water and then he walks, ploddingly, into the sea.

— I wonder how deep it is, at the deepest? How far out does it go? How many creatures does it contain, not just the little shells and the purple starfish and the kelp, but all the things that live a long way out? Deathly embracing octopus in the south waters, the white whales spouting in the only-half-melted waters of the north, the sharks knowing nothing except how to kill.

Duncan looks incredibly small on the rim of the ocean. But he keeps on walking outward until he reaches what he judges to be a decent and to himself acceptable distance. Then he turns and swims back to shore.

September, and the kids go back to school. Stacey, half ashamed of her own relief, waves at them from the veranda. The morning is warm, so she fetches a lawn chair from the garage and sets it up in the back yard.

Dad – it's such a lovely day, I thought you might like to sit in the garden for a while.

That was thoughtful of you, Stacey.

Stacey helps him down the steps.

— I never know whether he's being delicately ironic or genuinely grateful. If it's the latter, I ought to warn him. Thoughtful, hell, I just don't want him under my feet all morning, that's all. He pussyfoots behind me until I begin to feel he's my shadow, but a shadow that has to be spoken to, taken notice of, and then all I want to do is speak the unspeakable. Okay – so in some ways I'm mean as all getout. I'm going to quit worrying about it. I used to think there would be a blinding flash of light some day, and then I would be wise and calm and would know how to cope with everything and my kids would rise up and call me blessed. Now I see that whatever I'm like, I'm pretty well stuck with it for life. Hell of a revelation that turned out to be.

Stacey goes back into the house. Jen is in the kitchen and has dragged a chair over to the sink, climbed up on it and filled her plastic teapot from the tap. She holds it up for Stacey to see.

Hi, Mum. Want tea?

Stacey stares. Then, quickly, she recovers and manages nonchalance.

What did you say, flower?

Want tea, Mum?

Why – yes, thanks, Jen. I'd love some.

When she has drunk two plastic cupfuls of water, Stacey flies to the telephone in the hall. She speaks guardedly, glancing towards the kitchen, as though imparting top secret material to a co-spy.

Mac? That you?

Yeh. What's the matter, Stacey?

Nothing. It's Jen – she just talked.

Oh?

What d'you mean – *oh?* She *talked*, Mac. A whole sentence. A short one, mind you, but all the same

That's great, honey. I always knew she would.

Well, I just thought I'd let you know. Sorry for phoning you at work. So long.

So long, Stacey.

— What the hell. It may be nothing to him, but when you've listened to this child's garbled gargling for the past year, and all the other kids talked before they were two, then it's like brass bands and banners to me.

Flower, you're a genius.

Want tea, Mum?

Sure.

— Ye gods. What if she never learns to say anything else?

That afternoon, Katie comes home and goes into the back yard where Jen is playing and Stacey is reading.

Guess what, Katie?

What?

Jen talked – a whole sentence.

Katie picks up Jen and swings her high.

Hey – clever kid. What's your name, eh?

Jen.

That's right. My, my, such ability. You're the best two-year-old talker in this entire house. Hey – Mum?

Mm?

I'm going out tonight.

Who with?

Oh – just this boy.

Stacey fights the impulse to ask instantly for a total record – name, age, ambition, appearance, scholastic performance, religion (if any), principles, scruples, manners?

Oh? What's his name, Katie?

Don.

Don who? What's his last name?

How should I know?

— Good God. If it had been me, the name would be embossed on my mind in letters of silver, ten feet high. Maybe she's not quite so desperate to latch on and get the hell out as I was when I was her age? Or is that only my wishful thinking? She's always gone out before with a group of kids. This is the first time alone. It's been bugging her, too. Why, I can't think. At her age. Fourteen. To hear her, you'd think she was thirty and never been kissed. Oh, Katie, love. I hope everything goes well for you.

Okay Katie. Where you going?

Just to a movie. He's a funny kind of guy, in a way. His home background sounds all loused up. He was telling me about this pot party some of them had last summer, and his dad found out and actually took him to the police. Can you imagine?

You mean he smokes marijuana?

Well, he did that time. That wasn't what I was trying to say. Didn't you hear?

— Katie, I'm sorry. I guess I didn't hear. I only heard what was pertinent to you or what I imagined to be pertinent to you. In the same way that I used to wonder if my mother ever really listened to what I'd been saying. Sorry, Mother. Now I see why. I'm a stranger in the now world.

Sorry, Katie. Yeh – I agree. It seems a pretty low thing, for a person to take his own kid to the police. I guess the father felt desperate and worried and – you know – helpless. I don't know. You don't – you haven't – have you, Katie?

Stacey Cameron, standing very still in her blue dirndl skirt and yellow blouse, waiting to be released from the querulously probing voice. *Stacey, some of these boys drink – I know they do – all I hope and trust and pray is that you're not so foolish that you'd accept if one of them offered you a drink.* Of course not, Mother.

You mean have I smoked pot? No. But it's not up to me to judge what other people do, is it? That's his business. It's got nothing to do with me.

Well I guess I can't really argue with that

— It's odd. I believe her. But I guess my mother believed me, too, although I certainly wasn't telling her the truth. Do I know if this particular stuff will lethalize more than the tobacco and booze which are my cup of tea? No. I do not know. I, who may well expire from lung cancer or cirrhosis of the liver. It's partly fear of the unknown, this, with me. But it scares me all the same. I don't know what to tell Katie. I have the feeling that there isn't much use, at this point, in telling her anything. She's on her own, so help her. So help her. At least my mother had the consolation of believing herself to be unquestionably right about everything. Or so I've always thought. Maybe she didn't, either. Although I really do wonder if she ever saw her codeine and phenobarb in anything like the same terms. She always put such a patina of respectability upon them. Probably Katie thinks Mac and I do, too, with the gin and tonic. Ritualized props.

Stacey takes Jen and goes into the kitchen to start dinner. She turns the radio on and begins peeling the potatoes. The tune that is playing is "Zorba's Dance."

She is dancing alone. The café is in a village, a village of low whitewashed huts, surrounded by and threaded through with whatever kind of trees they have in Greece. Olive trees. Yeh, those. However they look. The café is small, and the band is only two or three men playing (unspecified string instruments). She starts slowly, following the beat of the music, her bare feet certain, confident.

*The sudden upswirling of the tune, and she is whirling,
wrists gyrating, possessed by the god. Swifter, swifter,
with the freedom of wild horses, the music races the wind.
Then he is beside her, the man who also is enabled to hear
the music, who also is directed by the god*

AND NOW A WORD FROM OUR SPONSOR   ARE YOU TIRED OF
WAXING FLOORS?

Stacey, immobile beside the sink, except for the
movement of the potato peeler in her right hand, laughs
with minimal amusement.

— I was wrong to think of the trap as the four walls. It's
the world. The truth is that I haven't been Stacey Cameron for one hell of a long time now. Although in some
ways I'll always be her, because that's how I started out.
But from now on, the dancing goes on only in the head.
Anything else, and it's an insult to Katie, whether or not
she witnesses the performance. Well, in the head isn't such
a terrible place to dance. The settings are magnificent
there, anyhow. I did dance at one time, when I could. It
would be a lot worse if I never had. Funny – I recall one of
my mother's bridge cronies in Manawaka, and every time
she came over, she'd ask my mother to put on a record,
and Mother would play the old-time one with a polka on
one side and a schottische on the other, and the old dame
would sit there as though under heavy sedation. Maybe
she was dancing in her head.

The next morning the letter from Stacey's sister arrives.
She tells Mac about it after dinner that evening, when he
has gone down into his temporary study in the TV room.

Mac – guess what?

What?

Rachel and my mother are moving out here. Here.
This self-same city.

Oh holy Jesus   that's all we needed

Yes. I know. But the fact remains that Rachel has had her all alone all these years. We can have them over for Sunday dinners, I guess, and pray it won't be much more than that. That's a fine thing to say about your own sister and mother, isn't it? But I can't help it, Mac. I just can't I don't want

I know. I know, honey. Well

Never mind. Maybe my mother will strike up a rewarding relationship with your dad.

Mac laughs.

I can just about see that happening, can't you?

Yeh. In a magazine story. Well, it'll mean a lot to her to see the kids. I can't begrudge her. She's had her troubles. As I know now. You know something, Mac? I'll be forty next week.

So you will. I'd forgotten. Do you mind?

To tell you the truth, I mind like hell. But there it is.

Yeh. There it is.

The butterfly priestesses flutter in winglike robes of pale mauve. The hairdryers sing whirringly like insects from another planet. Stacey flicks the heat control from high to medium.

— It's an ill wind and all that. At least since Tess's breakdown I can get my hair done again. There's a charitable thought.

She picks up a shiny-paged magazine and thumbs through until she finds the current pop psychology article. It is entitled "Mummy Is the Root of All Evil?"

What do you want for your birthday, Mum?

I don't know. I can never think of anything. What about a nice wheelchair?

Katie laughs obligingly.

No – we're saving up for that one next year.

Thanks, Katie. That's big-hearted of you.

But then Katie swings away, turns into herself.

Ah, drop it, can't you?

EVER-OPEN EYE STREETS IN CITIES NOT SO FAR AWAY ARE BURNING BURNING IN RAGE AND SORROW SET ABLAZE BY THE CHILDREN OF SAMSON AGONISTES VOICE: RIOTS ARE SAID TO BE WELL UNDER CONTROL IN

— I see it and then I don't see it. It becomes pictures. And you wonder about the day when you open your door and find they've been filming those pictures in your street.

On the bedroom chair rests a jumble of Stacey's clothes, offcast stockings like nylon puddles, roll-on girdle in the shape of a tire where she has rolled it off. On another chair, Mac's clothes are folded neatly, a habit he acquired in the army, as he has remarked countless times. Two books are on the bedside table – *The Golden Bough* and *Investments and You*, Hers and His, both unread. On the dressing table, amid the nonmagic jars and lipsticks are scattered photographs of Katie, Ian, Duncan and Jen at various ages. Above the bed is hung a wedding picture, Stacey twenty-three, almost beautiful although not knowing it then, Mac twenty-seven, hopeful confident lean.

Stacey is already in bed. Mac crawls in beside her.

Christ, am I ever beat.

You better get to sleep right away, then, Mac.

I've got to.

It's okay. I know.

— I can't very well say – look, don't worry, you're fine and what I'd really like from time to time is someone I've never been with before. No doubt he'd like that, too.

Well

Mac, it's okay. It's okay if you want to, and it's okay if you don't want to. Only – just talk to me sometimes when you can, eh?

What in heaven's name do you mean by that, Stacey?

Well   you know   like   about what's bugging you

They are silent for a moment. Then Mac turns to face her.

Stacey?

Yes?

What did you ever do with your dad's old revolver?

She sits up in bed and looks at him.

What?

The one you brought back that time from Manawaka.

How did you know?

I was looking for a tin of nails I'd stuck up on one of the rafters in the basement, and I found it. Couple of months later it was gone.

I chucked it into Timber Lake that summer. Why didn't you ever mention

I don't know. I didn't know what to say. I wanted to throw it away myself, but then I thought that might make you even more determined   if that was what was in your mind

What? What did you think I planned to do with it?

Maybe it sound crazy, Stacey. I was kind of afraid you might   you know   like Tess

Mac   that wasn't it at all

Slowly, Stacey tells him how she felt then and how she came to realize there was no use keeping the gun. She finds it neither easier nor more difficult to explain now than she did when she said the same thing to Luke. Mac scrutinizes her face.

You thought all that?

Yeh. Didn't you ever?

His voice is in low gear, with brakes on.

Yes. I guess. Sometimes.

She moves towards him and he holds her. Then they make love after all, but gently, as though consoling one another for everything that neither of them can help nor alter.

Finally, Stacey disentangles.

Mac, we better get some sleep.

I know. Good night, Stacey.

Good night, Mac.

> *Ladybird, ladybird,*
> *Fly away home;*
> *Your house is on fire,*
> *Your children are . . .*

— Will the fires go on, inside and out? Until the moment when they go out for me, the end of the world. And then I'll never know what may happen in the next episode.

As she tries to settle herself for sleep, Stacey feels a nudging pain like a fingernail scrawling fitfully under her ribs at the left side.

— There it is again. Should I phone Doctor Spender tomorrow? It's nothing. It'll go away. But what if it doesn't? What if it's the heart? Is the heart on that side? Well, so what? No one is indispensable. Maybe not, but it's myself I'm thinking about, as well as them. If I could absorb the notion of nothing, of total dark, then it would have no power over me. But that grace isn't given. My last breath will be a rattle of panic, while some strange face or maybe the known one hovers over me and says *Everything's all right*. Unless, of course, it meets me with violent quickness, a growing fashion.

She lies stiffly, listening.

— Maybe the trivialities aren't so bad after all. They're something to focus on. As I'm forty tomorrow, that would be a good day to start a diet. Not the banana diet – it's too repulsive. High protein. How would it be if I did myself a steak at lunch and then only had soup at night? Yeh, you do that, doll. You'll lose the same ten pounds you've been losing for ten years. All right. I know. It's not necessary to spell it out. I won't be twenty-one again. I'll never have a really decent-looking pair of hips again as long as I live. I don't claim that's any tragedy. I don't even claim it's anything except ludicrous. But it's enough to make me feel relatively lousy on occasion. Like today when I took the prescription into the drugstore to get more of the wonder pills. I hate getting them. I always think the pharmacist is looking at me and thinking *Who in hell would want to make love to that old cow?* On the other hand, they're a kind of proof that somebody still does. I would have liked to be a great courtesan, like that one in France who went on until she was about ninety-five. Still beautiful, it is said, although personally I find that hard to credit. Well, such was quite plainly not meant to be your lot, Stacey. Never mind. Give me another forty years, Lord, and I may mutate into a matriarch.

Stacey heaves over onto her side. The house is quiet. The kids are asleep. Downstairs in the ex-study, Matthew has been asleep for hours, or if not asleep, meditating. Beside her, she can already hear the steady breathing that means Mac is asleep. Temporarily, they are all more or less okay.

She feels the city receding as she slides into sleep. Will it return tomorrow?

Afterword

BY SYLVIA FRASER

Polemic proclaims its truths in black and white: "Since I am right, you are wrong." Fiction, by contrast, is a "yes, but" tapestry of extenuating circumstances woven out of every shade in the rainbow. It is the art of human frailty, of undiagnosable feelings, of facts that do not quite fit and details that frequently fail to add up to solutions.

In the United States, a country which seems to revere fact (defined as the provable, the photographable, the measurable) over fiction (often dismissed as elitist, trivialized as escapist and, in any event, denigrated as untrue), women shaped their post-fifties emergence with a powerful polemic that effectively redefined how North American society would see itself. In Canada, no equivalent female voices were raised. In Canada, the energy of the women's movement expressed itself more subtly and more characteristically through the power of its female fiction writers – Adele Wiseman, Alice Munro, Marian Engel, Margaret Atwood and, of course, Margaret Laurence.

Such was Margaret Laurence's enormous stature at the time of her death on January 5, 1987, that it is easy to forget that she began her career when describing one's self as a Canadian female writer from the Prairies was to seem to apologize three times. In the spring of 1969, when *The Fire-Dwellers* was first published, women were beginning to express their sense of generic, no-name frustration, but had not yet found a confident social voice, and the words "women's liberation" were just moving into general circulation. In North American literature, killing a tiger, having sex, and making war in the "macho" spirit of Hemingway, Miller, and Mailer were deemed the real stuff of greatness, whereas birthing a baby, yearning for love, and fearing nuclear disaster were labelled fodder for the women's magazines.

Across this tense, arrogant, unforgiving terrain, housewife-mother Stacey MacAindra – prairie-born, fearful, self-deprecating – had to make her precarious way as a literary creation. Her predictable slap down came on May 3, the very day of publication, by reviewer Barry Callaghan writing in the *Toronto Telegram*. Referring to the author, then divorced, as "Mrs. Laurence" in the quaint nomenclature of the times, repeatedly misspelling Stacey's name as "Staicey," and quoting expansively from Graham Greene to demonstrate what the content of novels "should" be, Callaghan dismissed MacAindra's aching loneliness as "the bleating of a dumb, starved, and boring lady of neither the night nor the day but of limbo." For Callaghan, Stacey MacAindra was that most tiresome of creatures, an unattractive female, "frowsy and flat-chested . . . a loser."

In her life and in her art, Laurence wisely eschewed all political or social labels while passionately working for what she believed in. She never wrote novels that were high-handedly didactic, though her characters – as profoundly moral creations firmly rooted in their worlds – wrestled with or reflected the dilemmas of their times. Her basic themes were universal – decent, recognizable people groping for understanding of themselves and others, struggling through lost innocence to maturity, through pain to wisdom and an acceptance of their unique, often humble place in the universe.

Perhaps more than any other of Laurence's novels, *The Fire-Dwellers* partakes of its time. Using sophisticated techniques which allowed her to pass easily from past to present, from reality to fantasy, from interior monologue to exterior observation, incorporating bits from television newscasts, clips from magazines and movies, Laurence recreated the kaleidoscopic sixties as experienced by Stacey MacAindra – a world of housewives and of breadwinners, of plastic kitchenware peddled as party-ware and vitamin pills as immortality, of governments threatened by the fires of nuclear holocaust and morals by the flames of illicit sex. It is not this historical view, however, which is most important for the reader. The compelling view is the one back through the kaleidoscope – into the acutely observing eye of Stacey MacAindra, into her wry and questing mind, into her nurturing yet defiantly yearning heart. Thus, twenty years after the novel's publication, it is Callaghan's kind of review that seems "bleating," antiquated and "of limbo" while Laurence's portrait of Stacey MacAindra shines through as a compassionate depiction of a woman caught at a particular time of her life, in a particular time of the female collective life.

Death, both symbolic and familiar, always lies close to the surface of Laurence's novels, even when she most open-heartedly celebrates life. The father of Stacey Cameron MacAindra (and of her sister Rachel in *A Jest of God*) was an undertaker, who worked matter-of-factly at his grim craft. The fire image that gives birth to the title *The Fire-Dwellers* comes jointly from a quotation by Carl Sandburg and the nursery rhyme, "Ladybird, Ladybird," both suggesting threat by fire. Fear that accident will claim one of her four children continuously nags at Stacey's consciousness – a fear made real by the recent death of one of their playmates. News broadcasts about nuclear holocaust seep like napalm out of Stacey's television set into her own living room. In interior monologue, Stacey, who once kept a revolver as an object of comfort, often speculates about death: "What'll it be like to die? . . . My father's dead face . . . and I thought his face had been dead for a long time before he died." The attempted suicide of a neighbour, the death through bravado of her husband's best friend and the near-drowning of one of Stacey's sons create the novel's triple-climax through which Stacey discovers the strength to rededicate herself more courageously to life.

Death touched Margaret Wemyss Laurence at an early age. Her mother died in 1930 when Margaret was only four, and her father died five years later. Thereafter, Margaret, her step-brother, and step-mother moved into the house of her autocratic grandfather, undertaker to the Manitoba town of Neepawa.

In a psychiatric treatise, I once read that persons who early lose a parent to death are called "blood" children because that shocking severance of the blood tie creates a psychic wound that time never heals. From my experience with creative writing classes, I know that such people are disproportionately represented there, as if early bereavement, with its sudden primal silence, hurls them into a private void of inner voices that clamour to be articulated.

Once, over breakfast in Margaret Laurence's Lakefield kitchen, I mentioned the blood-children theory to her. She remained enigmatically silent in the face of one more crude attempt to pigeonhole her, yet, whenever I saw her cry over the reported tragedy of someone whom she had never met, or out of sorrow for the threatened nuclear fate of this planet, I wondered if the tears she so generously shed for strangers were a kind of stigmata of the soul.

Perhaps this metaphor is overblown. Perhaps my theory of blood-children and their connection to literature is an idle one. I do believe, however, that Margaret Wemyss's precocious awareness of the fragility of life deeply informed the author's earthy, yet lyrical, compassion for mankind, for family, for friends, for her tribe of writers, for her fictional creations. This extraordinary compassion was Margaret Laurence's hallmark – a gift of wisdom and of magic and of caring that triumphs over her death.

BY MARGARET LAURENCE

AUTOBIOGRAPHY
The Prophet's Camel Bell (1963)

ESSAYS
*Long Drums and Cannons: Nigerian Dramatists and Novelists
1952–1966* (1968)
Heart of a Stranger (1976)

FICTION
This Side Jordan (1960)
The Tomorrow-Tamer (1963)
The Stone Angel (1964)
A Jest of God (1966)
The Fire-Dwellers (1969)
A Bird in the House (1970)
The Diviners (1974)

FICTION FOR YOUNG ADULTS
Jason's Quest (1970)
Six Darn Cows (1979)
The Olden Days Coat (1979)
The Christmas Birthday Story (1980)

TRANSLATIONS
A Tree for Poverty: Somali Poetry and Prose (1954)